Wraith Horizon
The CANZUK At War Series
Book 3

Table of Contents

Title Page 1
Wraith Horizon (CANZUK at War, #3) 6
Prologue 7
Chapter 1 19
Chapter 2 32
Chapter 3 40
Chapter 4 53
Chapter 5 70
Chapter 6 81
Chapter 7 95
Chapter 8 101
Chapter 9 112
Chapter 10 121
Chapter 11 130
Chapter 12 143
Chapter 13 152
Chapter 14 170
Chapter 15 179
Chapter 16 191
Chapter 17 212
Chapter 18 224
Chapter 19 235
Chapter 20 250
Chapter 21 264
Chapter 22 277
Chapter 23 284
Chapter 24 295
Chapter 25 304
Chapter 26 314
Chapter 27 330
Chapter 28 347
Chapter 29 361
Chapter 30 371
Chapter 31 393
Chapter 32 405

Chapter 33 416
Chapter 34 430
Chapter 35 441
Chapter 36 458
Chapter 37 470
Chapter 38 480
Chapter 39 494
Chapter 40 509
Chapter 41 523
Chapter 42 536
Chapter 43 553
Epilogue 561
Copyright 566
Afterword 567

Author's Note: CANZUK is an alliance comprised of **C**anada, **A**ustralia, **N**ew **Z**ealand and the **U**nited **K**ingdom.

Prologue

Undisclosed Location, Florida

—

Mitchell Spector, the President of the United Constitutional States of America, UCSA, stared at his image on the large screen that occupied much of the wall in the boardroom.

He looked exhausted because that is what he was. The war was proceeding well, but not as well as he had hoped, and this had meant long days and nights pushing his people to finish things in the north.

In the weeks after the fall of Washington, the Blues and their CANZUK allies had performed poorly. CANZUK in particular had not understood the concept of total war and had reeled at the things the UCSA regular army and militias were prepared to do to finish the conflict.

But as Andrew Morgan recovered from his double amputation and rallied the people of the Federation of the American States, FAS, CANZUK's militaries also began to turn on to the idea they needed to fight with their gloves off.

The challenge that now lay before Spector and his country was twofold. First, they faced the hugely challenging task of trying to take two fortified cities in upstate New York.

In the weeks after the fall of the District of Columbia, their enemies had lost battle after battle, and at one point it looked like they might suffer a complete collapse, but as Morgan recovered in the relatively safe confines of Minnesota, the man emerged as George Washington reborn.

Minus legs, the former VP of the Blues seemed to be everywhere, and whereas under Menendez he had been reserved and compliant, in the role of a wartime president, he channeled the type of leadership he must have exuded when he commanded one of the SEAL teams.

In public and on the frontlines, Morgan had been inspiring and courageous. Behind the scenes, Spector's intel people were advising that the Blues' new leader was intimately engaged in the faction's strategy-making and was said to be a shrewd tactician.

As if Morgan wasn't enough, the Martel woman from Canada continued to be an oversized thorn in his side. After surviving the latest attempt on her life, she had consolidated her hold on power with a ruthlessness he hadn't realized Canadians were prepared to accept.

Political opponents had mysteriously died, her inner circle had been overhauled with people prepared *'to do what had to be done to win the war,'* and she'd declared her intent to invoke the country's Emergencies Act, giving her a range of draconian powers.

And as recently as yesterday, Spector had read a report suggesting that Martel was seriously considering implementing a draft – conscription, as the CANZUK countries called it.

Whatever its name, with a population of nearly fifty million people, it could mean his country, the UCSA, might have to face hundreds of thousands more soldiers than they were now.

It was these reasons and others, that had driven Spector to participate in the conference he and his closest advisors were waiting to begin.

Without looking at the man to his right, he said, "Peter, we're five minutes past one, what's the problem?"

"It's the Chinese, Mr. President. The French are in the queue and waiting just like us. I'm not sure what the delay is. It's not the technology. Our tech people assure me the quantum connection is functioning perfectly."

Spector didn't reply to the update. Instead, he only released an extended sigh from a clenched jaw and then proceeded to crack the knuckles on both hands.

"Ah, here we go," said Peter Parr, his Chief of Staff.

As Parr made the pronouncement, the screen that the room's occupants were united in staring at came alive to show three panels, each featuring a small group of people.

The border of the stream featuring the Chinese delegation ignited in red as the Chinese President began to speak in Mandarin. As the near-instantaneous translation software began to do its job, Spector noted only the slightest delay between the movement of the Chinese leader's lips and the words registering in Spector's ears.

"President Spector and President Lévesque, my most sincere apologies for the delay. There was one issue I needed to finalize with my advisors in advance of our conversation. Please forgive me. I know you are both extremely busy."

The President of France, Marie-Helene Lévesque, beat Spector to a reply. Interestingly enough, the border around her panel remained green, signalling the woman had chosen to speak in English.

"It is no problem, President Yan. It is always better to have everything resolved with your people before these types of conversations start. I hope you are well, Mr. President?"

Lévesque then quickly added before Yan could reply, "And a good afternoon to you, President Spector. I trust you, too, are doing well?"

Not a complete ignoramus of how interpersonal dynamics worked, Spector deferred to President Yan so he could be the first to respond to the French leader's inquiry.

The Chinese leader said, "I am well, Madame President, and I am glad you and President Spector have agreed to this conference. As discussed in advance by our people, we have two items to discuss. I wonder if we might not dive into them immediately?"

Tired, Spector was more than happy to dispense with the personal pleasantries. Quickly, he responded to Yan's question and said, "Let's get into it then. Issue one on the table is an update on China's incursion into Vietnam. The floor is yours, President Yan."

"Thank you, President Spector," the Chinese leader replied, his voice sounding assured.

"As you know, for decades, the People's Republic of Vietnam has brutally persecuted ethnic Chinese within its borders, and while China has been historically stalwart in its respect for other countries' sovereignty, over the past year, we've received intelligence of the highest quality indicating Vietnam was increasing the persecution of its minority populations.

"The Chinese people only want peace. That is all we have ever wanted. But, where China and its people are threatened, we are not afraid to take action, and that is exactly what my country has done.

As the leader of China, I cannot and will not stand by and let countries like Vietnam humiliate their million-plus ethnic Chinese residents by taking their businesses and undertaking state-sanctioned pogroms."

The Chinese President paused briefly, no doubt for dramatic effect, and then said, "I would respectfully say to both of you that no country that has a claim to regional or global leadership can stand by and watch its people slaughtered in the thousands. China is a benevolent country, but we are also powerful. The government of Vietnam was repeatedly warned about its behavior of persecuting its ethnic minorities, but our cautions were ignored. And so, we had no choice but to do what we have done."

Mentally, Spector began to clap in response to the performance. In just over a minute, the leader of China had produced the largest load of verbal bullshit he'd ever heard delivered by a politician.

That the lie had been so shamelessly delivered had only increased the wariness Spector felt for the Chinese dictator.

He imagined it was the very same kind of deference given to a mob boss who was at the height of his power when he delivered some unbelievable excuse as to why he whacked someone who didn't deserve it. Only the biggest fool or a man with his own death wish quibbled or questioned this kind of power.

It was this type of thinking that paved the way for Spector to accept Yan Jiandong's explanation as to why his military had used tactical nuclear weapons to invade its much smaller, nuclear-free neighbor.

Spector, having spent time in China as the United States senior military attaché at the midpoint of his career, had been required to immerse himself in China's history and culture.

The result of this experience was that he was familiar with how China's invasion of Vietnam had gone back in 1979.

In truth, the People's Liberation Army had performed poorly against Vietnam, but anyone who knew anything about the conflict agreed that China had won a strategic victory. The arguable Chinese success of fifty years ago had forced the leaders of Vietnam to get wise to the idea that China could take Hanoi if it didn't properly defend its northern border.

They had gotten wise, and in the decades after the Sino-Vietnam War, successive Vietnamese governments had turned the northern reaches of their country into a gauntlet so severe that China had no choice but to use tactical nukes.

Of course, Spector was in no position to criticize. He too had recently used tactical nuclear weapons and with great military effect. In truth, his actions had paved the way for China to pre-emptively strike its neighbor.

Continuing with his opening statement, the Chinese leader said, "It is my most fervent hope that other countries in Southeast Asia will learn from the lesson that the People's Liberation Army is now teaching to the criminals presently running Vietnam. China and its people – those living in the Motherland and those living abroad, must be respected. China will not allow it to be any other way."

Yan paused, allowing the gravity of his words to fully connect with Spector and Lévesque. When neither of them offered any response to his declaration, he continued. "To you, our friends in North America and Europe, I want to make two things extremely clear in what remains of my opening statement.

"First, China's intelligence services are aware that other countries, specifically Thailand, are replicating the hostilities that Vietnam set upon its ethnic Chinese. As the leader of China, I cannot and will not let another genocide transpire. If necessary, we will extend our police action into Thailand, and in doing so, we will utterly destroy the Western militaries that are now building up their forces in that country."

And there it was, Spector thought. The rationale Yan would use to justify his country's ongoing effort to invade parts or all of Southeast Asia.

Because of the United States' collapse, the Chinese had been able to run amok in their part of the world. First, there had been the lightning-fast takeover of Taiwan. Then the Philippine island of Palawan, and now Vietnam.

That China would extend parts of its three-million-strong military into some or all of Thailand for its ample natural resources or to plunder the millions of female citizens between the ages of 15 and 35 to rectify the present-day disaster that was China's one-child policy was not surprising in the least. What China was now doing was choosing economic and demographic survival over collapse.

When neither Spector nor his French counterpart made any reaction to Yan's monumental claim about the Thais, the Chinese dictator continued, "The second and final part of my opening statement is thus. In undertaking these legal police actions, I believe China and each of your countries have a common cause.

"In the case of France, President Lévesque, you are faced with the problem of the Muslim. By our count, by the end of this calendar year, you will have reduced France's Muslim population by forty-two percent."

Lévesque interrupted. "By our count, Mr. President, we are closer to fifty percent, and if all goes well, by year's end, sixty percent of them will be removed."

The woman neither flinched nor hesitated as she confirmed her country's effort to displace millions of its citizens. A hard lady to be sure, thought Spector.

On the screen, Yan nodded at the French leader's update and said, "And, as we speak, five divisions of the French Army are moving to the border of the Netherlands, ostensibly to help that country's government deal with its own Muslim Problem."

Lévesque's chin raised slightly, and her eyes narrowed, giving her a defiant look. She said, "A coalition of politicians in the Dutch government has pleaded with us to lend whatever aid we can to find and destroy the terrorists who've fled France and Germany.

"President Yan, I can assure you and President Spector both, the fear of the people in the Netherlands is palpable, and the attacks that have been taking place in that country are real and will not abate until Dutch security forces begin to treat this threat seriously. And for the record, France will not allow one of its neighbors to harbor terrorists. My government and I will do what we must to keep the citizens of France safe."

From wherever he was in China, Yan nodded his head at Lévesque's statement and said, "As you know, President Lévesque, China too has suffered at the hands of the Muslim terrorist. I applaud your leadership and willingness to take a firm stand on this insidious and real threat, and even as China faces its own challenges in Southeast Asia, I want you to know that inside and outside of the UN, we are prepared to give France a free hand to do what it must to ensure Europe's security."

This time, it was Lévesque's turn to nod her head. "President Yan, my country thanks you for your staunch support. A strong and culturally united France free of those who would see my country on its knees is in the best interests of Europe and the rest of the world. For the support China has given to us, rest assured that we will support your noble efforts to protect ethnic Chinese in your part of the world."

Yan's fist gently pounded the table in front of him. "Very good. China and France are very much on the same page, which brings me to the common cause that China has with the United Constitutional States of America."

On hearing the UCSA's name in full, Spector's jaw tightened. Based on the political horse-trading he had just witnessed, a deal, or worse, a dictate, was about to come his way. Spector was no fool. When it came to China, the UCSA was the secondary power.

"President Spector, I have valued our relationship and the transparency with which we have conducted our business. Because I know and value your honesty, I am prepared to put my cards on the table so you can make a full evaluation of how our two countries might engage with one another once the two wars we are fighting come to an end."

"I'm listening," was all Spector said.

"You are winning your war, President Spector, but can you finish it in victory?"

Spector's eyes narrowed at the infuriating, but not untrue question and said, "We feel good about where things sit at the moment."

"Indeed, Mr. President," Yan said in a calm voice. "But your enemies are consolidating and are preparing to strike back, and because of the very real possibility of British nuclear reprisal, the use of any more tactical nuclear weapons is off the table – or it should be.

"And if my people's most recent intelligence reports are accurate, it would appear the political stance of the Neutral Faction is about to change and with it, perhaps, California."

After a brief pause, Yan asked, "How long might the UCSA be able to fight a two-front war, Mr. President?"

Spector felt the beginnings of a white-hot anger grow inside him. He wanted to lash out at the arrogant Chinese son of a bitch, but he controlled himself.

It was one thing to lose his shit in front of his people. It would be something else entirely to unload on another country's leader, particularly when that leader was only speaking the truth, as hard as it was to hear.

He took in a deep breath. On his exhale, he replied to Yan. "As much as it pains me to say it, your assessment is close to the mark. We are nearly five years into this civil war. My people are tired. To say the least, the potential change in the disposition of the Neutral Faction is disappointing. If California joins them... well, if that happens, the UCSA faces a difficult future."

His face sober-looking, Yan nodded in response to Spector's assessment. "As I said before, President Spector, I have valued your willingness to tell things as they are. It is for this reason that I called this meeting. China recognizes the challenge the UCSA faces, but with our help, we believe we can keep your country on the path to victory. But there will be a cost. A significant one."

To his credit, Parr had anticipated this moment, and though Spector had resisted the notion that the Chinese might dictate terms to him for their help, he had indulged his chief of staff in the conversation. Now, he was glad he had.

He might be furious at the notion of giving up American territory to secure Chinese support, but because of Parr's foresight, he was at least prepared to have the discussion.

"Tell me what China is prepared to offer, President Yan, and I will tell you what I might be prepared to give," Spector said.

To the man's tremendous credit, the Chinese leader's face did not provide the smallest hint that his country was on the cusp of making a deal that would solidify China as the world's premier nation for the next one hundred years.

"Quite simply, President Spector, my country is prepared to give whatever it takes to ensure your victory. Trucks, artillery pieces, and shells in the millions, armored personnel carriers, drones of all kinds, and more fifth-generation fighter planes. We are even prepared to send you some of our treasured automatons. China has these items in large quantities, and if necessary, we can produce more and quickly."

The offer of weapons was part of the puzzle to be sure, thought Spector.

The French had provided much of what the UCSA had needed in recent months, but with the prospect of war breaking out in Europe, the rate at which French armaments had been flowing across the Atlantic had been decreasing. Add to this CANZUK's efforts to bomb and sabotage his own country's factories, and it was a growing concern the Red Faction wouldn't have the war-fighting material it needed to win against the Blues, never mind the Neutrals and California.

But what was needed more than weapons were soldiers. Lots of them and in short order.

If the Canadians invoked a draft as was now being discussed, they could easily triple the size of their army by this time next year.

On the West Coast, California had been the biggest refuge for those in the US military who didn't want to fight in the civil war. Tens of thousands of active and retired service people had fled to the state.

Add to this California's huge population and that it had more than twice the number of military bases of the next largest state, and it was beyond clear the Golden State would be a big problem for the UCSA should it forego its neutral status. The Neutrals were much less of a problem.

All this being the case, Spector said, "If my country is going to win this war, we need to defeat the Blues quickly, but to do this, we need weapons and people."

Yan said, "China is prepared to offer you both of those things, but first, let us talk of what a victorious UCSA is prepared to do to compensate my country for the risk it would be assuming."

There it was. Spector had arrived at the moment he'd feared the most. The devil was in front of him and was preparing to ask for his soul.

When historians looked back on this moment, Spector knew they'd be cruel, but what choice did he have? He had discussed it with Parr and others, and they'd decided there was no choice. They had to win this war quickly, and to do that, they needed Chinese help.

Spector said, "Though it is not my place to give it, the UCSA will not contest China should it take parts or all of British Columbia beyond the already promised Vancouver Island."

He let the offer hang in the air for a moment, but when Yan made no indication that it was either interesting or satisfactory, he continued.

"Of the territories in the Pacific, we are prepared to relinquish American Samoa and the Northern Mariana Islands indefinitely. We will retain Guam, though we would pledge to demilitarize it for the next twenty-five years. Hawaii is off the table. It is too important to us strategically."

For the first time in the conversation, a frown began to crawl onto the Chinese President's face. But before it could fully emerge, Spector delivered the part of the deal that, in the eyes of many Americans, would be more controversial than using nuclear weapons on American soil. With great reluctance, he said, "We are prepared to offer the entire state of Washington. It would be on condition of a 99-year lease."

Quickly, Spector added, "The American people will not let me give away the land for time immemorial. If I did that, the moment the war was over, there would be immediate demands to take Washington back. It would be no different than what China would have done if the British had permanently held onto Hong Kong or Macau."

For a long moment, Yan said nothing. But then he issued a deliberate nod of his head and said, "I understand your rationale, Mr. President. You are wise. We are comfortable with this offer in general terms but with one alteration."

"And what might that be?" As the words left his mouth, Spector girded himself for an amendment he could not accept. He had gone too far already.

"Our previous agreement concerning British Columbia was that it would be subject to this 99-year lease we both seem to be so fond of. There will be no lease. When this war is won and our two countries are the victors, all of Canada's westernmost province will become Chinese territory. Forever."

Spector breathed a sigh of relief.

That Washington would eventually return to the US while British Columbia would become a permanent part of the Chinese empire was a development that would serve the UCSA very well.

In 99 years, whatever Chinese assets were in Washington could more easily be shifted north, while the permanency of the Chinese presence in Canada would make the temporary loss of the Evergreen State more palatable in the eyes of Americans. And, if, for whatever reason, the Chinese reneged on the deal and didn't want to leave Washington, it would be far easier to pry them from continental North America than it would be to evict them from somewhere like Hawaii.

Imperfect didn't begin to describe the arrangement, but it was the best outcome Spector could have hoped for.

Beside him, he could sense the stress from the other men in the room. No one was happy with what they had to do, and Spector least of all, but if they were going to win this war, they needed China's help. Cracking his knuckles again, he finally said, "In general terms, I accept your offer, President Yan. Our people will work out the specifics, but if nothing major comes up, I think we can make this deal."

The mouth of the Chinese leader flexed upwards into a smile. *And so he should, the son of a bitch,* thought Spector. He had just secured a permanent and prime piece of real estate for his nation on the other side of the world.

The Chinese leader said, "Indeed, we do have a deal. A deal that will allow us – China, France, and the UCSA, to dominate this planet for generations to come."

PART ONE

Chapter 1

Canadian Forces Base (CFB) Petawawa, West of Ottawa

―

The five-week-old baby cooed in the crook of Jackson Larocque's arm. When he looked down to take in the little man who was his son, the baby gave a lion-like yawn.

Beside him, he felt Madison reach around his waist and pull tight on his torso. When he leaned his head down to hers, she said, "I'm going to have to duck out in five to feed him, or he's going to go full demon during the ceremony. Give him to me."

Larocque did what he was told and gently passed over the football-sized human to his wife.

Gathering up the infant and her bag of supplies, Madison Larocque stepped into the aisle and as quietly as she could, made her way to the back of the small church.

Turning back to the ceremony, Larocque took in the padre who was officiating the non-denominational pairing of the young couple standing together on the dais to the right of the military chaplain.

Corporal Dune, who had since become Captain Dune of the Canadian Special Operations Regiment, CSOR, stood proud. Dressed in No.1s of the Canadian Army, the Aussie, now Canadian soldier, looked sharp.

Across his chest was the impressive row of medals the Australian commando had earned for his part in the numerous combat missions during the past year.

Next to the newly minted special operations officer was Dune's best mate from the 2nd Commando Regiment. Wearing his country's No. 1s, he'd stood apart for much of the day. Where the CSOR beret was tan in colour, the Aussie's headdress was a dark green.

Jeff Gretchen, recently promoted to sergeant and still in Canada on special leave, had his own parade of medals flowing across the left side of his chest.

Dune and Gretch, as the other man was called, looked as though they could have been biological brothers instead of the brothers-in-arms they actually were.

Both were tall, strapping, and sported sandy-colored beards that often caught second glances from any young lady who happened to be in the vicinity.

But where the two soldiers looked regal and powerful in their dress uniforms, it was the bride who dominated the scene.

Trisha Karvonen was a Canadian-Finnish stunner. Tall and blonde, she was an Edmonton-based emergency room nurse who had fallen for a cocky, handsome Australian non-commissioned officer who, on paper at least, was not in his soon-to-be wife's league.

By rights and by most people's uninformed assessment, Trisha should be hitching her wagon to some hugely successful doctor or perhaps a professional hockey player, but Larocque knew what most people did not.

Captain Mark Dune was an exceptional human being. Setting aside his good looks, the young Aussie was charismatic in the extreme, had an infectious effervescence for life, and possessed a streak of bravery that was peerless.

Dune, now an officer in the Canadian Army, was unlikely to make millions, but he would, without any doubt, make the beautiful gal staring at him a happy and proud woman.

Fifteen minutes later, the ceremony completed, he and Madison stood outside the quaint-looking church soaking up the summer sunshine, while Marcel lay quiet in Madison's arms, still in a milk-induced coma.

Hand in hand, Dune and the brand-new Mrs. Dune had been working the small crowd that had joined them for the ceremony.

Despite all that had been happening in Southeast Asia, Dune's parents and sister had been able to make the trek to Canada without much trouble.

All of it had come together perfectly. And with his son and wife at his side, Brigadier General Jackson Larocque was a content man.

Disengaging from a small group of Canadian paratroopers that had attended the wedding, the new couple made their way toward Larocque and his small clan.

The combination of the mid-afternoon sun and the soft breeze rustling the nearby trees gave the approaching pair an ethereal quality. Truly, God had given this beautiful couple his blessing, Larocque thought.

On reaching them, Dune released the arm of his wife and issued a precise salute. Free from baby Marcel, Larocque returned the gesture as the moment deserved.

"General, so good of you and Ms. Larocque to make it to our big day."

"Mark Dune, you will address me as Madison. I am not your teacher, and my hair isn't grey, thank you very much," Madison said sternly.

Dune didn't give a reply. Instead, he just stepped forward and enveloped Madison and the baby in a gentle bear hug.

When he stepped back from her, Dune's eyes were glassy with emotion.

"Oh no, you don't," said Madison. "Stop that with those big brown eyes of yours. I made it through the entire ceremony without ruining my makeup and there's still the dinner."

Without warning, Madison handed their son to Trisha, who gladly accepted the slumbering baby. Hands free, she reached into her purse, pulled out a tissue, brought it to her eyes, and began to dab.

"There, are you happy? Tears have officially been shed," Madison said playfully.

"In this moment, Ms. Madison, I've never been happier."

The hand not tending to her makeup lashed out and struck Dune's shoulder. "You're something else, Mark Dune."

The punch put a big grin on the Aussie's face. "This may surprise you, but I get that more than you might reckon. More often though, the words to express the sentiment are a touch more colorful. You know, something like, 'Mate, has there ever been a passing bloody hour where you didn't stir the shit?'"

Larocque couldn't help but smile as he took in the banter. He gestured to Trisha and the baby who was now on her hip. "That's a good look for you. Captain Dune informs me you just passed the first trimester. I guess there's another reason for us to celebrate."

If the new Ms. Dune was glowing before, the luminosity of her person increased as her free hand slipped down to her stomach. "We've decided to let everyone know tonight at the dinner."

"I approve," said Larocque. "Get it out there. With your move from out west, let's give every wife and partner on the base every reason in the world to give you a helping hand before CSOR heads out."

"Really, Jackson? I thought we weren't going to mention anything about the war," Madison said, making zero effort to hold back the annoyance she felt toward her husband.

"No wukkas," Dune said quickly, trying to draw Madison's attention away from her husband. "I can fight here in Canada against the Red Yanks, or head back to Oz and get shipped off to Nam to fight the Chi-Coms. Either way, I'm heading back to war."

"Stupid wars," Madison growled. "How is it that over the past five years, so many unhinged people have taken control of so many countries, including our own?" As she finished the statement, Madison delivered a hard look at Larocque.

Knowing Madison Larocque's unhidden dislike of Canada's Prime Minister, Merielle Martel, Dune threw a lifeline to the man and mentor who had done so much for him in the past year. "So, General, what does CANSOFCOM have you doing now that you're no longer commanding the Airborne? A cushy job worthy of a national hero, I hope?"

Larocque made a mental note to thank Dune for the intervention. "Madison will be staying here, but I'll be working out of Ottawa. I don't have all the details yet, but the gist of it is that I'll be a special operations liaison between the Prime Minister's Office and CANZUK Joint Operations Command."

"Meaning?" Dune said.

Unfazed by Dune's effort to shift the conversation, Madison responded on her husband's behalf. "Meaning, the CAF is hoping that Jaks here can help to rein in our increasingly authoritarian prime minister."

Dune's eyes widened at Madison's open criticism of the Canadian PM.

While Dune was a fighting man and had done very little to follow politics back in Australia or Canada, he was tuned in enough to know the various decisions Martel had made in the weeks since the Montreal assassination attempt had been controversial in the extreme.

He said, "Oi, well, if the PM needs a bit of managing, I can't think of a better bloke for the job than the legend himself, General Jackson Larocque."

Larocque threw his hands into the air, palms out. "Alright, alright, I should have never brought up CSOR's deployment. Today, we're celebrating the marriage of one of Australia's greatest soldiers to one of Canada's most beautiful and smart women."

"Instead of chatting about how batshit crazy the world has become, let's say we grab a drink or two and collectively pledge that for the next 24 hours, we only talk about things like love, babies, and the promise the future holds?"

One of Madison's eyebrows shot upward, but before she could contest his proposal, the baby mewled, drawing her attention.

She glided to the bride and her son, gently wrapped her arm around the emergency nurse's waist, and said, "Come with me, Trisha. You keep holding that baby. I need that drink my husband was talking about, and then I want to meet your mother. She's as gorgeous as you are."

As the two women stepped away, Madison Larocque called over her shoulder, "We'll give the general and the captain a few more minutes together to get things like war and politics out of their system."

As the distance between the now-separated couples made it so that Dune and Larocque could chat without Madison hearing, the young Aussie sized up the older officer and said, "No worries if I'm outta line, and feel free to tell me to bugger off, but are they moving you to Ottawa to keep an eye on the PM? 'Cause, if you don't mind me saying, you might be the best soldier this country has ever produced, but if there's one thing you're not, it's a bloody politician."

Larocque's lips thinned as he considered the question. Finally, he said, "I don't know what's going on in Ottawa, but my heart and gut are telling me that's where I need to be. Madison would like nothing more than for me to retire and for us and the baby to head back to Manitoba, where Ottawa and the war become far away places."

Dune gently shook his head at the statement and said, "All respect to you, mate, but I don't think retirement in Manitoba is where your head is at."

Larocque nodded at the newly minted officer's statement. "No, no it is not. Madison knows this, of course, so we've made a deal. She stays in Deep River and takes care of Marcel while I ship out to Ottawa and do what I can to make sure we win this war without becoming what we're fighting against. But no matter what, in two years, I'm done. I turn my back on the CAF and Ottawa and focus on raising my son. I won't make the mistake of putting my career ahead of my son like I did Lauren."

On invoking his daughter's name, an unwanted silence joined the conversation.

The death of Larocque's daughter had been a particularly sensitive issue for the two men. For Larocque, of course, the death of his daughter at sixteen was a memory that would haunt him forever.

For Dune, mention of the girl's name brought forward memories of shame. When he had first encountered Larocque, it had been in an MMA octagon, and amid their fight, he offered a cruel word about Larocque's misfortune.

That had been the type of man Dune had been. But with the fighting and the killing and all the time he'd spent with Larocque in just one year, he almost didn't recognize the man he used to be.

Sensing Dune's state, Larocque said, "So I heard a rumor CSOR and a third of JTF-2 is off to Guyana for some super secret meet-up with units from the UK."

"It's no rumor. We leave in five days," Dune replied.

Larocque slapped the younger man's back and, allowing for a big smile to jump onto his face, said, "Five days is more than enough time to enjoy Quebec City. It's a wonderful place for a honeymoon."

"We will enjoy it," Dune said, relieved the conversation had pivoted in a new direction.

"And don't worry about Trisha when you're away. In case you hadn't noticed, Madison is a lioness. She'll make sure she's treated well and has everything she needs here in Petawawa."

"I know she will, sir. She's a good and right sheila, your wife," said Dune.

"She is that," Larocque said, his smile growing at the endearing Aussie term for a woman.

"And for whatever reason they're sending you to Ottawa, I know you'll figure out a way to make a difference for us sods on the frontlines."

A look of sober concern replaced Larocque's smile, and he said, "If you can count on anything, you can count on me doing just that."

***

Somewhere in British Columbia, Canada

—

Sam Petit looked at the woman standing across from him. She was ten years his junior at least, but she carried herself like she was twice her age and had seen way too much of a world that was terrible and cruel.

As her hazel eyes met his brown, he cursed the people he reported to for what they had done to this woman. By rights, her first job should have been sitting in a cubicle somewhere in the depths of the Department of National Defence, DND, working as a junior planning officer for a team of mid-level officers planning some obscure part of the war.

But fate had chosen a different path for Sarah Hall.

Their eyes still connected, she asked, "You ready to get back at it?"

"Why don't you take a break and get out of here? I think we're close, and St. Jacques seems to have a knack for the work," Petit said.

Hall's response was quick and hot, "No. This was my gig from the get-go, and I'm gonna finish it. And as for St. Jacques, in fact, he's not cut out for the work. You can't always play the good cop, Sam. Somebody has to be the bad cop for the good cop angle to work."

"Sarah, you don't have to do this. You've been riding yourself hard ever since Montreal. You can take your foot off the gas.

We're now a hundred people or so. You have to let others do the work or you'll burn out or worse. Everyone has their limits."

Hall's hands moved to her hips, and her eyes narrowed. "Are you ordering me not to go back in there?"

"No," Petit said quickly. "I'm not there yet. I want you to recognize for yourself what's going on. For Christ's sake, think of all you've been through over the past month, never mind the shit you had to endure before that. What, are you even twenty-five yet?"

"Is that what this is about? My age?"

"No," Petit said insistently.

"Then perhaps it's because I'm a woman. Is it the case that women can't do the hard things, Sam?" Hall said.

"You know that's not how I feel." This time, when Petit spoke, there was a touch of heat in his words.

"Then what is it, Sam Petit?"

"It's your humanity, Sarah. You've done twice as much work as anyone else, and every time we walk into a dark room, I worry you're only five minutes away from a crash you'll never recover from. I know you're not a psychopath. What you're doing is eating you up inside, and I for one can't believe Aziz insists on putting you at the tip of the spear. It's not right. And I'm not saying this as the guy in charge. I'm saying it as your friend."

On hearing his final words, Hall's eyes softened, and she took a step in Petit's direction. Lowering her voice, she said, "Thank you for being honest with me, Sam. It's good to know where I stand in your eyes, but I'm fine. Really, I am."

A pensive look on his face, Petit said, "I won't stand by while you destroy yourself."

Hall took another step in his direction and on reaching Petit's personal orbit, she gently placed her hand on his forearm. Leaning forward, she whispered, "We're not friends, Sam. Friends and the emotions that come with them only get in the way of the work that has to be done."

When Petit made no effort to reply to Hall's stone-cold statement, she gestured over her shoulder at the shipping container thirty yards back in the dense forest behind the safehouse and said, "In that box is a woman who can give us the names of half a dozen Chinese agents and we have maybe another hour to get those names before those same agents know she's been compromised. Do I have that right?"

"Yeah, you got that right," Petit replied in a tone that refused to give any indication he'd been taken back by her brush-off.

"And was it not just a month ago that a pair of Chinese submarines sank half of our country's navy here on the West Coast, killing nearly four hundred sailors."

"Yes, but—"

"Don't *but* me," Hall said in a voice that had become heated. "You've missed the memo, Petit, and so has St. Jacques. Our country is on the brink of losing a war, so if you don't mind me saying, my humanity should be the least of your concerns. Your only concern in this moment should be getting results."

When he replied, Petit allowed his words to match her intensity. "I'm not going to let you torture her. It doesn't work. We're going to continue to lean on her hard, but we're not going to resort to torture. I don't care what Aziz's orders are. And if that means at the end of the day, we don't survive as a country, then I guess that's what I'm prepared to do."

As his position on the Chinese agent was made clear, Hall's eyebrows knitted together, giving her face an appearance of sadness. "I'm sorry, Sam. Truly, I am. This will only hurt for a moment."

Hall's eyes moved over his shoulder, and she gave a subtle nod.

Before he could begin to turn around to see what she was looking at, he heard a crackling sound behind him and then felt his body explode into pain as thousands of volts of electricity stormed through his body.

Falling into a heap on the ground, the pain-inducing current of the taser continued for what felt like an eternity. When it finally stopped, he was gasping for breath.

Opening his eyes, Petit looked to where he had last seen Hall, but she had moved. Instead, he heard her voice from behind him. "Bag him and put him with St. Jacques."

With the order given, Petit was grabbed by two pairs of hands, which forced him onto his stomach. Prone, the men above him grabbed at his wrists and wrenched them behind his back. With his muscles still like jelly, he made no effort to resist. Finally, somebody roughly grabbed at his hair, and with his face lifted off the ground, a black hood was reefed across his vision.

As he regained control of his body, a rage began to storm inside him. Yelling, he said, "Are you insane? For Christ's sake, Hall, we're not the Gestapo!"

He heard the crunching of booted feet walking across the gravel as someone moved in his direction. They pulled up their stride only a few feet from his now-shrouded face. Petit heard the rustle of clothing as the person lowered themselves to a knee.

"The people we report to don't think as you do, Sam." It was Hall's voice.

"We face a national emergency like none other in our history. We're not going to let any part of this country become Northern Ireland or the Donbas or whatever scenario the Chinese and UCSA have planned for us. Canada is at war, Sam Petit. For weeks now, I was hoping you'd come to that realization, but you're just too nice. You're just too... Canadian."

Slowly, Hall got back to her feet. "Goodbye, Sam. Hope we don't see each other again."

There was a flurry of sound around him. Without warning, several hands grabbed him and pulled him to his feet. Standing, someone delivered a heavy blow to his gut, driving the air out of his lungs.

Gasping, the hands then started to drag him in the direction of the white cargo van Petit and Hall had arrived in with the Chinese operative.

On reaching the vehicle, Petit felt himself go airborne as he was tossed into the cargo area. Grunting as he careened into something hard, he heard the doors slam shut and felt the van start to move.

After a minute of driving, someone spoke. The man's voice was scratchy and held a strong Québécois accent.

"I'll say this once. Say anything until you're told to speak, and I will put a bullet in the back of your head. And that's not a threat. That's a promise from the powers that be."

From next to Petit, he heard the voice of St. Jacques. "*Esti tabernac.* This is crazy. You guys, we're on the same side, eh? Pull over and I swear to God, this doesn't have to go any further. That soulless bitch you're taking orders from, she's crazy."

"Pull over," said the same man who had warned them to keep their mouths shut.

As the van came to a sudden stop, Petit heard the rustle of movement and then tensed every muscle in his body as he heard the slide and click of a semi-automatic weapon chambering a round.

Beside him, St. Jacques screamed, "Guys, don't! Guys, for Christ's sake, we're on the same side!"

When the gun fired, Petit knew straightaway it was sporting a good-sized suppressor because instead of hearing a deafening crack, his ears only registered a muted thud.

He listened carefully for some type of indication that the man who had been screaming seconds ago was still alive, but all he could perceive was silence.

Without warning, the hood covering his face was ripped away. As light from the afternoon sun dazzled his eyes, he could see a form lying on the van's floor only two feet away.

As his vision resolved, Petit could see it was St. Jacques. The man's eyes were lifeless, and bright red blood was still pumping out of the side of his head.

Petit shifted his vision to take in the man who had just executed the former RCMP tactical officer. Wearing a balaclava that exposed only his eyes, the man was staring back at him with the intensity of someone who had just committed cold-blooded murder.

"And now you know just how serious we are, Sam Petit of 4731 Rue Bélanger."

Petit gave no reaction to the address.

"Your girl. The pretty Haitian. It would be a terrible, terrible shame if something were to happen to her."

Again, he made no reaction to the threat.

"Good, I knew you'd play the game better than this piece of shit," the man said while directing the suppressor of his handgun at St. Jacques.

"We're closing out the second period of the game, Sam and the GM is making some personnel moves. Going into the third, he only wants those players on the team who truly understand what's at stake. You were on the bubble, and today, you finally showed your true colors."

While still staring at Petit, the man directed his next words at the driver. "Get us back on the road. We've got a schedule to keep."

The masked man stepped forward and got on one knee beside Petit. In a quick movement, the opaque hood was roughly drawn back over his head.

As the van started to move, he felt a knee drive into the middle of his back. "Not a word, Petit," the man growled above him. "That's the theme for today and for every day moving forward. You figure that out and you might survive this little cull to live a long and happy life. Choose to be a hero or tell someone – and I mean anyone – about us or what we're doing, and you and that pretty woman of yours end up like St. Jacques. Nod if you understand."

Petit nodded.

"Good," the man on top of him growled.

After one more dig of his knee into Petit's back, the executioner got up and returned to his seat.

Petit had agreed to silence because he needed to survive. He needed to survive so he could get Sabrina to a safe place, and because of what was happening to his country.

A national reckoning was coming. He could feel it in his bones.

As he lay there and listened to the drone of the van's engine, Petit had no doubt he was being spared because of his connection with Merielle Martel. He had saved her life once, and now she was saving his. They were even.

A clean slate meant the next time he encountered Hall or some other White Unit operator, he would be fair game, but he was okay with that.

For weeks, he had watched the White Unit hunt down, abduct and interrogate dozens of people suspected as Chinese, French, or Red Faction intel agents, and while he hadn't seen or participated in any extrajudicial killings, he was sure people were being killed.

As this had gone on, he'd been speaking with the men who were giving him orders about doing things differently. About connecting with CSIS and bringing the White Unit in from the cold. The idea that a rogue intelligence unit could operate long-term in a country like Canada was a dangerous, if not ludicrous, proposition.

He'd even spoken with Aziz. A week ago, over coffee in some mom-and-pop restaurant in the backwaters of the BC interior, he'd pled his case to the former special operations officer.

But now, as the cooling blood from St. Jacques's destroyed body began to seep into his clothing, he knew he'd been naïve. Something had snapped within the psyche of his country, and something had to be done about it.

So, for however many hours, he would stay silent and do what he was told, but once he was cut loose and Sabrina was safe, he was going to blow the whistle on the White Unit, even if that meant destroying his country in the process. Even if it meant he had to take a bullet like St. Jacques.

Someone had to stop Merielle Martel.

Chapter 2

Vietnam, 300 KM Northeast of Ho Chi Minh City

—

For what had to be the thousandth time in the past six hours, Captain Liam Hogan of the 1st New Zealand Special Air Service Regiment brought his binoculars to his eyes to scan the lush green golf course in front of him.

At precisely 1,678 meters, he spied one of the short-range tactical nuclear missile launchers the People's Liberation Army of China had successfully employed only a few weeks earlier to decimate and then roll past the extensive border defenses of the Socialist Republic of Vietnam.

As the Russians had done in Ukraine and the Red Faction Americans had done as recently as two months ago in Washington, D.C., the Chinese Communists, following a new and dangerous international precedent, had employed tactical nuclear weapons to prevent hundreds of thousands of casualties the PLA would have suffered had they invaded Vietnam conventionally.

Hogan and his six-man team had been led to this position by a similar number of Vietnamese recon soldiers from the 429th Commando Brigade, which was based just north of Ho Chi Minh City.

His outfit was one of two dozen Aussie and Kiwi SAS strike teams that had infiltrated in-country to identify and target high-value targets like the Chinese DF-11 road-mobile Short-Range Ballistic Missile.

Armed with low-yield, tactical nuclear warheads and high-explosive conventional munitions, these were the very same platforms that had devastated Vietnam's border defenses only a few weeks earlier.

Hogan's Battlefield Asset Management, or BAM, began to speak in the lone earbud he wore in his right ear.

Hogan had set the voice of his BAM to the still-stunning Sofía Vergara. "Incoming call from Raider 3," the perfectly synthesized Latina voice announced.

Raider 3 was Sergeant Steve Rigby. Even in the SAS, the man's bushcraft was legendary.

He'd sent the man forward to get as close as possible to the PLA units guarding the two missile launchers. "Accept the call," Hogan replied to the BAM's near-AI comms software.

"Boss, we have a problem. I've got eyes on a pair of trucks that just arrived. Hyenas are being unloaded, and they're going active."

"How many?"

"At least eight. No, make that ten. They're the hunter-killer versions."

Seconds later, Rigby added, "Hold one, Raider, something else has arrived."

Impatiently, Hogan waited for the sergeant to continue with his update. After a full minute went by, he couldn't stand it anymore and said, "Raider 3, report, mate."

Thirty seconds later, the SAS sergeant's update arrived in a careful whisper, "Wraiths, four of them. They're looking straight at me. Jesus, they're mean-looking things."

Not good, thought Hogan. The arrival of the four-legged and bi-pedal near-AI automatons changed the situation and dramatically so.

Hogan and every other special ops soldier had read the reports of the effectiveness of these killing machines in the hours after the Chinese nuclear strikes.

While radiation from the tactical nukes had made the various Vietnamese strong points along the border untouchable for China's human soldiers, it had not impeded the estimated two thousand Hyenas and Wraiths from crossing the border and wreaking havoc. Not in the least.

While Vietnam's frontline soldiers reeled from the nuclear bombardment and tried to consolidate themselves, the Chinese automatons stormed forward to seize key territory and create havoc among the surviving Vietnamese army regiments as they tried to organize a fallback.

Armored, bristling with weapons, smart, and programmed with the ability to differentiate between frontline soldiers and their officers, the units had unleashed an unyielding slaughter that only ended when the Chinese themselves had ordered the killbots to stand down.

If Hogan had to guess, it looked like these same units were now being deployed to protect the high-value targets that he and his fellow commandos had been neutralizing over the past four days. Not good.

"Raider 3, pull back," Hogan said quietly.

"Boss, I've got eyes on these things. I'm like a bug in a rug up here and..."

"Negative, Steve. You've seen the same reports I have. These things are like goddamned bloodhounds. If you stay where you're at, mate, they'll find you, and then we're buggered. Get out of there now. That's an order."

"Roger that, Raider," said Rigby, his voice sounding relieved. "Ex-filing now...wait, shit, a pair of the Hyenas are headed my way. They're making a beeline to my position. Jesus, the bloody things move fast."

"Steve, get out of there now," Hogan said as loud as he dared.

In the distance, Hogan heard an extended barrage of automatic gunfire.

Seconds later, the Latina voice of his BAM advised clinically, "The heart rate of team member Raider 3 has gone critical."

"Shit," Hogan said aloud.

"I do not understand that command?" the BAM replied.

"Patch in access to Raider 3's body cam, authorization Hogan-Romeo-Niner."

"Access granted," replied the BAM.

Hogan's eyes moved to his wrist to take up the screen of the oversized watch all CANZUK soldiers wore as part of the standard BAM kit.

Every frontline soldier wore two cameras on their person. One on their chest rig, the other on their helmet. Hogan selected Rigby's helmet cam, and through the camera's mic, he could hear the SAS sergeant's labored breaths.

Out of the dense bush perhaps twenty meters away, one of the X-5 Hyenas emerged and slinked its way into the small clearing Rigby occupied.

The green-and-brown pattern of the four-legged machine's exterior was a perfect match to the Vietnamese bush. The auto-turret on its back was pointed toward the wounded commando. The BAM's high-def camera caught the bright green targeting laser as soon as it started to emit from the turret on the Hyena's back. For a long moment, it danced across the image being captured by Rigby's helmet cam.

A flash of light burst from the Hyena's primary weapon. From his position, Hogan heard the sound of a single shot echo through the trees of the jungle.

"Raider 3's heart rate has gone terminal," advised his BAM.

"Shut off the connection with Raider 3."

"Connection severed."

"Connect me with Jupiter, priority designation, Hogan-Zulu-Six."

"Call connecting in three, two, one..."

"Jupiter, this is Raider Sunray. Our position has been compromised. We are ex-filing to rendezvous point Alpha-Bravo. What's the ETA on the delivery of your package?"

"Raider Sunray, the package has been delayed. Enemy air units have saturated your quadrant."

"You don't say, Jupiter. Nice of you to pass that along," Hogan snapped, doing nothing to keep the anger he was feeling out of his voice.

He felt a firm hand on his shoulder and turned his head to take in Staff Sergeant Watene, his 2IC for this mission. "Boss, those things are coming our way and quick-like. We think they have a bead on us."

Hogan cut the connection with the Australian special ops outfit coordinating the air strikes and Tomahawks for the Aussie and British nuclear boats lurking somewhere in the waters off Vietnam's coastline.

"Right, call in the lads and —."

Before Hogan could finish his order, a torrent of automatic gunfire erupted from the direction of the Chinese launch vehicles.

Except for the now-dead Rigby, each of his men was paired off with one of the Vietnamese commandos who had guided them to this location. At two o'clock from his position, he could hear the deeper-sounding chatter of the lone machine gun one of the Vietnamese soldiers had lugged with him.

Hogan activated his BAM, "All Raiders, with your locals, move to rally point Charlie. Now, people!"

"Boss, what about Rigby?" the burly SAS Māori commando asked, his face concerned. The big native Kiwi had been tight with the sergeant.

Before Hogan could give his reply, there was a loud crashing and snapping of the bush to his right. Together, he and Watene raised their Heckler and Koch 416s, pointed them toward the sound and waited.

From a wall of thick green jungle not fifteen meters away, a sci-fi nightmare slowly emerged.

With a wicked-looking rifle much too large for any normal-sized soldier wedged into its shoulder, the Chinese X-8 Wraith stopped its movement as its targeting system assessed the two humans standing before it.

At seven feet tall and lanky in form, the mottled black, green, and brown machine lowered its weapon slightly, then spoke English with an accent that wouldn't have been out of place in Britain's House of Lords.

"Enemy combatants, drop your weapons and surrender, or you will be terminated. This is your only warning."

Staff Sergeant Robbie Watene, 33 years old, a nine-year veteran of Level 2 rugby, a five-year man of the New Zealand SAS, and a bloke who didn't back down to anyone for any reason, didn't utter a word in the direction of the machine that had just addressed the two Kiwi commandos.

Instead, he opened up on full auto with his weapon, but before a third of his magazine had been expended, the Wraith's rifle levelled off at the staff sergeant and issued a burst of fire.

Hogan's head snapped to his left as the high-caliber rounds passed through Watene's body armor and drove the big man half a dozen feet backward onto the ground.

In Hogan's ear, the voice of his BAM advised him what he already knew. Staff Sergeant Watene was dead.

His eyes darted back to the Wraith. It was now only ten meters away, and its weapon was pointed squarely at his chest. Again, it spoke. "Drop your weapon and surrender, or you will be terminated."

Furious at the death of his two mates, Hogan did not comply.

Instead, the SAS officer threw down his rifle, and as though he was on a rugby field, he dodged right and left in the direction of the machine, and as he did so, his free hand went for one of the two grenades on his chest rig.

On his third jog to the right, he felt his right shoulder explode in pain as one of the rounds from the Wraith's assault rifle achieved a glancing blow.

Now stumbling, Hogan dove to the feet of the near-AI monster. On hitting the ground, he lowered his shoulder, tucked his head in, and executed a roll that brought him underneath the still-firing weapon of the auto.

Adrenaline coursing through him, the activated grenade still in hand, Hogan wrapped up his foe in a perfectly executed tackle and, with every ounce of strength he could muster, lifted the machine off its feet and drove them both to the ground.

When they made contact with the floor of the Vietnamese jungle, Hogan felt his left forearm snap under the weight of the Wraith. As he screamed in agony, he forced himself to concentrate on the F-1 fragmentation grenade still in his right hand.

Without warning, the Wraith rolled so that it was now on top of him. For a brief moment, Hogan's eyes stared into the largest of the three optical sensors that ran vertically along its face.

As he lodged the grenade into the space where the Wraith's hip connected with its torso, he bellowed, "Just another cheap Chinese knock-off. Die, you bastard!"

No sooner than the words left his mouth, the Wraith violently pushed itself upward.

Rolling onto his stomach, Hogan heard the crack of the grenade and felt a stab of pain in his buttocks as shrapnel tore into his flesh.

Rolling over again, he looked in the direction of where he had last seen his opponent. The Wraith was gone. As quick as he could, he used his good arm to push himself up so he could better survey the immediate area.

Ten feet or so away, he found the torso of the automaton. Its head was still attached, but the robot's legs were nowhere to be seen.

Gritting his teeth, Hogan began to get to his feet, but as he did so, his still-ringing ears managed to catch the sound of movement behind him.

Slowly, he turned, and through the same wall of jungle the first Wraith had burst through only a minute earlier, two more autos stepped into the clearing.

Hogan squared himself off to face his new opponents. As he did so, he strained to hear the sound of nearby fighting.

He and Watene had been caught flat-footed. It was his hope of hopes the rest of his men, along with their Vietnamese counterparts, had been able to extricate themselves from this disaster.

He couldn't hear any gunfire, but that didn't mean his lads hadn't survived.

His men. The SAS of the New Zealand Defence Force were some of the best-trained and toughest fighting men in the world. If anyone could survive this inhuman onslaught, it would be this group of tough-as-nails blokes.

"Enemy combatant, surrender, or you will be terminated. This is your only warning." The order was delivered in the same annoying posh English accent.

"A word, mate?" Hogan called out.

When neither of the Wraiths responded, he kept going. "That accent you blokes have is bloody rubbish. Seriously, if you're hoping us and the Aussies might be keen on buying whatever it is you're flogging, you can't go around sounding like the wankers who ran the show for the first third of our respective histories. It's just not on."

While delivering his unsolicited advice, he slowly moved his right hand in the direction of the Gen 5 Glock 17 in the drop holster on his right thigh.

As he made contact with the grip of the weapon, the two hunter-killers took a step forward, and from each of their assault rifles, a green targeting laser flared to life.

Hogan risked a quick look downward. A pair of green dots held inhumanly still at the center of his chest. Despite the pain and fear coursing through him, Hogan felt a surge of tremendous satisfaction.

As he'd done his whole life, he had done the very best he could and had managed to destroy one of the Chinese monsters.

With this feat captured by his BAM's body cam and transmitted back to the people who could do something with the information, he was at peace with what he was to do next.

As quick as he could, he moved to draw his sidearm, but before the Glock could begin to release from its holster, he felt his chest explode with a level of pain that dwarfed his earlier injuries.

Somehow, through the excruciating pain, Hogan felt himself stagger, then slam back-first onto the jungle floor.

As spots began to crawl across his vision, his two executioners interrupted his view of the placid late afternoon sky. Standing over him, each Wraith pointed the barrel of its rifle at his head.

On seeing targeting lasers begin to emit from each weapon, Hogan closed his eyes and said a brief prayer.

With his final breath, Captain Liam Hogan of the New Zealand Army opened his eyes and uttered, "Record this and pass it along. Whoever made you two spawns, I hope you go straight to hell."

Neither of the two autos replied to the statement. Instead, for the briefest moment, Hogan felt a shock of terrible pain and then nothing.

Chapter 3

The Yellow Sea

—

For the past sixteen hours, HMAS *Perth,* the third oldest of ten nuclear submarines of the Royal Australian Navy, had quietly worked its way to where it needed to be twenty-five kilometers off the coast of the Province of Shandong in Northwest China.

War or no war, on every day of the year, the Yellow Sea was one of the busiest bodies of water on the planet.

Situated between China's northeastern industrial heartland, the Koreas to the East, and Japan only a few hundred kilometers beyond the divided peninsula, this small enclave of the Pacific Ocean was teeming with vessels of every kind.

Small fishing boats, each doing their part to reduce the Yellow Sea's already endangered fishing stocks, numbered in the thousands, while the regional bulk carriers that moved the raw industrial inputs of China's economy were represented in the hundreds.

In smaller numbers were the gigantic international freighters and tankers that either exported China's endless finished products to markets across the globe or imported the oil and gas the communists needed to keep its gigantic economy driving forward.

Sixteen hours ago, the *Perth* received a message from the Royal Australian Navy high command that war between CANZUK and the geopolitical titan that was China had officially broken out.

Had she been asked by the admirals about the timing of the war, Captain Tessa Spann would have strongly advised that the RAN's submarine force should have been hunting down every Chinese naval asset in the Pacific the moment CANZUK had confirmed China had been the country that had attacked Canada's Westcoast navy weeks earlier.

Perhaps if they had started to eliminate Chinese vessels in the dozens, including those transporting their precious oil, China would have thought twice about storming Vietnam's northern border.

Whatever the reason, sinking Chinese navy and merchant marine vessels had not been her orders. Instead, the *Perth* had been stalking potential targets and gathering intelligence for the undeclared special forces mission evolving over the past two weeks in Vietnam.

But something had changed in the past 24 hours. What that change had been did not interest Spann. The only thing that mattered to her was that her boat and her crew had finally been given orders to take the war to the Chinese.

"Helm, bring us to a depth of ten meters."

"Aye, Captain. Bringing us to a depth of ten meters."

"Sonar, how are we looking?"

"Clear, Captain. There's a small flotilla of trawlers nine klicks east of us. Local time is 0420 hours."

"And subsurface?"

"Negative readings. If something is out there, they're doing a hell of a job to stay hidden. As best we can tell, there's no one in the neighbourhood."

In 2023, the Chinese navy had lost a sub in these same waters because it had gotten caught in an anti-submarine trap set to catch and destroy vessels like the *Perth*.

In the decade since the tragic accident, when fifty-five sailors had lost their lives, the Chinese had reduced their submarine patrols in the shallow waters of the Yellow Sea and had compensated by increasing the number of surface vessels and air assets that patrolled this congested part of the Pacific.

That the *Perth's* passive sonar was not picking up any of the patrol boats or corvettes that usually saturated these waters was not lost on her. Something was amiss. She knew it, and so did her crew.

"Weapons, be ready to launch the first salvo on my mark," Spann announced.

"Aye, Captain. The first salvo is ready to launch on your mark."

"XO, extend the communications mast. Let's have our last check-in." Quickly, she added, "When the message comes in, it is for our ears only."

"Aye, Captain. Comms mast being raised. Comms for our ears only," replied Spann's second-in-command.

With practiced efficiency, her XO manipulated the area of the ops table where he was standing, and within a few seconds, the *Perth's* near-AI said for all to hear, "Communication mast deployed. Incoming message received."

"Lower comms mast," Spann ordered.

"Aye, Captain. Comms mast is descending."

In her left ear, through the earbud that was ever present, *Perth's* communications software advised that a queued-up message was waiting.

"Play message," she said quietly.

As Spann listened to the update to her orders, her eyes connected with her XO. A solid bloke, if there ever was one, he made no outward reaction to the information they had both just heard.

The *Adelaide* and the *Newcastle-Maitland*, both City-Class nuclear boats, had been sunk. Like the *Perth*, they had been sent into the Yellow Sea to execute a series of cruise missile strikes deep into China's less protected hinterlands.

Despite the loss of the other two strategically critical and hugely expensive nuclear submarines, the message from RAN high command had been crystal clear. Proceed with the mission.

Without any outward indication of the news she and her XO had just received, Spann stepped toward the table-like display surrounded by the officers who would help her fight the boat she'd commanded for the past two and a half years.

Hands behind her back, she slipped into the sliver of space kept free for her at all times.

Looking down at the tactical display that was the nerve center for the sub's operations, she unclasped her hands, reached down, and pressed a large green square at the top right section of the display for her exclusive use.

As soon as her finger touched the screen's surface, a gentle female voice advised in her ear, "Vessel-wide comms channel open."

"Crew of the *Perth*, this is your Captain. We have positioned ourselves approximately twenty-five kilometers off the coast of Shandong province of China. Within the next minute, we will unleash the first of six salvos of our Tomahawks at four different targets in the province of Xi'An.

"In our effort to successfully put ourselves in a position to strike into the depths of our enemies' northern high-tech heartland, we're many kilometers from help. Nevertheless, we will fulfill our duty and make Australia proud. Together, we will win the day. That is all."

Her finger again pressed the green square, shutting down the connection. She then turned her head left and said in a clear voice, "Weapons, fire the first salvo on my mark."

Silently, Spann counted to five and then, in a calm and firm voice, said, "Mark."

Immediately, at his station, the weapons officer manipulated the screen before him. Perhaps two seconds later, she heard and felt the first of the American-built Mark V Tomahawk cruise missiles eject from the six launch tubes at the fore of her boat.

Thirty seconds later, the weapons officer confirmed the first salvo of missiles was away.

"Excellent. Advise me when salvo two is ready."

Five tense minutes later, the weapons officer announced, "The second salvo is ready, Captain."

"Weapons, fire the second salvo on my mark," Spann said, her voice still calm.

"Captain, we have a fish in the water." The urgent-sounding update came from her top man at Sonar.

"Report," Spann ordered, her voice sharp.

"It's bearing in on us 145 degrees. Speed 37 knots. Range, 2.1 kilometers. It had to be from the air, Captain. The data caught a splashdown right before the fish's engine kicked in."

"Does it have us?" Spann demanded.

"No, Captain. Its onboard sonar is actively searching, but it doesn't have us yet."

Suddenly, the sonar tech's right hand grabbed his headphone. Spann had worked long enough with the talented younger officer to know that critical data was about to come her way.

The lieutenant pulled his gaze from his station and locked his eyes onto Spann's. "Captain, two of the trawlers east of us have broken away and are making speed in our direction. They're moving fast. Real fast."

"Then they're not trawlers," Spann said in response to the new information.

"No, Ma'am, based on their engine signature, they're fast attack boats. It's a good bet they were riding in a saddle on the back of the trawlers."

"Range?" Spann asked.

"Just under nine klicks. At their speed, they'll be in range in just over seven minutes."

Another of the sonar techs spoke up. "We have another splashdown. It's three klicks to starboard. Preliminary data suggests it's an AHK, Porpoise-class."

Spann gritted her teeth. Controlled by a top-of-line near-AI, the Porpoise-class Autonomous Hunter Killer submersible, with its three onboard torpedoes and a powerful sonar suite, had just jumped to the top of her threat list.

"Weapons, fire the second salvo, now!"

"Aye, Captain. Tomahawks are ready to go. Firing now."

The sonar tech called out with another update. "Captain, the first torpedo has a lock on us. It's accelerating. It's now tracking at 53 knots. It'll be on us in just under two minutes."

For a brief moment, Spann canvassed the ops room with an intense gaze.

Every one of her people was focused on doing their job. This was the real deal, and while she hadn't practiced a scenario precisely like this before, every captain of a RAN submarine had to pass an intense crucible of training that would ensure they had the skills and know-how to survive the type of challenge she was now confronting.

"Weapons, I want the AHK targeted. Fire two torpedoes ASAP," Spann said and then snapped out another directive, "Countermeasures, release two Pixies when that first torpedo is sixty seconds out and not a second sooner."

"Aye, Captain," the lead officer at the countermeasures station replied promptly.

"Helm, the instant the last of the Tomahawks leaves the boat, get us down to thirty meters and get us out of here, extraction route Delta-Lima."

To her left, one of the other officers sitting at weapons said, "Captain, the last Tomahawk is away."

Spann's head snapped toward the *Perth's* helmsman, "Helm, get us out of here!"

The petty officer manning the sub's drive controls didn't acknowledge Spann's directive. Instead, she only felt the floor underneath her move suddenly. Grabbing for the operations table, she steadied herself as the last of the five Virginia Class submarines the Australians had purchased from the Americans under the AUKUS agreement began to knife through the water.

"Captain, the AHK has launched two of its torpedoes, and another torpedo has splashed down from the air. Both of the AHK's fish have acquired us."

On hearing the news, Spann's eyes met her XO's. They'd worked together for two years. They didn't have to exchange words. He only delivered to her the slightest of nods, confirming what she already knew — they were up to their necks in shit and were still sinking.

A distant boom suddenly enveloped the *Perth*.

Tearing her gaze from her XO, Spann looked down at the tactical screen. The first torpedo that had been set on them had disappeared. The Pixie countermeasures had done their job.

She ordered the release of four more anti-torpedo units to intercept the two torpedoes that had a lock on them from the AHK.

"Captain!" the cry had come from her man at sonar.

"Report," Spann barked.

"Enemy sub, bearing down on us at 047 degrees."

"How far?"

"Four klicks. It should be on your screen now. It's a Yuan class, diesel-electric. She's in an all-out sprint."

Looking down at the tactical display, she saw the enemy boat appear in the form of a flashing orange triangle. It had been waiting in the shallows.

"Weapons, as soon as the two fast attack boats are in range, unload with two torpedoes each. Let's give them something to worry about before they can get their torps in the water. We have the advantage of range."

"Aye, Captain. We've got them pegged. They'll be in range in another minute."

Another explosive reverberation slammed into the *Perth*, only this time the detonation was much closer. One of the two Pixies had claimed a victim, but the second and final torpedo from the

AHK had managed to survive and was still knifing through the water in their direction.

"Release countermeasures," Spann ordered, her voice tight.

Moments later, the senior tech at the sonar station reported, "The incoming fish didn't take the bait. Range four hundred meters and closing. Impact in twelve seconds."

Spann ignored the update. "Weapons, are those two fast attack boats in range?"

"Aye, Captain. Just."

"Then fire torpedoes," Spann ordered.

"Incoming fish at one hundred meters, Captain. Contact in six, five, four, three..."

When the Chinese Y-11 lightweight torpedo impacted the stern of the Australian submarine, the equivalent force of 243 pounds of TNT shredded through the compartment that contained the *Perth*'s nuclear reactor, which in turn produced a cascade of intense secondary explosions that ripped through the rest of the vessel instantly killing all aboard.

In the moment before its death, as it was programmed to do, the near-AI of the *Perth* released a buoy to the surface of the Yellow Sea to let the Royal Australian Navy know that it had just lost another of its ten City-Class nuclear-powered submarines.

***

Beijing

The President of China had always been an early riser. Without fail for the past three decades, his body awoke at 3:45 am.

So long as Yan's body got five hours of sleep, he could tackle each of his working days with the vigor of a much younger man.

It was this need for little sleep and his work ethic that had got him to the top of the ruthless political heap that was the Chinese Communist Party.

He had assumed power five years ago at the tender age of 55, an unheard-of achievement in a country where, except for Mao, each of China's leaders had been well into their sixties when they had assumed the presidency.

Without question, the decision to embrace the youth and the energy of Yan's leadership had been the right decision for the country.

Five years ago, China, more than ever, needed a leader who understood artificial intelligence and algorithms and had the know-how and connections to manage the vast and complex bureaucracy that pitilessly administered the country.

Yan, both a business titan and a CCP stalwart, had both of these skill sets.

He had been president only a year when the United States started to tear itself apart.

His country's invasion of Taiwan had come two months after the nuclear destruction of America's greatest cities. With the horror of millions of American deaths consuming news outlets and social media, China's brutal and perfectly executed invasion of Taiwan had been barely noticed.

Except in China, of course.

The final, glorious unification of the great Motherland had been a monumental achievement. An event so magnificent it would cement Yan's power for the next decade and his legacy for the next ten generations, if not longer.

No sooner had the Taiwanese victory been consummated than he had immediately set to the task of securing China's place in the world for the next hundred years.

With the American economy in shambles and China's male population furious at their inability to find a partner and start a family, Yan and much of the CCP leadership concluded that China must do what the Europeans, the British, and the Americans had done over the past three hundred years. Build an empire. An empire that would serve China's needs well into the next century, and if done properly for the century after that.

As empire building went, the first and most important objective of their effort would be to bolster China's ailing economy.

The Americans had been the epitome of this principle. From its invasion of Haiti in 1915 through to its intervention in Ukraine, the US economy had ridden the broad and strong back of the US war machine to unprecedented growth.

Starting with Vietnam, China would do the same.

And just as invasion would keep China's industrial base firing on all cylinders, the spoils of war would help to succor the discontent that millions of Chinese men held as it pertained to their chances for domestic bliss.

At last count, China had a surplus of thirty million men between the ages of 18 and 45. It was a demographic powder keg just waiting to explode.

Conquering countries like Vietnam, Laos, and even Indonesia wouldn't completely address the demographic situation his country was facing, but it would get them closer to where they needed to be.

Even if they could only find wives for five million of these desperate souls, Yan could look his people in the eye and honestly say that he'd done the best he could.

That would be enough. Of that, he was supremely confident.

But before any of this could happen, there was the small problem of this CANZUK outfit.

Unsurprisingly, the Australians and their pissant cousins, the New Zealanders, had decided that Vietnam would be the place where they would make their stand on continental Asia.

While the Kiwis were a non-factor militarily, this was not the case with the Aussies. As a much younger man, Yan had taken an interest in that country and had even spent time there while he worked for China's foreign intelligence service.

The Australians, all alone in their part of the world, had rightly seen the threat that China was and had armed itself accordingly. Size-wise, there was no comparison between China and the former colony of Britain, but in those areas where the Aussies could develop a strategic relationship or a technological advantage, the country had made many of the right investments.

Investments he and his generals were now determined to take off the board.

The People's Liberation Army could easily handle an Australian army division, whether it was in Vietnam or Cambodia. It was their air force and navy that were the problem. A problem that had grown significantly in the past week with the arrival of *HMS Queen Elizabeth* and the rest of her task force. In another week, a Canadian flotilla would be added to their enemy's numbers.

All together, it wasn't an insignificant force.

It was with all this information that Yan sat down at precisely 0530 hours to receive his first briefing from his generals on their plans to draw in and engage the CANZUK naval assets operating in the waters across Southeast Asia.

He had been delighted with the Army's efforts to root out CANZUK's special forces operating in Vietnam.

They hadn't caught all of them, but enough of their vaunted SAS soldiers had been found and executed to drive home the point that CANZUK's efforts to stand in the way of China would be costly and ultimately futile.

"Mr. President, first, I'm pleased to report that our efforts to hunt down and eliminate CANZUK's forces on the ground in Vietnam have continued to produce results. Since our last conversation, we believe we've captured or killed another six teams of SAS commandos," said General Wu Dezhi, the Chief of Staff of the Joint Staff Department of the Central Military Commission of the People's Liberation Army.

The general, knowing how Yan liked his briefings and knowing full well this conversation was to focus on the threat posed by CANZUK's naval assets, didn't dwell on the success.

In his typical monotone, the country's most senior military officer continued. "In the past four hours, Australian and British submarines and ships launched a series of cruise missile strikes on the Motherland. As the strikes were expected, the damage sustained was minimal, with a few key exceptions.

"In total, over the past four hours, CANZUK submarines and ships launched 314 Tomahawk cruise missiles at 47 different targets. As expected, most strikes focused on trying to hamper our peacekeeping operation in Vietnam."

"The exceptions, General?" As the question left his mouth, Yan injected a degree of curtness into his words. Quickly, he added, "And three-hundred-plus missile strikes greatly exceeds the number I had been told to expect."

Nodding respectfully, Wu said calmly, "The exceptions. Of course, Mr. President.

"In the south, our naval base in Zhangjian suffered multiple strikes. Half a dozen ships and one submarine in dry dock were lost. The damage to the base will have a moderate impact on naval operations in this part of the country for several weeks. I regret to report that our missile defenses in this part of the country did not perform to our expectation."

"But it's hardly a catastrophic loss?" Yan interjected.

"I agree, Mr. President. We shall shift resources and people quickly. We have contingencies for this very kind of scenario."

Yan leaned forward in his chair and glared at the old man sitting across from him. "What else? I know how you operate, General. Without fail, you save the worst news for last. On this occasion, you will rearrange the order of things. Give me the bad news. Now."

The sixty-something military man's lips thinned slightly. It was a rare emote for a man who otherwise gave zero indication of what he was thinking.

On observing the other man's tell, Yan said, "Tell me, General. Tell me now. Hold nothing back, or else I will become displeased."

"Xi'An, Mr. President. They were able to strike a couple of its factories. Regretfully, I'm advised they'll be offline for several weeks, if not months. We're still looking at the details of how one of their submarines got within range —."

The palm of Yan's hand slammed down onto the ancient table, cutting off the general mid-sentence. Wu, unflappable as always, maintained his face as though it were weathered stone.

His voice nearing a yell, Yan said, "General, you told me just last week that our factories in Xi'An were safe, and now you tell me they're not. We specifically put the automaton manufacturing in this location to prevent our enemies from damaging this critical capability. And now, in the first days of starting a war with a new enemy, you tell me they've been taken out for weeks, if not months. I trust you have answers as to how this happened?"

That Yan could send the old man to a prison camp or worse didn't seem to impact Wu's relaxed demeanor in these meetings. Like the veteran soldier he was, he just endured Yan's wrath whenever it came. "I have preliminary answers, Mr. President. The regional commander of coastal defenses in the Northeast sector elected to employ a passive defensive posture instead of an active one.

"In hindsight, it was the wrong call. Under questioning, the admiral confessed that he didn't think the Australians would risk sending one of their subs into the Yellow Sea, never mind so close to the coast that they could strike somewhere like Xi'An."

Yan snapped at the explanation. "Well, the man was a fool. I trust he's been relieved of his command?"

"Yes, Mr. President. Relieved and then shot," Wu said as though he was relating his score from his latest round of golf.

Yan nodded casually at the update.

Despite Yan's approval of summary execution by Wu and a handful of other generals, he realized that the misuse of this particular authority could do more harm than good to the rank and file of the military. But not in this case. A message needed to be sent. Gross negligence of this kind would not be tolerated in this new war with the West.

Vexation now gone from his voice, Yan asked, "I trust we made the Australians pay for this outrage?"

"We did, Mr. President," replied Wu. "Three of their City-Class nuclear submarines have been sunk."

Yan vigorously nodded and said, "Three. That's significant. This will be seen as a massive blow by the Australian people."

"Indeed, it will be Mr. President. They can't afford to lose more of these platforms lest they be unable to defend Australia itself."

Pleased by the news, Yan leaned forward in his chair and said, "And the planned strike on our enemy's homeland? The loss of capacity in Xi'an is hardly a reason for us to delay. In fact, it only reinforces the need for Operation *Shé Shí Zhě*. I trust all is ready?"

As always, Wu's façade was devoid of emotion when he replied. "All is ready, Mr. President. All we need to make Operation Snake Eater a reality is your order to make it so. We are ready to teach the people of Australia that war has consequences beyond their young people dying in far-off places,"

On hearing the general's assessment, a look of delight appeared on Yan's face. "I agree wholeheartedly. You have my permission to carry out the operation, General. This outrageous strike on our homeland cannot go unpunished. It is well past time we finally teach this arrogant Anglo alliance a lesson about how war will be conducted in a world where China is the predominant power."

Chapter 4

New South Wales, 100 KM South of Sydney

In the opinion of Fan Zhong, the toughest part of the operation was over.

In the early morning hours, he and his men had overseen the transfer of fifty automaton units from a specially designed compartment that had been built into one of the latest versions of the PLA Navy's Shang-class submarines.

Using a couple of barges his small team had rented from a company in Sydney, between the hours of 0200 and 0300, they had managed to unload two companies of X-8 Wraiths onto the barges and then disembark them at a secluded boat ramp two hundred kilometers south of Australia's largest city.

On shore, and with zero prompting or assistance from his men, each of the fifty units silently marched into the trailers of two Tesla autonomous semis his team had also secured.

As he watched the near-AI machines stalk through the moonlight, he marvelled at the combination that was their technology and firepower.

Most of the seven-foot-high robots carried hefty-looking rifles, but others carried things that looked like oversized shotguns or didn't carry a weapon at all. Instead, perhaps every seventh unit or so had various-sized 'packages' attached to their armored exterior.

In some cases, he suspected the added components were for communications or electronic warfare, but for others, Zhong had no idea what their purpose might be.

In truth, he did not care so long as the units performed as well in Sydney as they had in the jungles of Vietnam. By all accounts, the Wraiths and their four-legged brethren, the X-5 Hyenas, had been a complete surprise to CANZUK.

A surprise Zhong hoped continued to play out in the coming hours.

Despite the death toll that Australian and New Zealand special forces had experienced in the jungles of northern Vietnam, security forces here in Australia hadn't taken any steps to enhance the security of their VIPs or harden any of the physical locations where their leaders might gather.

Clearly, the cabal of arrogant and soft elites that ran this country and the other nations of the CANZUK alliance did not understand they were fighting a new kind of war.

The combination of tactical nuclear weapons and the wide-scale use of illegal autonomous hunter-killer robots was a new calculation the Australians and their allies had not yet made sense of.

But this had always been the central weakness of democracies. Rules. Human rights, the Geneva Conventions, the Rules of the Sea, the non-proliferation of nuclear weapons.

To their continual detriment, democracies treated these concepts or agreements as though they were god-like truisms that countries like China had to follow.

But China was not beholden to the West or its ideas. China was its own country and a powerful one. It made its own rules.

Tonight, his government, through people like him, would correct the imbecilic and naïve notions of the people of Australia and the pathetic alliance to which they belonged.

In the coming hours, the Wraiths would lay down the one and only truth that mattered in today's modern and fast-moving world. Strength.

The kind of strength the United States had exercised across the globe until the start of their second civil war. Now, it was China's turn. For the next one hundred years at least, it would be the strength of China that dominated the four corners of the world.

And there was nothing and nobody who would be able to stop them.

***

Downtown Sydney

—

"Crikey, can you believe this, Nicki? If I've said it once, I've said it a million times, we should've never let these things into the city without a driver," said the cop with the greying hair.

"Oi, and would you look at that, here comes another one!" he said again, pointing further down Willoughby Street where another of the battery-powered rigs had just turned the corner.

Leading Senior Constable Nicki Glass of the New South Wales Police Force watched as the oldest, but still very excitable member of the team she had been assigned to lead marched in the direction of the first Tesla Semi with arms gesticulating in the air.

A perfectly capable police officer, Glass watched and listened to her colleague unnecessarily bellow at the massive vehicle. While it was autonomous, Tesla hadn't given the machines the capacity to listen or carry on a conversation with the police should the need arise.

In his mid-fifties, Senior Constable Jimmy MacFarlane would never grow comfortable with the idea that cars – or in this case, a colossal semi-truck – could drive and navigate themselves across a major urban center like Sydney.

Positioning himself in front of the huge machine, MacFarlane was determined to make the autonomous semi-truck come to a stop.

"Jimmy!" Glass hollered as the nearly retired police officer finally took a breath to stop yelling at the Tesla.

As MacFarlane finally looked in her direction, she said, "Take a picture of the serial number on the door. We'll need that to talk to whoever owns this thing. Clearly, they didn't get the message that this part of downtown is off limits."

As the older cop waved his hand in the air acknowledging her request, Glass turned to one of the other nine officers standing by the road barrier she was in charge of and called out, "Brit, call this in and ask them to send a car or two of those brutes from the TOU."

With Australia now effectively at war with China and with CANZUK defence ministers gathering at Kirribilli House as a show of unity, the entirety of the Tactical Operations Unit of the NSW Police Force had been called in to shore up the security of this small but historic peninsula that jutted into Sydney Harbour.

"Will do, boss," the junior officer said as she moved to grab her radio.

Glass shifted her eyes to another pair of officers. "Danh and Simms, you're with me. Let's go give old man MacFarland a hand before he has a stroke. The rest of you lot, stay put and keep your wits about. I don't wanna hear any crap from the TOU saying we weren't looking the part."

By the time she was halfway to MacFarlane, she had been flanked by the two officers she'd called for. Glass had specified these two men because of the weapons they had been assigned. Danh, a third-generation Vietnamese-Australian, was carrying a Benelli Nova Tactical Pump Action Shotgun, while Simms, an entirely humorless Kiwi transplant, had a Colt M4 cradled in his arms.

On reaching MacFarlane, he was in the middle of taking a picture of the serial number displayed on the door of the gleaming white semi's cab.

As she pulled in beside the still-muttering older officer, Glass gestured to the back end of the Tesla's trailer and, looking at Danh and Simms, said, "You two, circle round and have a good look. Chances are these things got the wrong coordinates and are lost, but they're here now, so we might as well have a little walkabout."

Before either of the two cops could confirm her order, the huge left door of the semi's trailer swung open hard enough that it connected with the trailer's side, causing a loud bang that caught the attention of all four officers.

Instantly, Danh and Simms shouldered their respective weapons and pointed them in the direction of the trailer door that was now swinging back to where it had come from.

To her right, Glass saw MacFarlane step forward and place himself between her and the far end of the trailer. Slowly, he drew his service pistol, a Glock 22, and assumed a shooter's stance.

For her part, Glass reached for the radio handset clipped to her shoulder and activated it. "This is Glass of Team 6 at Elamang and Willoughby. Where's that TOU backup we called for? It needs to be here, like right bloody now. Please advise."

Glass didn't register the reply. Instead, her brain strained to focus on the thing that stepped out from behind the trailer's back end.

In the years just before the US civil war had started, human-looking robots had proliferated in large numbers into various industries and service sectors in the US, primarily in California. She had watched hundreds of videos documenting the incredible things those machines could do.

In those videos, robots, or automatons as the engineers who built them preferred to call them, were typically painted in bright colors and had none of the menace of the machine Glass was now looking at.

As another of the machines appeared and fell in beside the first, Glass recalled that only weeks before the start of the fighting in the US, the United States and most of the world's countries, including Australia, had signed an international treaty pledging that "automatons," like cluster bombs or chemical weapons, would never be used in war.

Without warning, there was a loud pop as the top of a rectangular compartment across both robots' chests ejected into the air.

From the exposed cavity erupted at least two dozen fist-sized drones.

For a long moment, the units floated in the air in front of the two machines, and then, without warning, each of them darted upwards and disappeared as they zipped in different directions.

"Nikki, what the hell is going on?" MacFarlane called over his shoulder.

Before Glass could answer the question, another two of the bipedal monsters came into view. Only this time, each was carrying a huge rifle, whose butt was buried into its shoulder.

As they walked past the unarmed units with what looked to be a near-perfect human gait, the synapses in Glass's brain finally began to fire off. What was coming their way was hugely dangerous. So dangerous, she wasn't going to risk ordering whatever the hell these things were to lay down their weapons.

As loud as she could manage, she yelled, "Open fire!"

Hearing her order, she heard the sound of MacFarlane's .40 caliber handgun begin to pop off rounds.

Then came the boom of Danh's shotgun and the chatter of Simms' M4.

Her own hand went for her sidearm, but instead of drawing the weapon, her eyes involuntarily took in the scene of violence that began to play out in front of her.

Unaffected by her colleagues' weapons fire, the armed robots aimed their weapons at Danh and Simms.

Glass registered the sound of suppressed fire being issued from the automaton's rifles and then caught the flash of bright red explode from each police officer's back as they were struck center mass by armor-piercing rounds.

As both men collapsed to the pavement, Glass saw one of the two machines shift its weapon toward MacFarlane. Before a scream could leave her mouth, the muzzle of the weapon flashed. She saw her friend's head disintegrate and felt something wet and sticky lash her face.

Blinded, Glass staggered back and found purchase against the side of the semi that had brought these mechanical monsters to downtown Sydney.

As fast as she could, she wiped her eyes to regain her vision. To her rear, gunfire erupted as the remaining members of her team at the barricade arrived to join the unexpected fray.

As her vision started to clear, her right hand stabbed downward for her Glock, and on making contact with the weapon's grip, she looked in the direction where she had last seen their inhuman attackers.

More of the machines were getting out of the back of the truck and more still were piling out of the Tesla Semi further down the street. Most of them were armed with rifles and were moving in teams of four or more.

Behind her, a female voice screamed her name, telling her to run.

But Glass could not flee. Instead, her eyes became transfixed on the first automaton that had left the truck.

It was walking in her direction.

At the halfway point of the trailer, Glass took note of the robot's right arm.

Protruding from underneath the mechanical appendage was a matte-black blade the full length of the thing's forearm.

Without thinking, Glass unholstered her sidearm, aimed at the machine's center mass, and unloaded the full contents of her pistol.

The bullets, some of which had hit her target, were useless. When it reached her, the automaton's arm flashed with inhuman speed.

Upon feeling a jolt at her elbow, her brain forced her eyes to leave her assailant and look down to locate the source of pain that had just set fire to her central nervous system.

From her elbow down, Glass no longer had an arm. Arterial blood was freely pumping onto the pavement from the stump.

Instinctively, she reached across her body with her remaining hand and clamped down hard on her bicep, instantly reducing the blood loss.

Blinking through the incredible pain, Glass looked up and found that the auto that had ruined her arm had moved on. It was further down the street, standing over an unmoving, uniformed body.

Beyond it were more of the machines and more dead colleagues and a real-life nightmare she would never be able to forget.

***

Sydney, Inside Admiralty House

Anne Watson did not have to force herself to watch the videos of Australian and New Zealand special operation soldiers being executed in the jungles of Vietnam.

She had been Great Britain's Minister of Defence for three years and, in that time, had seen her share of brutal videos emerge from the conflict raging in North America.

What made these videos unique, however, was that the individuals undertaking the slaughter of human beings were not humans at all.

Against international law, the People's Republic of China had unleashed a new hell on the world, as if their recent use of tactical nuclear weapons had not been enough.

As was the case with virtually all new robotics technologies over the past sixty years, it had been the high-tech sector in the US that had developed and eventually mastered the hugely difficult task of replicating the full range of biological movement.

Based on a generation of work coming out of MIT's Computer Science and Artificial Intelligence Laboratory, several companies had given birth to machines that could do the very same things an animal or human could do, only in most cases faster and better.

But it was only when the robots were uploaded with near-AI that the unethical scientists who created these incredible devices insisted they should be called automatons.

Her husband who was a professor of aerospace engineering at the Imperial College London, had regularly marveled at what the robots could do and how quickly they had come to replace the manual workforce in those places where automatons had become legal.

In 2026, *autos,* as the engineers had come to call them, had been a thing relegated to university campuses and the boasting of people like Elon Musk. But by the early 2030s, Amazon in the US had purchased enough of the machines that it was able to lay off eighty percent of its warehouse workforce and ninety-five percent of its package delivery agents.

Tens of thousands of people had been put out of work in California alone. But that's not what scared most people about this new and fantastic technology.

It was the idea of putting a weapon in the hands of something that could move and think faster than the average human that terrified anyone with half a brain.

In truth, you did not need to be Elon Musk or an engineering professor to understand the threat posed to humanity by armed robots who could think for themselves.

Hollywood had made billions off the trope, so it had been a welcome development when the Menendez government, in the year before the US civil war started, legislated strict product and technology export rules for all automaton technologies, along with a further pledge to undertake efforts to make sure this revolutionary tech was never militarized.

China, ever the gifted technological pirate, had made no such commitment.

In the dossier lying on the table in front of her, Watson had reports from Britain's MI6 indicating China had stolen robotics technology from the West and had been pumping billions into replicating the achievements of companies like Tesla, Honda, and the industry's golden child, the MIT Robotics Consortium.

But with China's invasion of Taiwan just two years ago, there had been no sign of an army of killer robots.

Yes, drones of all types had been employed, but if any of these new near-AI autos had been used in China's lightning-quick invasion of the island, its people had done a masterful job of keeping the capability a secret.

It was only with the assassination of Canada's prime minister just over a year ago that Western intelligence services had confirmed China was, in fact, producing militarized versions of the robotics platforms they had been displaying at their universities.

That the Chinese had sold a pair of their four-legged units to a Russian mercenary to assassinate another country's political leader spoke to how confident and brazen the PRC had become as a player in the murky world of international espionage.

Video shared by the Canadian Security Intelligence Service, CSIS, had shown the canine-like nightmares patrolling in front of the Canadian PM's residence on the night Robert MacDonald and his wife had been killed.

With turrets on their backs and grenade launchers fixed to the side of their bodies, the two four-legged autos had held off something like forty well-armed cops.

At the time of the assassination, CANZUK intelligence services had not been able to assure their respective political masters that China was not producing large numbers of robotic killing machines.

With the CIA hollowed out by the breakup of the US, the Five-Eyes intelligence arrangement had become a shadow of its former self, particularly as it related to China.

Britain and, to a lesser extent, Australia still had assets in the PRC, but their numbers and reach were minuscule compared to the Americans.

The videos the Australian and New Zealander governments had shared in the past week had confirmed CANZUK's worst fears. China had indeed mastered the automaton technology and based on the numbers of machines that had been tallied in Vietnam, they had thousands of them.

It was this new challenge that had brought the four CANZUK defence ministers to Australia.

"So, as you can see from these satellite images from thirty-six hours ago, buildings three, four, and seven have sustained catastrophic damage and will be out of commission for at least four months, likely more.

"Buildings one and five sustained significant damage that our people feel will keep them off-line for six weeks at least," said the Australian Minister of Defence.

The Aussie cabinet minister looked like a gargoyle, but Watson considered him the smartest person at the table.

She spoke up. "This is great news, Blaine, but how confident are we that this is the plant where they're building these things? Isn't it just a bit convenient that we got the intel on this location just as these things began to reveal themselves?"

The Australian shifted his eyes to look in her direction. "It's a great question, Anne, and the short answer is that we're extremely confident. For reasons you will all understand, I'm not prepared to share the specifics of our intelligence on this target in this forum.

"We'll have to narrow the group down to those who need to know, but for our immediate purposes, let me say that in the days following our strike on this location, a number of prime pieces of intel came into our system confirming this campus was, in fact, producing what the Chinese have called their X-series, which includes several variants of the X5 Hyena and X8 Wraith. The Hyena we were already familiar with. The bipedal Wraith is entirely new."

The answer annoyed Watson, but she let it go. She understood the man's caution. There were more than a few civilians in the room who had been brought in to help the generals and politicians better understand the capabilities of these new monsters, and while they all had clearance to be in the room, on the matter of the intel that led to the targeting of the Xi'An manufacturing plant, they didn't have a need to know.

Nodding her head in understanding, Watson started in on another question, but before she could finish her query, she and the rest of the occupants of the room became silent when their ears caught the far-off sound of what was most certainly gunfire.

Watson focused her eyes on the Aussie Defence Minister. "Blaine, any chance your people are undertaking some kind of exercise today?"

"Not bloody likely, but let me check," the Aussie said, his voice serious.

The Australian turned to the man sitting beside him. Before he could give instructions to find out what was going on, the large double doors to the meeting burst open, and a group of men Watson recognized as the heads of security for each of the four CANZUK nations walked into the room. Each had a look of concern on their face.

In the lead was the man she knew to be the senior officer from the Australian Federal Police, the outfit responsible for protecting Australia's Prime Minister and any political VIPs visiting the country.

Just as he was about to speak, an ear-splitting *BOOM* penetrated the dining hall where the meeting was taking place. The half-dozen large windows that ran along the wall Watson was facing shook violently in their frames.

"I need everyone to get up," the Australian policeman yelled over the explosive rattle. "We will be moving you to the harbor where we will put everyone on a waiting NSW patrol boat."

"A patrol boat in the harbor? Will, what in Christ's name is going on?" the Aussie defence minister demanded.

"Now isn't the time, Minister. Everyone needs to move —."

Another explosion — this one closer and louder — invaded the room, cutting off the police officer's instruction.

Suddenly, the head of her own security detail was at her side. Firmly, he placed one hand on her elbow and the other on her wrist and said, "Minister, you'll be coming with me."

With the unrelenting sound of gunfire reverberating throughout Admiralty House, Watson let herself be guided out of the meeting space.

As the head of her security detail took a step toward the doors the Australian head of security had burst through seconds before, she had to move quickly to keep pace with her protector.

As they reached the hallway, they took a right. Ahead of her, Watson could see the Aussie and Kiwi defence ministers also moving at a fast clip. Each was surrounded by a group of plainclothes police officers, of which half had drawn some kind of weapon. Her Canadian counterpart would be behind her.

On turning another corner, she saw another pair of doors being held open by a pair of uniformed police officers urging the politicians forward. Beyond them lay the gorgeous grounds that surrounded the home of Australia's Governor General.

"The patrol boat is just beyond that stand of trees, Minister. We'll be there in just a moment," the Met police sergeant said while his eyes darted back and forth, looking for danger.

Reaching the doors, Watson, the sergeant, and the rest of her small entourage began to jog across the fifty or so meters of pristine lawn toward where she'd been told their means of escape was located.

When she reached the concrete landing and stairway that led to the historic property's small peer, she saw the Kiwi Defence Minister, and her protection detail had already made it to the docking facility.

As Watson placed her foot on the first step to descend, she stopped and thrust her eyes skyward, having caught something at the top of her vision.

Almost immediately, the Met police sergeant was at her side and had latched both his hands on her right arm, but as he tried to pull her forward, she pulled back from the man's grasp, pointed into the air and yelled, "Drones!"

The police officer's eyes whipped in the direction Watson was pointing to find a pair of gray shapes descending from the sky toward the Kiwi delegation. On reaching their target, the two airborne units exploded with thunderous force.

As the flash of energy struck her, she and the police sergeant threw themselves backward and onto the grass.

As she lay on the ground, Watson kept her eyes shut, allowing her vision to recover from the bright ball of fire she had just been exposed to.

Only a few steps away, she heard the voice of her head of security. Somehow, the man had recovered from the detonation and was yelling orders she was having difficulty making sense of.

Without warning, the sergeant's bellowing was drowned out by a torrent of gunfire. Over the riotous shooting, Watson heard several men yelling out targets or issuing screams of terrible pain.

As the sound of gunfire relented, Watson forced herself to roll onto her side and open her eyes.

Her vision almost back to normal, she took in the scene playing out on the green space between her and the building she had just fled.

The lawn was littered with bodies, some dressed in police uniforms, others in civilian attire. It was in and amongst these bodies that Watson's brain registered who had done the killing.

Half a dozen Chinese bipedal autos — Wraiths, as she recalled from the briefing only moments ago —were slowly walking among the bodies. As they reached each lying form, the grey-colored machines aimed their shouldered rifles at the head of each body and pulled the trigger.

Incredibly, between her and the approaching Wraiths, Watson saw one of her staff taking in the scene. She was the only person still on her feet from the British delegation. Margaret Skye was a hugely talented policy wonk whom Watson relied on to decipher the inner workings of the Ministry of Defence, MOD.

"Margaret!" Watson called to the woman as she herself tried to stand.

Almost screaming, she said, "Margaret, you have to run! Get to the boat if you can."

After calling out the staffer's name three different times, the young woman finally turned to face her. When her eyes met Watson's, it was clear the analyst was terrified.

"Run, Maggie! Run to the boat, for Christ's sake. Down the stairs to the boat!" Watson urged.

As the words finally registered with the woman, the analyst tore her eyes from Watson's and ran in the direction of the steps that would bring her to the edge of Sydney Harbour.

On reaching the top of the stairs, the woman pulled up and looked down at the water.

Without warning, a single shot rang out.

Watson flinched as she witnessed the back of the heavy-set woman's head disintegrate.

Its biological command-and-control center eviscerated, the body of Margaret Skye collapsed to the ground in an unceremonious heap.

From the stairs emerged a pair of the Chinese autos. Both had shouldered weapons. While the first of the two Wraiths stopped its advance twenty feet back from Watson to take up an overwatch position, the other machine continued to stalk in her direction.

Standing alone, she straightened her suit jacket and lifted her chin to confront the approaching near-AI executioner.

As it approached her, she took the machine in. As robots went, it was a slick piece of engineering. Its exterior was smooth except for its joints, where you could see hints of servos and cabling. Its armor plating, a metal composite of some sort, looked thicker on those parts of its body that protected its key components. From head to toe, it was painted in a mottled grey camouflage pattern that stood out on the green of the lawn the auto was transiting across, but amongst the buildings of downtown Sydney, it would have blended in like a cheetah on the savannah.

When it stopped five feet in front of her, she investigated the Wraith's face. Long and rectangular, it had three different lenses stacked vertically. Watson focused her eyes on the largest of the three optics.

"Are you Defence Minister Anne Watson?" the Wraith asked with an accent that wouldn't have been out of place in London's financial district.

"Yes, I'm Anne Watson. To whom am I speaking?"

"It does not matter who I am. Only my message matters. It is a message you will take back to your prime minister and the other leaders of the CANZUK alliance."

Watson took a step in the direction of the auto. "Whoever you are, know that what has happened today is a declaration of war. China will rue the day it —."

In an inhuman blur, the Wraith's rifle swung up and fired something that thudded into Watson's midsection. Before she could look down to see what it was, her body exploded in pain as a storm of electricity consumed her.

Dropping to the ground and screaming in pain, she sizzled like bacon on a pan for what seemed like an hour.

Through wails of agony, she cried, "Jesus, it hurts! Stop! Please!"

When the pain finally relented and she opened her eyes, the auto was standing over her, looking down with its inhuman visage.

"You will not speak, Minister Watson, unless I give you permission. Nod your head if you understand."

Her body still reeling from the electrical fire, Watson nodded her head in submission.

"Excellent. Now, listen carefully.

"Within thirty days, the countries of the CANZUK alliance will desist in all military actions in Southeast Asia or the People's Republic of China will make it our unrelenting goal to visit total war on the country of Australia.

"And by total war, Minister, we mean that we will attack the Australian homeland, we will devastate its infrastructure, and we will make vast swaths of the country unlivable for its citizens."

Whoever was addressing her paused, allowing her to process the threat.

"Nod your head if you understand what I just told you?"

Still on the ground, Watson nodded at the machine.

"There is a reason we chose you to survive today's demonstration, Minister Watson. You are alive because Great Britain is the lynchpin of this pathetic alliance that refuses to understand that democracy has no place in the 21st century. China –."

Watson interrupted the speaker. "I'd like to stand if you don't mind?"

Following an extended pause, the auto finally said, "You may, but I'm warning you, this is not a negotiation. What I have told you will come to pass should CANZUK continue its efforts to support the war in Southeast Asia."

After slowly getting to her feet, a smile found its way onto Watson's face.

"You smile, Minister. May I ask why? Has today's demonstration not been sufficient enough for you to understand the seriousness of the challenge the United Kingdom and its allies face? I promised we would destroy Australia utterly, but rest assured, the rest of CANZUK will also be made to suffer if you don't do as you're told. Australia is just the closest of our enemies, but our reach is global. No country is safe."

Dropping the smile, Watson said, "I smile because the people who voted me into office have dealt with the type of government you claim to represent. Well, no one but the very old, and they would have been children at the time, but the point is that Great Britain will not bend its knee to tyranny. Whoever you are, you've made a grave mistake doing what you've done today."

As though it was human, the Wraith cocked its head to the side and said, "I was assured you were a highly intelligent person, Defence Minister Watson. Perhaps our assessment of you needs to be updated. If you're referring to World War II, I can assure you the PRC isn't Nazi Germany, just as the person who leads our great nation is hardly a madman. Today's actions are informed by rationality. It is a well-crafted exercise to drive home the point of how serious my country's threat is."

Watson reached down and plucked the saucer-shaped electrical shock unit that had affixed itself to her suit jacket and looked it at. Without any warning, she flipped the unit at the Wraith's head as though it were a flying disk.

The auto's left hand snapped upward and snagged the disc out of the air before it connected with its matte grey face.

"Good catch," Watson offered calmly. "My country and the whole of CANZUK will not be intimidated by your threats, rational or not. It's one thing for China to sail across the Taiwan Strait and brutalize a country of 20 million people. It is something else altogether for you to sail half the length of the Pacific to try and conquer 140 million. As we have always done, the CANZUK nations will stand together and oppose what you represent."

The Wraith's arm and hand extended toward the UK Defence Minister. The taser disc was sitting on its palm. Slowly, the machine's fingers and thumbs enclosed on the device.

Four feet away, Watson could hear the actuators of the machine's hand strain as it crushed the unit that had saturated her body with fifty thousand volts only a minute before.

When she heard a loud snap, the auto's hand opened. Gently, the Wraith tossed the destroyed device at Watson's feet and said, "Deliver our message to your prime minister and the other leaders of CANZUK. By way of today's events and our conversation, impress on her how very serious China's intentions are. CANZUK has thirty days, Minister — thirty days to choose between Australia's political survival or becoming this century's Carthage. We will not relent. We will be ruthless, and we will only stop when your ally is no more."

Chapter 5

Somewhere Over New York State

Captain Chris "Gravy" Williams banked his F-35A to the right, following his wingman as he undertook what had to be their tenth circuit of the figure eight they were transiting at twenty thousand feet ninety klicks east of Buffalo, New York.

Two other pairs of Royal Canadian Air Force, RCAF, F-35s were navigating the same circuit, waiting for direction from the RAF AWACS, which was loitering some two hundred klicks north and well out of reach of whatever interceptors the UCSA and French Air Forces could send their way.

On the ground at Canadian Forces Base, CFB, Trenton an hour earlier, every pilot from the 409 Tactical Fighter Squadron had received a detailed briefing indicating that today would be the day when the Red Faction military would try to force the Blue Faction forces and the Canadian Army out of Buffalo.

Over the past two weeks, the UCSA 3rd Army – some five divisions of frontline units and another three divisions of Red Faction militia – had been posturing themselves in such a way that they could assault the border town's southern and eastern reaches.

And they hadn't been hiding the fact. They couldn't even if they had wanted to.

While upstate New York did have its share of forests where you might be able to disguise the advancement of a division or two, this is not what the colossal Red Faction force had done. The Reds had not attempted to be quiet or crafty because there was no need for them to do so.

In the weeks since China had sunk a sizeable part of the Royal Canadian Navy off the coast of British Columbia, that same country had saturated the UCSA ground forces with the PLA's best long-range surface-to-air missile system, the HQ-9 Red Banner.

With a range of up to two hundred klicks, the Americans could now target CANZUK fighters the moment they took off from their forward operating bases in Southern Ontario and Montreal.

It also meant that the UCSA could now muster its forces for its attack on Buffalo without the worry of being harassed by CANZUK's numerically superior air forces.

As if the French Air Force and missile defenses hadn't been challenging enough, the appearance of the Chinese SAMs and the re-introduction of the dreaded J-31 6th-gen fighter had changed the situation in the skies above New York dramatically.

Within a week of their arrival, Canada alone had lost eleven of its F-35s, four of which had been from Gravy's own 409 Squadron. But as challenging as the loss of these planes and their pilots had been, it was the Royal Air Force shoot-downs that had turned CANZUK's status in the air from that of a hard-charging aggressor to that of tepid defender.

In all, nine of the RAF's precious sixth-gen Tempest fighters had been taken off the board along with twelve of their Typhoons.

Making it all worse was the exit of the Royal Australian Air Force.

The Chinese invasion of Vietnam had required the Aussies to send home their two AWACS Wedgetails and the entirety of their F-35s. Grudgingly, they had left a foursome of their EA-18G Growlers, giving their hard-pressed allies the ability to conduct electronic warfare action as the circumstances called for it.

Looking down at his fighter's primary data display, Gravy could see the entirety of the CANZUK strike group was now in the sky.

Each of the six fighter packages that would participate in Operation Eagle Scimitar was where they should be.

The operation had two main objectives. First, they would provoke the PLA Red Banner SAMs to reveal their positions.

In the next five minutes, a flight of eight RAF Typhoons would begin to make what would look like a classic attack run on the UCSA ground forces that had surrounded Buffalo, but instead of carrying a complement of ground attack weapons, each of the multi-role fighters was carrying a loadout of weapons designed to defeat the Chinese air defense system.

Each Typhoon was carrying three of the Japanese Phantom electronic warfare missiles. Until this mission, the Typhoons did not have the software to carry the sophisticated and hugely expensive EW weapon. This represented the first misdirection of Eagle Scimitar.

The moment the Chinese SAMs lit up the incoming fighters with their radars, the Japanese Phantoms would be launched, and on their own, they would do two things.

First, they would zero in on missiles launched by the HQ-9 batteries and would work to interfere with their independent targeting systems, forcing some number of them to drop their targets.

Second, some number of the Phantoms would move on to saturating the radars of those batteries that had revealed themselves and, for a time, would limit their ability to send more missiles into the air.

While this took place, the Typhoons would have already broken off their attack and would be racing west over Lake Michigan, where they would release the complement of Banshees they were carrying.

Like the Phantom, the Banshee was a new weapon for the RAF Typhoon. Once deployed, the Banshees would trail the eight fighters and employ a series of defensive measures that would confuse and stymie most of the pursuing Chinese SAMs.

As all this was playing out, ten Canadian F-35As would storm out of Quebec and together would launch forty AGM-88G Extended Range Advanced Antiradiation Guided Missiles at whatever Chinese Red Banner batteries had activated.

The AGM-88s unleashed, the largest element of Eagle Scimitar would then enter the fray.

In total, twenty-two F-35s and ten Tempests, now half of the RAF's inventory of its premiere fighter, would push into the airspace above New York. As each UCSA, French, and Chinese fighter jet revealed itself in response to the previous incursions, they would be set upon by the thirty-two CANZUK stealth fighters, each of which was carrying a full complement of air-to-air missiles in their concealed weapon bays.

With their enemies in the sky fully engaged and hopefully back on their heels, the next-to-final element of the plan would be revealed.

A strike force of RCAF F-35As and RAF Typhoons – some twenty fighters in total, each bristling with air-to-ground munitions

– would unleash hell on the Red Faction ground forces assaulting the Blue Faction and CANZUK forces trying to defend Buffalo.

And as a final coup de grâce — with the sky above upstate New York buzzing with activity, five RAF P-8 Poseidons flying out of Nova Scotia would unleash a barrage of eighty Block 3 Storm Shadow cruise missiles at various command-and-control and communication nodes helping to orchestrate the Red Faction assault on hard-pressed Buffalo.

In this complex ballet of looming violence, it was Gravy's job along with the five other F-35s flying with him above Ontario, to screen and protect the RAF Wedgetail flying its own holding pattern one hundred klicks north of their current position.

With its radar and hugely powerful near-AI battle management system, the Wedgetail's role in the coming operation was beyond critical.

As the importance of the vulnerable British AWACS aircraft entered his mind, the twenty-inch screen that was his plane's main display flashed to life. In the next second, dozens of red dots indicating enemy missiles appeared.

Before Gravy could begin to voice his concern about the data, an English-accented voice sounded in his helmet.

"Nomad One to Four, this is Nightmare Bravo, we have thirty-two incoming missiles. The data should be streaming onto your displays. Engage at will."

"Roger that, Nightmare Bravo. Nomads One through Four are engaging the vampires now," said the RCAF pilot leading Gravy's flight.

The AWACS's combat coordinator then addressed Gravy and his wingman. "Nomad Five and Six, we have hostile radar contacts two hundred klicks southwest of your position at forty thousand feet. These are your targets. Close on them and engage ASAP."

Looking down at his display, Gravy saw the six Chinese fighters designated as orange circles. They were just south of Detroit and well within what was supposed to be Blue Faction airspace.

These were the six fighters that had just unleashed a barrage of missiles at the RAF Wedgetail.

Having revealed themselves, they were now acting as bait. Somewhere close by, another two to four Chinese stealth fighters, their radars off, were waiting to see who would come out to play.

Before Gravy could acknowledge the order to close in on the six Chinese fighters, the RAF combat coordinator delivered another update. "Nomad Five and Six, be advised that four Blue Vipers are headed your way out of Wisconsin. They'll be able to engage in ten mikes."

"Nightmare Bravo, this is Nomad Five, we have a solid copy on that update," Gravy said. "Make sure to tell them to have their new Identification Friend or Foe on when they engage. It's gonna be one hell of a furball once they get on the scene."

"Roger that, Nomad Five. The IFF reminder has already been passed along. Give them hell. Nightmare Bravo out," the RAF combat coordinator said, his voice sounding nonchalant.

Not for the first time, Gravy took a moment to acknowledge the professionalism of the Brits. Had the data not been on his display, he would have had zero indication that the officer who had just updated him was flying in a plane that had thirty-plus missiles bearing down on it.

He put the RAF officer and the Wedgetail out of his mind and focused on the task at hand. "Vespa, let's move things along, shall we?"

"Lead the way, boss," replied the less senior officer.

"Roger that, Ves. Increasing speed to seven-fifty knots and bringing us up to forty thousand, on my mark in two, one – mark."

With thousands of hours of simulation time and well over three hundred hours of actual flight time in the cockpit of the F-35, Gravy gently pulled back on the flight stick, at the same time punching up the fighter's speed.

Of the six planes that had been screening the Wedgetail, it had been by design that Gravy and Vespa had been sent forward to prosecute the Chinese fighters.

Unlike the four RCAF F-35s that would launch missiles to intercept the incoming Chinese P-17 air-to-air missiles, Gravy and Vespa didn't carry missiles on their wings.

Had they done so, they would have been seen long before they got into range of the six enemy fighters they were now hunting.

Vespa's voice materialized in his helmet. "We're in range, boss. What's the plan?"

In their race to reach the six enemy fighters, Gravy had mulled several ways to engage their targets but had settled on the simplest. "Ves, take Dragons One and Two, and I'll take Three and Four. Two missiles for each. That leaves us with two for whatever surprise awaits behind door number one. When the Vipers get here, they can go after what's left."

"Keeping it simple. Love the plan, Gravy. Targets have been set. On your mark."

Before Gravy could give the order to launch their attack, the data feed from the RAF Wedgetail stopped, and his display went dark.

"Shit," Gravy said aloud. That they'd lost the targeting feed from the AWACS was not an encouraging sign.

Ignoring what the Wedgetail's absence might mean for the larger mission, Gravy said, "I'm turning on my radar. Bring yourself in tight with me and only fire two of your missiles. We need to make it look like I'm out here alone. If we fire eight, they'll know another fighter is with me. When my radar goes live, they'll come at me hard. Stay dark, close on them, and then when you're five klicks out, unload on these bastards. The Blue Vipers will be in range soon, so you'll have help. Got it?"

"Roger that, Gravy. I'm with you every step of the way," replied his wingman.

As soon as he saw Vespa's F-35 slide directly underneath his aircraft, Gravy turned on his fighter's powerful AN/APG-85 radar. Knowing where to direct its powerful search function, the Chinese J-31s were quickly reacquired. Seconds after that, Gravy had re-targeted four of the six enemy fighters.

"Fire missiles on my mark. Two, one, mark. Missiles away."

Having fired nearly a dozen of the air-to-air missiles in combat already, Gravy didn't bother to watch his four AIM-260s streak away from his aircraft. Instead, he intensely watched that part of the display that was his plane's radar.

Within seconds of them firing their six missiles, eight red triangles representing incoming enemy missiles bloomed on the display.

Close to where the P-17s appeared, there was now the radar signature of two new Chinese fighters. "Bingo!" Gravy said in triumph. He'd just found what was waiting behind door number one.

The entire border of his tactical display started to flash red as the advanced processor in his plane concluded that six of the eight incoming missiles had locked onto his radar signature. The other two would be searching the sky for any other CANZUK F-35s or Tempests that hadn't yet revealed themselves.

If Vespa played his cards right, they wouldn't find him, and when the Blue Faction F-16s arrived, he could launch his remaining four missiles at whatever Chinese fighters were still around.

At fifty klicks away, the latest version of the P-17 missile was fast and deadly accurate. Staying where he was, Gravy activated the electronic warfare mode of his plane's radar.

With the press of a button, the F-35's AN/APG-85 would send out waves of microwave energy to scramble the guidance systems of the incoming Chinese air-to-air killers.

Seconds later, one of the six missiles headed his way disappeared from the display. *One down, five to go,* Gravy thought.

"Ves, it's time to break. The Blue Vipers will be here in the next minute. Make those last missiles of yours count."

"Roger that, Gravy. I'll give 'em hell, and you stay alive, brother. Vespa out."

Hearing his wingman's confirmation, Gravy glanced at his tactical radar to assess the threat environment. The five missiles hunting him down were now just thirty klicks away.

It was time to make himself hard to kill.

He pushed forward on his flight stick, putting his fighter into a hard descent and, at the same time, increasing his speed. At not quite ninety degrees, he felt his body press back into his seat as his plane's afterburners ignited. He was now hurtling toward the center of Lake Huron at a speed of fourteen hundred kilometers per hour.

As the blue of the gigantic lake took up more and more of his canopy, Gravy scanned his radar to see where the four Blue Faction Vipers were.

While they had no stealth capabilities, the F-16 'E' variant or Viper was a nasty opponent in the hands of a skilled pilot.

As his altimeter passed five thousand feet, he saw a salvo of six missiles spawn from the J-31s who had been waiting for the Blue Faction fighter jets. In response, the Viper pilots launched their own missiles.

As he took in the burgeoning airborne battle, his own plane began to squawk at him. Gravy pulled out of his dive at two thousand feet, turning the nose of his plane north and west toward Lake Superior.

Checking his radar, he saw that three Chinese missiles were still in pursuit. The EW function of the AN/APG-85 had felled another two of the missiles. Manipulating his flight controls, he unleashed the full speed of his plane, reaching Mach 1.56, just a smidge below the F-35's top-rated speed.

"C'mon, baby. Give me everything you've got," Gravy said, the plea sounding strained due to the six g's of energy pressing into him.

As his display began to flash rapidly, signalling that the three incoming missiles were just a klick to his rear, his fighter passed from the deep blue of lake water to the emerald green of the thin band of Michigan forest that separated Huron and Superior.

As the proximity warning began to blare incessantly in his helmet, Gravy nudged his fighter closer to the earth so he was only a few feet above the tops of the trees.

"Just a little further! Just a little more, you son of a bitch!" Gravy roared inside his cockpit.

In the next few seconds, the closest of the three missiles would be within range to set off its warhead, sending forward a shower of supersonic metal ball bearings to shred his plane.

Through his canopy, he could see the end of the trees and the beginning of Whitefish Bay, the easternmost point of Lake Superior. Like a sparkling blue sapphire, the deepest and largest of North America's Great Lakes beckoned him and his fighter onward.

Clearing land, Gravy flew his plane ever closer to the earth's surface. While the missile proximity warning continued to batter his ears, another part of his display flashed green numbers at him.

In that section of the display that captured his altitude, he saw the number fifteen feet. With the hands of a surgeon, Gravy edged his fighter still closer to the water.

Risking a glance to his left, he perceived the blue smear that was Superior's surface, and for a second, he thought his brain registered the smell of fresh lake water. Goodness knows he was close enough.

Then, he did two things simultaneously. Almost violently, he pulled back on his yoke, telling the fly-by-wire electronics of his fighter that he wanted to invert its airframe as fast as it would let him.

Then, as the nose of his plane began to knife upward, his left hand triggered a barrage of flares and chaff to eject to intermix with the gigantic plume of lake water his fighter had just kicked up.

Streaking upward and straining against the forces of gravity assaulting his body, Gravy's left hand dropped down to the left arm of his seat, where he clumsily slammed down on a large red button that would release a series of powerful electromagnetic pulses in all directions from his plane's radar.

For what seemed like five minutes but was only a few seconds, Gravy squeezed his eyes shut and did nothing but wait to feel the white-hot pain of his body being torn apart.

When that didn't happen, his eyes snapped open to take in the cockpit's main tactical display. It was no longer flashing red. Also gone was the wail of the fighter's proximity warning.

Taking a deep breath, he focused on the specifics of the data on his display. The pursuing Chinese missiles were nowhere to be found.

"Hell yes!" Gravy bellowed.

His safety confirmed, his eyes then scanned the display for Vespa, the Chinese fighters, and the Blue Faction Vipers. In the time he had been trying to save his own life, a lot of things could have happened.

The first thing he noticed was that data from the Wedgetail was still not transmitting into his feed. At the edge of his radar, he could see two of the Blue Faction F-16Es. They were flying south, likely in pursuit of the fleeing J-31s.

He clicked on his encrypted link with Vespa. "Ves, I don't see you, brother. Where are you at?"

No reply came.

He switched frequencies. "This is Nomad Five. Nomad Six, are you receiving me over?"

Again, there was no reply.

"Nightmare Bravo, this is Nomad Five, do you copy?"

Nothing.

Before he could try the AWACS again, a new voice spawned in his helmet. "Nomad Five, this is Dreamcatcher Three. Do you copy?"

"I copy, Dreamcatcher. Where's my wingman?" Gravy snapped the question.

After a pause, the RCAF ground control officer said, "Nomad Six was shot down, as was Nightmare Bravo. We need to get you on the ground, son. The Reds and the Chinese have pulled a fast one on us. Get yourself to CFB North Bay, pronto. You'll get debriefed there while you're re-armed. Dreamcatcher Three out."

As he reeled from the news about his wingman and friend, Gravy didn't bother to confirm the order, but he also didn't waste any time in orienting his fighter toward where he'd been ordered to land.

CFB North Bay was a mothballed Cold War-era fighter base that had also been home to the "Hole," a massive radar and ground control facility burrowed deep into the granite formation known as the Laurentian Hills.

Both the air force base and the underground NORAD radar facility were closed in the late 90s, only to be hastily reopened a month ago as a logistics and staging hub for the growing war eight hundred klicks to the south.

Some fifteen minutes later, in the distance, he could see smoke rising from the location his display was telling him was his destination.

"Nomad Five, this is Dreamcatcher Three. We have a positive ID on your IFF. You are cleared to land on Runway Two. On touchdown, be advised you'll immediately be escorted to Briefing Room Zulu where you can get the latest. We'll have you topped up and rearmed in fifteen and you'll be back in the air in twenty."

"Roger that, Dreamcatcher. What the hell is going on?"

Just as the non-response was becoming too much for Gravy, the officer managing the airspace finally said, "The war just jumped over the 49th parallel, Nomad Five. The whole country is in the shit now and big time. Get on the ground, and we'll get you all the details that we have. Dreamcatcher Three, out."

Chapter 6

Buffalo, New York

From his perch on the roof of the southwest corner of Highmark Stadium, Major Nik Nikitas watched the last elements of the 2nd Battalion of the Royal Canadian Regiment, RCR, retreat from the outer perimeter defense that, until an hour ago, the Canadian 4th Division had been holding.

On its own, the Red Faction attack on the southern reaches of Buffalo had not been the cause of the Canadian Army's fallback.

As expected, an entire division of Red armor had raced forward into the myriad defensive works Canadian Army engineers had feverishly built around Buffalo in the two weeks CANZUK had been in possession of the city.

What triggered the massive retreat was the same thing that had placed Nikitas atop the complex where the Buffalo Bills had once played their home games.

"There they are, Major," the soldier beside him whispered.

"Where?" Nikitas asked as he put his binoculars to his eyes.

"The bastards are streaming out of the trees just west of the practice facility."

Through his binos, his eyes darted to the called-out area and immediately picked up on the movement of a handful of figures.

When he was forced to talk about what he did in the Army, without fail, Nikitas, or Nik Nik as his friends called him, would be modest about his skills as a Forward Observer, the trade in the CANZUK armies that called in artillery strikes.

But to himself and in his occasional chats with his cat, Scar, he knew he was the very best FO in the Canadian Armed Forces, CAF.

Because he was so skilled at calling in the army's big guns, Nikitas was one of a small group of CAF Army officers or senior NCOs who could also call in air support. In the whole of the CAF, there was no one person who could call down as much firepower as well and as often as he did.

"That's them all right," Nikitas said without pulling his eyes back from the binoculars.

His voice still low, the soldier beside him said, "Jesus, they just keep coming. Intel really messed this one up. How the hell did they not get word these things were in theatre? I mean, not even a week ago, fifty of the things showed up in downtown Sydney."

"Not our concern, Sergeant," Nikitas quietly rebuked the other man. "Our only concern right now is to slow down whatever comes into our sector. What's the status of the BAM?"

"Still down, sir. Whatever EW tech the Chinese have brought with them, it's nasty stuff."

"Still not our problem," Nikitas said.

His eyes never leaving the new threat, he reached toward the NCO who'd become his shadow since the fighting with the Reds and the French started four weeks earlier. "We'll do this the old-fashioned way. Your radio if you please, Sergeant Barnes."

By way of reply, Nikitas felt the handheld encrypted radio smack into his hand.

Suddenly, through his binoculars, a new threat emerged.

From the same place in the trees where the Chinese Wraiths had appeared, half a dozen of the four-legged X-5 Hyenas came into view at a trot. In seconds, double the number of canine automatons had overtaken the bipedal units.

"They're after what's left of 2RCR," Barnes said. Quickly, the NCO added, "If they find out we're here, they'll do to us what they did to 1st and 4th Battalion this morning."

Nikitas had heard the briefings and seen the videos. In less than an hour, the Chinese Hyenas achieved what should have taken the Red Faction at least a week.

Packed with high explosives and highly elusive, two to three hundred of the units had raced forward in the minutes before sunrise. As Red Faction artillery pounded the Canadian's lines, the Hyenas ran through minefields, jumped over razor wire and blew themselves up in hardpoints, trenches, and command posts, and all before anyone knew what was happening.

The attack had come as a surprise and had been devastating.

If they found out a platoon of Canadian soldiers was in the stadium, the Hyenas would explode their way into the structure and ruthlessly hunt down anything that had a heartbeat.

And what the Hyenas couldn't get to, the Wraiths would root out and destroy.

If the Hyenas were the shock troops, the Wraiths were the clean-up crew. There was nowhere they couldn't go and nothing they couldn't kill.

His mind clear on the threat that was coming their way, Nikitas said, "Tell the lieutenant to haul ass to the north gates and to take all his people with him. He's not to engage these things."

"And what about us?" asked Barnes.

As the other man's question registered in his ears, Nikitas perceived an undertone of concern.

"We need to slow them down, Sergeant. I can do that on my own. If you leave, I'll understand. You've got two little monsters. I have an unloving cat."

Barnes's reply was prompt and indignant. "Like hell. I'll be sticking around, thank you very much. We've made it this far together, and you, Major, seem to have an incredible reserve of luck. For my part, I want to see how far your good luck can take us. Damned far is my guess."

Nikitas pulled his eyes from his binos and looked at the older man. "You have to be lucky to be good, Barnsey. Now, get that order to the lieutenant, and let me do my job."

"Yes, sir," the NCO said.

Getting up from his prone position at the edge of the stadium's roof, Barnes scooted low in the direction of the ladder that would take him to the young lieutenant commanding the recce platoon who had been given the task of moving and protecting Nikitas.

Seeing Barnes disappear, Nikitas brought the radio to his mouth. "Wrangler Three, this is Rider Two. I have a fire mission priority destination pre-set Alpha-India-Seven. Break."

"Rider Two, we've been waiting on your call. Send mission. Break."

"Wrangler, I need every heavy hitter you can get your hands on and pronto. Map quadrant is Delta Niner. The grid is 7-8-9 by Romeo, Sierra, Tango. Intermix HE and AP. Break."

"Rider Two, we have your position on GPS. That's kind of close, isn't it? Break."

"Negative, Wrangler Three. Fire for effect. Fire now. Break."

"Roger that, Rider Two. Grab onto something. Both Wrangler Echo and Bronco X-Ray are in the hopper. Give them thirty seconds. Wrangler Three out."

It was more firepower than he had expected. Wrangler Echo was 'E' Battery from the 2nd Regiment, Royal Canadian Horse Artillery. Because of their range, they were across the Niagara River in Ontario. The Battery was armed with eight CAESAR 155mm self-propelled howitzers.

French-made, the 'truck with an artillery system' had proven to be an exceptional piece of kit. As CANZUK had slowly retreated north from where they had first engaged the Red Faction, Nikitas had as many as three of the RCHA's CAESAR batteries dialled in and striking at their pursuers.

The combination of their mobility, accuracy, and destruction made him feel like Zeus, as though, at any moment, he could place his hands on the reins of a thunderstorm to unleash hell.

Bronco X-Ray was 3RCR's mortar platoon. Unlike the rest of the battalion, now falling back from their enemies' early morning assault, the mortars were already ensconced inside CANZUK's second and final line of defense that ringed downtown Buffalo.

The platoon's eight tubes of 81mm wouldn't have anywhere near the destructive firepower of the CAESARs, but he wasn't trying to slow down or stop a charging Red Faction armored brigade.

What he needed to neutralize the approaching Chinese kill bots was coverage. They might be fast, smart, and deadly, but the sophisticated components that made up each machine made them susceptible to the type of concussive attacks that the CAESARs and mortar platoon were about to deliver.

With his naked eye, Nikitas could now see twenty of the Hyenas moving forward in the long but narrow Lot 1 of Highmark Stadium. The parking lot was surrounded by a good-sized urban forest and fenced suburban homes. The barriers were serving to funnel the approaching autos, as he had heard them called in several recent intel briefings.

Suddenly, torrents of gunfire erupted somewhere close by. He couldn't tell if it was coming from within or outside the football stadium.

"Not good," Nikitas said aloud. His hope that young Lieutenant Kay's recce platoon would escape their position unscathed began to fade as he heard more explosions coming from the north of the stadium.

Hyenas – some that had come from an altogether different direction – were behind them and had most likely fallen on Kay and his men as they raced for their vehicles.

The thought of what might be happening to the young officer and his thirty soldiers evaporated from his mind as he heard the first telltale sounds of the artillery strike he'd ordered.

The banshee-like scream of the incoming 155mm shells from the CAESARs was music to Nikitas' ears.

As the targeting salvo from the battery struck three hundred meters out from his position in a line perhaps two hundred meters wide, the sound and concussive energy enveloped him.

As the echoes of the big shells reverberated in the stadium bowl, the smaller shells of 3RCR's mortar platoon began to arrive.

The barrage struck the earth fifty meters beyond the furthest Chinese auto. As one, the Wraiths stopped their advance and turned to take in the plumes of destruction behind them.

Nikitas pressed the button on his radio. "Wrangler Three, you are aces. Roll it forward at pace, Lima, and let'er rip with everything you've got. Rider Two, break."

"Roger that, Rider Two. Rolling forward at pace Lima with everything we've got. Wrangler 3, out."

The order given to unleash hell in the form of a rolling barrage in the direction of the south end of the football stadium, Nikitas turned his attention back to the parking lot and the growing number of Chinese hunter-killer machines.

As the whistle of incoming artillery shells once again began to fill the air, the Wraiths turned back to the stadium, and in perfect unison, the dozen or so of the bipedal autos, raised their heads to look upwards into the sky.

"Jesus, the goddamned things can sense something's coming."

As if to confirm Nikitas' hypothesis, as one, the Wraiths lowered their heads from the sky and began to sprint forward in the direction of the stadium, as did the more numerous Hyenas.

It was as the Chinese autos reached their full speed that the 'E' Battery's rounds began to fall amongst them.

As the combination of 155mm high explosive and fragmentation rounds impacted the rear guard of the sprinting autos, those units in the immediate vicinity disappeared in the explosive energy that each munition delivered.

Those autos outside the immediate kill zone were either tossed to the ground or wobbled like a punch-drunk boxer as their software attempted to recalibrate their balance so they could continue their advance.

The incoming artillery from both the CAESARs and the mortar platoon was now coming in continuously, and as directed, it was quickly being walked to Nikitas' position.

Back in WWI, the Royal Canadian Horse Artillery had been one of the first outfits to master the rolling artillery barrage. At the Battle of Vimy Ridge, hundreds of Canadian guns, along with those of the British, had performed the technique brilliantly and, in doing so, had made a major contribution to Canada's most significant victory of the war, if not its greatest national triumph of all time.

As the devastation of the assault reached within fifty meters of his position, Nikitas brought the radio receiver to his mouth, depressed the transmission button, and said, "Wrangler Three, this is Rider Two, cease-fire. I say again, cease-fire."

"Roger that, Rider Two. Ceasing fire."

Seconds later, the comforting sound of exploding artillery and mortar shells came to a stop.

From his perch on the roof of the football stadium, Nikitas had not taken his eyes off the unfolding destruction of their enemy.

Surveying the ruin he'd called down, Nikitas was beyond satisfied.

Where a company of the mechanical monsters had been moments before, there was only a handful of the autos left, and they were unmoving.

Best of all, in the tree line some four hundred meters away, no more of the nightmares were emerging.

With the sound of gunfire and shelling echoing in other parts of the city, Nikitas had not heard Barnes clamber up the metal ladder they had used to gain access to this section of the stadium. Instead, he caught movement out of the corner of his eye.

Keeping his profile low, he turned to speak to the man who had done as much as anyone in the past month to keep him alive. "Sergeant, you missed one hell of a show. I'll never get tired of seeing those CAESARs unleash hell..."

Where his friend, the RCR sergeant should have been stood one of the Wraiths. At just fifteen meters away, Nikitas could see the auto's huge assault rifle pointed at his chest.

"Crafty devils, aren't you?" Nikitas said as he stood tall.

He took a half step backward and felt his rear end bump into the half-wall that he had been looking over to watch the annihilation of the Chinese machine's brethren. To heave himself overboard was a seven-story fall and death.

Better to go down fighting, Nikitas thought.

Just as his hand was about to flash down to the Sig Sauer P323 on his thigh, a hissing object landed directly in between him and the auto. Instantly, the Wraith's trio of 'eyes' zeroed in on the new threat.

As blood-red smoke began to billow out of the smoke grenade, Nikitas moved left, pulling his sidearm from its drop holster. The Wraith, recognizing the smoke was harmless, moved its weapon to reacquire him, but Nikitas had already begun to send rounds down range.

On the third squeeze of his weapon's trigger, he dove to the ground.

Through the smoke, he couldn't see the Wraith but heard the distinct crack of its rifle as it sent a short burst of 6.8mm rounds through the space he had just occupied.

Scrambling to his feet, Nikitas resolved that if there was any chance he was going to survive this encounter, it would only be by getting up close and personal with his near-AI opponent.

If he could get his hands on it, maybe he could yank some of its wiring or damage some other critical part. Dodging as he moved forward, more bullets ripped past him.

Plunging into the wall of red smoke, he caught a glimpse of the Wraith. Less than ten feet away, he could see the machine had its weapon lined up with his chest.

Without a doubt, this was the end. The auto had him dead to rights.

As the Wraith once again disappeared in the red haze, Nikitas issued a guttural war cry, pumped his legs, and drove forward toward his attacker.

Two steps forward, a burst of gunfire sounded off in Nikitas' ears, but he felt no pain.

Another three strides forward in the hellish smoke, and he could once again see the Wraith. Its weapon was still firing, but it was pointed in the direction of the tar paper roof.

Wedged into the arm holding the stock of its assault rifle was a bright red fireman's axe. Holding the axe's haft was none other than a determined-looking Sergeant Barnes.

Wrenching the weapon from the auto's arm, Barnes, an outdoorsman who loved camping with his kids, raised the axe into the air, unleashed a savage war cry, and levelled a mighty blow that connected with the Wraith's neck.

By design, a fireman's axe is not sharp. It is a smash-and-bash tool used to break through walls and doors. But on this occasion, the implement worked well enough as the sheer force of the sergeant's swing tore through the Wraith's neck, sending its head tumbling through the smoke-filled air.

Headless, the machine stood unmoving until Barnes delivered another vicious blow, this time connecting with the kill bot's right knee, crushing the joint inward to form an inhuman angle.

Rushing forward to join the melee, with both hands, Nikitas grabbed the other side of the Wraith and, with all his strength, forced the auto's weight toward its damaged knee. Decapitated and with its knee joint destroyed, the machine keeled over like a felled tree.

Coiled and waiting for their enemy's body to settle on the roof, Barnes brought down one final blow on the Wraith's oversized weapon, crushing its barrel and rendering it useless.

Breathing hard but looking extremely pleased, Barnes' eyes connected with Nikitas', and he said, "This was the only one I saw on my way back to you, but if I had to guess, more are on their way."

He thumbed over his shoulder in the direction of the ladder. "The goddamned thing climbed up the ladder like it was a ten-year-old on a jungle gym. I tried shooting it as it climbed, but the rounds didn't even register."

"Yeah, well, it almost got me. Thanks for coming back. I owe you one, Barnsey. Big time." As Nikitas said the words, his gloved hand reached in the direction of the sergeant.

Locking into a firm handshake, the RCR sergeant said, "The colonel would have my ass if I didn't bring you back. And —."

A burst of static opened up on Nikitas' BAM, and then he heard the voice of Brigadier General Bell, the CO for 5th Brigade.

As the two soldiers released their handshake, their eyes met as they listened to the first message to come through the BAM since the Red Faction had begun its attack.

"All units, all units, this is Outrider Sunray. We are executing standing order Pegasus Bravo, verification code Seven-Alpha-Seven-Kilo. I say again, we are executing the standing order Pegasus Bravo. Everyone, stay primed on the BAM for further orders from your respective commands. We're confident we can maintain the BAM connection, but if it cuts out, we'll operate on tac frequency Niner-Delta. Outrider Sunray out."

"We're evacuating Buffalo?" Barnes said, a look of disbelief on his face.

Nikitas nodded. "The bastard Chinese have screwed us again, Sergeant. Those Hyenas must have done one hell of a number on our command and control."

Barnes spat on the unmoving Wraith and said, "So Buffalo falls within hours. Folks back home are going to have a shit-fit. Do you think they'll cross the border?"

As Barnes asked the question, his look of disbelief became one of concern. The sergeant's wife was from Southern Ontario. If the UCSA did cross the border, his in-laws could be caught up in the fighting.

Nikitas shook his head and, injecting confidence into his voice, said, "I don't think they'll cross. We knew this could happen, so preparations have been made along our side of the river. Getting across the water wasn't easy in 1812 – it'll be harder now. If they do come, it won't be for weeks or even months. My best guess is that there will be lots of time to move people about and get ready."

"Maybe they'll cross at Syracuse?" Barnes said. "It's closer to Ottawa, and the water there isn't as challenging. If the Brits fall —"

Nikitas cut his friend off and said, "Let's not bother with the hypotheticals, Barnsey. The first thing we need to do is get back to our lines to get across the border."

The RCR sergeant nodded and said, "Right, makes sense."

Hefting his axe onto his shoulder, Barnes then motioned his head toward the ladder and said, "After you, Major."

Nikitas stepped toward their escape but stopped, looked at his friend and said, "Where did you find that thing, by the way?"

"What, this thing?" Barnes said as his left hand caressed the axe's bright red handle.

"Yes, the big red axe."

"Major, you can thank God, the Buffalo Bills, or both. When the rounds I was putting into that thing's ass weren't having an effect, I looked to my right and lo and behold, there was an emergency station with an extinguisher and this here wonderful axe."

"And the rest is history?" Nikitas offered.

Barnes's eyes finally left the implement and reconnected with Nikitas. "Yes, sir. The rest is history."

***

Moscow, The Kremlin

Russian President Pavel Dadanov stared at the group of men in front of him.

The silence that pervaded his advisors had been going on for nearly a minute, but being familiar with how he conducted his business, no one's face showed any concern.

In the domestic media, he was labeled as a thoughtful plodder. He much preferred that to the most frequent description offered by the international press.

Overweight dullard was only half correct.

Yes, he was overweight. By a hundred pounds, if the doctor from his last medical was to be believed. But he was no dullard. That someone took time to carefully consider all the facts did not make that someone an idiot.

While his Western peers who were still democratic had to play to the media and public opinion, Dadanov did not. He didn't have to offer quick, witty quips or stand in front of a lectern and have it out with reporters on live television.

No, there would never be any of that. He, along with his closest advisors, sat behind closed doors and did what Russians had always done. They carefully plotted.

In the history of Russia over the past one hundred years, such an approach had served the country well. Not always, but mostly.

Slowly, his hand reached out to take up the glass before him. On reaching his lips, he took an extended sip of the cool water.

Refreshed, he placed it back on the table and continued his earlier train of thought. "So, the latest from America is that the Chinese re-entry into the war could mean a rapid collapse of CANZUK. The Red Americans, you say, could be in Ottawa within three to four months. Is that correct?"

He paused, waiting for one of his advisors to validate his assessment. On cue, Sergei Kulikov, his man in charge of the SVR, Russia's foreign intelligence service, said, "Correct, Mr. President."

"And we're now confident that the Chinese have an agreement with Spector to give them some part of North America's Westcoast, plus we're highly skeptical CANZUK can prevent the Chinese from gobbling up most or all of Southeast Asia. Is that also correct?

"Correct, Mr. President," Kulikov repeated.

"And while all of this is happening, our ancient enemy, the French, are waving their little French dicks in Europe, threatening to invade Holland and others if they don't comply with their scheme to unload Western Europe of its fifty million or so Muslims. Is this too accurate?"

"Yes, Mr. President," the SVR man said again.

Dadanov issued a contemplative "Hmmm..." to the group, his usual sign that he would be taking his time to issue his next words.

But on this occasion, his decision had come to him quickly.

"My fellow patriots, it is my view that we are watching the end of democracy as we know it. As it was with the Greeks and the Romans, it has once again been proven that the concept of one man, one vote is not all that it was claimed to be.

"We will – no, we must – act decisively if Russia's interests are to be advanced. We have sat on the sidelines long enough."

Dadanov reached for the glossy red pack of Prima cigarettes sitting on the conference table in front of him.

Tapping the pack twice on the massive table, his large fingers nimbly pulled one of the cigarettes from the pack, lit it, and took a long, satisfying drag.

Expelling the smoke from his lungs, he continued, "We will finish what my predecessor should have finished almost a decade ago and secure the lands we need to ensure our children's children never have to worry about the West. We will not permit the conditions for a neo-Napoleon or a modern-day Barbarossa. Not under my watch."

For the first time in the conversation, Russia's most senior general spoke.

As generals went, he was on the younger side, but the man held his position because he was competent, just like the rest of the men around the table. The general said, "So, you are approving Operation Brush Fire, Mr. President. All of it?"

Dadanov nodded his head. "Yes, General. All of it. You will sweep through what remains of Ukraine as the Chinese have done to Vietnam, and we'll correct the mishandling of our two wars against these cursed people. As other countries have done in the past year, we too will be ruthless in what must be done to secure our future."

He took another long drag of the cigarette, exhaled, and continued. "And when you have wrapped up Ukraine in a tight little bow, we will give the Poles the fight they've wanted since they were humiliated in '39. As Poland is a NATO member, I understand that tactical nukes will not be available to us, but without the Americans to reinforce and re-arm them and with trouble brewing in Western Europe, they will succumb within a year, just as your people's analysis suggests. How much further we go beyond the Poles, we shall see."

Dadanov gestured to the general with the hand that held his half-finished cigarette and said, "But you know all of this, Ivan. Your people wrote the plan. This is your baby I'm talking about."

The senior commander said, "It might be my baby, Mr. President, and it may be a bold plan, but it is filled with pitfalls and dangers."

Dadanov waved off the other man. "I know this. We all do, but like our enemies, we, too, must be bold. As China makes its grand play, so must we. With the bastard Putin in his grave, we – the men at this table – have worked tirelessly to reforge our country. We are as strong as we've ever been. If we do not act now, Ivan Varmalov, when?"

When the general gave no reply, Dadanov pressed his cigarette into the ashtray in front of him. With his next craving thirty minutes away, his eyes swept the room.

Eight men, excluding himself, and not one of them was there because they had bought or corrupted their way into their position. That had been his predecessor's greatest weakness.

It had been a flaw he swore he wouldn't repeat. Yes, corruption was still all too common in Russia, but he had been pitiless in keeping it out of his inner circle.

"Steel yourselves, gentlemen. The Poles are the only lions left in Europe. They will resist and there will be hard days, but once they fall, who will stop us?"

When no one moved to answer his question, he continued, "Not the Germans. Despite the recent ravings of this fellow some are calling the Fuhrer Reborn, they remain a country that is too focused on its past. No, for the foreseeable future, the German people will remain fickle and soft.

"The French? They'll be of no help to the Poles. As the French often do, they will see the writing on the wall and look to reach a deal to secure their part of Europe.

"The Scandinavians? As long as we leave them be, they'll do the same to us. With but one exception in the past three hundred years, that is what they've done. This will not change."

Dadanov reached for the small glass of vodka positioned beside his water. Raising the glass to his lips, he slugged the entirety of the substance down his throat and, for a handful of seconds, savored the taste of Russia's most sacred of liquids.

As the liquor fortified him, he continued, "And what of NATO? There is no United States, so there is no NATO. Europe is naked and ripe for the taking, and I say we take what we can, just as the Chinese are doing in their part of the world."

Dadanov placed his strong, if pudgy, hands on the arms of his chair and pushed himself upward. Despite his unwanted heftiness, he was powerful and spry for a man of sixty. As a much younger man, he had participated in two Olympics as a freestyle wrestler. It was this previous life that gave him the energy and determination to secure Russia's future in the present.

Now towering above his still-seated advisors, Dadanov made his final pronouncement. "Six weeks, gentlemen. In six weeks, we remake Europe as we see fit. Do you understand?"

As one, the eight men gave their reply, "*Da*."

"Good, then I'll leave you to your business. You all have much to do."

Chapter 7

Colorado Springs, Colorado

Rachel Anders-Maxwell looked back at the man sitting across from her. She had spoken with him several times via a secure quantum connection and had seen him in many dozens of news reports in the months leading up to the election he'd recently won.

In those conversations, she had been able to confirm that the Governor of California did indeed have the charisma and intellect talked about in political circles. But in person, even at 4 am and under the harsh fluorescent lights of the Cheyenne Mountain NORAD boardroom where their meeting was to take place, the man sitting across from her was something else entirely.

Ricardo "Ricky" Sanchez was the third governor of the Golden State to make a name for himself in Hollywood, and like the first two, in person, he was larger than life.

Not only did his charisma increase two-fold when he was physically present, but as a man who had won an Academy Award and starred in some of the greatest movies of the past forty years, Sanchez's personal magnetism was off the charts.

For what had to be the tenth time in the past twenty minutes, Anders-Maxwell chided herself for not already getting past the fact that the man sitting across from her was a walking and talking legend.

In fact, he was just a man, if an exceedingly handsome one at the age of sixty-two.

Pulling herself together, she said, "Governor Sanchez, I'm glad you've made the time to visit us here in Colorado. Based on our recent conversations and developments both here in the US and in Southeast Asia, we have much to discuss."

"Please, call me Ricky," replied Sanchez. A transplant from Texas, the man's voice maintained just enough drawl for it to be obvious he wasn't a native of the state he now led.

"If you ask me, Rachel, all this pomp and circumstance of elected office is one of the things that has got our country in the mess it's in. If politicians had been a bit humbler and carried themselves as regular folk instead of all-knowing kings who send out orders from on high, perhaps the country could have been saved."

Sanchez paused, then flashed his brilliant smile across the table. "But could haves and should haves is not why we're here, is it?"

Not able to help herself, Anders-Maxwell returned the man's smile.

Too late to catch her reaction, she cursed herself for acting like a twenty-year-old fan girl. Jesus, only two years ago, she'd ordered nuclear strikes on UCSA military targets in retaliation for their strikes on five Blue cities.

Hollywood and the vain people who came from that world only made movies about the things she'd done.

Her self-chiding complete, she replied to Sanchez's question. "I agree, the past is not why we're here. We're here because both of us are sick to death with what's happened to our country and the rest of the world. The recent invasion of Vietnam by China is but the latest disaster to befall what remains of the old order."

At her mention of the world's newest conflict, the smile on Sanchez's face disappeared. Continuing, Anders-Maxwell said, "In fact, it is the developments in Southeast Asia that prompted me to ask you to come here at this un-godly time in the morning.

"Spector's casual use of tactical nuclear weapons has made it okay for any country with similar weapons to use them whenever and however they see fit. Both of us know where the frivolous use of tactical nuclear weapons ends."

Sanchez's brown eyes were unflinching as he listened to her words. When he said nothing, she moved forward with her analysis. "We were both on the call with President Morgan and saw the intelligence on the Reds. Spector would never admit it, but the UCSA is strained."

"But Buffalo?" said Sanchez.

"Yes, Buffalo fell, but at the same time, the food and gas shortages and the riots in the UCSA have only grown. And then there's this deal with the Chinese. Respectfully, Ricky, if giving up part of the continental United States is not an act of desperation, I don't know what is. The Reds may have won a victory in pushing

CANZUK and the Blues out of Buffalo, but you heard Morgan. The Blues will not give up, and you've seen the growing numbers of oil tankers CANZUK has sunk. The Reds' fuel reserves are already dire.

"The balance is starting to shift away from the UCSA. That's why Spector made the deal with the Chinese. To do otherwise would be to lose the war."

Sanchez nodded his head at her words and said, "This deal with the Chinese is a problem, but to be honest, my people and I are as convinced as ever that we shouldn't come within a thousand miles of any war.

"No matter what happens, California is not rejoining whatever replaces the United States. With most of the Pacific fleet in Californian ports, we have more than enough nukes to fend off any future threats, whether they're from the Chinese or the Reds or whatever political Frankenstein is manufactured in DC whenever this damn war ends."

Sanchez gestured across the table at Anders-Maxwell and said, "And the same goes for Colorado and the rest of the Neutrals. You have hundreds, even thousands of nukes. Whether you like it or not, they're your guarantee. If you don't have to engage in this orgy of violence, why would you?"

"Because the world is bigger than us, Ricky," Anders-Maxwell replied hotly. "What happens on other continents will affect us. Maybe not you and me, but our kids are going to have to face the music. Surely, you must see that?"

If Sanchez was concerned about the Governor's impassioned words, he gave no outward indication of it. Calmly, he said, "If I do what you're suggesting, Rachel, I'm putting every citizen of my state at risk. And for what? I was clear with Californians during my campaign. We don't need to get involved. Our economy is booming, and we're safe. If we keep our heads down, the storm will pass us by."

Anders-Maxwell's eyes almost popped out of their sockets. "So, you're prepared to watch the world burn to the ground while you remain cozy and safe in your little slice of the world?"

When Sanchez didn't give a reply, she rolled on.

"In case you hadn't noticed, Governor, with our former country on its knees, the rest of the world is becoming more dangerous by the minute. In weeks, Vietnam will fall to the Chinese. CANZUK won't stop that. In Europe, the Russians look to be on the move again, just as France grows more belligerent and fascist by the day. And if all of this wasn't enough, the Iranians are massing on Iraq's border.

"As things currently stand in your isolated world of bliss, there is nothing and no one to stop the ayatollahs from sweeping through the whole of the region. Tell me, Ricky, how long will it take for the Israelis and the Saudis not to use their nukes? Tell me again how this doesn't affect California?"

Sanchez shook his head and said, "What if this is how it's meant to be, Rachel? What gives the United States the right to regulate how the world does its business? What do we care if China invades Vietnam or Russia sweeps into the Baltics or Poland?

"Maybe after all of these moves are played out, we have a world that's more stable than when we were running things?"

When Anders-Maxwell gave no reply, he continued. "The truth is we don't know how things will end up. No one does. The one thing I can say with certainty is that it was our constant meddling in other country's affairs that led to our own country's destruction.

"Perhaps if we'd paid more attention to what was going on here in the US, we could have done more to manage the Red-Blue divide.

"The US cannot be all things to all people, Rachel. When the Roman Empire fell, it led to the Dark Ages. When the British Empire collapsed, we got World War I and II. The American Empire has collapsed and what comes next, I do not know. What I do know is that the United States of America is no more and it's not coming back, no matter how much we wish this wasn't the case."

With a sad look on her face, Anders-Maxwell finally gave a shake of her head and said, "I didn't think you were this naïve, Ricky."

On hearing the other politician's assessment, Sanchez's eyes narrowed, and he said, "You may call it naivety, but how I see it and what the people of my state see is prudence."

Her tone chiding, Anders-Maxwell exclaimed, "Oh, come on, Governor! If Spector defeats the Blues, democracy—and everything that comes with it — will be extinct in the next two to five years.

"You're a smart man, Ricky Sanchez, you must see that. California won't be safe, no matter how much you keep your head down. The UCSA, the Chinese, or both will come for the Neutrals. And when they're done with us, they'll come for you."

Sanchez shook his head at the supposition. "I see many possibilities and none are as clear as you make them out to be. And to suggest otherwise is to demand that I start making policy by reading tea leaves. That's not going to happen."

Anders-Maxwell stared at Sanchez for a long moment. With his salt-and-pepper hair, smooth tanned skin, and fashionable attire, he looked every bit the movie star he was.

The movie-star-turned-politician had made millions playing the hero. And though he wasn't acting very heroic at the moment, Anders-Maxwell's gut told her the man sitting across the table couldn't have made all those movies without caring about doing the right thing when the moment called for it.

Breaking the silence, she said, "Spector and the people around him know they can't bring California to heel through physical force. To the contrary, he'll build up political opposition in each of our states, and one by one, we'll fall. The Rocky Mountains, nuclear weapons, and the US Navy will not save you.

"It may take two years or ten, but know this, Governor Sanchez – the UCSA is us. They speak our language, we share the same culture, Christ, we even share families – tens of thousands of them.

"If the Blues fall, the Reds will find a way to convince or cajole each of us to join their side, and when that happens, the light of democracy leaves this world. This CANZUK outfit is plucky, but they can't do it alone."

Anders-Maxwell took in and released a couple of breaths and let Sanchez chew on her words.

When it was clear he wasn't going to accept her way of thinking, she sighed and said, "Listen, I know this is going to sound hokey, and I know we're not in a movie but isn't the promise of democracy worth saving? Doesn't it have to be saved? At least here in North America where it has a chance of surviving?"

Sanchez slowly shook his head and placed both of his hands down on the table that separated the two politicians. With a kindness in his eyes that seemed genuine, he looked at Anders-Maxwell and said, "I'm sorry, Rachel. The people of California elected me to keep their great state out of the civil war, and that's what I plan to do. Democracy, if it's meant for this world, is going to have to find a way to survive without my state's help.

And, if I might add, what good is the will of the people if their newly elected leader ignores it? No, the people of my state have spoken, and I don't see a reason to turn my back on them."

Seeing Anders-Maxwell's face become crestfallen, Sanchez, a man who'd spent his professional life trying to make people's lives better by making great films, quietly added, "I'm sorry Rachel, but it has to be this way. California has given me a mandate and I can't think of a reason for me to change my mind. Maybe a reason comes, but I don't see that happening any time soon."

Chapter 8

Ottawa, National Defence Headquarters (NDHQ)

This had only been Larocque's second meeting attending Merielle Martel's inner circle of war planners and so far, he had done little but listen.

He had been impressed by the tandem of the Chief of Defence Staff, General Kaplan, and General Gagnon, the man who had command over the expeditionary force that had entered the United States just over a month ago and was now back on its heels along the Canadian-US border.

He'd also been impressed with Merielle. Her command of the issues facing the country was strong, as was her personality.

Interestingly enough, both times she had come into the room to meet with this group of serious men, she ignored the empty chair at the head of the table. Instead, for both meetings, she seemed to randomly select one of the other free chairs.

Today, she was sitting directly across from Larocque. She was pissed, and rightfully so, in his opinion.

Terse, Merielle said, "So, the bottom line is that the counterattack coming out of Michigan *is* going to happen, and we're not going to be delayed by the Chinese strikes we had no idea were coming?"

As the PM issued her questions, she was staring at General Gagnon, but the second part of her inquiry had been meant for the Director of CSIS, James Plamondon.

Martel had been fit to be tied when Chinese cruise missiles had struck military and key infrastructure targets across Ontario and Quebec.

CSIS, who had hundreds of operatives and thousands of informants across the Red Faction states, had received zero warning of the Chinese buildup and now Merielle was paying a price in the media and politically.

In particular, the political elites in Quebec had gone ballistic. Eric Labelle, Merielle's nemesis and the province's highest-profile separatist leader, had not let the dead bodies of the attacks get cold before raging on TV and social media about how Merielle was single-handedly leading the country to its demise.

On the same day hundreds of the Chinese Wraith and Hyena automatons had helped to crack open Buffalo's defenses, the Chinese had unleashed over one hundred Longsword cruise missiles on targets as far north as Ottawa, CFB Petawawa and CFB Dwyer Hill, the home of Canadian Special Forces Operations Command.

With the limited air defenses operated by the Canadian Army and CANZUK's air forces otherwise occupied, the missile strikes had been all but unopposed. The destruction had been catastrophic.

Across Ottawa, strategically important buildings had been hit or levelled entirely. National Defence Headquarters had been hit no less than five times, while CSIS HQ and the HQ of the Communication Security Establishment, Canada's equivalent of the National Security Agency, had taken two missiles each. Aside from the damage to infrastructure, hundreds of critical people were now dead.

In the day's only good news, the British and Aussies had held Syracuse. They, too, had been pounded by newly arrived Chinese weapons, but they had not faced the horde of Hyenas and Wraiths that had stormed Buffalo's outer defenses.

That Merielle was supremely vexed about the situation and had taken a shot at the man leading CSIS seemed understandable to Larocque.

The Canadian Security and Intelligence Service, the country's domestic counterterrorism and international intelligence-gathering agency, had dropped the ball on the Chinese entry into the war and big time.

As Larocque saw it, the PM had every reason to be displeased with the Service's Director, Plamondon.

Ignoring Merielle's statement lambasting CSIS's massive intel failure, General Gagnon addressed the PM's question about the CANZUK-Blue counterattack gathering steam in Michigan. "Madame Prime Minister, our attack out of Michigan will happen. In fact, because of yesterday's events, we're working to move up the timing of the counter-offensive.

"Based on what we're seeing, the Reds weren't expecting the results they achieved, so a significant gap has opened up in their force posture. They know this, of course, and are trying to correct it, but if we move quickly, we can take advantage of their sloppiness and sever their 3rd Army into two pieces. If we can achieve this, it would force the Reds to pull back some number of the forces they've sent to bolster their attack on Syracuse.

"With the forces the Blues have pulled in from Wisconsin and Minnesota along with our 3rd Division, we will be able to deliver one hell of a punch to the force that just took Buffalo. I know with all that's happened, it's hard to believe, but the Reds are in a vulnerable position. We need to take advantage of this opportunity."

Merielle's jaw clenched as Gagnon finished his proposal. Across the table, she looked at Larocque. "And what do you think, General?"

Larocque had been ready for the question. What kind of fool would he have to be to sit in this room and not be up to speed on Gagnon's plans to salvage Canada's greatest defeat on the battlefield since WW II?

Injecting authority into his voice, Larocque said, "It's the right plan, Madame Prime Minister. Aggression is what this moment calls for. And for what it's worth, it is one of those rare times where my experience and gut are in complete agreement."

Merielle only nodded at his statement. Her eyes then shifted from his to the Director of CSIS, two seats to Larocque's left. When the PM spoke, her words were measured. "Jim, we've worked together for over four years and during this time, I have valued your advice and respected how you've conducted your business."

Merielle let her statement hang in the air momentarily, allowing the tension already in the room to thicken.

"But yesterday's intelligence failure is the last straw. I know your organization well. Never have I seen so many people so well-paid achieve so little."

"Madame Prime Minister —," Plamondon began to say, but Merielle's hand thrust forward, palm out, silencing the bureaucrat. "No, you will listen. I will not let you make any more excuses for your people. I regret the losses your agency has experienced in the past twenty-four hours, but everyone has suffered. And in my view, they are suffering mostly because your people dropped the ball."

Merielle got up from her seat. At a normal pace, she moved to the head of the table and stopped behind the seat that Larocque knew had sat empty in memory of the country's most recent PM, Robert MacDonald. She sat down.

Now at the head of the table, Merielle's eyes began to canvass the whole of the room. After connecting with each set of eyes, she said, "Our country stands only meters before a precipice that is a massive and dark chasm.

"If we continue to close the distance to that gap by doing more of the same, we will lose everything. Democracy and freedom — the very core of what and who we are. It will be gone."

Deliberately, Merielle's gaze re-acquired the spy chief. Casting a withering stare at Plamondon, she said, "With all of this going on, do you know what I'm told about your organization, Jim?"

Larocque did not know James Plamondon personally, but he knew enough about the man to predict he wouldn't respond to the question. Like everyone else in the room, he understood that his fate as a senior bureaucrat and leader was about to be decided.

"I'm told, Jim, that people in your organization have refused to go into the U.S. because they're not being given enough danger pay, or that once in the U.S., they are refusing orders because *'this isn't what they signed up for.'*" As Merielle delivered the last part of her statement, her hands rose to form air quotes.

"Jim, I know you are a competent person, and you and I have repeatedly discussed how CSIS, over two generations, has softened into a risk-averse talk shop instead of a well-honed operational outfit. I hate to say it, but we have a spy agency whose spies care more about the car they show up to work in than whether or not the country they've sworn to protect becomes enslaved."

Finally, the CSIS Director came to his own defense. "Madame Prime Minister, you're not wrong, but we are making the transition. We now have ten Direct Action teams, and my efforts to weed out those whom you describe... well, it takes time."

Merielle shot back, "We are out of time, Director, and I'm of the view a change in leadership is needed, and not just in CSIS."

Merielle rose from her seat, leaned forward, and placed her hands atop the polished surface of the conference table. With her soft brown eyes, she surveyed the politicians, agency leads, and bureaucrats in the room.

Finally, her attention shifted back to Plamondon. "I'm sorry, Jim. You deserve better than what amounts to a public execution, but today, things are going to change in this country, and you and several others are going to help me communicate this change."

Merielle's gaze pulled back from the intelligence boss and took up the rest of the room. She said, "When the Americans entered World War II, and they weren't used to making war, its four services were replete with senior officers who had gotten their positions because of who they were and who they knew and not because of how they performed on the battlefield. The result was that in their first two campaigns of the war, a lot of good men died because the wrong people were in leadership positions.

"Jim, if we had more time, I believe you would be able to whip your agency into shape, but we are out of time."

Merielle's eyes snapped across the table to take up the Clerk of the Privy Council, the country's most senior bureaucrat, Lyse Rancourt.

Without any verbal prompt, the rotund senior bureaucrat opened a folder on the table in front of her. Efficiently, she removed a small stack of paper and began to distribute the legal-sized one-page document in opposite directions.

As the document was passed from one person to the next, each individual's eyes took up the words on the page as though they were about to read of their own death sentence.

Because of his positioning at the table, Larocque was one of the last to receive the document.

There were two columns. On the left was a list of names of persons in current high-level positions across government. On the right, was the same list of positions but in all cases, a new name was listed.

Among those people on the move was the Minister of Foreign Affairs. Shiv Chandra, Merielle's loyal and hawkish Foreign Affairs lead, would move to National Defence.

The politician was in the room. Larocque's eyes darted toward Chandra. He looked satisfied.

The crucial portfolio had been managed by the junior Parliamentary Secretary for DND since the brutal assassination of the Minister in Australia two weeks earlier.

Further down the list were senior military roles, various agency leads, and several ambassadorships. Jim Plamondon's name was noted beside the position of *Chargé d'Affaires*, State of California.

When Larocque's eyes fell on the person who would lead CSIS, he stared in disbelief.

Flabbergasted, he slowly raised his eyes upwards and began to look around the room. Not everyone but most of the attendees were staring at him.

When his eyes finally connected with Merielle's, he saw a look of determination.

They stared at each other for several seconds. Finally, Merielle's eyes moved back to Plamondon. "Jim, see that the transition happens smoothly. It's my expectation you will remain in the building for the next two weeks, and you will do everything in your power to make sure that General Larocque gets everything he needs to affect the kind of change we've discussed today."

To the man's tremendous credit, his reply to the PM was prompt and without any hint of emotion. "Of course, Madame Prime Minister. The General will be able to count on my full support for the next two weeks and beyond."

"I know he will. You're a good man, Jim, and I'm sorry this had to be done and done in this way, but circumstances have compelled me."

The now-former director of Canada's intelligence service nodded solemnly and replied, "I understand."

Merielle pushed herself away from the table she had been leaning on, stood to her full height, and crossed her arms under her chest. "The information on the document in front of you will be released to the public at noon. The swearing-in ceremony for the Cabinet shuffle will take place at three at Lake Harrington, but that won't be disclosed to the public.

"It goes without saying this information is embargoed until that time. Questions?"

Still in her power pose, Merielle again took in the whole of the room. When no questions came, she returned her eyes to Gagnon. "General, everyone in this room still has a role to play if a different one than five minutes ago. Let's use the time we have left to get a briefing on your plans for that counterstrike against the Reds. If there's an opportunity to take advantage of our recent misfortune in Buffalo, I suspect you'll want direction sooner vs. later?"

Gagnon didn't hesitate with his reply. "Yes, Madame Prime Minister. Every extra hour you give us to shape our next move is going to make a difference in this next critical phase of the war. The UCSA has played its hand and now that we can see its cards, we need to take action. We can turn this war around, Madame Prime Minister, but we have to move quickly."

Merielle nodded and slowly lowered herself back into the chair that had most recently belonged to her political mentor. It was hers now.

Her eyes still zeroed in on Gagnon, she said, "Then let's hear your plan, General. Tell us how we're going to turn this nightmare around and fast."

***

As the last person left the boardroom, Larocque turned his eyes on Merielle.

She smiled at him and said, "Surprise."

"Madame Prime Minister —."

Merielle interrupted, "None of this Madame PM bullshit when the rest of the heavies aren't around. It's Merielle, if you please."

Since the Whiteman mission, Larocque and Merielle had become legitimate friends. For different reasons, they had both been shoved into the national spotlight and each had endured their own traumas.

If Larocque was being honest, it had helped to have occasional chats with the woman because when they were finished, his problems seemed more manageable.

"Okay, Merielle, we'll play it your way. I'm honored that you would think so highly of me to take this task on, but I'm just a soldier."

Merielle's lips thinned, and she shook her head. "You're not just a soldier, Jackson. You're a national hero, you have a history of getting things done, you were tasked with pulling the Airborne out of its most recent cultural decline, but most important, you don't owe anyone anything in the viper's nest that is CSIS. If anyone can whip that organization into shape, it's you. And that's exactly what you're going to do for me."

"But surely Jim was the right guy for this role. He lived and breathed CSIS his entire career and I've heard you mention he was making progress. Jesus, Merielle, CSIS isn't a bunch of meatheads trying to kill things. It's complex. It's subtle. It'll be like racing in the Monaco Grand Prix instead of the Dakar Rally. They're two totally different things."

One of Merielle's eyebrows raised. "I don't get the racing reference, but I think I know what you're saying, and you're right and wrong."

"But—" was the only word Larocque could get out of his mouth before Merielle pushed on.

"Yes, Jim knows the organization and where all the bodies are buried, and yes, he was making progress, but we've run out of time.

"Our enemies are quite literally on our doorstep, and do you know what the chief concern of the rank and file of Canada's spy agency was just last week?"

"What?" asked Larocque.

"Parking."

Larocque's forehead knitted together and repeated the word as a question, "Parking?"

"Yes, parking," Merielle said, sounding thoroughly annoyed. "You see, because our country is at war, we've had to draft more people into CSIS's ranks and in doing so, our veterans of the service – the very same people who missed the arrival of hundreds of Chinese cruise missiles and killer robots – were more concerned about how far they have to park their Tesla from work instead of making sure the CAF had the intel it needed to hold a city we should have held for months."

With a look of incredulity on Larocque's face, he asked, "Jim brought that forward to you?"

"No," Merielle snapped.

Larocque, knowing the PM well, let the intemperate one-word answer go.

Taking a deep breath to calm herself, Merielle continued. "Jim wouldn't bring that forward, but when it comes to the CAF, CSIS, and CSE, I keep my ear to the ground, and people I trust have been feeding me bullshit like this for months."

Merielle delivered a hard stare in Larocque's direction. Again, knowing the politician as he did, he met her eyes and waited for the words that would come next.

"There is an Order In Council ready to go. It will pass next week and give you, the Director of CSIS, extraordinary powers to do what must be done to get our country's intelligence service to cut weight and get into fighting form."

A former Canadian middleweight amateur boxing champion, Larocque signalled his appreciation for the metaphor with a smile and asked, "Can I see it?"

"Of course. But in a nutshell, the Order will enable you to suspend whichever internal processes you need to reconstitute the Service."

Larocque nodded and asked, "This gig you've thrust on me – it doesn't sound like I have a choice about whether or not I can take it?"

The PM's face softened. "I know Madison is not my biggest fan, Jackson, and I can't say I blame her."

Larocque started to protest, but Merielle shushed him. "I'm a fifty-three-year-old woman, who was also a cop for twenty-one years. I know when another woman doesn't like me. But it's okay, because she knows what I know."

"And that is?" Larocque asked.

"That you're the right person to do what I'm asking you to do. And that you'll do what it takes to keep this country safe. You'll make the tough calls so that Madison and Marcel can live in a safe country free of the tyranny that will surely come if we don't win this war."

As Merielle mentioned his son's name, a warning flashed inside Larocque's brain. In deciding to attach himself to the woman sitting across from him, it had not been lost on him that dark rumors continued to swirl around Canada's 26th prime minister.

He tamped down the concern for the moment. He would discuss it with Madison when he got home and they'd make what plans they could. Perhaps it was time for her and the baby to head west to Manitoba. His mother would be thrilled to have Marcel under her roof.

"So, you'll do what I've asked?" Merielle said.

The question snapped Larocque's attention back to the present. "I'll do it," he said with conviction. "I can't promise miracles, Merielle, but as you say, I do know a bit about changing culture, and if I'm to take your earlier comment about getting CSIS into fighting form literally, that is a world I know very well."

"Good. Now I'm more confident than ever that I've made the right decision."

The prime minister pushed back her chair and got to her feet. As she did so, Larocque moved to do the same. Standing, Larocque towered over Canada's leader, but in that moment, in no way did he feel like he had any physical power or advantage over the tenacious former cop from Montreal.

Merielle Martel had come into her own by leading a country at war and making life-and-death decisions. She was as powerful and in command as any Canadian politician had ever been. She was five-five in height, but it was her political power that made her seem the giant in the room.

Merielle said, "I have to get to my next meeting. We'll reconnect in three days. I'm going to do a tour of the damaged CSIS HQ."

She gestured with her hand to his uniform. "Do you own a suit?"

"A couple," said Larocque.

"Make sure you're wearing it tomorrow when you arrive at your new job. You'll need a few more. You might want to take care of that today."

"Right. Good advice," said Larocque as he glanced down toward his combats.

Merielle took a step toward Larocque and thrust out her hand. As he accepted it, he was surprised by the strength of her grip, and to signal as much, he gave her a curious glance.

"Impressive, I know," Merielle said with a smile. "I learned a long time ago you can throw off men with a grip that's stronger than their own. It helps to establish dominance – or at least that's what I've been told."

Larocque returned the woman's smile and said, "Well, there's no need to show me who the big dog is in this relationship. We've been through a lot, you and I, and by now, I have a good understanding of how you operate. I promise I'll do my best to get CSIS going in the right direction and firing on all cylinders if that's what you need me to do."

"It is," Merielle said as her smile dropped away. "And I need you to do it quickly and, if necessary, ruthlessly. You and I aren't here to make friends, Jackson. We're here to save this country."

Chapter 9

West of Houston, Texas

—

"Pull!" Spector bellowed.

On his command, the first of the final two targets streaked into the air from his left.

Raising his already-leveled Beretta over-under, Spector pulled the trigger, instantly destroying the clay target.

To his right, the low trap house issued the round's last target. Again, the President of the UCSA aimed his shotgun, and when the skeet was directly in front of him, he let loose.

"Goddamn!" Spector hollered, missing the final skeet.

"Clear range!" the man acting as the Rangemaster yelled.

Spector lowered his weapon, engaged the safety, and turned toward the small audience observing his performance.

Overweight to the point that it was the regular go-to topic on the few late-night talk shows still on the air, Spector strode slowly toward the group of men who were his closest advisors.

"Twenty-two is respectable, Mr. President. I almost believe you were as good as you say," Peter Parr announced as his boss neared the gathering.

"Well, it's as good as I'm gonna get. Gone are the days when I had the time to make regular visits to a place like this," Spector replied to the younger man's observation.

Stopping in front of the group, he added, "It was a great idea to come out here, Pete. It's exactly what I needed. Yes, my shooting's shit. There is no denying that, but damn if having a shotgun at your shoulder isn't a great way to clear the mind."

He pointed to a large, unoccupied pavilion fifty yards away. "Follow me, gentlemen. We'll have our meeting there."

As he started to move, one of the two orderlies present matched Spector's pace and took the big man's shotgun. "Thanks, sergeant. While you're at it, have some coffee brought out for us. I think you know everyone's order by now?"

"I do, Mr. President."

"You're good man, son."

"Thank you, sir," the Air Force NCO said as he peeled away in the direction of the private members building of the Houston Cedars Gun Club.

Reaching the outdoor seating area, Spector didn't seat himself but instead leaned his bulk against one of the pillars helping to keep the roof of the covered space aloft.

Gesturing to the group following him, he said, "Sit or stand as you please. I'm feeling good, so I'm gonna stay on my feet for a bit. The coffee should be here in five, but let's not waste time. Who's first?"

A tall, square-jawed man with a healthy dose of grey hair raised his hand and said, "If others don't mind, why don't I start with the latest from New York?"

Spector nodded at General Spellings, the Army's Chief of Staff and the man he relied on most to run the war against the Blues and their new CANZUK allies. "The floor is yours, General."

Stepping apart from the group of advisors, Spellings began his briefing. "The Canadian 4th Division and what remains of the 10th Mountain and 28th Division are across the border. As of six hours ago, Buffalo is officially ours."

Behind Spellings, applause broke out, and several of Spector's inner circle called out words of congratulation.

As the clapping and praise died down, Spellings continued, "We don't have precise estimates of casualties, but we think we chewed up at least thirty percent of their fighting strength. The bulk of their casualties came from having to wait to cross the bridges we left standing. Had we brought them down, I suspect we could have destroyed all three formations entirely. It might have been a bloodbath—maybe even the end of this war."

In making the last part of his statement, Spellings made no effort to keep the bitterness out of his voice. He had kicked and screamed to level the two spans that joined Buffalo to Southern Ontario but had been overruled by Spector based on the notion that UCSA forces might need those same bridges if CANZUK didn't come to its collective senses and sue for peace.

Spector wasn't having any of it. "Get over it, John. We took Buffalo in less than three days instead of months, and in the process, we saved tens of thousands of our soldiers' lives. Jesus Christ, man, sometimes you put the Grim Reaper to shame."

For a brief moment, Spellings glared at Spector, but he was far from an idiot, so he pushed on to the next part of his update.

"As expected, the collapse in Buffalo has accelerated the counterattack CANZUK and the Blues have been staging west of Cleveland.

"As best we can tell, they plan to charge the length of Lake Erie and try to catch us unprepared as we sort out our posture in Buffalo."

"Not a very good plan if you ask me," Spector said, interrupting the other man. "With all the tech our new Chinese friends have given us, they must know we'll be able to see them coming. There's another shoe to drop. What is it?"

Spellings shook his head. "We don't know. At least not yet. The Canadian 2nd Division is in the process of crossing into upstate New York west of Montreal. They'll have two ragtag Blue Divisions with them from New England and New York. This group's objective will be to try and relieve the Brits and Aussies at Syracuse."

"Try?" asked Spector.

"Yes, Mr. President. As you know, we now have Syracuse surrounded, and the intelligence we're able to pull out of the city suggests the defenders are short of everything and growing desperate.

"The order I've given to the 3rd Army is to press the city as much as possible. If Syracuse does fall before the relieving force can arrive that could be the straw that broke CANZUK's back. I've told my people Syracuse is their top priority."

Spector, himself a three-star general before a bloodless coup d'état that put him in his current position, looked at Spellings and said, "Syracuse ain't gonna fall, John. We both know the Brits and Aussies are made of tougher stuff than some give them credit for. As each week of this war passes, you can see the backbone of CANZUK get stiffer. I hate to say it, but it's almost like they're coming out of some deep sleep.

"And the French didn't do us any favors by trying to off that Martel woman. What the hell were they thinking? Had they just left well enough alone, she might still be fighting for her political life. Instead, we have Wonder Woman reborn, and the Canadians are now talking about a draft."

Parr's voice cut into the dialogue. "The same can be said of the Chinese and their stunt in Sydney. Everything coming out of Britain and Canberra is that both countries are furious. Even the go-along-to-get-along Kiwis are hopping mad. I'm hardly an expert, but it doesn't look like any kind of surrender is in the cards at the moment."

On delivering his assessment, Parr and Spellings locked glares on one another, but before the battle could be joined, Spector growled, "Don't even start, you two. Keep your eyes on the prize. There are more positives than negatives, as I see it. If the Canadians want to come at us again, let them. We kicked their ass back to the border, and we'll do it again. Our on-again friends, the Chinese, may not have many more of these killer robots to give us, but we're back to even Steven in the sky, and the artillery they've put into play will only make the job of killing our enemies easier."

Spector focused his eyes on Spellings and said, "Tell me I'm wrong, John?"

Grudgingly, the general tore his eyes from Spector's chief of staff. "You're not wrong, Mr. President. So long as we can ramp up production of the needed ammunition type, the Chinese artillery is going to make a difference. And yes, knowing the Canadians are coming gives us a tactical advantage, but I'm concerned about the bigger picture. Our people are tired. Exhausted, in fact.

"They've been fighting for almost four years, and now we're seeing signs that the Russians are on the move and that the Neutrals are having a change of heart.

"If the Russians move on Poland or the Baltics, France's support could dry up quickly. Without their fighters, our new status in the air becomes iffy once more. And if France is looking to Eastern Europe, it means the British can afford to send over more of their air force to North America, including the F-35s put on loan to them by the Norwegians and Danes. We're still in the thick of this fight. And if all this wasn't challenging enough, this Sanchez son of a bitch has this ill-timed meeting with Anders-Maxwell. Mr. President, if the Neutrals and California decide to join the war —."

"Hold up there, John," Spector said, nodding in the direction of a pair of orderlies approaching the pavilion with the coffees that had been ordered.

Reaching the stairs, the two plainclothes airmen efficiently circulated amongst the gathered group of men distributing beverages.

On receiving his, Spector removed the cup's top, took a preliminary sip of his latte, and then turned his eyes on the Air Force sergeant. "Michael, tell the ladies inside I approve. This thing is scalding."

"I will, Mr. President. Is there anything else you need?"

"No, we're fine for now. Someone will holler if we need anything."

"Yes, sir."

On word of their dismissal, the two orderlies turned and began to make their way back to the clubhouse.

With the NCOs gone, Spector prompted Spellings to continue. "The movie star – you were saying."

"Maybe it's best if Director Christoff gave the latest," Spellings said, gesturing to one of the other men standing in the loose circle that was Spector's war cabinet.

In the years long before the civil war and the creation of the Consolidated Intelligence Branch, CIB, Dave Christoff had been a well-respected CIA officer who had vast experience doing clandestine work in several countries.

At the outbreak of the conflict, he had held an Assistant Director role in the vast bureaucracy that was the CIA. From Vermont, he was one of the many Blue State natives who had recognized the political cancer that had infected the United States and chosen the side that promised to remove the disease no matter the cost.

Like the rest of his key advisors, Spector had elevated the man to his role because of a combination of competence and an innate ruthlessness to do what it took to win the war.

Leaning against one of the large cedar tables that occupied their impromptu meeting space, the man looked and dressed as though he had taught high school geography. It was the classic nondescript spy look if there ever was one.

"Well, Dave, what's the story on the pretty boy and his flirting with the Neutrals?" Spector asked after taking his first real sip of his drink.

Christoff pushed himself up from the table so he was standing. "First, Mr. President, I think it's important to say that in our library of assets across the world, California is one of the few places where we're spoiled for choice. Between our in-state field officers and our network of informants, not much can happen in the state without us knowing about it."

"Good, then let's get the details. Do we need to be worried about Sanchez or not?" asked Spector, allowing a touch of impatience to come through in his voice.

"Unfortunately, Mr. President, the answer to that question is, I don't know."

One of Spector's eyebrows arched upward. "What do you mean you don't know? You just told me we had California covered."

"The state is covered and this is just one of the reasons why I'm becoming increasingly concerned about Sanchez. On almost any other issue, we've been able to get a sense of where he stands, but on this, we've heard nothing. Despite the recent meeting with Anders-Maxwell, we've heard nothing from him or our informants about what his intentions are."

"Sanchez not saying anything doesn't mean he's changed his mind, Dave," Spector said, chiding his senior intel man. "I mean, he repeatedly said during the election that California would mind its own business. What makes us think he might change his mind?"

Christoff shook his head and said, "The fact that he's not saying anything." After a long pause, the CIB Director continued, "As you might expect, we've done a profile on him, and when he goes silent on an issue, it doesn't necessarily mean he's moved on. The model we've produced indicates that when Sanchez goes quiet, there's a twenty-seven percent chance he'll flip his opinion."

Spector snapped at the other man, "Jesus Christ, Dave, he's only been a politician for a few months. He can't have made that many decisions, and what do you mean by model? I thought you frowned on near-AI to do this profile stuff?"

Christoff nodded and said, "As you know, Mr. President, Sanchez has had a long career in the public eye, and he's never been afraid of giving his opinion. When you scan his career, there's quite a bit of data to mine. Based on our analysis, I can tell you that in more than one in four times, the man shifts his stance after he's taken a position publicly. Further, where that topic is highly controversial, that percentage increases to forty-three percent. To put it mildly, sir, he's a fair-weather politician, and like most politicians of that ilk, he tends to go where the political winds are blowing."

Christoff raised his coffee to take a quick swig and then continued, "As for using near-AI to construct the Governor's profile, I don't pass along anything to you, Mr. President, that my best people haven't chewed on."

"On this one, my best folks and gut are telling me Sanchez is a risk to waffle. As soon as Colorado and the other Neutrals get involved, he won't be able to help himself. He's played the hero in too many movies. This is his natural inclination. Whether it's six months or twelve, we should count on California and what remains of the Navy joining the fight."

Spector gave the CIB Director a long, hard stare. Just as the dynamic was becoming uncomfortable, he said, "I take it you think we should get out in front of the problem?"

"I do," said Christoff without hesitation. "We'd hardly be the first to make a play of this kind. The assassinations in Sydney were just the latest examples of state leaders being neutralized."

"And you have a proposal?" Spector asked.

"We do. Peter and his team have been invaluable in helping pull a package together. What they've accomplished since Operation Sunlight kicked off is nothing short of remarkable."

Parr made no outward effort to acknowledge the compliment.

By every measure, Operation Sunlight had been a resounding success. It had been just a month since the fall of Washington and the start of the UCSA's ambitious effort to purge the Blue Faction of the people who acted as its ideological foundation.

In all, in those Blue territories the Reds now controlled, nearly five thousand deserving social media types, academics, and politicians had been liquidated. And all of it had been under Parr's precise and unforgiving direction.

Christoff continued, "Mr. President, with the assistance of Mr. Parr and his team, on your order, we have a contractor who's signed on to a mission we're calling Operation Golden Silence."

Christoff turned his head toward Parr. "Pete, would you like to take it from here?"

Nodding at the intel boss, Parr took several steps forward, putting him near the center of the President's circle of advisors. For an unnatural amount of time, he let a silence grow amongst the gathered men.

It was a bit of theatre, but as his successes grew, Spector had given him an increased license for the boardroom theatrics he had mastered in his past corporate life.

Just as Spellings was about to growl something, Parr said, "Mr. President, how much do you want to know?"

"As with most things to do with Sunlight, give me the broad strokes," Spector said casually.

Nodding as though he was expecting this reply, Parr continued, "We don't know the time or place as yet, but when we do, I can assure you the contractor we've brought on to do the job is the very best. He and his team have taken down some of our hardest-to-reach and most elusive targets. Quite simply, Mr. President, this man and his methods have the body count that gives us the confidence we need to recommend this course of action."

Spector's eyes narrowed, signalling he was thinking something through. Then he said, "This contractor, he's that good? Because Sanchez is now the governor of a state of forty-five million people. He's gonna be a tough nut to crack. The amount of protection around him will be significant."

Parr nodded vigorously and said, "Mr. President, there is no doubt in our mind. What this man and his people can do – well, it verges on incredible. No matter how well protected Sanchez is, I rate our man's chances of success as very high."

One of Spector's meaty hands lifted to his face and rubbed at his mouth and chin, his eyes taking on a thousand-yard stare.

Finally, his hand dropped from his face, and his eyes re-focused on Parr.

Still staring at his chief of staff, Spector said, in a loud voice, "Any objections, people? Is there anyone here who doesn't think we should go in the direction Dave and Peter are proposing? You all know the methods that will be used, so you know how messy this could get."

When no one moved to speak, Spector's eyes canvassed each man under the pavilion. After looking each of them in the eyes, he said, "Gentlemen, hearing no objections, I think it's time the people of California and its leader got a taste of the hell the people in our part of the country have been force-fed for the past four years."

His gaze then moved back to Christoff and Parr. "What did you call the operation?"

It was Christoff who replied. "Operation Golden Silence, Mr. President."

"I like it. Damn poetic, if you ask me. Make it happen. Let's take this Sanchez son of a bitch off the board before he puts his too handsome nose where it doesn't belong."

Chapter 10

Toronto, Ontario

Irene MacPhail was dog-tired. In fact, she had been in a near-continual state of exhaustion since she had been elevated to the position of Canada's Deputy Prime Minister.

The role was a funny one in Canadian history because the position – whether it existed or not – was entirely at the whim of the Prime Minister.

Further, the power and scope of the role was also at the discretion of the PM. Over the past fifty years, there had been as many powerful Deputy PMs as there had been figureheads or sometimes, no Deputy PMs at all.

As she strode down the hallway of Toronto's Sunnybrook Hospital after visiting with more victims of the recent UCSA missile attacks, there was no doubt what type of Deputy PM historians would apply to her.

While Merielle focused on running the war, Irene MacPhail had been given the task of overseeing the Conservative government's domestic agenda. If it didn't directly pertain to the war, it was her problem to solve or her event to attend.

Today was one of those occurrences where domestic issues and the war had collided.

The Chinese missile strikes had killed hundreds, wounded more, and sent parts of Canada's economy and health care system into shock.

Within less than forty-eight hours after the attacks, the Prime Minister's Office had tasked MacPhail and the man striding beside her to get on the road and undertake a full-court press to assure Canadians that their hospitals had the capacity needed to care for the wounded.

The man keeping in step beside her was Michael Oyinlola, the federal Minister of Health. Ten years her junior, not for the first time, she thanked whoever needed thanking, Health was his portfolio and not hers. Even before the missile strikes, Canada's healthcare system was a disaster. Now, it was a shambles.

For seventeen hours straight Oyinlola answered question after question from the ever-present media pool about the capacity of the health system to respond to the emergency.

And when they weren't in front of the cameras being quizzed or berated but were instead secluded with victims and their upset families, he had repeatedly demonstrated his skill as an exceptional small-'p' politician.

On each occasion, he knew the right times to listen, to speak, to comfort, and when necessary, to deliver the message that while the war was an awful thing, now was the time for the country to pull together.

On one occasion, she'd heard him say to a man who'd almost been crushed to death, *"Freedom was never free. Even here in Canada. And as terrible as things are now, they'll get worse if we don't stand up for ourselves."*

To his full credit, when the man said the words, he made you feel like he believed it.

"You're quiet," Oyinlola said, interrupting her appraisal of his good works.

Releasing a sigh, MacPhail said, "I'm not gonna lie, Michael, I'm totally bushwacked. I feel like I've worked a triple shift at the fish processing plant back home. Mary, Mother of God, I don't know where you get the energy, but I, for one, am grateful for it. You did well today. As well as any politician I've seen in action."

"You didn't do so poorly yourself, and if you're tired, that didn't come through in this last visit," he replied, his voice deep and pleasant.

"Yes, well, it wouldn't look great for me or our government if I was caught on camera dozing off or uttering insensitivities to some over-the-top husband whose wife has a broken bloody toe."

When the words MacPhail had just said registered in her exhausted brain, she began to apologize, but Oyinlola shut her down.

"Never mind that. I felt the same way. He was being a dick and was way out of line. For Christ's sake, there was a child with a crushed skull in the bed next to them. The man was a full-on prick."

MacPhail allowed herself a quick laugh and then said, "He was a prick, wasn't he? But I should still be careful with what I say. I trust you, Michael, but you're one of a few."

Fifteen feet ahead of them, four of the six RCMP officers that had escorted them around the hospital reached the entrance that would bring MacPhail and Oyinlola to their separate vehicles.

In pairs, the four bodyguards stepped into the warm night air to join the officers and vehicles waiting for them.

Suddenly, MacPhail felt Oyinlola's hand grasp at her elbow. Firmly but gently, he slowed the two of them down to a stop.

Though fatigued, when something unexpected happened to MacPhail's well-tested fight-or-flight system, it had no problems kicking into a higher gear.

With a look of inquiry, she glanced at Oyinlola's face but could see his attention was focused on his phone.

Seeing the man was otherwise occupied, her eyes darted to the two RCMP officers trailing them.

Both had pulled up their strides and were warily looking forward and back, trying to ascertain the reason for their charges' sudden lack of movement.

Just as quickly as it had come, Oyinlola's hand left her elbow, and his light brown eyes met her's. "I trust you too, Irene. I trust you enough that I know the information I'm about to tell you will stay with you and only with you."

As Oyinlola's words registered in her brain, MacPhail's heart started to gain speed. For the love of Peter, she thought, would other people's bloody secrets and machinations stop storming into her life?

Sensing the man's urgency, she said, "I'm a Newfoundlander who made her name in journalism. In the world I come from, it doesn't get any more trustworthy than that. What's up?"

He took a step closer to her. "Within an hour of your return to the hotel, a man will come to visit you in your room. Let him in and listen to what he has to say. The two officers stationed outside your room will not be there. Don't be alarmed. Your conversation won't take ten minutes, and it will be off the record."

One of MacPhail's eyebrows arched higher, and she said, "Michael, I don't meet strangers when I don't know what they're coming to speak to me about. It's that simple."

"The White Unit," he said quietly.

"I'm sorry, what did you say?" MacPhail said, making no effort to lower her own voice.

"You heard me, Irene. I can't say anything more. Talk to the gentleman who'll visit you tonight. That's all I can say."

Out of the corner of her eye, MacPhail saw one of the two RCMP officers trailing them begin to walk in their direction.

She felt Oyinlola's hand grab hers. His grip was firm. "Will you meet with him, Irene?"

Just as the officer arrived and cleared her voice to announce her presence, MacPhail looked at Oyinlola and said, "Goddamn you, Michael, yes, I'll meet with him."

***

Nearly ninety minutes later, MacPhail heard a knock on her door. On her second tea and wearing casual clothes, she was as ready as she was going to be.

Reaching the entrance to her hotel room, she opened it without hesitation and saw a man who rivaled Mr. Oyinlola's looks, though he was younger and had lighter skin.

That he was wearing a loose-fitting hoodie over his head, no doubt to protect his identity from the hotel's CCTV system, endowed the man with a dangerous feel.

She only stared at him.

Finally, in a voice that held the slightest hint of a Québécois accent, the stranger said, "May I come in?"

"Sorry. Yes, of course. It's been a very long day. I was told to expect you. Please come in," MacPhail said.

Stepping aside, the hooded man walked into the room. On reaching the foot of her bed, he turned and pulled back the cowl to expose the whole of his face.

"Thank you for agreeing to meet with me, Madame Minister. I believe we can help each other."

Straight to the chase, MacPhail thought. Good. The less time he's here in the room, the better.

"I've taken this meeting at Minister Oyinlola's request. He said you had something important to tell me. I'm exhausted and have to be up in four hours, so it's best you're efficient with the time you have with me."

If the stranger was concerned about her abruptness, he gave no sign of it. Instead, he fired off a series of questions.

"Are you aware that in the past two weeks, at least eight Chinese intelligence operatives have been found dead in BC, while another three have been found murdered here in Toronto?"

"You mean gang members?" MacPhail said, and then quickly added, "The Triads have been pushing into the Big Circle Gang's territory in BC and Ontario. Everyone knows that. As it's been told to me, Big Circle is a nasty bunch."

"And you believe that?" the man scoffed.

MacPhail, quite unwilling to jump to the stranger's tune, gave no reply.

The stranger issued another question. "Are you aware that Canada, on the direct orders of its prime minister, abducted, tortured, and then eventually killed the director of France's foreign intelligence service?"

MacPhail's eyes narrowed as she gave her reply. "A vicious and fantastical rumor. More likely, the man is sipping margaritas somewhere in South America counting the millions he allegedly embezzled."

The stranger took a step in her direction.

As he did, the stern look on his face transitioned into something approaching anger.

His next question came off more like an accusation. "You are aware that only six weeks ago, Merielle Martel gave orders to assassinate Yvette Raymond?"

No wilting flower, Irene MacPhail stared back into the accusatory eyes locked onto her. Icily, she said, "Listen to me carefully, whomever you are – Canada isn't in the assassination business."

The look of anger on the man's face disappeared. Just as quickly, it was replaced by what might have been pity or sadness. He then said, "Oyinlola thought you might play things this way. He has taken a huge risk in connecting us. We hoped that you might choose to help us save our country, but it looks like that hope was misplaced."

After one final penetrating stare, he dropped his gaze and began to walk towards the door.

Stepping out of his way, MacPhail watched the stranger reach for the door. As loudly as she might, she said, "Wait. I know about the White Unit."

The man's hand atop the door's handle stopped, but he did not turn around.

MacPhail continued, "I don't know anything about any Chinese or French spies, but I do know that Raymond's death was unnatural, that it's likely some paramilitary group killed her, and this group is in some way linked to the PM. I've used all my resources to get more details – I've taken risks myself, but no one will talk with me. As best I can tell, people are supportive of what's going on, or they're scared."

Over his shoulder, the man said, "So you understand that Martel is more than what she seems?"

"She is," MacPhail said firmly. "But I can't prove anything. And even if I could, what could I do? Christ on the bloody cross, we are in the middle of a war. A war we could lose. If the PM is having people killed, maybe she's right. Maybe this is what the moment calls for?"

The stranger slowly raised his hand from the door handle and turned back to face her.

"On the matter of proving things, Minister, I can help. When the time comes, I can get you the evidence you'll need to expose the PM."

"How?" MacPhail said in a harsher tone than she would have liked. Tired and treading on dangerous political ground, her frayed nerves were revealing themselves.

Unconcerned by her forcefulness, the stranger, perfectly calm, said, "Until two weeks ago, Minister, I was in the White Unit, and I was there the night Yvette Raymond was assassinated, and by my own hand, I killed – no, assassinated – Education Secretary Roberta Hastings."

MacPhail's eyes narrowed as she tried to recall the details that surrounded the name she'd just heard. Finally, it struck her, she said, "Hastings of the Blue Faction? She resigned just before Washington fell. She's in hiding, not dead. You killed her? Why?"

As the questions tumbled out of her mouth, they sounded skeptical.

"She is most certainly dead," the man said calmly. "And I know she's dead because I put two bullets into her chest and one into her head in a CSIS safe house in Connecticut.

"I also killed one of the two US Marshals protecting her. When the time comes, I can show you where their bodies are buried. But that's just the tip of the iceberg."

He took a couple of steps back into the room and said, "On the matter of Hastings, she was killed because dead bodies can be trusted not to tell their secrets, or in this case, to tell how Canada directly manipulated the politics of another country."

"Entirely unbelievable," MacPhail said. This time, her skepticism came through loud and clear.

"And yet, it happened," said the hooded man. "Canada and the UK manipulated the FAS political scene together to help Morgan get rid of Menendez. Conveniently for Merielle Martel, any interest in Canada's role in helping to overthrow the legitimate leader of another country disappeared the moment the Reds took Washington."

The stranger took another step in MacPhail's direction. With his intense brown eyes locked onto hers, he continued, "The PM and a small group of operators are manipulating this country from the shadows, Minister. I know you know this. Help me, Oyinlola, and others stop this despotic nightmare before it's too late."

"Despotic?" MacPhail said, almost sneering.

"I know all of it sounds crazy, but I've seen the rapid growth of the White Unit. I know what it can do. I know who's leading it, and I know what he's capable of. And if you don't think Canada can become a tyranny, Minister, then maybe you are not as in touch with reality as I was led to believe."

A look of annoyance claimed MacPhail's face and, in an icy tone, she said, "You don't know the first goddamned thing about me."

Then it was her turn to take a step forward. Her intense green eyes blazing, she continued, "Maybe Merielle is right? Maybe we need this White Unit? Maybe we should be killing people like Chinese intelligence agents. For Christ's sake, just over a month ago, they killed over four hundred of our sailors, and only two days ago, they killed hundreds more with these bloody missile strikes. I saw the charred and destroyed bodies, some of which were children, by the way. Not five hours ago, I saw a baby who had two bloody stumps where her legs used to be. Who the hell are you to question Merielle's methods? Maybe she's going about it the right way?"

Unfazed by MacPhail's use of graphic imagery, the stranger pushed forward with his argument. "Tell me, Minister, under what circumstances is it justifiable for a Canadian prime minister to order the murder of a Canadian citizen?"

When MacPhail did not reply, he continued, "Who's to say you're not the next person to die? The White Unit is growing, and with each passing day, they're getting better at their work.

"Soon, if they're not stopped, this country is going to have its own homegrown version of the Gestapo or FSB – pick whatever secret police you want. Within the year, they'll be everywhere, and the bounds of their terror will know no limits. History shows these types of things don't take long to become entrenched, but it doesn't have to be this way. Help us, Irene."

For a long moment, MacPhail's gaze took in the man who, five minutes earlier, had revealed himself as the murderer of Roberta Hastings. Now, he was asking her to trust him to take down the leader of her country. It was madness of the highest order.

Finally, she said, "I won't commit to anything that will take the PM down until I've got a fuller picture. I'm sympathetic to your position, but I need to be convinced. There's too much riding on this war. I need more information."

He gestured in the direction of the chairs and table situated by the room's large floor-to-ceiling window. "Let's have a seat. We have twelve minutes before the officers on this floor are replaced by people we don't trust."

Moving to the furniture, MacPhail asked, "We? Who are you, by the way? And don't you dare give me a fake name because if we get caught doing what you're proposing, aliases won't make a lick of difference."

Reaching the pair of leather-backed chairs, the stranger turned to face MacPhail and slowly offered his hand.

Looking into the man's face warily, after several heartbeats, she accepted it. His grip was firm but not overly so.

"My name is Sam Petit, and only a few weeks ago, I was part of a small team that saved Merielle Martel from certain death in Montreal. It is because I saved her that I'm still alive and can have this conversation with you."

When Petit gestured to her seat, they both moved to sit down. Seated, he glanced at his watch and said, "And over the next ten minutes or less, I'm going to convince you to help me take down the leader of our country."

Chapter 11

Guyana, Camp Low Wood

As the CH 525 Roc skimmed over the jungle canopy, Dune eyed the helicopters west of their position.

As planned, the five British Army Wildcats and the soldiers riding in them had flanked the Canadian assault team. The Brits would land on the north part of the airfield.

With dawn having just arrived, he could see the five UK helos with his naked eye and could make out that, like the Canadian Special Operations Regiment soldiers riding in the RCAF Rocs, the Ranger Regiment soldiers in the Wildcats had cast the doors of their rides wide open. It was almost go-time.

Together, the five Wildcats were carrying nearly fifty operators, each loaded with the kit needed for a lightning-fast takedown. Along with the commandos in the four Canadian Rocs, just over one hundred fifty CANZUK special operators would descend on the morning's designated target.

As he shifted his gaze to one of the nearby Canadian choppers, Dune's BAM came alive in his ear. "Dagger Teams Alpha and Bravo, listen up," the British-accented voice said, its tone severe.

"We have new intel from the target area. Local militia forces have just arrived on the scene and have doubled the size of the defending force. Our mission proceeds as planned. We'll only get one shot at this. Air assets will suppress the LZ on our arrival, but expect the opposition to be tougher than our briefing. When our boots hit the ground, keep your heads on a swivel and listen to your BAMs. If we need to make adjustments, we will. Be sharp, people. Dagger Sunray out."

As soon as the British officer's update finished, the helicopter Dune was riding in dropped itself closer to the treetops and, in the process, drove his stomach into his throat.

He hadn't been with CSOR long, but in that brief period, he had come to know that the men and women who flew the helicopters of the 427 Special Operations Aviation Regiment were a daring but also highly competent lot.

Another voice, this one more familiar and Canadian-accented, popped into his earbud. "All right, Dagger Team Bravo, I hope you've enjoyed the flight. We're three minutes out. As Dagger Sunray just said, we have additional baddies to deal with, but the plan remains unchanged. It just means more bullets to dodge, CSOR. Our specialty. As always, stay cool, practice good comms and fight hard. Dagger One Bravo, out."

As Major Linden's instructions registered in Dune's ears, his eyes moved to the helicopter his company commander was flying in. The moment his eyes connected with the Roc, the voice of his BAM – the raspiest, sexiest version of ScarJo that could be found in the BAM's voice-over database – said, "Priority call from Dagger One Bravo."

"Accept call," Dune said instantly.

"Captain Dune."

"Yes, Major."

"Dollars to donuts, these new party crashers will be around the target, so be ready to move when I give the word. If Brant and Chipper can't gain access to the aircraft in the first two minutes, you and your boys will wedge in and make it happen. This plane does not get off the ground, is that clear, Captain?"

"Understood, Major. The lads and I will get it done when the time comes."

"Damn right you will. Dagger One Bravo, out."

Outside and to the front of Dune's racing helicopter, multiple small explosions lit up the horizon. In the dull grey of the pre-dawn light, the roiling fire would be seen for kilometers.

As had been the plan, one of the two RAF Protector RG Mk1 drones surveilling the target area had unleashed all four of their JAGM missiles.

At least two had struck the pair of short-range air defense units the enemy had set up only hours earlier.

"Dagger Team Bravo, we are thirty seconds out and starting our approach. Hold tight, people, 'cause we're coming in fast," said a voice Dune recognized as the pilot of the Roc he was flying in.

In the next helicopter over, Dune caught a burst of light emanating from one of the two door-mounted miniguns the Canadian helicopters had brought to the fight.

Even with the ferocious wash of the rotor blades spinning a few feet above his head, he heard the *brrrrrrt* sound of an M134D minigun unloading hundreds of 7.62mm rounds into what would now be a fully wrecked target.

As the canopy of trees below them suddenly disappeared, without warning, the pilot again dropped their helicopter.

Ahead and to the right, Dune could see a small commercial jet at the midpoint of a single runway. Because of the JAGM strikes, enough light bathed the airfield that he could easily make out that something close to a dozen military vehicles were around the plane. And running around those vehicles were men carrying weapons — lots of them.

As the four Canadian Rocs elevated their noses into the air to slow their descents, Dune shifted his weight, increased the strength of his grip on the handhold above him, and bellowed, "Hold tight, you bloody bastards!"

Beside him, Sergeant Butch Rochefort issued a rare smile onto his thickly bearded face.

"What?" Dune yelled over the blare of the helicopter's engines.

"You didn't use the c-word when addressing the boys. Well done, Captain."

"Yeah, well, the mission ain't over yet, mate, so hold your praise for the moment."

Canadians, like Americans, rarely, if ever, bandied about the word that was a commonplace term of endearment in most parts of Australia.

It had taken several months, but between his new wife's cajoling and the patient prompting of people like Rochefort, he'd mostly banished the word from his lexicon. Mostly.

When the four RCAF Bell 525s landed, Dune and his platoon were the furthest back of the four machines. As the wheels of their Roc connected with the grass surrounding the airfield, Dune and his men leaped out both sides of the helicopter.

As the designated reserve force of Dagger Team Bravo, Dune and his twenty-two soldiers formed the rear echelon of the assault group so they could watch the main attacking force's flanks and be ready to be called forward if the main attack faltered.

As the four heavy-lift helicopters began to rise into the air, Major Linden's voice re-emerged on his BAM.

"Team One and Two, advance and close the distance with the group of vehicles, ten o'clock to my position. Shut those bastards down!"

As two quick "Rogers" were given, the commandos of Team One and Two climbed to their feet and started running in the direction of a clutch of military-style vehicles firing at the four Rocs as they rose into the air.

As Dune looked on, both teams stopped running and, as one, raised their weapons and let rip in the direction of the vehicles and men they were about to assault.

This went on for ten seconds at which point half the commandos started to run forward while those remaining continued to fire their weapons.

At thirty meters, the running group of soldiers stopped, got low, and opened up again with their weapons while the group who had been covering them jumped to their feet and stormed forward. It was a classic cover-and-fire maneuver.

At the north end of the runway and four hundred meters from the plane, the Ranger Regiment was unloading from their five Wildcats.

In under a minute, the half-company of British special operations soldiers was replicating the leapfrog attack of the CSOR commandos approaching the objective from the north and east.

Around the airplane, defending soldiers were on the ground or behind vehicles, spraying their weapons at the Canadian and British attackers.

To their credit, on seeing the two sets of incoming helicopters, the defenders had split up and put themselves and their vehicles in between the approaching enemy forces and the airplane.

Getting within fifty meters of the vehicles defending against the Canadians, what remained of the first wave of CSOR soldiers was advancing at a crawl.

The heart rate of twelve members of Team One, fully half of Captain Chip's men had gone offline during their advance. The soldiers of Captain Brant's Team Two hadn't fared much better. A third of his men were dead or seriously wounded, according to the data flying across Dune's BAM wrist unit.

BOOM! A large detonation went off near one of the airport's outbuildings.

As Dune's eyes came up to take in the bright tower of light illuminating the early morning sky, he saw a group of men emerge from the building that had been designated as the airport's terminal.

They were moving in a circle formation toward the airplane with what looked to be two men at the center.

Dune activated his BAM. "Call Dagger One Bravo, priority Dagger Zulu-Seven."

"Priority call is in the queue," the simulated voice of ScarJo advised.

"Crikey!" Dune yelled in frustration.

Looking to his right he saw Rochefort staring at him expectedly. He, too, had seen the VIPs.

"Sergeant, get the lads ready to move," Dune said to his right hand.

The man with the dense beard only nodded and then started to yell orders at the twenty commandos surrounding their position.

"Dagger Seven!" the voice of Major Linden spawned in his earbud.

"Sir, VIPs just left—."

"I know," Linden barked, cutting Dune off. "Take your guys northwest. You're gonna meet up with some of the Rangers, and then together, you'll drive forward to the plane.

"They've done well to move most of their men to both ends of the runway to meet our attack, but if we move quickly enough, you and the Rangers might find a mushy middle."

"We're on it, Dagger One. Dagger Seven out,"

When Dune's eyes reconnected with Rochefort, his hand stabbed in the direction he'd been given. "That way, Sergeant, about two hundred meters. And fast like the bloody wind. Keep your eyes open for a gaggle of Rangers. Once we connect with them, we assault the plane. Move!"

Rochefort didn't acknowledge the order. Instead, he bellowed, "CSOR 3rd Platoon on me! On me!"

In seconds, all twenty of Dune's commandos were charging forward on Rochefort's flanks. Getting up off his one knee, Dune moved to follow them.

By the time he had caught up with Rochefort, the leading elements of his men had already connected with the Rangers.

Arriving, Dune instantly found his equivalent standing beside Sergeant Rochefort. Captain Dowd, easily as well-muscled as the Canadian standing beside him, stood out because he was one of the few Black men in either of the Rangers or CSOR.

Affable and with an Irish-like ability to drink alcohol, Dowd had quickly become a favorite of the Canadian officers since arriving in-country.

Pointing toward the plane, he said in a North English accent, "They've seen us. They're moving folks to cut us off, but not enough of them, I'd wager."

Looking in the direction the Brit was pointing, Dune saw a handful of men running to get in position. He also saw the airstairs truck beginning to move toward the plane. Whoever was managing the VIPs had been caught with their pants down. That the truck wasn't already at the plane was a huge cockup.

"How do you want to do this?" Dune said to the Brit.

"We'll go first, but when this is said and done, mate, you and your lads are buying drinks for us."

"How many?" Dune said, with more than a hint of outrage in his voice.

"The first three rounds," Dowd said with a huge smile.

"Outrageous, mate!" Dune called back instantly.

"You need this win, Dune and if you don't get it, you won't catch Fielder. And I know you hate that prick."

"Get down!" Rochefort bellowed beside them. "The bastards finally figured out how their weapons work."

Hearing the order, the combined group of Ranger and CSOR commandos lowered themselves to the ground—all except Dune and Dowd, who continued their negotiation, seemingly oblivious to the incoming enemy fire.

"Christ, Dowd, we're talking three rounds. Some of your lads can't even drink that much!"

"Yeah, we'll see about that. It's three, and you get a shot at taking the top prize and passing Fielder and his lot. I know you,

Dune. I know guys like you. Make the goddamn deal, mate, it's not getting any better."

"You're a real son of a bitch, you know that?" Dune said, the tone of his voice suggesting incredulity.

"And my men love me for it. Do we have a deal or no?" the Brit asked.

Dune's eyes moved from Dowd to Rochefort. Despite the glower on his face, the sergeant nodded.

When Dune's eyes returned to the Rangers', Dowd's smile was even bigger than before. "Say it, Dune."

"It's a deal. Three rounds."

Dowd pivoted away from Dune and roared at the soldiers around him. "Rangers, on me!"

As one, the twenty or so British special operators got to their feet and in seconds, they were charging toward the airplane.

As Dune watched them go, two men to the right of Dowd stumbled and fell to the ground.

He turned to Rochefort. "We swing to their right and put the landing gear between us and the VIPs. We get in close and do what we do best. Is that clear, Sergeant?"

"Yes, sir."

"Then lead the way."

With his face grim, Rochefort turned, yelled, "On me!" and started to jog toward the plane.

Less than one hundred meters later, and down only one soldier, Dune and the rest of his commandos had reached the plane's wings.

Despite the Rangers' losses, Dowd and his men were well on their way to putting down the last of the soldiers that had raced forward to prevent their advance onto the tarmac.

Swinging to the Rangers' right and keeping the plane's landing gear between themselves and the detail protecting the two VIPs, Dune and his men began their assault with alacrity.

As their rate of fire intensified, the two men, who were their targets, broke from their circle of protectors and began to sprint up the airstairs.

With less than thirty meters between his men and the fleeing VIPs, Dune moved to the front and center of his men and, firing his weapon prodigiously, yelled, "Advance, advance, advance!"

Superbly trained and with a two-to-one advantage, Dune's men quickly began to dominate what remained of the VIP's protection team. For every one of Dune's men that got waylaid, two of the defenders fell.

Never stopping their forward movement, Rochefort, Dune, and two other commandos reached the stairs, formed a line, and began to ascend.

Reaching the plane's door, the first of their number was cut down, but the second commando dispatched the sole combatant between the CSOR assaulters and the two older gentlemen standing in the plane's only aisle.

Both were fit and wore neatly trimmed mustaches.

With nothing between them and the Canadians, both men slowly raised their hands in the air. Keeping their rifles aimed at the VIPs, the remaining CSOR soldier and Rochefort moved to the side, allowing Dune to step forward.

He stopped at the incapacitated soldier lying in the aisle and stared into the faces of the two VIPs. "Going somewhere, gentlemen?"

Hearing Dune's question, a grin broke out on the face of the taller of the two men, but he did not speak.

Instead, it was the stouter soldier who addressed Dune.

His accent was Canadian, and when words came out of his mouth, it sounded like he was in the throes of a terrible throat infection. "Well done, Captain. I believe this puts you in front of Captain Fielder. I suspect he will be rather displeased by this turn of events."

"My thanks, General. My lads and I are now up two points on the good captain, but it's gonna cost us at the mess, so it's a victory, but an expensive one. Pints here on this base ain't cheap."

Major General Day, the Commanding Officer of CANSOFCOM, Canadian Special Operations Force Command, raised one of his eyebrows as though he was about to ask a question but instead said to the man beside him, "Shut it down, Colonel."

On hearing the Canadian officer's order, the taller and still-grinning VIP said with a light Scottish accent, "Open channel Dagger Force Omega, priority code McIntyre-Romeo-India."

After a brief pause, he continued, "Dagger Force, this is Dagger Alpha. Exercise Sapphire Bronco is terminated. I say again, endex, endex, endex. All units can stand down and barring any official protest, five points are awarded to 3rd Platoon, 2nd Company, CSOR."

Dune felt the heavy hand of Rochefort come down on his shoulder. "Nice work, sir. I can't wait to see Fielder's face. He's gonna be super pissed."

***

Flanked by Rochefort and his company's senior warrant officer, Ram Sahoo, Dune strode in the direction of the building where all company commanding officers and their two designated senior noncoms had been ordered to attend.

On returning from the exercise six hours ago, Dune had been able to get three solid hours of sleep, a decent meal, and a twenty-minute conversation with Trisha before the call had come in for CSOR, the Rangers, and the two countries' Tier-1 units to gather in the largest building on the bursting at the seams military base.

Lost in thought about the latest updates from his wife's new life on CFB Petawawa, Dune was jolted back to reality when one of Rochefort's hands reached out and roughly grabbed his shoulder, forcing him to come to an abrupt stop.

"What the f..." he began to say but then realized why Rochefort had manhandled him.

Standing in front of the double doors that would lead to the space they'd been ordered to rendezvous in was none other than Captain Fielder.

Flanked by a lieutenant and a scowling senior NCO who had the look of an attack dog, the man who ran the Ranger Regiment's intelligence unit had his arms crossed and was doing nothing to hold back the look of contempt on his battered face.

"Oi, if it isn't Captain Fielder," Dune said in as cheery a voice as he could muster. "I see that pleasant face of yours is healing up nicely."

"Cut the shit, Dune. I'm putting in an official protest. That son of a bitch Dowd shouldn't have let you take the prize. It's bollocks, and you know it. Buying drinks to get to the front of the line. Isn't that just what a snake like you would do? You Aussies just can't help yourselves. You're as dishonest as the day is long, the whole bloody lot of you."

The smile on his face growing wider, Dune said, "Come now, Captain. Gone are the days when we can stereotype an entire people. For example, I know better than to walk around telling people that the entirety of England is a country full of drunks with bad teeth and tiny dicks, but then I meet you and your lads, and I wonder if some stereotypes aren't stereotypes because they're true."

"Vishnu save us," Sahoo muttered from behind Dune. The big Indian-Canadian added, "The briefing, Captain."

Dune ignored the warrant officer and took a step forward. "My deal with Captain Dowd was fair and square, mate, so you're wasting your time with any protest."

"Dowd's a prick and ought to have known better," snarled Fielder.

"That's funny, that's what he said of you. That you're a prick, that is."

Fielder uncrossed his arms and took a step in the direction of Dune, but before the burly Brit could say or do anything, someone bellowed in French-accented English, "Fielder! Dune! *Esti*, you two jackasses clear a goddamned path!"

Together, the two men looked to see a group of senior officers striding in their direction. At the head of the group were none other than the sergeant majors of CANSOFCOM and United Kingdom Special Forces, UKSF.

As though they were two halves of the Red Sea, Dune and Fielder stepped apart and gave the approaching entourage space enough to enter the building. Rochefort and one of Fielder's men moved to hold the doors open.

As the group of senior officers approached, Dune recognized all of the men and women from his three weeks on base except for the officers wearing a camo pattern he was unfamiliar with.

Interesting, he thought.

On walking by them, the two sergeant majors delivered baleful glares toward Dune and Fielder.

Without a doubt, before the day was done, he knew he was going to be called out on the carpet by CSOR's regimental sergeant major, if not the colonel himself. This thing with Fielder had already gone too far.

As the last of the group passed by them, Dune's gaze returned to the dead blue eyes of the Ranger intel officer. The two men held each other's stares until Dune grandly gestured to the doorway and said, "Losers first."

Fielder started to growl a reply, but the sergeant with the attack dog face grabbed him by the arm, pulled him in the direction of the door, and muttered, "We'll deal with it later, Captain."

After a short walk, the two groups of commandos entered the crowded room where the briefing was to take place.

It was packed with fit men and a few women in their late twenties to early forties. As Dune stood at the entrance looking for a place to squeeze in, he recognized many of the faces.

Operators from each of the UKSF units were present. Perhaps two score of SAS, SBS, and Rangers were scattered about the room. In equal numbers were operators from Canada's two main unconventional forces, JTF-2 and Dune's own CSOR.

But off in the front of the seated area, there were perhaps a dozen soldiers wearing the same unfamiliar camo pattern he had seen moments ago.

They were spec-ops to be sure. Those few standing certainly looked the part. Each one of them was fit and square, and while they looked affable enough talking amongst themselves, there was no mistaking the aura of violence that surrounded these blokes, wherever they were from.

Moving from the strangers, his eyes found one of the CSOR company commanders he got along with best. Captain Ho waved him over with his ever-present smile.

Knifing between the groups of broad-shouldered commandos, Dune and his two designates arrived at Ho's location.

Just as the two company commanders fist-bumped, a British general Dune didn't recognize walked in the direction of the podium located to the left of the small stage.

On his arrival at the microphone, he leaned forward and, in a clipped voice, barked, "Attention!"

As one, every man and woman in the space, whether seated or standing, became ramrod straight.

After a count of two, the general said, "Rest easy and find your seat if you've got one."

Thirty seconds later, the general began his address. "For those who don't know me, my name is Major General Leslie Dunbar. I'm currently the Chair of the MOD's Operations Committee, which is why very few of the younger folk in this room will know me.

"For the past five years, I've spent far too much time in Whitehall, but once I was like you. For a decade, I was at the tip of the spear, and though it's been many years, I still remember what it's like to kick in a door or jump out of a plane."

From near the back of the room, Dune saw several of the older soldiers nod their heads at the man's words.

"But this isn't about me. I'm here to tell you we've done enough training and that this special task force the UK and Canada have pulled together is getting back into the fight."

Dunbar gestured to the men and women sitting in the front row wearing the camo pattern Dune hadn't been able to place. "And as we get back into the fight, I'm pleased to let you know we have new friends to help us win our war against the Red Faction and their allies. As of forty-eight hours ago, the Neutral Faction has shed its neutral status, and with us today are representatives from the newly formed Western Alliance's joint Special Forces Group."

Raising his voice several octaves, the British general said, "Let's give our new friends and allies a big CANZUK welcome!"

The room ignited in roaring applause as the gathered UK and Canadian special operators let loose their appreciation.

As the room regained most of its quiet, the Brit resumed his address. "For the next week, we will integrate with what will now be called the Western Alliance SFG. Together, we will work hard and diligently to ensure our communications systems, protocols, and procedures are as tight as they can be in the short time you will have."

The general paused and scanned the whole room with his eyes and then said, "Our comms, our procedures, and our relationships will need to be tight because, by this time next week, the whole of this joint task force will be heading to Western Alliance territory, where we'll be helping our new friends open a second front against the Reds.

"CANZUK Special Forces Task Group Bravo, you're going back to war."

Chapter 12

CSIS Headquarters, Ottawa

—

There was a knock on Larocque's office door. "Come in," he said without hesitation.

Looking up from his desk, he took in his Assistant Director of Operations as she strode through the doorway. She was not happy and hadn't been since he'd promoted her to the position three weeks earlier.

Monique Tomic was a striking woman.

She wore her raven black hair short and seemed to prefer makeup that accentuated her already severe Eastern European features. Had she not chosen a career in the intelligence business twenty-five years ago, her distinctive looks could have easily secured her several lucrative modelling contracts.

Stopping in front of his desk, she looked down at the Glock 26 handgun in front of him and said, "So, you finally convinced the right people, eh?"

Larocque pointed to the weapon and said, "You mean about this?"

"Yes, that. To my knowledge, you'll be the first Director to carry one on his person. Not even our IOs carry a weapon domestically, though I'm beginning to wonder if we should change that."

She threw a red folder onto his desk beside the handgun. "A car bomb in Manila killed two more of our people. Both had families. My people are screaming at me – literally screaming at me – to pull them out of the Pacific. The Chinese outnumber us ten to one in the field, they have more resources, and most importantly, they're ruthless."

The killings of foreign-based intelligence officers had started just before Larocque's arrival. The two names lying in the folder on his desk would bring the number of dead IOs to eleven.

And CSIS hadn't been the only service to lose people. Each of CANZUK's intelligence services had experienced casualties, though not as many as Canada had since the Chinese had gone lethal.

Tomic crossed her arms across her chest and delivered a withering stare in Larocque's direction. "Whoever or whatever is killing the Chinese here in Canada has to be found out and stopped. The organization you're now running isn't a military unit, Director.

"We're not soldiers, despite what my dick-swinging male colleagues might say about our origins. If we don't somehow manage to stop the killing of Chinese agents here in Canada, you're not going to have an organization to run in about a month. Just today, I received another four resignations. Resignations of highly trained, reliable people. There aren't so many of us that this can go on for much longer."

Larocque returned the woman's hard stare.

He was not of the intelligence world and, therefore, had limited experience to draw on when it came to finding and stopping the people killing Chinese intelligence assets across the country.

The French intelligence service, the *Direction Générale de la Sécurité Extérieure*, had also suffered casualties in Ontario and Quebec, but for now, the DGSE hadn't struck back at CSIS domestically or in Europe.

Dropping his eyes from Tomic's relentless gaze, Larocque said, "And there's nothing new on who might be doing this. Just this amorphous White Unit that no one seems to know anything about?"

"We have nothing," Tomic said, her voice now frustrated. "There are only whispers this group is out there and that it's growing. In twos and threes, retired CSIS IOs, RCMP officers, and small numbers of military people with specialized skills are suddenly disappearing. Their families, if they have them, don't have a clue where they've gone, and we can't find them. Not a single goddamned trace. It's like every one of them has disappeared off the face of the earth."

Larocque pointed to one of the seats in front of his desk. "Have a seat, Monique."

"Thanks, but I like standing," she replied, her voice icy.

When Larocque arrived at CSIS, it had taken no less than fifteen minutes to realize just how pissed off the organization was that an outsider had been brought in to try and 'correct the culture and better operationalize' Canada's intelligence service.

His first conversation with Jim Plamondon, the director Merielle had fired in Larocque's presence, had been cordial enough, but the moment he'd walked out of Larocque's office, his new assistant had walked through the door and with an ugly scowl on her face placed no less than twenty-two resignation letters on his desk, including her own.

With the country at war, the timing of the departures verged in the direction of treasonous, but in preparing for the task Merielle had given him, he had known people were going to have to be forced from the organization. He just hadn't realized it would be on their terms and that it would happen so fast.

But Larocque had done this kind of thing before. When the Airborne had been reconstituted in the weeks after the Haiti hostage rescue incident nine years earlier, the Regiment had got off to a rough start.

As they had in the eighties, Canada's regular army regiments had cast off too many of their problem soldiers and officers to their parachute companies, and these had formed the core of the born-again Airborne. In two short years, the testosterone-heavy and poorly led unit was on the verge of being shut down for a second time.

It had been CANSOFCOM and Larocque who had turned things around. To reduce the superiority complex the Airborne had developed relative to Canada's regular army battalions, it was brought under the thumb of Canada's Special Operations community, and Larocque, one year into a 2IC stint with the Canadian Special Operations Regiment, had been fast-tracked to full colonel and given orders to whip the Canadian Airborne Regiment back into shape.

And he had. Within six weeks, half of the Regiment's officers had been shipped out and nearly two-thirds of its soldiers sent back to their substantive regiments with unwritten orders that each one of the bastards should be driven out of the CAF.

Three years later, Larocque had re-forged the CAR into a fifteen-hundred-strong outfit on par with the UK's Parachute Regiment.

It had nearly cost him his marriage and, in ways his mind still refused to explore, had contributed to his daughter's suicide.

Those costs, particularly the latter, had almost been too much. He had given so much for his country, so as he sat across from the woman who had just refused his request to take a seat, he decided now was the time to do what he did best.

His plans to remake this organization, such that they were, needed to be implemented – starting right now.

Annunciating each of his words, Larocque said, "Monique, I said sit the fuck down. Now."

As the words registered with her, the stare the veteran IO had been levelling at Larocque dropped away. Sternly, she said, "I won't be talked to this way. This isn't the military, and —."

"Now!" Larocque boomed, cutting her off. Yelling, he continued, "You will sit down *now*, and you will listen or, so help me God, I will ask for your resignation, followed by the resignation of every last executive in this building until I get to someone who has the wherewithal to turn this damn organization around."

Tomic was once again staring into Larocque's eyes, only this time, it was a look of shock.

Slowly, she took a step to her right so she stood in front of the chair and then began to lower herself.

As her posterior hit the chair's seat, Larocque grabbed the matte-black handgun on his desk by the barrel, offered it to the person who was effectively his second-in-command and said in a normal tone, "This isn't mine. It's yours."

Dropping her eyes from his face to the handgun, she made no move to take the weapon.

"Assistant Director Tomic, I know you spent time in Russia and Belarus as an IO, so I know you are qualified on a similar version of this weapon. Take it, it might be that you're going to need it."

"What are you talking about? Domestic Intel Officers don't carry weapons, never mind executives. We never have. It's against the law."

"Not anymore. Effective midnight, an Order in Council will come into effect allowing CSIS officers to carry weapons and make arrests in Canada."

He gestured to her again with the weapon, and this time she reached out to take it.

Larocque then grabbed a piece of paper off his desk and handed it to her. Taking the document, she began to scan it.

"I'll save you the time," he said. "On that document are the names of one hundred and thirty IOs who are in Canada and who were at one time weapons-qualified. Within the next three days, all of them will be requalified. Within seven days, all of them will have completed a two-day intensive urban tactical weapons course at Dwyer Hill using the Glock 19 and the Heckler & Koch UMP. The course will be taught by JTF-2 instructors.

"During this course, you and I, along with representatives of JTF-2, will interview some or all of these IOs, and from them, we will select up to fifty for a new unit we'll be creating."

"Wait, what new unit?" asked Tomic.

"You're familiar with the Direct Action Teams operating in the US?" Larocque asked.

"Of course, but they're not of CSIS. They're operating out of the CAF."

"Correct," Larocque said. "We will duplicate these teams domestically, and CSIS will begin to operate two to three of them until we figure out who the hell is killing foreign intelligence assets across our country."

With a questioning look, Tomic asked, "Don't tell me you got permission to create these units as well?"

"No, I didn't," Larocque said plainly.

A look of outrage jumped onto the woman's face. "I'm sorry, you didn't get permission to create what amounts to a new domestic police force?"

"I don't need anyone's permission on how CSIS IOs are used, Monique. It's now legal for our people to be armed and carry out arrests. How we use them is up to us."

"Jesus Christ," Tomic said, "To what end? And before you answer that, let's be clear – these aren't *your* people. You've been here for three weeks. They're *my* people, and I'll be damned if I'm going to let you use them recklessly."

For a long moment, Larocque said nothing. Instead, his eyes bore into Tomic. To her credit, the woman did not back down.

Finally, he said, "I'm going to put *your* people in harm's way, Monique, but I'll never be reckless with them. I may not be of your organization, but I've led people for a long time, and I know the cardinal rule of leadership in war is that you never ever waste your people doing something reckless. Dangerous, yes. But never reckless."

Larocque allowed a long silence to predominate and then slowly, his right hand moved to one of the drawers in his desk and opened it.

When his hand reappeared, it was holding another handgun, this one a Glock 19. Gently, he placed it on the desk's surface in front of him. Taking his gaze off the weapon, Larocque's eyes reacquired Tomic's.

He said, "One more operational update. Though I'm Director and my place is behind this desk and taking meetings on the Hill, that's not my style. At least it won't be for the next few months.

"I'm going to track down this White Unit, and I'm going to speak to who's running it, and they're going to answer my questions. Do you think you and *your* people will be okay with that?"

"It doesn't sound like we have much of a choice," Tomic said, in a tone that suggested she was less than okay with this new direction.

It wasn't the reply he was hoping for, but he didn't have the time to play Tomic's game, whatever that was. She would get in line, or she wouldn't, and when the time came, he'd deal with the cards she was playing close to her chest. For now, Tomic was the last and best senior operator in the Service, and he needed her.

Pushing back from his desk, he got to his feet, grabbed the handgun, and, in a well-practiced movement, placed the weapon in a holster at the small of his back.

Looking down at the still-seated Tomic, he said, "Starting today, you and me – we're going to fix this organization, and in doing so, we're going to make sure that CSIS is the only outfit in this country to conduct counter-espionage operations domestically. Are you with me, Monique, or not?"

On hearing his question, Tomic's façade turned contemplative. After a half minute of silence, her eyes found Larocque's, and she said, "Don't screw my people over, and I'm with you until I'm not, Director."

Larocque nodded and said, "Good enough. Now, grab your weapon and follow me."

This time, Tomic followed Larocque's direction promptly. As she got up from her chair, she tucked the Glock into the waistband of her pants underneath her jacket. "Where are we going?"

"During this little chat of ours, several people would have found out they've been promoted. Some others would have received new assignments. Like you, those who understand what needs to be done are waiting for us in the Clark Room. We're going to meet with them now."

An elevator ride and two long hallways later, Larocque pulled up short of their destination and turned to face her. "When we walk into the room, two things are going to happen. First, we're going to get rid of anyone who we think isn't in line with the direction I outlined to you in my office. I tried my best to get the right people for what needs to be done, but I don't know these folks like you do."

Nodding, Tomic said, "I can help with that. What's the second thing?"

"I want the beginnings of a new plan – a solid one to find this organization no one seems to know anything about."

"You mean the White Unit?"

"Yes," Larocque said, his voice firm. "I'm going to get answers to my questions, Monique. And faster than you, the PM, or anyone else might think. Our country is at war, so from this moment forward, myself and the organization I'm leading – there's no more screwing around. This White Unit is now our number one priority, and you may not want to hear it, but that means things around here are going to change real quick like and radically. For too long, the people in this building have wanted to ignore the fact Canada is fighting for its life. Today, one way or another, they start to get that message."

***

"I told you it was a bad idea to put him in charge. Of course, he's going to try to turn the organization around. The man can't help himself.

"And if this wasn't bad enough, you went along with this scheme to let them carry weapons and give them powers of arrest. Jesus Christ, Merielle, it's almost as though you want to go to prison."

For a long moment, Merielle stared at Colonel Mustapha Aziz through their quantum connection.

"It's a calculated risk, Colonel. I need for CSIS to be turned around and quickly. We could be fighting this war for six more months or six more years. The organization needed to become leaner and meaner, and Plamondon was moving too slowly. Way too slow."

Aziz growled, "Yeah, well, slow was good for us. Dodging and staying ahead of the police is challenge enough. Now, we're going to have to look over our shoulders for people who are specifically trained to look for and stop the kind of work we're doing.

"I've got nearly two hundred people working for me. At some point, someone's going to trip up or get caught. What then? And don't tell me you've got everything under control because I'm far from an idiot. This country may be at war, and people might be scared, but there are still laws, and people are required to enforce them. And you aren't some all-powerful dictator. Should things start to unravel, Merielle, it will become very difficult for both of us and quickly."

Aziz moved his face closer to the screen and said, "What game are you playing, Madame Prime Minister?"

Unfazed by the directness of his inquiry, Merielle didn't hesitate with a reply. "I know you are not an idiot, Mustapha, and while I understand your concerns, all I can tell you is that you are going to have to trust me. At least for the next several weeks. You may not believe it, but things are developing as I had hoped."

Aziz nodded his head slowly. "Trust you. Oh, I do trust you, Merielle, because under your direction, the people who report to me have interrogated no less than twenty-six people, of which thirteen are no longer of this world."

Aziz paused on delivering this fact, waiting to see if Merielle would offer some kind of reaction, but when she said and did nothing, he continued, "I'm keeping track, Madame Prime Minister, and should the time come, whether I'm dead or alive, the right people will know what I know if you betray me or the people who've placed their trust in me.

"You and I, Merielle, whether we like it or not, we're in this together, and there's no turning back."

"Who said anyone was turning back?" Merielle snapped. "Have you not been watching the news?"

"I watch it constantly," replied Aziz calmly.

"Then you'll be familiar with the fact that only two days ago, Chinese missile strikes killed fifteen hundred Canadian citizens. Fifteen hundred people on my watch. And it will get worse if this country doesn't get with the program the rest of the world is running on."

Merielle paused and narrowed her eyes to stare daggers through the display. "You tell me you've eliminated thirteen Chinese intelligence agents. Fine. We eliminate as many as we have to. Canada is at war, Colonel, and I won't apologize – not once, not ever, for doing what needs to be done to keep Canadians safe."

She took a deep breath, forcing herself to moderate her tone. "Everything I do is for something bigger than myself. I know this now, and I fully understand that things could go very poorly for me. But this is the path I have chosen, and I will not turn from it."

Merielle's eyes narrowed yet further, and she repeated, "I will not turn from it. Do you understand?"

Aziz nodded. "I understand, Madame Prime Minister, and I trust you. We are both under a lot of pressure, we are alone, and there is so much at risk. But I trust you know what you're doing, even if you cannot share all the details."

Her face softening, Merielle said, "I do know what I'm doing, Colonel. My actions in time will show that to be true. And believe me when I say that one way or another, Jackson Larocque and the Canadian people will come to understand the choices I have made are the right ones. As you hear my voice, I promise they will come to understand and support my vision. Of that, I am one hundred percent certain."

Chapter 13

Northwest of Canton, Ohio

―

BOOM! Nine hundred meters in the distance, a Red Faction JLTV exploded into a grey and then orange-and-yellow fiery mess.

"Bingo!" Sergeant Bets, the Leopard 2A7 gunner, yelled in triumph on seeing his target's destruction.

"Nice shot, Bobby," Major Allan Lange of the Royal Canadian Dragoons said via his tank's internal comms system. "Number four for the day, and we're just getting started. Keep your eyes peeled while I update the boys."

"Roger that, Major."

Lange activated his BAM. "Open Channel Alpha-Bravo."

"Channel open," advised the male voice of the near-AI comms software. For today, he'd chosen the synthesized voice of Patrick Stewart. He was a Trekkie through and through, so the idea that Lange was fighting his tank with the help of none other than Jean Luc Picard was a feeling beyond excellent.

"Mako Team Bravo, all units, all units, this is Mako Bravo Sunray. Keeping our line of advance intact, all units are to advance eight hundred meters toward Point Charlie. Engage anything and everything that gets in our way.

"The latest intel indicates there's a battalion of Red regulars coming from the north, and by all accounts, they're hot to trot. The data indicates at least a dozen Abrams are charging in our direction, so shit is about to get real 3rd Squadron.

"Oh, and air support is inbound, so by the time we make contact with the Reds, there should be fewer of them, and they should be frazzled, so keep your spacing and make sure you have everything you need for a sustained bout of kick ass. Mako Bravo Sunray out."

From his position in the command seat, Lange looked down into the A7's guts and yelled, "Jamil, put us beside that JLTV. I want to get a good look at Bobby's handiwork. I think these are the guys who were riding us hard yesterday."

Lange didn't hear his driver's reply. Instead, the engines of one of the world's most modern and dangerous machines roared to life. In the next moment, it, along with the ten other Leopards in Lange's 3rd squadron, began to advance and tear up the soybean field that was part of the loose battle front which had formed between the Ohio cities of Canton and Youngstown.

As they approached the burning JLTV, he could see the charred head and shoulders of the body that had been operating the armored vehicle's mounted Javelin system.

During the Red's retreat from the Canadian-Blue counter-strike out of Michigan, this same vehicle and its crew had single-handedly destroyed three Canadian Tactical Armored Patrol Vehicles, TAPVs, and one of the Dragoons' older Leopards.

Above the front wheel well, Lange made out eighteen kill strokes.

"Finally ran outta luck, eh, you bastards?" Lange said aloud to himself.

Because of America's extended civil war, the Javelin system had become a rare sight on the battlefield. The French and now the Chinese had brought in and distributed their own versions of the weapon, but with things growing hot in both Europe and Southeast Asia, their numbers on the battlefield here in Ohio had been markedly less than what CANZUK had faced in their retreat to Buffalo and Syracuse.

The burning JLTV crew had been pros.

Time and again, they would pop over a ridge or around a corner, fire, and then retreat. But what this crew hadn't realized or, more likely, had chosen to ignore, was the all-but-invisible Reaper drone Lange had made a special request for an hour ago.

With the commencement of the wars in the US and now Vietnam, CANZUK's drone resources had been stretched thin.

That the Reaper that helped destroy this crew had been assigned to his regiment had been a surprise, but a surprise he and his boys had put to good use.

The MQ-9 Reaper had been tracking the retreating Americans for the past forty minutes and Lange himself had flagged the missile team behind the ridge the JLTV was now burning on.

The instant the vehicle exposed itself, Sergeant Bobby Bets was ready and tagged the JLTV, ending the lives of the prolific foursome of American soldiers.

With the still-cooking armored coffin only fifteen feet away, Lange peered through his tank's optics system to survey the ground before him.

In the late '20s, after much debate about whether or not the CAF should continue to operate tanks, Canada had ordered one hundred and twenty of the latest version of the German Main Battle Tank.

The optics in the periscope system that each Leopard had was a godsend to every one of the Canadian tankers that rode in the armored behemoths.

Through it, Lange could see for kilometers with crystal-clear clarity. Combined with the tank's targeting software, the periscope automatically identified definite and possible targets for each tank's commander or gunner.

At just over a thousand meters away, he could easily make out what was left of the Red Faction units they'd been playing a cat-and-mouse game with for the past hour. By the looks of them, they were no longer much of a threat.

They had been fighting a determined rearguard action since they first encountered the Royal Canadian Dragoons tearing through the southern suburbs of Canton.

The fighting within the city had been vicious and determined, but it had also been short. Canton, it turned out, had no shortage of people still in the city who were prepared to let CANZUK know where the Red Faction forces were located.

Waves of Reaper and attack helicopter strikes had been all that had been needed to start the Red pullout from the city.

Once exposed and under pressure, the combination of the Leopards' main guns, the brigade's anti-armor drones, and the occasional attack run from the dozen Super Griffons assigned to the fight had quickly decimated those Red platforms that could hurt and slow down the advancing Canadian mechanized division, of which Lange was the leading element.

Based on intelligence from interrogated Red soldiers from the city, the brigade that Lange was now evaluating through his optics had been ordered to slow the CANZUK and Blue Faction forces charging out of Michigan so that the main elements of the UCSA's 3rd Army in Buffalo could finalize their defensive positions.

Pulling his eyes from the tank's optics system, Lange rose higher and looked right and left.

Arrayed beside him was the full strength of the squadron he commanded.

Including his machine, they were eleven of the forty-seven Leopard tanks that represented the entirety of the heavy armor capacity of the Royal Canadian Dragoons, which until 24 hours ago, had not been involved in any of the fighting with the UCSA.

The Lord Strathcona Horse and their Leopards out of Edmonton had fought the Reds in Kansas during the Whiteman operation and had performed well, but, ultimately, they had been required to leave the field before a true victor could be named.

More recently in Pennsylvania, CANZUK's generals, in their infinite wisdom, had decided against the deployment of Canada's heavy armor.

Had the Dragoons, along with the British Army's Royal Tank Regiment, been allowed to bring the full might of their machines to bear on the Reds five weeks ago, the disastrous retreat to the Canadian border might not have happened. But it had, and now it was up to the Dragoons and their Leopards to try to turn around the disaster of a war CANZUK had been fighting against the UCSA.

Try was the operative word, Lange reminded himself.

Beyond the brave but inadequate Red Faction force that stood opposing him a kilometer away was the full might of the UCSA Army, which had received dozens of tanks and other weapons from its on-again Chinese allies in the past two weeks.

But while the Reds might have new weapons and more soldiers than CANZUK, the newly formed Canadian 6th Division rolling east across northern Ohio would not be alone.

They would be joined by three Blue Faction divisions, one each from Minnesota, Wisconsin, and Michigan, and combined, it represented a formidable force.

Lange activated his BAM. "Team Mako Bravo, it looks like our friends have indeed been told to make a stand. Target and engage all vehicles or flagged hard points. On my word, we advance and push past them. The boys in the LAVs will mop up whatever we don't put down."

Lange paused to look down at the rightmost display of his command station to take in the battlefield map and made note of their position relative to the city they had left an hour before.

His unit, along with the Dragoons' other two Leopard squadrons, were about seven klicks west of the city they had stormed through at dawn.

Lange had earned his undergrad degree in history from the Royal Military College. Based on his knowledge of historians and how they did their work, he suspected that Ohio's state capital was close enough to serve as the geographic reference point for what history would call the Battle of Canton. A battle he and his boys were winning.

"Bobby, you have a target?" Lange called left to where his gunner was waiting for the order to unleash hell.

"I do. Just say the word, Major," the farmer's son from Saskatchewan said.

"Fire!"

***

"How's it looking?" Major Vihaan Varma asked his copilot, sitting next to him in the Bell 212 Super Griffon.

"We won't lack for choice. The queue had seven priority missions. All of them are Red heavies. Any preferences?"

"Nope," Varma said, his voice business-like. "We'll do the first four in pairs. Give the order, and then let's get this party started."

"On it," the lieutenant said as he began to manipulate the trackball located on the tactical console to the right of his seat.

Seconds later, the copilot confirmed, "Targets have been assigned. We're good to go."

Varma activated his connection with the other seven helicopters. "Harpoon Flight, this is Harpoon Sunray, targets have been assigned. The angels above us have done their best to clear the sky. Stay on the lookout for SAMs. We know the Chinese have delivered a shipment of their MANPADS and they're working their way through the Red's logistics chain, so stay primed for that type of threat. Good hunting, people. Harpoon Sunray, out."

At no more than fifty feet above Lake Erie, the eight Super Griffons had flown east two kilometers out from the shoreline of Ohio and were making one hundred and ten knots over the sapphire-blue water of North America's sixth largest lake.

Their targets assigned, in four pairs of two, the gunships kept their altitude and turned south where the leading elements of the Canadian 6th Division and FAS 9th Division were in the midst of slugging it out with a brigade's worth of heavy armor units the Red Faction had rushed forward.

Knowing the helicopter's near-AI flight software would keep at altitude and on course, Varma looked down at his instrument panel and took in the display with the map of the area they were now racing over.

A clutch of bright red triangles was where they were headed. A Reaper or, more likely, one of the 6th Division's smaller Blackjack drones had tagged thirteen different vehicles, five of which were tanks.

These had been fed into the targeting app within the BAM system, which, in turn, had made them available for Varma and his flight.

As they left the blue of the Great Lake, endless green patches of farmers' fields and irregular-sized forests dominated his field of vision. Ahead and to the right, his eyes caught a loose convoy of vehicles racing through a cornfield.

His copilot's voice came alive in Varma's helmet. "Looks like a Red recon outfit. They've seen us. Whoa! We've got incoming!"

As the warning registered in his ears, Varma manipulated the helicopter's flight controls to bank the Super Griffon left and skyward.

At the same time, the Griffon trailing a couple hundred meters behind Varma kept low and banked in the direction of the enemy vehicles that had opened up on Varma's helicopter.

As the initial barrage of tracer fire whipped past his machine, the door gunner on the trailing Griffon maneuvered his minigun, aimed at the first vehicle of the recon force, and unloaded with a long burst of 7.62mm rounds.

As he leveled out his Griffon, Varma craned his head to the left and out of the corner of his eye, caught the fuel tank of the targeted pickup truck detonate. A huge ball of fire jumped into the sky.

"Boss, our target package is ahead, six klicks."

Varma grunted to acknowledge his copilot's update and asked, "How's Da Silva?"

"She's right where she should be."

"Goddamned reckless is what she is," Varma replied hotly.

"Feel free to tell her that when we get back on the ground," his copilot said.

"I plan to. There's not so many of us that we can afford to be shooting up random bloody pickup trucks. Her orders are clear – no attacks of opportunity, and we fight in pairs. This Lone Ranger bullshit she pulls has got to end."

"Roger that Major. But that explosion sure was pretty," said the younger man sitting to Varma's right.

"Stuff it, Robins. Commentary like that will only encourage her."

Six years ago, when the Canadian Army had purchased the Super Griffon as its next-generation medium-lift helicopter, it had also elected to purchase thirty-eight Rafael SPIKE Extended Range, ER anti-armor missile kits to create three squadrons of gunships that could take on enemy armor.

During CANZUK's tilt with the Reds in Pennsylvania and New York five weeks ago, two of the three squadrons had been thrown into the fighting and had made a difference at several critical junctures in the retreat north.

But in making this difference, they had lost nine helicopters – almost an entire squadron of the crucial stand-off armor-busting gunships.

"Target package is now at four klicks," his copilot said

"Roger that," Varma said as he brought the nose of his Super Griffon upwards and began to gain altitude.

Levelling out at fifteen hundred feet, he could now see for kilometers. Ahead, he picked up what had to be a dozen or so columns of black smoke.

"I hope that's the Reds and not us?" Varma said.

Robins, his copilot, ignored the question and said, "I have three good targets flagged via the on-station Blackjack."

"Fire," Varma said without hesitation.

Using the Canadian drone's targeting feed, three of the four SPIKE Non-Line-Of-Sight missiles ejected from their tubes on the left side of the helicopter, ignited their engines, and after a brief, bright flash of light, the missiles began to tear through the clear morning sky toward their designated targets.

About half a kilometer to his right, he saw Da Silva's Super Griffon perform the same feat, but unlike Varma's gunship, his wingmate only carried one set of four SPIKEs while he carried two.

As per RCAF doctrine, the Super Griffons operated in pairs where one of the two helicopters carried a minigun for sustained ground suppression, while the other carried two sets of pylons with eight SPIKEs.

Together, a pair of Super Griffons didn't come close to matching one of the RAF's fully loaded Apaches, but as armed utility helicopters went, they were as mean as they could get.

Ahead on the ground, Varma's eyes caught detonations.

"Three kills confirmed, boss," Robins said. "I have two more ready to go, but after that it looks like we're going to have to get up close and personal to do the targeting ourselves."

Just as Varma was about to signal his agreement with the plan, their helicopter's defensive systems started to blare.

Not far away from where he had seen their SPIKEs explode, he saw a pair of smoke trails emerge from a copse of trees.

"Hang on," he said calmly, knifing the nose of their chopper downward.

As Varma's stomach leaped into his throat, he felt two anti-SAM drones eject from pods affixed to the underside of the Griffon.

Korean-built, each of the drones would instantly spool up and then race to meet the incoming surface-to-air missiles, and when their on-board targeting systems told them to, they would detonate, sending thousands of ball bearings in the direction of the approaching threat.

Halfway to the earth's surface, the Griffon's onboard near-AI gave a monotone update on their impending demise. "One incoming SAM has been destroyed. Releasing additional countermeasures."

Another of the two anti-missile drones popped from their underside cradles. They only had two more.

Reaching the treetops, Varma coaxed the Super Griffon to give them as much airspeed as possible. Immediately ahead was a line of massive transmission towers.

The voice of the near-AI again spoke in his helmet. "Countermeasures ineffective. Incoming missile strike is imminent. Estimated impact in eight, seven, six ..."

"C'mon, baby, get us there, you son of a..." Varma said, urging on his Griffon.

Running parallel to the transmission wires, with every ounce of skill available to him, Varma violently banked his helicopter underneath the power lines and at no more than ten feet from the ground, weaved around one tower and back again around the next.

When a flash of bright white light lit up behind them, he pulled back on the chopper's collective and shot higher into the morning sky.

"Incoming hostile missiles have terminated their pursuit," the monotone voice of the Griffon's near-AI advised.

Looking to his right, he saw Robins still hanging on tightly to his flight controls. The younger man was looking at him with eyes wide open. "Holy shit. That was some flying, Han Solo."

Varma smiled. "Nope. Solo himself couldn't have done what I just did."

"Jesus, you might be right. Certainly, I couldn't have," Robins said in a voice that might have been filled with awe or terror, Varma wasn't sure which.

"Give me a sitrep on the flight. How's Da Silva?"

Robins pulled his hand off his flight controls and moved his eyes to the larger display with the map and battlefield overlay. After a few seconds, he reported in. "Seven helos are still flying. Three, including us, still have weapons to unload."

"Who's down?" Varma demanded

"Sorry, Boss, it looks like they got her. There's a note from Harpoon Three flagging where she went down."

Before he could begin to ask for the coordinates, a high-priority message via the BAM sounded off in his helmet. "Harpoon Sunray, this is Trident Alpha. We have a high-priority action for you. Targeting should be on your screen now."

"Negative, Trident. We have a downed bird that I need to check on."

"Harpoon, SAR is on its way for the downed bird. Engage with targeting data pronto. They need your help ASAP."

A growl started in Varma's throat, but instead of rejecting the order, he said, "Roger that, Trident. We see the data. ETA is four mikes. Harpoon Sunray out."

"Bloody hell!" Varma roared. "That goddamned woman! I tell you, Robins, when we get back to base, she's done. No more missions for Ariana Da Silva. I'm her CO, and she's grounded!"

Knowing Varma needed a minute to get past his personal feelings about the woman he was not-so-secretly sleeping with, Robins finally said, "Boss, I've connected with the unit that needs help. It's the Dragoons. It sounds like they're deep in the shit. Anything we can do to help, they'll take it."

Varma grunted and moved his eyes back to the targeting data. Robins had designated the Canadian armored unit in a yellow circle.

"Tell them we're on our way and tell them not to laser anyone until we say so. I don't need these Red pissants being tipped off that something is coming their way."

"Roger that. Anything else?"

Without looking, Varma thumbed in the direction of the cargo space of the Griffon. "Are Mac and Mo still with us?"

"We're both still here, boss. But just barely," replied the more senior of the two door gunners.

"Good," Varma said via the Griffon's internal comms. "Cause we're going in tight and that means we're going to get our hands dirty. I want the two of you to keep an eye out for anything that looks like a SAM. As it turns out, the Chi-Comms MANPADS have arrived. If you see anything that looks like one, spray it."

"Will do, boss. Any other special requests?"

"Do you two pray at all?"

"Not me, sir. But Mo here prays all the time. The guy can't seem to get enough of it."

"Glad to hear it. Private Mohammed," Varma said, speaking to the other soldier.

"Yes, Major," the nineteen-year-old soldier replied, his voice still holding the tone of respect that fresh personnel used when speaking with an officer.

"Kid, if you are praying in the next few minutes, it might be a good idea to put in a good word for all of us because things are about to get real dicey."

"Allah is always with me, Major Varma, and when I am with you, God is with us. *Allāhu Akbar*."

"Works for me, Private," said Varma as he manipulated the gunship's flight controls so they could gather speed.

Once again flying at the height of the tree tops and pushing his gunship to its physical limits, Varma said, "Everyone, be ready to get mean in three mikes. We've got a bit more of hell to deliver."

***

At a near yell, Lange said, "Mako Seven, Eight, and Eleven watch our left flank. I just got word from one of the Griffons they saw more of those Hyenas. At least ten of them are headed our way. Stay away from the trees, at least fifty meters, otherwise they'll be on you too quickly."

"Roger that. We're ready," came the clipped reply over the BAM from the senior tanker in that area of their advance.

Looking to his left and right, Lange saw LAV VIs and TAPVs intermixed around his seven remaining tanks. Each one of their autocannons and soldiers in their top-side hatches were keeping their eyes peeled looking in all directions for the four-legged automatons.

As if the Red Faction Abrams and other armored vehicles hadn't been enough of a challenge, twice in the thick of battle, the Chinese suicide machines had scampered out of culverts, from behind cars, or from a collection of trees to explode beside one of his tanks or underneath one of the LAVs or the TAPVs.

They didn't carry enough of an explosive charge to destroy one of the Leopards, but they had damaged wheel tracks, and now one-third of the regiment's MBTs were out of the fight.

No sooner had the tally registered in his mind than voices came across the open BAM channel with warnings. "This is Mako Six, I've got Hyenas at my ten o'clock. Engaging now."

Using the footholds that allowed him to elevate his entire torso above the lip of the commander's position, Lange craned his upper body to look forty-five degrees to his left.

There, loping across a field in the direction of the Leopard that had just made the call, were eight of the fast-moving Chinese autos. They were less than a hundred meters out.

Atop the tank, the gunner had already opened up with the C-6 machine gun that each Leopard had affixed to its turret.

Meters ahead of the Leopard, a troop-carrying version of the LAV VI opened up with its own pintle-mounted C-6 while a pair of soldiers standing in the vehicle's rear hatch let loose on full auto with a pair of C-9 machine guns.

As the storm of 7.62 and 5.56mm rounds tore up the field of hay grass the Hyenas were running through, the autos began to succumb to the firepower.

Two, then five, stumbled and eventually collapsed to the ground while the remaining three charged toward the tank.

Suddenly, the tank's driver took a hard right, swinging his vehicle away from their pursuers. Over open terrain and at full speed, the Leopard could reach seventy klicks an hour, while the Hyenas had been clocked at one-ten.

As its pursuers gained ground, the tanker's topside machine gunner rotated his weapon and poured hot lead into the sprinting autos.

At six hundred meters away, Lange could only watch as the distance between the Hyenas and the lone Canadian tank shrank.

The tank's gunner cut down another of the four-legged pursuers, but as his C-6 began to unload on his next target, Lange saw the man lift off the machine gun's feed tray. He had run out of ammo.

Lange clicked his tank's internal comms system. "Jamil, left twenty degrees. Get us closer to them. Bets, it's gonna be a long shot, but do what you can."

Jamil didn't reply. Instead, Lange felt the 70-ton vehicle pick up speed just as his tank's gunner shouldered his C-6 and aimed the weapon at the two remaining Hyenas.

As Lange's brain calculated distance and speed, he let loose with a vicious curse.

Like a fool, he had watched the scene develop as though he were a passive third party. In a few more seconds, his lack of action would cost him another of his squadron's tanks.

As though reading his mind, Bets opened up with his weapon, but at four hundred meters and with his targets on the move, it was a futile gesture.

As Bets momentarily paused his firing, the closest of the Hyenas reached the rear end of the Leopard.

On disappearing under the tank's chassis, Lange saw a small explosion, but the Leopard didn't falter. Via the BAM, Lange reached out to the other tank, "Mako Six, are you good?"

With relief in his voice, the other tank commander said, "The bastard gave us a jolt, but we're still in the fight."

Now less than two hundred meters away from the last racing auto, Bets again opened up with his weapon. At the same time, the gunner in the hunted tank had reloaded his C-6 and, at close range, unleashed a torrent of rounds.

At less than ten meters behind the Leopard, the last Hyena began to slow, falter, and then stop altogether.

Pumping his fist in celebration, Lange felt his own tank turn to take up a parallel course to the right and behind the surviving tank.

BOOM! Without warning, a blinding flash tore through the landscape as Mako Six exploded.

Only a hundred meters away, Lange flinched at the unexpected surge of energy.

"CONTACT, CONTACT, CONTACT! We have multiple vehicles, including at least two Abrams, in that subdivision up ahead," someone yelled across the BAM.

WHOOMP! Fifty meters in front of them, one of the four-wheel TAPVs tasked with helping to screen Lange's squadron vanished into a blinding burst of orange flame. As the armored vehicle rolled to a stop, twisted and burning metal began to shower down on Lange's Leopard, forcing him and Bets to take cover.

Safe in the turret, Lange began to deliver a series of quick-fire orders. "All units put down a wall of smoke across the front of that subdivision. All Makos undertake evasive maneuvers, find a target, and engage. Fire, advance, fire. All other units get on thermal and look for anything that looks like a missile team and unload. Move, people!"

Deactivating the connection, Lange popped upward to better survey the battlefield. Yelling across the turret, he asked of Bets, "I thought the recce guys had cleared that neighborhood?"

"They did. Not twenty minutes ago!" Bets replied over the cacophony.

"Well, they did a piss-poor job."

"I've got something on thermal," the gunner said excitedly.

"Hit it," Lange ordered without hesitation.

WHOOSH! The Leopard's main gun unleashed an HE round at whatever Bets had seen through his targeting aperture. With thick white smoke starting to boil everywhere in his field of view, there was no indication the round had hit anything.

To Lange's right, another vehicle exploded. This time, it was an Infantry Fighting Vehicle version of the LAV VI.

Yelling into the tank, he said, "Step on it, Jamil. Get us into the houses now! That's the only way we're gonna survive. We're sitting ducks out here. At least in the subdivision, we can put houses between us and whoever is in there!"

As the engine of their tank whined, drawing more power, Lange activated his BAM and said, "Message for Trident Seven, priority designation, Lange Alpha-X-Ray-Two."

"Priority designation confirmed. You're number two in Trident's queue," Patrick Stewart's calm voice advised.

While he waited to be connected, he tagged the outermost part of Salem, Ohio, on his main tactical screen and designated their current position.

"Mako Bravo Sunray, this is Trident Seven. How can we assist?" said the officer who was responsible for coordinating air support missions for the brigade."

"Trident Seven, my squadron has been ambushed. You should see data point Charlie-Two on your screen now. If you have air support, we need it and pronto."

"Data point confirmed. Hold, Mako Bravo Sunray."

Again, his tank's gun fired. As the pungent smell of propellant of the anti-armor round saturated the air, he heard Bets yell in triumph, "Got a Stryker. Nailed him flush, the bastard!"

Below, he heard the fourth member of their crew, the wiry Private Kojo, run through the commands of loading another round into the Leopard's breech-loader. As the next round was set, the Torontonian bellowed, "Ready up!"

A voice in his helmet cut through the sound of his crew making war. "Mako Bravo Sunray, we have three Harpoons on their way to your position. Do not laser targets until the Harpoons ask for it. I say again, do not laser targets until directed to do so."

"Roger that Trident. No targeting until asked. What's their ETA?" Lange said, trying his best to remain calm in the madness of the knife fight he and his squadron had just rushed into.

"Five mikes, Mako Bravo Sunray. Hold tight and stay alive. Trident Seven out."

***

As Varma approached the western edge of Salem at an altitude of a thousand feet, he listened to his copilot's conversation with the hard-pressed tank commander slugging it out in the wealthy neighborhood ahead of them.

Between and around houses and the beautifully landscaped properties, he could see a deadly game of cat-and-mouse playing out. Tanks and armored vehicles of all kinds were firing their weapons from one position and then scooting forward or backward in an effort to find cover. It was chaos.

With their remaining four SPIKEs and the three that the other two Super Griffons had, Varma thought they had enough firepower to make a difference.

The Dragoons had pushed past the initial line of the ambush and were now engaging the secondary elements of the Red Faction force. Working in pairs, six Leopards were leapfrogging deeper into the enclave, but they had been overzealous and were now at risk of being cut off from the rest of their unit.

Beside him, Robins said, "Mako Three and Mako Seven, laser any priority targets you have to your north and east."

Immediately, the exercised voices of the two tank commanders confirmed their targets had been painted.

On the tactical display in front of his copilot, an eight-wheeled Stryker with a mounted four-tube Javelin system came into view.

No sooner had the enemy's machine appeared than one of their SPIKEs ejected into the air, ignited, and began its sprint to the target.

Seconds later, a small column of fire erupted at the front of the twenty-ton vehicle as the missile's penetrator easily cut through the Stryker's protective armor.

There was no dramatic explosion. Instead, oily black smoke began to roil from all parts of the now-destroyed vehicle.

Not wasting a second to celebrate the kill, his copilot reached forward, grabbed the flight controls of the Super Griffon and said, "I have control."

"You have control," Varma confirmed, allowing Robins to fly the gunship so as to more effectively maneuver the aircraft as he hunted down the remaining targeted vehicles.

With his copilot in full control, Varma took in the full scene of the battle taking place only two kilometers away.

In the distance, he could see one of the other two Super Griffons swooping from the sky in the direction of what looked to be an approaching convoy of Red Faction militia.

Having seen the Canadian helicopter's approach, several of the pickup trucks came to a quick stop and, from out of nowhere, produced what looked like half a dozen M240s, the American's general-purpose machine gun.

Mesmerized by the action, Varma watched as the Griffon's door-mounted minigun opened up on the closest truck.

Within seconds, the pickup and the men riding in its flatbed had been shredded.

But no sooner had this happened than the remaining militia trucks opened up with their weapons, sending a storm of gunfire at the lightly armored Canadian helicopter.

The fascination Varma had experienced only seconds before turned to horror as the Griffon failed to pull out of its descending strafing run.

As though in slow motion, he watched the Bell 212 slam at speed nose-first into the two-lane road leading into the subdivision.

On connecting with the ground, the Super Griffon, which would have had just under half of its fuel, ignited into a spectacular fireball that lit up the mid-morning sky.

Beside him, Robins raised his gaze to take in the explosion but didn't say a word. Instead, he immediately went back to manipulating his flight controls so he could maneuver their own gunship to unload its final missile.

As the last of their missiles struck the rear end of a javelin-armed JLTV hiding behind a four-door garage, Robins said, "No more SPIKEs. Control back to you, Major."

"I have control. Good work, Lieutenant. Hopefully, it will be enough."

***

At close to forty klicks an hour, Corporal Jamil drove their Leopard into and through the flatbed of a filthy Ford F-150, sending the men in the back of it flying in all directions.

Behind and to both sides, Lange heard the pulsating, welcome sound of the numerous LAV VI Bushmaster chain guns and the more rapid chatter of the TAPV's autocannons as they helped to suppress the militia convoy that had been trying to reinforce the Red Faction armor unit that Lange and his squadron had just bested.

Now down to five from the original eleven Leopards he had started with in the morning, he would have to hand off their advance to lighter armor elements of the brigade.

It would be up to others to push on to their objective of Youngstown where they would refuel and resupply.

From there, what was left of the Royal Canadian Dragoons would form a corridor between Youngstown and New Castle, Pennsylvania, that would allow the rest of the Canadian 6th Division, along with two Blue Faction heavy armor brigades from Wisconsin, to undertake a flanking maneuver on two Red divisions that had positioned themselves in a wide north-south arc just east of Cleveland.

Jamil finally stopped their battered tank beside the smoking wreckage of the Super Griffon that had been shot down at the apex of their fight with the UCSA.

Lange hadn't seen what had brought the helicopter down. He had only watched the distressed machine perform a near-perfect nosedive, where on its violent contact with the ground, it turned into a column of fire.

Whether by coincidence or because they had been infuriated by the loss of their comrade, it was around this moment of the battle that the remaining two Super Griffons unleashed several missile strikes, which had turned the close-quarter fighting within the subdivision in the Dragoons' favor.

The gunship's charred frame was compacted by its impact with the asphalt. As he stared at the melted and still-burning gunship, Lange stepped into the footholds that would elevate him high above the lip of his position in the turret.

With friendly automatic weapons firing only a few dozen meters ahead of their position, his hand came up to issue a sharp salute in the direction of the Griffon's cockpit.

He held the gesture of respect for four long seconds.

Satisfied he had shown the RCAF flyers the battle honor they deserved, he settled back into his seat and activated his BAM.

"Mako Team Bravo, this is Mako Bravo Sunray. I've designated a new rally point. All units are to fight on to Point Echo, where we will undertake a brief standdown. Mako Team Alpha and Charlie will take up the push toward Objective Romeo. Outstanding work, Dragoons. Mako Bravo Sunray, out."

Chapter 14

West of Houston, Texas

As Parr approached the elevators that would bring him to the complex eighty meters below the billionaire's incredible half-billion-dollar compound, where the president and his closest advisors had been operating for the past two weeks, he put the memories of Maryland out of his mind.

As it had been throughout his professional life, the bottom line for Parr was that he got results. And in Maryland, he'd delivered, and big time.

After a short descent, the elevator doors opened up to the main conduit, which was the spine of the thirty-thousand-square-foot facility.

While it was technically a bunker, had you been unaware of the complex's underground location, you would have thought you were in a modern office suite.

Stepping into the hallway, Parr saw several people on the move. Due to the facility's size, some four hundred people were living in or close to the billionaire's extravagant above-ground estate and were working their tails off to help Spector, Parr, and the other senior officials of the UCSA government finish the war.

Of these four hundred, at any one time, a quarter of that number was in the buried complex, beavering away on whatever issues Spector or his inner circle of advisors prioritized.

In Parr's estimation, it was this rotating Tiger Team approach, along with the UCSA's ruthlessness, that was going to win the war.

As Parr strode down the hallway, he made sure to make eye contact and greet everyone he encountered. The generals who surrounded Spector might loathe him for his methods, but that wasn't the case for the policy and operational people who made the country work.

Parr understood as well as anyone that while a leader could be a monster in the boardroom if that same person could be a pleasant human on the shop floor to the worker bees who actually got things done, much could be achieved.

Reaching the door to the boardroom where the president took his morning briefings, Parr lifted his wrist upwards and checked the time. He would be arriving ten minutes late.

Just one more thing to endear him to the president's inner circle, he thought.

Taking a deep breath, he opened the door and entered the room.

"There you are, you son of a bitch."

The heat-laden words had come from General Spellings, the UCSA's Army Chief of Staff.

Parr ignored the pissed-off general and focused solely on Spector.

"Sorry I'm late, Mr. President. My flight leaving Washington was delayed."

Spector gave Parr a long look and said, "Welcome back, Peter. Have a seat. We were just talking about your success in getting Maryland and the rest of the holdouts to sign their declarations of surrender."

"Thank you, Mr. President," Parr said neutrally.

Standing behind the seat Spector had gestured to, Parr cast his eyes toward Spellings and said, "I take it not everyone is pleased with how these results were achieved?"

From across the boardroom table from where Parr was standing, Spellings pushed back his chair and stood to stare back at Parr.

A tall, well-built man, Spellings looked every bit the commander of men he was.

The general's hand came up and pointed an accusatory finger toward Parr. As he began to speak, the man's face began to take on a reddish hue. "Mr. President, this man and this goddamned Operation Sunlight... I'm telling you, sir, if we continue to —."

Still seated at the head of the boardroom's massive oblong table, Spector's hand rose upward, signaling for Spellings to slow his roll.

Slowly, Spector's eyes moved back and forth between the two men. When he was confident Spellings was going to continue to bite his tongue, he said, "It's true that not all of us in this room like

Peter's methods, but you can't argue that they haven't got results. They have, indisputably so.

"I wonder, General if you would be so willing to call out Peter if the Army's efforts weren't floundering as much as they are."

Spector quickly added, "And not just the Army. The Air Force is just as guilty."

Spellings rounded on Spector, and in the process, his face had become an even darker shade of red. "Mr. President, the war in New York is in hand. Over the past two days, we've spent six hours with you running through our plans to finish the Blues and Canadians in Upstate New York and Northern Ohio."

Nodding, Spector replied, "Yes, John, you've walked me through the plans, and I agree that what I saw was solid, but we've had good plans before. Over the past two weeks, we haven't lacked good plans. What we've been missing is execution. Our supply lines are shit, and because of that, we've run low on everything from fuel to food. Logistics wins wars."

"We're operating in hostile territory," Spellings said forcefully. "We're starting to see success against the Blue Faction irregulars attacking our supply lines, but this will take time. As we speak, we're receiving another shipment of the Chinese Wraiths and Hyenas. They excel at counterinsurgency. In another week or two, we'll have a protected corridor going north, and our people will have everything and more they need to finish off what's left of the Blues."

Spector nodded slowly and said, "In two weeks, you say? Well, of everything we're running out of, time is the thing we can afford to lose the least."

Spector turned away from the still hot-under-the-collar general and looked at the UCSA's Navy Chief of Staff, Admiral Briggs. "We are running out of time because why, Admiral?"

Not called on often, Briggs cleared his throat and said, "Mr. President, in the past two weeks, CANZUK submarines have sunk just over one million tons of shipping destined for our ports. They've given particular attention to any tankers out of Nigeria and Venezuela.

"As you know, because of the Royal Navy's strikes against our refineries early in the conflict, our capacity to process our oil has been reduced. As a result, we've had to turn to places like Africa and South America to replenish our reserves. CANZUK is aware of this shortage, of course, and has done everything in its power to make it worse. Presently, we suspect five Canadian, two British, and at least one Australian submarine are working the shipping lanes out of both Nigeria and Venezuela."

Spector's head moved back in the direction of Spellings. "I know you know this, John, but I will make the point anyway because it relates to Mr. Parr and his recent trip to Maryland.

"Americans, particularly those living in the UCSA, need to drive their trucks and cars. This is what they do. Gas is as much their right as it is for them to bear arms. But to drive, they actually have to be able to buy gas."

Spector pulled his gaze from Spellings and looked to the back of the room. "Regis, the video please."

Behind Spector, from four feet from the floor to the ceiling, a display embedded in the wall ignited with a video.

To the fifteen or so people in the room, Spector's voice boomed, "We'll watch this because I find it instructive. This video, more than anything I can say, will impress upon you why we have to end this war as soon as possible."

Turning back to the screen, Spector pronounced, "Regis, Let's see the nightmare."

In the video's frame were dozens of vehicles lined up at a huge BP gas station. Intermixed with the cars and trucks were two groups of people.

The larger group was made up of mostly Whites, the smaller one of Blacks.

Whoever was operating the camera moved closer to what had the look of a standoff.

A heavy-set Black woman with dreadlocks and a skinny white guy wearing a wifebeater that showed off two arms covered in poorly done tattoos were screaming at one another.

Wifebeater said, "I'm not telling you again, bitch, I was next in line, so you better move that there car of yours, or I'm going to take those keys from your fat hands and move it myself."

Dreadlocks stepped toward Wifebeater, raised her hand in the air and dangled her keys between two fingers. "Listen, you skinny punk piece of white trash, I'm telling *you* for the last time that I was here before you rolled up in that bitch-ass truck of yours."

The keys still out in front of her, she took another step toward the man and announced loudly, "I ain't goin' nowhere. Here's my keys. Why don't you go ahead and try and take'em?"

The person controlling the camera shifted right and zoomed in on Wifebeater's face. The man had a crazed look in his eyes. For a hugely tense moment, the pair stared at one another, not saying or doing anything.

Finally, the woman lowered her keys and said, "That's right. You got nothing to say 'cause you know I'm right. Now get the hell outta here before I whoop your skinny White ass."

In the group behind Wifebeater, someone yelled, "Don't be a pussy, Shad!"

Off camera, a male voice yelled, "Shut the hell up, man, else I'm gonna come over there and shut yo honkey mouth!"

Police sirens started to wail in the distance.

A man about the same age as Wifebeater suddenly appeared at his side and said something in his ear.

Nodding, Wifebeater slowly moved his right hand to his back.

As the camera operator pulled back to take in more of the scene, Wifebeater's right hand emerged with a revolver.

On seeing the weapon, people from both groups began to scream, creating a wash of panicked noise.

The same man who had given Wifebeater the gun again leaned forward to speak into his friend's ear. Clenching his jaw and looking down the pistol barrel, Wifebeater pulled the trigger.

For an instant, the sound of a single gunshot overwhelmed the chaos.

Moving quickly, the camera jolted to frame in Dreadlocks. The woman hadn't been struck. Instead, she stood fixed in place with a shocked look on her face.

As people on both sides of the confrontation began to run in all directions, Wifebeater yelled something incomprehensible and then unloaded three more shots.

At the mid-point of the barrage, Dreadlocks staggered backward and fell to the pavement.

The person filming surged forward, making the woman the sole focus of the recording. Just above her right breast, an ugly blotch of red had bloomed on her creamsicle orange t-shirt.

Hearing a wild scream, the camera jolted back to the shooter. He had moved closer to Dreadlocks and had assumed a two-handed grip on his weapon, but before he could pull the trigger, a series of gunshots erupted off camera.

As he stumbled backward, a bright red circle appeared near the center of Wifebeater's stomach. Reaching down, he touched the wound and then held his blood-soaked hand high in the air and screamed, "Ricky man, they shot me, dude! Jesus, I'm bleeding! I'll kill her! I'm gonna kill that bitch good!"

With a crazed look in his eyes, Wifebeater looked at Dreadlocks from across the parking lot. With one hand pressing against his wound and the other holding the half-raised gun, he ran forward screaming.

Reaching Dreadlocks, he levelled his pistol at her and roared, "You fucking —."

He didn't get to finish the sentence as another bullet struck him, only this time it tore through the left side of his throat, sending a red slash of blood through the air.

For the first time, the person recording the unfolding disaster spoke. He had a strong Latino accent. "Shit, man! Fucking *puto* got it."

As Wifebeater's knees buckled and he collapsed to the ground, the smartphone operator shifted his aim to canvas the broader scene of chaos.

Among the collection of gas-starved vehicles, a dozen people — a mix of Black and White — had weapons and were unloading wildly in each other's direction.

The camera suddenly shifted from the melee to focus on a woman seated on the ground in front of a stack of green windshield washer fluid jugs. Several were in the process of emptying from tiny holes.

As the camera zoomed in, the woman was sobbing uncontrollably.

In her arms was a tiny body. As she stroked the child's face, the whole of her arm and hand were covered in bright red blood. As the woman's eyes looked directly into the camera, she unleashed a long, keening cry of anguish, and then she screamed, "They killed my baby! They killed my baby!"

"That's enough," Spector's voice boomed over the woman's haunting cries.

The image of the screaming woman holding her dying or dead child remained on the screen.

Spector's gaze moved back to Spellings. "You had seen the full recording?"

"No," the general said soberly.

"Understandable. You have a war to run. I, on the other hand, have to keep this country together, and I can tell you that after four years of fighting and the death of millions, the people of our country do not feel they have the luxury of time."

Spector turned his eyes from Spellings and looked up and down the table. His voice sounding grave, he continued, "Not only are we short on gas, but now, for the first time since the beginning of the war, grocery shelves are not being stocked."

"Worse, this delightful incident caused race riots in no less than thirty cities. As we speak, Atlanta and Jacksonville are still burning."

Without warning, Spector's hand shot up and he leveled a finger at Parr.

For what seemed like an eternity, he pointed and said nothing. Finally, in a quiet voice, he said, "I understand and appreciate why people on this committee might not like Mr. Parr's methods, but realize we do not have the luxury of time.

"What Mr. Parr did in Maryland is get results, and as much as anything, right now, that is what we need. We are so close to the finish line, people."

He paused and after two calming breaths, his gaze moved back to Spellings. "John, I appreciate that you have the balls to speak up. I know there are others who don't dare to speak as you do. It's a quality I respect.

"But I need you to understand that the world we currently live in is devoid of things like honor, kindness, the rule of law, and freedom of the press. All these things are secondary to victory.

"In time, when the struggle is over, I promise we'll dust all these things off, but for now and until we have utterly destroyed the FAS, the only thing I want to hear out of anyone's mouth at this table when we get a win is praise."

Spector again jabbed his finger at Parr. "Peter here went to Maryland and, in three days, got three conquered Blue states to sign declarations to join the UCSA. Now, you might not like how it was done, but it got done."

Slowly, Spector retracted his finger and lowered his hand to the table. With his eyes still on Spellings, he said, "So, from this moment on, I don't want to hear any more of this horseshit about how Peter or anyone else does their business. I want results, and I want this war won. That is our sole focus, that is your only mandate, and if you can't deal with that, then put in your resignation."

Spector's jawline visibly tightened as his eyes bore into Spellings from across the table. "Is that understood, General Spellings?"

"Perfectly understood, Mr. President."

"Good, then we have one more issue to discuss."

Spector moved his gaze to Christoff, the Director of the CIB, the UCSA's combined version of the FBI and CIA, and said, "Dave, you were letting us know about the buildup of CANZUK special forces in Nevada and New Mexico. I think we all agree that type of force at those locations is not something we're comfortable with. I liked it much better when they were down in that shit hole in South America. If you have a plan to neutralize this threat, we'd like to hear it."

Pointing to the screen that still held the image of the distraught mother, Christoff said, "If I may use the tech, Mr. President?"

"It's all yours," Spector said, waving at the brutal image.

As all heads turned back to the screen at the front of the room, they saw the images of the X-8 Wraith and X-5 Hyena.

Christoff said, "Gentlemen, as we've become more experienced in using these remarkable machines, we've come to realize their best use is long-range, high-risk missions where there is a strong possibility regular soldiers or even special forces would not make it back."

"Suicide missions, like Sydney," one of the other generals at the far end of the table said.

"Just like Sydney," Christoff agreed. "We now understand that the Neutral Faction or Western Alliance, as they are now calling themselves, is preparing to join the war. This explains why upwards of three thousand CANZUK special operations soldiers have shown up just west of Texas. But what we don't know is how these forces are going to be used."

"We don't give them a chance," Spector said, interrupting the briefing.

Christoff nodded vigorously. "Correct, Mr. President. Just as we plan to do with the Governor of California, whatever CANZUK's intent, we will bring the war to them and not the other way around. As Mr. Parr did in Maryland, we will take the initiative and be ruthless in doing so."

Chapter 15

Quantum Call

"So, are we agreed?" the British PM, Susan Richardson asked her CANZUK colleagues on the quantum encrypted video call.

The Australian PM, Brian Hanson, responded first. "It's a gamble, to be sure, but we've seen all the reports. The UCSA is as fragile as it has ever been. The riots in Atlanta and other cities have been heart-wrenching to watch, but they are as good a sign as we've seen that Spector's grasp is starting to loosen. My vote is that we go for it."

"I agree," said New Zealand's leader, Nigel MacCrimmon. "The plan your people have put together, Susan and Merielle, is an audacious one, but my people and I think it can work.

"And like Brian said, things are spiralling in the UCSA. Spector's people have done their damnedest to scuttle the rumor he's made a deal with the Chinese for Washington, but it persists, and the people of the Red Faction are not happy about it. I can't say I blame them. It's an outrageous proposition if it's true. Some pressure on the leadership could be just what is needed."

"Merielle, what's your take?" Richardson asked of the Canadian prime minister. Uncharacteristically, Merielle had been reserved during most of the conversation.

After a brief silence, the Canadian PM spoke up. "It's risky, but, as I mentioned earlier, even if it's not successful, it'll give Spector something else to think about. The man is not an idiot, that's for sure, but it's our best guess he's operating at his outer limits. If we can secure the target, it could put the Blues over the top. If we miss, we send a shockwave through the Red's leadership. Perhaps that's the straw that breaks the camel's back. My vote is yes."

On-screen, Richardson nodded and said, "My vote is also to move forward. I agree with Merielle. If we can take the target, it does nothing but help us. If we're unsuccessful, it's one more thing to shake the UCSA's already wobbly foundation."

***

Vancouver, British Columbia

—

From twenty meters down the hallway, Larocque and Tomic watched the team of six newly created CSIS Direct Action Team, DAT officers get ready to breach the entrance of the suspected interrogation site they had received a tip about only twenty-four hours earlier.

As he watched the five men and one woman stack to the right of the door, Larocque felt the beginnings of what he recognized as pride.

Despite Tomic's skepticism that it couldn't be done as quickly as he'd arranged, ninety percent of the IOs they had sent to become weapons-qualified had agreed to put their names forward for the new domestic-focused DAT program. Of those, they selected thirty-nine men and twelve women.

On achieving their requals, the newly selected team had remained at Dwyer Hill and, under the supervision and guidance of a team of JTF-2 operators, drilled on a host of urban warfare tactics, including the room entry procedure they were about to undertake.

"Now," a voice said in the earbud in Larocque's right ear.

On hearing the team leader's order to breach the room, the biggest IO on the team stepped away from the wall to reveal the battering ram he was carrying at his side.

Moving to the door, he opened his stance, shifted his weight to his back foot, and glided the forty-pound cylinder backward.

Extending the ram as far as it could go, the man issued a grunt and drove the head of the implement into the door with as much force as he could muster.

As it made contact, there was a sharp crack of the doorframe breaking. Stepping back from the door, the other five members of the team stormed into the room, their submachine guns at the ready.

Thirty seconds later, the same voice that had given the order to breach the door gave the 'all clear', indicating the room was secure. "You're welcome to join us, boss. There's nothing here," the voice added.

A minute later, Larocque and Tomic entered the room. Standing at the center of the space were the six CSIS officers. On their faces, he could see looks of determination but could also sense their frustration.

This was the third site in the Greater Vancouver Area they had raided only to find nothing. Someone who knew about the White Unit had been feeding them the locations.

The source knew something about their target because he knew of the outfit by name and seemed to have some idea of what the rogue unit had been doing.

But in each location his people raided, they found exactly what they'd found in this room — nothing.

He walked over to a table at the side of the room and slid his index finger across its surface. No dust. Not a trace of it. Whoever had been here had been here recently and had cleaned the place to perfection.

It had been the same with the other two locations.

The man who had been designated as the leader of the DAT, Marc Blondin, looked in Larocque's direction and asked, "The same?"

"Clean as a whistle," Larocque said, allowing just a hint of the same frustration the DAT was feeling to taint his response.

As Blondin's mouth parted to say something, Larocque's earbud signaled an incoming call. Pointing to his ear, he turned from the IO and made his way to the room's now-wrecked entrance.

As Tomic followed in his wake, he activated the connection with the caller.

"They were gone, I presume?" the caller asked.

"You don't get to know that kind of information," Larocque said, his voice icy.

"I have other locations, but those too will be empty. Somebody on this new team of yours is tipping them off. You have a leak."

"So you say. It could also be that you're jerking our chain. For all I know, you're running the outfit we're looking for," Larocque replied, his tone sounding matter-of-fact.

"I'm not because I've told you who that person is, and I know you're trying to figure out who on your team is leaking to the White Unit. You were smart to break down this new team into smaller isolated parts. Now you'll know it's one of what...ten people? Very likely, it's one of the people you were in the room with only thirty seconds ago. Or, perhaps it's the person standing beside you."

With that comment, Larocque pulled up his stride and turned to look at Tomic. As a look of thunder stormed onto his face, coldly, he said, "Quit it with the fucking games."

Still calm, the stranger said, "I think it's time we met in person, Director, but let's be cool when it happens."

After a pause, the man spoke again, "I'm right here." This time, Larocque didn't hear the stranger's flat and pedestrian voice via his earbud. Instead, the words that echoed down the length of the hallway were both deep and resonant.

Larocque's hand quickly moved to the gun on his hip. Drawing the weapon, he pointed it in the direction they had been walking seconds before. There, standing in the middle of the hallway, was a man. He was Black with lighter-toned skin and a physique that suggested he frequently saw the inside of a gym. To Larocque's relief, both of his hands were in the air.

He stared at the newcomer for a long moment and then said, "Why would I want to speak with you? So far, your information has been useless. It's that, or you've been playing us for some reason. Whichever it is, you're not much use to me, whoever you are."

Tomic was now to his right, and further behind him, he could hear the shuffling of the breaching team as they left the room to investigate why Larocque was speaking in a heated tone.

Behind him, he heard Blondin call out. "Hey, Petit, you bastard. What are you doing here? It's been a while."

The stranger nodded his head at the man standing behind Larocque. "Good to see you, Marc. I'm here to take a meeting with the new director."

On hearing the stranger's name, bells began to ring inside Larocque's head. Petit. The man had been somehow involved with Merielle in Montreal, and there was something else.

And now he was standing in front of him, asking to talk.

"Petit, is it?" Larocque asked while lowering his weapon.

The man did not confirm his identity. Instead, he thumbed over his shoulder in the direction of the building's exit. "Let's go for a walk, Director. There's a trail not far from here that meanders along the Fraser for a few klicks. I think you'll enjoy it."

Petit's eyes shifted from Larocque to Tomic. "And you can bring her. I'm almost certain she's not the person you need to be concerned about. Almost."

"Sam, it's been a while," Tomic said coolly. "Last I heard, you'd been sent down south. And what, pray tell, is it that you're almost certain about as it pertains to me?"

From the way they spoke to one another, Larocque could tell there was a history between the two. Whether that history had been personal, professional, or both, he would find out soon enough.

"Marc," Larocque called over his shoulder.

"Yes, sir."

"Bring in the forensics team and see if they can find anything. We'll give it the old college try. Once they're finished, pack up and head back. The Assistant Director and I will be taking a meeting with your friend here."

"Roger that, boss," Blondin said promptly.

His eyes never leaving the interloper who had appeared from nowhere, Larocque said, "Lead the way, Sam Petit."

***

'The trail' Petit had referred to was, in fact, a paved pedestrian pathway that ran some distance along the great Fraser River.

The threesome had walked for several hundred meters and were approaching what looked like a sharp turn on the path.

Larocque, as adept as anyone at scanning his surroundings for threats, had not perceived anything out of the ordinary, so as they'd walked, he'd been happy to listen intently to the man's extraordinary story.

"So you were on this White Unit, you left it for what amounts to ethical concerns, you think you're still alive because you saved Merielle's life, and you think it is none other than the PM who is directing the actions of this said rogue unit. Do I have this correct?"

"In a nutshell, yes," Petit replied.

As they reached what looked to be a hairpin turn in the trail, Larocque pulled up his stride, turned to face the man, and said, "Why are you assuming it's Merielle tied into this outfit? She's not dumb. Far from it, actually. Why would she risk her position and the power she wields by doing something as crazy as setting up a rogue intelligence unit that does, among other things, political assassinations?"

Petit smiled at Larocque.

"Is something I said funny, Mr. Petit?" Larocque asked.

"No, it's not funny, Director — if that's what you'd like me to call you?"

Lifting his chin slightly, Larocque said, "I'd prefer you used the title, yes. When we're done with this little chat of ours, I'm going to have your file pulled, and I suspect it's going to tell me you're still active with CSIS, and we're paying you a salary."

When Petit made no response to his supposition, Larocque continued, "As you know, I'm not far removed from the military, and I've always found it good practice for my subordinates to call me by my rank, no matter how long I've worked with them. To do otherwise makes it more of a challenge when I have to send those same people off to do something that might get them killed."

On hearing the explanation, the smile that had been on Petit's face disappeared. "Then 'Director' it shall be."

Petit gestured to the path. "Shall we continue our stroll?"

"Let's," Larocque said.

As they resumed their pace, Petit said, "Is it not a universal maxim that absolute power corrupts absolutely?"

"If you're talking about Merielle, her power is hardly absolute," said Larocque. "I mean, yes, a Canadian PM has outsized power relative to most democratic leaders, but there are still many checks in the system. And I know there are people in her cabinet who wouldn't allow her to do what you're suggesting, even if I did think she was capable of creating this White Unit outfit."

Beside him, Petit nodded his head. "So you say, but what will you do should you find evidence that our PM is connected with the White Unit?

"No, let me be more clear, Director. Let us say you find evidence that she is not just connected with this White Unit, but she is actively involved in its day-to-day operations. What if the PM has blood on her hands?"

When Larocque did not provide a reply, Petit continued, "When the Nazis were looking across the English Channel, how many people did the British kill in the dark of night between the years of 1941 and 1945, Director Larocque?"

After briefly contemplating the question, Larocque said, "I'm not sure."

"No one knows the number, but we know it wasn't zero. And across the Cold War and in the War on Terror, how many people did MI6 and the CIA have a hand in killing?"

This time, Larocque had some idea and said, "Many."

On hearing the reply, Petit nodded and said, "So, you're prepared to admit that democracies similar to Canada's have killed people through extrajudicial means?"

"I said as much, didn't I?" Larocque replied quickly.

"Just one more question along this line of thinking, Director."

When Larocque didn't tell him to stop, Petit said, "Is it not the case that in the United States, presidents have sat in the White House's Situation Room and watched–no, actively participated in– the assassination of America's enemies?"

When Larocque again made no reply, Petit said, "We know for a fact that six months before the American civil war, Gloria Menendez oversaw and gave explicit direction for a US Air Force drone to target and destroy a building on the outskirts of Baltimore being used by the Patriot Front. The strike killed sixteen Americans."

"What's your point, Petit?" Larocque growled.

"My point, Director, is that when countries are at war like Canada is now, is it so fantastic or unbelievable to think that a leader of a democracy couldn't get directly involved in the assassination business? In fact, one could argue that due to their ultra-sensitive nature, political leaders couldn't help but be hands-on when it came to this kind of operation."

Without warning, Petit came to a stop.

To their left was an actual dirt path. Well-trodden, it led into the dense forest that hemmed in this side of the Fraser.

Larocque eyed the pathway warily.

Petit said, "No tricks, Director. I have someone I want you to meet."

Larocque turned to Tomic. A frontline intelligence officer by trade, she looked intrigued at the offer to move off the beaten path. When their eyes connected, she said nothing.

He was the Director. It was his call.

He turned his eyes back to Petit. "Lead the way."

As the CSIS intelligence officer stepped onto the trail, Petit resumed his questioning. "So, has CSIS begun its implosion since you've arrived?"

"No," replied Larocque. "There have been resignations, but these people needed to go anyway. They've done the organization a favor. It will make the transformation easier, not harder. And I still have changes to make."

Over his shoulder, Petit asked another question. "Across your professional career, Director Larocque, have you failed at anything?"

Larocque's reply was quick-fire. "No. I've been far from a perfect leader, but I know how to get things done. I lead people to where they need to be. That is what I do."

"So, it's fair to say that you're honing CSIS into a machine that, if needed, could on its own hunt down and capture people and make those same people disappear."

Larocque grunted at the question, then said, "I don't know about the disappearing part, but give me six months, and there won't be anyone in the whole of this country we won't be able to find and nobody's door we won't be able to kick down."

Perhaps fifty meters in, the narrow trail suddenly opened into a large clearing with a bench at its center.

A single person wearing sports attire similar in fashion to the dozen or so people who had passed them on the walkway was seated at the bench. With the hood of the person's jacket up, Larocque couldn't make out any of the stranger's features.

To his rear, he sensed Tomic flank him. No doubt, her hand had slipped to the weapon she too was carrying.

Slowly, the figure began to stand, and as it did so, the person's chin came up, and with their hands, they pulled back the cowl covering their face.

The fabric removed, Larocque instantly recognized the face framed in by curly, bright red hair.

When Irene MacPhail spoke, her voice was clear and held the accent of someone who had spent most of her life living in Canada's easternmost province. "The prime minister knew exactly what she was doing when she placed you in your current position.

"She knows full well that you are going to remake CSIS into the organization she thinks it needs to be to win against the Reds, the Chinese, and whatever other threats come our way. The world, it seems, is getting more dangerous by the day."

Petit moved to stand beside Canada's Deputy Prime Minister. Together, the mysterious CSIS officer and the politician stared at Larocque as though they were trying to get a read on his soul.

"Merielle Martel is playing a dangerous game because she feels she has to," continued MacPhail. "That you will prove this, I have no doubt.

"Where my doubts lie and why I am here to meet with you today is to tell you there will be a time in the future – perhaps soon – when you will have to make a choice. A choice between saving Canada's imperfect democracy or letting it drift toward something else. Something very different. Something dangerous."

Larocque did not like ambushes, particularly political ones. He delivered a hard stare in the direction of MacPhail, and when he spoke, there was a noticeable heat to his words. "Merielle has my trust and my loyalty because she's made the hard decisions, just as I have. Decisions, I would add, that have cost her dearly. We're at war, Minister. In war, you have to be prepared to do terrible and difficult things."

Larocque turned his gaze onto Petit. "Isn't that what you had to do in Haiti? Hard things. Things of national consequence?"

When Petit gave no reply, Larocque said, "Yes, I know who you are. You were one of the first files given to me when I started. You are an interesting and complex person, Mr. Petit."

His eyes reacquired MacPhail's. "I appreciate you coming here, though I'm not sure all this cloak and dagger bullshit was needed, but –."

Her voice sharp, Canada's second most important politician interrupted him. "Listen, you don't think I know our country is in a tough spot? For Christ's sake, not two weeks ago, the Chinese government assassinated three CANZUK ministers of defence – one of them a close friend of mine – with bloody killer robots. I get that things are bad, Director, and I know that tough choices have to be made, but I'm worried for Merielle and I'm worried for this country.

"I know she has your loyalty, but I think I know the type of person you are, and I'm sure the oath of loyalty that you gave to the Queen all those years ago wasn't for nothing."

MacPhail's finger came up and pointed at Larocque's chest. "All I'm saying, Director Larocque, is that as you learn more about what's going on, it will be important for you to think about the type of country you want Canada to be when this war ends. What type of country do you want your son to grow up in?"

"Leave my family out of this," Larocque said in a near snarl.

Stepping into Larocque's personal space, MacPhail's index finger made contact with the center of his chest. Boring her eyes into his, she said, "Tell me, Jackson Larocque, when your son finds out you died in the dead of night by a CSIS death squad you had a hand in creating, and he joins the underground movement to overthrow the same government that blew his dad's brains out - will that matter to you?

"Because that's the kind of scenario this country will face if people like you don't make the right choices in the weeks and months ahead."

As the hypothetical scenario played out in Larocque's mind, he chose not to reply. Instead, he moved his eyes to MacPhail's index finger and said, "You'll want to move that."

While she continued to stare, the politician held her finger in place for a second more and then pulled it back. With a slight smile, she said, "Good, I have your attention. Now listen to my words, Jackson Larocque. In the near future – I don't know when, but soon, you will have to make a choice. You, and a few others.

"Those of you who have the guns and the authority to use them will have to decide what type of country Canada is to become. On behalf of every politician alive or dead, I came to see you today to ask you to make the right choice, Director. It may be that others try to pull you in another direction, but as I stand before you, I say to you: remember your son, remember your oath, remember what the men and women under your command fought and died for. We're counting on you, Director."

Slowly, MacPhail's haunting green eyes turned from Larocque and took up Petit. "I've said what I've needed to. I'll leave at the other end of the trail just as planned."

The IO only nodded his head.

As the politician walked past Larocque, his hand shot out and grabbed the woman by the arm. Again, his cloud-grey eyes locked onto hers, and he said, "I've done some terrible, terrible things, but I'm a good person."

MacPhail gave him a nod of her head. "I know you are, Director. That's why I fought on the side of the Prime Minister to get your appointment to CSIS approved. Help us figure out if Merielle truly is involved with this White Unit, and if she is, help us steer her in a direction that doesn't destroy this country."

"And if I don't, and I side with Merielle?"

MacPhail looked over Larocque's shoulder at Tomic. "How many of your officers have been killed in the Pacific in the past two weeks?"

Tomic's reply was immediate. "Too many."

MacPhail's gaze reacquired Larocque's. "You can release my arm, Director."

Larocque's jaw tightened noticeably, but he did as he was asked.

As he released her, MacPhail's hand came across her body, rubbed at the place he had been holding, and said, "Setting aside things as banal as saving the soul of our country, you are losing good people because someone has gone off the reservation. For the moment, Director, let's set aside the motivations of the PM and concentrate on getting fewer of your people killed. The bigger stuff will come in due course. Of that, I'm certain."

MacPhail started walking again, and when she was five feet past him, Larocque turned and called to her back, "I won't do anything that will lead to us losing the war. I won't have us live under the boot of someone like Mitchell Spector. Whatever Merielle may or may not have become, the Reds are worse. Much worse."

MacPhail, without pulling up her stride and without looking back, said, "The White Unit, Director. Find them and stop what they're doing. What happens after that, we shall see."

Chapter 16

South China Sea, 150 kilometers off the coast of Vietnam

—

Rear Admiral Yin Jian stood beside the senior captain who had command of the *Fujian*, the first of three Chinese aircraft carriers that made use of the American-invented electromagnetic catapults.

The senior captain had been giving and amending orders to get the first strike package of eight J-15s into the air so they could begin to lay waste to the forward operating bases the Australian, Thai, and now Japanese air forces were using in central Cambodia to hammer the PLA forces fighting tooth-and-nail against what remained of the Vietnamese Army.

"Finally," the senior captain uttered. "A hell of a time for the catapult system to go on the fritz. They're all in the air now and on their way, Admiral."

Yin chose not to rebuke the man. The catapults had been finicky since before they were installed. That they had chosen this moment to go lame was an engineering issue, not an operational one.

From an operations perspective, Yin had few complaints about Senior Captain Bai's performance. In fact, the man's body of work until this very moment had been sterling.

"It's unfortunate timing, to be sure, but the delay will not matter. You and your people will launch hundreds of strikes over the next several days. You will make up the time."

"We will, Admiral. You can count on it," the senior captain said confidently, knowing that every officer and sailor within listening distance in the Operation Center would hear his reply and report it to their mates across the ship.

"Then I will leave you to organize the next strike package, Captain."

"Yes, Admiral. My people are already on it."

Yin turned away from the aircraft carrier's commander and walked toward the large table-like display that sat at the center of the ship's OC. By way of his experience on other vessels, the space that was the operational hub of the *Fujian* was positively cavernous.

Arriving at the table, he took in the large map and digital overlay of information that told him everything he needed to know about the eleven surface ships in the task force he was in command of.

His one and only condition on taking this mission was that his flotilla would be assigned additional anti-submarine warfare ships.

The PLA naval command had assigned two additional vessels, giving him five destroyers that specialized in ASW. But despite the additional capacity, they hadn't yet picked up any enemy submarines, which concerned him greatly.

At the midway point of his career, he himself had commanded a Type 054A+ for two years. The outfit of the four-thousand-ton vessel had been the ASW version of the platform, so Yin had an expert-like understanding of the game of cat-and-mouse playing out in a concentric circle around his flagship.

As if the CANZUK sub-threat hadn't been enough, the danger lurking underneath the waves had recently increased with Japan's unexpected entry into the war.

Personally, Yin had thought it was the assassination of the CANZUK politicians in Sydney that had put Japan over the top.

The outrage that followed the extraordinary attack had been palpable. Both the British and Australian prime ministers gave Churchillian-like speeches, and massive anti-Chinese rallies took place in many of CANZUK's major cities.

At the time, Yin had understood the purpose of the attack.

Brazen and brutal, the message sent to the Anglo alliance had been clear - China's military power and technology were indeed awesome, and now was the very best time to come to the table to strike a deal.

But that had not been the reaction of CANZUK.

In the days after the automaton attack, Australian and British subs and surface ships had sent no less than four hundred Tomahawk missiles into all parts of China, striking all sorts of critical infrastructure.

For the war planners in Beijing and the near-AI models helping to formulate their strategies, the level of violence and destruction wrought on the homeland had been anticipated and deemed acceptable.

What the generals and admirals and their near-AI servants hadn't foreseen was the personal impact of the Sydney killings.

In losing colleagues and friends in such a callous way, CANZUK went on a full-court press politically. Instead of returning to Britain, the lone surviving Defence Minister from the attack, Anne Watson, flew to Japan and, in twenty-four hours, had done the impossible. Anti-war Japan and its modern military had been convinced to help fight the Chinese 'war machine.'

It was in response to Japan's decision that Beijing's war planners had determined it was time to send a message to the world that China was not afraid of its ancient rival or any other navy, for that matter. That message was the *Fujian* and its task force.

"Sir," Yin heard a voice from across the table. He raised his eyes from the table-top tactical display he'd been staring at to focus on the officer who had addressed him.

"Yes? What is it, Commander?"

"We have radar contact with two hostile planes two hundred kilometers south and east of our position. They've lit up their radars. The bulk of the task force is being painted."

"Those would be Australian F-35s. Just out of range from our SAMs but just close enough for them to tag us for a missile strike. They are coming earlier than I would have guessed. No matter, we are ready," Yin said confidently.

"Sir, we have a pair of fighters screening that quadrant of the task force. Shall I assign them?"

"Yes, Commander. Remind them there will be more than the two F-35s on radar. The two that have revealed themselves are guiding the missile strike already on its way. They will keep their radars on, but more F-35s will be in the vicinity to protect them. It's a standard tactic, as you know."

Suddenly, Senior Captain Bai was beside him. He too was staring intently at the horizontal table display.

"I trust the next package of fighters is ready to go, Captain?" Yin asked of the other man.

"Yes, Admiral. Shall I order them to engage the enemy fighters or send them on their mission?"

"No, keep them to their original purpose. Their outlay will be of minimal assistance for what is to come, but once they're off, the next six planes should be for air-to-air," Yin said without hesitation.

His attention returned to the Battle Watch Commander, BWC, across the tactical display. The man's eyes were poring over the huge screen, no doubt trying to anticipate where the impending missile strike would come from.

The Australian F-35s didn't carry the American AGM-158C Long Range Anti-Ship Missile, LRASM, but RAAF's Super Hornets and their P-8 Poseidons did.

Each Aussie F-18 could carry four of the ship-killing units, while the P-8 could carry six of the missiles.

The LRASM was a highly sophisticated weapon with several capabilities that helped it avoid a ship's missile defenses. For instance, on seeing an incoming threat, the missiles could autonomously line themselves up front to back to ensure the rear-most missiles could hit their target.

But as smart as the LRASM was, it wasn't fast and CANZUK didn't have an endless supply of them.

Looking down at the map on the display, it was Yin's best guess the RAAF had launched their strike force from Southern Thailand instead of somewhere closer like Cambodia, where it could be picked up by PLA ground-based radar and be shot down by Chinese SAMs.

Because of the distance from their launch point across the Gulf of Thailand, the Australian Super Hornets would have to launch their missiles from what would be the LRASM's maximum range.

While fuel wouldn't be an issue for the Aussie P-8s, to maximize the barrage of missiles that could be sent at Yin's ships at one time, the Poseidons would launch their missiles at the exact moment the Hornets did.

All of which meant that it would be another full minute before the radars of the task force's outermost ships could zero in on the low-flying missiles and begin to shoot them down.

It was more than enough time for them to react, and if Yin was being honest, it was more than a little disappointing. He had expected more from his enemies. He hadn't even needed the assistance of the *Fujian's* near-AI to help him devise his enemy's strategy.

When Yin next spoke, his voice was filled with confidence and authority. As the flotilla's overall commander, it was his job to direct its collective defense. "Sound the general alarm. All ships and helos are to go live with their radars. Advise ships Echo-1 and Echo-4 to concentrate their radars to the west of their immediate positions. They should start to see incoming hostile missiles sometime in the next sixty seconds."

As the orders left his mouth, the BWC and several other officers around the OC tactical table began to give sub-orders or tap out directions on various parts of the tactical display. As they did so, the lighting in the ops room switched from standard white to tactical red.

As Yin listened to his people expertly conduct themselves, he crossed his arms and mentally admonished his enemy. During the first two weeks of the war, the Australians and the British had exercised a degree of guile and bravery he couldn't help but admire.

It had cost them dearly, but these quick victories had set back the PLA's charge southward in Vietnam by shredding parts of the army's supply chain and bringing the production of the Wraiths and Hyenas to a standstill.

This most recent attack might well be brave and might have come earlier than he expected, but in his professional opinion it lacked any of the cunning CANZUK had demonstrated earlier in the conflict.

Across the display, the BWC coordinating the task force's defensive posturing gave an update. "Sir, all radars and all weapons are online, charged, and ready. The moment something shows up, it'll be tagged and splashed."

Pleased with the update, Yin announced, "Very good, Commander. Today, our enemies will find out just how impotent they are."

As the pronouncement left Yin's mouth, the border of the tactical table began to flash an urgent red, but instead of hostile missiles appearing to the west where Yin had expected them, a single missile designated as a red square appeared less than a hand's length from the southernmost ship of the task force.

Across the table, the BWC's hands flew across the screen, and a quick moment later, the display was divided into two even parts.

On the left remained the data overlay of the task force's overall footprint with the *Fujian* at its center. To the right, the overlay had zeroed in on the new threat from the south, but instead of one missile, there was now a half dozen. Beside it flashed a new data point – TO-5-A, which was short for the Maritime Strike Tomahawk.

The British are coming, thought Yin. They were the only nation that operated this version of the legendary American missile.

With a tone of appreciation in his voice, Yin said, "Well played, CANZUK. Of course, you would try to hit us from multiple vectors."

Because anti-ship missiles flew so close to the water, a ship's radar would only be able to pick them up at a maximum of forty klicks out from their target.

In this case, the radar of the southernmost ship of the task force, a Type 055 destroyer, had only managed to identify the incoming threat at thirty klicks from its position.

But identify the threat the destroyer had, and in the next instant, the powerful near-AI that collectively managed the multifunction phased array radars of the task force sprang into action, taking over those systems it needed to put down the new British threat.

In a perfectly orchestrated firestorm, the southernmost Type 055 sent forth thirty-six missiles from its one hundred and twelve vertical launch cells to intercept the growing number of Tomahawks. Their number meant at least two British subs were in play.

Yin took a deep, calming breath and listened to the operations room. It was surprisingly quiet. Just fifteen years ago, as the commander of a strike force such as the one he now commanded, he would have been barking out orders to adjust their defense in real-time, but those days were long gone.

With the near-AI of the HHQ-9 maritime missile defense system, he looked on with satisfaction and relief at the growing swarm of green triangles that would intercept the incoming Royal Navy attack.

Without a command, the screen narrowed to improve the scale of the two fast-closing missile groups. Between the two different bodies, a timer appeared. Its countdown started at fifteen seconds.

As the timer hit nine, the border of the ops room tactical table flashed yellow three times in quick succession.

With all the mental toughness he could muster, Yin tore his eyes from the impending collision of the two missile groups and looked in the direction of the team of officers and sailors who manned the ops room sonar station.

Flashing yellow meant only one thing.

"Torpedoes in the water!" the senior officer from the sonar station called out.

"Details, Commander," Yin demanded of the BWC.

"On screen now, Admiral," the talented officer said, his voice calm.

The display was now divided into quadrants. Yin's eyes flashed to the bottom left to see the data stream listing the number of Tomahawks still in the air. Twenty-two.

The HHQ-9 system would have already designated more missiles from other ships to bring down the incoming British attack. That threat was no longer worth his time.

Quickly, he looked to the top right square where he had anticipated the original attack from the Australians.

Not to be disappointed, a collection of red squares was emerging. Sixty-five missiles and counting, only twenty kilometers out. Again, the near-AI of the air defense system would assign the required number of missiles to address this new threat.

In rapid succession, Yin scanned the bottom left and top right quadrants and decided the top right was the priority. Eight torpedoes designated as orange squares were perpendicular to the broadside of the *Fujian*. They were coming from the direction of Vietnam's coastline. The lead torpedo had just passed the two-thousand-meter mark. The others weren't far behind.

"Sonar, where did they come from?" demanded Yin.

"We have a track now, Admiral. Japanese *Taigei* class. It must have been hiding in one of the crannies that run along the coastline."

Beside him, Senior Captain Bai began to issue orders to protect his aircraft carrier from the new threat.

"Weapons, ready countermeasure package Alpha-Foxtrot," Bai called out.

"Aye, sir, countermeasure Alpha-Foxtrot ready."

"Release the countermeasure."

"Countermeasure released, Captain," confirmed the senior weapons officer.

Turning his head to another part of the Ops Center, Bai called out, "Officer of the Watch, come hard left, steer 225, increase full ahead."

"Aye, Captain, coming hard left, maximum speed, heading two-two-five degrees," the officer confirmed the order in a clipped tone.

As soon as the words left the helmsman's mouth, Yin felt the enormous power of the aircraft carrier's engines come to life while the deck underneath his feet shifted slightly as the massive ship undertook its new course. All around him, anything that wasn't locked down skittered across surfaces or fell to the floor as the massive ship began to heel.

Ignoring the chaos, he pulled his gaze from Bai and quickly surveyed each of the four quadrants on the tactical table.

The British Tomahawks were no more. To the west, there remained too few of the Australian LRASMs. In that direction, a single Type 053 ASW destroyer had been hit. The incoming damage report scrawling across the bottom of his side of the display suggested the vessel would not survive.

In the quadrant Yin had chosen to ignore moments earlier, he could see another salvo of torpedoes chasing down a Type 054A frigate.

The furthest north and weakest ship of the task force, the vessel had been given the rearguard responsibility of screening for any submarines or Vietnamese missile boats that might try to take the task force from behind.

In serving its purpose, it, too, would die.

A pair of torpedoes, fired by another Japanese sub, had defeated the frigate's last batch of countermeasures and were now seconds away from exploding underneath the hull of the four-thousand-ton ship.

From across the room, Bai's senior sonar officer delivered an update on the six torpedoes chasing down the *Fujian*.

In response, the officer at the weapons station called out, "The first anti-torpedo drone is set to engage the lead torpedo."

Yin's eyes once again took in the top right quadrant. At the center of the screen, the first of the Y-7 Blackfish anti-torpedo drones appeared to collide with the lead Japanese Type-18 heavyweight torpedo.

For a too-long moment, there was no report from anyone to suggest that the Chinese drone had defeated the threat.

Finally, to Yin's right, the senior officer from the sonar station gave a report. "Japanese torpedo destroyed."

Beside him, Senior Captain Bai silently pumped his fist.

Over the next forty-five seconds, the remainder of the Blackfish drones also found their marks.

When the final orange square on the display disappeared, Bai called out in a loud voice that made no effort to hide the relief he was feeling, "Excellent work, everyone. Now, find me the sub that thought it was a good idea to try to sink my ship."

Across the table, the BWC advised, "We have two ASW helicopters on the way, and a third will be in the air in five minutes. We'll track it down, Captain."

Bai turned to Yin. He had an ecstatic look on his face. "A good test, Admiral. One, I'd say we've passed with flying colors."

"Indeed. Well done, Senior Captain Bai. Please resume our schedule to launch our fighters. This morning's events demonstrate more than ever the importance of our mission. The quicker we can degrade CANZUK's forward air bases, the fewer opportunities they'll have to direct these attacks at us."

"And the British subs to the south?" Bai asked.

"Leave them to me, Captain. In revealing themselves, they have lost the initiative, and hunting subs is something at which I excel.

"Get your planes in the air, and I'll oversee the effort to hunt the foreign devils down. Today, our enemies underestimated our defensive capabilities. Now, we will show them that the Chinese navy is the preeminent power in the Pacific Ocean."

From across the table, Yin once again heard the voice of the BWC. "Admiral, we have a new contact out of the northwest."

Yin's gaze took up the eyes of the younger officer. "Yes, and what is it?"

"The track suggests they're hypersonics. Twenty units, sir. They're flying low. Preliminary data suggests they're British."

"Range?" Yin demanded.

"They've just passed within thirty klicks of the Nanchang to our northwest. The Nanchang is engaging them now, Admiral."

"Sloppy and late, wouldn't you say, Commander," Yin asked.

"Very late, Admiral. Only five minutes sooner, and they might have given us more than we could have handled."

Yin nodded at the assessment and said casually, "Perhaps, but not now. Once again, the British have fumbled the ball. Admiral Nelson must be rolling in his grave."

The BWC's fingers danced across the table's surface, and the tactical display became a single large-scale map that showed the southern half of Vietnam. A collection of red squares was just east of Ho Chi Minh City.

Between the *Fujian* and the incoming British missiles was the Nanchang, a Type 055 guided missile destroyer.

Green triangles appeared on the display on the starboard side of the vessel. Upon receiving the data on the new threat, the destroyer's HHQ-9 air defense system instantly came to life to unleash a barrage of its own missiles.

Across the table, the BWC looked up from the display and locked eyes with Yin. There was a new look of concern on his face. "Sir, the data coming in suggests that some of the British missiles could make it through to the Nanchang. She's at risk, Admiral."

"Not a problem," Yin said dispassionately. "The Nanchang has served its purpose and given us advance warning. However many of the hypersonics make it past the Nanchang, we will be able to handle them. That is what is important."

When Yin next spoke, he made sure to raise his voice so that the entirety of the OC could hear his pronouncement. "This Anglo alliance and their new Japanese friends have been found wanting. If the Nanchang falls, it and its crew will be heroes celebrated by our great nation for generations. And China, through the *Fujian* and the full might of its navy, will make CANZUK and the Japanese, and whoever else comes before us, pay and pay dearly for the wrongs they have inflicted on our great nation."

As Yin finished his speech, he looked around the ops room to see that most of the officers and sailors were looking at him. To the last, their faces beamed with confidence.

And so they should, Yin told himself.

Quietly, from across the tactical display, the BWC provided a new update. "Admiral, the Nanchang has been struck. A single hit based on the data. Four contacts continue in our direction."

"Four is nothing, Lieutenant. Shoot them down, and let us be done with this part of the day's events," Yin crowed.

"Yes, Admiral. Our missile defense systems are activating."

On hearing the update, Yin felt the slightest shudder reverberate through the ship's massive steel bulk as the *Fujian's* onboard HHQ-9 system launched over a dozen missiles in the direction of the four remaining British hypersonics.

A minute later, when the announcement came that the incoming threat had been neutralized, a grin lit up on Yin's face. His voice once again loud, he said, "Excellent work, everyone. Commander, relay orders for –."

"Sir, new contacts!" the BWC said, cutting Yin off.

"Northwest, at forty kilometers, twelve, no make that thirty-eight unidentified planes flying at thirteen hundred kilometers an hour. They're coming straight at us."

"Unidentified?" Yin said in an outraged tone. "Tell that damned near-AI that we need to know what's coming our way and now."

The BWC's eyes came up from the tabletop and connected with Yin's.

"MiG-21s, sir,"

"MiG-21s? Is that a joke, Commander?"

"No, sir. That's what they are. It took the near-AI an extra moment to identify them, but it's certain now. Thirty-eight MiG-21s are coming our way, Admiral. And fast."

Before Yin could decide to believe or contest the update, he heard the *Fujian's* air defense system again come to life.

His eyes darted downward as the screen in front of him expanded to show a close-up of their position relative to the new threat.

Now just twenty kilometers north of their position, Yin took in the individual blue triangles that represented the ancient Soviet-built single-seat fighters and began to laugh.

"They must have been flying only a few feet above the water. The British missiles were timed in such a way to help mask their approach," the BWC explained over the sound of Yin's continuing guffaws.

Finally, Yin managed to get out, "And what is this new threat armed with? If my recollection of history is any good, the MiG-21 was an interceptor and only had air-to-air missiles."

"That's correct, Admiral. The Vietnamese Air Force MiG-21s carried both radar-guided and heat-seeking missiles. It also has a cannon."

Beside Yin, Senior Captain Bai spoke. "Whatever they might have, they'll fall into the sea the moment they're launched. Our EW systems will fry whatever our SAMs don't bring down."

"Speaking of which," Yin said, pointing at the huge display. On-screen, the HHQ-9 missiles fired to intercept the MiGs started to appear as blue dots.

Three minutes later, in threes and fours, the enemy fighters, pathetic in every way, began to disappear.

From across the tactical display, the BWC spoke, "Six have made it through. The HHQ-10 battery and EW systems will now engage."

Less than a minute later, the tactical display zoomed in to show two remaining planes.

At just three kilometers out from the ship's broadside, the *Fujian's* final close-in weapon system, a single Type 730 seven-barreled 30mm rotating gun, began to pour thousands of rounds at the lead fighter.

Seconds later, one of the two targeted MiGs disappeared from the screen.

Outside the operations room, through the steel and insulation that was the carrier's innards, Yin heard the blare of the rotating gun as it tried to pick up the last Vietnamese fighter.

On the screen below him, he could see that the angle of the weapon in relation to its target was not favorable.

The Type 730, like all similar weapons, was most effective when a target had to fly into an elongated spray of supersonic bullets. It was much less accurate when it had to lead a target. Particularly one flying as fast as the incoming MiG.

As Yin reached down to grab the handles that ringed the tactical table, he heard Bai quietly utter a word under his breath that he himself had not contemplated.

"*Kamikaze.*"

***

When the formal request had come for volunteers to fly the handful of Soviet-era MiG-21s to try and damage the Chinese aircraft carrier, Major Trung Ha had been the first to raise his hand.

Nearly two hundred pilots had been brought together in a single hangar on Vietnam's southwest border to hear the plan described by the Air Force's most senior general.

As with the rest of Vietnam's military, the Air Force had not fared well against the Chinese juggernaut. Their planes had been too few and too old. Not as old as the MiG-21 he was now flying, but old and ineffective relative to the hundreds of sleek fighters China had employed to crush his country's much smaller air force.

That it had taken all of three days for China to destroy Vietnam's frontline airplanes was the reason why there had been so many pilots available for the mission he was now leading.

The speed and violence with which China had undertaken its invasion had meant that many of Vietnam's fighter jets had been on the ground when they'd been destroyed.

So complete had the Chinese victory been in the air that pilots in Ha's squadron had been leaving in ones and twos to join their brothers and sisters fighting the Chinese horde and their futuristic robots on the ground.

As one of the senior officers in his unit, he'd resisted the temptation.

Ha had held out on the hope that some other military in the region would donate their unwanted fighters to Vietnam's cause just as several countries had done for Ukraine during their war against the Russians.

That he would be flying one of the still-working fighters his country had used to shoot down American warplanes seventy years ago was not how he'd envisioned his contribution to the war, but that's precisely what he was doing as he flew his MiG a few feet above swollen rice paddies at nine hundred kilometers per hour.

The general that had asked for volunteers for the mission had been explicit. Vietnam would not ask its sons and daughters to purposely destroy themselves to help save their country.

Instead, he had explained that, along with nearly forty MiG-21s, the air force still had an inventory of the missiles carried by the plane and that it was with this armament that the Chinese aircraft carrier could be disabled.

When the distinguished-looking former pilot had made the statement, Ha had been relieved that no one in the briefing had balked or gasped at the outrageous suggestion.

The missile in question was the K-13 Atoll. Last produced in the late 1970s, when launched, the heat-seeking K-13 could, in theory, identify the *Fujian's* power plant and with god-like good fortune, could make it past the ship's short-range defenses and strike the carrier, leaving the pilot and his plane with just enough fuel to make it back to land.

It was a fantastical proposition and Ha and every other pilot who had heard the old general's proposal was no fool.

The chances that any one of the thirty-eight planes to go on the mission would even make it to the point where they could fire their missiles at the carrier was all but inconceivable.

The PLA Navy's modern radars had been designed to pick up incoming low-flying missiles. At the very latest, he and his fellow pilots would be flagged at twenty klicks out from their target, at which point they would need to try and survive a wall of lightning-fast and hugely accurate air defense missiles the *Fujian* itself would launch.

Then, at no less than two kilometers out from their target, flying at speeds nearing fifteen hundred kilometers an hour, whatever pilots remained would need to convince their plane's rudimentary targeting system to somehow lock on to the ship, all the while avoiding the tens of thousands of 30mm rounds the aircraft carrier's close-in defenses would be throwing at them.

It was, in truth, a mission impossible.

With the futility of the strategy understood, in the two days they had had to prepare for their mission, Ha, the most senior officer of the volunteers, had gathered his fellow pilots together to talk about the one and only way they would be able to make a difference in this war.

During the short meeting, he had only spoken for himself. Dispassionately, he'd spoken of his love for his family and his country and gave voice to the concern that everyone had about what the Chinese would do to the peaceable and increasingly prosperous country Vietnam had become in the decades since the end of the American war.

Ha had ended his speech by indicating he had no intention of trying to execute the ridiculous suggestion of trying to send a pair of sixty-year-old missiles into the aircraft carrier. One way or another, he had said, he was not coming back from this mission. He would die with honor and, if God willed it, with a victory that would inspire generations of his countrymen for the next five hundred years.

There had been no discussion following his brief remarks, only the nodding of heads that bore thoughtful looks.

As his fighter transitioned from the green-and-brown of farm fields and jungle to the azure blue of the South China Sea, Ha discarded the memory of his address and focused on the modern-day tactical pad affixed to the cockpit's instrument panel by a team of CANZUK technicians that had quietly materialized on base less than twenty-four hours ago.

Somewhere in the sky high above him and his fellow pilots were one or more Australian F-35s using their plane's radar to paint their target.

According to that incoming data, their first test of the day was just sixty kilometers away.

As per standard naval doctrine, the person commanding the Chinese task force had placed its strongest defensive assets between the *Fujian* and the area that represented the greatest threat to the aircraft carrier. In this case, Vietnam itself.

Flying no more than ten meters above the waves, the radar of the Type 055 guided missile destroyer would begin to detect Ha and his fellow pilots at about thirty kilometers out.

For the first time during their short flight, he activated the MiG's obsolete VHF radio. "Tiger Squadron, this is Tiger Lead. Stay in formation and at current speed until I give the word. We should be seeing the package any moment now."

Just as he finished the statement, a bright yellow square appeared behind Ha's flight of MiGs. Fired minutes earlier and over three hundred kilometers away, the British hypersonic missiles had shown up on time.

Traveling at Mach 5, twenty Perseus missiles fired from five RAF P-8 Poseidons would in theory give the defensive systems of the Chinese destroyer all it could handle.

As his eyes moved back and forth between the tactical pad and the crystal-clear horizon, the British hypersonics gained ground on them.

As they approached the thirty-kilometer mark where the Chinese radar should have picked up the low-flying MiGs, Ha caught several grey streaks moving past him to the right and left.

He glanced down at his instrument panel. Doing just over a thousand kilometers per hour, the British missiles had passed him like he had been standing still.

The border of the tactical pad flashed red. Ahead, missiles started to emerge from the Chinese missile destroyer. With one hundred and twelve vertical missile cells at the ship's disposal, a wall of red appeared on the starboard side of the vessel.

Ha once again activated his radio. "Tiger Squadron, increase speed to twelve hundred. Tiger Team Bravo. If Target Echo remains operational, that is your objective. Tiger Lead out."

Low on the horizon in front of him, a series of flashes erupted as the British Perseus missiles encountered the SAMs from the Chinese HHQ-9 system.

Developed by the MBDA corporation, the Perseus had several technologies beyond its prodigious speed to maximize its chances of hitting its target. Equipped with a powerful near-AI, each missile had its own radar and maneuvering system that would allow it to evade whatever defensive system was trying to prevent it from reaching its target.

Ahead of Ha, at perhaps fifteen kilometers, a massive explosion erupted on the horizon. As the destruction of the Chinese destroyer registered in his mind, Ha executed a violent fist pump.

But his moment of celebration was short-lived as he realized that at least some of the missiles from the Chinese ship's defensive volley had ignored or missed the British missiles and were seconds away from hitting his people.

Ha's eyes flashed to the CANZUK tac pad and saw that the border of the unit was strobing a red warning. He activated his radio, "Tiger Squadron, defensive maneuvers on my mark."

He counted down two seconds and calmly said, "Mark."

On his order, all thirty-eight MiG-21s began to juke as best they could at low altitude. Flying no more than thirty feet above the waves and not wanting to reveal themselves to the radar of the aircraft carrier, each pilot did what they could to avoid being hit while staying low and flying fast.

As Ha executed his own subtle movements and shifted the profile of his MiG, he perceived several bright flashes to his right and left.

As the red on the tac pad faded away, he saw there were still thirty fighters with him.

Looking up, he saw the Chinese missile destroyer was burning.

One of the British hypersonics had struck the ship just below the fore superstructure. Black smoke engulfed the entire center portion of the vessel.

Toward the stern of the ship, his vision caught a flash. His eyes darting to that location, he saw one of the destroyer's close-in defense weapons was still operational. Seeing it wasn't pointed in his direction, he made no adjustments to his flight.

Now approaching the MiG's top speed, he passed over and through the dark smoke pouring out of the warship.

Glancing at the tactical pad, he noted that four of the British hypersonic missiles were still skimming across the South China Sea in the direction of his squadron's prize.

Flagged by the *Fujian's* missile defense system, a swarm of red dots appeared on the tactical pad's screen and began to make their way to the approaching RAF missiles.

An optimist by nature, Ha told himself the hypersonics would do the remainder of his squadron a massive favor by temporarily emptying out the aircraft carrier's limited number of vertical launch cells, leaving the Chinese ship with fewer missiles to fire at him and his fellow pilots once they realized the MiGs were part of the assault.

On the screen, the four Perseus missiles suddenly blinked away, and what remained of the red dots that represented the HHQ-9 SAMs continued in their direction. A quick count told them there weren't enough of them to bring down all of Ha's squadron.

In a moment of silent triumph, he realized at least some of their number would get to lay their naked eyes on the floating airfield.

Another salvo of red dots emerged from the starboard side of the carrier, signalling the Chinese task force had finally flagged their approach.

He didn't bother to count the SAMs. Without a doubt, there were now more highly advanced missiles in the sky than there were of the seventy-year-old interceptors.

Without thinking, Ha clicked on his radio and as he began to speak, he realized this would be the last time another human being heard his voice. "Tiger Squadron, we have incoming. Lots of them. Pour on as much speed as you can and do what you can to make it to the objective. May God favor our efforts on this day and may the Fatherland achieve victory over the filthy Han. Vietnam, live forever. Tiger Lead out."

Quickly, Ha looked at his instrument panel to check his speed and altitude. Instinctively, he knew he couldn't squeeze more juice out of his plane, and there was no sense trying to get closer to the ocean below him.

The highly sensitive radar of the Chinese carrier had them now. The only tactic he and his fellow pilots had left was hope. Hope that their speed and numbers might allow at least one of them to reach their target.

Pulling his eyes back from his instruments, he saw a pair of MiGs begin to edge out in front of him. As his airframe began to endure the wash from the two fighters, he had to reduce his speed slightly.

Falling back from the two planes before him, another pair of fighters came into view to squeeze in behind the first two ancient interceptors.

Thirty seconds later, three-quarters of what remained of his squadron had forced themselves in front of his fighter.

It was halfway through this spontaneous re-arrangement of their attack that he realized what his people were doing. They had formed a vanguard.

The sixteen pilots in front of him would give their own lives so that he might be able to strike a righteous blow against their enemy. Despite the very long odds he still faced, in that moment, every molecule in Ha's body felt encouraged. They could do this.

Letting out a deep breath, he looked ahead to where the leading edge of his squadron would meet the incoming missiles.

Without warning, two explosions flashed well ahead of him. Seconds later, another two planes disintegrated before his eyes, only they were closer.

Perceiving something coming his way, Ha juked upward, bringing his fighter several hundred feet up. Elevated, he saw a flash as one of the carrier's SAMs exploded where he had been only half a second before.

Still supersonic, he rolled his fighter and brought the bottom of his plane within twenty feet of the ocean's surface, once again placing himself behind what remained of the pilots escorting him to the aircraft carrier.

Ahead, he could now see the *Fujian* with his naked eye. Its size on the horizon told him he was about six kilometers out.

Immediately to his front, another MiG exploded, this time in a spectacular orange fireball.

Jerking hard on his flight stick, Ha desperately weaved around the conflagration and, in the process, heard a terrible clanking sound as something from the disintegrating plane connected with his fighter.

Several yellow-and-red buttons on the MiG's instrument panel lit up, trying to tell Ha what was wrong. Having only flown the '60s-era fighter for three days, he had no idea what the flashing buttons meant.

Gingerly, he maneuvered left and right. No problems there. It was when he tried to gain altitude that he found out what the issue was.

When he tried to pull back on the flight stick, he heard the unwelcome sound of metal tearing at itself from the MiG's left side. In what time he had left, he could no longer ascend.

Gently, he set the flight stick back to its natural position and took stock of his altitude. Eighty-two feet. Too high.

"Get low, you son of a bitch," Ha said as he again pushed his flight stick forward.

When water from the ocean rushed up to meet him, he quickly levelled off the fighter at twenty-five feet.

Hugely relieved he was back at an altitude that wouldn't see him fly uselessly over the deck of the quickly growing ship, Ha glanced at the tac pad and saw that only three planes remained ahead of him.

As yet another fighter exploded, this one out of his flight path, he did some quick math and realized the aircraft carrier's short-range defensive missile system had run out of time.

The single HHQ-10 launch system on the starboard side of the ship took nearly ninety seconds to reload its twenty-four cells, and for the moment, there were no angry red dots on the tactical pad between the remaining fighters of Ha's squadron and their prize.

Flying at thirteen hundred kilometers an hour and only four klicks out from the *Fujian*, now the only thing that could stop them was the carrier's point defense systems.

Just as the thought crossed his mind, hundreds of tracer rounds enveloped the lead MiG-21 and before Ha knew it, the plane began to disintegrate and pinwheel through the air.

Flaring his fighter to the left to avoid a collision, water sprayed across his canopy as the destroyed fighter connected with the ocean.

As the final two fighters ahead of him began to bob and weave in the hopes of drawing fire for as long as possible, all the intuition and experience he had gathered in his thirteen years of flying fighter aircraft kicked into high gear and screamed at him to push his plane as fast as it could go.

Steadily, so as not to overwhelm and stall out the timeworn engine, Ha increased the MiG's speed.

To his left, the last of the two planes that had been ahead of him broke up and ignited into a ball of fire as the carrier's only starboard-side high-velocity cannon found its mark.

Ripping past the explosion and only two klicks out from his target, several other smaller weapons underneath the carrier's deck began to open up on him.

With a storm of bright red tracers consuming his vision, Ha waggled his fighter left and right in a desperate effort to stay alive for another few seconds.

As he pointed the plane's nose in the direction of the *Fujian's* hanger deck, where he prayed his fighter would find tens of thousands of liters of jet fuel, his canopy began to disintegrate.

With every bit of concentration he could muster, Ha's hands remained faithful and firm on the MiG's flight controls.

As chunks of glass from his fighter's canopy tore into his flesh, Ha did not feel pain. Rather, in his final seconds alive, he experienced something approaching existential joy as he perceived the moment his supersonic fighter connected with the outer hull of the Chinese aircraft carrier at speed.

For a nano-second, his joy transitioned to pure ecstasy as he felt his body compress and transform as the force of his jet's engine penetrated steel and tore into the guts of the crown jewel of China's navy.

Chapter 17

Beijing, China

—

For what had to be the twentieth time, President Yan watched the incredible footage of the last moments of the *Fujian*. The video came from the periscope of one of CANZUK's submarines.

A propaganda godsend, CANZUK had released the damaging video to the world's media less than three hours ago. And like a lightning strike in a tinder-dry forest, the story had blazed its way across the planet in minutes.

Of course, the near-AI that China employed to censor all parts of the internet on behalf of its citizens had prevented the news from reaching the mainland.

And thank goodness, thought Yan. Had the 1.4 billion people of his country had the opportunity to see what he was seeing, he was not sure he could have contained their outrage.

As it was, it was becoming difficult to manage the tens of thousands of protesters who showed up daily to march and chant slogans at each of the CANZUK embassies.

In truth, the agent provocateurs Chinese domestic intelligence had seeded into the leadership of the pro-war movement had limits on how much control they could exercise over the protests. They were students for the most part, and young people could be unpredictable.

Had the video of the *Fujian* and the subsequent news of the destruction of its task force found the eyes and ears of the impassioned young people who led the city-wide protests, Yan was certain the police would not have been able to prevent a storming of the four countries' embassies even if he had wanted them to.

No, he told himself. As satisfying as it might be to see a handful of middling diplomats torn to shreds by throngs of revenge-fueled Chinese nationalists, Yan understood that any such actions would not advance his program.

When his people had spoken with the Defence Minister of Great Britain nearly four weeks ago and had delivered his ultimatum of coming to reasonable terms with China in thirty days, it had been an honest gesture.

Yes, the automaton attack that had killed the CANZUK politicians had been egregious, but at the time, he had wanted to push the Anglo alliance into quick action. He had hoped they would see the futility of escalating the conflict and start negotiations, but he had also prepared himself for the opposite response.

That the opposite reaction had been the destruction of the *Fujian* meant that the democracies of the CANZUK alliance did not appreciate just how determined China was.

The loss of an aircraft carrier and its three thousand sailors along with the rest of the task force had been an audacious and mighty blow that Yan could appreciate. But in smiting one of his country's national treasures, the four little countries had consented to what happened next.

China had been explicit and precise in the language it had used with Anne Watson, the UK's Defence Minister. The words 'total war' had been stated to the politician for good reason.

In the annals of history, the practice of total war had, in many instances, resulted in entire countries ceasing to exist. Carthage and the Aztecs were two of the most well-known examples. Germany and Japan had narrowly avoided this fate eighty years ago. Yan had studied each situation closely and understood the conditions that had led to each country's demise.

CANZUK could not say they weren't warned.

His finger moved to the digital pad sitting on the massive conference table in front of him and pressed the green square at its center.

On connecting with the button, the large ornately carved double doors of the conference room opened, allowing nearly two dozen senior military officers and advisors to quietly enter the room.

Within a minute, they were seated at their usual positions and were staring in the direction of their leader.

Yan embraced their gazes while at the same time perceiving the nervous energy practically oozing from the pores of the twenty or so men who were hard-bitten veterans of the one-party political system of which Yan was firmly in control.

Just two hours ago, Vice-Admiral Song Feng, the man in charge of the command that had drawn up the plan to send the *Fujian* to its untimely destruction, had been found in his office with a self-inflicted gunshot wound to his right temple.

That rumors were circulating that a pair of men in dark suits had entered the Vice-Admiral's office only twenty minutes before the gunshot had been heard were unfortunate.

Unfortunate in that Yan took no great pleasure in artificially setting the conditions that would ensure China achieved the destiny he had spoken to this group of men about so many times before.

There had been no real consequences after the CANZUK missile strikes several weeks earlier.

Yes, senior people had been demoted, and more than a few egos had been bruised, but in time, those types of career-oriented consequences could be recovered from.

Career rehabilitation would not be an option for Vice-Admiral Song.

As was his way before he began an address, Yan placed both hands palms down on the table and locked eyes with the most senior general of his country's armed forces, the PLA's current Chief of Staff.

He would start his address by focusing on General Wu Dezhi because the man was a linchpin in the hierarchy that Yan needed to control the military.

Clearing his throat, he said, "In the time I have been our country's President and the Chairman of our great Party, I have done all I could to support China's armed forces. Rarely have I said no to a funding request. Rarely have I denied a strategy to advance our country's geo-strategic position in the near abroad. I hope all of you in this room would agree, I have been your greatest advocate, your greatest ally."

He paused, allowing the room to confirm or deny his statement. No one spoke.

"I want to be transparent with those of you in the room who I suspect are not fully behind the program I have put forward. I have heard that some of you do not think we should be so ambitious. That we should not start wars with countries half a world away or that in order to be great, China does not need to take the lands of others. China is already vast, it is said."

Keeping his gazed locked on General Wu, he continued, "And then there are others of you – the historians in the room – who have mentioned that with the return of Taiwan, China now controls the same territories it held when it was at its political zenith. Why do we need more territory, these same amateur scholars ask? Who are we to say that we are better than our own history?"

Yan paused for a moment, shifting his gaze from Wu to randomly survey the other faces in the room. Like the PLA Chief of Staff, theirs were faces of granite. Serious and unmoving.

His eyes finally stopped on the man who many suspected would eventually replace General Wu.

As Yan would have expected, Admiral Xi Fenghui returned his gaze as though he himself was an emotionless robot. "As all of you sit here before me, you will be asking yourselves how I know the things you are saying or thinking. But in truth, the answers to these questions do not matter. The only thing that matters is what I am about to tell you."

Still staring at the PLA Navy's most senior officer, Yan did something he had never done before. Slowly, he pushed his chair back from the table and stood.

Automatically, the military men around the table moved to follow him to his feet, but in a sharp tone, he said, "Stay seated."

As the words registered in their ears, as one, the generals, admirals and advisors froze their ascents and began to look at one another for some type of collective reassurance.

Finally, after a too-long moment, both General Wu and Admiral Xi re-seated themselves and together set their eyes back upon Yan.

"Gentlemen and my fellow patriots, I stand while you sit because I want this moment to stand out in your memories. Today, an accomplished military man and beloved husband and father chose to take his own life because of the shame he felt. The shame of an entire nation. It is a shame I share."

Yan started to pace counterclockwise around the table. As he moved, the eyes of his people began to track him as though they were loyal hounds.

"This is a rhetorical question, so I do not expect... no, I don't want an answer.

"Do you know why I am the president of our beloved country?"

He took a few more steps and reached the end of the table furthest from his own seat. Stopping, he said, "I am president for many reasons, but the chief factor is that I look into the future. With regularity, I look six months, two years, or even five years into the future. There are even moments when I look forward twenty or even fifty years to see where our great nation could be."

He took another five steps. "And when I look into the future, colleagues, do you know what I see?"

He stopped his tour of the enormous briefing room behind General Wu and continued his speech over the man's shoulder.

"I see a world that will continue to be fractured and weak. A world that will continue to argue over ridiculous things like whether a man can menstruate. A world that will continue to fight for pieces of land that are hardly worth fighting for. A world where two straight generations of young Western minds have become dumber, lazier, and more handicapped by record levels of things like depression and anxiety. Never have our enemies been weaker. Never have they been more divided."

He stepped forward and placed his hand on the back of Wu's chair.

"General Wu believes now is the time for China to expand. He has a brilliant mind, you know. I respect him for it. Do you know that just last week, he and I spent nearly two hours talking about of all things, Mars?"

Yan repeated the planet's name for emphasis. "Mars. You heard that right."

"We are in the mid-2030s. The great Elon Musk wanted to have the beginnings of a city on Mars by this time. But there are no people on that planet. They are not even close."

Yan pulled his hand off Wu's chair and resumed his stroll.

"Listen to my next words very, very carefully. The war I am asking you to fight on behalf of the people of China is not about adding a few countries under our thumb. It is not about giving us a strategic advantage over our enemies so that China as a nation cannot be threatened by a resurgent United States. It is not about expanding our economy. It is not even about bringing more women into our country so that millions of men can have the opportunity to start a family, though I feel particularly strongly about this part of our collective effort."

Yan stopped again, this time behind Admiral Xi.

"The war we are fighting is about setting the conditions for China to dominate, to utterly dominate the entirety of this world for the next one hundred years.

"It is China and its 1.4 billion citizens who will control and use all of Southeast Asia for its own purposes. It is China's aircraft carriers and submarines that will dominate the South China Sea, the Indian Ocean, and the Persian Gulf. It is Chinese leadership in the fields of AI and quantum computing that will drive innovation and economies across the world. It is Chinese spacecraft and Chinese astronauts who will establish the first settlement on Mars, and, in time, it is Chinese colonists who will grow this settlement into a city.

"China, my dear friends, needs to think about where it wants to be in the twenty-second century, not where it was in the thirteenth."

Yan snapped his fingers, causing more than one of the men around the table to jump in their seats.

As the echo of the sound died away in the ancient high-ceiling chamber, the double doors that the generals had come through ten minutes earlier swung open.

Standing at the entrance were two X-8 Wraiths, their usual mottled-gray camouflage replaced with a glossy, almost lacquered black.

On the upper left part of the chest of both Wraiths was a red star about six inches point-to-point, while along their right arm and right leg, there seemed to be red slashes that, upon closer inspection, were claw marks.

On the right thigh of both autos, sitting in an affixed holster, was the assault pistol that each Wraith carried as a part of its standard weapons complement.

Yan gestured in the direction of the two menacing automatons. "I know many of you in this room are uncomfortable with the technology represented by these near-AI machines, but it is the future, and it is a future I am determined to have China embrace."

Raising his voice slightly, Yan said, "Bravo-Seven. Would you join me, please?"

The moment the command left Yan's lips, the Wraith engaged the hundreds of servos used to manipulate its body and smoothly walked toward the Chinese President.

On its arrival, Yan took a step back from the Admiral's chair and, in the process, put the Wraith between himself and the PLA Navy's highest-ranking officer.

When Yan next spoke, his voice once again became louder so as to address the whole of the room. "I have a confession to make, and the confession is this.

"I lied when I said I felt some of Admiral Song's shame. I experienced none of what that man felt in the moments before he shot himself. And he did shoot himself.

"He blew out his own brains when he was presented with indisputable evidence that he and Admiral Xi had conspired to provide our enemies with the precise coordinates of the *Fujian*."

On hearing the accusation, the eyes of the military men Yan could see widened and stared in the direction of the officer he was standing behind.

His voice still loud, Yan continued, "Why would Admirals Song and Xi conspire in such a matter, you are no doubt asking yourselves? It is a good and fair question, my dear comrades."

Nodding, Yan added, "Bravo-Seven, execute Order Ten."

Without warning, the Wraith grabbed the back of Admiral Xi's chair, pulled it backward hard, and in the process pulled the chair's seat from underneath Xi's posterior. A heavy-set man of perhaps sixty years of age, Xi grunted loudly as his body met the floor, but before the man could begin to make any kind of protest, the auto was on him.

With speed and strength well beyond any human, the Wraith grabbed the front of Xi's uniform and hoisted him into the air so he was standing on his toes.

Finally, the admiral managed to get words of defense out of his mouth. "This is an outrageous accusation — a fantasy! Of course, I supported Song's plan to send the *Fujian* south. Yes, the mission had risks. So much so I countermanded Song's decision not to increase the number of ships in the carrier's task force. The man was arrogant, but he was no traitor, and neither am I. We took a calculated risk and were beaten by our enemies. That is war.

Sometimes, your enemies win, no matter how well you plan, no matter how well you fight. Now, put me down. Now!"

On hearing Xi's explanation, Yan nodded as if to signal his agreement with the admiral's argument, but then he said, "Bravo Seven, play Recording Three."

Emanating from the Wraith's three-camera face, came the voice of Admiral Song. *"This is a dangerous game we're playing, my old friend. A terribly dangerous game. If we're found out, you know what it will mean for us. And not just us, but our families too. We will condemn the next three generations."*

When the next voice spoke, it was that of Xi. *"Not three. Four at least, but my family will forgive me knowing what I have tried to do. This war goes against everything our country stands for. With the return of Taiwan, China is whole. This idea that all of Southeast Asia must bend its knee to us and give us their women. The notion that we must gain a foothold in North America. These robots, and using them to assassinate other countries' leaders - they are the fever dreams of a madman. A man, I might add, who somehow avoided military service of any kind. He is sending our sons and grandsons to die because he has no idea of what it means to sacrifice.*

"He must be stopped and if that means we have to sacrifice every one of our carriers, then we should do so. Ships can be rebuilt, our sons cannot."

When the recording ended, Yan took a step toward Xi.

"You recognize those words, of course?" Yan asked in a neutral tone.

"I do not," the admiral said forcefully. "Voice replication is a technology of ten years ago. It proves nothing and more importantly, I deny it. I am a patriot in service to the Motherland. I would never betray our great country."

Yan stared into the other man's eyes for a long moment. To Xi's credit, he did not flinch or look away.

Finally, Yan said, "You know, Admiral, you were right about the number of generations impacted by your treason. I will not live to see the twenty-second century, but neither will your family. None of them. Not a single one. And when they leave this world, you can take comfort that you will be there to greet them and will be able to explain how your abiding patriotism accounted for their shortened lives. I'm sure they will find eternal solace in your words."

Yan snapped his fingers again. Like a well-trained dog, the Wraith, with its hands still gripping the front of Xi's dress uniform, pivoted its weight to its left foot and, in an incredible feat of strength, swung the admiral around its body and whipped the large man through the air in the direction of the stone wall of the conference room.

On making contact with the wall's rock-solid surface, Xi issued a cry of pain and promptly collapsed to the floor.

As every pair of eyes around the table stared at the fallen and moaning military man, the Wraith advanced several steps toward its victim, paused, and placed its right hand on the grip of its weapon. Standing nearly seven feet tall, the mechanical monster loomed over the now-sputtering naval officer.

Yan's voice emerged from behind the machine. "What was it you said about me, Admiral? That I was Hitler incarnate? That my actions and my choices would lead to the destruction of the Motherland? Those were your words, weren't they? I can play them if you need me to."

Gingerly, Xi began to push himself off the floor. With a grimace and stifled cry of pain, he managed to erect his upper body to lean against the wall.

When his eyes finally met Yan's, they narrowed just as a sneer lit up his face. "You are mad and I'm no traitor! If you kill me and kill my family, it will be you who goes to hell and sooner than you might think."

Yan took a step forward and placed himself beside the Wraith. "This is your one and only chance, Admiral. Admit that you and Song were taking action against the State, and I promise that your children, your nieces and nephews, and all of their children will get to live normal lives during what will be the golden age of Chinese society. The things they will see and do, Admiral. It will be magnificent, and they will make you proud. All I'm asking is that you speak the truth."

For a long moment, there was silence.

After what seemed like an eternity, Yan turned his head toward the Wraith and said, "Bravo-Seven, complete Order Ten."

Its hand already on its weapon, in a fraction of a second, the Wraith's oversized handgun was pointing at Xi.

"Stop! Stop!" yelled Xi.

"Hold, Bravo-Seven," Yan snapped at the auto.

"Go ahead, Admiral. You have something to say?"

Sputtering, Xi said, "Yes, I did conspire. I did work with Song. We provided the task force's coordinates to the British. But it was just us. We had hoped to bring in more of the senior command as it became clearer that our enemies are not the impotent fools you claim them to be. You are going to destroy us, and for what? Some megalomaniac dream that would see China own Mars?"

On saying the word Mars, the admiral began to laugh, and then, through his laughter, added, "You are a little man with a too-big chip on his shoulder, Yan Jiandong, and whether you are prepared to admit it or not, that is the opinion of men in this room – at least those who have half a brain."

Putting an end to his laughter, the admiral went on, in a grave tone, "And it is not me who will be the one to stop you, but it will be someone in this room. We will not let you destroy our country."

As though he had just been updated on the day's weather, Yan said, "You made the right choice, Admiral."

Turning from the broken man, Yan strode back to his seat at the head of the massive table and called over his shoulder, "Bravo-Seven, complete Order Ten, if you please."

The words *if you please* weren't heard by anyone who wasn't within five feet of Yan.

The Wraith's gun was already drawn and aimed at Xi. Upon hearing the first part of the Chinese president's directive, a single gunshot rang out, filling the confines of the cavernous room.

Yan did not look in the direction of what would have been a real-life horror show. Instead, his eyes quickly canvassed the faces of the remaining officers in the room.

There were a variety of reactions to take in. Surprise, disgust, and anger were all present. But the one reaction he hoped would be most prevalent was on enough faces that he felt his actions in the last five minutes were justified. Fear, the unadulterated kind, marred the faces of half the men at the table.

In ones and twos, the eyes of the generals and admirals of the Central Military Command returned to Yan.

As the final officer managed to tear his eyes away from Xi's body, Yan took his seat. "Thank you for indulging me in that difficult but necessary exercise, comrades. I will not hold you much longer in this room with our former colleague. I have but one more message to deliver to you."

One of Yan's hands rose into the air and pointed to his right in the direction of an officer wearing an Air Force uniform.

"Two weeks ago, General He provided a thorough and impressive presentation on the concept of total war and what this kind of strategy would look like should China make good on the threat we delivered to British Defence Minister Anne Watson.

"When this presentation was finished, my words to this group were that your respective commands should make immediate and detailed efforts to be prepared to implement these plans should you be asked."

Yan's still elevated hand shifted to the other end of the table, where the PLA's senior general was sitting.

"I am pleased to report that General Wu has advised me that in all cases – even in the case of the Navy – we're in a position to affect ninety percent of the plans outlined by General He."

Yan's hand dropped back to its normal position.

"In seventy-two hours, together with the full military and economic might of our great and everlasting Republic, we will escalate the nature of this war and fulfill the promise made twenty-five days ago to our enemies in Sydney.

"Gentlemen, as you leave this room, take one final look at what remains of Admiral Xi. Look upon his destroyed body. Take in the smell of the blood and codify in your memories how very serious I am about winning this war."

He paused his address, allowing his words to bury themselves into each man's brain.

Continuing, he said, "Recall this image when you see reports of Sydney and Canberra burning in a hell storm caused by our missiles. Remember it when your wives show you footage of gaunt and dying white children who are starving because we have prevented Australia from feeding itself. And remember it well when our vast and indomitable military land on the beautiful shores of the Australasia continent and we begin to depopulate that land and eviscerate anything and everything that Australia and its people hold dear.

"That is what you are going to do, gentlemen. Do not fail me, and do not flinch from what needs to be done. They will suffer so that others choose not to. Total war is now our policy."

Yan slowly cast his eyes over the faces of China's military leadership, and seeing only sober, clear-eyed looks, he announced, "You are dismissed."

Chapter 18

North of Las Vegas, Nevada

—

The well-muscled Black man smiled at the back of the skinny, pale kid sitting in front of the bank of six large monitors.

He had tried to keep up with the images on the screens, but each time he watched the Savant orchestrate the six hundred hunter-killer anti-personnel drones at his command, it sent his linear mind into a tailspin.

No matter how hard he tried to follow along, it was information overload, and he'd said as much to the drone operator's business partner, the fast-talking Indian who said he was British but certainly didn't sound it.

Reynolds turned to his right to face the man with the brown skin.

"So, is he ready or not? We're running out of time."

The Indian continued to watch the pasty drone operator as he guided something like eighty drones through a maze of rooms in a long-abandoned casino.

Without taking his eyes off the screens, the Indian said, "It was tricky trying to slave-in the sixth near-AI unit, but I think we've done it. As far as I know, five blocks is the most anyone has done with the kind of resources we have access to. When you get to six, you pass the theoretical threshold of what each unit's quantum core can manage without generating the occasional error. And by occasional, Mr. Reynolds, I mean thousands per minute. Like a tired old star, the coordination program can't keep up and it collapses in on itself."

Reynolds grunted and said, "Save the poetic explanations for the next conference you attend, professor. The question is: are you ready?"

In front of them, the usually silent drone operator spoke in a voice that sounded like it could use some water. "Watch Screen Three."

Reynolds, not having heard the Savant speak while seated at the bank of displays, immediately stepped forward and focused on the monitor that had the number three in its top right corner.

It was the camera feed of a drone perhaps ten feet back from a pair of double doors. Down the hallway past those same doors, Reynolds could see an uncountable number of drones of various sizes.

Without warning, the drones shifted in a wave-like pattern as a larger unit approached and positioned itself at the left side of the entrance.

The camera zoomed in on the machine that had a chassis a touch bigger than a basketball.

An arm with a hook-like apparatus at the end of it extended out from the drone's face and eventually reached the door's handle.

Reynolds watched in fascination as the unit adjusted some of its fans and began to try and pull the door open.

Ten seconds later, he declared what the problem was. "It's locked."

Just as the words left Reynolds's mouth, four drones the size of someone's head emerged from the gaggle of flying units down the corridor.

Quickly, they made their way to the four hinges of the double doors while the larger unit positioned itself directly in front of the entrance's central locking mechanism.

Without any warning, there was a bright flash, and when the drone's camera came back into focus, the five breaching drones and the two doors were gone.

Those drones waiting in the hallway were now surging through the smoking hole that had once been the entrance. As they did so, an orchestra of loud noises began to emit from the space the drones were pouring into.

The drone with the camera feed began to move. Zipping forward, it whipped through the destroyed entrance, allowing Reynolds to see firsthand what was causing the racket.

Four men were firing handguns at the swarm of drones that had encircled them on three sides while two other men were behind them at another double door, engaged in what looked like a ferocious argument.

Curiously, the drones were not attacking the men randomly firing their weapons.

Reynolds turned to the Indian and growled, "What the hell is going on? I can't make heads or tails out of this mess."

"Monitor One," the Savant said in his quiet voice.

Reynolds' eyes darted to that screen and saw a different angle of the room with the six men.

It was a huge space that looked like it had been set up for a banquet. Throughout the room, dozens of tables with hundreds of chairs had been set up, and in what had to be half of the seats were unmoving figures that Reynolds guessed were mannequins.

To the left of a good-sized stage at the front of the space was the group of surrounded men.

The four men with handguns seemed to be protecting the two still arguing at the doors to the left of the stage.

The camera zoomed in closer to capture the profile of one of the four armed men.

The guy was homeless. Of that, Reynolds was certain. His clothes were filthy, and his hair looked like it hadn't been washed in months. To top off the man's pathetic look, he was holding his gun with both hands, wildly moving it from one drone to the next.

In his deep voice, Reynolds said, "Why haven't they left the room? Is the door locked? That's hardly a realistic scenario."

It was the Indian who replied, "Those men who remain have elected not to leave the room, Mr. Reynolds. Look at Screen Four, if you please."

The former Green Beret from Northern California did as he was instructed and, on the screen, he saw two destroyed bodies lying on the ground. The bloody corpses appeared to be lying only a few feet from yet another set of double doors.

"Are those the same doors I was just looking at on Monitor One?" Reynolds asked.

"Yes, but on the other side," said the Indian.

After a pause, the brown man continued, "You wanted to see if the updated system works. Well, I can now tell you that it does. Nearly perfectly based on today's performance. We still have a few more tweaks to make, but with this sixth unit slaved in, we can control up to twelve hundred units. It will be more than enough for the mission."

Reynolds grunted at the Indian's update, pointed at the screen, and said, "Dude, these guys are homeless pieces of shit. Look at them. They're hardly a professional protection detail. That one guy just pissed his pants."

"You're not wrong," the Indian said casually. "We did our best to get participants with some kind of military or police experience, but the pickings were slim. The bottom line, Mr. Reynolds, is that the sixth block is working within its expected parameters. As far as I'm concerned, my associate and I are ready to move forward."

Reynolds turned his gaze on the Savant, and in a voice that demanded a response, he said, "Is that true?"

In his quiet and scratchy voice, the pasty drone operator said, "He said it's good, so it's good."

"Finally!" Reynolds exclaimed, his voice sounding triumphant. "This target is gonna be a tough nut to crack, but between my guys and you two, I think we've got a real chance. A chance that'll make us thirty mil, and all of it in crypto."

The phone Reynolds had been holding burped a notification.

Bringing the screen to his eyes, he smiled when he read the update.

"Good news, I hope?" the Indian asked.

Reynolds's eyes rose from his phone, and looking at the Indian, he said, "Now, there's timing for you. It looks like we just got new intel on the target. He'll be in public in the next few days and in a location that will work for us. Jesus, it's almost as though the universe wants us to take him out."

Reynolds gestured to the Savant's wall of screens. "Time to wrap this shit up. We need to be in L.A. in two days."

"Not a problem, Mr. Reynolds," said the Indian.

Turning to the drone operator, the pudgy man with the thick foreign accent said, "Finish the ex, my friend."

"And these guys?" the Savant said, nodding to one of the screens that held what remained of their 'paid actors.'

To keep his conscience clear, the Indian had already given the eight homeless fellows half of their payment, allowing them to fill their veins or lungs with whatever pleasures they wanted in the days leading up to the demonstration.

When he had made a deal with each of the men, he knew they would die. Still, when they did, it had been his sincere hope that each man would perish with the hazy memories of whatever poison or debauchery they had availed themselves to in the days leading up to today's exercise.

Instead of answering the drone operator's question, the Indian's gaze took up the brown eyes of the thick American. "Would you like to watch, Mr. Reynolds?"

A look of disgust leaped onto the mercenary's face as he replied, "No, I don't want to watch. Just get it done and be ready to move in two days."

With that, Reynolds turned to leave the room. As he did so, the Indian turned back to the bank of screens and focused on the single man who had a wet stain on his crotch.

Jeremy had been his name. A long time ago, before he'd become addicted to fentanyl and crack, he'd been a cop on the Los Angeles County Sheriff's Department. He had lowered his weapon and was now staring forward blankly. Fresh tears streaked down the pathetic man's filthy face.

The Indian walked over to the Savant, gently placed his soft hand on the younger man's shoulder, pointed to Jeremy, and said, "Start with this one. But this time, do it slowly. Very, very slowly."

***

Vancouver, British Columbia

—

Larocque stared at the middle-aged man through the one-way mirror.

Denis Rouloux looked like the Hells Angel he was. He sported a goatee dusted in grey, was well-muscled, and his arms and neck were covered in a riot of colorful tattoos.

Without taking his eyes off the biker, Larocque asked, "So, what's his story, and why do we think he's linked with the White Unit? He's too high profile if you ask me. The moment somebody sees this clown walk by, you can't forget him. That's not the White Unit's style."

"His story," said Tomic, "is that he's been a full-patch Hells Angel for five years, and in that time, he's been one of the organization's top earners. Racketeering, drug distribution, prostitution. And if that wasn't enough, the Guns and Gangs Task Force here in BC have him attached to three different murder-for-hire schemes."

Larocque finally removed his eyes from the thug and looked at Tomic. "And he's ex-RCMP?"

"Yes, and apparently, he maintains many helpful connections to the Force."

"No doubt that's served his career change well," Larocque said.

Nodding, Tomic replied, "It has. It's also helped to keep him out of jail. According to his file, on no less than eight occasions, witnesses that have been prepared to testify against this scumbag have recanted their stories after receiving a visit from one of Mr. Rouloux's 'associates.'"

"Don't tell me," said Larocque, interrupting Tomic. "Someone in the police is leaking their names to the bad guys?"

"Of course," Tomic said, making no effort to hide the annoyance she felt toward Canada's national police force. "We've seen the same thing with a handful of our investigations. You would be doing the country a huge favor if you convinced the PM to burn her former employer to the ground and create provincial police forces. The Mounties are too bureaucratic and filled with too many political types who are prepared to keep losers like Denis 'The Pig' Rouloux, a free man for one bad reason or another."

Larocque nodded at the suggestion and said, "I agree something does need to be done about the Mounties, but that's for another day. Today, I need to understand how Rouloux is linked with what we're after and how that info is going to help us."

"Fair enough," Tomic said and then handed Larocque a data pad with a map that had Vancouver at the center of it. In the city and outside it were dozens of red dots.

"If you zoom out, there are more data points. A lot more."

"What are they?" asked Larocque.

"The dots are properties owned by a Chinese holding company. Said company has Canadian assets worth around three hundred million. In British Columbia, all registered foreign holding companies worth over fifty million must have at least three directors sitting on their boards who hold Canadian citizenship."

"And Mr. Rouloux is one of their directors?" asked Larocque.

"Bingo," Tomic replied quickly.

"And the White Unit is involved with Rouloux and the holding company how?" Larocque enquired.

"With data provided by Petit, we know at least six of the White Unit's sites have been located in properties or on lands owned by the holding company. That can't be a coincidence."

"What about the other two board members?" Larocque asked.

"They're squeaky clean," said Tomic. Nodding her head at the Hells Angel, she added, "Along with ourselves, the nerds in CSE have thrown all we have at this guy. He's crafty, but someone involved in as much criminal activity as Rouloux can't hide everything. We've got him dead to rights, I promise."

Larocque grunted and said, "So we've got leverage on him, and he's still not talking?"

Tomic shook her head and said, "He's a former cop, so he knows the business. We've had him sitting there for the past two hours, and my best people have leaned on him hard. The only words he's said to us are that he wants his lawyer."

Larocque smiled at Tomic, his first of the week.

One of her eyebrows arched at the gesture. "Is there something funny you want to share, Director?"

He didn't answer her question. Instead, he said, "In the next fifteen, a man named Javier will be joining us. He'll have four of his associates with him. He'll call your phone. When he does, bring them to this room and wait for me."

"And where will you be going?"

Larocque pointed in the direction of the biker. "I'm going to have a heart-to-heart with our friend."

Hearing his plan, Tomic immediately moved to stand in front of the entrance leading to the interview room. "I can't let you do that. You're the Director of CSIS. Nowhere in the world do directors of national intelligence services meet with scum like Rouloux. *Nowhere.*"

In the past five days of keeping tabs on Tomic and her people as they tried to nail down a credible lead on the White Unit, Larocque had become convinced they were a well-meaning group.

But for all the manpower and technology CSIS had thrown at the problem, they hadn't produced anything actionable.

Despite what had happened in Australia and the attention that ongoing disaster demanded of him, Larocque had made time to come out to BC when he'd heard Tomic's team would bring Rouloux for questioning.

Taking up her intense gaze, Larocque said, "Monique, I know you are only trying to protect me, and I know that in almost any other situation, it would be crazy for me to walk through that door, but you're going to have to trust me. At least for the moment, we're going to have to do things my way."

Tomic shook her head vigorously. "Your way? And what way is that? Now, I'm definitely not moving. If you walk through that door and you talk to that man, you are undermining my authority, but worse, you're jeopardizing our investigation. I won't let you do it."

Larocque took a step in the direction of the slender CSIS executive. Despite having three inches and at least sixty pounds on her, she made no move to back up or stand aside.

In a low voice, Tomic said, "Take one more step toward this door, and I walk out of this building. I'll resign. There is so much chaos in the world right now. I'm not going to let it infect my team or this organization. You've brought enough change as it is. There are rules and expectations for how we do investigations. If I let you walk into the room, you are tossing that aside. I won't be a part of it."

As she delivered the threat, Tomic's phone began to ring, but she didn't move to pick it up.

"Take the call," Larocque said, his voice calm.

She didn't move.

As the ring cycle started again, Larocque's hand snapped forward and grabbed Tomic's suit jacket. Ripping it open, he grabbed her phone and activated the speaker option.

"Javier?"

The man who spoke had a thick Spanish accent. "Ah, Director Larocque. I was not expecting you to pick up. Is everything all right?"

"Everything is fine. As planned, my associate is on her way to gather you. She'll be down in five minutes."

"Not a problem, my friend. Your lovely colleague here at the reception is getting my associates and I some coffee. You can collect us at your leisure."

Larocque cut the connection.

Through a look of righteous fury, Tomic asked, "Who the hell is that?"

"An old friend, but more important, he's someone I trust."

"Trust to do what?"

"People are dying, Monique. As of yesterday, six thousand people in Australia. In the next hour, that man," as he said the words, he pointed emphatically in the direction of the fallen RCMP officer. "That piece of human garbage is going to tell us what we want to know."

Tomic didn't look in the direction of Larocque's pointing finger. Instead, she looked him in the eyes and said, "You didn't answer my question. What is your friend going to do, Director? This is Canada and there are laws and rules which need to be followed."

Tomic herself gestured at Rouloux. "Give me three hours and I can get you a Security Certificate. It'll be a game-changer. We can hold him indefinitely. We can freeze his assets. If we let him talk to a lawyer, they'll tell him he's screwed, and the best thing for him to do is to give us what we want."

"When?" Larocque demanded.

When Tomic said nothing, Larocque repeated the question, except this time it was at a half yell. "When will he talk, Monique? Thirty-six hours? Seventy-two? A week? We don't have that kind of time, and you know it."

If she was cowed by the volume of his voice, she didn't show it. Instead, maintaining her gaze with Larocque, "We don't use torture in this country."

"No one is going to be tortured," Larocque said forcefully.

"Then what is your old friend Javier here to do? Tell me so that I might help you."

Larocque moved to hand back Tomic's phone. As he held it out in front of her, he said, "Back when I was boxing, I had several fights against Javier Cruz. He beat me at the Pan Am Games and went on to win the gold for his country. He was a ferocious fighter, but he was also cunning — an exceptional tactician.

"In between those fights, I had the chance to train with him. I can assure you, Monique, the man you are going to collect downstairs is the smartest man I have ever met inside and outside of the ring."

Tomic made no effort to take back the proffered phone. Instead, she continued to deliver a hard stare into Larocque's eyes.

Finally, when he realized the skeptical and pissed-off woman standing in front of him would need some details as to what was about to happen, Larocque continued, "Many were surprised when Javier didn't turn pro. I wasn't. He was way too smart to put his body through a career in pro boxing. In just six years, Javier Cruz graduated from the top of his class at Harvard Medical. From there, he went on to the field of neuropsychiatry, where he has become one of the world's leading minds on neuro-integration."

Slowly, Larocque reached toward Tomic's left hand. As gently as he might, he grabbed her wrist and slid her phone into her fingers.

As she accepted the device, Larocque said, "We are one-third of the way into the twenty-first century. There are other ways – more civilized ones – to make people tell you what you want to know."

"You're going to use drugs?" Tomic asked.

"Yes, but not in the way you think. It's best if I let Javier tell us what he will do."

Larocque motioned his head to the door. "Please, Monique, collect Dr. Cruz and bring him here."

Tomic said nothing for almost a minute but then said quietly, "Fine, but I better have a good understanding of what he's going to do before he does it."

"He'll walk you through it. He loves to explain the process," Larocque said, sounding relieved.

"Wait, you've seen him do this before?" she blurted out.

Another smile crossed Larocque's face. "Sorry, it's classified."

As an intense look of annoyance flashed onto the CSIS officer's face, Tomic asked, "You're serious?"

"Entirely."

"And you still want to have a word with him?" Tomic said while thumbing over her shoulder at the gangster.

"Yes. It won't take long. By the time you return with Javier, I might be wrapped up, but if I'm not, just keep the doctor and his people company. Understood?"

Still very much annoyed, Tomic replied, "It's not understood, but I'll go get your doctor. You have five minutes without me in the room."

After one final hard stare, Tomic stepped around him and moved to leave the space.

As the door to the interview suite closed behind him, Larocque moved forward and placed his hand on the door that contained the thoroughly bored-looking Hells Angel captain.

It was time for him to have a heart-to-heart with one of Canada's biggest scumbags.

Chapter 19

Los Angeles, California

"So, welcome back to the show," said the muscular man wearing sunglasses.

"Always good to be with you, Max."

"If producer Mikey is right, this is our sixth time talking since the civil war broke out."

"If Mikey says it's six, then it's six," the guest said in a somber voice.

"Civil war, man. Every time I say those two words together, I can't believe I'm saying them."

"It's crazy," said the guest in agreement. "I can't believe it myself."

"Except now, we're looking at what everybody is calling World War III. It's wild, man. Wild!"

Grabbing and then lighting the cigar that was in the chest pocket of his shirt, the guest said, "I think I might have mentioned things were ready to spiral out of control the last time I was here."

"Yeah, man. Which is why I brought you back. You've got this amazing ability to pull the strings together and explain it in a way my audience appreciates. It's a real skill."

The guest shrugged his shoulders and said, "Thanks, brother. Always happy to help."

The podcaster brought his own cigar to his mouth, took a drag and then gestured across the table. "Listen, before we get too far into this, why don't you remind those who are new to the show what you bring to this conversation."

Emptying the smoke from the hard-to-get Trinidad Colonial from his lungs, the fit man with the greying ponytail said, "So, the name is Jake Taylor. I served twenty-two years in the US Army, with seven of those years as an operator in the US Special Forces. In those twenty-two years, I spent operational time in fifteen different countries.

"After I got out, I worked as a contractor for the CIA for five years. Where I went and what I did remains classified, but I want your listeners to know that every night I close my eyes to go to sleep, I sleep well. Everything I did, I did to keep Americans safe. I have a clear conscience, brother."

"And now, what do you do?" the podcast host asked.

"Let's just say I'm in the security consulting business."

"And how's that going?"

"There's a civil war going on, my friend. Business is very good."

The podcaster nodded his head emphatically. "Good to hear it, and things are getting crazier by the day. I want to discuss it all with you. Your insights, dude, they're just the best."

The guest took another drag of his cigar. "I've cleared my whole schedule for you, Max. We can go as deep and as long as you want to go."

"Dude, I want to get into all of it. But just in case anyone has been living under a rock and for reasons of posterity, let me summarize just how crazy things are."

From across the table, the guest gave a thumbs-up and said, "Set the table, brother."

"Yeah, so like in Europe, the Russians have invaded Estonia and Latvia, while the Poles have positioned their military in Lithuania and the border of Belarus. Poland has told Russia if it crosses into Lithuania, they'll declare war.

When the guest nodded, confirming the assessment, the podcaster continued. "In Western Europe, you have this crazy situation where France is trying to bully the Dutch into doing what, I'm not exactly sure?"

Exhaling another cloud of cigar smoke, the guest said, "The French are in an interesting situation. I've got lots to say about them."

"Good, cause I gotta say, man. Of everything that's going on, they're the country that I'm having the toughest time figuring out. I mean, dude, the French have some balls pushing their weight around. From everything I can see, the country is in turmoil, it's an economic mess, and this woman who runs the country – what's her name?"

"Lévesque," supplied the guest.

"Yeah, this Lévesque lady. Man, just look at her. She looks crazy with those nails. I mean, it looks like she should be running a brothel, not a country."

"Ouch," the guest said, offering the podcast host a mild chuckle. "You know, I've met her."

"Who, Lévesque? Get out!" the podcaster almost shouted his reply.

"Ya, twice. She's an interesting lady. And I gotta tell you, man, I was impressed. People think she's crazy and she is, but crazy like a fox, if you know what I mean."

"Like No. 47 crazy?"

"Something like that."

The podcaster made a face that looked like he wanted to pursue the French angle, but as was his erratic style, he shifted the conversation to another topic.

"And then there's the Chinese. Dude, in front of my nine million listeners, I want to apologize."

The guest's face became quizzical. "Apology? For what?"

"You know what for, you son of a bitch. When you were last here, you told me in no uncertain terms, China was going to use tactical nuclear weapons to start a war in Southeast Asia, and I told you you were full of shit. No way were the Chinese that crazy, I said. No way, because China doesn't have a history of invading other countries."

"It became inevitable the moment Spector nuked Washington," said the guest.

"That's what you said. You said the CCP could no longer stand by while Vietnam, Thailand, and the region's other economies continued to take away Chinese manufacturing jobs and that the UCSA's casual use of nukes would open Pandora's box in Southeast Asia and other places."

The guest took another drag of his cigar and blew the smoke high into the air.

"Dude, are you inhaling that stuff?" inquired the podcaster.

Ignoring the question, the guest said, "I would advise the good people of Poland to be careful in the next few weeks."

The host nodded as a huge smile erupted on his thickly bearded face. "Dude, did you see that video of that Vietnamese pilot fly his plane into that fucking carrier. That guy or gal – whoever it was – they just laid waste to that thing. The explosion was incredible!"

"It was spectacular, wasn't it?" the guest said, wearing his own big smile. "A one-in-a-million shot, I'm told. The pilot had his plane going so fast, the steel of its engine penetrated through the carrier's hanger and hit one of its aviation fuel cells."

"Boom!" the guest said as his hands lifted into the air and spread out to mimic the explosion. "That's what fifty thousand gallons of jet fuel looks like when it cooks off in under a second."

"Brother, I was telling my wife that I thought I heard the bang while jogging. What's the South China Sea to LA? Ten thousand miles?"

The guest shrugged. "Something like that."

"Props to CANZUK for pulling it off, man. What a mic-drop moment. Do you think they can win the war?"

The guest shook his head. "Not without more help. The Japanese will give CANZUK a temporary boost in the South China Sea, but China is just too strong. They've got too many people and ships they can throw at their opponents. Unless the US Navy gets off its ass, it's just a matter of time."

"Yeah, man, explain what's happening with the US Navy. You got into it during our last chat, but maybe rehash the details for those listening."

"It's pretty simple, actually. At the outbreak of the civil war, about ninety percent of the Navy's officers, and I want to say about seventy percent of the enlisted, decided they weren't going to pick sides.

"The admirals aren't stupid. They know the secret to American hegemony is the American Navy, and whether you agree with them or not, they collectively decided they would sit out the war so that when it was over, they could go back to serving America and dominating the world's oceans."

The podcaster interjected. "But they thought the Blues would win, didn't they?"

"I can't say for certain, but that's what a lot of people think. Just like our first civil war, a lot of people thought it would be over in a few weeks. Everyone underestimated the Reds and their ruthlessness."

The podcaster's hands mimicked an explosion and said, "Nukes, dude. What the hell? Big ones and small. But the Chinese and the Reds' hands are tied as long as the British are in the fight."

The guest nodded at the statement. "Yeah, Richardson, the UK's prime minister, has been clear. Use nukes on any CANZUK soldier and the Brits retaliate. It's why Aussie and Kiwi troops are fighting on the front lines with the Vietnamese. It stays China's nuclear hand."

"And it's the same here in North America with the Canadians and Brits?" offered the podcaster.

"The very same thing. When the Brits eviscerated Soldier Key ten miles east of Miami, Spector, the Chinese, and the rest of the world were put on notice."

Slipping into an English accent, the guest said, "Use nukes on our lads, old chaps, and we send parts of your country back to the stone age."

"Which brings us back to the US Navy," the podcaster prompted. "What do you think of the rumors they're getting ready to get involved? I mean, they could make a real difference, couldn't they?"

The guest took another drag from his cigar and said, "They could, but they won't unless California changes its tune on the war."

"Explain that," said the podcaster. "How is it that the US Navy is now attached to what California does? I thought the admirals had chosen independence over politics?"

"They had four years ago, but with each year, they've grown closer to the Californian government. That's where the senior admirals are and where most of the Navy is. Even ships from the East Coast and Europe went there.

"The US Navy isn't political. It prides itself on its apolitical nature. It's why it chose not to get involved in the war. But the Navy has always had a political master. Before the war, it was Congress and the President. In response to the chaos, the admirals have slowly allowed themselves to take on a new master."

"California and Ricky Sanchez," the podcaster said, interrupting his guest. "That's wild, man! How crazy is it that a movie star is in control of the US Navy? But the more important question is, what is he going to do with it?"

The guest shook his head. "Control's a bit of a strong word, but everyone knows the US Navy wants to help end the civil war. They feel it's been going on too long and as it's been told to me, with CANZUK, the French, and now the Chinese getting involved, they also want in."

"So why don't they? I mean, what's stopping the admirals from sending a couple of aircraft carriers to the East Coast to start to bomb the Reds?"

The guest smiled. "Ah, there you go, my friend. You always ask the right questions."

The podcaster's mouth shifted to the far left of his face, a physical tell he wanted more information.

"It's like this, Max. The US Navy has held itself together because it didn't choose sides. The moment it does choose a side, the Navy itself will split up. The admirals can't make the decision. If the US Navy is going to go to war, that decision has to be made by the people who direct the Navy, and in this case, after four years of most of the Navy sitting in San Diego, that political force is..."

"Ricky Sanchez!" the podcaster exclaimed.

"Bingo," said the guest, snapping his fingers. "Only Governor Sanchez has the ability to order some or all of the US Navy to unleash hell, and as it stands right now, he has no intention of getting California involved in any wars, whether that's to join the civil war on the East Coast or send ships into the Pacific to help CANZUK fight the Chinese."

The podcaster said, "Rumor has it Sanchez met with Anders-Maxwell and she leaned into him to join what's now become the Western Alliance."

The guest gave a subtle nod of his head. "She did, or that's what my sources have told me."

"And he said no?" supplied the podcaster.

"That's the rumor, but I can't help but think there's a part of him that wants to get involved. I mean the guy played a hero in how many movies?"

Nodding slowly, the podcaster took a long haul on his cigar and blew a huge cloud of smoke into the air. "So, you think he could change his mind?"

"I don't know the man, brother. But I'll say this – right now, he's a man with a lot of power, and in my experience, men with power have a real tough time not using it."

"So, Ricky Sanchez is the man who gets to decide if WWIII kicks off if we're not already there? That's a lot of power for a man who used to make movies," the podcaster said.

"It is," replied the guest.

With the hand holding his cigar, the podcaster gestured across the table. "If you were talking to Sanchez, what would you tell him to do? I mean, who knows, maybe he listens to the podcast. He probably does."

"What would I tell him?" the guest said, confirming the question.

"Ya, dude. You know the world and how it works. If you were talking to Sanchez right now, what message would you give him?"

"Honestly?"

"Of course, dude. Your honest opinion. What would you say to him?"

The guest turned his eyes to look directly into the camera recording the conversation and said, "Ricky, my man, California has a good thing. War is hell. Trust me. Screw the admirals and screw the war machine. Keep California safe, and when all of this madness has past, you and California will be king."

***

Vancouver, British Columbia

—

As Larocque opened the door to the interview room, he tossed an energy bar to Rouloux.

The man caught the food and immediately set to tearing it open. Ravenous, he took two full bites before he looked at Larocque. When he finally did, his face had a look of fury.

As Rouloux took his third bite, Larocque turned to the CSIS intel officer tucked away in the corner of the room.

"You can leave. And don't stick around on the other side. I'd like to have a short private chat with our guest."

The stocky intel man gave the biker a hard stare but said nothing and moved to leave the room.

As the door closed behind him, Larocque grabbed one of the two seats across the table from the biker and sat down. When his eyes once again took up the Hells Angel, the man had finished the energy bar.

Rouloux tossed the wrapper onto the table's surface while staring daggers at his new visitor.

Larocque pointed to the wrapper and said, "You're welcome."

A smile came to the other man's lips.

"A smile, eh? Is that because of the food, or is it for another reason you'd like to share?"

Slowly, Rouloux brought his cuffed hands from where they'd been on his lap and placed his elbows on the table. Short sleeved, both of his arms were heavily tattooed. His hands, also tatted, were balled into meaty, imposing fists.

Larocque knew hands well and could tell that in his time as a biker, Rouloux hadn't only been using his brains to make bank for the Hells Angels. Scars, some of them recent, littered his knuckles.

Larocque issued forth his own friendly smile. "C'mon, you're dying to say something. I can tell. And from everything I've been told about you, once it gets going, you can't keep your mouth shut."

When Rouloux said nothing, Larocque moved closer to the table and quietly said, "Let's make a deal, you and I, Denis. For the next five minutes, nothing you say will be held against you. Whatever you've got bouncing around in that steroid-addled brain of yours, now's the time to let it out. I'm giving you a free pass. Let it rip and get it out of your system. Be as bad as you want to be, Mr. Full Patch, Hells Angel. And then, when you're done, maybe we can have a chat and we can help one another. What do you say?"

The index finger on Rouloux's left hand pointed at the interview room's entrance. "The biggest mistake you've ever made in your life was to walk through that door."

Larocque's eyes flashed wide open. "Really. How so?"

"Unlike all of the other idiots I've dealt with today, I know who you are."

"And who am I, Denis? Tell me more. It's all good, my friend."

"Let's cut the bullshit. I may look like some meathead, but I'm not. You're Jackson Larocque. Canadian fucking hero, who as of what... three weeks ago? You were put in charge of CSIS by that bitch, Martel."

The biker paused for a moment, no doubt hoping his salty language would get a rise out of the other man.

When Larocque didn't take the bait, Rouloux added, "It looks like she loves to suck dick. Any truth to that rumor?"

One of Larocque's eyebrows arched into the air, but he said nothing.

Rouloux chuckled and said, "No comment, eh?"

Leaning forward in Larocque's direction, the biker said, "Let me tell you how the next few months are gonna work, you lapdog piece of garbage.

"I'm gonna sue the government and you personally, and I won't settle. You can't pay me enough money for me not to tell the story of how you infringed on my Charter Rights. You'll be in court for years. Don't forget, I was once a cop, so I know exactly what I'm entitled to. You're breaking the law, and you know what happens in this country when the Feds do something stupid?"

"Tell me, Denis," said Larocque.

"You pay, man. Big time. Millions!" As he shouted the word 'millions,' his cuffed hands rose into the air and came down in a pumping motion, and he added, "Ca-ching, you fucking loser!"

After a pause to let the echo of his voice fall away, the Hells Angel spoke, only this time, his voice was barely audible.

"But I'm a reasonable guy who understands the reputation of a Canadian hero is something worth protecting. If you let me walk out of this place right now – not in an hour, not in ten minutes – right now, I promise I won't say anything about this. It will be like it never happened. How's that for a deal?"

One of Larocque's hands came up to his face and massaged his chin in a display of faux contemplation. Finally, injecting as much reasonableness into his voice as he could, he said, "I appreciate that you're looking out for my interest, but I don't make deals with traitors. You're aware of what happened in Australia?"

"Ya, but dude, I don't give a shit. That's not my problem."

"Six thousand people are dead," Larocque countered. "There's nothing about that number that resonates with you? Nothing that makes you want to help your country?"

Rouloux scoffed, "Dude, why should it? I had nothing to do with it. I'm a legitimate businessman with businesses in BC. What do I care what happens to a bunch of funny-talking losers on the other side of the planet?"

The biker made a quick brushing motion toward the door and said, "We're done. I gave you a chance to get yourself out of this mess. I'm not saying one more word. Get the hell out of my sight. You're a joke."

Slowly, Larocque pushed back his chair and got to his feet. While doing so, he glared at the Hells Angel and said, "We know about your dealings with Sunshore Corp. We have enough information that we can get a Security Certificate and keep you locked up for at least six months before you get to see a judge. And because you were once a cop, you know that under the Certificate process, it's the government who assigns you legal counsel. That'll take at least two months to arrange. Maybe more. Things in the world are moving fast, Denis. It would be a shame if they passed you by while you were locked in a cell."

Rouloux only returned Larocque's gaze with a contemptuous glare.

"Denis, think of all the earned money you won't be making. All the strippers you won't get to control. All the coke you won't get to shove up your nose. Think of the competitors who will take what's yours. It doesn't have to stop. We're not interested in any of that."

Larocque paused, hoping his words would sink in, but still, the gangster said nothing.

It was time to try his final gambit. Larocque said, "Sunshore Corp. Tell us about it. Just a few questions and we part ways. It couldn't be easier. Make the right choice, and you get to walk out of this building not only a free man, but I'll also put three million into a bank account of your choosing.

"Three million, Denis. Three million dollars for doing the right thing. I know you remember doing the right thing at one time. You can do right again, except this time, it would be in a big, big way."

On mentioning the sum of money, one of the Hells Angels' eyebrows flexed upward, and when Larocque stopped speaking, he said, "Wow. That's a lot of cash."

Quickly, Larocque added, "I can even do it in crypto – completely untraceable."

While nodding at Larocque's words, the look on the biker's face transitioned from interested to something that was some combination of dangerous and nasty. "I remember from all the press about you that you have a wife. I betcha she was a smoke show back in the day. I betcha she's still a nice piece. It would be a real shame if anything happened to her."

"Your five minutes is up. I would begin to tread carefully, Denis," Larocque said quietly.

"Oh, I'll tread where I please, Mr. CSIS," Rouloux said mockingly. "You don't scare me. Not one little bit. I tell you what. You hold on to your three million. I'd rather use my own money to pay the guys I'm gonna use to beat you down and then make you watch as they ruin your whore wife."

On hearing the gangster's threat, Larocque clenched his fists and stepped in the man's direction, but before he could take a second, the door to the interview room opened.

He rounded on the interruption, ready to tear a strip off Tomic, but instead of seeing the veteran IO, his eyes took in a man that was his height, build, and age.

The moment the newcomer's espresso-brown eyes connected with Larocque's, the man said in a warm, Spanish-accented voice, "Jaks, my good friend, it has been much too long. How is Madison? How is the baby?"

As he struggled to process the personal questions, Javier Cruz moved toward him and took Larocque into a gregarious and genuine embrace. Slapping his back roughly, the man continued loudly, "I know you know this, my friend, but Fernanda and I, we pray for you and Madison all of the time. You are in our hearts, always."

Before Larocque could say anything to his friend and former opponent, he looked toward Tomic, who had followed into the room on the heels of Cruz. Before he could say anything about not letting Cruz into the room, his friend released him and said, "She told me not to come in, but I know you, and I know how these little chats can go when they start to get personal."

Cruz's gaze moved from Larocque to Rouloux and, with a look of disdain, said, "You were right to call me Jaks. These gangsters – no matter the country – are the worst kind of scum. But they are surprisingly resilient to typical interrogation methods."

"Who the hell are you?" Rouloux said in a voice that held a sliver of concern.

Cruz didn't answer the question. Instead, he clapped his hands twice, loudly.

No sooner had the sharp sound dissipated than two huge men walked into the room, each carrying a suitcase suitable for a short journey.

Without instructions, they placed the suitcases on the floor and advanced toward Rouloux.

His eyes blazing, the Hells Angel began to unleash a stream of profanities, but they soon turned into cries of pain as the two big men launched forward and began to pummel him.

Quickly overwhelmed by the attack's ferocity, the biker found himself in the corner of the room, desperately trying to protect his head and face from the onslaught.

Behind him, Larocque began to hear Tomic scream for the beating to stop, but the two henchmen were undeterred.

It was only when she strode past him that Cruz snapped off the word *"Alto!"*

Like well-trained hounds, the two men stepped back from the gangster.

"Get him seated," Cruz said, this time in English.

Again, the two burly aides descended on Rouloux. Grabbing the man, they dragged him to the chair he had been sitting in for his conversation with Larocque.

Slamming him down together, the aides wrapped their thick arms around the gangster's shoulders. Pressing him downward, the man on the biker's left grabbed a fistful of hair and reefed on it brutally.

Without warning and through cries of pain, the gangster managed to unload a gob of spit. As a shiny red missile connected with Larocque's shirt, Rouloux howled, "I'm not going to sue you, man! You're dead! You hear that, Larocque. You're a fucking dead man!"

Without taking his eyes off the biker, Larocque said to Cruz, "The last time I saw you do this, I don't remember it being so physical. In fact, I remember the whole thing being rather civilized."

With a sober look on his face, Cruz said, "Ah, yes. Normally, this is the case, my friend, but as you know, I am a man of passion and great honor."

Cruz gestured in the direction of Rouloux. "When he threatened your beautiful wife, I told my associates here to have their way with him. Where I come from, scum like this makes the lives of everyday people a misery. Were I not in your naïve country, I would end his life and do so gladly."

"But we won't be doing that," said Tomic, interjecting herself into the conversation. She had moved to stand behind the two brutes holding the biker.

Cruz's eyes met with Tomic's and, in a friendly tone, said, "We'll do nothing of the sort. We will get the information you are seeking and we will wipe his memory. The worst that can happen to the subject is a permanent episode of unresponsive wakefulness syndrome."

Rouloux yelled, "What the Christ is that?"

Cruz's eyes took up the Hells Angel. "It's more commonly known as a vegetative state. A terrible way to live the rest of your life by every account, but you will not die."

Rouloux struggled against the iron grip of the men holding him and said, "This is bullshit. Whatever this asshole is up to, it's crazy illegal. Whatever career you two once had, it's gonna be over. Over! Do you hear me?"

Tomic made no reply to Rouloux. Instead, the career intelligence officer's jawline tightened perceptibly as she delivered a hard stare at Larocque.

Cruz clapped his hands again, this time not as loud.

On hearing the sound, both Larocque and Tomic looked to the room's entrance. Two stunning Latina women, identical twins in fact, walked into the room and moved to grab the suitcases the two men had brought in.

With practiced grace, they grabbed the cases, set them down on the interview table, and opened them to reveal a myriad of engineered components and a dozen vials that held liquids of various colors.

Seeing the contents, Rouloux roared something unintelligible and began to strain mightily against his two captors.

Calmly, one of Cruz's female assistants reached into the suitcase she had placed on the table and removed a piece of delicate-looking equipment designed to fit atop someone's head.

Stepping around the man who had a hold of the gangster's hair, she placed the high-tech crown over the top of his head and uttered something in Spanish.

As the muscle-bound aide removed his hand, the woman deftly placed the headset onto the biker.

The instant the unit made contact with Rouloux's skull, the man's yelling and straining came to a blissful end.

"Jesus, that's better," said Larocque.

The sound of Tomic's heels filled the now quiet room as she circled around Rouloux. Seeing the gangster's face, she asked, "Is he in pain? What are you doing to him?"

"He's experiencing what you would understand as a seizure," explained Cruz.

"But he's not shaking?" said Tomic.

"He is, it is just very subtle. You will have to trust me - the subject is perfectly safe."

Cruz then said something in Spanish. Whatever order had been given, the two men released their hold on the biker as the twins began to remove items from the suitcases.

Cruz turned to look at Larocque and Tomic. "You are welcome to stay and watch, but much of the work I'll be doing in the next hour will be delicate and will require all of my attention.

"Neuro-interrogation has come a long way since the CIA first started playing with Musk's Neurolink, but it is not without risks. I'll be totally honest with you. There have been times when the information I've gathered from a person's mind has not been usable. I would say it's one in fifteen."

Before Tomic could say anything, Larocque said, "You have our full trust, my friend. Proceed as you need to."

"And we'll stick around," added Tomic quickly. "If only so I can give a full debrief to the Crown when I'm charged with whatever is about to happen."

One of Cruz's female assistants handed him a long white cylinder.

Taking the object in his hand, he began to spin it casually. On stopping the tool's rotation, the whine of what sounded like a dentist's drill filled the room.

When the noise stopped abruptly, Cruz, still in a friendly tone, said, "We have to drill into the skull to insert several microelectrode arrays. It is all but harmless to the subject."

Her face alarmed, Tomic rounded on Larocque and said, "Jesus Christ, what the hell are we doing? We're gonna go to jail for this, you know that, right?"

Larocque nodded at the statement and, in a sober voice, said, "Yes, I'd say there's a very good chance we'll go to jail. For what it's worth, I'll take the rap for it as best I can.'"

"And you're okay with this?" exclaimed Tomic.

Larocque's reply was immediate. "People are dying under my command, our country is fighting two wars, and the homeland of one of our allies is in the throes of an actual firestorm."

After briefly pausing to let his synopsis sink in, Larocque added, "Have you seen the images coming out of Australia, Monique? It's a goddamn nightmare. How many more thousands will die if we don't do what needs to be done?"

When Tomic gave no reply, he continued, "We've tried the CSIS way, and it's not working. At least, not as quickly as we need it to. I know you don't like it and you probably think I'm a monster for what's about to happen, but if we don't start to chalk up some wins, going to jail will be the least of our concerns."

Larocque returned his eyes to Cruz and said, "Do it."

Chapter 20

Anaheim, California

"And so, my fellow Californians, as I finish my address, I want to reiterate that we will not involve ourselves in any wars. With your support and collective wisdom, I know, and I believe, that California can and will remain prosperous and independent if it maintains its neutral status."

Sanchez, standing at the center of the large stage behind a formidable-looking podium designed to protect its speaker from any number of threats, looked left and right at the faces that had come to the Anaheim Convention Center to hear his speech.

As he quickly canvassed the crowd, his confidence was buoyed. To the last, he saw only faces of approval.

They could do this, he thought. He could do this. They could stay out of the fire now consuming the world and when it was all said and done, California and its 46 million people would be well-positioned to do many wonderful and great things, including becoming its own country.

He brought his eyes back to the camera platform at the center of the convention hall's floor and with the most earnest look he could muster, said, "War is a terrible thing, and we grieve for our democratic friends across the world as they confront their respective challenges. But California will run its own race, and it will survive, and we, as a people and as an economy, will thrive!"

Throwing one of his hands into the air, in a louder voice, Sanchez said, "Bless our free and soon-to-be independent California!"

Staying in place, he raised his other hand into the air and waved at the capacity crowd as they began to roar their approval.

"Do not step away from the podium. Your detail will be there in thirty seconds," a firm voice said in the comms device in his right ear.

Sanchez didn't acknowledge the order but also didn't step off the small dais the podium was set upon.

After another thirty seconds of pointing, waving, and yelling back to the closest members of the audience, six men in dark suits walked onto the stage and surrounded him.

Giving one final swing of his arm, Sanchez turned and stepped off the platform. Within three strides, the six California State Troopers had fully enveloped him, and together, they walked off the stage toward where his political team was waiting.

Arriving off stage, he was greeted by the man who had spoken in his comms device, directing him not to leave the protective bubble of the Israeli-designed VIP protection unit they had installed specifically for this event.

Jim Schafer was a former Secret Service agent who had been given the task of updating the California State Police's training and methods as they pertained to VIP protection.

"Well done, Governor. Or should I start calling you 'Mr. President'?"

Sanchez smiled. "Not yet, Jim. We still have a lot of work to do."

"Indeed, let's get you back to Sacramento, then."

The Secret Service man half-pivoted and gestured to the designated bank of doors that would take Sanchez to his waiting motorcade.

As the two men started to move, Schafer peeled away enough to allow Sanchez's chief of staff, Tracy Crawley to file in beside her boss.

"So, how did I do?" Sanchez said to the pretty thirty-something woman.

Looking down at the phone in her hand, she said, "You rocked it, boss. Insta-polling suggests people think you were genuine – no surprise there. The numbers went through the roof every time you mentioned the words 'neutrality' and 'economy.'"

"Glad to hear it. I was worried that with all that's happening Down Under, people might begin to waver, but it might be that the Aussies' disaster will help our cause. They could easily be us," Sanchez said casually.

As a group, they reached the doors leading out of the still-buzzing convention hall.

Through the doors and into the concourse, an additional dozen plainclothes state troopers surrounded them, but unlike the six officers who had walked Sanchez off stage, this second group was bearing an assortment of larger weapons that couldn't be hidden underneath a suit jacket.

As the reinforced entourage began to make its way along the massive glassed central thoroughfare of the convention center, the public that had come to the event began to crowd the line of stanchions and uniformed police officers put in place to give Sanchez and his security detail a clear path to and from the hall.

As they walked past what had to be a couple thousand people, Sanchez did his best to quickly respond to those of his supporters who called out to him.

Halfway to the safety of his armored SUV, Sanchez gestured into the throng of milling people and said, "Jesus Christ, Tracy, is that Mrs. Horowitz?"

"Like, *the* Nancy Horowitz?" his chief of staff asked.

"Yes, that Nancy. She's waving at me. You can't miss her," Sanchez snapped, pointing toward the elderly woman who was the single biggest private donor to his campaign.

Sanchez stopped moving, gesturing to the woman to confirm he'd seen her. "Look at her, Tracy, the poor woman looks exhausted."

Seeing the woman for herself, aghast, Crawley said, "Jesus, that is her. What the hell is she doing here? She never reached out to us. Where are her people?"

"I don't know," Sanchez said, sounding frustrated. "But we can't leave her there. Look at her, the woman is confused. It's all over her face. The poor thing."

His arm flew into the air as he called out, "Nancy! Nancy! Ms. Horowitz! Yes, yes, I see you, Nancy. No, stay right there. I'm coming over to speak with you."

As he moved to step under the thin barrier into the crowd of people calling to him or recording him on their smartphones, Sanchez felt a strong pair of hands roughly grab him from behind and then heard the voice of Schafer say, "Sir, under no circumstances can you leave the detail. We need to keep moving."

As an actor, Sanchez prided himself on being kind and supportive to every crew member he had ever worked with, no matter their role. From the director to the folks who cleaned his dressing room, everyone got his time and respect.

But there had been moments where, because he was stressed or because he was dealing with a genuine dickhead he felt it necessary to draw upon that power that all A-List actors had to be a self-righteous asshole.

To be sure, he liked Jeff Schafer. The man had a good sense of humor, and his service had been nothing short of professional and exact, but truth be told, Sanchez had always chafed at the people who provided security. They were always making things out to be a bigger deal than they were, and Schafer had been worse than most.

Perhaps it was because he was a former Secret Service agent, but the man saw danger and death around every bloody corner. It had become grating weeks ago, but at this precise moment, it had been too much.

Pulling from the man's grasp, he whipped around to face the head of his protection detail and brought up his finger so it pointed into the taller man's face. "Do not touch me. When I want to talk to someone, I will damn you. I'm the boss, and you're the help. You got that?"

Having spent years protecting presidents and more movie stars than Schafer could remember, he accepted Sanchez's outburst gracefully and looked to solve the problem. That was the only sure way to get them moving again. "Governor, I can see you're stressed about something. Tell me what's going on, and I'll see if I can have someone take care of it."

"Not someone – me." Again, Sanchez tried to lower himself to step underneath the barrier, but before his upper body could move more than an inch, Schafer's hands again grabbed Sanchez's arm, preventing him from moving. This time, the man's hands were like iron.

Now irate, Sanchez snarled, "Now, you listen to me –."

But his words were cut off as Crawley somehow managed to wedge herself between the two men. In a strained voice, she said, "Governor, I'm with Jeff. You can't go out there."

Moving her gaze to Schafer, she said, "Just over there is Mrs. Horowitz. She's the Governor's biggest donor, she has low-level dementia, and she's here. Why she's here, I don't know, but she needs help."

"Show her to me," Schafer demanded.

Still wedged between the two men, Crawley pointed out the old woman.

Schafer nodded his head and then yelled, "Simpson, Starr. On me!"

Two of the state troopers who had come onto the stage to retrieve Sanchez pulled their eyes from the gawking crowd.

Schafer's hand knifed out in the direction of the old lady. "That is Mrs. Horowitz. She is a close friend of the Governor's. As though she were your own grandmother, you will collect her and ensure she gets home safely."

"I'll go with them," Crawley said as her body emerged from between the two men.

Turning to Sanchez, she said in a low voice, "I'll take care of Nancy, and I'll speak with the half-dozen people who just recorded your little outburst. Not a good look, Governor."

Sanchez cinched his lips at the admonishment, blew a huge gust of air from his lungs and said, "Sorry. I've just been feeling so much pressure with this decision to stay out of the war. Jesus, the videos out of Australia. They're just incredible."

"You made the right decision, Ricky," Crawley insisted. "Now, go with Jeff and get to the airport. I'll meet you there."

Turning from him, she and the two hulking state troopers stepped under the barrier and made their way to the old lady.

As Sanchez pulled his eyes from the trio negotiating their way through the crowd, he found Schafer staring at him. The man's face gave no hint of what he might be thinking. Instead, with a hand, he gestured down the concourse to where their motorcade was waiting, and said, "Governor, that way, if you please."

"Jeff..." Sanchez started to say, but his words trailed off.

"It's not a problem, Governor. We'll discuss it on the way to the airport but for now, we need to get moving."

Again, the security man's hand gestured up the concourse.

Nodding to signal his compliance with Schafer's direction, Sanchez started forward and within a couple of strides, was once again surrounded by the whole of his protection team, less his chief of staff and the two officers who had been sent to help that lovely old woman.

***

"They've stopped."

"Why?" asked Reynolds.

"Not sure. Wait. It looks like the target is giving it to his head of security. Oh yeah, he's pissed about something. The dude's face is red. He's not happy."

"What else is happening? Keep talking," prompted Reynolds.

"The chief of staff has swooped in. She's way hotter in person, by the way."

"Stay focused," Reynolds said, doing his best to keep his temper from flaring.

"Dawg, I'm just saying she's lost some weight and is looking fine. *Real fine.* What a shame."

Before Reynolds could begin to scold the lone operator he had in the convention center's concourse, the man called Grady provided another update. "She's leaving the detail with two officers. Headed in the direction of Bravo."

"What about the target?" demanded Reynolds.

"He's on the move again. It looks like the chief of staff will deal with Mrs. H."

In the small boardroom three blocks down from the Anaheim Convention Center, Reynolds nodded as though he had expected that Sanchez wouldn't take the bait he'd worked so hard to put in place for this moment.

He had sunk a lot of hope and money into the idea that human cunning and not technology would win the day. Nevertheless, he was confident the old woman would still serve a purpose in what was to come.

He looked to the other side of the room where the Savant had set up a bank of eight giant screens. The young man with the ghoulish skin was sitting at a customized desk that had everything he needed to oversee the thousand-plus drones that had been clandestinely positioned in the area around the convention center over the past two days.

While the Savant's back faced Reynolds, the Indian, standing at the drone operator's right shoulder, was staring at him intently.

As their gazes locked onto one another, the Indian's coffee-dark eyes widened in anticipation.

"Stay cool, *Kemosabe*," Reynolds said to the brown-skinned tech just as his hand dropped down to his wrist unit. Without looking, he activated the comms channel that would connect him with the five members of his team positioned in various locations around the convention center. "All units, we are a go for Hurricane Romeo. I say again, we are a go for Hurricane Romeo. Execute, execute, execute."

Before he had finished giving the order, the Indian had turned away from him to take up the screens now filled with images Reynolds knew were a predetermined selection of feeds that would give the Savant the information he needed to tweak or, if necessary, override, the near-AI software program that had already begun its hunt for the Governor of California.

***

The officer's radio burped from where it was attached to his chest rig. "Shakespeare is on the move again. We'll be arriving at the departure location in three mikes. All units, standby."

Satisfied the update about the Governor meant he could continue to do as he was doing, the senior officer of the four LAPD cops standing watch over the convention center's loading dock resumed the conversation he'd been having thirty seconds earlier.

"So, as I was saying to you two jackasses, I don't know how we got stuck watching this entrance, but it's not for me or you to ask questions. And let's be clear, neither of you has so much brainpower that you can afford to contemplate why the sergeant put us where she put us. You should consider yourselves lucky you get used at all, considering your most recent fuck-up."

"It was a good shoot, Jonesy. A good shoot, and you know it!" the shorter of the two officers exclaimed, throwing his hands in the air.

The senior cop, Jones, rolled his eyes as dramatically as he could, and as though on cue, his partner García, a petite but tough-as-nails Latina, took up the prosecution. "You shot a chihuahua, Mikey."

"It was dark and it was raining, and just two weeks earlier, Rodriguez got tagged on that same block. Anyone in my position would have done the same thing. It was a good shoot, I'm telling you."

Their faces dead serious, Jones and García started to bark in their best impression of a high-strung chihuahua.

"Go to hell! The both of you. That lady should have never let her dog out. I'm telling you, it was dark, it was rainy, and the shadows... it made that thing look huge."

"Oh ya, huge, eh, Mikey?" García manage to squawk through her laughter.

Beside his partner, Jones, now on the verge of laughing hysterically, wheezed out, "Big like a dragon, eh, Ferino?"

For the first time during the conversation, the fourth cop spoke up with a clear sense of urgency in his voice. "Guys, hold up. Up there."

Picking up on their colleague's tone, the other three cops managed to pull themselves away from the banter and look in the direction the youngest of their group was now pointing.

"What the hell is that?" Ferino said.

Across a huge parking lot and atop a six-story parking garage, each of the four officers laid their eyes on what had to be dozens, if not a couple hundred, dark specks floating in the air.

All four of the police officer's radios came alive, "All units, all units, be advised that multiple airborne objects have been picked up on the RADTACT. Report any sightings or strange activity ASAP."

Ferino looked in the direction of Jones and said, "You gonna call this in?"

"Yeah, I think I might, kid," Jones said, keeping his eyes on the growing number of black specks on the horizon. His hand went to the handset on his left shoulder and activated it. "Romeo Alpha, this is unit 043. I'm seeing upwards of a hundred drones on the west side of the center above parking structure..."

"Seven," his partner, García, said.

"Above Parking Structure Seven."

When no acknowledgment of his update came from the ops center, he activated the handset again.

"Romeo –"

"Shit, look out!" Ferino cried as he lifted his Benelli M4 Super 90 Tactical shotgun straight into the air and started to fire. *BOOM!*

Above where the four officers were standing were an uncountable number of drones, many of which were zipping toward them.

With each blast of Ferino's weapon, one of the drones disintegrated, but just as Jones placed his hand on the grip of his service pistol to draw his weapon, one of the drones dropped quicker than the rest and, positioning itself near García, it exploded.

As a flash of brightness invaded his eyes, Jones felt himself fly backward and skid over the concrete of the loading area.

Somewhere to his right, he heard a terrified scream. Just as he was about to call out García's name, there was a second bang followed by silence.

His face hot with pain and his eyes struggling to see anything but a swirl of beiges and greys, Jones screamed, "Lucy! Lucy! Talk to me, Lucy. Talk to me, damn you! Are you okay?"

Just as he began to perceive shapes, shotgun blasts started to once again fill the air. Directing his eyes to the sound, Jones finally comprehended what his eyes were seeing.

With a blood-soaked face and a crazed look in his eyes, Ferino was pouring round after round from his Benelli into a huge group of drones hovering outside the two massive doors used to accept everything and anything the convention center needed to run its business.

Tearing his eyes from Ferino, he searched the immediate area for his partner. When he found her, the pounding of his heart went into overdrive.

He took several steps in her direction so he could verify the horror show that his frazzled brain was trying to comprehend.

Still half a dozen feet away from the body, Jones pulled up his stride. He was now close enough to confirm that, in fact, his rock-steady partner of the past three years was now headless.

Growing up Catholic in Lancaster, California, he made the sign of the cross, quietly uttered the words, "God have mercy on you, Lucy," and then reached for the FN 509 service pistol on his hip.

Drawing the weapon, Jones turned back to the swarm of drones to see the two loading doors begin to rise.

Only a couple feet into the air, the drones began to whip into the building.

Placing the reticle of his pistol on the closest of the flying machines, he began to put rounds down range, but it was no use. Between the distance and how badly his hands were shaking, his barrage of half a dozen shots had been useless.

He bellowed a curse and turned his attention back to Ferino. The diminutive Italian-American was in the process of feeding shells into his shotgun.

Jones ran to the other man and, on reaching him, said, "García is gone."

Feeding the last round into his weapon, Ferino worked the pump action and said, "I know. I saw it happen. They did the same thing to Ng."

As the two doors of the loading bay reached their summit, the last of the drones disappeared into the maw of the building. With the buzzing of so many drones no longer in the vicinity, Jones could hear gunfire in the distance. "Jesus, they're everywhere."

Instead of answering, Ferino took a step in the direction of the loading doors, but before he could get out of reach, Jones's hand snapped forward, grabbed the man's shoulder and said, "Where are you going, man? García and Ng... They're gone. We've gotta..."

His words trailed off because he didn't want to finish his sentence.

"We gotta what, Jonesy? Watch their bodies bleed out? Screw that, man. I'm still breathing, so I'm going in there," Ferino gestured with his shotgun at the entrance where the drones had disappeared, "and I'm gonna get some payback. You can come, or you can stay, but I'm going in."

Jones released the man's shoulder and allowed his eyes to dart to where Ng's body lay. Like García, the body of the officer lay in a pool of blood, but his head was still attached. But there was so much blood, there was no way Ng could still be alive.

Jones's right hand once again moved to his service pistol. It had been useless only a minute before, but he knew he wouldn't be able to live with himself if he didn't follow Ferino on his crusade.

Finally, he said, "You're right. I'm with you, man. Let's go get some payback."

***

In the time they had walked a hundred yards of the vast glassed concourse to the entrance where his motorcade was waiting, Sanchez had come to realize just how much of a jackass he'd been.

As the protection detail approached the huge glass doors that were the main entrance to the facility, he said, "Listen, Jeff, I want to apologize. It's just that I've been feeling a lot of pressure around this decision not to get involved in the war. It hasn't been easy. You may not know this, but I actually have family living in Australia. It's just been a heck of a time for me and my wife to see the images and..."

Sanchez stopped talking and moving when he again felt Schafer's hand grab at his arm.

As his eyes darted down to take in Schafer's big hand, every molecule of Sanchez's self-discipline began to scream at him not to lose his cool.

Forcing himself to keep his voice calm, he said, "Jeff, if we're going to continue to work together, this grabbing thing you've been doing – well, it's gotta stop. You see –."

Before he could finish the sentence, a series of sharp popping noises grabbed his attention.

Looking through the glassed façade of the concourse's entrance, Sanchez saw flying debris ejecting into the air from the two Air Defense Anti-Drone vehicles.

Hugely expensive and difficult to get from their manufacturer in Turkey, Schafer had made their purchase a requirement of his employment contract.

As Sanchez watched dozens of drones eject from the top of each vehicle and fly higher into the air, his eyes moved back to the head of his security team.

Quietly, as though he'd been the only one to see the drones leap into the sky, he said, "Jeff, what's happening?"

One of Schafer's hands was at his ear. Undoubtedly, the man was getting an update from someone.

Around them, as one, each of the state troopers raised their assault rifles or drew handguns and started to actively scan the area looking for something to shoot at.

Having seen the drones deployed and noticing the change in posture of Sanchez's protection detail, the public milling around the area began to pull back. Even they could sense something was about to go down.

As people began to try and exit through the bank of doors not set aside for Sanchez's departure, he heard a series of loud bangs.

Outside, dozens of people began to point into the air, and then in ones and twos, they began to yell and then scream.

Without warning, a low buzzing began to overwhelm the sound of panicked voices that were now rushing to exit the building. Sanchez forced himself to look away from the devolving scene and back at Schafer. This time, when he spoke, it was a yell. "Jeff, what the hell is going on?"

Schafer pointed in the direction of Sanchez's armored SUV and said, "We're under attack."

Following Schafer's finger, Sanchez looked toward his waiting motorcade.

The door to his SUV was open and standing in front of it was a female plainclothes state trooper he recognized. Shaunda was her name.

Despite the chaos around her, the cop's face remained focused on the entrance that Sanchez would be emerging from at any moment.

Finally, Sanchez couldn't take it anymore and said, "Why aren't we moving?"

When the Secret Service agent didn't reply, Sanchez yelled, "Schafer, you son of a bitch, why aren't we moving? The SUV is right there. Let's get the hell out of here!"

Schafer spun on Sanchez and said, "We're safer in here. They're everywhere. RADTACT is being jammed. The last data we have is that nearly a thousand drones are converging on this position. A swarm is coming."

"A swarm? What the hell is that?" Sanchez demanded.

But before Schafer could offer a reply, there was another series of bangs outside. These were louder and reverberated through the huge wall of glass that was the exterior of the building.

Just as debris started to fall from the sky, those members of Sanchez's protection detail outside with the motorcade raised their weapons into the air and began to fire.

The moment the gunfire erupted, mass panic ensued inside and outside the building.

In slow motion, Sanchez's eyes were drawn upward as some uncountable number of drones appeared in his field of vision.

The first wave of drones was brought down by a furious fusillade of gunfire being put into the sky by the state troopers and LAPD officers outside protecting the motorcade, but as a second and larger wave arrived, the dodging drones began to find their targets.

Sanchez's eyes darted toward the state trooper who had been faithfully guarding the door to his SUV. At some point, Shaunda had stopped looking in the direction of the convention center's doors, drawn her service pistol, and was firing wildly into the air.

Just as her weapon ran out of rounds, a drone, perhaps the size of a softball, arrived at her position and exploded without any warning.

As Sanchez's brain tried to make sense of the horror he'd just witnessed, a second and much larger drone arrived at the door of his SUV. It quickly tucked itself into the vehicle and detonated.

BOOM!

Because of the SUV's bullet-resistant windows, the bulk of the energy from the explosion shot out of the open door like a cannon and struck the entrance Sanchez was standing in front of.

Glass, shattering inward, shredded everything in its path.

Hammered by the wall of energy, Sanchez screamed in pain as he was thrown backward.

As he stumbled back and fell to the concourse's floor, it felt like his face was on fire. Instinctively, he put his hands to his face and pulled them away and saw they were covered in fresh blood.

Because most of his movies had been of the action variety, Sanchez had taken several advanced first-aid courses and knew to go straight for his jugular veins. Patting his neck down, he was relieved when he felt no spurting fluids.

Satisfied he wasn't dying, he put his hands down to push himself up, but before he could start the process, two sets of strong hands grabbed him and yanked him upwards.

With mass confusion all around him, Sanchez took heart at the sight of Schafer and the state trooper who had manhandled him onto his feet. Miraculously, neither of the two men seemed to have been touched by the implosion of glass.

As a new surge of gunfire erupted to his right, Sanchez kept his eyes on the head of his security detail. If he was going to survive the next few minutes, something deep inside his brain was telling him it would be because he did exactly what this man told him to do.

Over the cacophony, Schafer bellowed, "Listen up, people. We are leaving via Exit Zulu, the emergency exit on the west side of Convention Hall C, the space we just came from. LAPD's SWAT is en route, and they will secure that exit. As quickly as possible, that is where we need to be."

Schafer pointed at Sanchez. "This is the principal. He is alive. Keep him at our center. This is your only priority."

The Secret Service agent's hand cut in the direction of a pair of state troopers. "Miguel and Gates. You're on point. Anything that is flying take it down.

"The rest of you. Form up with me at your center."

Drawing his pistol from the holster at his belt, Schafer set his eyes on Sanchez and said, "We're getting out of here. Follow me."

Chapter 21

Anaheim Convention Center, Los Angeles

—

"Shit!" Jones cried out as he moved to charge after Ferino.

The Italian-American was at least ten years younger than him and had a level of fitness that matched a guy who was still keen on being a cop, plus he was single and had wanted to stay fit for the ladies.

It was because of these characteristics that Ferino easily climbed up the loading dock the drones had streamed through only thirty seconds earlier.

Jones, not so much.

Though slower and with much less grace, he did scale the same obstacle.

Once a fanatic softball player, now forty-six and with two bad knees, he spent most of his leisure time running the LAPD's massive and complex coed league.

Jones loved competition and at one time took pride in his athletic abilities, but as it had turned out, he was a better administrator than he had been an athlete. His personality and ability to get people to agree to compromise had reversed the league's fortunes to the point where they now had to refuse new teams.

Breathing hard but securely on the concrete platform of the loading dock, Jones yelled after the younger officer, "Ferino, you dumb son of a bitch, wait!"

To his surprise, the other man came to a stop and turned to face him. "Keep up, old man. I'm not going to stop again. We've already lost them!"

Jones pointed in the direction of the long, oversized hallway the swarm of drones had flown into. "Listen, man, I think I know where they might be headed. About five years back, I did some calls here for a bunch of break-ins. Before it got handed to Commercial Crimes, security took me all over the building. This tunnel we're in is the service conduit for the whole facility. There are a few twists and turns, but I think I might be able to remember how to get where we need to be without too much trouble."

Ferino looked in the direction Jones was pointing and said, "Fine, but you said you know where they might be going. Where?"

"On the TacNet, I just heard them declare the Governor's motorcade is a no-go. My guess is that they'll go back to where he gave the speech. The only other road access point to the Center is at the far end of that space. If they want to drive him out of here, that's where they'll need to take him. It's their only other option."

Ferino nodded and said, "Fine, let's go."

But before the younger cop could take a step, Jones's hand snapped forward and latched onto the other man's bicep.

Feeling the contact, Ferino turned and levelled an angry gaze at the older cop and said, "Jonesy, what the hell? We gotta get going, man."

"Dude, let's think this through for a moment. There are two of us. There are hundreds of those things. You saw them. We need more bodies. Lots of them."

"So what? What do you want me to do about it?"

"I need you to help me get people to meet us along the way. There were a hundred of us here, and some of us had to survive. Between the two of us and our phones, maybe we can direct enough of them here so we can make a difference."

Ferino, a dedicated officer but not the brightest cop in the precinct, said, "Why not just use the radio?"

"Dude, even if it's working, whoever has done this has to be monitoring TacNet. We gotta work our networks, man, and fast."

For two full seconds, Ferino's pissed-off eyes stared at Jones, but he finally relented and said, "Fine, let's do it. What do you need me to do?"

Jones exhaled a relieved breath, released Ferino's arm, and turned his eyes back to the tunnel the drones had disappeared into.

Taking a stride forward, he said, "Follow me and start sending messages to anyone and everyone from the briefing this morning. Tell them to rally to the kitchen on the south side of Hall B, and tell them to be there in no less than five minutes if they want to have a chance to open a can of whoop-ass on whoever thought it was a good idea to try and mess with us today."

Following Jones, Ferino whipped out his smartphone, brought up his message app, and started typing. Hitting Send on his first message, his eyes reconnected with Jones, and he said, "And what are you gonna do?"

His phone out, and while typing furiously over the display, Jones said, "Besides rallying the troops, assuming we can find the Governor alive, we're gonna need a way to get out of here."

"Dude, half the force will be here in the next fifteen. There will be plenty of rides."

Jones looked at Ferino skeptically, "Seriously, if you think upper management will be able to pull its head out of its collective ass in time to organize a way out of here, you really are the dumbest cop on the force."

When a hurt look popped onto Ferino's face, Jones, starting to half-jog, said, "Jesus Christ, Ferino, I'm kidding. Keep texting people and just try to keep up."

***

Sanchez, a veteran of over eighty-six major motion pictures, told himself over and over that the gunfire, the explosions, and the blood he was seeing were the result of an incredibly talented special effects team.

With him at its center, the protection detail was moving quickly down the concourse in the direction they had come from only five minutes earlier.

Behind them, he could hear the blast of shotguns and automatic weapons fire as his protection detail and a collection of LAPD officers continued to engage with the drones coming through several of the shattered windows near the convention center's entrance.

Ahead of them was pandemonium.

When the attack had started, the audience that had come to watch his speech was still in the process of exiting.

Now, these same people were running wildly in all directions as they stormed and clawed their way out of Hall C. Those security staff and police he could see had given up all efforts to try and manage the bedlam.

A familiar voice called his name, "Ricky! Ricky!"

Still moving forward, Sanchez searched the frantic crowd and finally laid his eyes on his chief of staff.

In the sea of panicked faces that surrounded her, Crawley was a pillar of calm. She was still with Mrs. Horowitz and was holding the elderly woman's hand.

To his relief, the two state troopers that Schafer had assigned to help gather up the old woman had their weapons drawn and were guarding over the two women like a pair of hyper-vigilant guard dogs.

He reached forward and grabbed Schafer's shoulder, but before he could say anything, the head of his security team said, "I see them. We're not stopping."

Sanchez's grip tightened on the former Secret Service agent's shoulder, but the man tore away from him and before he understood what was happening, two of the heftier state troopers had flanked him and grabbed his suit jacket. Together, they began to push and drag him forward.

As he understood what they were trying to do, he tried to resist but was no match for the adrenaline-infused strength of the two highly fit men.

After a dozen or so steps of being dragged forward, he stopped resisting and looked to reacquire his chief of staff and Mrs. Horowitz. As they passed by them, as best he could, he would tell Crawley to keep her elderly charge safe and that they'd connect later.

His eyes found the pair. They were navigating the crowd, making their way to the advancing protection detail, but the officer leading the two women came to a stop and brought his free hand to his ear so he could better hear whoever was speaking to him.

Sanchez's eyes flashed to Schafer and sure enough, the Secret Service agent seemed to be talking into the air.

Still moving forward, Sanchez yelled in Schafer's direction, "You son of a bitch! They can make it to us."

Schafer gave no sign that he heard Sanchez's words. Instead, he started speaking urgently.

Sanchez's eyes once again moved to Crawley and the old woman.

The state trooper who had been speaking with Schafer suddenly rounded on his two female charges, and, in a flash of movement, inexplicably grabbed at Mrs. Horowitz's blouse and tore it open.

Cinched around the flummoxed woman's stomach just underneath her bra was a black object of some kind.

Sanchez was now ninety degrees and maybe twenty meters distant from the two women.

For the briefest moment, his gaze connected with the terrified eyes of his chief of staff. Then Ms. Horowitz exploded.

***

It might be the case that Helen Horowitz was experiencing the early stages of Alzheimer's, but three hours earlier her brain had fully comprehended what would happen if she didn't attend the Sanchez speech and make her best efforts to get within ten feet of California's governor.

Reynolds had been confident the elderly woman would comply the moment he saw her face when he walked her granddaughter and her two small children into the boardroom just across the hall from where he was now standing.

A high-functioning psychopath, Reynolds had always appreciated the degree of callousness he could bring to bear in any situation.

In truth, it was the one trait more than all others that gave him the ability to do extraordinary things like cutting off the pinky fingers of an eight and ten-year-old.

As he held his knife over her youngest grandson's dainty finger, Helen Horowitz had sworn up, and down she would do everything he wanted to help kill Ricky Sanchez.

Reynolds had wanted to believe her, but there was thirty million in crypto on the line, and that was a shit-ton of money.

The two fingers had come off with far too much squealing, but when it was done, whatever lingering doubts he had that the old woman would do what she had been told to do had disappeared.

Helen Horowitz might have been a fan of Ricky Sanchez and had become one of his biggest political donors, but foremost, she was a woman who deeply loved her family.

After shooting her up with a cocktail of drugs that would stimulate her brain function for the next several hours, Reynolds had personally dropped her off at the convention center.

Getting out of the Mercedes Benz, he had rushed around the sedan to open her door for her. When she extricated herself from the back seat, their eyes locked onto one another.

"You're going to go to hell for what you've done today," she said quietly.

Reynolds, wearing clothing that made him look as though he was the elderly woman's chauffeur, smiled and replied, "I punched my ticket to that place a long time ago, Mrs. Horowitz. You're just the latest notch on my headboard."

Still offering a grand smile, his hand tapped his ear. "Be sure to have a listen when I talk. We'll have lots of eyes on you in there. Do exactly as I say, and everything will go fine for your granddaughter and her kids."

The ancient widow stared into Reynolds's face with a look of unadulterated hatred but said nothing.

As she turned and began to walk away, Reynolds had not been able to help himself. Calling after the stooped woman, he said, "Goodbye, Helen. Best of luck to you."

Some thirty minutes later, Reynolds stood well back from the Indian and the Savant. Through the smart glasses he was wearing, he watched the scene Grady was streaming from inside the convention center.

Amid the chaos of fleeing civilians, gunfire, and shattering glass, Reynolds watched in growing delight as Sanchez's security detail fled from the destruction of the governor's motorcade back in the direction of where they had left Mrs. Horowitz.

To say that he was thrilled that his part of the plan was coming back into play would have been an understatement.

To her full credit, Helen Horowitz had insisted to anyone who would listen that she had to do one, and one thing only – speak with her dear friend, Ricky Sanchez.

The police she'd spoken to initially had blown her off, figuring her to have escaped a local old folks' home. But determined to save her great-grandchildren, she had slipped the first pair of officers she'd spoken with and had tried to get Sanchez's attention directly as he had left his speech. That this had almost worked had convinced Reynolds the nine-fingered children and their terrified mother could live.

He wasn't a complete monster.

When it was clear Sanchez's entourage would be rushed by the now thoroughly frazzled old woman, Reynolds said, "Grady, take cover. You have three seconds."

When the video streaming from Grady's smart glasses was nothing more than tiled floor, he pressed the single red button on the screen of his smartphone and said, "Good bye, Mrs. Horowitz."

***

As Sanchez's body was hurled through the air, the neurons of his brain chiselled in the memory of Tracy Crawley the second before she was consumed by fire.

Instinctively raising his arms to prevent his skull from being crushed, he felt his body skip once along the floor and then hammer into something solid.

With his faculties in play, Sanchez perceived the precise moment when his collarbone snapped in two. The pain was beyond excruciating.

Lying on the ground for what could have been one minute or ten, Sanchez willed his eyes open.

Unlike most of incestuous Hollywood, Sanchez had made it into the acting business because of talent, good looks, and a few good breaks, but mostly because of his work ethic.

He had only made his first movie when he was twenty-five. Before that, he had paid his bills working at some of the worst jobs that could be found in L.A. in the early nineties.

He arrived from Texas to California at just eighteen, and for seven years, as he took acting lessons and auditioned for bit parts, he worked long, hard hours. It had been a challenging but formative experience that had instilled in him the power of getting back on your feet.

Now at sixty-five, that willfulness was so ingrained inside him that he easily ignored the pain in his shoulder and, with his one good arm, started to push himself off the ground.

He got halfway into a seated position before he sensed someone beside him. Turning his head, he saw Schafer. His face was blackened and there was an ugly cut on his forehead, but otherwise, he seemed unharmed.

As he lowered himself onto one knee, a grimace of pain overtook the former Secret Service agent's face. Through gritted teeth, Schafer said, "We have to move. The drones just keep coming. Are you hurt?"

Wincing from the pain, Sanchez replied, "My collarbone is broken. If there's more, I can't feel it."

As the sound of gunfire started anew, Schafer nodded that he understood, got back to his feet, and yelled two names Sanchez didn't catch.

As Schafer stepped away and began to fire his own weapon into the air, a pair of wide-eyed but determined-looking state troopers reached his location, and without warning, they grabbed his shoulders and heaved into the air.

Sanchez howled in pain as the quick movement jarred the shattered bone in his shoulder to rip into flesh and muscle. As his vision blurred, he caught Schafer yelling at what remained of the security detail to move in the direction of Hall C.

As they arrived at the bank of doors that led into the space where he'd given his address, a pair of female LAPD officers were urging them forward. Both had shotguns at the ready.

As Sanchez was carried past the two officers to re-enter the cavernous event space where he'd been on stage only minutes ago, he saw Schafer sprint forward. Watching the man, Sanchez saw what had to be a dozen heavily armed LAPD SWAT officers running in their direction.

The two groups met each other at the front of the stage. The bright lights, still on from his address, laid bare just how much of a bloody mess his protection detail was.

Along with the state troopers holding him up, the remaining police officers from his detail formed a tight circle while the SWAT officers quickly formed up around them. The LAPD's legendary tactical team had their weapons locked into their shoulders and as one, were scanning in all directions.

Suddenly, shotgun blasts came from the doorway where Sanchez had seen the two female LAPD officers only seconds ago. Turning his head to the sound, he saw one of the two cops running in their direction.

She was only a dozen feet past the entrance when the next wave of drones appeared.

Like a hound that had just laid its eyes on its prey, the first unit through the door raced to the fleeing officer and exploded near the small of her back.

Through the flash, Sanchez caught the woman's limp body fly into the outermost chairs of the seating area like a bowling ball colliding with pins.

Those SWAT officers on that side of their defensive circle opened up with their weapons as dozens of the flying machines surged past the destroyed policewoman.

Shotguns and automatic rifles delivering short accurate bursts began to have an immediate effect on the charge of drones, and within seconds, they had brought down this first wave of attackers.

Behind him, Sanchez heard a voice he didn't recognize yell, "We have a pair of armored trucks waiting for us outside. Stay tight, everyone. Keep the governor at our center. Let's move, people!"

Just as the two state troopers holding him turned his body in the direction they'd been told to advance, Sanchez heard the buzzing of more drones.

Around him, voices were yelling out new threats and firing their weapons.

One of the two men carrying him uttered, "Jesus, they're coming in from all over!"

The voice of the SWAT commander bellowed encouragement, "Move, people! Move and engage. Move and engage. This ain't our first rodeo!"

Finally moving in two tight concentric circles, his detail and the SWAT team started to make good progress toward the doors where the rest of the LAPD's tactical team and their vehicles were waiting.

From the direction of that entrance, there was a new and furious barrage of automatic gunfire. Halfway to their escape, Sanchez could make out a handful of SWAT officers outside the building firing their weapons into the air.

BOOM!

A massive explosion tore through his vision, forcing Sanchez to momentarily close his eyes.

On opening them, where there had been a contingent of SWAT officers holding the entrance they'd been trying to reach, there was now only a smoking, jagged hole and the scattered remains of broken and burning bodies of police officers in tactical gear.

Averting his gaze from the dreadful sight, Sanchez watched in horror as drones in the dozens began to pour through the shattered entrance and cut off their escape.

Though they continued to fire their weapons, the protection detail was forced to come to a stop.

Behind Sanchez, someone cried out in a strained voice, "We're surrounded!"

Without warning, the smaller of the two state troopers that had been helping to carry him released Sanchez and drew his pistol from underneath his jacket. Over the cacophony, Sanchez heard the man yell, "Carry him on your own, Sammy."

As the state trooper began to fire his handgun, the other cop swung Sanchez into a bridal carry. Now, every officer, except the one carrying him, was shooting their weapon. In the confines of the conference space, the sound was deafening.

Despite the pain and noise, Sanchez craned his neck as far as he could.

In every direction was a wall of drones. Most were no bigger than a softball.

As one, the drones had stopped advancing and were hovering about fifty feet back from the outer ring of SWAT officers. Those drones closest to the still-firing cops were randomly dodging back and forth in an effort to avoid being hit.

"Cease fire! Cease fire! Cease fire!" the SWAT commander roared from the group's center.

Slowly, the rate of fire from the surrounded police officers relented.

As the echo from the last fired round petered out, the hum of the drones became the new dominant sound.

As a weapon, drones had come into their own during the Russo-Ukraine conflict. During the four years of that terrible war, both sides had purchased or built hundreds of thousands of drone units and used them for everything from reconnaissance to undertaking assassination missions in places as far away as Moscow.

With the arrival of near-AI and advancements in battery performance, drones had become smarter, more dangerous, and as quiet as the laws of physics would allow.

In effect, in the past ten years, the special effects of the movies he had acted in had become the living nightmare Hollywood had been warning people about for generations.

"Put me down," Sanchez said to the state trooper still carrying him.

When it was clear the officer wasn't going to follow his direction, Sanchez snapped, "Put me down, son. And that's a goddamned order."

It was only after the state trooper got a nod from Schafer that the big man gently set Sanchez on his feet. For a second, the police officer hovered over him to make sure he would be able to stand.

"I'm good," Sanchez said, loud enough to be heard over the hum of the countless flying machines.

He took a step in the direction of Schafer and the SWAT commander, but before he was halfway there, a deep voice that sounded highborn English boomed from all directions, "Governor Sanchez!"

Sanchez pulled up his stride and turned to face the wall of drones directly between the protection detail and the doors they had been trying to reach. Yelling, he said, "To whom am I speaking?"

"It does not matter who I am. The only thing that matters is the life of your people. They do not have to die, Governor. Too many honorable people have died today."

After a long pause, the voice continued, "You must now realize you cannot escape. Step away from your protectors and I promise they will live. Stay with them, and I will kill them. Every last one. That too is a promise. You have sixty seconds."

"But –"

The voice boomed louder than before, cutting him off. "There are no buts. No negotiations. You have fifty-five seconds, Governor."

Sanchez closed his eyes and within two seconds made his decision.

He took a single step in the direction of the drones, but before he could take his second, he felt a hand firmly grab at his good shoulder. Turning his head in that direction, Sanchez wasn't surprised to see Schafer.

"Where the hell do you think you're going?" the Secret Service man said.

"There's no time for this, Jeff. Whoever this bastard is, he's right. Too many people have died."

"You're not going anywhere," Schafer said. "Everyone of these guys knows what they signed up for, including me. We can do this. TacNet is back up and they're telling me this is all of them. We can hold."

"It's not your decision, Jeff, and I know bad odds when I see them." As Sanchez delivered his reply, he gritted his teeth, raised his good arm, and placed his hand atop Schafer's. He gave it a gentle squeeze, lifted it off of his person, and began to move forward.

Just as he passed the inner ring of California State Troopers, his peripheral vision caught the rush of motion to his extreme left.

He stopped and half turned his body where he had caught the movement.

In the darkened area behind the stage, just beyond the wall of drones in the area of the hall, were something like three dozen LAPD officers, who, except for a single officer at their center, were carrying a semiautomatic rifle or shotgun.

At perhaps seventy meters apart, Sanchez's eyes met the sole officer holding a handgun. He was Black, a touch overweight, and looked to be in his mid-forties. On his face was a look of determination. They did not need to speak for Sanchez to glean what the officer's intentions were.

As a final group of officers joined this new firing line, Sanchez realized that every camera on the hundreds of drones surrounding him and what remained of his protection detail was focused on him and him alone.

Always the focus of the camera, Sanchez thought. Even in this state of chaos and death, people wouldn't let him not be a movie star.

The voice boomed again, filling the cavernous space. "You have ten seconds, Governor. Step away from your officers in that time, or every single one of them dies. There will be no extensions."

On hearing the final ultimatum, Sanchez slowly turned back in the direction he had been looking when he'd first heard the drones' overlord speak.

As his eyes passed over Schafer and the SWAT commander, he could see they were aware of the new officers. No doubt, they too had seen the same look of determination Sanchez had seen on the face of their leader.

Amongst the wall of drones, Sanchez set his eyes on one of the larger machines and as though he was on a sound stage about to deliver a line he knew was going to be a hit with the audience, he raised his one good arm into the air, pointed, and with his best stage voice said, "Ladies and gentlemen of the LAPD and California State Police, give these bastards hell!"

Chapter 22

Anaheim Convention Center

The moment Sanchez delivered his line, Schafer and the SWAT commander simultaneously yelled, "Open fire!"

On giving the order, a storm of gunfire erupted from the circle that surrounded him.

For the first few seconds, Sanchez watched as the closest drones began to fall from the air. But for every one that fell, it seemed two or three more took its place.

To his right, there was a sharp crack and a flash of light.

His eyes darted in that direction and saw a pair of SWAT officers lying on the ground. A grapefruit-sized drone tried to fly into the gap, but it was met by the assault rifles from a pair of state troopers who quickly brought the unit down.

Moving forward, one of those same cops moved up to the position of the destroyed SWAT officers and filled in the breach.

Sanchez felt a hand grab his good shoulder. Turning from the action, he saw that it was Schafer and the cop who had been carrying him moments before.

Over the storm of noise, Schafer pointed to the newly arrived group of LAPD officers. "We're going to try to link up with them. Stay close to us."

Sanchez only nodded and stepped between the two men.

As one, his protection detail and the SWAT officers began to move past the right end of the stage in the direction of the line of cops, each of whom was firing a weapon.

Sanchez heard someone scream, "Take the big ones! Take the big ones, now!"

Ahead of him, he saw a pair of state troopers track a drone that appeared to be a touch larger than a basketball. The unit was gliding along the ceiling of the structure in what looked to be an effort to avoid detection.

Without warning, it stopped and began to drop.

At a range of what might have been twenty meters, the two troopers tracking the unit opened up on full auto to unleash a chain of lead at the descending machine.

One-third of the way to the floor of the convention hall, a round tagged the drone, sending it into a wobble.

It was then that the drone began to free fall. At the top of his lungs, Schafer screamed, "Take cover!"

Sanchez did not see whether the drone exploded in the air or when it made contact with the ground because both the state trooper and Schafer flung themselves on top of him.

Contained within the confines of Hall C, the sound was deafening. On the ground and overlapped by his two protectors, Sanchez's ears rang while his broken shoulder surged with jolts of cataclysmic pain.

But before he knew it, he was back on his feet, as were half of his protection detail and most of the SWAT officers.

Schafer's hand knifed in the direction of the waiting LAPD officers. He roared, "Keep moving!"

From the line of officers that were waiting for them, many were on the ground and out of the fight, but most remained standing and were firing their weapons with a cool fury. An eye for visuals that would resonate with audiences, Sanchez recognized the LAPD cops for what they were – a badass posse that was standing firm in the face of an inhuman and relentless enemy.

As he staggered forward with what was left of his protectors, for the first time, he noticed a golf cart near the oversized set of doors the LAPD officers must have emerged from.

A dozen ragged steps later, they made it to the firing line of uniformed cops. As they passed through them, the officer Sanchez had locked eyes with earlier fell in beside Schafer and yelled, "Get him to the golf cart. I know this place pretty well. I'll get us out of here."

Schafer only nodded. Turning to the big officer who had been at Sanchez's side through the whole ordeal, Schafer said, "Grab him and put him in the front seat. Now! Move!"

Before Sanchez could utter any kind of protest, the thick state trooper scooped up his frame and started to run in the direction of the cart.

Reaching their ride, as gently as he could, the trooper slid him into position. Beside him, the Black officer practically flew into the driver's seat and slammed into Sanchez, forcing him to issue a pained yelp.

"Sorry!" the cop said.

With officers still firing their weapons behind them, Schafer jumped into the back rear-facing seat along with the SWAT commander.

A pair of men from the protection detail also perched themselves on the sides of the main seating area. While one of their hands grabbed a handhold on the roof of the cart, in their other hand, they each held their weapon, their barrels smoking.

Without waiting for an order, the LAPD officer hit the pedal of the golf cart, scooting it forward. In seconds, the vehicle was racing at its top speed and was past the doors and into what looked like a service corridor.

As their getaway driver negotiated a corner, he yelled over his shoulder, "Are we being followed?"

"A few have made it through. They're coming," replied Schafer.

"It's okay. I can lose them. Everyone, hold on tight!"

With his good hand, Sanchez reached forward and grasped the crash handle in front of him and not a second too soon.

Without warning, the driver took a hard left down a short corridor and smashed his way through a pair of swinging doors into another tunnel, which had much less room due to stacks of supplies along the right side.

"Hang tight!" the cop roared.

He took a hard right and stopped in front of a large pair of doors that had standard crash bars, allowing them to be opened. Without asking, one of the two state troopers leaped from the side of the golf cart, raced forward and pushed one of the doors open.

Carefully, the cop navigated the vehicle through the doorway, which put them into one of the convention center's massive halls. It was empty but for the echoing gunfire.

As Sanchez heard the door close behind them, he managed to get a peek at the officer's name tag on his chest rig. It read "Jones." Letting go of the cart's crash handle, he offered his hand to the policeman, who was watching the state trooper return.

It was when the trooper got back onto the cart that Jones noticed Sanchez's proffered hand. Seeing the gesture, the officer's hand shot forward.

Before Sanchez could begin to offer a word of introduction, Jones spoke. "Great to meet you, Governor. Love your movies. Shaft No. 7 is my fav, bar none. You were robbed of an Oscar for it. A goddamned travesty if you ask me."

Before Sanchez could offer any type of reply, Jones raised his voice and said, "Okay, listen up, everybody. We're going back on the concourse, and we're going to the far end of the facility, where I've got detectives and half a dozen unmarked cars waiting for us. As of one minute ago, there were no drones on the concourse, so we're going that way and we're not stopping for anything. Everyone give me a 'hell yeah' if you understand."

In unison, everyone on the cart gave a boisterous confirmation.

"Good, then let's get the hell outta of Dodge."

With that, Jones's foot hit the accelerator, shooting the cart forward in the direction of the doors that would open out to the concourse, which, if all went as planned, would result in Sanchez surviving a day he shouldn't have survived.

As they approached the doors, and as the same state trooper rushed forward to prop the entrance open, Sanchez quickly thought of his wife and family. When he saw their faces later today, he knew his love for them would go supernova.

They were his everything. He had taken on the governorship because he believed that by keeping California out of World War III, he could keep his family safe.

When it came down to it, this was the primary and entirely selfish reason he'd rebuffed Anders-Maxwell and the admirals who would come to see him twice a week, repeating all the reasons California and its adopted navy should join the war.

Just thirty minutes ago, he was fully convinced that if California stayed out of the world's problems, the world would let California and his family be.

Perhaps, if he'd delivered his speech proclaiming his administration would stay out of the war a week earlier, the people who did this would have backed off.

Perhaps, if he hadn't met with Anders-Maxwell, they wouldn't have had a reason to suspect California would throw in with the Western Alliance.

Or perhaps all of his equivocations and excuses for avoiding the war had been a signal of weakness, and today had been a message to the other weakling states of the world: stay in your own lane or else.

Or perhaps, or perhaps, or perhaps, the voice inside Sanchez's head screamed.

It did not matter what the 'perhaps' was now. Whoever had tried to kill him had wanted to take him from his family. He had worked assiduously to try and convince people he and California were not a threat. That he and his state did not want war.

But war had come all the same, and in coming, so had a revelation. It was the same revelation that had struck the British in 1939 and the United States in late 1941. Sometimes to save the people you love, you have to do bad things to bad people.

Years ago, he had discreetly purchased a compound in the far northeast of the state where, if things went pear-shaped in the south, he and those closest to him would have a place to go.

By this time tomorrow, his family would be there. But he would not join them. He would not even acknowledge they'd left. He would stay in the south and do what needed to be done.

Over his career, time after time, in his movies, he'd dealt with evil men and had come out on top. In life, he had always been a winner. And today, despite incredible odds, it looked like he was going to come out on top yet again.

With the door open, the other state trooper, Schafer, and the SWAT commander stalked into the concourse with their weapons raised. Seeing it was clear, Schafer gestured to Jones to drive the cart forward.

Gingerly, the LAPD cop edged their ride into the glassed, wide-open space.

Looking up and down the concourse, Sanchez saw scores of dead bodies and the wounded being comforted by other civilians or being treated by first responders.

Not ten feet away, an elderly man was holding an old woman in his arms. She was unmoving, and his shirt was covered in drying blood. When their eyes connected, the man's pain transcended time and space and filled Sanchez with a terrible grief.

His gaze was forced to leave the old man as Jones started to drive the cart in the direction of Sanchez's still-smoking motorcade.

With Schafer and the rest of the cops back on the cart, they raced past the destroyed exit and more bodies and eventually came to the end of the convention center's main thoroughfare. There, they found a pair of plainclothes LAPD officers with shotguns holding open yet another set of doors.

Slowly, Jones navigated into another hallway, and then, after a few more twists and turns, he stopped in front of a nondescript set of double doors with another pair of shotgun-wielding plainclothes cops.

Jones gestured to the doors and said, "Through those doors, Governor, is every detective from the closest three precincts. Quietly, they'll take you to wherever you want to go."

Sanchez looked back at Schafer and the former Secret Service agent said, "There's a heliport an hour south of here. We'll have the Navy send a chopper from San Diego and then we'll get you to Coronado. It won't get any safer than that. At least not until we figure out what happened today."

Nodding his head, Sanchez said, "Make it happen, Jeff."

Turning his gaze back to Jones, Sanchez reached out and shook the officer's hand. "You did great today, Jones. Tell your people they did great too. All of you are heroes. We'll be seeing each other again soon enough."

With that, Sanchez moved to get out of his seat. Standing on his own, the two remaining state troopers from his protection detail, Schafer and the SWAT commander, surrounded him.

His shoulder still on fire, he walked forward through the doors and saw the dozen or so unmarked police cars and the determined faces of the men and women who would get him to where he needed to be.

He was going to get out of here. That was now clear. Thinking of his revelation from moments before, he called out to Schafer. "Would it surprise you, Jeff, if I told you my opinion on the war changed all of a sudden?

Looking over his shoulder, Schafer looked at Sanchez and said, "And what is your opinion now, Governor."

"We're going to war, Jeff. California and the US Navy – we're going to war."

PART TWO

Chapter 23

Gatineau Park, Lake Harrington, Northwest of Ottawa

—

As Merielle looked down the hallway in the direction of the bedroom, she struggled to keep the P320 Sig Sauer raised. She could feel her heart pounding in her chest as though she were on the last kilometer of a marathon.

She knew what lay at the end of the hallway. She had seen it all before. But she was compelled. She took one step forward and then another. Inside her brain, she released a mental shriek, telling herself she had to move faster. But no matter how fast she pumped her legs, the door ahead did not get closer.

"Merielle, please!" a pained voice cried out loudly. "Help me. I need your help!"

"I'm coming!" she screamed.

She lowered her pistol and forced herself to run faster.

Then, without warning, she was in the room. Her eyes widened as she realized where she was.

It was the master bedroom of the Prime Minister's residence at 24 Sussex, and she was looking at the bed, but there was no one there.

Wildly, her eyes moved to the rest of the room. At the opposite end of the space was a seating area with two regal-looking wing-backed chairs and an intricately carved coffee table.

In each of the chairs was a man she recognized.

Slouched in the left seat was Bob MacDonald, her mentor and the man who had been Canada's prime minister before Merielle.

His skin was an unnatural grey, and his eyes were yellowed and sickly-looking.

As Merielle took in the man, the corpse raised its finger and pointed it at her accusingly.

When it spoke, the voice hit Merielle like a slap to the face. In life, Bob MacDonald's voice had been like the sound of tearing paper — rough and emotionless. But the voice that struck her now was equal parts mewling and insufferable. "My wife. My wife. You killed us, Merielle. You killed us."

The putrefying thing tried to push itself out of its seat, but after a brief straining effort, the body resumed its defeated and slouching posture.

She turned her eyes to the other chair. Asher Lastra had been the lead of her RCMP protection detail and, for several months, had been her lover.

He had been so strong and confident. A rarity in the shallow pond of single, older men in the dating scene that was Ottawa.

And while most women might not think so, she had found him to be beautiful. It had been the combination of his well-muscled chest and the gemstone-light brown eyes that dazzled in the low light of the few safe places they could make love.

Staring at her, he looked the complete opposite of the despoiled corpse that was his to his left. She smiled at him and said, "Asher, my love."

He smiled at her, raised his hand into the air, and beckoned her forward.

An intense warmth ignited inside of Merielle's chest. She took one step forward, but before she could take a second, the image that was Lastra opened its lips.

As they parted, blood began to gush forward, streaming onto the fitted white t-shirt he was wearing.

Stopping in her tracks, both of Merielle's hands came to her mouth as she took in the horror of the bright red liquid vomiting from her former lover's mouth.

"No!" she howled.

The voice of Bob MacDonald found her ears again. This time it boomed. "You did this, Merielle! You did this, you incompetent bitch. How many more will you let die? Hundreds? Thousands? Millions even?"

Merielle turned to face the zombie. Somehow her pistol was back in her right hand. Taking the weapon into both hands, she aimed the weapon at MacDonald's center mass and screamed, "You're dead! You're fucking dead!"

The ghoul's lips slowly turned upward so that the former prime minister was wearing a hellish smile. Peeling back his lips to reveal blood-soaked teeth, he said, "Indeed, we are the dead. We died to make you, Merielle. Never forget that. Ours was a sacrifice of blood. A sacrifice to create what you must become, child."

Tears began to well up in Merielle's eyes. "I can't. It is too much. It is all too much. I don't want any of this."

The nasty smile that had been on the former prime minister's face disappeared and before Merielle's eyes, the walking corpse transmuted into a hale version of her political father figure.

Quietly, Merielle uttered, "Please stop this. I can't do this anymore. Why are you doing this to me?"

She caught movement to the ghost's right. A bloodless version of Lastra stepped in beside the older man. His brown eyes drank in all of Merielle's body.

His voice clear and strong, MacDonald intoned, "God creates angels for a reason. Among the living walk demons. Stay the course, Merielle. Be the angel. Like Gabrielle, you must be strong. Strength will bring victory, my child."

"STOP!" Merielle shrieked. "I'm scared. I'm alone. I want this to be over. Do you hear me? I am no angel, and there are no demons. This is just a dream!"

As she had done every time before, Merielle lifted her gun and shifted her aim so it landed on the forehead of the former prime minister. Without word or warning, she pulled the trigger.

As though they were on an earthly plane, the back of the older man's head exploded outward just as his body began to fall to the floor.

Merielle turned the weapon on Lastra. Both of the spectre's hands came up, his palms out, his eyes pleading. Her voice growling, she said, "I am no angel. Angels don't do the things I have done."

When she pulled the trigger, Merielle didn't see the destruction of her former beau. Instead, her eyes ripped open to find herself looking up into the face of a forty-something-year-old woman.

The woman was shaking her shoulder gently. "It's time to get up Madame Prime Minister. He's here. I've put him in the sunroom as you asked."

As she blinked her eyes, trying to get them to focus, Merielle said, "How long was I asleep?"

"At least two hours. That's when I first checked in on you and found you dozing."

"Jesus, sleeping at my desk. Don't let the press get a hold of that fact. On top of all the other bullshit they write, the last thing I need is a headline, 'PM, caught sleeping on the job.'"

"It's 2 am, Merielle. Your first meeting yesterday started at 7 am. Yes, the press is soulless, but I suspect even they might give you a pass for nodding off after an eighteen-hour work day."

Merielle pushed her chair back and slowly got to her feet. Tell him I'll be there in five. I just need to freshen up a touch."

Her personal secretary nodded her head and, in a kind voice, said, "Of course. When you arrive, I'll have coffee ready for you."

Merielle's gaze hardened, "I thought you said all staff would be sent home?"

"They were sent home as directed, Madame Prime Minister. Six hours ago. I, your personal secretary who speaks five languages, with my twenty-five years of experience in Canada's foreign service, will prepare your coffee. I believe your guest takes tea."

Merielle's hard look turned into a sheepish one. "Sorry, Shawna. Of course, you sent everyone home as I asked. I'm just a bit frazzled, is all. I had that same bloody dream."

The other woman gave Merielle a concerned look. "Are you feeling okay? I can send him away and reschedule."

Quickly, Merielle said, "No, I have to take this meeting. I can't delay it any longer. With a bit of coffee, I'll be right as rain. Tell him I'll be there in five."

***

Refreshed, Merielle walked to the sunroom on the east side of the Prime Minister's Herrington Lake residence. For almost half of his time as PM, Trudeau and his brood had lived in this out-of-the-way summer home because of the dilapidated state of the Prime Minister's primary residence at 24 Sussex before its massive renovation six years ago.

Nestled on the shores of an oh-so-Canadian lake deep in the middle of the Gatineau Hills northeast of Canada's capital, outside of Trudeau's extended residency, the cottage had only ever been used sporadically by other Canadian leaders.

In light of the failed attack on the California Governor, Merielle did not have any difficulties convincing her people that working for a week or two outside of Ottawa wasn't a bad idea.

While the Herrington Lake residence was isolated since the French attack on Merielle in Montreal two months earlier, the RCMP's Protection Division had grudgingly accepted help from CANSOFCOM, and now, several more robust layers of electronic, cyber, and other undisclosed physical protection elements were a part of her everyday security package.

If someone wanted to attack her now, Merielle had been assured her people would see it coming and that the response from the security people surrounding her would be devastating.

Having this knowledge, she confidently strode into the sunroom where her single guest had been waiting for her.

Entering the room, Merielle noted the blinds for the space had been drawn. That they had been lowered for this early hour and that a steaming cup of coffee was waiting for her again reminded her that she had scored big in landing her new personal secretary.

Shawna knew nothing about the man sitting in the room waiting for her but had been perceptive enough to know that Merielle wouldn't want anyone from her security team to see who she was meeting with at this late hour.

She didn't go for her coffee, nor did she acknowledge her guest. Instead, without a word, she turned her back on the man and closed the double French doors that served as the only entrance to the room.

Hearing the locks of the doors click into place, she turned and let her eyes take in the face of Colonel Aziz.

If the man was tired, he didn't show it. He was alert as ever.

As their eyes met, he gently placed the cup of tea he'd been sipping on the table in front of him and said, "Normally, I would stand when the prime minister of my country enters the room, but I know you loath that kind of bullshit. I presume that remains the case?"

"It's still the case. Good to see you again in the flesh, Mustapha."

"We'll see if you feel that way in a few minutes, Madame Prime Minister. I applaud your courage in agreeing to meet me in person. I wasn't sure you'd take the meeting in this format."

"Courage or stupidity, Colonel. Throughout my life, I've more or less demonstrated equal parts of each trait. This morning, I've convinced myself it's courage that's winning the day."

A smile appeared on the large man's face. "For both our sakes, let's hope it is the former."

Reaching the table, Merielle pulled back her chair, sat, and then took up the coffee. Putting it to her lips, the French roast tasted like a small miracle. She was up to six cups a day, but it had been at least five hours since her last drink of the stuff. With her tastebuds recharged, she allowed herself a second wonderful sip before re-engaging in the difficult conversation that was to come.

As she lowered the cup back to the table's surface, Aziz spoke. "You are aware of the pressure being put on our operations in BC?"

"Yes," Merielle said.

"Then you know you have put me and the people who've agreed to work for me... no, let me correct that. The people that have agreed to work for *us* – you've put us in a very difficult position, Madame Prime Minister."

"I am aware of that, Colonel."

"I'm glad to hear you say that because, until this moment, I wasn't sure you appreciated that fact."

Aziz leaned forward in his chair, placed both his elbows on the table, and locked his hands together. In the silence of the room, a single knuckle within the man's huge hands cracked, sounding like a small caliber pistol. His voice a low rumble, he said, "Let me remind you that you and I are linked together, and intimately so. On a dark day only two months ago, you sat me down and told me you were prepared to do anything to keep this country safe. I have kept my end of the bargain, and what has been done cannot be undone."

Merielle raised her chin slightly and said, "I understand our agreement, and nothing has changed."

Aziz nodded in agreement with her statement and said calmly, "Then why have you allowed Larocque to run amok? Are you aware that he's trying to poach dozens of operators from CANSOFCOM?"

Merielle's response to the question was instantaneous, "I am. I cajoled Cabinet to approve it."

"Why!" As he barked the word, Aziz's right hand turned into a fist, and like a meteor striking the earth, it crashed into the table. On hitting the polished surface, the tea he'd been drinking moments before leaped into the air, fell, and made a jarring sound.

Merielle did not flinch at the man's voice, the sudden movement of Aziz's descending fist, or the crashing of the China. Instead, her eyes narrowed, and she stared into the man's dark brown eyes.

"Why, Merielle?" This time, Aziz's voice was normal. "Help me understand your thinking so that I can go back to my people and assure them you have a plan that doesn't see nearly two hundred patriotic Canadians spend the rest of their lives in jail, if not worse. Sooner or later, you won't be prime minister, and when this war is over, people will come to understand what we have done, and they will come for us.

"You know the Laurentian Elite, Madame Prime Minister. You know they are the real power of this country. You know they loathe you. What they did to the truckers will be quaint compared to what they will do to us. They will be relentless should they come back into power and understand what we've done. That is, of course, unless you have a plan?"

Aziz paused and slowly lowered both of his huge hands to the surface of the table and rested them palms down. "I do not have to share it with my people, but I have to assure myself there is some method to the madness of placing Larocque in charge of the country's intelligence service and then giving him the support and tools he needs to cut us down before we've accomplished the task you've given to us."

Aziz, twice a member of JTF-2, Canada's only Tier 1 special forces unit, and a man who had killed in cold blood because that's what needed to be done to keep the country safe, stared at Merielle's face with pleading eyes.

Annunciating each word, the leader of the White Unit said, "Merielle, what is your plan?"

While accepting his stare, Merielle again raised her coffee to her lips, ingested a double dose of the liquid, and in an entirely un-lady-like fashion, issued a loud gulp as she forced the hot substance down her throat.

Indeed, Merielle did have a plan. But as she contemplated Aziz's state, she once again reminded herself she was no master strategist.

Until only a few years earlier, she was a cop. A good one to be sure, but at no point in her policing career had she ever been tapped to look years into the future on any given issue and come up with a grand plan to fix whatever challenge the RCMP brass had wanted fixed.

To the contrary, her strength as a cop and as a politician had been and still was solving the problems of everyday life. Across her whole life, Merielle had thrown herself into the hugely satisfying challenge of solving short-term problems.

You solved one problem and then moved on to the next, and over the course of a year, five or ten, you had a body of work that told the higher-ups you were a person who got shit done.

But since becoming Canada's prime minister she had been forced to look at the big picture.

In the weeks following her survival of the Montreal assassination attempt and the vicious Chinese attacks on Canada's Navy and the CANZUK politicians in Sydney, Merielle had come to the stark realization that the world would not be returning to the civilized state it had been in the years following WWII through to America's second civil war.

No, even if the Americans reconcile and CANZUK somehow manages to contain the Chinese in the Pacific, she was convinced the world would be a very different and dangerous place for many years to come. Perhaps for a generation or more.

The absence of American hegemony meant all bets were off. China and Russia's belligerence would persist. France's machinations would only continue to grow. The nightmare of nuclear weapons had become a reality. Some thirteen million Americans had been killed in their civil war. Perhaps millions more would die before it was all said and done. And these were only the issues consuming Canada and CANZUK. In her estimation and the smart people she talked to about such things, the world would remain a wild and dangerous place for years to come.

It was this environment that had infiltrated Merielle's dreams and honed her strategic thinking. In the midst of this perilous world, she was determined not to let Canada become soft again.

She refused to let her country endure the same fate as the devastated Ukrainians, or suffer like the Baltics and Dutch were now suffering due to their larger, more ruthless neighbors.

No, Merielle Martel most certainly had a plan to make Canada hard enough to withstand what the world would be for the next decade, and the White Unit and its current mission were a critical element of the political transformation she was determined to facilitate.

Merielle's eyes flashed down to her watch. Aziz would have to be on his way by no later than 0400 hours.

The man had a sharp mind and a strong grasp on the country's power structures. Outside of his willingness to do hard things, it was this intellect and knowledge that had made him the obvious choice to lead the organization that was going to help her reshape the country she loved so much.

When her eyes reacquired Aziz's face, she said, "I do have a plan, Colonel. And it is a plan that requires more than the White Unit can provide.

"It is a plan that requires the state itself to do things differently. Very differently. At least for several years, and I'm convinced Jackson Larocque and women and men like him will come to see this vision the way we do. In months or, if necessary, in weeks, my plan will change the face of politics in this country. It is risky, but as I see it, it is better than the alternative of doing nothing and letting those we both despise re-claim power."

"Good. Then you have a plan. I'm all ears, Madame Prime Minister. Tell me more," the special forces officer said.

Merielle reached into the inner pocket of her suit jacket and withdrew a folded piece of paper. Slowly, she put it on the table on the other side of her coffee.

"On paper. How quaint," Aziz said.

As a genuine smile rose to her lips, Merielle reached forward and launched the document across the polished surface.

Once the paper stopped its glide, Aziz reached forward and took up the document. Unfolding it, he began to read.

Within the first thirty seconds, he had begun to nod. At the one-minute mark, he issued what Merielle thought was a scoff. At just over two minutes, the man removed his eyes from the document and directed them toward Merielle.

"Your thoughts?" she asked.

"Who else has seen this?"

"Only you."

"Good. I don't have to tell you this, but I will anyway. If you have this saved anywhere, destroy it."

Merielle's eyes narrowed. "It is not saved anywhere. I'm not an idiot. Answer my question."

Aziz's lips scrunched to the left of his mouth as his brain worked to formulate a reply. Finally, he said, "It lacks detail in key places, but under the circumstances, I can see why. In this case, less is more. It's also brazen, but most certainly, that's what the moment calls for. But most important, I think it can work. Luck will have to factor in at some point, but that would be the case with anything this complex."

He paused for a moment and moved his eyes back to the document to re-read something. Seconds later, they flashed upward and reconnected with Merielle.

As their eyes locked, Merielle said, "You said you think it can work. Does that mean you're willing to be part of it? You and your people?"

As she waited for an answer, images from her recurring nightmare stormed into her mind's eye. As she fought to tamp down the terrible scene of recrimination, she assured herself that the words written on the paper that Aziz now held in his hand were not a response to her own traumas and loss.

What was on the paper was so much bigger than her. Tens of thousands of lives were at stake. But more than that, the independence and the collective freedom of the country she loved were on a knife's edge. Merielle had to push Canada's institutions in a direction that would allow the country to survive what was to come.

Now was not the time to bend a knee to the rules, laws, and elites that nearly ruined Canada a decade ago. The United States had been destroyed by these same forces. She would not let the same happen to her country, not when Canada was surrounded by ravenous and cruel wolves. She would do the hard things that needed to be done. She, too, would be cruel.

Her eyes narrowed and she re-asked her question of the dangerous man sitting across from her. This time when the words came out of her mouth, there was an edge to them. "Are you in, Colonel, or do I need to find someone else to help me save our country?"

Aziz flexed his jaw and returned Merielle's stare. "I'm in Madame Prime Minister. I was always in, but until I saw this document, I wasn't sure about you. I see now that you're prepared to do what it will take. We're with you, Merielle. All of us. Every step of the way."

Chapter 24

Bến Phà Mỹ Hiệp, Western bank of the Mekong Delta, 100 km west of Ho Chi Minh City, Vietnam

—

In the distance, Colonel Simpson Kelly of the 2nd Cavalry Regiment of the Australian Army's 3rd Brigade of the 1st Australian Division listened to deep echoing booms of the Chinese 75th Army Group and the Vietnamese 4th Army Corps exchanging titanic amounts of artillery fire.

After three weeks of intense and heroic fighting, the Vietnamese had finally found their mettle and managed to slow the People's Liberation Army's advance down the length of their country, starting from the east side of Ho Chi Minh City.

The Chinese hordes that had pushed across the border following a series of tactical nuclear strikes had been unstoppable until they had reached the dense urban sprawl of Vietnam's largest city.

Once called Saigon, the city had been renamed after the Vietnam War to honor the man who had been the ideological and strategic leader of Vietnam's fight against the Western imperialists until he died in 1969.

A vibrant metropolis of nine million souls, Ho Chi Minh City, had served as an eleven-day meat grinder for the Chinese 74th Army Group. So much so, that it had needed to be relieved by the 75th Army on the second-to-last day of the fighting to take the city.

By all accounts, the struggle had been the second coming of Stalingrad, only with terrible bouts of heat and humidity replacing Russia's brutal cold.

In all, it had been estimated the Chinese suffered one hundred and fifty thousand casualties in trying to take the city. In eleven short days, the PLA had lost twenty times the number of soldiers they had lost in six months of fighting to retake Taiwan.

Critically, in fighting as doggedly as they had, the generals commanding Vietnam's defense had not only blunted the Chinese advance but also given CANZUK and its growing list of allies time to ready themselves to get into the fight.

By day seven of the Battle of Ho Chi Minh City, the entirety of the Australian Army's 3rd Brigade, the 11th Infantry Division of the Royal Thai Army, and two mechanized battle groups from the New Zealand Army had crossed into the southernmost military district of Vietnam to backstop the formidable line of defense the Vietnamese had built up along the east side of the Mekong Delta.

During this same period of fighting on the ground, the Royal Australian Air Force, along with F-35s of the Royal Navy's *Queen Elizabeth*, had been joined by no less than three fighter squadrons from the Japanese Self-Defense Force, including forty Block 4 F-35s.

Flying out of hastily constructed airfields cut into the jungles along the Thai-Cambodian border, upwards of one hundred CANZUK and Japanese fighters had been fighting for air supremacy with twice as many high-end fighters from the PLA Air Force for the past five days.

The CANZUK experience of battling the J-31 in the skies of North America months ago had made a difference in these clashes, but the real difference-maker in the air had come from underneath the Yellow Sea.

The arrival of what had been reported as twelve US Navy fast-attack nuclear submarines had been the ultimate game-changer.

Combined with the remaining nuclear subs operated by Australia, the Royal Navy, and a number of conventional boats being operated by Japan and Canada, China's Navy had suffered catastrophic losses in the two short weeks since Governor Ricky Sanchez had ordered the US Navy into the Pacific war.

Though China had put a large number of diesel and nuclear submarines out to sea to control its territorial waters, the less technologically advanced Chinese submarine force had been no match for the undersea full-court press the Americans had unleashed.

Using a highly advanced Underwater Wireless Optical Communication system that only the Virginia-class sub possessed, the US Navy's submarines were able to communicate with each other in real-time over distances of a few hundred kilometers.

This near-magical advantage meant that whatever number of US subs were operating in the Yellow Sea could easily share information about their enemy and, when the moment called for it, act in unison against any given target.

In being able to communicate as though they were operating underwater radios, the US Navy had re-instituted some of the tactics German U-boats had used to devastating effect during the early parts of WWII.

The result was that wolfpacks of submarines were once again prowling the world's oceans.

The first victims had been China's submarine force. Overmatched by teams of Virginia-class subs, the Chinese had been forced to withdraw what remained of their nuclear and diesel platforms within a week of the Americans' arrival.

But it was in the second week of fighting that the war underneath the waves began to impact the fighting in the air and on the ground.

Together, the US, Japan, and CANZUK submarines began to prioritize attacking those Chinese vessels equipped with the highly effective HHQ-9 missile defense system.

With a range of up to 300 kilometers, ships with the HHQ-9 had made the sky above the whole of Vietnam a one-sided shooting gallery for Australian and British pilots during the first two weeks of the war. So much so that they had to stop flying all but the most critical missions over the country.

But as the allied submarines off the coast began to whittle down China's missile frigates and destroyers, and as Vietnamese special forces supported by thousands of citizen soldiers became proficient at destroying whatever SAM batteries the Chinese Army brought across the border, the air above southern Vietnam became increasingly hospitable.

The American subs had been so devastating that at the mid-way point of the struggle for Ho Chi Minh City, CANZUK's admirals had agreed to send a flotilla of Type-26 frigates to the southern coast of Vietnam to replicate the surface-to-air coverage the Chinese had enjoyed for the first two weeks of the war.

Armed with the latest version of the Aegis Combat System and air defense missiles that could reach out to tag a Chinese fighter at two hundred klicks, no less than eight Type-26 frigates from

Australia, the UK, and Canada were prowling off the southern tip of Vietnam working hand in glove with CANZUK and Japanese fighter pilots to turn the tables on the PLA's Air Force.

As though to emphasize this dramatic turn of events, a pair of RAAF F-18 Super Hornets roared over Kelly's position low in the sky, their wings heavy with eight Australian-made BLU-111 500-lb GPS-guided bombs. It was only in the past three days that CANZUK fighters had begun to undertake close-in air support missions for the Vietnamese Army.

As it was, Kelly had been assured a full squadron of F-35s from the RAAF's No. 75 Squadron would be available to him and the leading elements of 3rd Brigade as they moved to flank and then bite into the rear echelons of the 75th Army Group's 31st Heavy Combined Arms Brigade.

Only forty-eight hours earlier, the Chinese army would have seen the whole of his 2nd Cavalry Regiment coming, but with the change in the skies above southern Vietnam, CANZUK had unleashed hundreds of near-AI drone-hunting drones and had severely compromised the 75th Army's ability to anticipate 2nd Cavalry's movements.

And it wasn't just the Australians getting the jump on their enemies. At other points along the forty-kilometer-long Mekong Line, reserve armored regiments of the Vietnamese 6th Army and two armored brigades from the 11th Infantry Division of the Royal Thai Army were undertaking similar forays into what was now a degraded Chinese offensive.

The near-AI voice of Kelly's BAM came alive in his headset. "Incoming call from Osprey Seven."

"Accept call," Kelly said.

"Hammer Sunray, be advised there is a column of enemy armor advancing approximately three klicks east of your current position."

"Type of vehicles and numbers? And can I get the drone feed up on my screen?" Kelly asked, his voice sharp.

"The feed should be on your screen now, Hammer. Number of vehicles is about thirty. They're evenly split between the Type 99 MBT and various types of APCs."

Without any hesitation, Kelly said, "We'll take them, Osprey Seven. Relay fire mission to Scaffold. I want them to pound these bastards with everything they've got until I say so."

"Roger that, Hammer Sunray. Fire mission is being relayed to Scaffold. Will pass along confirmation as soon as we receive it," said the female Aussie officer helping to manage the flow of data from the half-dozen surveillance drones prowling the skies above the CANZUK ground forces and their allies.

"Good, keep me posted, Osprey Seven. Hammer Sunray out."

Without missing a beat, Kelly moved to his next task. "Open channel Hammer Group Charlie."

"Channel open," advised his BAM.

"Hammer Group, this is Hammer Sunray. On your screens, you should be seeing a feed from Osprey Seven. Using formation Delta, we will attack this force. Your primary and secondary targets will be flagged in the next minute.

"It is our turn, diggers. We've been watching the good people of Vietnam take it on the chin for three weeks. It is payback time, 2nd Cavalry. Today, we make history – we go to war. Today, we make Australia proud. Hammer Sunray out."

***

16 Field Regiment, Royal New Zealand Artillery, 161 Battery, West of Mekong Delta

---

Lt. Colonel Gus Robertson stood underneath a ten-by-ten army green pop-up tent, watching a pair of his soldiers work through targeting data being fed to his unit from an Australian Army Ghost Bat drone.

At an altitude of seven thousand feet, the Aussie-built drone had spied and tagged seventy-three percent of the formation the 2nd Cavalry Regiment was about to take on. It would have to be enough, Robertson thought.

"Targeting status?" he asked, loud enough that the two soldiers sitting in front of him could hear the question over the sound of distant artillery fire.

The captain seated to Robertson's right replied, "Data has been confirmed. Targeting has been set. The battery is ready to go on your say-so, Colonel."

Hearing the confirmation, he raised his eyes upward to canvass the eight M777s and their crews. Each stood ready, waiting for his order to unleash a fiery hell.

His one-time mentor, Major General Kate Galbraith, had fought tooth and nail for the New Zealand Army to upgrade to the M777 system.

At the time, she had rightly argued that if New Zealand wanted to make a meaningful contribution to security in the Pacific region, it would need kit and systems that could be seamlessly added to the capabilities of its allies, of which Australia was the closest.

The Aussies and Canadians operated the M777, and so should New Zealand, Galbraith had pleaded to Cabinet. She had won the argument only to unexpectedly pass on a year later in a freak car accident.

Knowing Galbraith as well as he did, Robertson knew that she would be aghast at the madness that had consumed the world, but amid this insanity, she would be supremely proud of New Zealand's big guns and the men and women who operated them.

"Captain, give the order for a salvo of sixteen rounds from each gun, every fourth round is anti-personnel. Adjust targeting data as it comes in. Repeat order."

"Colonel, sixteen rounds of sustained fire per gun. Every fourth round is AP. We adjust targeting data as it comes in."

Robertson nodded his head at the younger officer and said, "Order confirmed. Make it so, Captain."

Within seconds of the order to fire leaving Robertson's lips, the lead NCOs for each of the battery's eight 155mm howitzers began to bark orders at their respective crews.

In another minute, for the first time in over sixty years, the guns of the Royal New Zealand Artillery opened fire on an enemy on the battlefield of Vietnam.

***

"Fire!" Kelly roared the moment the reticle of his Abrams' main gun squared up on the Chinese Type 99 MBT just over six hundred meters to their front.

BOOM!

The high-explosive armor-piercing round struck the Type 99 where its turret connected with its tracked base. A bright flash forced Kelly to momentarily close his eyes. Opening them, he saw that the Chinese tank had been decapitated and that orange fire and black smoke were pouring out of the machine's chassis.

Activating the tank's internal comms system, Kelly addressed his crew. "Bell, slow advance five hundred meters. Nobre, tag anything that's made of steel. Keep your eyes peeled, mates."

He heard a pair of double clicks in his headset confirming his order.

As their tank began to move forward, Kelly's eyes were drawn into the air as a pair of RAAF AH-64E Apaches from the 1st Aviation Regiment passed over them.

The chin guns on both helicopters were unleashing a firestorm of 30mm rounds at something he couldn't see from his perch in the command seat of his tank. Whatever destruction they were sowing, he was thrilled the attack helicopters seemed to be operating with impunity.

Their assault on the Chinese heavy armor battalion had been nearly textbook.

It had started with an RAAF F-35 casting an electronic smear of energy over the area, hampering the enemy force's ability to communicate. Then came the Kiwis' artillery barrage. It had been shorter than Kelly would have liked, but what did arrive had been pinpoint and deadly.

It was at this point that the whole of Kelly's 2nd Cavalry raced forward through the half-dozen pre-determined routes their Vietnamese Army liaisons had selected to get them through the maze of rice paddies between them and their Chinese opponents.

By design, Kelly and his soldiers had unveiled themselves along a solid one-kilometer stretch of agricultural space. With overlapping fields of fire, the regiment's Abrams and Boxer IFVs quickly unloaded several salvos at the hurt and confused Chinese armour.

In the twenty-minute tilt that followed, they had lost a single tank and a trio of Boxers.

Arriving where he had instructed his driver to take them, Kelly stood higher in the commander's position and surveyed the battlefield.

Burning and shattered Chinese armor lay in every direction. Their enemy had been utterly surprised and had paid for it.

"Open channel, Hammer Group Bravo, priority Kelly-Two-Uniform."

"Channel open. All units are connected," replied the female voice of his BAM.

"This is Hammer Sunray. Brilliant work, people. All credit to each of you. Today, and for however long it takes, is payback for what these bastards did to Canberra, Sydney, and the rest of the country.

"Intel coming is suggesting the 75th Army Group is starting to implode. It turns out you're not so tough or organized when you've got five-hundred-pounders falling from the sky every five minutes.

"So we are pushing on. Check your screens. Eyes in the sky are telling us that Point Yankee could be the 75th Army's forward HQ. That is our next objective, 2nd Cavalry. It's about thirty minutes away as the crow flies.

"Word from the top is that 2nd Commando will be conducting an airborne assault on their HQ. We are going to lay our hands on a general. It is our job to interdict any reinforcements from reaching 2nd Commando once they land. Our route has already been laid out for us. If there are any questions, type them into the chat and I'll address them as we're on the move."

Kelly paused his update as the two RAAF Apaches he'd seen earlier flew overhead. The weapons stations on both helicopters were absent some of the Hellfires they'd been carrying only minutes earlier.

As the blare from the low-flying helicopters subsided, Kelly resumed his address. "We move in two minutes, people. When we're on the move, keep your eyes peeled and heads on a swivel. Osprey Group is doing its best to stay out ahead of us, but they can't see everything. The 75th might be on the ropes, but there are still ninety thousand PLA soldiers on this side of Ho Chi Minh, and we've yet to see any of those bloody Wraiths or Hyenas. Those are coming, people. Count on it, so be ready.

"Hammer Sunray out."

Chapter 25

Vancouver Island, British Columbia

―

Lai Shan's people had bought most of the materials for the rudimentary but powerful bombs from gangs operating out of Seattle.

It was the only city on the western half of the United States that had been nuked three years ago by the UCSA. And like Chicago and New York, gangs and other nefarious actors had become the predominant powers within the former metropolis.

Since Seattle's destruction, it had become the main conduit China used to smuggle people and materiel into Western Canada.

When Lai had been first instructed to assassinate the provincial leader of British Columbia weeks ago, his superiors had been advised that one or more truck bombs should be used and that humans – humans like himself – would be required to deliver the fully laden vehicle to its final destination.

That the destination would be heavily protected and would likely mean the death of several of his operatives was not a concern that registered with his masters in Beijing. They had been direct: the mission must be successful, no matter the cost.

Vietnam was the reality currently driving events in China. Thousands of his countrymen had been dying on the battlefields of that insignificant country. By comparison, the death of a half-dozen intelligence operators in Canada was inconsequential.

It was this harsh calculation that had made the arrival of the Wraiths so welcome.

It was only four days ago that he and his team had finalized a plan to deliver the truck bombs. At a minimum, the plan allowed that the two drivers of the trucks would be severely injured. Much more likely, they would be killed.

But then he'd received an encrypted message to rendezvous with a dilapidated fishing trawler on the wharf of an obscure fishing village on the far west coast of Vancouver Island.

There, he had watched in amazement as four X-8 Wraiths had silently climbed off the trawler's deck, then walked to the two waiting cube vans, where, without any help or direction, they lifted the doors to the van's cargo areas, climbed in and closed themselves in with the three thousand pounds of fertilizer each van was carrying.

"Damn, are those things scary or what?" he said aloud to the three other men that would help him drive the vans to the provincial capital two hundred kilometres to the south.

Regardless of how the war was proceeding in Southeast Asia, Lai and his team, and teams just like his in the other CANZUK nations, had a mission to accomplish. They were to exploit, cajole, and, if necessary, force the ethnic Chinese community to answer the call of their ancient homeland.

That so few of their marks in Canada had been willing to entertain China's overtures, generous or otherwise, had driven the higher-ups in the Ministry of State Security to deliver a message to every Chinese person in Canada that there were consequences for inaction.

Consequences even for the most powerful of the ethnic Chinese community.

***

Victoria, British Columbia, Government House

—

"So, how do you like the place?" said the young man through the iPad Shirley Chin-Edwards was holding on her lap.

"Oh, it's grand enough, but it's just too big. I was just saying to your father that I feel terribly guilty living in what, for all intents and purposes, is a palace, while only a few kilometers away, there are ten thousand people who live on the street. Not a day passes where your dad doesn't tell me to expropriate all that gorgeous land the university owns and plop down twenty thousand affordable units."

"It's not a bad idea, Mom. Have you had anyone look into it?"

"You are your father's son, aren't you? It's a political idea that has disaster written all over it. Don't underestimate the power of NIMBYISM, Felix. Were I even to make the suggestion, in one 24-hour spell, our polling would go from winning every riding in Vancouver to political disaster. It's just not on."

The handsome twenty-something man on the tablet's display paused. After about ten seconds of silence, Chin-Edwards, British Columbia's Premier, prompted her oldest son to speak about what was actually on his mind.

"I'm your mother, Felix. I know exactly when you want to say something you don't want to say, so let's get it out there. Let's hear it, young man?"

Her son's mouth shifted to the right of his face.

Chin-Edwards waited patiently. She recognized the tell, even if it was through video. When her son's lips released, whatever question or statement he wanted to ask would come. He was both a sweet and predictable young man.

"I know this is going to sound crazy, Mom, but I want you to hear me out. Elizabeth, Stefan, and I have talked, and we think you should resign."

The politician's eyebrows shot upward while her mouth tightened, and she said, "Were you talking to your father? Did he put you up to this?"

"Dad? No. We talked this morning, and Dad wasn't involved. This is all us. Did he tell you the same thing?"

Her face resumed its default look of serenity. "He mentioned it last night, and I'll tell you what I told him without the swearing. I'm not resigning. I don't care about all of the anti-Chinese sentiment that's out there. I may look Chinese, but I'm Canadian, and I'll be damned if I'm going to let some small-minded racists and losers chase me from the position I've worked so hard for. Not only that, but more than ever, the people of this province need to see a competent Asian woman in charge of things. We can't engage in this game of 'othering' that's taking place across this country. Now, more than ever, we need to lean into our diversity."

"Mom –."

She cut him off. "Felix, I have to confess, I'm surprised by you and your siblings. I thought..."

Outside Chin-Edwards heard a noise that sounded like a raft of fireworks going off.

"What was that?" her son said, hearing the sound through their electronic connection.

Her husband appeared from the kitchen, which was connected to the east end of the cavernous family room. He was immediately followed by a pair of plainclothes RCMP officers.

"Shirley, we have to go to the safe room," he said, his voice vibrating with concern.

"What's going on? Are those gunshots?" she said, doing her best to tamp down the fear brewing inside her body.

Before her husband could offer a response, one of the police officers interjected, "Madame Premier, as your husband just said, we have to get you to the safe room. Now, please."

When she didn't move to get off the couch, the same cop who spoke to her leaned in her direction and, without warning, grabbed her wrist and firmly pulled her to her feet.

As she rose into the air, she lost her grip on her tablet. As it collided with the floor and made a loud cracking sound, there was another cascade of sharp sounds from outside, followed by the squealing of tires.

"Mom, what's going on? Dad, are you there? What the hell is happening?" her son said urgently from his new position on the floor.

Chin-Edwards tried to pull her wrist from the cop, but the man's grip was like iron. Her eyes narrowed in on the RCMP officer. "Let me go, I need to talk to my son."

"Honey, listen to him. We have to go. I'll grab the tablet. Just get moving!" Chin-Edwards' husband said urgently.

Government House was a spectacular Tudor Revival-inspired mansion built at the turn of the 19th Century. Located at the heart of BC's provincial capital, Victoria, it was a stunning testament to Britain's colonial rule.

The size of the residence was rivalled by the grounds that surrounded it. Thirty-six acres in total, the property was a popular tourist destination when it wasn't being occupied by its regular resident, the province's Lieutenant General.

A constitutional figurehead that represented the Crown's largely symbolic role in Canadian politics, the current Lieutenant General had been moved out to allow Chin-Edwards and her substantial security detail to move in.

With the Chinese submarine attacks off the coast and suspected Chinese intelligence agents operating across the province, the consensus of the security people was that Government House was the best place for the Premier to live if she was going to insist on conducting business as usual.

Before Chin-Edwards could take her first step in the direction of the stairs that would take her and her husband toward the safe room that had been set up in the property's basement, her eyes were drawn to the four large windows facing the crescent driveway that was the only way to reach the residence.

Just after ten in the evening, it was dark outside, but dozens of lights ensured the grounds were well-lit. Through the far-left pane, she spied two moving trucks racing up the driveway.

As she watched the cube vans get closer, she felt the RCMP officer loosen his grip on her wrist only to transition into hoisting her off her feet and into a bridal carry. Though the officer wasn't a big man, he was strong, and in two strides, he was racing forward.

As she began to bounce along in the police officer's arms, something inside Chin-Edwards screamed at her not to protest the indignity of what was happening.

Leaving the family room, the RCMP officer dashed through the kitchen and then rounded a corner into an airy hallway that had stained glass windows evenly spaced along its length. At the end of the hallway was the doorway leading to the basement and the safe room.

It was just as the officer was setting her down so she could navigate the stairs on her own that the explosions from the tightly packed truck bombs detonated.

In 1995, the truck bomb that devastated the Alfred P. Murrah Federal Building in Oklahoma contained just under five thousand pounds of fertilizer.

Together, the two cargo vans, each driven by an X-8 Wraith, carried three thousand pounds of ammonium nitrate.

When they hit opposite ends of the colonial-style home, the resulting explosion unleashed the equivalent of five tons of TNT.

In a nanosecond, energy and fire consumed Government House, obliterating it and everyone inside — including British Columbia's first Chinese-Canadian premier. Utterly.

***

Global National News Studio, Ottawa

—

The news anchor, dressed in somber colors, turned in her seat toward her in-studio guest.

"Dr. Lloyd, thank you for coming in today. I've always found your analysis of national security matters to be well-informed and absent speculation."

"That's kind of you to say, Shreena. These are grave times for our country. I'm happy to try and help," said the rotund, balding academic.

"Speculation is rampant. Yesterday evening, the Premier of British Columbia, her husband, and part of her security detail were assassinated in a massive truck bombing in Victoria. This morning, only four hours ago, the RCMP released a statement that the leader of the New Democratic Party was found dead in her Ottawa apartment. Initial reports seem to suggest there was foul play.

"And only twenty minutes ago, off-screen, we watched the Prime Minister deliver a statement that the government intends to invoke the Emergencies Act, a measure, I might add, she pledged she would not take at the height of the most recent election.

"Speaking on behalf of Canadians across the country, Professor, I feel like things are spiraling out of control and in a direction Canada might regret. Help us make sense of what's going on if you would."

Lloyd, a professor from the Norman Patterson School of International Relations at Carleton University in Ottawa, steepled his fingers together in front of his chest and, with a sober look on his face, said, "In perfect honesty Shreena, the PM should have invoked the Emergency Measures Act in the hours after the first UCSA missile attacks twelve days ago. That she didn't and continued to tie the hands of our security services was a mistake, in my informed opinion."

One of the anchor's eyebrows shot into the air on hearing the academic's statement. "So you support the invocation of the Emergencies Act?"

"Entirely, Shreena, and I only regret that it wasn't brought into force earlier. It will give the RCMP, our country's other police forces, and CSIS the authority they need to begin to counter the outrageous espionage currently taking place in our country. Even now, until the Act is passed, they've been operating with one hand tied behind their back."

"But what about overreach? Or the militarization of CSIS? I recall from one of our earlier conversations you expressed concerns about the fact the Prime Minister had moved General Larocque into the Canadian Security Intelligence Service, and now we're hearing reports of a personnel purge in CSIS and that members of Canada Special Operations Command are being drafted into the organization. Isn't this all a bit concerning, Professor? Are there not examples in history where the cure might have been more deadly than the disease itself? I'm thinking of McCarthyism in the '50s or, more recently and worse, the weaponization of the FBI and CIA in the years leading up to the US civil war. Are we not heading down a similar path with these recent moves by the PM?"

As the anchorwoman finished her statement, a look of concern emerged on the academic's face. Nodding his head, he said, "I understand your concerns, but I feel compelled to remind you that in the past sixteen hours, the premier of one of our country's provinces was assassinated – most likely as an intimidation tactic by the Chinese government.

"And if that wasn't enough, the Leader of His Majesty's Loyal Opposition has been killed. Again, most likely the victim of assassination. And these actions are over and above the Chinese attacks on our navy and commercial shipping on the West Coast, never mind the brutal missile and sabotage attacks by the UCSA just two weeks ago."

Lloyd leaned forward in his seat. "You said it feels like the country is spiraling, and I agree with that assessment. But for our descent to stop, our prime minister has to get serious about our country's internal security. This notion that she wouldn't invoke the Emergencies Act because some extreme part of her political base will scream she's acting like Trudeau in 2022 is the Prime Minister giving into her worst political impulses. Canada is not facing some hokey political protest being run by amateurs. By any definition, the country is at war, and in war, difficult decisions about civil liberties need to be made."

The reporter interjected. "But isn't this a firm step in the direction of authoritarianism? Just this morning on another news panel, I heard one of my colleagues – and a perfectly moderate one, I might add – suggest on air that now might be the time to suspend Parliament until such a time that the country's safety can be assured. He said the PM and her Cabinet shouldn't have to deal with something so unimportant as being held accountable by their political opponents. These were his words. I –."

"Shreena, if I may..." Lloyd said, himself trying to interject, but the reporter rolled on.

"I want to hear your reply, Professor, but before you do, I want to remind you and our viewers that not once, not ever, did Britain's Parliament not sit during their struggle against the Nazis. The Emergencies Act, an indefinite suspension of parliament, the military leading civilian agencies, rumor and innuendo about political assassinations, and not just the most recent ones. Something dangerous is happening in Canada, Professor, and the media in this country has to do its job by calling out what we're seeing."

Lloyd cleared his throat and then said, "May I?"

"I'm sorry. Yes. Go ahead. I got carried away. It's just..."

Nodding his head gently, the academic said, "I understand. It is an emotional topic. Democracy is indeed a fragile thing, and I, too, am concerned with recent developments, but I would put to you that never in its darkest moment was Great Britain ever at serious risk of invasion by the Nazis.

"Instead of Churchill, think instead of Lebrun, the man who ran France from 1932 to 1940. This is a man who equivocated when he should have been strong. A man who proposed signing an armistice with one of history's most evil regimes so that his people would not be made to suffer unnecessarily. A man whose nation had endured nine million casualties at the hands of Germany only two decades earlier.

"I would remind you, Shreena, that France too was a democracy, but instead of making hard choices and doing hard things to maintain their government, France's freedom, along with their national dignity, was taken away from them. It did not have to be that way. France in 1939 could have chosen to be strong and –."

"But the costs, Professor?" said the journalist, cutting him off. "We have gained so much over the past seventy years or more. If we become a dictatorship or something worse, what does that mean for the rest of the world?"

Lloyd vigorously shook his head at the question. "You are referring to a situation where the United States was the predominant power. Their supremacy afforded us the gains you are referring to. This world no longer exists and may not for decades to come.

"As I see it, we have a choice. Canada, with powerful enemies on its borders and their agents inside our country, can choose to do the things that must be done so we can remain a sovereign country and decide our fate in this new and dangerous paradigm. Or, we can choose to go the way of France in 1939 and succumb to whatever foreign tyranny is prepared to do the things we ourselves are not prepared to do.

"Democracy, if it is Canada's birthright, will find a way to survive, but only if we can find a way to remain in control of our destiny. You only have to look at Taiwan and Ukraine. They are only the most recent states to have their sovereignty ripped from them. It looks like the Baltics will be next."

With a look of outrage on her face, the anchor snapped at her guest, "So you think, under the current circumstances, a Canadian dictatorship would be justified?"

Despite his annoyance with the journalist's attempt to bait him into an exchange that would earn her ratings, Lloyd dipped into the reservoir of wisdom he had earned from his thirty-six years as an academic. Forcing a pleasant smile onto his face, he said, "There's a saying that goes like this. 'Hard times create strong men, strong men create good times, good times create weak men, and weak men create hard times.' We live in a time where several bad men and at least one bad woman are making hard times for our country and our allies. I, for one, am glad someone as strong as Ms. Martel is in power instead of the man you worked for when you were still in politics. How is your former boss, by the way?"

For a brief moment, the anchorwoman glared at Lloyd, but whether it was her initiative or at the prompting of the producer pleading in her earpiece, she turned to the camera and said, "I want to thank Dr. Lloyd for joining us today to help us make sense of the bigger picture that Canada and the world are facing during these extraordinary times. We'll be back after these messages from our sponsors."

Chapter 26

Vancouver, British Columbia

—

When Cruz had finished with the Hells Angel, they had identified sixteen possible locations the White Unit could be using for their operations.

Using their own data, sources, and analysis, Tomic's team had further narrowed it down to eight spots, all of them in BC.

Breaking their Direct Action Team, DAT, into sub-units of four to six members and giving them access to the capabilities of the Communication Security Establishment's – CSE – field operations unit, they had got it down to three suspected locations.

One just on the edge of Vancouver's Downtown East Side and two to the east of Canada's second-largest city.

Larocque looked down at his BAM wrist unit. It was nearly two minutes until 'go time.'

Unsurprisingly, CSIS intel officers didn't use the BAM system or a similar type of product, so just as he had the members of the DAT requalified on their weapons, each member of the team had also been given a crash course on those parts of the BAM system needed to run the types of operations they were about to execute.

Tomic's voice came alive in his earbud. "All units, this is your two-minute warning. Conduct your final check."

"Alpha Team ready," replied the IO leading the team that would storm the eighth and top floor of the office building in Vancouver.

"Bravo Team ready," replied the team lead assigned to a greenhouse complex northwest of Vancouver.

On cue, the senior officer from the third and final team reported in, "Charlie Team ready." This group was to raid an automotive shop just east of Chilliwack in the BC interior.

Planning out the three locations' takedown, Tomic and Larocque had agreed not to bring the Vancouver Police Department or the RCMP into the mix other than to give trusted contacts in each organization a heads-up that something would happen somewhere in their jurisdictions sometime this morning.

In what Larocque considered an impressive operational feat, the DAT had moved quickly after the Rouloux interrogation.

The gangster had regained consciousness in a spectacular executive suite at the Aria in Vegas. The twelve thousand-a-night room had been strewn with enough cocaine, gambling chips, and panties to suggest Rouloux had been on the bender of benders.

To add to the ruse, they had arranged for an attractive twenty-something IO to play the role of call girl to visit the biker's room the moment he awoke to seed memories of what he'd been up to during the past seventy-two hours.

Among the other bits the young IO had put into play to convince the gangster he'd actually been in the Sin City partying was a collection of impeccably rendered deep-fake pictures and videos on Rouloux's phone showing him having the time of his life.

Bank accounts had also been doctored showing to the penny how the biker had blown through no less than six hundred thousand dollars and change at three casinos and fifteen different restaurants.

Larocque had thought the single fifty-seven-thousand-dollar charge at the Emerald Lounge in the MGM was over-the-top, but when he'd been shown video of Rouloux lecherously pouring a seven-thousand-dollar bottle of Cristal down the throats of a pair of AI-generated escorts, he had become a believer.

Convincing Rouloux he had been in Vegas had become a necessary and crucial part of the plan the moment they had found out the degree the Hells Angel was involved in the White Unit's activities. In addition to providing them with properties to operate from, Rouloux had fronted them cash and even made arrangements for them to receive a delivery of weapons and explosives from Eastern Europe.

The consensus on Tomic's team was that the White Unit could go up to three days of not hearing from Rouloux without becoming suspicious. Further, at the end of those three days, when the biker did speak to whoever his contact was, he would have to have some kind of believable explanation for why he had gone dark, otherwise, the White Unit would suspect something was up, move to sever its connection, and would itself go dark, leaving CSIS back where it was just three days ago.

Standing beside him in the operations hub of the CSIS BC regional office, Tomic said, "One minute."

Together, they were standing behind a single long table that had six people sitting at it. Each person had a laptop open in front of them and was wearing a headset that included a microphone.

On the wall of the room that everyone was facing were eight screens. On five of the screens were the bodycam images from each team that would storm the locations as soon as Tomic gave the order.

The remaining screens were divided into halves. Each section featured the live stream from one of the ten drones that CSIS was using in support of the operation.

Without turning to look at Larocque, Tomic asked, "Thirty seconds, Director. Are we still a go?"

In Larocque's professional opinion, in the past three days, they had done everything right. Yes, they had bent rules and taken extraordinary risks, but in the time they had been observing these locations, they had identified several individuals CSIS had flagged as being possible White Unit operators.

In the past three days, he and his people had taken the initiative. The ball was now in their court. And now, finally, they were going to get some of the answers he needed about this elusive White Unit.

"We're a go," Larocque said.

Tomic brought her wrist unit up to her chest and pressed the comms app with her finger. "All teams, we are a go. Execute, execute, execute."

***

Blondin was last in the first stack of four IOs outside the filthy doorway. A second and third stack of four armed CSIS officers would follow him once they breached the entrance and cleared the first room of the business suite that they'd been surveilling for the past two days. Inside, they would find at least two people.

Within the first two hours of putting the building under surveillance, the techs attached to the DAT had hacked the building's rudimentary security system and gained access to the lone camera that kept an eye on the eighth floor.

They had seen a total of six different people enter the eight-room suite over the past forty-eight hours, but as of three hours ago, the only people who should be on the other side of the door they were about to bust down were two disgraced former cops.

Blondin, himself a former police officer who had joined CSIS nearly ten years ago, had been thrilled to be able to put his old training back to use.

As a patrol cop on the streets of Winnipeg for seven years, he had done his share of high-risk forced entries, and until he had been recruited onto the DAT, he had forgotten how much of a charge he got from doing dangerous fieldwork.

For what had to be the tenth time in the past minute, he looked down at his wrist unit. They were ten seconds out on their two-minute countdown.

At minus six seconds, Tomic's voice flared inside his earbud, "All teams, we are a go. Execute, execute, execute."

On hearing the go-ahead, Blondin instantly slapped the back of the IO in front of him, giving the signal for the breach to kick off.

From behind him, the two strongest men on his twelve-person team silently came forward with a sixty-pound battering ram.

With the precision that had come with hours of practice, the two IOs placed the tapered end of the ram against the door's locking mechanism and, without warning, shifted the breaching tool backward and, with two muted grunts, drove the steel pillar forward.

Upon making contact with the door, a satisfying crack filled the air as the entrance to the office suite buckled inward.

At the top of his lungs, Blondin yelled, "Move! Move! Move!" while the IO directly in front of him bellowed, "Police, put your hands up!"

With their weapons drawn, the first four CSIS officers entered the room.

Looking through the red dot sight of his Sig Sauer P320, Blondin perceived no threat in the reception area of what had been at one time the office of a successful husband-and-wife law firm.

Hearing the other three members of his team yell, "Clear!" Blondin's hand knifed in the direction of the door on the left.

According to the city's floorplans on file for the building, the room on the other side of the door he was pointing at was the suite's only boardroom, the largest room in the space by far. If the White Unit had any Chinese nationals in their possession at this location, Blondin and the rest of his team had concluded this was the room where they'd be.

Shareen Abdulla, one of two women on his twelve-person team, padded up to the closed door and put her free hand on the lever.

"Open it," Blondin commanded.

Twisting the handle and pushing the door inward simultaneously, Abdulla stepped into the boardroom and then, without warning, stopped.

Just as Blondin was about to reprimand her for blocking the doorway, his attention was drawn to the reason Abdulla had stopped in her tracks. Two men, Chinese by the look of them, were tightly bound in a pair of chairs. Both of them had terrified looks in their eyes.

Blondin's eyes dropped down from the two men and took up what was clearly a bomb. He had seen enough C-4 in his career to know what he was looking at, but the explosives weren't his primary concern.

Behind the bomb was a screen, and on the screen was a descending number, and it had just cleared thirty-five seconds.

His eyes darted back to the bound men. Despite their tightly gagged mouths, he knew exactly what they were saying. It took him two long seconds to make his decision.

As loud as he had ever yelled in his life, he gave the order to evacuate the floor.

Still stunned by what she was seeing, Blondin grabbed Abdulla's chest rig and drove the woman through the door they had entered. The two other four-person teams had already entered the suite and had been in the process of clearing the other offices when Blondin's urgent order had been given.

Following Abdulla into the reception area, he saw the first members of the other two teams begin to emerge from the space they had been assigned to clear.

As they ran by, Blondin counted five men and one woman. The final two men who emerged were the assigned leaders of the second and third breach teams.

Johnson, the senior of the two, said, "There's two women back there. They're tied up. One's been beaten –."

Blondin cut him off and fired his thumb over his shoulder. "I don't give a shit. We have fifteen seconds before a bomb goes off. Move!"

Johnson, an empath if there ever was one, made to argue with Blondin, but the practical former Winnipeg cop growled, "Ten seconds. Move. Now!"

Finally, the IO turned, and together, the three men dodged through the door, and with all the speed that each could muster, they ran for the stairwell at the far end of the hallway.

Holding the stairwell door open and urging them forward with a repeating frantic swing of her arm was Abdulla.

The bomb, which in Blondin's estimation had been five pounds of plastic explosive, detonated just as Johnson reached the threshold of the door.

Ten strides behind the younger and much faster man, he perceived the energy of the explosion pick him up like the hand of a giant and toss him forward in a blur of movement.

After a nano-second of flight, he clipped the doorframe that Abdulla was no longer standing beside and felt the bone structure of his left shoulder disintegrate.

Undoubtedly, that grievous injury had been the factor that saved his life because instead of hitting the concrete wall at the far side of the stairwell at terminal velocity, he connected with only so much force that it knocked the wind out of his lungs.

As he struggled desperately to draw breath, with an incredible force of will, he raised his body so he could look down the stairs.

It was filled with a thick haze of dust, but through the miasma, he saw a single, unmoving body. It was Abdulla.

Even if he had the breath to draw to call out the woman's name, Blondin would have refrained from the futile act. She was dead. The neck of the well-regarded IO, who had just finished back-to-back postings in East Africa, was set at an impossible angle.

Disaster thought Blondin. What a bloody goddamn disaster.

***

Larocque watched in horror as the same scenario played out at all three locations.

His mind began to race as he listened to the frantic conversations over the BAM. Tomic was doing her best to give direction and calm people at the same time, but the magnitude of the disaster had overwhelmed the woman's operational experience or competency, or both.

It struck him in that moment that he'd made a terrible error in thinking he could convert CSIS into a military outfit in such a short period.

Under similar circumstances, the men and women of the Airborne Regiment would have been upset, to be sure, but they wouldn't have let that distress compromise their ability to problem-solve.

That was the miracle of the soldiers who had served in the CANZUK militaries since the time of the Boer War. No matter how bad things got, no matter how many of your mates went down, you fought and functioned as a disciplined unit until the person giving you orders told you to let up or you were dead.

His wrist unit vibrated. It was the fourth such buzz in the past five minutes. Bringing his hand upward, he glanced down and saw the name Shareen Abdulla. The IO's wrist unit was no longer tracking a pulse.

He lowered his hand, ground his teeth, and reminded himself that the CANZUK nations were at war.

Not three months ago, the Chinese had killed nearly four hundred Canadian sailors, not two hundred klicks from where he stood, while in the past week, that same country had ruthlessly firebombed Australia, killing thousands.

In New York State, things were only slightly better. After a week of intense fighting, Canadian, UK, and Blue Faction troops had fought the Reds to a standstill on the American side of the border.

In the last update from the New York front, something like eight hundred Canadian and UK soldiers had been killed or wounded. It was a harsh assessment, but as tragic as the loss of four CSIS intelligence officers was, the losses had been needed so as to complete the total transformation of Canada's national intelligence service.

He activated his BAM and said, "Communications override, channel three, cease all comms except my voice, authorization Larocque Zero-Five-Lima."

The near-AI synthesized voice of the BAM said, "Channel three is open and ready. All other communications have ceased."

Across the room, Larocque heard Tomic begin to raise her voice as the conversation she had been having with the senior IO at the greenhouse location went dead. She slammed her hand down on the table she was standing beside, making the closest operations coordinator jump out of her seat. She spun in the direction of Larocque, but before she could begin to complain about how the BAM system cut out, he began to speak.

"All units, all units, this is Arrow Sunray. Effective immediately, each team is to grab any wounded and evac to their respective rally points. Any team member designated KIA is to be left where they are. They will be retrieved by local assets who are on their way to your locations."

From across the room, Tomic's face took on a murderous look. "Like hell! You can't leave my people there. I won't let you!"

Larocque ignored her and continued to speak through the connection to the three teams. "Our mission is compromised. If the local authorities arrive and take you into custody, our ability to carry out our mission to catch the people who have done this to us ends. We become ineffective and we are off the board. This cannot happen."

Tomic began to walk in his direction. Her voice nearing a yell, she said, "My people aren't leaving. This is the fuck-up of all fuck-ups. We are not the army. We are not machines. They will stay with the dead, and those who are wounded will wait for medical treatment."

Knowing the BAM system was exceptional at keeping any sound that did not come out of the operator's mouth from transmitting, Larocque understood Tomic's insubordination would remain confined to this room. At least for now.

As she reached his position and opened her mouth to issue further defiance to his order, his right hand, already in a fist, delivered a quick blow to the woman's chest right underneath her diaphragm.

At less than fifty percent of a full punch, it was more than enough force to expel every last bit of air from Tomic's lungs.

With a shocked look on her face, the slender CSIS executive staggered backward until she collided with one of the IOs sitting at the coordination table.

As Larocque watched Tomic gasp for air, he resumed his address of the three sub-teams of the DAT. "I know this is difficult, but the people who've left us will be cared for. I have already sent messages to each of the police forces that are on their way to your positions. We are at war, people. If you didn't know this five minutes ago, you do now. Gather yourselves and get to your rally points. We didn't win today, but I can assure you we will. We'll debrief in ninety minutes. Arrow Sunray out."

On the screens beyond the winded Tomic, Larocque began to see movement at each of the three locations. That they were moving and not standing in place arguing with one another was a positive sign.

"Re-engage communications except Arrow One, authorization Larocque Niner-Seven-Lima."

"Communications have been reestablished, excluding Arrow One," advised the BAM in his earbud.

Tomic, now standing on her own and beginning to breathe normally, was staring at Larocque with eyes blazing.

Taking a step in her direction, he saw her hand move to the pistol holstered on her hip.

"Don't be foolish," he said in a calm voice.

Her hand still on the grip of her weapon, she spat, "Not a foot closer, or I swear I'll do it."

"It's okay, Monique. It's over. I know you fed information to the White Unit about this mission."

Tomic barked a short laugh. "You're completely unhinged. You kill good people without a care. You torture people without hesitation. And now, when things go to shit, you blame me for what? For being a traitor to my organization? For having a hand in the death of my colleagues, my friends? I was a fool to trust you, but not now. Now, I'm going to do what's right."

While Tomic's right hand remained on the grip of her weapon, her left hand came up, and she pointed her index finger at Larocque's chest. "This is my organization. For twenty-six years, CSIS has been my career. Every one of those people who died today was my family, and you have the audacity - no, the unmitigated gall to blame me for your recklessness and failure.

"This was your mission. Beginning to end. Don't you dare blame me for what's happened today. As the people in this room are my witness, it is your incompetence and recklessness that have led to this disaster. You're going to jail, Jackson Larocque. Not even the PM can stop that now."

A sad look fell onto Larocque's face. He said, "There are only two people in our outfit who knew the three locations we were going to hit and had enough time to pass that information along to the White Unit."

Slowly, Larocque's hand came up and tapped his chest. "I knew." His hand rotated and pointed in the direction of Tomic. "And you knew."

Tomic laughed again. "Oh my god, you're unbelievable. We gave the full DAT three hours' notice on the takedown. If you don't think the folks we're chasing can pull off the stunt we just witnessed in that amount of time, then you are more dense than I thought. There are now over a hundred people on the DAT. Any one of them could have leaked the takedown info to the White Unit."

Larocque shook his head. "I didn't say the details of our takedown were leaked in the past three hours. We've been watching each location like a hawk for almost three days. The members of the DAT only learned of our plans for the takedown of each location at 0700 this morning, and from that time through to the moment we breached each space, not a single person was seen entering or leaving the three locations. Unless the materials used to kill our people were teleported into each space, they had to come at an earlier point. And how did the operatives in each location disappear? There were supposed to be seven White Unit operators at the three locations, but there were none. Remarkable, wouldn't you say?"

Tomic scoffed and said, "So the bombs came in earlier. Who's to say it isn't their standard practice to rig each of their rooms in this fashion? And talented operatives can easily disappear. It happens all the time. As I stand here, Director, I can think of another dozen explanations as to how they were ready for us, and none of them involve me leaking information."

Tomic took a step in the direction of Larocque. "You might have been a great soldier, but two weeks as the Director of CSIS doesn't make you Columbo. You're in over your head, Larocque. You always were. Give me your weapon. Slowly, mind you."

When Larocque didn't make any move for the holstered weapon on his hip, Tomic spoke again, but this time, her voice was low and menacing. "I'm not going to ask again. Today, you stop destroying our organization.

"Give me your weapon, and I promise we can end all of this quietly. You can retire and spend time with your family. I know you miss Marcel. I see it in your eyes every time you mention his name."

Slowly, Larocque took his eyes off Tomic and, to no one in particular, said, "BAM, play recording Three-Alpha on an external speaker authorization, Larocque Uniform-Tango."

The voice of Larocque's BAM system replied instantly in his earbud, "External speaker found, playing the recording in three, two, one."

Tomic's voice filled the operations room. *"You have to give my people at least sixty seconds to get out of the room, longer if possible. We've lost too many people already."*

Another voice, also female, replied, though it sounded like she was several feet away from the recording device. *"We know what we are doing. You only have to do your part."*

"I'll do what I have to when the time comes," Tomic said insistently.

"Will you?" said the other woman.

"Yes. This last debacle with Rouloux – it was the last straw. My people don't want what he's selling. What the PM was thinking in putting him in charge is beyond me. If you and whoever you work for want to go around rounding up Chinese and French nationals, that's fine by us. We understand there's a war going on, but the rank and file didn't sign up to put our lives on the line. We'll give you space. But we're done. Enough people are with me."

There was a long pause, but finally, the distant voice of the White Unit agent said, *"We don't care what your reasons are. When the time comes, do what needs to be done."*

Her voice clear and determined, Tomic said, *"One way or the other, he'll be gone."*

The synthesized voice of the near-AI said, "Recording has ended."

"A deep fake. Anyone can make them," Tomic said dismissively.

His voice still calm, Larocque said, "You know it's not. It's as genuine as the remarkable micro-recording device you'll find installed in the weapon your right hand is currently wrapped around."

Tomic's eyes narrowed as Larocque's revelation struck her.

Slowly, she drew the weapon from its holster and levelled it at his chest. Holding it steady, her eyes went from his face to the weapon searching for some kind of indication the weapon was bugged.

As a look of disappointment took over his face, Larocque said, "It's there, Monique. I only activated it when I couldn't find out who was tipping off the White Unit to our raids before we got our hands on Rouloux.

"Petit had been joking when he said he was almost positive it wasn't you tipping off the White Unit, but when I couldn't nail down who the leak was, I activated the listening device. For what it's worth, I understand and sympathize with why you've done what you've done. I know rebuilding CSIS into a paramilitary organization is difficult for you and many others to support, but it must be done. Gone are the days when the people in this organization could sit behind a desk or rely on others to do the dirty work. For the foreseeable future, CSIS IOs will have to get their hands dirty, and that means people will have to die."

After a pause, Larocque added, "Remove your hand from your weapon, Monique. Whatever coup you were planning – it's over."

"Like hell it is," Tomic said quietly. She then snapped the fingers of her left hand. As the sharp sound resonated in the ops room, the six IOs that had been operating behind the laptops got to their feet and turned to flank her. At least two of them had placed their hands on their still-holstered weapons.

Tomic took a step forward and, in an icy tone, said, "As it turns out, Director, someone in the White Unit is as concerned about your leadership as I am, though I'm certain their reasons are different than mine. Whatever their reason is, the important thing is that we're united on the need to see you resign or..."

"Or what, Monique?" Larocque prompted.

Tomic's eyes shifted right, and firmly, she said, "King."

One of the IOs drew his handgun and pointed it at Larocque's chest.

When her eyes returned to Larocque's, she said, "Or, we take you off the board, and we feed the PM and whoever else cares some bullshit story that you were shot doing something stupid – you know, like personally getting your hands dirty leading a raid on a Chinese safe house."

After a pause, Tomic smiled and added, "An entirely believable story, wouldn't you say, Director? Important people can die too when they lead from the front, as you're so fond of saying."

Larocque shook his head slowly and said, "Please don't do this, Monique. Enough people have died today."

Tomic scoffed. "Yeah, *my* people, and you talk as though it's you who's pointing the gun at me. My God, you have to be the most arrogant son of a bitch I've ever met. Is that what commanding dozens of people to their deaths does to somebody? Does it give you this superiority complex that lets you flaunt the rules and kill people on a whim? Even now, with a gun pointed at you, you think you can dictate to me how this is going to end.

"We're so done with you and your cowboy ways, Larocque. To hell with you and the PM and her schemes, whatever they are. My people and I – we want none of it. Canada's intelligence service isn't some amateur outfit you can use and abuse. We are professionals who follow the rule of law. We're not thugs and assassins out of some Hollywood movie."

Her eyes narrowing, Tomic continued, "So what's it going to be, Director? A quiet resignation, where you pack your things and take your wife and baby out West and live a quiet and happy life, or option number two. Decide right now. My people are ready to implement either scenario."

Larocque's reply was firm and immediate. "Neither."

"Neither," she repeated the word incredulously. "For Christ's sake, Larocque, this isn't a fucking game. I'm going to count to five, and when I get to five, you're going to tell me you're going to resign, or King and I are going to shoot you."

Her eyes blazing with anger, Tomic slowly started the countdown, "One. Two. Three –."

Behind him, Larocque heard the ops room's only doorway crash open just as he heard the roar of voices bellowing for everyone in the room to put their hands into the air.

As Tomic's eyes widened in surprise and darted over his shoulder to take in the commotion, Larocque lunged toward her and grabbed her pistol. Much stronger than the slight CSIS executive, he easily ripped the weapon from her hands and violently shoved her backward into the table of laptops the six IOs had been working on minutes earlier.

As Tomic crashed into and flipped over the workspace, Larocque's ears caught a snap followed by the distinctive sound of crackling electricity.

Looking to his left, he saw the IO King lying on the ground, shaking violently. When the disabling energy finally came to a stop, two men wearing civilian clothing fell onto the intel officer, disarmed him, and then flipped him over and slapped flex cuffs onto his wrists. Scanning the remaining five IOs, he saw that each had their hands in the air and were looking warily at the men and one woman pointing the carbine version of the C-71 at each of their chests.

To Larocque's right, a familiar voice said, "Sorry about the delay. Getting into the building wasn't as smooth as I was expecting."

Petit tilted his head toward the splayed and now moaning Tomic and said, "She had my access pass cancelled. We had to wait for someone to leave the building, if you can believe it. It's only by pure luck we got here when we did."

Nodding his head, Larocque turned to Petit and said, "You got here, and that's what matters."

Larocque barked, "Sergeant Major Bear! Disarm these people. Strip them of anything they can use to communicate with the outside world and put them in boardroom four. Take Assistant

Director Tomic to boardroom two. Keep a close watch on all of them."

"And Sergeant Major."

"Yes, sir," the stocky NCO snapped his reply.

"If anyone so much as whispers, you have my permission to rap their knuckles. Hard."

"Roger that, General."

Turning away from the grizzled First Nations paratrooper, Larocque turned his attention to the lone female soldier who was still pointing her carbine at the other intel officers. "Major McCaul, get your people up here and get them going on these laptops. We have a mission to clean up. Your verbal authorization is McCaul Six-Alpha-X-Ray-Seven-Seven. I've been assured everything will slide to you when you take the helm."

"On it, sir."

He turned his gaze back to Petit. "Thanks for helping to make this happen. Your gut was right."

"I still can't believe she did this," Petit said, gesturing to where Tomic still lay on the ground moaning groggily.

Larocque turned to follow his gaze, and with a pitying look, he said, "There's something wrong at the heart of this country, Sam. Rank and file Canadians don't trust the government, and the people in government don't trust Canadians. Monique just couldn't wrap her mind around the reality that the person elected by the people had the power to tell her organization what to do. The deep state, it's here in Canada, and as it turns out, she was one of its most resolute champions."

Quietly, Petit said, "She could have resigned like the others. She could have gone to the media. It didn't have to be this way."

As commandos from the Airborne's intelligence platoon entered the room and began to seat themselves behind the six laptops, Larocque said, "She could have, but clearly, she didn't want to leave. Going covert was who she was. She'll have to be dealt with severely, but I respect that she stayed on the inside and played the game as long as she did. I only wish she got on board. She was talented, and people respected her."

Releasing a sigh, Petit said, "Yeah, well, that respect means that another healthy number of IOs and executives will have to be sent packing. I'm not sure the Service can suffer a house cleaning like the last one. We're already pretty thin."

Nodding, Larocque said, "We'll find the people we need, Sam. And when we do, we'll reforge this outfit into the White Unit's worst bloody nightmare."

Chapter 27

Las Vegas, Nevada

"Shit, you've got to be kidding me," Dune said as he looked down the Strip and laid eyes on Captain Fielder, the 2IC for the Ranger Regiment's Intelligence group. The stocky Brit was flanked by six other men.

Within a week of the visit by the politicians to Guyana to address the CANZUK special forces group, the entirety of the force had been shipped to Nevada and New Mexico. The Neutral States, and now California, it seemed were finally getting serious about the war.

To keep CSOR and the Rangers under wraps, both units had been sent to the Nevada Test and Training Range, otherwise known as Area 51. A massive, remote area, there had been lots of space for CSOR to train, though it had to be done at night.

Six days ago, the Commanding Officer of CSOR had let the lads know that groups of forty at a time could have up to 48-hours leave to go wherever they liked on the condition they kept a low profile. That Dune and Captain Fielder had been released on the same leave cycle was either bad luck or stupidity of the highest order. Whichever, it didn't change the fact his unhinged nemesis had locked in on him and was coming his way.

"Tabarnak," Sergeant Rochefort said to Dune's right. Quickly, the well-built man added, "You know I hate to say it, Captain, but I think we should get out of here. These guys just aren't worth it."

Beside Rochefort, another CSOR sergeant, Derek Finlayson, said, "He's right, sir. These guys. Look at 'em. They're loaded to the gills. The guy beside Fielder can barely walk."

Dune took in a long haul of the city's dry night air and exhaled like a small explosion had lit off in his chest. All of the synapses in his brain were screaming at him to turn, walk away and dismiss the grief that would come the next day after Fielder told everyone how he had high-tailed it into the safety of the Venetian.

How the bitter pissant had made it through the Ranger's officer selection process remained a mystery to Dune.

Back home in Aus, there was no doubt in his mind that a bloke like Fielder would have never made it into Special Operations. What that said about the British Army, he wasn't sure, but as Fielder and the men with him swaggered cocksure in his direction, it didn't much matter. What mattered was that he and the two men standing beside him manage not to get the piss kicked out of them or, worse, get arrested by the LVPD for causing a disturbance.

The world might be going to hell in a handbasket, but that was outside the municipal confines of fabulous Las Vegas.

At all points during America's second civil war, the people of the great state of Nevada had been abundantly clear. When you came to Vegas, you left whatever shit you had behind you, and for however long you were in town, you acted like a good and normal human being – at least as good and normal as Vegas allowed – and only when you left would you resume whatever life you had been living, with all of its violence and bitterness.

Fail to follow this unwritten rule and the local police would come down on you hard. Everyone had seen the videos of SUVs filled with Vegas police officers and K-9 units storming onto the pedestrian portion of the Strip to separate and then brutalize anyone who did not follow these perfectly reasonable terms.

But in the end, Dune had decided that he couldn't run. Fielder was a bully, and in his young life, he had never – not once – backed down from a tormentor like the one standing in front of him.

The seven Rangers stopped a couple paces in front of Dune, Rochefort, and Finlayson.

"Well, well, well. If it isn't everybody's favourite golden boy, Captain Dune." As Fielder said the words, it was clear the man didn't have all of his faculties. Dune could easily smell the alcohol on the intel officer's breath as he spoke.

Determined not to be the one to start anything, Dune said in a friendly enough tone, "Oi, Fielder, good to see ya, mate. You and the lads make any money tonight?"

"Me and the lads?" the Ranger officer said, slurring his words. "You hear that, I think our friend here with the funny accent wants to make friends. Did we make any money, lads?"

"Oh, loads of cash, Captain," roared one of the soldiers who was having trouble standing. "Hickey here just blew up at the craps table at the MGM and darn near won a million. A million, I say! Fucking loaded we all are now."

The drunken intelligence officer took a step toward Dune. As he did so, the rest of the British soldiers moved to surround them. Leaning forward, Fielder called out loudly, "Does that answer your question, pretty boy? Have you got any more questions about our night? Would you like me to tell you how I paid for a young lass at a strip club who I could have sworn had the face of your pretty wife?"

An ugly smile bloomed on Fielder's face. "Yeah, that's right, mate. I've seen pictures of your little miss online. A delicious little thing she is. So much so the lads and I have arranged for this lass at the club to come back to our hotel. When she's sucking me off, Dune, it'll be your wife's name I use when I finally relieve myself. Trisha, isn't it?"

Despite the Brit's egregious baiting, Dune saw the punch coming. Leaning back, he felt the wind from Fielder's punch as it passed by his chin.

Taking a step back to avoid Fielder's follow-up blow, he felt one of the Rangers crash into him from behind. In a tumble of bodies, Dune, Fielder, and whoever had hit him from behind careened to the Strip's pavement in a heap.

Caught between the backstabber and cement, the air in Dune's lungs was driven out of him.

As his rear attacker rolled off his body, Dune flipped over only to have Fielder straddle his chest and begin to rain blows down on his face.

By way of instinct and training, Dune's guard came up, and for the next few seconds, all he did was try to protect himself and get air back into his lungs.

But Fielder, himself an accomplished MMA fighter, was relentless. It felt as though Dune had been transported back into the trenches at Whiteman Air Force Base, where he'd engaged in brutal hand-to-hand fighting with a squad of Red Faction soldiers trying to take one of the Airborne's trenches.

The look on Fielder's face easily matched the savagery on the faces of the UCSA soldiers he had fought to the death all those months ago.

With his chest compressed and the beating only getting more intense, black spots began to fill Dune's vision. No matter how hard he tried, he couldn't get enough air into his lungs. But just as the darkness seemed to reach the point where he would lose consciousness, he heard what sounded like automatic gunfire.

Suddenly, the weight on his chest was gone, and air – the sweet, dry air of the desert – flooded into him.

Gasping, Dune's vision quickly began to clear. Looking upwards into Vegas's starless night sky, he again heard the sound of automatic weapons. This time, he also perceived yelling and screams of pain.

Taking one final quick breath, he turned on his side to see the bloodied body of Captain Fielder lying beside him. Raising to his elbows, Dune saw the man's chest was riddled with bullets.

"Crikey!" Dune yelled.

More gunfire filled the air.

Staying low, Dune flipped over onto his stomach and looked in the direction where he thought he'd heard the gunfire.

On the ground in front of him were more dead bodies. Finlayson and two of the Rangers were bloodied and unmoving.

His voice ragged, Dune called out to Finlayson, but the CSOR sergeant gave no reply or indication he was still of this world.

Beyond the waylaid soldiers, movement caught Dune's eye.

Perhaps thirty meters away and moving in his direction was a threesome of terrifying figures he instantly recognized. Each of the Chinese Wraiths carried the huge assault rifle Dune had seen on the dozens of intel recordings CSOR had been shown in recent months demonstrating the capabilities and supposed weak points of the near-AI killing machines.

A targeting laser from one of the Wraith's rifles suddenly danced across Dune's vision. Dropping his head, he rolled in the opposite direction from where he had seen Fielder's body just as he heard a burst of automatic gunfire.

"Captain! Captain! Over here!"

Dune flashed his eyes to where he had heard the French-accented voice. It was Rochefort and two of the Rangers. They were at one of the entrances to the Venetian Hotel and Casino. All three were waving at him wildly.

He didn't hesitate. Like a scared cat, Dune leaped to his feet, undertook a quick shimmy as though he was dodging opposing players on a footy pitch, and then sprinted with every ounce of speed he had in the direction of the men hailing him.

Near misses of gunfire tore through the air as he ran. Halfway to his destination, he juked once more and, again, felt bullets zip past him.

Reaching the entrance, Dune sprinted past Rochefort and the two Rangers, who had themselves hit the deck to avoid the incoming fire.

In the casino, he saw a huge fountain that had, at its center, several massive interlocking circlets burping water while twisting in a mesmeric pattern. Reaching the structure, like an American baseball player, he slid behind the fountain's concrete base, putting himself out of harm's way, if only for the moment.

After taking two quick breaths, Dune looked over the lip of the fountain's bowl and saw Rochefort and the two Rangers come dashing through the entrance. Only a few strides beyond the threshold leading into the casino, the glass behind them began to disintegrate as a hail of indiscriminate gunfire chased after them.

Amid their dramatic entrance, one of the two Rangers lost his footing and crashed to the ground. With a hailstorm of bullets still peppering what turned out to be the Venetian's VIP check-in area, Dune got up from his location, raced to the prone man, grabbed him with two hands, and with everything he had, began to drag him to the safety of the fountain.

He had made it halfway there when the second Ranger joined him. Dune released one of the man's hands, and together, they frantically pulled the heavy-set British commando to cover.

Reaching the relative safety of the fountain, they found Rochefort, down on one knee looking in the direction of the Wraiths.

"They're still coming. We have to run," said the Quebec soldier.

Dune cast his eyes in Rochefort's direction and saw the three machines stalking forward, their guns at the ready.

In the far right of his peripheral vision, Dune caught movement. Shifting his gaze, his eyes found a group of women who looked to be a bachelorette party. Their hands linked, as one, they were running to the entrance Dune, and the others had just come through, no doubt in a confused effort to escape whatever nightmare had just befallen them.

"STOP!" Dune screamed as loud as he could.

When they did not stop or even acknowledge that someone was bellowing at them, Dune started to get to his feet, but before he could take a step in the direction of the doomed group, Rochefort grabbed him and pulled him back.

"It's too late," he yelled into Dune's ear.

As he strained at the vice-like hold the Quebecer had put on him, Dune and the other three soldiers watched in abject horror as the gaggle of beautiful young women walked into the path of the approaching killing machines.

Sensing a potential threat or acting on instructions to deliver mass casualties, the three Wraiths opened fire.

"Fuuuuck!" Dune roared as the women, all of them his wife's age, were brutally cut down.

As bullets again began to rip past them, Rochefort muscled Dune to the floor.

Yelling, he said, "Captain, we have to get out of here. They're after us, for whatever reason. If they're after us, we need to bring them away from the Strip, so fewer civies get tagged."

It took a moment, but eventually, Rochefort's words registered with the Aussie-turned-Canadian commando.

"Okay, okay," Dune finally said, nodding his head. "I agree. Let's take these bogans for a ride. We were here earlier today. Let's move further into the casino and head west. We'll get to the other side, and go from there. Maybe as we're on the move, we'll get the chance to give these bastards a bit of payback."

The Ranger who had helped Dune drag his mate to safety called out, "They're getting close. We need a plan. Like now!"

"Let me up. All's good, mate," declared Dune to his bigger friend.

Giving the Aussie a quick nod, Rochefort finally released Dune from his death grip.

Getting to his knees, Dune looked over the lip of the fountain and saw the robots passing over the bodies of the women they had just slaughtered.

He glanced in the direction of the check-in counter, which was now devoid of staff. They would need to keep the fountain between them and the Wraiths if they had any chance of escaping.

Dune knifed his hand in the direction of the posh marbled area with the signage that indicated VIP Clients and Check-In, and loudly said, "Right, follow me, lads. Over the counter and then into the guts of the hotel. We move west as fast as possible. Let's see just how fast and smart these bastards actually are."

***

Lieutenant Volk was proud of his service in the UCSA's still-growing intelligence service. In his time in the US Navy, he had been an officer of middling talent. He had earned a physics degree at the US Naval Academy and promptly been assigned to the less-than-exciting world of undersea imaging.

For Volk, the civil war had been a godsend, the excuse he had needed to leave the Navy and do something with his life that held meaning.

It had not been difficult to choose the Red Faction. For as long as he could remember, he had understood that the woke ideologues and the sheep who brayed for them were the diseases that would kill the United States. He'd been so confident of the country's disintegration that he had put money down with a bookie service in the UK. His girlfriend at the time had called the stunt a stupid waste of money, but when the first shots of the war had been fired, he'd collected and big time.

For the first six months of the war, like most of his fellow naval officers, he had sat on the sidelines and watched in horror and growing frustration as the country tore itself apart. A smart enough fellow, he could understand the reasons the Navy brass was choosing to stay out of the fighting. But eventually, he had been compelled to jump ship, if not literally.

It had taken the better part of another six months, but with the persistence of someone who truly wanted something, he had worked his way into the UCSA agency that had combined the mandates of the FBI and the CIA.

Officially called the Consolidated Intelligence Branch, the CIB had had a tumultuous start to the war. As one could imagine, the *Great Sorting* that took place across all government departments once the actual fighting started had been equal parts confusion and opportunity.

Mass firings, ideological purges, and eventually, extrajudicial killings had been the order of the day during the war inside the war that had consumed the United States once proud and capable intelligence agencies.

It was in this hot mess that Volk had received his training and first few assignments.

As it turned out, unlike his performance in the Navy, he was no middling talent. In the opinion of the six different bosses he'd worked for during the three years of the civil war where he'd been a CIB agent, he was 'excellent' at what he did.

It was Volk's affinity for technology and his willingness to get into the field that had opened doors for him. Within a year of his first assignment, he had been running a full team of counter-intelligence officers identifying and, when necessary, liquidating FAS double agents who had stayed on with the UCSA. This had been painstaking but hugely satisfying work.

At the end of his second year, he was shifted to Europe. Proficient in German, he had spent most of his time in Germany and the continent's other German-speaking regions, surveilling and, in a few cases, assassinating FAS intelligence or diplomatic officers. This, too, had been a rewarding use of his skills.

Volk had been brought back to North America once the Spector regime came to power. As it had been explained to him, the country's new leader wanted every single asset the country owned dedicated to one thing and one thing only: defeating the FAS in North America.

For a short period, he had taken the skills he had honed in Europe and put them to use in Washington and Boston. It had not been easy work. It never was when you operated in enemy territory, and on two different occasions, he had come as close to dying as had ever been the case in his thirty-five years of being alive.

He had been relieved when Washington had fallen. The use of tactical nuclear weapons had been the right call, and it had been a terrible shame that Andrew Morgan had slipped from their grasp. Killing the FAS's vice president would have left the Blues leaderless, and most certainly within weeks, if not days, America's second civil war would have ended.

To Volk's consternation and the dismay of everyone he'd talked to in the CIB, CANZUK had somehow managed to pull victory from President Spector's grasp by saving Morgan, and in so doing, had made everything much harder than it needed to be.

CANZUK was why he was in Las Vegas. Despite their attempts to keep their operation in South America a secret, CIB intelligence had discovered that Great Britain and Canada had located large parts of their Special Operations commands to the backwater of Guyana only to have them most recently arrive in several locations in Nevada and New Mexico.

Two thousand highly trained soldiers doing a shitty job of playing secret in the jungles of an entirely different continent was one thing. Having those same soldiers less than a thousand miles from some of the UCSA's great cities and allegedly within striking distance of the President's current base of operations was something else entirely.

Since their spunky operation to remove the nuclear weapons from Whiteman AFB, the UCSA had underestimated CANZUK. No more. They were a legitimate threat, and now it was his job and that of the CIB to take this special operations group off the board so they couldn't implement whatever plans they had cooking.

Sources in both of the Neutral Faction states had given the CIB the precise location of CANZUK's people, and in turn, the higher-ups had given people like himself access to no less than two hundred Chinese X-8 Wraiths and half that many of the X-5 Hyenas so they could storm each of the four locations harboring the CANZUK commandos.

At Area 51, for example, four of his colleagues driving two tractor-trailers would haul fifty of the Wraiths and some smaller number of the Hyenas into the desert, drop them off within five kilometers of the base, and let the near-AI machines do the rest.

Together or alone, the Wraiths and Hyenas excelled at infiltration and the destruction of soft targets. And while it was true that Area 51 was a protected facility, it was also a fact the Chinese automatons, operating with their near-AI programming and being guided by experienced handlers, had pulled off dozens of missions at least as complex and dangerous as the task of laying waste to what was nothing more than a glorified airport.

As Volk thought about his task, he was reminded of how unfortunate it was that China only had a few thousand of these near-AI killer robots and not tens of thousands.

To be sure, the Wraiths and Hyenas weren't perfect. For example, he'd been told the autos' software struggled to manage more than forty units at any one time, and intel reports from the battlefields in Vietnam had confirmed their armor had been found wanting against 7.62mm rounds. Those issues aside, these incredible pieces of tech had changed the way warfare and covert ops were being conducted.

Which brought his mind back to his current mission.

Including himself, twelve other CIB operatives had each been given a van and up to four Wraiths and sent off to Las Vegas.

Independently, it was each operative's job to track down and set upon CANZUK soldiers on leave across Vegas the moment the assault on the four bases commenced.

The direction to hunt down and kill the British and Canadian commandos anywhere and everywhere in the adult playground that was Vegas had come straight from the top. In allowing CANZUK's soldiers to take up residence in their state, the leaders of Nevada had forfeited Vegas's informal neutral status.

Whatever Nevada's intentions were in receiving the foreign soldiers, Spector or someone in the President's office had given the order to make it clear to the people of Nevada, the other Neutral Faction states, and the rest of the world that there were consequences to throwing in with the UCSA's enemies.

For six straight hours, Volk had tracked a group of seven men from the UK's Ranger Regiment, and in that time, whatever sympathies he might have held for the marks he was going to eliminate on this evening dissolved within the first hour of his pursuit.

Being a product of the US Navy, Volk was, of course, familiar with shore leave and the types of shenanigans men could get into when they let loose. But shenanigans weren't what this nasty bunch was into.

Fit, large, and mean, for nearly every minute he had observed this posse of troublemakers, they had acted like modern-day Vikings braying and bullying anyone who crossed their path. But it was the leader of the group whom Volk had come to loathe most acutely in the brief time he'd been following this unprofessional lot.

About two hours into his shadowing, he had been able to get a clear shot of the leader's face and had sent it into mission ops asking for any details they could find on the man.

Fifteen minutes later, the brute's details had come in.

Captain Branson Fielder III was presently the 2IC of the Enhanced Intelligence Team of the Ranger Regiment. As Volk read the briefing on Fielder, the behaviors he had been observing started to make sense.

As an American, Volk could never truly wrap his mind around the concept of the British aristocracy. That there was this special class of people who, because they were born to certain parents, received all kinds of formal and informal privileges was of the exact same madness that had been the DEI movement in the fifteen years or so before the civil war.

In both systems, you received things you didn't deserve or that you weren't qualified for because of biological status and not how you performed.

In Fielder's case, the brief dossier sent by the mission control team seemed to suggest that Fielder Senior, himself a retired general, had used his influence to shoehorn his son into the Rangers. That must have been the case because the younger Fielder's record of service in the British Army was somewhere between regrettable and downright appalling.

In the intensive course Volk had taken only two days earlier to become a qualified handler of the X-8 Wraith platform, he recalled the function of being able to upload the facial image of a particular target and then issue orders to have said target put at the top of each auto's hit list.

He had gladly done this for Captain Fielder and then issued a secondary order to brutalize the man's body once he'd been eliminated because the Wraith's software allowed for that too.

340

Volk tended not to be a vindictive man, but this Fielder character pushed all the right buttons. Among his other escapades, he had watched the man loudly berate a scantily clad street performer who was a touch on the hefty side.

The woman, clearly no wilting flower, had stood up to the Brit, but as she was doing so, one of Fielder's crew snuck up behind her and, with the quick flick of a blade, sliced the back strap of the performer's top, exposing her ample breasts to hundreds of people walking by.

As they howled more obscenities at the humiliated woman and began to walk away, Volk looked down at his watch. Only thirteen more minutes to go until things kicked off. It wouldn't be easy, but he would force himself to wait that amount of time so that he could properly dispose of this despicable man and his small band of modern-day marauders.

***

As Dune, Rochefort, and the two Rangers ran through the administrative area for this part of the casino, he saw other people on the move and witnessed staff running into rooms and closing the doors behind them.

As he dodged around a corner, he heard screams and the distinct sound of the Wraith's assault rifles firing. At least one of the autos had pursued them past the check-in desk.

"Left! It'll take us to the casino floor," Rochefort yelled from behind him. The administrative space was a maze, and once already they had had to double back from what had been a dead end. They couldn't afford to do that again.

Reaching a T-junction, Dune did as Rochefort suggested. The Quebec soldier seemed to have a knack for direction. Running down the hallway, on reaching the oversized door with a sign on it reading 'Casino West 1-B', Dune pushed on the door's release bar without hesitation. With way more force than he should have, the door swung open and loudly collided with the casino's wall.

Bursting onto the gaming floor, Dune's gaze was filled with the faces of terrified people. A few casino patrons and staff raced across his vision, but most of everyone he saw was huddled behind something solid, whether it was one of the slot machines immediately in front of him or one of the concrete Roman-style pillars that was the signature motif of the massive complex.

And to the last of them, every panicked soul had positioned themselves in such a way the object they were hiding behind was between them and a pair of seven-foot-tall gun-toting robots making their way up the casino's main thoroughfare.

Hearing the crash of the door Dune had just muscled through, the elongated heads of the Wraiths simultaneously shifted so that the three lenses on each unit's face found him.

For what was a second but felt like five minutes, Dune locked eyes with the two machines overtop a field of slot machines.

The butt of their weapons already in their shoulders, both Wraiths shifted their bodies, raised the barrels of their 6.8mm rifles, and unleashed a long barrage of rounds at that part of Dune's body that was exposed.

"Shit," he cursed as he snapped his head and shoulders downward so that a half-dozen rows of slot machines were between him and the automatons.

As soon as his profile was no longer exposed, the gunfire and the riotous explosion of slot machines stopped.

An Aussie who'd left his country only because he had met the woman of his dreams, Dune had kept in close contact with all of his mates back home and, in so doing, had heard a great deal about these Chinese Wraiths and their performance in Nam.

Without a doubt, the two Wraiths they had encountered on the casino floor would be advancing to flank their position. They had to move fast.

Looking back at the three men who had also lowered their profiles, he raised his hand and knifed it in the direction of the corridor of space that flowed between the casino's exterior wall and what seemed like endless rows of the Venetian's slot machines.

When the three men acknowledged his direction, silently, Dune darted forward in a hunched run and, at twenty meters ahead, dodged left into a row of slot machines.

Stopping, he turned to face Rochefort and the two Rangers. He still didn't know their names.

Whispering, he said, "We don't have much time for a plan. Ahead and at the end of the casino is an escalator. I remember it from this morning. I say we break into pairs, give them multiple targets, and move up the escalator and get to the second floor. From there, we can move onto the Monorail."

"What then?" asked one of the Rangers.

His voice still low, Dune said, "Don't know, mate. Let's get there first."

Canvassing the three men's faces and seeing no hint of disagreement, he said, "Right, you two, that way, we'll take the center. Go."

Still hunched, Dune and Rochefort moved down the line of slots in the direction of the gaming area's central walkway. In doing so, they passed a group of petrified elderly women. Without asking for permission, Dune snatched away a huge purse one of the ladies held while whispering quickly, "Sorry!"

The woman issued a panicked yelp, but Dune pushed on to where the row of slots ended.

As quick as he might, he looked into the carpeted aisle and saw the two Wraiths. They were advancing slowly as they checked each row for their quarry.

Pulling his head back, he said to Rochefort, "Get ready to run."

The Quebec commando only nodded.

With both hands, Dune opened the woman's purse, looked inside, and said aloud, "A right good Sheila."

The purse had been heavy, and to his relief, he confirmed that it was filled with a wide assortment of junk and several dozen gambling chips.

Standing, with as much force as he could manage in the confined space, Dune threw the purse like a flying disc so that its contents showered in every direction.

Within a second of the bag leaving his hand, a storm of gunfire erupted.

"Move!" Dune cried as he launched himself into the gaming area's main transitway. After sprinting maybe fifteen strides, he zigzagged twice and then found himself in an open space where he spied the escalator he'd remembered from their earlier visit.

Reaching the escalator's landing, he turned and urged Rochefort upwards. To his left, and from around a corner of slots, the two Rangers appeared. Together, the two men sprinted in his direction.

As the two Brits reached him, the single Wraith that had pursued them into the hotel's admin area appeared from the same place the Rangers had just emerged and opened fire.

Together, Dune and the lead Ranger threw themselves upwards and onto the moving steps of the escalator.

As rounds zipped overhead and punched into the steel of the escalator's metal framing, Dune looked back to the casino floor and saw the second Ranger crumpled into a fetal position only a couple feet from where the escalator's moving steps emerged from the floor. The flank of his torso had been torn open, and his white button-down was soaked in blood.

Beside him, Dune heard the anguished cry of the sole remaining Ranger, "Dodger! No, Dodger!"

Halfway to the second level, the British commando got to his feet, but before he could start in the direction of his mate, Dune grabbed him and, with all the strength he could bring to bear, pulled him down.

Just as they disappeared behind the protection of the escalator's right-side balustrade, a stream of bullets ripped past where their upper bodies had just been.

Dune hugged the frenzied commando until they reached the escalator's apex, where Rochefort was waiting for them. A powerhouse of a man, the CSOR sergeant easily took control of the much-leaner Brit.

Freed from holding down the distraught soldier, Dune got to his feet, looked down the length of the escalator and saw all three Wraiths walking toward the moving stairwell, their weapons raised upward and scanning.

Dune turned to Rochefort and the Ranger, but before he could announce they needed to haul ass, his eyes caught movement in the direction of the Grand Canal.

Perhaps the most popular feature of the Venetian Resort was its Grand Canal shopping district, a spectacular indoor replication of the world-famous canal system in Venice. In response to the gunfire and the terrified people who would have fled the first-level melee, the shops and restaurants were practically empty except for one rather large man riding what Dune assessed to be a four-wheel miracle.

Without saying a word, Dune raced toward the obese American and sturdy scooter that had been tentatively edging out from one of the Canal's many restaurants.

As Dune got closer to the gentleman and saw the man's eyes widen in terror, he was struck with a not-so-kind idea of how he might get his hands on the man's ride.

Skidding to a halt in front of the bloke, Dune put his right hand into his shirt at the small of his back and, with the best Arabic accent he could muster, screamed, "Get out of your seat, mate, or I'll fill your noggin with lead like the people I just off'd down on level one."

And then, in his Aussie accent, he quickly yelled, "Allahu Akbar!"

It was the Arabic words that did the trick. Hearing the reference that so many Hollywood movies had abused, the man stammered, "Okay, okay. You can have it."

With all of the speed of a geriatric sloth, the terrified man began to turn his huge body so as to extract himself from his ride. The man was about halfway out of his seat when Dune heard Rochefort call to him, "Captain, they're halfway up the escalator - what's the plan?"

"Shit!" Dune said, and then turning his eyes back to the heavy-set American, he put both of his hands on the man's back and pushed as hard as he could.

As the man crashed onto the marble floor and grunted in pain, Dune cried out, "Crickey, sorry, mate!"

The seat of the heavy-duty scooter now free, Dune leaped on board and, using its joystick controller, sent the machine rolling forward toward the escalators.

Within a half-dozen paces, Dune had the machine up to its top speed, which had to be at least fifteen klicks per hour. Through the unit's off-road tires, he got a feel for its weight. A solid piece of kit, he guessed his momentary chariot to be at least four hundred pounds. It would do the trick.

To his left, he saw Rochefort and the last Ranger. Both of them were looking at him as though he had gone bat-shit crazy. As he whizzed by them, he heard Rochefort yell something he didn't understand in French.

Ahead in the direction of the mouth of the escalator, Dune spied the first of the Wraiths. Seeing only the first of the auto's vertical row of eyes, he kept his arse firmly planted on the powerchair's seat and willed the bloody thing to move faster.

It was only when the Chinese automaton's rifle came into view that Dune finally bailed.

Throwing himself to the right and rolling the moment he hit the polished floor, he heard a long string of gunfire erupt and felt a sharp pain in the lower part of his right leg as one of the Wraith's bullets grazed across his flesh.

Though yelping in pain, Dune still managed to perceive the sound of gunfire being replaced by that of something heavy and mechanical being hurled down a flight of at least two hundred unforgiving steel stairs.

The combined sound of heavy clattering and things breaking was music to Dune's ears.

Opening his eyes, he took in both Rochefort and the Ranger standing at the edge of the escalator, looking down in the direction of where he'd last seen the first of what he'd hoped had been all three of the Chinese terminators.

Together, with wide smiles on both of their faces, the Canadian and British commandos turned their eyes toward Dune. It was the Ranger who spoke first. "I don't care what Fielder says about you, Captain. You're a bloody CANZUK legend."

Chapter 28

Ottawa, CSIS HQ

"So, we're certain the Chinese did it?" Larocque asked.

"There is no doubt," said Petit. "You saw the footage yourself. Those were Chinese Wraiths driving the trucks. The method of using a truck bomb is new, but employing those machines to conduct assassinations has been going on for weeks."

"And we think more Chinese agents have come into BC just in the past few days?"

Petit nodded his head. "There's no doubt. Our assets in the Chinese-Canadian community have been unequivocal. They're seeing new faces every day. Current estimates are that an additional two to three hundred Ministry of State Security assets have entered the country just in the past week."

Larocque paused his questioning of Petit and cast his eyes to the twenty or so empty seats in the boardroom. Empty because after the Tomic-led mutiny, he'd undertaken another full house cleaning of the country's national intelligence service. Fully two hundred IOs and another twenty-six executives had been put on paid leave or outright fired from their jobs.

At this rate, Larocque wouldn't have an agency to oversee, never mind having meaningful conversations about how to address the growing Chinese threat or the menace that was the White Unit.

It hadn't been lost on him that while CSIS was unloading people, Canada's enemies were bringing in assets in the hundreds and growing bolder by the day.

But there had been no choice. Once Tomic's treachery had been exposed, he had to suspect anyone who had worked with her in the past five years.

Employing a specially designed near-AI program that had been created by a team of techs from the Canadian Security Establishment, Larocque had given the order to pull tens of thousands of internal CSIS emails and have those documents passed through an algorithm that would score how likely it was the author of the email would be sympathetic to or even a supporter of the Assistant Director.

The analysis completed, a purge had followed.

As Larocque's gaze returned to Petit, he offered a silent prayer this latest cull would be the last. "So, we know it was the Chinese who killed Chin-Edwards, and we know more of them are coming into the country every day. Making all of this worse, we still have the White Unit out there disappearing Chinese agents."

"It's a terrible mess," offered Petit.

Larocque nodded at the other man's statement and said, "Yes, it is, Sam, and now you're the Assistant Director of Operations and one of a handful of people I can trust in this organization. So, what's the plan?"

"Well, as we sit here and chat, I've got folks we trust promoting and reassigning people from across the organization. Within forty-eight hours, all of our critical positions will be filled."

Larocque interrupted. "Including those who we're pulling in from the outside?"

"Correct," Petit said. "CANSOFCOM isn't happy about it, but with your cajoling, they've agreed to loan us just over one hundred and fifty bodies. Mostly from their intel and signals units, but there are a good number of people who can affect direct operations. On that front, between these new folks and those you pulled in from the Airborne, we're actually quite a bit stronger than we were before this whole debacle kicked off."

"And the police?" said Larocque.

"We've had to be a bit more choosey with the RCMP and other forces because we lack personal connections with these outfits, but with the help of a few people I trust on the domestic intel side of our business, we've submitted nearly sixty names of people we want to bring in. We suspect three-quarters will agree to sign on."

Again, Larocque nodded his head in approval, then cast his eyes down at his BAM wrist unit. It was Madison's birthday today, and he hadn't been home in over ten days. His wife, understanding all that was going on, was being a patient and supportive partner, but everyone had their limits. "I don't want to rush you, Sam, but I have a hard stop in thirty mikes. In that time, I want to know what we're going to do about the Chinese and this goddamned White Unit."

If Petit was thrown by the truncated briefing, he didn't give any indication of it. "Not a problem, Director. I'll start with the White Unit and then move to the Chinese as answers to that problem will take more time to explain."

"Go in whichever order you'd like," said Larocque.

"The solution to the White Unit is simple. With yesterday's announcement to invoke the Emergencies Act, I instructed Legal to start the paperwork to freeze the assets and bank accounts of everyone we suspect is a part of the White Unit plus their immediate families, including their parents and siblings."

"Jesus, we're going after their families," Larocque exclaimed.

"It's heavy-handed and won't stand up to a court challenge, but we think it's the quickest way to crimp their operations. If those closest to the White Unit can't access their bank accounts, the people at the top of the organization will hear about it almost immediately."

"Indeed, they will. And then what?" Larocque asked.

"We offer immunity and agree to turn their financial taps back on. It'll be a trickle at first, but we think the numbers will grow quickly enough. Two weeks, maybe three – my guess is that by then enough people will be willing to inform on Aziz, his whereabouts, and other critical parts of their operation. The moment we can get our hands on the Colonel and his lieutenants, things start to get easier."

"And Legal's on board?"

"They are as soon as the Emergencies Act gets passed. Draconian as it may be, it'll be a game changer for us," Petit said, sounding confident.

For several moments, Larocque remained silent as he processed what he'd just been told. As his brain ran through various scenarios, the fingers on his right hand tapped out a beat. Finally, he said, "Okay, it's a good plan, Assistant Director. Now, I'm even more interested to hear what you have on tap for the Chinese."

***

Five hours later, with a beer in his hand, Larocque sat contently on the sofa in his family room watching the Blue Jays play the Yankees.

Despite the civil war and the destruction of large swaths of New York City and Chicago by UCSA nuclear strikes just over two years ago, Major League Baseball teams located in the American Northeast and Great Lakes region had continued to play.

He heard footsteps moving in his direction. Lifting his heavy eyes from the television, he turned his head to find Madison and Trisha Dune standing at the threshold of the room where he had been digesting the birthday dinner his wife had cooked. Trisha, now showing the hint of a belly, was holding a sleeping baby Marcel on her chest.

As he had found out during the discussion over dinner, Captain Dune's wife had been spending a fair bit of time with Ms. Larocque. The two women were clearly fond of one another, and as she'd promised on the Dune's wedding day, Madison had made sure Trisha had been exposed to anything and everything that was positive or family-oriented on CFB Petawawa and the surrounding community.

In truth, Trisha had not needed Madison's help with her transition. As an emergency room nurse, she quickly found a position at the local hospital, which was hopping due to the fighting south of the border.

There, the combination of her nursing skills, delightful personality, and killer good looks had her new colleagues and patients alike singing her praises.

When Larocque's eyes met Madison's, one of her eyebrows arched, and she said, "Is it General or Mr. Director? Or perhaps as you sit your butt in that sofa and allow us to cook and clean, the proper title should be none other than Lord Larocque?"

With a mischievous smile blooming on his face, he said, "Lord Larocque, eh? It has a bit of a ring to it if you ask me."

Madison rolled her eyes and, with a sarcastic tone, said, "The cake's ready, *Jackson*, so haul your ass off the couch and come join us in the kitchen."

Still smiling, Larocque pushed himself to his feet and said, "I would love to join you for cake, my queen. Is it somebody's birthday?"

As Trisha's eyes widened, Madison's right hand came up from her side and, in true spitfire fashion, gave him the bird.

Larocque's only response was to blow her a kiss.

On reaching the kitchen, he took in the butterfly-inspired cake with the number forty-one sitting atop it.

It was charming, but before he could offer a compliment or ask who had made it, there was a polite knock at the front door.

Larocque froze.

With everything going on, CSIS had assigned two pairs of protection officers to follow him everywhere he went when he left the Service's main campus.

Since getting home, one pair would have been in their car parked at the only turn-off leading to his residence, while the other pair would have tucked themselves into a secondary laneway to the left of his house that the previous owners had used to store boats and jet skis.

The closest pair of officers couldn't place eyes directly on Larocque's home, but if they got a warning from their colleagues down the road, they could quickly move to block access to Larocque's laneway or, if needed, could use a path through the trees, enter Larocque's house, and help to defend the property or evacuate Larocque and his family.

Larocque and Madison lived on the edge of the town of Deep River, which was about ten klicks west of Petawawa. They had neighbors to their left and right, but unless you knew they were there, the trees surrounding their property made it seem like the residence was in the middle of nowhere.

On top of that, they were hardly close to either neighbor. Larocque dug through his memory, and the last time he could remember either of them stopping by unannounced was a few weeks after Lauren's funeral. Mr. and Mrs. Knoll, long-retired teachers, had stopped by with a casserole and bouquet of flowers. That had been nearly three years ago.

Understanding where Larocque's thoughts were going, Madison's eyes locked onto her husband's.

Sensing something might be wrong, Trisha broke the room's silence. "I take it you weren't expecting anybody?"

There was another knock on the door. Again, polite but firm.

Larocque lifted up his arm and looked at his BAM wrist unit. The border of the display was red, signaling the network was being jammed.

The CAF had invested billions in telecoms hardware to ensure the BAM could not be jammed easily. Since getting the kit, Larocque could recall only a handful of situations when the system had been forced offline.

He took two strides in the direction of the fridge. Reaching over it, he opened the left cupboard, pulled out his Sig Sauer P365 compact, and chambered the first of its 9mm rounds.

Turning to his wife, he said, "Go to the back door. If I give the word, gun it for the trees and get to the river just like we practiced. Paddle to the base and connect with Bear, St. Pierre, or Mallory. Only those three. They'll know what to do."

Tears started to well up in his wife's eyes. He reached for her, but before they could make contact, there was a third knock at the door. This time, it was heavy, even aggressive.

Flicking his head to the back of the house, Larocque said, "Go. Now."

He did not wait to see if Madison would follow his direction. He knew she would because, above all else, Madison would protect the baby.

Reaching their home's foyer, Larocque went to the large bay window overlooking their front yard. It was dusk. Looking right at a sharp angle, he could see what looked to be a single man standing at their front door. Whoever he was, he was burly and appeared to be alone.

Taking one more careful look into his yard to see if he could identify anyone else and seeing nothing, he moved to the entrance.

Tucking his weapon into the small of his back but leaving his hand on its grip, he reached out with his other hand, turned the door's handle, and slowly opened it.

Immediately, he recognized the huge man standing in front of him.

"Director Larocque," the man said in a deep voice. "I'm very sorry to have disturbed you here at your home. I understand it's your wife's birthday today, so no doubt my visit is even more of an intrusion."

"Colonel Aziz. I would have never thought." Larocque said plainly, quickly adding, "I trust my people are well?"

Slowly, both of Aziz's huge hands rose into the air, his palms facing outward. "Your people down the street and next door are fine. Not their pride so much, but tonight will be a good lesson for them."

As the Special Operations officer lowered his hands, he nodded his head to the interior of the house. "And I am only here to talk. Your wife, her friend, and your son are not in any danger."

Ignoring the reference to his wife and Marcel, Larocque asked, "Then you're here for a friendly chat?"

"I am," said the visitor. "May I come in?"

"No," Larocque said firmly. He gestured to a pair of Muskoka patio chairs on a landscaped area to the right of the stairs leading up to the house. "Grab a seat. I'll be back in under a minute."

Aziz didn't look back in the direction of the chairs. Instead, the smile on his face dropped away, and he said, "I'm not a vampire, you know. By letting me into your house, you're not making yourself any or more or less vulnerable to what I am."

Larocque took a step in Aziz's direction and, making sure to lower his voice, said, "In all honesty, I'm not sure what you're trying to achieve by coming here, but I'm glad you came. The conversation you and I are going to have is long overdue."

Lowering his voice another octave, Larocque added, "But know this, Colonel, should you or anyone who works for you take one step inside this house or even on this property after our conversation is over, I will hunt you down, and I will end you. Do you hear me, Aziz?"

As a smile returned to Aziz's lips, he stepped to his left.

Without warning, a pair of green targeting dots emerged on Larocque's chest. Through the increasing darkness, he could see the lasers emanating from separate locations in the trees across from his property.

"I'll sit and wait for you, Director, but before you go, a word of advice, if I may?"

Forcing himself to rip his eyes from the two green pinpoints on his sternum, Larocque moved his gaze back to Aziz's face.

When it was clear that Larocque wasn't going to indulge the White Unit's leader with permission to give whatever advice he had on offer, the barrel-chested man said plainly, "I'll see you in under one minute, and when you come back, don't even think of threatening me again, Director. Ever."

***

It had been four days since Petit had left CSIS HQ. In the aftermath of Tomic's treachery, his assumption of her role, and the cleanout of another tranche of intelligence officers, he had been working twenty-hour days. But coffee, energy drinks and a handful of two-hour power naps could only take you so far. Following Larocque's lead, he had decided he would sleep in his own bed tonight.

As he exited the elevator to the underground garage where the Service kept its fleet of surveillance vehicles, he found the black SUV that had been assigned to him in the pick-up zone with its engine running. Standing in front of the up-armored vehicle were its driver and a second CSIS Protection Officer.

In the hours after the White Unit ambushes that had killed the Intel Officers in BC, Larocque had mandated off-property protection for those CSIS executives responsible for running domestic and international operations.

As the Assistant Director, Operations, Petit had been given the coveted and hugely challenging role of overseeing both the domestic and international sides of Canada's national intelligence service. At forty, he was young for the role, but so many of the old guard had left on their own or been pushed out by Larocque's effort to ensure the executive ranks of the organization were reading from the new playbook.

And truth be told, he checked all the requirements for the position. He had seven years of international postings and four years of domestic ops, and to the best of Petit's knowledge, he was the only person in all of the Service who'd actually worked inside the White Unit.

Yes, that last role had splashed blood onto his hands, but that was something he would come to terms with when the country and the rest of CANZUK had pulled back from the precipice of disaster they were now facing.

"You two again. You guys have all the luck," Petit said to the two Protection Officers – POs – as he arrived at the SUV.

There was a pool of the POs that rotated through a handful of responsibilities, of which the two most common were patrolling key government buildings like the CSIS campus and providing VIP protection service as was being done now.

In the past two days alone, Petit had been downtown, attending meetings on five different occasions with various government higher-ups. On three of those trips, it had been Maurice and Gaetan who had got him to and from where he needed to be.

"All the way to Montreal tonight, eh, Sam?" It was Gaetan, the older of the two men, who had posed the question.

The man was in his mid-fifties but had taken care of himself over the years. Mostly quiet, in their short time working together, he had regaled Petit with more than one good story from a tour he'd done in Afghanistan with the Vandoos back in the late 2000s.

Smiling at the former soldier, Petit said, "My place is on the west side of the Island, so it won't take us more than an hour with the way you drive."

The PO smiled at the light jibe making reference to his lead foot, but true to form, Gaetan said nothing. Instead, he turned and made to get into the driver's seat of the vehicle.

The other PO, younger and nowhere near as reserved as his partner, called to Petit, "I know you're a bigwig and all now, Sam, but if you don't mind me saying, I think it's a good thing you're going home. If you're asking, and I know you're not, it looks like you should use what's left of today and all of tomorrow to catch up on some of your sleep."

As Petit put his hand on the handle of the passenger door to open it, he called back to the PO now making his way to the SUV's passenger seat and said, "Did you just say I look like shit?"

As both men opened their respective doors and climbed into their seats, the PO replied, "Listen, far be it from me to tell the number two guy of our national intelligence service he looks like garbage. As Gaetan is my witness, it was you who said you looked like shit, not me. I only remarked it looks like you need some sleep."

As the SUV began to move, Petit raised both hands in mock surrender and said, "Alright, Mom. I've got the message, loud and clear."

Using the buttons on the right side of the seat, Petit began to make adjustments to lean back so he could catch some shut-eye as he made the trip home.

Whatever the reason, for the moment, his inbox was quiet, so there was no good reason for him not to have a catnap. His seat reclined to the proper angle, Petit said, "While I start to get my beauty rest, can I leave you two gentlemen to find your way to West Montreal?"

"Roger that, Boss," said Gaetan. "It's just after eight. If traffic is kind, we'll be at your place in just over an hour. One of us will give you a wake-up call when we're ten minutes out."

Petit looked at the other PO, who said, "Sweet dreams, Boss."

***

He was woken by the steady pulse of his BAM wrist unit. He was wearing the smaller version of the tech more suitable for civilian-facing work.

Blinking his eyes, Petit brought the wrist unit forward so he could read the display. Not recognizing the name, he didn't immediately pick up. Instead, he said, "Maurice, where are we at?"

The PO in the front passenger seat turned his head to look at Petit and said, "Just passed into Quebec. Another thirty minutes. Traffic is light, and our driver this evening is Max Verstappen in spirit, if not the flesh. We could make it shorter if you wanted?"

Petit shook his head. "No, that's okay. It looks like I need to take a call."

The PO flashed Petit a thumbs-up and turned back to the road ahead.

With enough of the synapses of his brain firing, he raised the back of his seat and placed the BAM's earbud into his ear.

'Terri Dunlop,' the name flashing on his wrist unit, wasn't a name he'd heard of before, but there seemed to be an entire legion of self-important officials in the Prime Minister's Office who wouldn't hesitate to call after hours. "Stupid staffers," he said quietly, and then after taking a deep, calming breath, in a louder voice, he said, "Accept the call."

"Sam, it's me."

As if struck by high-voltage electricity, whatever parts of his brain were not yet in motion instantly came alive. Hearing Sara Hall's voice invoked a flood of memories, none of them good.

As casually as he might, Petit turned his head left and right to see if there were any vehicles around them that were a threat. Seeing none, his eyes moved to the display affixed to the dash in front of Maurice.

Because of the use of drones as a tool for assassination during the Ukraine-Russia war, CSIS and a handful of other security-focused departments had purchased a few hundred drone defense kits that could easily be mounted on any vehicle. The screen that monitored the kit's activity read as normal.

"Sam, I know you can hear me."

"I can hear you," Petit said, making sure to keep his voice calm.

"You are a complicated man."

"Oh? How so?" Petit asked.

"I've not called you to play games. You know the choices you've made, but more importantly, you understand that with every choice a person makes, there are consequences."

Before he could ask what consequences Hall might be referring to, their vehicle started to change lanes and slow down. Ahead in the distance, Petit could see an off-ramp approaching. Gaetan, the driver, signaled they would be taking the exit.

Tamping down the alarms going off in his head, Petit, still in a calm voice, asked, "Gaetan, where are we going?"

But the driver did not answer. Petit's eyes then flashed over to the passenger seat. There, he found Maurice unsmiling and holding his service pistol with its barrel pointed at his center mass.

Hall's voice once again invaded his earbud. "This time, I couldn't save you, Sam. I hoped you would walk away, but a part of me knew you wouldn't be able to. But even if there was a part of me that wanted to give you another chance, I've gained enough wisdom in my young life to know that you'd burn me again."

As the SUV approached the stop at the end of the exit ramp, he drilled his eyes into Maurice and said, "You don't have to do this.

Whatever they've told you. Whatever they're paying you, we can work it out, Maurice."

"He won't talk with you," Hall said. "The only thing he'll do is fill your chest full of lead should you do anything stupid, like make a move to release your seatbelt or reach for your weapon. Just sit still, Sam. You're almost to where you need to be."

Ten minutes later, in near darkness, the SUV turned off a rural road onto a gravel roadway hemmed in by trees on both sides.

The SUV stopped at a clearing where there was a dilapidated farmhouse. A single vehicle, an SUV similar to the one Petit was riding in, was parked in front of the overgrown property. A lone person was standing beside it.

When the SUV came to a stop, Gaetan immediately exited and moved to open Petit's door. His gun drawn, he said, "Hands where I can see them and get out. Slowly."

Doing what he was told, Petit undid his seatbelt and slid from his seat.

With no engines running, he heard the crunching of gravel as Maurice approached him from behind. Roughly, Petit felt the protection officer reach for and relieve him of his handgun.

He then heard what sounded like metal sliding across metal. Just as he was about to turn his head to identify the sound, an explosion of pain erupted at the back of his knees.

As he began to yell in pain and protest, he was struck in the same place. This time, his knees buckled, dropping him to the ground.

"Fuck!" he yelled as the combined pain of the take-down strike and his knees connecting with the hard ground surged through his body.

Weaponless and immobilized, the two men retreated from him. As the two POs came to a stop, Petit again heard the sound of gravel being tread upon.

Looking over his shoulder, he wasn't surprised to see the face of Hall.

As she arrived in front of him, they took a moment to stare each other down.

Finally, Petit broke the silence. "You look the same."

"It's only been a few months. What were you expecting?"

"I don't know. A bit of weariness, maybe. It's got to be tough killing people in cold blood for weeks on end. You'd think that would begin to take its toll."

Hall didn't reply to Petit's unvarnished assessment. Instead, she lowered to her haunches so her hazel eyes could be level with Petit's brown.

Speaking softly so as to prevent her words from being heard by the two nearby POs, Hall said, "Before I kill you with my own hands, Sam, I wanted to give you the dignity of knowing why you're going to die tonight."

"Besides the obvious reasons, of course," Petit retorted.

"As we speak, your new boss is having a conversation with my boss."

When a look of panic leaped onto Petit's face, Hall continued, "Not to worry, Sam. He won't be happy about the visit, but Larocque will be fine. He'll be offered a deal. A deal, I hope, for our country's sake, he takes."

Petit nodded. "Larocque isn't unhinged like Aziz or you. The only thing you'll accomplish by visiting him at his home is to add more fuel to his fire. He's going to catch you, you know?"

This time it was Hall's turn to shake her head. "Don't forget, Sam, that I know Larocque too. And yes, he will be most unhappy with our visit, but it is also the case that the Director is, above all other things, a practical operator who loves his country."

Petit said, "And you're going to make him a deal he can't refuse? Just like the deal he was offered by Tomic? And how is it that my death fits into this deranged proposal? If you kill me, he'll only come after you harder."

For a long moment, Hall only stared at Petit. Her eyes were pitiless. Finally, she said, "You, Sam Petit, are the exclamation mark of our offer. You will be the example of what happens should Larocque refuse to work with us. If we can get to you, we can get to him. No one is safe, Sam. No one."

For the first time during their conversation, Petit raised his voice. "What they're doing to you is not right, Sara. They're using you. What they're doing to you and to this country – it's not right, and it's going to make things worse, not better. Open your eyes! It's so goddamned obvious. All you have to do is open your eyes to it."

Hall shook her head and said, "You've tried this angle before, Sam. It didn't work then, and it won't work now."

Rising from her haunches, a pistol appeared in Hall's right hand. Now standing, she raised the weapon and pointed it at Petit's chest. "I understand that you, Sam Petit, live in a naïve world where kind words and gestures and things like 'soft power,' diplomacy, emotions, and 'doing the right thing' are notions that still have currency. And one day, far into the future, these things might matter again, but not right now.

"Right now, our country and our prime minister need to be given the time and the space to do the hard things that need to be done. We know who you've been speaking to. We're not just sending a message to Larocque but others as well.

"Goodbye, Sam. For the record, you were warned."

Instinctively, Petit's hands came up into the air. His palms out, he said in a pleading voice, "Sara, it doesn't have to be like this."

When she gave no hint of a reply, he screamed, "SARA!"

The first round struck Petit at the center of his chest.

As though he had been struck by a well-swung sledgehammer, his upper body flew backward so that he was lying flat on his back.

Staring into the sky, Petit's eyes were drawn to what looked to be the night's first star. Hearing the crunch of gravel and seeing Hall's dark form standing over him, he drew as much breath as he could manage into his lungs and then, gasping, said, "God, forgive me for all that I have done."

As Hall levelled her handgun in the direction of Petit's head, she took a long moment to stare into his eyes. Finally, quietly, she said, "You just weren't strong enough for the time we live in, Sam. If God does exist, perhaps he can explain that to you."

Then she pulled the trigger.

Chapter 29

Deep River, West of CFB Petawawa

—

After a brief conversation with Madison to inform her the plan of escape remained the same, he returned to the front of the house where Aziz was now seated.

The leader of the White Unit looked out to the well-manicured front yard and said, "This is a nice place. Both times I was here at Pet, I lived in Pembroke. I grew up as a big city kid so when I did have free time, I would drive into Ottawa. It's hardly what I'd call a big city, but it's certainly not like this place."

Aziz turned his head to look at Larocque. "It's the quiet that's the worst part. Where I grew up in Montreal, there's this constant unnatural hum that comes with three million people and everything it takes to keep them comfortable. But not here. The vibe here is different."

Pausing, Aziz canted his head and listened to the sound of nature as it made the transition from a busy summer day to the sedate sound of night.

"I'm fifty-two now, Larocque. Perhaps, in my old age, I might come to appreciate a place like this. If you've found your peace, I'm glad for it."

"I'm afraid there will be no peace for you, Colonel, or however it is you'd prefer me to address you?" Larocque asked in a tone that contrasted sharply with the quiet resignation Aziz had just offered.

After releasing a tired sigh, Aziz said, "I still have my commission, so you can call me Colonel or Mustapha. And you're right, there will be no peace for me. That is not the path I've chosen. On the path of sacrifice, peace only comes at the end, when you are no longer of this world. And even then, it may be that peace for me is not assured."

"What is it that you want, Colonel? Why are you here?"

"I'm here to offer you a partnership."

Larocque's eyebrows jumped upwards in surprise, but before he could say anything, Aziz carried on.

"But before I make my offer, I want to apologize for that misunderstanding with Assistant Director Tomic. Until recently, I thought it might be best if you weren't leading CSIS, but I've since been convinced it would be best if you stay where you are. I see now that your resourcefulness and determination should be leveraged, not disposed of."

Larocque snapped angrily, "A 'misunderstanding' – is that what you called that disaster? You killed four good people. People with families."

Aziz shrugged his massive shoulders and then reached into the light jacket he was wearing and pulled out a pack of cigarettes. Opening the package, he drew a smoke and placed it to his lips.

As he moved to light the cigarette, he said, "Care for one?"

"Don't ignore me, Colonel. You killed four CSIS officers and have indirectly killed countless others with this campaign you're waging on the Chinese."

His voice still casual, Aziz said, "I did you a favor, Larocque. Yes, good people died, and I regret that, but with this disaster, as you call it, you wouldn't have been able to smoke out Tomic and the other resisters. The way I see it, you owe me one."

Ignoring the look of outrage on Larocque's face, Aziz took another long drag of this cigarette and said, "You and I both know the world isn't going back to what it was before the Americans started killing themselves. At least for the next five years. Even if the Chinese get pushed out of Vietnam and even if the Americans somehow manage to reconcile, the world is going to remain a very dangerous place."

When Larocque only continued to give Aziz a hard stare, the bigger man scoffed and continued, "C'mon, Director. Rome has fallen. Our country can't afford to return to the type of thinking that ran Canada for the past sixty years, and you and I can't get hung up on the death of a few people, as tragic as those deaths may have been. Because if we do get hung up on them, the country we both love will get eaten alive."

"I don't think we're being eaten alive now," Larocque finally spoke, his voice hot.

"And why is that?" Aziz asked.

When Larocque gave no answer, the White Unit leader said, "For just one minute, I want you to indulge me. Think of the world as it exists today and then think of a certain washed-up trust fund loser once again leading our country. Worse, think of the man they are getting ready to re-install as the leader of His Majesty's Loyal Opposition."

After a pause, Aziz said, "How will Canada fare under the leadership of one of these men? Or worse, both? It's happened before, and it was a disaster."

Aziz paused his narrative to take another drag of his now half-finished smoke.

"Tell me, Larocque, how does that scenario end in your mind? Does it end with President Yan agreeing to pull his people out of BC because he was delighted by our leader's choice of socks? Or maybe Mitchell Spector agrees to stop murdering thousands of political opponents because the leader of Canada stands up in Parliament in his Armani suit and Rolex and hectors about the man being a white supremacist bigot?"

Larocque interjected, "The Conservatives and Merielle just won a majority. They're in power for the next four years. A lot can happen in that time. They could win the next election. The opposition parties could come to their senses and not recycle old garbage. I trust Canadians, Aziz. Not just the ones who I know think like me. People aren't stupid. They see what's going on in the world, and they'll vote accordingly. That's the beauty of our system."

Aziz issued a quick chuckle and then said. "Jesus Christ, Larocque, I didn't think you were that gullible. Can't you see what's going on?"

"Enlighten me," Larocque said.

"The Laurentian Elite is what's going on. As we speak, they're circling Merielle, and they are getting ready to pull her down. That woman, Tomic, was just the first. They can't stand that they're not pulling the strings. I know you've had conversations with some of them, and I know they've whispered in your ear that Merielle is fast-tracking this country toward authoritarianism and that she must go.

"I know you know Merielle well, Larocque. You know where her heart is and what it is she's trying to do, and most importantly, whether you want to admit it to my face or not, you know our current PM is precisely what this country needs for the next four years, if not longer."

Larocque exhaled loudly. "And my support for Merielle means our country's national intelligence service should partner with a rogue agency that is disappearing Chinese nationals?

"Do you know, Aziz, that as of two days ago, CSIS is no longer operating in Malaysia and the Philippines?"

When the other man gave no reply, Larocque continued, "We're no longer operating in those countries because for every Chinese operative the White Unit takes off the board, as many as two to three of our people are found with a bullet in their head, drowned, or worse."

On hearing the revelation, Aziz only stared back at Larocque.

When it was clear no response would come, Larocque rolled on. "Tell me you're not so stupid to think that the actions of your people don't have consequences in other places. We never worked together, Aziz, but I know your reputation, and never once did anyone mention you were a fool. What's your damn play?"

Aziz took one final haul from his cigarette. Exhaling and flicking the butt onto the grass, he said, "How can the elite of this country replace the prime minister if she's responding to assassinated opposition leaders and blown-up provincial premiers, never mind two wars?"

Not waiting for Larocque to reply, Aziz said, "They can't. They wouldn't dare."

"The wars won't go on forever," said Larocque. "Even now, in the Pacific and in New York, there's hope where there was none even two weeks ago."

Aziz shook his head, "The world is not returning to the way it once was, Larocque, and to think otherwise is a fool's errand.

"First look to Europe. Russia is as strong as it has ever been. The Poles are well-armed and determined, but like the Ukraine, they cannot prevail. To the west, France remains determined to deport every Muslim in Europe. In the Middle East, Iran, as ever, wants to wipe Israel off the map and now they have the weapons to do it. Another nuclear war is in the offing.

"In Africa, the north seethes because Europe has sent them tens of millions of people who may look North African but who are two or even three generations removed. Of course, the rest of the continent burns and starves per the norm.

"In the Pacific, within three years, China will have Taiwan's microchip factories back up and running. Even if we were successful in pushing them out of Vietnam, tell me how the Chinese become anything but stronger. They will learn from their mistakes, they will adapt, and they'll try something else. You can't stop 1.4 billion people."

Aziz paused his tour of everything wrong with the world to light another cigarette. Blowing smoke into the air, he said, "You've seen war firsthand, Larocque. You know how vicious and brutal the world can be. The thin veneer of civilization has been pulled off. I know you can't be so naïve that you think this mess we're in gets fixed by the end of Merielle's mandate, assuming she's allowed to finish it."

Larocque let the other man take a long drag of his cigarette and said, "You mentioned a partnership. What is it you're offering, and why should I consider it?"

In between drags, Aziz nodded at the other man and said, "Good. I'm relieved that you're listening and that you're prepared to hear me out. Knowing what I know of you, Larocque, that's all I can ask."

In the distance, a loon on the Ottawa River issued its call into what was now late evening. As the two men listened to the bird's haunting cry, Larocque maintained a poker face and kept his eyes on Aziz.

Finally, as the call of the bird faded into the night's calm, the other man said, "I need a steel-clad commitment from you. One that binds you and the whole of CSIS."

"A commitment to what?"

"Merielle needs another mandate. She cannot fix what needs to be fixed in four years. She needs two mandates. Two mandates, and she walks away. She resigns, and whoever wins the next election gets to call the shots. If she can't sort out what needs sorting in eight years, then it's beyond her, but she needs to be given that opportunity."

Considering all of the information that had been shared with him by Petit, MacPhail and others, Larocque was only half-surprised the request had come. He said, "You want CSIS to rig an election?"

As though he was commenting on the day's weather, Aziz said, "Not exactly."

When the White Unit leader didn't move to provide more details, Larocque said, "If you're asking me to thwart Canada's democracy like the KGB or the CIA, you're gonna have to give more than a 'not exactly.'"

Still standing, Aziz uncrossed his huge arms from his chest and moved them down to his hips. The look on the man's face suggested he was negotiating with himself as to what he should say next.

Finally, he said, "We know there's an effort underway to remove Merielle from power. These elements exist within the Conservatives themselves. We know these elements have approached you and have made the suggestion that as you hunt down the White Unit, you should look to establish a link between our organization and the prime minister.

"Let me save you some time, Larocque. The PM has nothing to do with us. That is a fantasy that's been concocted by people who themselves want to run this country. Let me suggest to you that these people are playing a dangerous game."

Larocque shook his head vigorously and said, "Cool your jets on the conspiracy thinking, Colonel. We're hunting you because you're a rogue outfit killing people in a country that has never – never in its entire history – ever contemplated the idea of assassinating people. It's that simple."

With a hint of disdain in his tone, Aziz said, "You can deny it all you want, Larocque, but we know people are actively working to take down the PM."

His voice calm, Larocque said, "Is Merielle directing the White Unit?"

When no reply came, he posed another question. "Did Merielle put me in charge of CSIS hoping that in my respect and sympathy for her, I would help her stay in power? Has this game of cat and mouse that's killed dozens of my people been nothing more than an effort to convince me I should help subvert our country's democracy?"

Slowly, Larocque got to his feet, all the while staring at Aziz. "What you're asking me to do is treason. You have to give me something to help me understand why I should do what you're asking me to do."

"You have all the information you need, Larocque. You know what's taking place in other parts of the world. You know what's happening here in Canada, and I know you know people are trying to take Merielle down.

"The White Unit is filled with patriots. Jackson. We won't let this happen, just as we won't let the Chinese, the French, or the UCSA take what is ours. Even if we lose the war, we will continue to fight. If it comes to that, we will put the IRA and mujahideen to shame with our deeds. While you and others may deny it or might say I'm overstating the threat, the fact of the matter is that the White Unit is Canada's insurance policy. This is who we are, and this is why our two organizations should work together."

Aziz's right hand came forward and pointed toward Larocque's heart. "In that place, you, more than anyone, understand the challenge that confronts this country, and know that it is only Merielle who can navigate these times. She and people like you are what this country needs for a half-dozen years at least. Two full mandates would be better."

When Aziz finished delivering his proposal, he and Larocque stared at each other wordlessly. Finally, breaking the silence, the White Unit operator said, "I have given you the information you need to make a decision. Think of everything we've discussed and think about the offer that's on the table. You have three days to decide."

One of Aziz's hands moved to his pants pocket, pulled out what looked like a business card, and handed it to Larocque. "In three days, use that address and inform us of your decision. It's encrypted. Your response will be limited to fifty characters. We don't want an essay. We want an answer."

Without another word, Aziz turned his back on Larocque and began to walk down the laneway. It was now twilight, and out of the reach of the interior lights of the house, the man CSIS had been working so hard to find in recent weeks grew into a hulking shadow.

Aziz was at the end of the laneway when he stopped and called back through the still night air, "I was serious earlier when I said there are people close to the PM who are working against her. Tonight, we've taken one of those actors out of the game. On a permanent basis, I'm afraid."

Larocque called back, "I still don't know what you're talking about. If there's a conspiracy, I'm outside of it."

"Perhaps," said Aziz, "But as you get word of what has transpired, know that in this country, the liars and political hustlers who claim to support Merielle but who, in fact, work against her will be found out and will be treated accordingly. Our days of ignoring this threat are over, Larocque. We will protect the leader of our country, no matter the cost."

"What the hell does that mean?" Larocque called back to the other man, but instead of answering him, Aziz turned to face down the street.

From that direction appeared a set of headlights and the sound of a moving vehicle.

Beyond Aziz on the other side of the road, Larocque caught two figures emerging from the tree line. With the illumination of the approaching vehicle, he could clearly see the outline of the rifles they were carrying.

As an SUV rolled to a stop at the end of his laneway, Larocque watched as the sharpshooters got in the back seat while Aziz opened the front door.

As the vehicle undertook an unhurried three-point turn to extricate itself from Larocque's cul-de-sac, he felt his BAM wrist unit vibrate gently.

Looking down, he saw that the red border had disappeared. He was relieved to see that there was no stack of calls waiting for him. Raising the wrist unit to his mouth, Larocque said, "Open channel to Scabbard One."

The female voice of his BAM instantly replied, "Channel open."

"Scabbard One, are you there?" Larocque said urgently.

He counted to three and repeated the question, "Scotty, are you there, kid?"

When the lead officer from his protection detail finally spoke, his voice sounded relieved. "It's good to hear your voice, Boss. Is everyone okay? I'm sorry. We're sorry. They snuck up on us from the trees. My BAM went offline, and the next thing I knew, we were both looking into a pair of suppressed barrels."

"We're fine, Scotty. Are the rest of your people okay?"

"Lillian and I are good, if a bit shaken. I need to check on Fahad and Bronson."

"Do that, and then all four of you can come to the house. We'll have cake."

"Cake, sir?" the PO said, his voice sounding confused. "Shouldn't I call for the military police at Pet? They can be here in under five. And shouldn't we put a call out for a drone to track that SUV? We've got one on standby back at the base."

"That's a negative, Scotty. Come in for food and, if you're up for it, a stiff drink. And don't rush to get here. Just come straight in through the door and be cool. We'll be in the kitchen. For tonight at least, I think the threat is over."

"Roger that, Boss. We'll see you in five."

"Make it ten, Scabbard. I've got to make a few calls before I head in. Scabbard Sunray out."

On hearing the connection drop off, Larocque said, "Priority call to Petit, Samuel, authorization Larocque Seven-Yankee-Two."

"Priority call has been placed. There is no queue," advised the BAM.

After five seconds, his BAM said, "The call recipient is not picking up."

His voice calm, Larocque said, "Repeat call."

Ten seconds later, the BAM update was the same.

"Locate Petit, Samuel, call sign Wildcat Alpha, authorization Larocque Niner-Hotel-Bravo."

"Authorization confirmed. Location of Wildcat Alpha is confirmed."

Larocque tabbed his wrist unit and brought up the tactical map featuring a red dot denoting where Petit was. He zoomed out, and on seeing the location, issued a quiet string of profanities.

"Confirm Wildcat's health status," Larocque said to the BAM.

"Wildcat Alpha's health status is negative."

"When did it go negative?"

The BAM, in a feminine but sterile voice, said, "Wildcat Alpha's heart rate ceased precisely fourteen minutes, seventeen seconds ago."

Chapter 30

White Sands Missile Range, Holloman Air Force Base, New Mexico

---

In the hours following the Wraith attack in Vegas, Dune had come to find out the extent of the UCSA attacks on CANZUK forces in Nevada and New Mexico. In a word, they had been extensive.

In all, something close to a hundred of the Chinese automatons had assaulted three military bases where CANZUK and California special operations forces had been gathering. Limited in the amount of destructive power the Wraiths could bring with them to assault each location, like Vegas, the bipedal robots had focused on soft targets.

Between base personnel, special operators, and civilians, nearly three hundred people had been killed. In Vegas, a staggering five hundred and thirty civilians and CANZUK military personnel had been cut down.

In the eyes of CANZUK's military leaders, it had been an epic security and intelligence failure and had rightly brought into question the plan to launch an attack on Spector's current headquarters to the west of Houston.

To the relief of Dune and others, that plan was no longer on the table. Privately, he had been concerned about the distances involved. The former United States was a big place, and though New Mexico and Texas were beside one another, from their mission take-off point in the east of New Mexico, the CANZUK-Western Alliance task force would have had to fly over a thousand kilometers of hostile territory to be able to assault the Red Faction leader's compound.

But in the days since the Wraith attack, it had become clear to Dune the brass were now cooking something else up.

He had been in no less than four meetings where he and the other junior officers from CSOR and the UK Rangers had been directed to re-organize and drill their people so that they would be primed and ready to fight in as short a time as possible.

With their CO and 2IC riding everyone's ass, in the last four days, each of CSOR's companies had conducted no less than four heliborne assaults, a fifteen-klick ruck march, and, as a Regiment, had expended what must have been over a million rounds at two separate extended range shoots. And all of it had taken place underneath the unrelenting sun that blazed over the Nevada desert.

Having spent nearly six months with CSOR as an officer, Dune was now prepared to admit his new unit was as tight as 2nd Commando. But even his former regiment, used to the scorching heat of the Outback and the stifling jungles of Indonesia, would have wilted in the face of the relentless training program that CSOR and the Rangers had been subjected to in recent days.

As he walked into what would be the fifth meeting to report on how his command was coming along, he promised himself that he wouldn't permit the Regiment's senior people to so casually blow off the growing concerns about their brutal training.

Yes, they were special operators, and yes, Dune understood that in response to the trauma of the recent attacks, they needed to keep their people busy enough they wouldn't have time to process what had happened to their mates. But too much was too bloody much.

As he walked into the same room that had been used for the previous briefings, Dune noticed there were more officers, including soldiers who weren't CANZUK special forces. At the front of the room were the Rangers and CSOR Commanding Officers and a stocky man that Dune recognized as a senior spec-ops officer from the Western Alliance.

Like the rest of the officers in the room, Dune moved to find a seat. Arriving only a minute before the briefing was to start, he opted to slide into a single free seat beside a hulking bloke whose uniform was devoid of any markings.

Seated, Dune offered his hand to the man and cheerily said, "G'day, mate. The name's Dune, Canadian Special Operations Regiment."

The soldier, who hadn't acknowledged his arrival, finally looked in his direction and narrowed his eyes. Ignoring Dune's proffered hand, he said, "Dude, what's with the accent?"

Dropping his hand, but still in a cheery tone, Dune said, "Ah, you see, mate, that's a bit of a story. Maybe after this here briefing, we can grab a java, and I can tell you how an Aussie like myself got in with a bunch of Canucks, and you can tell me why your uni doesn't have any markings. Sound like a fair trade?"

Before the soldier could answer, there was a call to attention from CSOR's CO, Colonel Beliveau from the front of the room. "All right, everyone, listen up. For the CANZUK people present, I know we've been working you hard. Very hard, in fact. But in all cases, you've stepped up.

"As some of you might have guessed, the recommendation to keep you busy came from the docs. Well, I'm pleased to let you know that the docs have signaled we can let up on our push. Which is good because, as of this afternoon, we have a new mission."

The CSOR CO looked to his right and said, "This is Major General Bryce Sato of the Western Alliance 2nd Special Operations Group. He's going to tell us about a joint op CANZUK and his people are going to partner on, so give him your full attention.

"General Sato, the floor is yours."

Sato was a squat man who had some Asian heritage running through his veins. On stepping up to the lectern that Beliveau had just vacated, the large display on the wall behind the general came alive with an image of a man whom Dune instantly categorized not as handsome but as pretty.

Pointing to the screen, Sato said, "Ladies and gentlemen, this is Peter Ian Parr. Those of you who watch the politics of the former United States may know that this man is the chief of staff to President Spector. He is Spector's closest and most trusted advisor. He is also the mastermind behind Operation Sunlight, a program that some of you in this room may have already been briefed on."

Lowering his hand, Sato's eyes left the screen to again take up the soldiers in the room. "Based on estimates, in the past five months, Operation Sunlight has liquidated something in the range of five to seven thousand Red Faction political opponents across the FAS. It's also believed that Operation Sunlight operatives were the ones who attacked Governor Sanchez at the Anaheim Convention Center."

The image on the display transitioned to another adult male, but where Spector's chief of staff had the looks of a movie star, the man now occupying the screen had the dreaded combination of being overweight and homely. "This is the Governor of Missouri. Missouri, you will recall, joined the Red Faction after CANZUK's Whiteman operation, but with all of the drama that followed this op, Missouri never signed a formal declaration that it was joining the UCSA. Our intelligence tells us that the Governor of Missouri is resistant to making his state's relationship with the UCSA official.

"Recently, we received intelligence suggesting Parr had been sent to Washington to strong-arm the states of Virginia, Maryland, and Delaware to sign their own UCSA declarations. With recent developments in the war here in North America and the Pacific, Spector is looking to shore up his political situation at home."

The screen behind the general transitioned again to show a rather uninspiring turn-of-the-century mansion. Pointing to the box-like structure, Sato said, "This is the Missouri Governor's official residence, and based on information we believe to be accurate, Mr. Parr will be meeting with Governor Reginald Powers at this location. It is here where Parr will ensure Missouri officially comes into the UCSA's fold."

As Sato leaned forward and placed both hands on the lectern, he said, "We do not care if the State of Missouri signs a formal declaration to officially join the UCSA. What we do care about is being able to take Peter Parr into custody so that Mitchell Spector can no longer benefit from his counsel, but more important, we want this person in our custody as a warning to Spector's other advisors and cronies that there is no safe place for them in the whole of the UCSA."

After he finished his statement, a pair of mid-ranking officers on both sides of the room began to hand out a document.

As the package reached Dune, he read the cover page: OPERATION JUSTICE SERVED – TOP SECRET.

Once the document had been provided to every officer in the room, the Western Alliance general continued. "Over the next ninety minutes, we will walk through our plan to visit Jefferson City and take into our possession Mitchell Spector's chief of staff and, in so doing, arrest or terminate a man who a year ago was a nobody, but who is now one of the world's great war criminals."

***

The plan had several moving parts.

To convince the UCSA's spies watching them in New Mexico and Nevada that Spector's compound in Texas was their primary target of interest, elements of CSOR, a contingent of SAS, and the whole of the Ranger Regiment had conducted a heliborne feint in the direction of the massive billionaire estate and underground bunker west of Houston.

Twenty-four hours before this ruse had taken to the air, the rest of CSOR, accompanied by two Navy SEAL platoons from Coronado and an Operational Detachment of Green Berets from the Western Alliance, had, in the dead of night, driven deep into the White Sands Missile Range.

There, Dune and four hundred other soldiers had boarded eight RCAF Hercules transports and flown north to Montana. From Montana, they'd turned east, then south, and ultimately, the assault force landed in the mid-sized city of Springfield, Illinois.

An hour before dawn, with trucks waiting for them, the force had driven an hour southwest until they arrived at a collection of unused farmer's fields that had been cut into the middle of a dense forest that ran along the Illinois-Missouri border.

The northern suburbs of St. Louis were twenty klicks south, while Jefferson City and their objective was only one hundred and twenty klicks west.

Dune's brain came alive as he got out of the ancient army transport truck he and his platoon had been riding in and saw the two dozen transport helicopters and a smaller collection of gunships arrayed across the field. "Oi, now there's a sight. Our chariots await," he said aloud as his soldiers began to unload their gear.

Beside him, Sergeant Rochefort pointed into the trees. "That's where we wait until things kick off."

Dune looked to where Rochefort was pointing, saw the movement of people and spied a well-concealed tent.

He glanced at his BAM wrist unit. It was 0654 hours. If everything went to plan, he and his men would be boarding their assigned helicopters within three hours, heading west to Jefferson City.

Taking a few steps off the road, Dune turned to survey his still-unloading commandos. To the last man, he knew they were ready.

Reaching down to pick up his light operations ruck, without a word, he started walking in the direction of the staging area where he would get his final orders for today's op.

***

As Parr waited for his door to be opened by the Secret Service agent who had been riding in the front passenger seat, he again glanced around the grounds of the Governor's Mansion. He had been told the Governor had learned an important lesson from the Whiteman debacle and that was to be ready for anything.

State police cruisers, SUVs, and more than a few Missouri National Guard trucks with machine gun turrets on the top of them were everywhere he looked. By way of an insurance policy, he had brought double the number of Secret Service agents with him.

As he had prepped for the meeting that would officially cement Missouri into the UCSA, there had been no intelligence to suggest that the trip to the Show-Me State was going to be a problem. Despite gains CANZUK and the Blues had made in recent days in the north and the relative proximity of Illinois to Jefferson City to the Blue Faction, he had come to trust the UCSA's intelligence apparatus.

Time and again, they had proven their worth, with the most recent example being the audacious attack they'd been expecting on the president's base of operations.

A trusted source had sent word that the Western Alliance and CANZUK were furious in the extreme with the recent automaton attacks and had been insistent about being able to strike into the UCSA's heartland. That Spector was unlikely to be at the billionaire's residence didn't matter. Their enemies wanted to send a message that they could strike into the heart of UCSA territory, not just from the Northeast but now from the West.

Knowing of the pending attack and that the president and his team had moved to another location, Parr had given direction to proceed with the Missouri visit. He would show the UCSA's impotent enemies that he would do whatever and go wherever he pleased.

As the door to the armored Tahoe opened, he stepped onto the pavement and took in the entrance of what could be the country's most unremarkable governor's residence. Parr wasn't sure who the architect for the bland and square structure was but hoped for the good people of Missouri that the man's talents had come through on the interior of the building.

As he walked up the steps, he saw Governor Reginald Powers and a handful of state officials through the open double doors. Despite being overweight and looking like a gargoyle, Reginald Powers was known to be a happy-go-lucky man. And indeed, as their eyes met, Missouri's governor was wearing what seemed to be a genuine smile.

As Parr strode into what was an airy and regal-looking foyer, the governor addressed him warmly. "Good morning, Mr. Parr. It is truly an honor to have a man of your caliber and distinction visit our great state. Knowing how busy and important you are, it is not lost on me or our state's legislators that you have taken the time to visit us in person."

Taking the governor's outstretched hand, Parr said, "Governor Powers, I appreciate the kind words, and I fear your estimation of my importance is overstated. Nevertheless, it's been some time since anyone greeted me with a smile and warm words. It makes me feel good."

"Well, here in Missouri, we pride ourselves on things like courtesy, and as the saying goes, Mr. Parr, honey is almost always more effective than vinegar when it comes to getting deals done."

Parr didn't know if the Governor's statement was a reference to his efforts to cajole Maryland and the other states to sign their declarations or if it was just the man being his usual folksy self.

Whichever, Parr chose to move the conversation toward the reason he was here. He'd booked only an hour for the meeting and had every intention to keep his schedule.

"Governor, we have much to discuss, and regretfully, my time with you today is limited. So, whether it's honey or vinegar, by the end of the hour, you are going to sign the declaration you've repeatedly committed to signing. In truth, today is nothing more than a formality."

"Of course, of course, Mr. Parr," Powers said while gesturing into the building. "We'll meet in my office. Please follow me. I feel very good about our discussions."

***

The SEALs, Green Berets, and CSOR were already airborne when word came in that their target had arrived at the Governor's Mansion. At that exact moment in New Mexico, the SAS and Rangers had begun to board sixteen Marine MV-22 Ospreys that would carry them in the direction of Houston.

In Jefferson City, the plan was straightforward. Staying low and moving fast, four Apaches would lead six Black Hawks with nearly fifty SEALs and Green Berets to storm the governor's residence and take the objective.

Landing on the mansion's expansive grounds, the Western Alliance and California commandos would surround and advance into the Governor's mansion to secure the target and then extricate themselves under the cover of the lurking gunships. All in all, from the moment they touched down on the grounds, the extraction shouldn't take more than ten minutes.

In pulling the mission together, it hadn't been lost on the planners that Missouri had implemented a range of security measures to better protect key infrastructure across the State, including the Governor himself.

If the SEALs didn't progress as quickly as planned and if Missouri sent a rapid reaction force to help fend off the raid, it was the job of the two hundred soldiers of CSOR to make sure these reinforcements couldn't get within a few hundred meters of the residence grounds.

All of CSOR's soldiers except Dune and his men.

To his disappointment, the two Black Hawks he and his platoon were flying in had drawn the responsibility of being the assault force's reserve. While the rest of the strike force put their boots on the ground, he and his twenty-five commandos would stay airborne and wait for direction from the higher-ups.

Like the rest of his men, Dune hadn't liked the assignment, but he was an officer now, and that meant he needed to be a team player.

Seated where he could see into the Black Hawk's cockpit, Dune watched in admiration as the pilot flew the helicopter only a few meters above the Missouri River. Well ahead of them, he caught two Apache gunships rise quickly into the air from atop the same river to reveal themselves to anyone in Jefferson City who happened to be looking north.

They were quickly followed by those helicopters carrying the SEALs and Green Berets. Together, the two gunships and six Black Hawks commenced the run toward the objective.

Without warning, Dune's eyes caught something streak from the ground far ahead. In the air, he saw a stream of flares burst from the underside of both Apaches, but the missile, if that's what it was, wasn't fooled and slammed into the gunship on the right.

Struck, the armored helicopter wobbled for a brief moment and then dropped to the ground. As the gunship disappeared into the trees of what would have been the far north end of the city, the female pilot to Dune's left let loose with a string of savage curses.

Ahead, the Apache that had not been targeted unleashed a salvo of its Hydra rockets while also firing a long burst from its cannon. What it was targeting, Dune could not see.

At that moment, the two Apaches that had circled around Jefferson City so as to descend on the Governor's mansion from the south, revealed themselves by knifing high into the air.

Though they were kilometers away, Dune couldn't miss the bright flare that issued from one of the gunships as it unleashed one of its Hellfire missiles. Seconds later, something on the ground he couldn't see exploded into a pillar of bright orange flame and oily black smoke.

Beside him, the pilot said, "Hang tight. It's our turn to get into the sky."

No sooner had she spoken than the line of helicopters carrying CSOR began to rise upward, but where the Black Hawks and Chinooks ahead of him levelled out at three hundred feet, the Black Hawk Dune was riding in continued to climb. At six hundred feet, the pilot finally leveled off her machine.

Without saying a word, he turned and moved into the cargo area with his men. At this altitude, they would circle the combat zone, relay what they saw to those fighting on the ground, and wait to get the call.

Taking a step to the open cargo door, Dune grabbed one of the canvas handholds above him and craned enough of his upper body outside the helicopter to be able to see the six Black Hawks from the main strike force fly past the downed Apache. Black smoke was roiling into the sky from where it had crashed into the ground.

As all six of the main force transport helicopters maneuvered to land, Dune watched in horror as a JLTV appeared from one of the many leafy side streets that surrounded the Governor's residence and began to unload its 20mm remote-controlled cannon on the closest Black Hawk.

At a distance of fewer than two hundred meters, the helicopter didn't stand a chance as hundreds of armour-piercing rounds instantly shredded the UH-60 and everyone inside it.

As the Black Hawk fell to the ground trailing black smoke, the remaining Apache covering the strike team opened up on the JLTV with its 30 mm cannon, but the armoured truck scooted forward, dodged around a corner, and disappeared among the trees.

Activating his BAM, Dune said, "Call Roughneck Two, Priority Dune Alpha-Kilo-Six."

"Call has been placed. You're number four in the queue. Expected wait time three minutes," the voice of his BAM advised.

His eyes darted back to the mansion. The five remaining Black Hawks were now on the ground unloading their commandos. From his vantage point, Dune could see SEALs and Green Berets exchanging fire with the police and soldiers who had arrayed themselves around the building.

As best he could tell, there were twice as many of the defenders as there were attackers. The soldiers on the ground didn't have three minutes. They needed more bodies now.

Just as he was about to give the pilot the order to land his platoon on the west lawn of the property, there was a flurry of movement at the grand entrance of the home.

As a dozen men in suits stormed out of the front door, three black SUVs raced up the property's driveway. As they came to a halt, red tracers from heavy-caliber rounds began to lash the lone Apache providing air support to the attackers.

Through the canopy of trees, Dune spied what could have been the same JLTV unloading its topside 20mm gun into the Apache. Just as the gunship was aligning its own cannon on its attacker, grey smoke started to emerge from the drive shaft that spun the helicopter's rotor blades. Before it could begin to unleash its own weapon, the nose of the machine dipped, and the Apache began to slide away from the fight.

As Dune turned his eyes back to the drama on the ground, his BAM said, "Priority incoming call from Roughneck Actual."

"Accept the call," he instructed the near-AI software.

"Wrangler Nine, do you copy?" It was the voice of Sato, the Western Alliance general in charge of the entire mission.

"Solid copy, Roughneck."

"The target has been extricated from the property," Sato advised calmly.

On hearing the update, Dune's eyes darted to the trio of SUVs now racing away from the Governor's Mansion. Just outside the property's gated entrance, a pair of JLTVs, each sporting a remote-controlled turret, were waiting for the small convoy.

"I see the three SUVs on the move," Dune confirmed.

"They will head for the airport," the general said. "It's just a four-minute drive across the river. We want you to meet them at the airport and take the target or delay it until reinforcements can arrive."

From their altitude, Dune could easily make out the Jefferson City Airport just across the Missouri River to the east. His eyes then moved to the dual bridges that spanned the river. The Senator Roy Blunt Bridge was an arch truss span about two hundred meters in length.

Focusing his gaze on the east side of the bridge where its spine of steel trusses ended, Dune knew exactly what move to make. "Roughneck, that's a negative on the airport. We're going to take them on the east side of the bridge. If they get to the airport, who knows what supporting forces will be there? If we hem them in on the bridge, they're alone. I'm gonna need the two remaining Apaches to take out those JLTVs if we're going to make this work."

After an extended silence, Sato's voice spoke in his earbud, "That's an affirmative on the bridge, Wrangler Nine. Air support is being redirected. Give 'em hell. Roughneck Actual out."

***

"So, we're agreed?" Parr said to the man sitting on the other side of the dark wooden desk.

"Yes, we're in agreement, Mr. Parr. I appreciate your understanding as it pertains to our delay in signing the declaration. It's been busy for all of us since the attack on Whiteman. But I can assure you, it was never our intention not to sign on with the UCSA."

Parr nodded in agreement and said, "It's been an extraordinary time, Governor. Would you like to sign the declaration here in your office, or would you prefer something more public? Perhaps downstairs where your staff can look onto this historic moment?"

Before Powers could give his answer, his head tilted in the direction of the office's large bank of windows. Just as Parr was about to ask the man if anything was wrong, the Governor's gaze returned to him, and he said, "Helicopters. Can you hear them?"

Parr looked straight ahead and concentrated all his faculties on listening. Immediately, he heard the whomping of helicopter blades. His eyes reconnected with the other man. "I do hear them, and it sounds like more than one. Were you expecting any?"

Powers shook his head. "No, there's an army aviation depot at the airport, but that hardly gets used."

The hefty governor pushed his seat back, and with speed Parr wouldn't have thought possible, the big man all but bounced out of his seat and said, "Excuse me a moment, Mr. Parr. Let me just pop out for a moment so I can speak with my people. You just can't be too careful nowadays."

But before Powers could take a step in the direction of the office's door, there was a cracking sound Parr couldn't identify, followed by a distant boom.

The next sound that invaded the walls of the space was a series of loud explosions. These were much closer. Then, they heard the unmistakable sound of gunfire. Parr wasn't a military man, but even he recognized the chugging sound of a heavy-caliber gun being fired.

As he leaped to his feet, the door to the office swung open. It was the lead agent from his protection detail. His face wore a look of concern. His eyes found Parr and he said, "We're under attack. We don't know who it is, but most likely, they're coming for you. We have to leave."

Before Parr could do anything, a massive explosion rocked the building. Outside the room, Parr could hear people screaming. His eyes darted to Powers, and he asked, "This isn't your people?"

Powers gave him a shrug. "If this is my people, which I highly doubt, it's being done without my knowledge."

As more gunfire erupted outside, the Secret Service agent moved toward Parr, grabbed his arm and said, "It doesn't matter who it is. We have to leave. Now!"

Allowing himself to be pulled along, Parr found a quartette of agents waiting for him outside the office with their weapons drawn. As he cleared the doorway, they surrounded him, and as a group, they hustled in the direction of the mansion's main staircase.

As they began to descend the stairs, the agent pulling him along raised his wrist to his mouth and said, "Good work, Kenny. An armed escort will help. Just let them know we're gonna move fast. And, yes, we'll head to the airport. Tell them I want to be wheels-up the moment we get there. Longmore out."

As they neared the main floor of the building, a powerful explosion rocked the east side of the mansion, causing two full stories of windows to disintegrate and transform into a shower of sharp and fast-moving fragments.

Parr shouted in pain as he felt something bite into the right side of his head. Instinctively, his hand flew upwards in response to the injury, but on doing so, he lost his footing.

The Secret Service agent, who still had a hold of his arm, tried to prevent him from stumbling down what remained of the stairs, but he too lost his footing, and together, Parr and the other man careened in a jumble down what remained of the curving staircase.

Completely unprepared for the fall, Parr was unable to make any effort to protect himself. At what might have been the halfway point of their descent, his left elbow exploded in horrendous pain as it slammed into the unforgiving hardwood stairs.

Then, as his body reached the floor, that same part of his head that had been struck by shattered glass rebounded off of slate tiling. As his body finally came to a rest, Parr's vision flickered several times as his brain tried to remain conscious.

He didn't know if he'd been lying on the floor for five seconds or five minutes, but just as his vision started to right itself, someone grabbed at him and yanked him upright. The quick upward movement made him want to empty his stomach. Opening his eyes, Parr saw what he recalled as one of the bigger agents of his protection detail straining to carry him in his arms.

Out of his field of vision, someone yelled, "The SUVs are here."

Another voice bellowed, "Move! Move! Move!"

Looking ahead, Parr saw two policemen holding open the mansion's double-door main entrance, and beyond those were more stairs. On the driveway leading up to the entrance, he saw the three Chevy Tahoes of his motorcade waiting with their doors open. Police officers and more Secret Service agents, all with automatic weapons, surrounded the three SUVs.

Grunting, the agent carrying Parr navigated the stairs as best he could. Reaching the sidewalk, the big man issued a curse and pumped his legs in the direction of the second SUV's open door.

Inside the vehicle, an agent was waiting. His arms were fully extended as he waited for the man carrying Parr to reach him so he could pass off his charge.

Reaching the door, the agent turned his body so that Parr was perpendicular to the SUV. Without any warning and with a huge grunt, the linebacker of a man tossed Parr through the air in the direction of the man waiting inside the vehicle.

For a split second, Parr felt his body go light. Then he felt the waiting agent's hands and arms embrace him as he took on Parr's full weight. With a mighty exertion that Parr both heard and felt, the agent roughly placed him on the floor between the two seats that made up the vehicle's second row of seating.

Grabbing his upper arm, the agent gave Parr a violent shake and yelled, "Stay on the floor!"

When Parr's eyes connected with the man yelling at him, the agent's hand snapped forward and pressed a thick white bandage into one of his hands and said, "Keep this pressed to the side of your head as best you can. You're bleeding like a stuck pig. We'll deal with it when we get to the airport."

"My head?" Parr said, his voice sounding groggy.

The agent took Parr's hand with the bandage and pressed it against the right side of his skull. He then brought his wrist to his mouth and said, "Limiter is secure. I repeat, Limiter is secure."

No sooner had Parr's code name been spoken than their SUV started to move.

As it did so, Parr heard what he thought were bullets impacting the side of their vehicle.

The two agents driving the Tahoe yelled at one another as they called out threats.

"There! Ten o'clock. Six of them."

"Shit, they've got an RPG!"

"Stevie, watch out!"

BOOM!

There was an explosion right in front of them. Parr couldn't see what had detonated, but from where the sound and light had come from, he guessed it was the lead SUV of his protection detail.

In the seat to his right, the agent who had carried Parr out from the mansion bellowed, "Stevie, get around them, or we're fucking dead!"

The driver didn't reply. Instead, he slammed the Tahoe into reverse. Tires screeching, it moved backward and stopped. Shifting the transmission into drive, the engine revved hard as it leaped forward. Almost immediately, the driver jerked the SUV wildly to the left as he dodged what had to be the struck vehicle of the motorcade.

As another hail of bullets found the exterior of the vehicle, the Secret Service agent in the passenger seat said, "Take a right at the gate. That's Capital Ave. But when you get there, Stevie, slow down. The National Guard is gonna give us an escort. Let the first JLTV get in front of us. It'll take us to the airport."

Before the agent named Stevie could protest at the prospect of reducing his speed, the agent beside him said, "Look around, there's still fucking choppers in the air, and our rides don't have any anti-air defense. We need their firepower."

"But –."

"Just do it!" the other agent roared.

As the SUV began to slow down to take a right onto the street that would allow them to escape the ambush, the agent that seemed to be in charge said, "See, there they are, and the lead one is already moving. Just slip in behind them, Stevie."

Above him, Parr heard a window begin to come down.

Looking in that direction, he saw the agent who had given him the bandage raise the entirety of his upper body out of the window. After what might have been ten seconds, he came back inside and reported, "There are still two Apaches in the air. One is coming our way. It'll be on us in moments. If there are more of them out there, I can't see them."

"It doesn't matter," said the lead agent. "The airport is just across the river, and we'll be there in less than five. If it's CANZUK or the Western Alliance coming after us, they won't blow up a plane. Not when it's filled with civvies. When we get there, we'll have as many airport staff on the plane as there are available seats, and we'll broadcast that to everyone who's listening. If they shoot us down, they'll kill upwards of thirty innocents."

"And if it's the Blues?" said the driver.

"If it were the Blues, they wouldn't have bothered to send commandos. They would have blown up the residence the moment he walked in the front door," the senior agent said, gesturing toward Parr. "No, whoever is after us cares about their reputation. It's those CANZUK bastards, I'm sure of it. This thing smells just like the Whiteman operation."

"We're coming up to Highway 54 and the bridge," said the driver. "We're gonna make a right at speed, so hang on."

Parr felt the SUV make a hard right and then accelerate.

His brain, now reset, raised his upper body from the floor so he could see where they were going. A quarter mile ahead, he took in the steel trusses of the bridge they had taken earlier in the day. The airport wasn't three minutes past the other side of the span.

As the SUV passed underneath the bridge's steel girders and the prospect of escape began to swell inside of him, the lead agent unleashed a torrent of curses and then screamed at the driver, "Stop, Stevie, stop!"

The Secret Service agent driving the SUV hammered the brakes, bringing them to a screeching halt.

With the momentum of the vehicle propelling him forward, Parr got to his knees, and his eyes stabbed in the direction that the three agents were looking.

Through the windshield and beyond the lead JLTV that had also stopped, Parr's eyes found what had elicited the hurricane of curses from the agent-in-charge.

For the first time during their effort to escape, Parr spoke, "Turn around. We don't need to go to the airport. We can drive home if we need to. Get us out of here."

"We can't," said the driver.

Parr snapped at the agent, "What do you mean we can't? Just turn around and drive!"

The agent didn't reply to Parr's question, he only gestured with his thumb in the direction from which they came.

Turning, Parr looked through the bullet-riddled rear windshield and only said, "Shit."

***

Dune had given the pilot instructions to approach the one and only bridge crossing the Missouri River from the east and to stay low over the water. In doing so, he'd hoped to keep their movement secret from the fleeing convoy until it was too late.

His BAM was connected to the Apache shadowing the convoy. The gunship pilot said, "Wrangler Nine, they're turning on the highway that will bring them onto the bridge."

"Roger that, Mustang, "Dune replied. "When we set down. I need you to hit those two JLTVs."

"Negative, Wrangler. I can't take the shot. The trusses will be in the way."

"Bullshit, Mustang. If you don't take the shot, we're screwed, and we lose the target, so find a way to make it happen. I don't care how. Wrangler Nine, out."

Dune then tapped the shoulder of the pilot of the Black Hawk he was flying in and yelled, "Put us down now!"

As the pilot nodded her head, the Black Hawk's engines powered up, lifting the helicopter up into the air and then forward over that part of the bridge span where its trusses came to an end. She then dropped the helicopter down fast, landing hard on the left side of the bridge's asphalt.

Only thirty meters behind them, the second Black Hawk carrying the rest of Dune's platoon landed on the right side of the highway. Together, the two helicopters would form a barrier the approaching motorcade would have to choose to barrel past or fight through.

As his feet hit the pavement, his soldiers were already forming a line of attack across the road. "Open Channel Dune Team Alpha."

"Channel Open," advised the voice of his BAM.

Ahead, the two SUVs and two JLTVs came to a halt almost at the center of the bridge.

"Nobody moves," he said calmly. "When I give the word, we rush forward as one. Team One will take the SUV on the left, Team Two will take the SUV on the right. We take the target alive."

As he'd given the orders, his eyes had remained focused on the two JLTVs' auto turrets.

At a distance of about seventy meters, if they started firing, they would turn Dune and the rest of his lads into red mist, but instead of unloading on his exposed platoon, together, they spun the barrels of their cannons in the direction of the lone Apache lowering itself to the road on the other side of the bridge.

Before either turret could fire on the gunship, a single Hellfire shot forward from the Apache and slammed into the right-most JLTV, turning it into a bright orange ball of fire.

As energy from the nearby explosion slammed into Dune, he took several steps back and almost lost his footing.

His eyes were drawn back to the vehicles on the bridge as he heard the sound of the cannon on the remaining JLTV open up. But just as the 20mm tracer rounds from the remote-controlled cannon began to find the hovering helicopter, a second missile issued from the gunship's right side.

This time, when the anti-armor missile impacted the JLTV, Dune was ready for it. Turning his face from the white-hot energy of the exploding vehicle, he leaned into the wash of destruction that struck him and his men.

Turning his face back to the scene at the mid-point of the bridge, he saw the SUVs starting to move in their direction.

With the threat of the JLTVs neutralized, through his BAM, he said to his men, "Advance! Concentrate on their engines. Open fire!"

On giving the order, each of Dune's commandos opened up with their weapons at the fast-approaching vehicles.

Like Dune, most of the men in his platoon were armed with the Canadian Army's standard C-71, 5.56mm rifle. And though the C-71 was considered one of the world's newest and best assault standard infantry weapons, the rounds the majority of his men were pouring into the up-armored Chevys were ineffectual.

But amongst the men of his command were other weapons.

Affixed to eight of his lads' rifles was the Army's standard grenade launcher, and in the hail of gunfire being unleashed, he heard a handful of *thunks* as light armor penetration projectiles were sent down range.

In full credit to their skills, the men driving the Tahoes managed to avoid the incoming 40mm grenades. As they raced forward, both vehicles had violently swerved back and forth making them difficult targets for the single-shot weapons.

In the end, it was the four .50-caliber K-59 Centurion assault rifles that had wrecked the engines of the two SUVs and brought them to a standstill only ten meters to Dune's front.

The K-59, designed and built by the Knight's Armament Company of the UK, had been rushed into service across CANZUK in response to the Chinese Wraiths and Hyenas, which had been designed to resist the NATO-standard 5.56mm round.

As tendrils of grey smoke poured out of the engines of both SUVs, Dune bellowed, "Cease fire, cease fire, cease fire!"

As the cacophony of small arms came to an end, Dune surveyed both vehicles. All parts he could see were riddled with bullet holes, including their windshields, which were now largely opaque due to the amount of hits they'd suffered.

The voice of the Black Hawk pilot materialized in his BAM's earbud. "Wrangler Nine, word is in that we have company coming from the direction of the airport. Ten or so police vehicles and a few military. We've got maybe two minutes before they're on us. We'll give it to them with our door guns, but we won't last long."

"Roger that," Dune said.

Aloud, Dune yelled, "Theissen and Theriault, I want charges placed under each vehicle. Make it three pounds. Go!

"The rest of you surround your assigned vehicle, and if any windows or doors open and you see a weapon, let'em have it.

"Move, people!"

As soon as he barked the order, two sets of twelve commandos advanced in the direction of the two SUVs with their weapons at the ready.

The two men Dune had assigned to set the charges pulled off their packs and readied the explosives they'd been ordered to prepare.

With the two Chevys surrounded, Dune walked forward and put himself at the midway point of the immobilized SUVs.

Bellowing, he said, "Occupants of both vehicles, I hope you can hear me because, in less than one minute, your vehicles will be detonated with an explosive charge that is being placed underneath each SUV.

"We will not permit you to stay alive long enough for whatever force you think is coming to save you. Our orders are clear. If we cannot take Mr. Parr alive, he is to be eliminated.

"To this end, I address Mr. Parr directly. Exit from your vehicle now so that you can save the lives of the men who have tried to save you. Do the honorable thing, mate."

Dune's eyes darted back and forth between the two soldiers setting the charges. Within five seconds of one another, they gave the thumbs-up they were ready to go.

"You now have one minute before we detonate both vehicles. I repeat, you have one minute before we blow both of your vehicles into the trusses above."

Dune turned to Rochefort. "Sergeant, take half the lads and reinforce the helos. Make sure we can get off this bridge when the time comes."

"On it, boss," the Quebecer said.

Dune turned back to the SUVs and yelled, "Thirty seconds, Parr."

Activating his BAM, he said to the remaining CSOR commandos who had their weapons trained on the doors and windows of the disabled vehicles, "Stay primed, lads – if they are going to do something stupid, it'll be in the next few seconds. Remember, if they do show themselves, we want Parr alive, but should anyone start shooting, tear into them."

At what he felt was twenty seconds, Dune gave the order for everyone to move back to a safe distance. He trusted that the two soldiers who had set the charges had done so in a way that the bulk of their energy would drive upward into the SUVs and not in the direction of their mates.

At fifteen seconds, he said, "Theissen and Theriault, when I say so, send these blokes into their next life."

As loud as he could, Dune then started a countdown from ten. At eight, several of his commandos joined him.

At five, one of the passenger doors facing Dune opened. As he yelled out the number three, the rest of the doors, except one, began to open. Slowly, men with their hands in the air exited the two vehicles.

Dune quickly scanned each man's face, but none matched their person of interest. Peter Parr's good looks made him an instantly recognizable bloke.

With his weapon trained on the Red Faction operative closest to him, Dune moved forward. When he was five feet away, he said, "Parr, where is he?"

The man's right hand thumbed in the direction of the lone door that hadn't opened. "In there. He doesn't want to leave."

Without saying a word, Dune's hand came off his rifle's pistol grip and motioned in the direction of the open door.

Behind him, four commandos – all of them hulking – rushed the SUV with their weapons at the ready.

On reaching the vehicle, the senior NCO began to yell a series of well-practiced commands. When the occupant of the vehicle didn't respond, the sergeant turned to his left and tapped the biggest man of the foursome and said, "Bowser, drag that bastard out of there, pronto."

Handing his weapon to the sergeant, all six-four, two-hundred and thirty pounds of Corporal Trip Bowser tore open the door, and without a moment's hesitation, he dove into the SUV.

The struggle that followed took less than ten seconds.

In a violent flurry of movement, Corporal Bowser dragged his prize out of the back seat of the SUV and, with a scream of anger, slammed the adult male he was manhandling into the bridge's pavement.

No sooner had the man's body connected with the asphalt than one of Bowser's booted feet came crashing down on the subject's upper back, driving the man's chest and face into the ground.

As the burly commando removed his boot from the subject's back, two other commandos rushed forward to place flex cuffs on the man's wrists, and together, they grabbed the subject's shoulder and yanked him to his feet.

"Bring 'im here," Dune yelled.

As the two soldiers dragged their prisoner toward Dune, Rochefort's voice sounded in Dune's BAM, "Boss, the cavalry has arrived. It sure would be helpful if we could get that Apache at the other end of the bridge in the air to help us out."

"Consider it done, Sergeant."

When the two commandos arrived with their prisoner, Dune's hand snapped forward and grabbed the man's chin. The face was covered in fresh blood. It looked like Bowser's kick had knocked out one of the man's front teeth, but through the gore, Dune recognized the man he was looking at. "Peter Parr. Good to make your acquaintance, mate."

Parr moved to say something, but Dune slapped the man with a quick and mighty blow. As Parr cried out in pain and staggered backward, Dune said, "Bag this son of a bitch, get him onto my ride, and let's get the hell out of here."

Chapter 31

Vinh, 300 KM South of Hanoi, Vietnam

Kelly had insisted on seeing the bombardment with his own eyes. The 2nd Cavalry Regiment and the rest of the 3rd Brigade were three kilometers back from where they would cross the Cả River, but he had driven forward with the regimental sergeant major, leaving his 2IC to make the final preparations for the river crossing. Under no circumstances was he prepared to miss the show about to start.

He still had to pinch himself that they had made it this far north. In just twelve days of intense and often times brutal fighting, Vietnam's army had mercilessly driven the Chinese invaders back an incredible thirteen hundred kilometers.

On day five of the drive north, the Chinese 75th Army Group had been pushed back to the city of Tuy Hòa, where after only one day of bombardment from the air, land, and sea, they capitulated. Twenty-two thousand soldiers had surrendered.

Two days later, the same fate befell the 74th Army Group at Huế. Famous for the intense month-long battle that had taken place during the Tết Offensive in 1968, the exhausted Chinese forces that had retreated to the city had lasted only forty-eight hours.

And Kelly couldn't blame them. The shellacking the PLA had taken from the CANZUK and Japanese air forces and the US Navy's two aircraft carriers now off the coast of the southern part of Vietnam had been unrelenting and severe. Strike after strike of F-35s, Super Hornets, and the sixty-plus attack-capable drones the growing alliance had rushed into the theatre had devastated their opponents in every way.

The Chinese war planners simply hadn't foreseen a scenario where the US Navy and its submarines would involve themselves in the conflict to take away their air superiority. And now they were paying for it with ungodly amounts of their soldiers' blood and equipment.

This had been the state of affairs until the Vietnamese 4th Army Corps began to approach Vinh. Just three hundred kilometers south of Hanoi, Vinh was on the very outer edge of the Chinese air defenses that CANZUK and its allies would not breach with their aircraft.

Would not, because the US Navy and the Japanese Self Defence Force had been given explicit orders that under no circumstances were they to attack anything on the Chinese side of the border.

The result of this policy had been for China to move a huge number of their most advanced air defense batteries to the border along Vietnam and to the western side of Hainan, the Chinese island province just across the Gulf of Tonkin.

From these locations, the PLA's HHQ-9 surface-to-air-missiles could reach out and tag CANZUK fighters and drones flying under five thousand feet in the Vinh area, meaning that CANZUK and their allies would need to be more selective in the types of missions they put into the air to support people like Kelly and his 2nd Cav as they began to push into the northernmost part of Vietnam.

But those challenges were for tomorrow when the 3rd Brigade began to cross several temporary bridges that a combined team of Australian and New Zealander combat engineers had been working on so they could cross the fast-moving and wide Cả River.

With Chinese air defenses back in play and shorter and better-defended lines of logistics across Vietnam's northern provinces, the PLA had funneled several fresh divisions into the fight and elected to make the city of Vinh and the north side of the Cả River the place where they'd slow down or stop the Vietnamese-CANZUK advance.

According to intelligence reports, the PLA's build-up of Vinh's defenses had started on the same day the second battle of Huế had kicked off. In the time it had taken Kelly and the rest of the alliance's soldiers to move from reclaimed Huế to the southern part of Vinh, Chinese sappers had created a nightmare of trenchworks, minefields, razor wire, and hardpoints along the banks of the Cả in support of the PLA's reinforcements.

On the south side of the Cả, just down from where the third and final temporary CANZUK bridge would be assembled in the morning, Kelly had plunked himself down on a huge pile of gravel at the center of a massive sandlot that had been deserted by the locals.

Behind him, Kelly heard the outbreak of laughter. Shifting his body so he could look in the direction opposite of the river, he looked down the slope of gravel and caught a group of Aussie and Kiwi soldiers standing around a trio of barrel BBQs, talking and laughing as though they were back home in someone's backyard.

He did not ask where the Diggers got the BBQs, but he was glad for them. Tomorrow would be a difficult day, so the generals had given their blessing to those blokes and Sheilas who could take a break and find a way to unwind without compromising their readiness for the river crossing to take place in eight hours' time.

Below, he saw 2nd Cav's RSM and several other senior NCOs from other units circulating among the soldiers, making sure everyone was following the rules that had been set for alcohol. Whether the soldiers were from the 2nd Cavalry or not, they needed to be minded closely.

Not one of the outstanding men and women he was looking at in that moment hadn't suffered the loss of someone close to them, so the pressure to have a few too many bevies would be hugely tempting. Best not to let that happen, he thought.

The war had been intense, so much so that the CANZUK governments had sanctioned the creation of a burial site in a section of a military graveyard in Ho Chi Minh City. With every transport plane needed for war materiel and the walking wounded, there had just been too many bodies to ship home.

Beyond the gaggle of commiserating soldiers, a pair of up-armored utes pulled into the sandlot's parking area and disgorged a handful of senior officers.

A few minutes later, four of the new arrivals were making their best efforts to scale the small mountain that Kelly and a few other officers had already conquered. Two of the officers were Australian, while the other two were Kiwis. He immediately recognized the two Aussies as senior officers from the 4th Regiment of the Royal Australian Artillery.

As they neared his position at the summit, the four men got down on their stomachs and elbowed their way the last half-dozen feet or so. Reaching him, the senior of the two Aussie officers said, "Colonel Kelly, so nice to see you again, sir. Mighty nice of you to pass along the invite."

"Glad too, Colonel. You and your people have been standup lads for us every step of the way. I've run out of fingers for the number of times your batteries have saved our bacon. I wouldn't have anyone else for this occasion."

The artillery officer gestured to the men on his right. "This here is Major Rankin, the lead for 4th Regiment's Operations Support Battery, and these two fine gentlemen are Lt. Colonel Angus Robertson, the CO for 16th Field Regiment, and his 2IC, Major Manu."

Kelly's eyes sparkled at the introduction of the two New Zealanders. Without warning, he swam forward and extended his arm to Robertson. "What a great pleasure, Colonel. Your people have been superb. Better than that, actually, but I can't think of a better word. If your lot hadn't stepped in during that surprise counterattack back at Da Nang, my regiment would've been shredded, and I reckon I would've carked it."

The other officer let out a quick chuckle and said, "Call me Gus, Colonel. And whenever we Kiwis can lend a hand to pull our Aussie mates out of a dodgy situation, rest assured we'll give it heaps."

"Indeed," said Kelly as he slithered back to his spot.

Reaching his original position, his ears caught the droning sound that had brought him and the rest of the officers and soldiers to this elevated location.

Turning his head to the southeast sky, he saw several formations of planes with huge wingspans. Bringing his binoculars to his eyes, Kelly could easily make out the first of the B-52s that had flown out of Northern Australia.

Before the civil war, the bulk of the United States B-52 fleet resided at two bases: Barksdale AFB in Louisiana and Minot AFB in North Dakota.

In the first year of the conflict, the Red Faction used their half of the ancient bombers to devastating effect. But between changed

Blue tactics on the ground and the shoot-down of the planes in the air, by the end of year two of the war, the UCSA's strategic bomber force had become a non-factor.

The other half of the former United States bomber force had been in the possession of the Neutral Faction in North Dakota, and besides doing routine maintenance on the twenty-seven planes in their possession, the fleet had not left the ground — until now.

It had taken the Neutrals, now the Western Alliance, and CANZUK the better part of two weeks to find enough pilots and crews, but they had done it, and thirty-six hours ago in the dead of night, twenty-five of the flying behemoths had flown north into Canada, then west to the Pacific, where they turned south and east and flew directly to RAAF Base Amberley in Northern Australia.

Arriving with 84 GPS-guided Mk 82 500lb bombs in each of their bellies, the multinational team of pilots and crews refueled their machines, got their final briefing, and retook to the skies to fly north to undertake Operation Tighthead Prop.

With the full support of the Vietnamese government, two waves of B-52s at twenty thousand feet would drop nearly one million pounds of high explosives on the unsuspecting defenses the PLA had built along the Cả River.

It was this orchestration of god-like violence that Kelly had come to see.

His BAM vibrated, as did those of the rest of the soldiers on the tiny gravel mountain. As one, the officers and the senior NCOs present looked down at their wrists and saw the warning that the bombardment would commence in two minutes.

Looking backward, he took in the scene of the BBQs. Everyone but the lads doing the cooking had disappeared from view.

For their own protection, the Aussie and Kiwi soldiers had been ordered to stay behind the massive hill of gravel lest a PLA mortar team or a keen-eyed forward artillery observer spot them.

But Kelly, along with the COs for the 3rd Battalion of the Royal Australian Regiment and 1st Battalion of the Royal New Zealand Regiment, had agreed that their soldiers could take in the display at the last moment so long as they tried to remain inconspicuous.

He looked forward and down and saw several dozen soldiers crawling in the direction of the river bank. "Goddamned bogans," Kelly said loudly. "They're doing a piss-poor job of staying out of sight."

But before he could start to scream for someone to get control of the situation, he heard the Kiwi artillery officer, Robertson, say, "It won't matter, Colonel. Even if someone does see them, they won't have the opportunity to call in the fire mission."

Kelly looked at the Kiwi, who promptly pointed to the late evening sky and said, "It's begun."

He looked high into the air, and sure enough, with his naked eye, he could see the line of the first flight of Stratofortress bombers not quite directly above Vinh. From Kelly's vantage point, it looked like they were southeast of the city and too far to release their weapons.

"They don't look close enough," he said as his eyes picked up the movement of dark specks falling downward through the sky. There were hundreds of them, and as they got closer to the ground, he could easily hear the clacking sound that precision-guided bombs make as they adjust their flight path.

Kelly had heard the distinctive precursor many times before as CANZUK and US Navy fighter-bombers had used precision-guided munitions to strike targets Kelly himself had flagged, but he had not heard hundreds of the munitions descend from the sky at the same time.

Between the roar of the B-52s' engines, the cacophony of menacing clacking, and the scream of over a thousand bombs as they tore through the sky, Kelly was taken aback by the spectacle.

Across the river, more than one klaxon began to sound, but it was too late.

CANZUK and the Western Alliance had made every effort to ensure this attack would be a surprise, and as Kelly looked along the river, he could see men and vehicles moving haphazardly to try and find cover.

And then the bombs struck.

In rapid succession, over one thousand GPS-guided 500-lb bombs struck a narrow one-kilometer-long rectangle that started eight hundred meters from where Kelly lay.

The noise of that many bombs going off so quickly was violence of the highest order.

As the thunderous shockwave of the explosions rolled over him, Kelly felt the mountain of gravel underneath him shake, just as the organs in his body resonated and hummed from the incredible sonic force of just over five hundred thousand pounds of explosives lighting off in a twenty-second span.

Opening his eyes, Kelly took in the destruction that had been carved along the banks of the Cả River and a couple hundred meters back into the city of Vinh itself. Besides the pall of brown dust and black smoke thrown into the air, columns of fire were burning in dozens of spots where vehicles or structures had been struck.

Slowly, Kelly got to one knee, and as he did so, he performed the sign of the cross over his chest and said aloud, "I hope to God the people in that city listened to their government and got out of there."

As he heard some cheering from below, his eyes moved to the Aussie and Kiwi soldiers who had moved to the river's edge to catch the bombardment. Most of them were standing, and more than a few were embracing in a transparent show of emotion. How could they not after witnessing such terrible destruction?

It struck him that this is how senior officers in the Australian Army must have felt when they received news of the first atomic bomb falling on Japan. News of the enemy's destruction would mean that fewer of their lads would have to die.

That's how Kelly felt now. The B-52s would fly back to Northern Australia, where there would be enough bombs to re-arm all of the massive planes.

After a two-hour turnaround in Amberley, the flying monsters would return to the skies above Vinh, and they would again pound the Chinese just as CANZUK engineers started to assemble their bridges that would allow Kelly and his people to again close with their enemy.

But that was tomorrow. For what remained of today, he would join his soldiers and eat what he expected would be the greatest Australian BBQ he had ever tasted.

***

Somewhere in Beijing

—

For the past five minutes, General Wu Dezhi, the Chief of Staff of all branches of the People's Liberation Army, looked down at the tablet atop the large table where he was sitting. Like two lasers, his eyes focused on the red square that would start a dialogue that, until two weeks ago, was an impossibility.

Once his finger pressed the red square and it became green, Wu could not turn back. It would not matter what the substance of the conversation was. His fate would be sealed the moment the quantum comms systems connected.

Despite the risks, he would press on. He had no choice.

His journey to this point started in the seconds after Wu had watched Admiral Xi's brain get blown out by the robotic abomination President Yan had used to execute his long-time colleague.

Wu had not been aware of the Admiral's machinations to sacrifice the *Fujian* and its task force, but as he bore witness to the true brutality of China's leader, the seeds of treason had come to dominate his mind.

The last straw had been the ongoing destruction of the 72nd Army Group and, with it, Yan's demand to once again employ tactical nuclear weapons.

With the 75th Army Group's total loss and the quickly approaching destruction of the 74th, Yan had ordered the 72nd Army Group to cross the border into Vietnam and hold the north of the country no matter the costs.

In leading up to the order, Wu and his fellow generals had been clear with President Yan. China could not win the war in Vietnam and were they to use tactical nukes on Vietnam's military, there could be no guarantee that Great Britain would not retaliate in kind.

To their full credit, CANZUK and the US Navy had solved the monumental challenge that was the PLA's air defenses, and unit by unit, kilometer by kilometer, the 72nd had been pushed back to the outskirts of Hanoi, where it was instructed to hold the city and strategic points along the Red River.

Raging at Wu and his fellow generals, President Yan had insisted that every piece of ground east of the Red River would be held and that they should make obvious preparations to use tactical nukes against any large concentrations of Vietnamese forces that came within five kilometers of what Yan had described as 'Chinese territory'.

Savaged with every step of its retreat from the city of Vinh to Hanoi, the 72nd had lost over forty percent of its soldiers. Altogether, in just four weeks of fighting, the People's Liberation Army had suffered nearly two hundred thousand casualties. They were troubling losses, even for a country the size of China.

But in the end, it was not the number of dead or wounded soldiers that had prompted Li's actions. He had prepared for the possibility of war his entire adult life and had seen the casualty estimates if China were to fight a war against the Americans or even the Russians. Their current losses in Vietnam were but a fraction of how bad things would get if China had to fight a land war against one or both of these great powers.

The factor that had forced the hand of Wu and his fellow conspirators was the notion that China needed to expand its territories beyond the Motherland. This idea that China should control some or all of Southeast Asia was misguided policy at best. The idea that China should take control of places as far away as North America and even further afield were the ravings of a madman, a madman Wu was now convinced needed to be put down.

As the time on the tablet arrived at 0700 hours, without hesitation, his finger pressed the red button on the display to establish the connection.

Instantly, the faces of the prime ministers of Australia and the United Kingdom appeared in two separate boxes.

As he had arranged the meeting, Wu was the first to speak. Knowing his first words would help to set the tone for the conversation, he had decided to use the same voice he used when he was speaking with one of his teenage grandchildren – respectful and kind.

Allowing the resentment and anger he felt toward these two people and the alliance they represented to come through in his words would do nothing in the service of his objective. Despite the countless deaths they had caused, he needed their help. "Good evening, Prime Minister Richardson. Good morning, Prime Minister Hanson. Thank you for agreeing to this meeting."

The Prime Minister of Australia didn't reciprocate Wu's salutation. Instead, the politician said forcefully, "Prime Minister Richardson and I are willing to take the call with you, General, because our two nations are interested in one thing and one thing only, and that is peace. Is it because of peace you've taken the risk of connecting with us?"

Wu cleared his throat and said, "First, Mr. Prime Minister, I want to start our conversation with an apology to you and the people of Australia. The recent devastating attacks ordered by my country's president are an affront to the parts of the People's Liberation Army that I am representing.

"Since ancient times, China has never sought to physically dominate countries as far away as yours, and even in the near abroad, our military efforts have been limited. And while it is true we are likely to see Australia as a competitor for years to come, we also recognize that we can have relations that are productive and fruitful for both of our great nations."

His tone now harsh, the Australian PM interrupted Wu and said, "The attacks may be an affront, General, but it was the same military you oversee who attacked my country and killed nearly seven thousand civilians. It is a damned outrage, and to be perfectly frank, if it wasn't for cooler heads like Prime Minister Richardson, I'd tell you to go to hell, and we'd continue to hand your asses to you in Nam."

"What you say is indisputable, Mr. Prime Minister," Wu said in a somber tone. "And for whatever time I have left on this world, I will have regret for what has been done, but I am a practical man. I solve problems, and I have a problem that I believe only your two countries can help with."

It was the British PM who spoke next. "We'll get to your problem in a moment, General Wu, but before we do, we want you to answer the question as to why you insisted this meeting include only ourselves. CANZUK is a four-country alliance, so anything you share with us will be shared with our partners."

Wu nodded and replied, "It is a good question, Madame Prime Minister, and the answer is linked directly to the problem I need your help with, so if I may, why don't I tell you about the challenge I face and how you might be able to help me bring an end to this terrible war?"

The UK PM said, "As Prime Minister Hanson already stated, General, peace is our goal. That being the case, tell us what this challenge of yours is and why you think we're the only ones who can help with it."

Wu took in a deep breath and reminded himself that he had already signed his own death warrant by arranging this call. If the President's internal security services had somehow gotten word of this clandestine conversation or, worse, were doing the impossible and listening in real time, he would be dead by the end of the day, if not sooner.

For better or worse, he was at peace with what he was about to do, and so he said, "Madame Prime Minister, I need the help of both of your countries to eliminate President Yan."

Wu let the words hang in the air for several seconds. To the credit of the two politicians, neither gave any kind of reaction to his extraordinary statement.

Choosing to interpret their silence as a positive sign, Wu continued, "And as to why I only contacted your two countries, it had crossed my mind that the assassination of China's president is something those involved might want to keep close to their chests. I appreciate that you have close and longstanding relations with the Canadians and the New Zealanders, but their militaries do not possess the capabilities I believe are needed to undertake the task I have mentioned. Yours do. And considering my proposal, it is my strong view that the involvement of two countries is preferable to four, no matter how close their relationship."

On delivering his explanation, Wu decided it was his turn to remain quiet.

Just as things were becoming awkward, the Prime Minister of Great Britain opened her mouth but then quickly snapped it shut. The Australian Prime Minister, a brutish-looking man, only stared into the camera feed with a look of defiance.

Concluding that the two politicians were gobsmacked by his proposal, Wu finally said, "I know what I've just said is incredible—perhaps even unbelievable, but I can assure you that the offer to work together to replace President Yan is both genuine and well thought out. But before I can tell you about how we might be able to work together, I will need you to confirm your interest in working with me to make this happen."

For the first time since announcing his intent to carry out what was an international conspiracy to assassinate the leader of the most powerful country in the world, the PM of Great Britain said, "General, Prime Minister Hanson and I will need to speak privately to discuss your proposal. Might you give us ten minutes?"

"I will give you five, Prime Minister. As you can appreciate, every minute I'm on this call with you is another minute my country's security services have to discover my intentions. You must appreciate the extraordinary risk I am taking."

"We do, General. We shall return to the call in five minutes."

With that, the screens of the two CANZUK leaders went dark.

Four minutes and fifty-two seconds later, the two heads of the Western politicians reappeared in their respective squares. Without any prompt from Wu, Richardson said in a voice level and clear, "General Wu, if the United Kingdom and Australia can help with the People's Liberation Army's effort to install a new president, we would like to know how."

Chapter 32

St. John's, Newfoundland

She couldn't believe the dumb luck of it.

Things in Ottawa were on the precipice of disaster, and it was at this moment her mother had decided to have a stroke. MacPhail couldn't wait to see the eighty-two-year-old woman to give her a piece of her mind.

On receiving the news of her mother, MacPhail had booked the first flight back home. She'd spoken to the physician in charge of her mother's care and been advised the stroke hadn't been life-threatening, but as her mom wasn't in the greatest health to begin with, it might be best for her to make the trip back to St. John's, 'Just in case.'"

Of course, she didn't need to be emotionally cajoled by the doctor. Her mother, a shrew of a woman, had always supported and loved her in her own way. MacPhail, in turn, had loved the woman back, if only in short bouts and mostly when it was convenient to her career.

But a stroke, even with all of today's modern medical interventions, was no small thing for an octogenarian, and on the off chance something did go awry, she would never forgive herself if the old bird did pass. MacPhail hadn't been there when her father died and had beat herself up for it for years afterward.

The drama playing out in Ottawa would just have to survive without her for at least 24 hours.

Politically and militarily, the past week had been a whirlwind inside a hurricane.

Everything had kicked off with the Sanchez assassination attempt. It had been a spectacular effort and a miracle the man had survived, but in surviving, Sanchez's mind had been made up about California's role in the war. Along with the Neutral Faction, Sanchez and California were now all in.

Within hours of leaving the Anaheim Convention Center, the UCSA had been identified as the culprit behind the attack. In turn,

Sanchez had secured an agreement with the US Navy in California and in the Pacific to begin supporting the CANZUK war effort against the Chinese.

If the Chinese were aiding and abetting the UCSA in North America with war material and soldiers, then it stood to reason California should support the people fighting the enemy of California's enemy in Southeast Asia.

The subsequent warpath trod by the US Navy's submarines in the South China Sea and the more recent entry of two aircraft carrier strike groups had been devastation beyond CANZUK's wildest dreams.

With control over the skies of South Vietnam and supplies and reinforcements being choked off in the north of the country, the on-the-ground coalition of the Vietnamese, Thais, and CANZUK had steadily pushed the PLA beyond the DMZ line that had separated Vietnam during its mid-twentieth century conflict with the Americans.

Not satisfied with these indirect attacks on the UCSA, Sanchez also gave orders to California's various army units and the 1st Marine Division out of Camp Pendleton to begin supporting the war efforts in North America.

Within days of the order, California's special operations group joined the Western Alliance and CANZUK special forces, and together, they concocted the mission to grab Spector's chief of staff. The mission in Missouri didn't go quite to plan, but in the end, they had secured the man whom intelligence sources identified as the UCSA President's most influential advisor.

As if these developments weren't coming fast enough, events in Europe were also galloping forward recklessly.

The Poles, seeing a Russian invasion as inevitable, had sent their tanks East to take possession of the Kaliningrad Oblast and were actively building up their mechanized forces along its border with Belarus.

Fighting the tenacious Nordic Alliance in the Baltics, Russia's President had vowed a swift and terrible response against their ancient Polish rival. Having already used tactical nukes to end the war in Ukraine, CANZUK intelligence, using the alliance's most powerful near-AI models, had estimated a fifty-seven percent chance nuclear weapons would again be used on European soil in the next six to twelve months.

To the West, in the Netherlands, France had finally taken the gloves off.

In the previous two weeks, the French Army had tentatively probed into Dutch territory, hoping the smaller country's politicians would see the writing on the wall and agree to the terms French President Marie-Helene Lévesque had proposed.

On their fourth refusal and with the war in full bloom in the East, France had unleashed the full weight of its military on the Dutch and was now in the final stages of wholly occupying its brave but much smaller neighbour.

Finally, there was Germany. 'Europe's wild card,' as Merielle had labelled them.

For years now, the Germans had resisted Lévesque's anti-Muslim program, and in so doing, that country's coalition of centrist politicians had opened themselves up to attack by the far-right nationalist movement now in charge of France.

Looking to capitalize on its long-time rival's weakness, France and its intelligence services had undertaken a massive effort to destabilize Europe's largest country so that it might be replaced with one that would join France's increasingly brutal effort to cleanse Western Europe of its Muslims and treat seriously the threat that was the Russian Bear.

With all of this going on, you could forgive Canadians if they forgot just how crazy things had gotten in their own backyard.

In the past week, four CSIS intelligence officers had been killed by three explosions in British Columbia, the leader of Canada's official opposition had been found dead, and last but not least, the Premier of BC had been blown up by Chinese automatons.

And just yesterday, one of the few people MacPhail trusted to help her understand and head off the growing disaster that was Canada's prime minister had been found on a rural side road with a bullet in his head.

MacPhail had only been working with Sam Petit for just a month, but in that short time, she had grown to trust the man. In speaking with him and reading his reports, it had become clear his motivations aligned with her own. Petit, like her, wanted to see the country successfully navigate the current mess it was in, but not at the expense of the nation's soul.

Based on his last update, it sounded like he and Larocque were starting to make progress in bringing this elusive White Unit to heel. Petit himself had been confident that CSIS was now free and clear of people who would be working against Larocque and his plans to reorganize the Service to better support Canada and the two major wars it was fighting.

As Petit described it, these same changes would also help Larocque's efforts to pin down and, if necessary, take down the White Unit so that Merielle couldn't use it to effect whatever plans she seemed to be concocting.

Regarding the prime minister, during this same time frame, Merielle had taken various steps to protect her status and power in Ottawa.

Within two days of invoking the Emergencies Act, she announced a surprise cabinet shuffle replacing several ministers, all of whom at one point had pushed back against Canada's involvement in the US civil war. A slew of deputy ministers, those powerful senior civil servants who ran the country's bureaucracy, had also been replaced.

In both cases, the promoted people were known to be supporters of the PM, if not unabashed partisans.

That MacPhail herself hadn't got the boot was a mystery she was still trying to figure out.

While she had problem-solved for Merielle and knocked down one problem after another in her role as Deputy PM, on more than one occasion, MacPhail had vigorously resisted Merielle's proposals on the wars and domestic issues.

Whatever her status in the eyes of Merielle and regardless of Petit's death, MacPhail was as determined as ever to figure out what game the PM was playing because as sure as MacPhail's hair was red, Merielle Martel was up to something.

The cab she was riding in from St. John's International Airport to the Health Science Center, located on the Memorial University campus, stopped at the entrance she'd been given directions to.

Normally, someone from her constituency office would have picked her up at the airport and drove her to wherever she needed to be, but her mother was a proud woman and had been sure to tell the physician who had spoken with MacPhail that she didn't want anyone to know about her predicament.

Getting out of the cab, she saw a middle-aged Black man standing in front of the entrance of the facility. She had done an internet search on the doctor who had been taking care of his mother and had found Dr. Mascoll. From Nova Scotia, he had spent twenty years as a medical generalist in the Canadian Armed Forces before giving up his commission and taking a teaching job at the local university just two years ago.

As was a prerequisite for all full-time lecturers at the medical school, he was required to have a caseload or conduct regular rounds at one of St. John's three medical facilities, and by chance, he had been the physician to evaluate her mother when she arrived at the hospital two days ago.

As she reached the doc, she held out her hand. "Dr. Mascoll, very nice to meet you. Thank you so much for taking care of my mum. I hope she's been kind. She can be a bit rough when she's stressed."

The physician chuckled and said in the same deep and calming voice she had heard over the phone, "Your mother is a lovely woman, Minister MacPhail. I only wish more of my elderly patients had her grace."

One of MacPhail's eyebrows arched upward. "Okay, two things, Doctor. First, we're not in Ottawa, so please don't call me 'Minister.' It's Irene, if you please. Second, are you sure it's my mother who you are taking care of? Because, in all of my years of being that woman's daughter, I've not heard anyone, and I mean not a single bloody person, mention Nancy MacPhail and the word 'grace' in the same sentence."

A smile cropped up on the physician's face. His expression radiated kindness. Combined with the soothing sound of his voice and his not-so-bad looks, MacPhail could see why this man had won over her mother.

Dr. Mascoll pivoted and gestured to the doors of the hospital. "Minister... sorry, Irene, why don't I take you to your mom?"

"Lead the way, Doctor."

After one elevator ride and navigating several long hallways, they reached their destination. "I managed to secure her a private suite. She seemed quite pleased with it," the physician remarked.

By now, Mascoll's baritone voice and pleasant bedside manners had won MacPhail over. As they stood in front of the suite's entrance, she wondered if he might be interested in grabbing coffee once she was done visiting her mom. After all, he wasn't wearing a wedding band, and she would have time to kill before she caught a flight back to Ottawa.

Giving the door two quick knocks, Mascoll pushed it open and moved into the room.

MacPhail, gladdened by the pleasant conversation she had with the doctor on their journey through the hospital, followed him into the room with a genuine smile on her face.

Her smile dropped like a lead balloon when she saw the person seated on the edge of the bed.

Before she could ask any questions, the room's only occupant said, "Minister MacPhail, good to see you again."

***

With an exhausted look on his face, Spector looked at the giant digital screen that featured the map of the Northeast portion of the former United States.

To say that the retreat of the UCSA forces from New York and parts of Pennsylvania had been a disaster was the kind of understatement that could only come from someone who didn't understand war."

Whatever it was, it had been caused by two main factors. The first was the UCSA's inability to employ tactical nukes. When employed in support of a ground attack, low-yield nuclear weapons were a game-changer.

With just a handful of tactical strikes, an enemy's defensive lines, including any minefields, could be annihilated, leaving huge gaps for mechanized forces to advance through in as little time as twenty-four hours.

This is what the Russians had done in Ukraine years earlier and what the UCSA had done to take Washington. And it is what the Chinese had done along the border of Vietnam. When used, low-yield nuclear weapons were the ultimate advantage.

But these weapons only gave you leverage so long as the country you were fighting didn't have nuclear weapons of their own.

To Spector's ever-growing regret, the United Kingdom did have nukes, and so, by default, did the whole of CANZUK. North in Canada, the Brits had shipped in a dozen strategic weapons and a larger number of tactical munitions.

To put a point on the UK's willingness to use their doomsday weapons, Prime Minister Richardson hadn't gone a day in the past week without mentioning her country's willingness to lay waste to one or dozens of industrial or military targets in the UCSA if the Red Faction used their tactical nukes anywhere within two hundred miles of a CANZUK military unit.

The second factor had been fuel or the increasing lack of it. In recent days, CANZUK submarines in the Atlantic and Gulf of Mexico had been joined by some undetermined number of submarines from the US Navy's West Coast fleet.

Following a massive cash payoff to the Panamanian government, a battalion of paratroopers from the UK's Parachute Regiment had air-dropped into the Central American country to oversee the transit of at least seven US Navy subs as they made their way into the Atlantic.

With the destruction of the bulk of its own submarine force at King's Bay two years ago, the UCSA had few options available to them to prevent the sinking of the fuel tankers and cargo ships the country needed to keep its war machine going.

Slowly but surely, as less fuel had been available to move north and as more gasoline stations across the country had gone dry, the UCSA, a juggernaut only six weeks before, was retreating en masse and facing the real possibility of both a military and societal collapse.

On top of it all, CANZUK, along with Sanchez and Anders-Maxwell, had managed to get their hands on Parr.

Pulling his eyes from the tactical map, Spector turned his gaze back on his advisors.

Exhaling a deep breath he didn't know he'd been holding onto, he said, "So, if I can summarize, in the Northeast, we consolidate Army Group Three in Morgantown, West Virginia while the rest of our forces retreat into DC where we prepare both cities for a siege. Is that correct?"

It was the Army Chief of Staff, General Spellings, who answered the question. "That's correct, Mr. President. Both cities have natural defenses, and if our troops are static, we can save the fuel that we do have for the western front."

"The West," Spector growled. More quickly than he would have thought possible, the western flank of the UCSA had become a problem. A big one. "What's the latest there?" he asked wearily.

Again, it was Spellings who delivered the update. "Well, Mr. President, intelligence as recent as this morning informs us that advance elements from the 40th Infantry Division out of California have been seen setting up on the outskirts of Albuquerque while the 1st Marine Division has been seen doing the same at Holloman Air Force Base. To the north, in Colorado, we're seeing a slower but steady buildup of units from several National Guards, including those of Colorado, Utah and Nevada.

"At the current rate of buildup, we expect that the California Army could be ready to take offensive actions within two weeks while the Western Alliance force would be ready in four to five. If nothing else, their presence limits our options to reinforce our people in the Northeast."

Spector pushed his chair back from the table and slowly got to his feet. The rest of his advisors, long used to his habit of standing at random times, did not move to join him. He walked in the direction of the huge screen and said, "Adjust the map so I can see the United States from Washington, DC to Amarillo, Texas."

Instantly, the map shifted to show the requested landmass. Stepping closer to the screen, with his index finger, Spector traced a red arc from Washington to the city in the far west of Texas.

Taking a step back, he took a long moment to observe the line.

Perhaps a full minute later, he turned back to the eleven men he had been relying on to help him run the UCSA and win the war against the Blues. His voice measured, Spector said, "I know we are losing this war, and I know if we continue down the path we're on, we lose it completely. For reasons we are all familiar with, we cannot fail. As I've said before many times, losing is bad for us and me, but more importantly, it is terrible for our country.

"None of you needs a lecture on the way things used to be. And if you think for one minute that a reconciliation under someone like Andrew Morgan might not be so bad, just stop and think back to every time that bastard stood behind Valeria Menendez and smiled while she announced yet another policy that tore this country apart.

"For all his talk of reconciliation and finding a new way, we all know what this man and his people believe. They are no longer Americans. Andrew Morgan is a post-national ghoul who would love nothing more than to finish the job that Menendez started."

He took a number of steps forward so that he was once again behind his chair and said, "But we need time. We need time to reconstitute our military and bring peace to our cities. This enterprise called the United Constitutional States of America has fought, won, and survived some of the hardest fighting this world has ever seen. We can survive the next four months and the next four years if we need to, but we have to make the right moves in the coming days and weeks."

Spector turned his gaze onto General Hoffman. "How goes Operation Preservation Midnight?"

The Vice-Chief of the Air Force looked as tired as everyone else in the room, but when he spoke, his words came across as confident and clear. "Mr. President, we're now up to sixteen weapons of forty kilotons and seven of ninety kilotons. But perhaps more importantly, with the plans we were able to obtain from Pakistan, we're just a few weeks away from operationalizing our first batch of mobile launchers capable of sending these warheads as far as five thousand miles away."

Spector nodded his head and asked, "And five thousand miles puts us in range of where, General?"

"From the East Coast, it will allow us to drop as many as ten devices at one time on Southern England."

"Good. Very good," Spector said in a quiet voice.

When Spector's eyes left Hoffman's, he canvassed the rest of the faces in the room.

On each was an unvarnished look of worry. The very same concern he felt. "Gentlemen, the next few weeks will be critical for us. Until we can demonstrate our ability to melt the capital cities of our enemies from afar, we are vulnerable, and we'll not be able to negotiate terms that will allow us to live to fight another day if that's what the future leaders of our great country wish to do.

"It may be that it's not us who unite the former United States. Our new objective is to set the table for those who come after us. We need to give the UCSA time."

He let his statement stew for a moment. Around the table, he saw a few looks of relief and more than a few nodding heads.

Continuing, he said, "So we need to do two things. First, until those mobile launchers and the missiles they carry are operational, we need to fight like hell. We need to hold the territory that we now have in the Northeast, and under no circumstances will I permit us to lose one single yard of the Western front. Texas and Kansas must remain whole. Is that understood?"

In their own ways, each advisor sitting at the table confirmed his direction, whether it was through a boisterous "Yes, Mr. President" or the determined nodding of a head. To the last man, they were on board.

Spector raised his right hand into the air and made a fist. "We can do this, people."

Following another round of head nodding, he continued, "The second thing we need to do is move our base of operations."

Locking his eyes on his Intelligence Director, Spector asked, "The Californians have moved a batch of GBU-28s to Holloman AFB in New Mexico – is that correct, Dave?"

Christoff, the CIB Director, said, "It's been confirmed, Mr. President. Eight of them, at least. That bomb, even one of them, will crack any of our protected facilities asunder and easily. I suggest we move further east and put ourselves out of range."

Nodding at the intel man's update, Spector said, "Gentlemen, I think it's time we took what is rightfully ours. We will be moving to Washington, where I will be taking up residence at the White House, and we will begin to hold our meetings in the West Wing.

"No one and nobody is going to risk hitting those buildings, and I will be damned if I'm gonna leave that piece of real estate unoccupied any longer so that it can be used as a bargaining chip for whatever deal we make to end this war. Mark my words: the White House is UCSA territory and will remain so forever and a day."

After a pause to let his words sink in, he added, "Everyone should be ready to leave in two hours. At 1700 hours Washington time, we'll meet again in the Situation Room, in the West Wing."

Chapter 33

St. John's, Newfoundland

—

When MacPhail's eyes found Larocque sitting on the edge of the bed where she'd expected to see her mother, her eyes narrowed, and she felt the furnace of her Irish heritage begin to fire up.

She turned in the doctor's direction and, in a heated voice, said, "Where is my mother? Did she even have a stroke?"

"She is well. She is at home and safe and sound," Mascoll said in the same tone of voice he'd been using for their entire conversation.

MacPhail wheeled back to Larocque, "What the hell is going on? In case you hadn't been keeping up on the news, there's no shortage of high drama taking place back in Ottawa. Jesus on the cross, Larocque, you've wasted the better part of two days and added stress to my life when I didn't think I could take anymore."

She took a step in Larocque's direction and pointed her finger at his chest. "Start talking, Director, before I completely lose my shit, and we lose whatever pretense of secrecy you were hoping for in arranging this little rendezvous."

Larocque got up from the bed, and as he did so, his height and frame towered over Canada's Deputy Prime Minister. His eyes left MacPhail's and found the physician's. "Thanks, Barry. I owe you one."

"Not a problem, Jaks. It was good seeing you again, my friend. Be safe."

The doctor then turned his eyes on MacPhail. "I'm sorry, Irene. Jaks and I go back some years, and I trust him as much as I trust anyone. If he says it was important to get you here based on a ruse and all you lost is a couple of days in the viper's nest that is Ottawa, then I was okay to help. Whatever discussions you need to have, I hope you two can help sort out this country because, from my perspective out here on the East Coast, things aren't looking so good."

With those words, Mascoll turned and left the room.

As the door closed behind the physician, MacPhail and Larocque reacquired one another.

"So, you know that guy from before," MacPhail asked, making a determined effort to keep the heat she was feeling out of her voice.

"I do. He delivered our daughter, and for a couple years after that, I taught him how to box at the fight club in Pembroke when we were both stationed at Pet."

"And how is it that you came up with the idea to have him get me out of Ottawa?"

"It wasn't my idea. It was my wife's. It's a bit of a story, but the long and short of it is that the White Unit visited me at my place two nights back."

MacPhail interrupted Larocque and with concern in her voice, said, "They did? Is your wife okay? Did they do anything? Jesus, you're here, so they must have done something."

A grim look dawned on Larocque's face. "Except poor Petit, everyone's fine, but things have come to a head, and I needed to get you out of Ottawa so we could speak face to face. Knowing you were from St. John's, my wife mentioned to me that Barry – Dr. Mascoll – was out here and that he might be willing to help.

"As you can imagine, there was just no way I could arrange for us to meet anywhere in or near Ottawa without it getting back to the wrong people. I'm now convinced that the White Unit is bigger and more connected to the government's infrastructure than I would have thought possible. Even getting you to come here under the pretense of your mother being unwell is a risk."

Before MacPhail could interrupt again and ask about her mother's health, Larocque pushed on. "Your mother is fine. She has no clue she was a part of the ruse. She's sitting at home, clueless about all of this.

"The nice thing about your home province is that there are only a few ways to get here. I've got people watching the airport, the ferry, and a few other angles. Everyone in Ottawa will know that you came here for your mom – more importantly, none of these people will know you met with me."

"This is quite the production," said MacPhail. "I thought you said this White Unit was better connected than you thought. What's to say they don't know you're here?"

Larocque shook his head. "I've taken certain steps to tighten things at the Service. I'm now convinced I have a solid core of people on my side. If we're going to act against this White Unit like I think we need to, I now have the right people. And I think we have to do something fast. We're running out of time, Irene."

After blowing a massive gust of frustrated air from her lungs, MacPhail said, "Yes, we are running out of time, but I hope you're not looking to me for any answers on how to proceed. Merielle has turned over those parts of her Cabinet that she felt weren't loyal enough. The woman has surrounded herself with yes-people, and she's done the same with the bureaucracy. For a woman who's a former cop, she's one hell of a crafty politician. You'd think she'd lived and breathed the machinery of Ottawa her entire life."

Larocque nodded and said, "This is why she keeps winning. Everyone underestimates her, and she uses it to her advantage, but there's one part of this narrative she can't control."

"And that is what exactly?" asked MacPhail.

"Early next week, there's a bill to be voted on that will amend the budget. It's inconsequential because no one expects your party to vote against a bill that will provide more money for the war effort. But because there's funding attached to it, it's a motion of confidence. If it doesn't pass, the Martel government falls, and if it falls, it can be replaced with a unity government."

MacPhail's eyes widened as Larocque's proposal struck her. "You want me to work with the opposition parties to bring down the government? The same government that I'm the Deputy Prime Minister of?"

"Yes, and by next Tuesday," Larocque said, his face deadpan.

"And you want me to do this in such a way that Merielle and her people don't find out about it? In five bloody days?" MacPhail said incredulously.

Larocque said nothing and only continued to stare back at the politician.

"For Christ's sake, Jackson, you can't be serious?"

Without warning, Larocque's face darkened, and he took a step in MacPhail's direction, forcing her backward.

Though she was tall for a woman, the former soldier-turned-spy towered over her and, in a voice almost a growl, said, "At last count, nearly three thousand Canadian soldiers, airmen and sailors have died fighting a war *your* government decided to join. In the past three weeks, CSIS has lost forty-eight people. On the same night the White Unit came to my home and put my family under threat, these people killed your man."

Larocque took another step forward, forcing MacPhail to back into the room's only door. "Sam is dead, and a lot more people are gonna die if we don't do something to stop the train that is Merielle Martel. Because once she is finished reshaping government, and she and her people have a full head of steam, you and I and people like us are going to have to go along for the ride – or more likely, we'll be thrown from the train."

Clenching his jaw, Larocque continued, "Everyone's got skin in this game, Irene, especially politicians. You came to see me about the problem that was Merielle Martel, and I'm now telling you I need your help to stop this country from turning into what might be its first dictatorship. So yes, I am serious, Minister. Terribly serious."

For a long moment, they stared at one another. Finally, dropping her eyes, MacPhail said, "You're right. You're right. We have to do something. It's just every time I've tried to make a move, it's gone nowhere, or it's been countered. Christ, in most cases, I've chosen to do nothing because I'm scared."

Her eyes shot back to Larocque's, and she said, "I'm not a soldier like you. I haven't killed anyone. Jesus, I'm a reporter from bloody Newfoundland who's somehow found her way into being the Deputy Prime Minister. Yes, I'm good at my job, but leading what would be a coup? What you're proposing, Larocque, has never been done. Never."

"There's a lot of *nevers* happening, Irene," Larocque said, his voice calmer than it had been moments ago. "Civil wars, tactical nuclear weapons being tossed around as though they were mortars, killer robots conducting assassinations in far-off lands, a two-front war no one in this country could have foreseen five years ago.

"Yes, it's all unbelievable and scary. And Merielle is doing what she's doing because she feels she has no choice. She's a practical, patriotic woman who is prepared to do bold things in response to extraordinary events. But if we're going to prevent her from doing something that could alter the political trajectory of our country for a generation or more, we also need to be bold and we need to act before it is too late."

MacPhail closed her eyes and took in a deep breath. As she counted to five, the image of her father appeared in her mind. He was staring at her from behind the laptop kept on the table in his office. His face was kind as it always was when he spoke with his daughter. In her mind, she could hear him say, *"You're not a reporter anymore, kid. It's okay to become the story. Do what's right, and give 'em hell."*

She released her breath, looked into Larocque's face, and said, "All right, it sounds like you have a plan. Let's hear it."

***

The Yellow Sea

While the CANZUK and US navies owned the South China Sea, that was not the case in the narrow enclave of water located between China and the Korean Peninsula.

Though it seemed a decade or more in the past, just weeks ago, the Royal Australian Navy had lost one of its submarines in these same waters.

At the time, as it was now, the shallow waters of the Yellow Sea were teeming with Chinese ASW frigates and destroyers relentlessly searching for any hints of an enemy submarine.

Upon first receiving the order for their current mission, Captain Maggie Alcock of *HMS Agincourt* had taken time to review the data the *HMAS Perth* had released in her death throes.

When the war was over, she hoped the captain and crew of the *Perth* got the medals they deserved. That they had gotten so close to China's coast, been able to launch two full salvos of Tomahawks, and severely damage factories deep within China, had been a feat verging on the miraculous.

Their own journey had been perilous. On four occasions, they had been required to go ultra-silent, fall to the sea floor, and wait several hours as one ship or a whole flotilla of PLA Navy vessels passed them by.

Despite the delays, they had made it and within the time mandated by what were the sparsest orders she had yet received during the war.

Their orders had been: arrive by this date, by this time, four hundred kilometers east and south of Beijing, and once there, be ready to act offensively, and as tactically feasible, every half hour extend the communications mast of the *Agincourt* above the water to receive further directions.

Well, they were here, and this would be the eleventh time they had exposed themselves without receiving any new orders.

Alcock looked at her watch and saw that it was coming up to 0900 hours. The idea that they would breach their comms mast in broad daylight in these waters went against all her training and suggested someone in Whitehall had a death wish for her and her crew.

Ignoring the angst she felt in the pit of her stomach, she said calmly, "Sonar, what's the latest, if you please?"

"Same as before, Captain. Nothing within forty kilometers on the surface. Sub-surface, our last contact was six hours ago, one hundred five klicks to the east. We haven't picked up anything except local wildlife since. Without sending up the periscope and taking a look around, I think we're as clear as we can be."

Alcock moved her gaze to the woman currently driving the boat. "Helm, bring us up to a depth of seven meters."

"Aye, Captain, reducing our depth to seven meters," confirmed the helmswoman.

"Comms, be ready with the comms mast. Twenty seconds and no more."

"Aye, Captain, comms mast is ready on your order."

"Captain, we are holding steady at seven meters," advised Helm.

"Thank you, Ms. Smythe."

"Comms, raise the mast."

"Aye, Captain, comms mast being raised."

Ten seconds later, the officer at comms reported, "Mast has breached the surface."

When she heard they'd become exposed, Alcock turned her attention to the stopwatch she was holding and started counting down.

When it got to twelve, her XO called out, "Captain, new orders have arrived."

"Excellent, XO. You have the bridge. Send them to my ready room, if you please. Come see me when we're tucked away."

"Aye, Captain," the XO said.

On reaching the space that served as her office and the place where she and her senior officers discussed matters privately, she immediately took up the tactical pad sitting on the room's small table and saw that she had a high-priority message waiting.

Taking a seat, she opened and quickly scanned the new orders, then said aloud, "Jesus, they can't be serious?"

She re-read the order, this time more deliberately. As she finished scanning them a second time, she heard her XO's knock.

"Come," Alcock said in a voice lost in thought.

Opening the door, her XO strode into the small space and said, "What's the good word?"

She didn't answer her second-in-command. Instead, she handed him the tablet.

Raising his eyes from the display, the XO let out a puff of air and said, "This will make things interesting."

"That's an understatement if I've ever heard one. Every helo, plane, and ship within two hundred klicks will come at us like bloody gangbusters. The *Perth* didn't last fifteen goddamned minutes once they pegged her."

Her XO, a happy-go-lucky chap from Manchester, said, "Well, nothing against the *Perth*, Captain, but if there's anyone in the Royal Navy's submarine service who can get us free and clear of the Yellow Sea, it'll be you. At my last count, there are at least a dozen submarines in this part of the world that could have been selected for this mission. And last I checked, the Navy didn't do suicide missions. If they sent us here, it's because they think we can make it out."

Alcock looked at the rail-thin man who had been her go-to confidant at every moment of the war. "I think you missed your calling, XO. You should have become a therapist. You always know the right things to say and when to say them."

"I'm not sure my ex-wife would agree with you, Captain, but if me telling you you're a great submariner is what it takes for us to survive the next few hours, then I'm willing to channel as much

Counsellor Troi as much as I'm prepared to be your Commander Riker."

Quickly, the XO added, "And it's true, by the way."

Alcock's eyebrows furrowed, "What's true?"

"You're a great captain, Maggie. I would have thought the last five weeks would have made that clear, but I guess that's one of the things that makes you excellent at your job."

This time, Alcock arched one of her eyebrows and asked, "And what *thing* would that be?"

"That you're humble, almost to a fault."

Nodding at the XO's words, Alcock said, "Be less humble. Got it."

Gesturing to the door, she added, "Let's end the therapy session, shall we? As of five minutes ago, we have a government to overturn."

***

Yantai, Shandong, China

The border of the tactical display of the HHQ-9 battery started to throb red just as the alarm within the trailer started to blare loudly.

Run by a near-AI, the HHQ-9 missile defense system could run independently of the humans in the trailer nearing the end of their eight-hour shift. For better or worse, China's leadership was not yet prepared to allow highly intelligent thinking machines to make the mistake of blowing up a civilian airliner.

For all of their sophistication, it remained the case that near-AIs weren't yet deemed to be sentient, could not be put on trial, and, if needed, could not be executed for whatever decision they had made or not made.

In the end, when something went wrong, and there needed to be accountability, humans needed to be in the chain of command, even if their role in that chain was nothing more than pressing a button.

"Sir, radar has picked up what looks like six sea-launched missiles. Most likely Tomahawks."

At the other end of the trailer, the major quickly walked down to the radar technician's position and looked at the display.

"Sir, the missiles have been confirmed as Tomahawks. The system has locked onto them. Permission to fire?"

"Permission denied, Corporal," the major said firmly.

"But, sir, the missiles are vectoring in the direction of Beijing." As he said the words, the NCO pointed at the screen and added, "We only have twenty more seconds before our missiles are out of range."

Keeping his eyes focused on the screen, the major said, "Take no action, Corporal. That's an order."

In the direction where the major had come from, one of the other two radar techs piped up, his voice concerned, "Sir, we have a second launch of missiles from the same location. The system is actively flagging them. We have a lock."

The officer didn't look in the direction the new report had come from. Instead, his gaze remained locked on the first radar tech, who had edged his hand forward so that it was within reach of the large green square on the display that would send a dozen of their battery's missiles toward the incoming Tomahawks.

"I said don't, Corporal," the major said, injecting as much authority into his voice as he could manage.

In a voice of protest, the corporal said, "Sir, we're running out of time. It's been confirmed they're enemy missiles."

As the two men stared each other down, the major's hand slipped to the pistol holstered on his hip. The movement drew the radar tech's gaze. Seeing the officer's hand begin to wrap around the grip of his sidearm, the NCO's face flared into a wild look just as he reached for the button on the tactical display.

But before the NCO's hand could make contact with the green launch toggle, the major's booted foot came forward and kicked the radar tech's chair, driving the corporal away from the control panel.

Ripping his pistol from his holster, the major pointed its barrel at the younger man's chest and, without hesitation, shot him twice.

With the echo of the shots still reverberating in the tiny space, the major spun in the direction of the two remaining radar techs and pointed his weapon at the man who'd given the warning about the second salvo. The NCO, also a corporal, held his hand a few inches above the launch toggle.

Calling out sternly to the soldier, the officer said, "Don't, Heng. Don't make me do this. I'm just following orders. Please!"

From the corner of his eye, Heng saw the timer on the display counting down the window of opportunity to shoot down the incoming missiles. They would be out of range in ten seconds.

When the countdown reached five, Heng's eyes widened, giving him a panicked look.

His voice cold, the major said, "Heng, you stupid piece of shit, don't. I'll shoot you down. I swear I'll do it."

At two seconds, Heng's eyes snapped shut, and just as he shifted in the direction of the launch button, a gunshot rang out.

The pain that followed was excruciating.

Instinctively, with both hands, Heng reached toward that part of his body that was in agony. Looking down, he pulled his hands away and saw they were soaked with blood.

As his brain struggled to comprehend what had just happened, it was shocked back to reality as two more gunshots rang out.

Behind him, he heard an extended howl of terror.

Turning in that direction, the third radar tech and his friend, Cai Lang, was on the control room's floor, propped up on the wall that was beside the only entrance into the trailer. He'd been shot just underneath his right shoulder and was gasping for air as though he were a fish out of water.

From behind him, another gunshot rang out. This time, the round struck his friend between the eyes, creating a gory red mess on the metallic panelling.

Still in his chair and still being waylaid by waves of pain, Heng heard a faint footfall. Slowly, he swiveled around to find the major standing over him with his pistol pointing at his head.

The officer, an at-all-times pleasant man he'd enjoyed working with for the past year, had a grim look on his face.

His voice low and determined, the major said, "I'm sorry, Heng. I didn't want it to be this way. I'm just following orders."

As tears began to well up in his eyes, Heng managed to get out, "Don't. Please. I won't say anything. This never happened. I promise, Major. Not a word."

With a sad look, the major shook his head. "It's too late now, Corporal. Dead bodies don't tell secrets. For what it's worth, I'm sorry."

As the major's finger tightened on the trigger, Heng's world slowed to a crawl. His mind clung to every detail: the glint of the pistol's barrel, the grim determination etched into the major's face, the sharp tang of blood and gunpowder filling the air.

In that last fragment of awareness, Heng felt a brief torrent of pain and then only darkness.

***

Beijing

"Where are Generals Wu and Qiu?" demanded Yan.

"I've just heard from Wu's Chief of Staff, Mr. President. They were both held up by traffic from the suspected terrorist attack this morning. Apparently, the entire western half of the city is snarled with traffic. Even emergency vehicles are struggling to get through."

Yan glared at the general who'd given the update. "Terrorist attack. Unbelievable. In Beijing. I won't believe it until I see the evidence."

Yan wheeled on the senior man representing the Ministry of State Security. Pointing at the senior party official, he demanded, "Where is Wang?"

The Deputy Director for MSS stuttered and then finally said, "He elected to attend the national headquarters, Mr. President. He felt it would be best if he could get first-hand knowledge of the attack. He's been sending me regular updates every ten minutes or so."

"And?" barked Yan.

With a confused look on the replacement's face, he said, "And, Mr. President?"

Yan threw his hands in the air and all but screamed, "You are a fool, Chen. How did you ever secure your position? *And,* who carried out the attack, man?"

"Right, of course," the Deputy Director said hurriedly. "As of this moment, we don't know, Mr. President. Initial indications are that it was a cell of Vietnamese terrorists. We've caught several operating in the southern provinces, but all of the intelligence we've seen to date has poured cold water on the idea they could operate this far north.

"In the south of the country, there are enough similarities in the look of the people that their more talented operatives can blend in. At least for a period. Here in Beijing, they would stick out like a sore thumb."

Yan snapped at the man, "So if it's not the Vietnamese, then who else could it be?"

The second-in-command from China's national intelligence service turned his palms up, gave a slight shrug of his shoulders, and said, "Mr. President, as I already advised, we're unsure of who carried out the act, but our very best people, including Minister Wang himself, are on the problem. In an hour, maybe two, I'm confident we'll have an update for you with hard evidence."

Just as Yan was about to continue to verbally thrash the MSS deputy, the double doors to the boardroom swung open wildly, and eight officers from the Central Security Bureau rushed in to immediately surround Yan.

The leader of the protection detail approached Yan and whispered in his ear. "We've received reports missiles are on their way to Beijing, Mr. President. We do not know their targets. We are taking you to safety."

Without allowing Yan to speak, the two largest of the men who had entered the room jumped to his side, grabbed his arms, and began to hustle him to the entrance. Yan, having grasped the seriousness of the team leader's words, moved to keep pace with the two agents.

Reaching the hallway, they took a right, and with two protection officers leading the way, as a group, they jogged at the quickest pace Yan's sixty-one-year-old body could manage.

At his direction, the morning's meeting had taken place in Qinzheng Hall, the ancient and magnificent structure that served as Yan's residence and a gathering place for some of the Party's most important meetings.

"Where are we going?" Yan finally managed to yell as they turned another corner, and he laid his eyes on the doors that would take him to his limousine and the rest of the vehicles that made up his motorcade.

Over his shoulder, the lead of his protection detail started to yell back a reply, but he was cut short by an extended burst of fire from what Yan thought might be one or more of the anti-aircraft batteries that surrounded the Forbidden City.

Together, the two beefy security agents on either side of Yan picked him up by the arms and legs and began to sprint with the rest of the security detail to the doors leading to the building's exterior.

Ahead, a pair of black-suited agents, each holding one of the massive wooden doors of the entrance, were urging them forward. Yan didn't think it was possible, but somehow, the two men carrying him picked up speed.

Just as they crossed the entrance's threshold and his two protectors began to navigate the stairs that would bring him to the protective confines of his armoured limo, he was engulfed by an incredibly intense flash of light and a blast of heat that ripped through his suit as though he'd been wearing nothing.

In an instant, the energy that flooded his body unleashed a pain beyond anything he had ever known, a torment so intense it defied description. Excruciating didn't even begin to capture the agony as his skin started to liquefy.

In his last hazy memory, he felt his body fall through the air and strike something hard. Opening his eyes, he saw that he was on the ground and that his limousine was engulfed in flames. Here and there around him, he saw the bodies of his protection detail and a few of the minor officials who helped him run the country.

All were dead or on their way to dying.

Somewhere behind him, there was another massive explosion.

As the ground shook beneath him and burning debris fell from the sky, his destroyed ears somehow perceived the dual sound of more anti-aircraft gunfire and a single person screaming hysterically.

It sounded like war. It sounded like hell.

It was at that moment he felt his body begin to shut down. The amount of pain coursing through him made it abundantly clear his end was near.

What a terrible shame. There had been so much more to do. And worse, he would never find out how his enemies had struck him down.

The realization was a helpless feeling for a man who had held so much power. But he could fight no longer. At sixty-one, Yan Jiandong, China's 9th President – the man who had finally united the Motherland – accepted his fate and died.

Chapter 34

Yellow Sea

—

"Captain, we're being actively pinged."

Alcock turned to the sonar station. "Source?"

"Dipped sonar. Almost two kilometers west of us."

Her voice in full command mode, Alcock said, "Helm, get us down as deep as you can and set a speed of fifteen knots, take pre-set route Lima-Bravo."

"Aye, Captain, bringing her down to within eight meters of the sea floor, setting speed at fifteen knots, proceeding on route Lima-Bravo."

"Helm, make it so," said Alcock.

Turning to her XO, she said, "More helicopters will be coming. There have to be at least two more from that grouping of ships we flagged a couple of hours ago."

She looked down at the large table display that was the *Agincourt's* near-AI combat information system and pointed to the five-ship flotilla to their east. "They're thirty klicks away. By the time they get their helos in the air, it'll be thirty minutes before they get here."

"Captain, we've registered a second dipped sonar. It's gone active. It's ahead of us at eighteen hundred meters."

"Roger that, Sonar," Alcock said without taking her eyes off the tactical display.

Across the table, the XO said, "Considering how loud we were, I'd say two helos is a blessing."

Before Alcock could tell her second-in-command not to jinx their good fortune, the voice of the senior petty officer and her best sonar operator called out urgently, "Torpedoes in the water."

"Details?" Alcock asked sharply.

"Hold one," the sonar operator said from his station.

After what felt like an eternity, the petty officer said, "We have a second torpedo in the water. They're both active. Bearing on our position at one-nine-four degrees. The estimated time to impact at the current speed for Fish Alpha is two minutes, nine seconds. Fish Bravo is two minutes, forty seconds."

"Countermeasures, start jamming them," ordered Alcock.

"Aye, Captain," replied the lieutenant leading that three-person station.

"Helm, maximum speed. Keep our course steady," Alcock ordered, her voice calm.

"Aye, Captain, maximum speed, stay on course," replied the helmswoman.

Two red triangles appeared on the tactical display at the stern of her boat. In between the two torpedoes and her vessel, a countdown had commenced.

As she felt the *Agincourt's* Rolls-Royce nuclear power plant begin to surge to get the Royal Navy sub to its thirty-knot maximum, the numbers on the display began to tick down at a slower rate, if only slightly.

Chinese naval helicopters carried the Yu-8 torpedo, a lightweight anti-submarine weapon that had come into service in the past five years.

Almost certainly derived from the Italian A244-S torpedo, data from the war confirmed that the unit's maximum speed was fifty-seven knots. It wasn't the PLA Navy's fastest or most powerful torpedo, but it would easily kill the *Agincourt* if one of them got close enough.

She moved her eyes ahead of their charted path. At their current speed, the helo ahead of them would definitely get a fix on their position.

At fifteen knots or less, the Astute Class was as quiet as any submarine in the world's navies, but once you passed this speed, none of the vessel's stealth technologies could prevent it from being lit up by an active enemy sonar.

But stealth wasn't what Alcock was going for. She was playing a numbers game. Two helos meant a maximum of four torpedoes. In the next twenty minutes, she and her crew needed to do two things. The first was survive the four torpedoes that would be sent against them.

Once this was done, her second task would be to drop the *Agincourt* to a much quieter speed and then try to put as much distance between themselves and their current position before more helicopters arrived.

From the sonar station, an urgent voice called, "Captain, two more torpedoes in the water ahead of us. Bearing zero-one-eight degrees. Estimated time to contact is one minute, seven seconds."

Alcock pulled her eyes from the tactical display and placed them on the back of the helmswoman. Snapping her words, she said, "Helm, set a new course at zero-five-five degrees, maintain speed, maintain depth. Make it so."

"Aye, Captain," replied the twenty-something woman responsible for physically steering the one-billion-dollar vessel.

Immediately, Alcock felt the interior of the submarine shift as its state-of-the-art pump-jet propulsion system initiated the tight turn.

In the older Trafalgar-class, where she had first cut her teeth in the Royal Navy's submarine service, this type of maneuver would have resulted in the submarine's propeller creating obnoxious amounts of cavitation and, thereby, enough noise to let every vessel within a thousand klicks know that a Royal Navy submarine was on about something.

It was not so with the Astute-class. While Alcock and the rest of the crew braced themselves as the floor of the sub tilted some twenty degrees to starboard, the *Agincourt* cut through the water as though it were an organic life form birthed in the sea.

As the submarine began to level out, her eyes refocused on the tactical display and saw the countdown for the second, closer pair of torpedoes, which had reached thirty-two seconds. "Countermeasures, release four Pixies, now!" Alcock said, all but shouting the order.

"Aye, Captain. Pixies are away."

As they had learned from the death of the *Perth* and several other CANZUK subs, it was best to release the Type-57 Autonomous Anti-Torpedo System in pairs for each torpedo hunting you.

With both hands, Alcock reached forward to manipulate the tactical display so she could zoom in on the countermeasures as they raced toward the closest Chinese torpedo.

Understanding what she was trying to do, the near-AI of the *Agincourt's* combat information system started a countdown between the red triangles of the two torpedoes and the four blue squares that were the sub's primary defensive tool.

As she watched the display, panic rose within her as she began to suspect she had released the Pixies too late.

Just as the countdown reached six seconds, a massive *BOOM* erupted, sending waves of energy into the port side of Alcock's boat. As lights within the bridge began to flicker, the petty officer at sonar said at a near-yell, "The closest two fish have been killed, Captain. The remaining two fish at our stern are now forty-seven seconds away from contact."

"Understood, sonar," Alcock said, her own voice still elevated.

Across the tactical display, her XO said calmly, "That was close."

With a sheepish look and under her breath, Alcock said, "A bloody stupid move on my part is what it was. I waited too long to release the Pixies."

She pulled her eyes from the XO and shouted, "Countermeasures, launch four more Pixies and give the order to load four more."

"Aye, Captain. Pixies have been launched, with four more being readied."

The XO had already manipulated the tactical display to show the final two Chinese torpedoes. Just as the countdown reached twenty, four blue squares appeared at the sub's stern.

Ten seconds later, when the countermeasures met the two torpedoes, there was another explosion, only this time, the shockwave from the detonation was milder than the one a few minutes before.

As a collection of hoots and hurrahs died down across the bridge, Alcock said, "Helm, bring us down to twelve knots. Let's take a good listen to what's going on around us. Sonar, let me know if those dip sonars are still in play."

As Alcock watched the speed of the *Agincourt* begin to reduce on the table-sized tactical display, she closed her eyes, took in a deep breath, and in her mind, told herself they could do this.

Even if the Chinese helicopters were still searching for them, they were out of torpedoes. All they needed was twenty minutes of skulk time, and their airborne pursuers would reach their bingo fuel limit and leave, or they'd lose them in the deepening waters of the Yellow Sea as they moved further south. She didn't care which. They just needed a bit of time.

"Captain, we have a new contact," the petty officer leading the sonar team announced, causing her eyes to snap open.

Turning to that part of the bridge where the sonar team worked, she said, "Report."

"It should be coming up in the data now, Captain. It's at least one AHK, but if they follow SOP, at least five more will splash down over the next two minutes. It's one klick southeast of us."

Alcock looked down at the tactical display and saw the single near-AI Autonomous Hunter Killer denoted as an orange square.

"A second one has dropped, Captain. It's a half-klick to the starboard of the first unit," the sonar man advised.

Whether they dropped six or ten of the AHKs, the Chinese strategy was clear. They were trying to cut off her escape.

It didn't take her long to decide on her approach. They would run as quietly as they could manage and pray they could slip underneath the screen of near-AI sub-killers coming their way.

The helicopters had lost their track of the *Agincourt* because of the earlier explosions, otherwise, the two AHKs in the water would have already unloaded their torpedoes.

Their pursuers knew their general location, but in submarine warfare, that could mean they were anywhere in a three-by-three-kilometer square of the ocean. They'd have to get more precise than that if they were going to unleash the three torpedoes each autonomous unit was carrying.

Her voice quiet, Alcock said, "Helm, bring us down to four knots, get us as close to the bottom as you can. Stay on your current heading."

"Aye, Captain, reducing speed to four knots and bringing us to a depth of three meters."

"XO, not that they need it, but send a message to all hands that we are to remain ultra-quiet until they're told otherwise."

"Aye, Captain, the message is being sent now," the XO said.

For a full minute, no one on the bridge moved or said a word as the British submarine glided through the shallow waters of the Yellow Sea.

When the petty officer at sonar interrupted the stillness, a sense of dread ripped through Alcock's body. "Captain, we have multiple torpedoes in the water... I think."

Inside her brain, she screamed, 'I think' – what the hell does that mean, Bradley? But aloud, and in the most professional voice she could muster, she said, "Details, sonar."

"The track is coming from behind the AHKs, Captain, but it's faint. Wait, hold on, the signature is clarifying... there, we have it," the petty officer said with a hint of triumph in his voice. "We have a clear signature – Spearfish torpedoes – eight of them are tracking in the direction of the AHKs. Their speed is sixty knots. Estimated time to contact is three minutes. They're ours, Captain. Someone east of us is lending us a hand."

"Bloody brilliant! God bless the Aussies or Royal Navy, whichever – I don't care – they've done us a huge solid." Quickly, she added, "What are the AHKs doing now?"

"They haven't picked them up yet. They will soon, and then they'll start to move evasively, and by the looks of it, we'll be passing under them just as the mess begins."

Alcock turned toward her XO and asked, "Stay the course then?"

The XO nodded and said, "It's what I'd do."

Nodding, Alcock, speaking as loudly as she dared, said, "Helm, bring us up to ten knots, but be ready to punch it to full speed if I give the word."

"Aye, Captain. Speed increasing to ten knots, and warp speed on standby."

"Weapons," Alcock said, turning her head to the other side of the ops center.

"Aye, Captain," replied the petty officer working that station.

"Make sure all of our tubes are loaded up and ready to go. If any of those AHKs survive what's coming their way, we're going to send those bastards to the bottom of the sea. I'm not risking any of the survivors tracking us down. That done, and if the gods of the deep continue to favor us, then and only then, we run like hell."

***

Camp Pendleton, California

As Sanchez looked at the man hanging from the ceiling by a rope wound around his bloody wrists, he felt neither pity nor regret for the man's condition. The animal before him was getting everything he deserved.

Clearing his voice, he said, "Well, you asked for me, Mr. Parr, and here I am. Apparently, you're a lot tougher than your pretty face might suggest. That's what I'm told, at least."

Parr's face was unrecognizable from the many videos Sanchez had seen of the man on the news and in social media. Most of it was a collage of purples and yellows, with the exception of a solid black circle around the war criminal's closed left eye.

A long groan issued from Parr's mouth, and then he said, "Let me down, and I'll talk."

"Fine by me. I think you're getting what you deserve, Mr. Parr, but I can't say I take pleasure seeing you like this."

In a loud voice, Sanchez said, "Let him down and bring in some water."

As soon as he gave the order, the door leading into the interrogation room opened, and a pair of solidly built men in civilian clothes entered.

As one of the guards operated a manual winch to lower Parr, the other quickly placed a pair of chairs and a folding table in the space between Sanchez and the former chief of staff.

As Parr's feet hit the ground, the man who had arranged the furniture grabbed Parr from behind and shoved him into the chair. The guard at the winch stopped providing slack the moment Parr's hands rested on the table, effectively limiting his ability to reach for Sanchez.

Sanchez himself doubted the man now sitting in front of him could do much of anything. Peter Parr was a destroyed man. He didn't need to be an interrogation expert to know that.

Without saying a word, one of the two minders handed Sanchez two bottles of water, and then, he and his colleague left the space.

Sanchez placed the two bottles on the table. He opened one and pushed it across to Parr, whose one good eye was staring at the liquid intently. "It's all yours, Peter. And the second one, if you want it."

Without a word, Parr snatched the bottle from the table, put it to his lips, and began to drink ravenously. Within seconds of finishing the first bottle, he gestured to the second. Without pause, Sanchez opened it and passed it to the broken prisoner. With this one, Parr only drank the first half of the bottle's contents.

Slowly, Parr set the bottle back on the table and, with his one good eye, looked at Sanchez and said, "I know I deserve everything I'm getting. I know what I've done, and I know what I've got coming. But I and the people who worked for me never treated people worse than animals. Yes, I've given orders to kill hundreds of people, thousands even, but that's war. In war, people die. But never once did I tell anyone to do what you've done to me."

Sanchez shrugged his shoulders and said, "Peter – I'm going to call you Peter if that's okay?"

When Parr didn't answer the question, Sanchez continued, "When you were first brought to us, I believe you were given a choice. Provide us with information that could help us defeat the UCSA. Any information, mind you, and we'd treat you like any other prisoner of war.

"We also told you that if you chose not to help us, we'd get the information out of you using whatever methods we thought appropriate. Is that an accurate summary of the proposal outlined to you?"

He waited for a reply, but when none came, Sanchez continued, "But you haven't helped us. Not one little bit. Instead, you've surprised everyone with this insane ability to resist pain and deprivation. I mean, I'm just an actor, so I know nothing about what it takes to resist the kind of abuse you've endured this past week, but I, for one, have been impressed."

Without warning, Parr began to laugh. In seconds, his laugh turned into what sounded like an unhinged cackle. This went on for nearly a minute, and just as Sanchez was about to call in someone to help manage what he suspected was a full-on mental breakdown, Parr's laughing came to a sudden stop.

"Care to share what's so funny?" Sanchez asked.

As the smile he'd been wearing dropped from his face, Parr said, "You mentioned I've been here for a week. That can't be right. I've been here for a month at least. Maybe two. It can't be just a week. That's not possible."

Sanchez leaned back in his seat, crossed his legs, and stared back into the one good eye now staring at him. "Peter, it's important that you listen to my next words very carefully. Can you do that for me?"

When Parr returned Sanchez's question with only silence, the politician said. "Why have you insisted on bringing me here? The people overseeing your stay have been given every authority they need to arrange a deal with you. As far as I can see, there's nothing you can say or offer to us that does not result in you getting the end you deserve."

"I don't want to die, Governor," Parr said quickly, almost yelling the words.

Sanchez cocked his head to the right and said, "So you've mentioned before. But we all die, Peter. It just so happens you'll know the date and time of your death. For many, I understand that can be a great comfort."

Without any warning, Parr howled in rage, straining his still-bound hands across the table. With a wild look on his beaten face, he screamed, "I will live, Governor. I will live because you and I are going to cut a deal. A deal that gives me what I want and what you need. We both win, Governor, but only if you make the deal I want."

As he finished making the pronouncement, Parr was breathing heavily and rocking to and fro in his seat. As Sanchez watched the man seemingly trying to soothe himself, he elected to continue with whatever game the broken man in front of him was playing.

"Okay, you want to live. It's officially on the table, but you will never ever get to be a free man. Every single day God gives you will be in a four-by-six cell. That's all you'll ever get. There is no world where a monster like you can walk free."

"I understand," said Parr.

"All right, what can you give us?"

"Give me six hundred million in crypto and pardons for up to one hundred people, and using the same system I used to kill thousands of the UCSA's political opponents, I will arrange a contract to kill Mitchell Spector."

Sanchez leaned forward in his seat. "How? Surely, they must have taken your access away from whatever system you were using to manage that nightmare of a program."

"There's a backend that only I can access. I had it built as a form of insurance. In case things for whatever reason didn't go my way. And before you ask, the people who do this work don't care about politics. They don't care about Spector, you, Morgan, the country's future. None of it. They care about one thing and one thing only."

"Money," Sanchez said, nearly spitting the word out of his mouth.

"In crypto, yes," Parr said, nodding.

For a long moment, Sanchez stared at the pitiful man sitting across from him. Finally, he said, "I don't understand. You've resisted for so long. Why not put this on the table at the beginning? And why would we ever believe you'd do this to Spector? By every account, you were his most loyal soldier. You've killed thousands for his cause. By all definitions, you're a fanatic."

An ugly smile emerged on Parr's already hideous face. Leaning forward, Parr said in a quiet voice, "I'll let you in on my little secret. It was never about the cause or Spector. It's always been about me. My career and my rise to the top. I'm no patriot, Governor. I'm just a media consultant who saw a way to be close to one of the most powerful people in the world. And I was. For a short and glorious time, I was."

Parr then sat back and spread his hands apart as far as they could go. "And who knows? When that fat son of a bitch was gone, maybe I could be the next president. Stranger things have happened in our lifetimes."

His hideous façade still in place, Parr said, "That's who I am. It's always been about me, Governor. Always."

Sanchez gave Parr a quizzical look. "We'll do this, Peter, but I must know why you waited so long. Why go through all the pain and deprivation?

Parr shrugged his shoulders. "Just as you took me, Governor, I thought the UCSA could take me back. We're winning, or we were – it's not an impossibility. How much more would I be in

Spector's good graces if I could resist the inhumanity of the savages who work for you?"

Sanchez shook his head, and with a sad look on his face, he said, "Your ego is so big that you thought the UCSA would rescue you all the way here in California? Well, I'm sorry to say, Peter, that you're not nearly as important as you think."

When Parr didn't respond to Sanchez's assessment, the politician said, "You know you're a disgusting human being, don't you?"

"I am, but I also have an overriding drive to continue to breathe. Hell can't have me yet, Governor. Not yet, and not for a long time. And who knows, stranger things have happened in politics than a man like me going free. Jefferson Davis eventually became a free man, and he split the country apart and caused the death of nearly two million people."

Sanchez scoffed. "Peter, if what you say comes to pass, and you somehow go free, you'll be dead within the week. When people discover what you've done, nowhere will be safe. Nowhere."

Parr winked his one good eye. "Maybe. But at least now, I'll get to wait and see."

Sanchez reached across the table, grabbed the half-full bottle of water and got to his feet.

Looking up, Parr spat, "Hey, I was gonna drink that!"

"No, you're not. Instead, you're going to speak with a few people about this backend you claim you still have access to, and if you can convince us you can arrange a hit on your former boss, maybe, just maybe, we'll make a deal that lets you 'wait and see.'"

After a long pause, Sanchez added, "And then, and only then, maybe you can have some more water."

Chapter 35

The Ready Room, the White House

—

"Pause it there," said Spector from his seat at the midpoint of the long table.

On the screen of the large display at the end of the room was the face of General Wu Dezhi. Turning from the still image, he turned his gaze to the Director of the CIB, "So, Dave, your people have had a couple of hours to sniff around. What do we know of him, and what, if anything, do we know of the attack that killed Yan? If it was a CANZUK missile strike as is being reported, color me skeptical. There is an actual forest of SAMs around Beijing. It had to be something else. Maybe this Wu fellow did it?"

Spector gestured to the display. "He certainly looks like he could order the assassination of his president. I know the Chinese people, and if you told me there was a more spiteful-looking member of their race, I wouldn't believe you."

While most of the others in the room snickered at Spector's dig, Christoff's face remained sober while keeping his gaze fixed on the UCSA leader. "Mr. President, we dug as deep as we could get but there's very little on the general other than the various commands he's held.

"And as per your earlier question, as it pertains to our agreement with the Chinese, Wu had no involvement that we're aware of. We've reached out to our contacts in the Chinese military, but we've not heard anything back as yet."

Spector grunted, then said, "What about the rumors about this being a CANZUK missile strike – do we have anything solid on that?"

Before the CIB Director could begin to answer Spector's inquiry, General Hoffman spoke up. "Mr. President, I'm sorry to interrupt. I just got a text from one of my people saying that Wu has just appeared on the Chinese state news and is making a statement."

Spector's big hand thumped the table. "Well, let's get it on the screen so we can hear what the good general has to say."

At the far end of the room, one of the two analysts Christoff had brought with him to the meeting began to fiddle on his laptop. A few seconds later, a video featuring the head and shoulders of an older Chinese man in military uniform appeared on the Ready Room's main display.

"... the terrorists who struck in Beijing this morning and who killed President Yan have been found and, as we speak, are being interrogated by our security services. In the hours and weeks to come, China will get to the bottom of this plot, and those individuals or organizations who have committed this heinous act will face retributions they could have never anticipated. Citizens of China and members of the Party, I assure you, for as long as it takes, we will be relentless in bringing justice to the perpetrators of this outrageous crime."

The general paused and turned over a piece of paper on the desk he was sitting at. Without looking down, he continued. "In the immediate hours after the attack that killed our beloved and respected leader, I met with the Standing Committee of the Political Bureau of the Central Committee, and with their full support, I have agreed to take on the role of Interim General Secretary of the Communist Party for the next twelve months."

Wu paused for a moment to give emphasis to his next statement. "I want to thank the members of the Politburo Standing Committee for their wisdom, counsel, and willingness to act quickly. China is at war and, as its interim leader, it is my promise to my fellow esteemed Party members that I will lead our great nation to a victory that will secure China's place in the world for the next century."

Wu turned over another of the papers in front of him and said, "To China's enemies, I say the following. There is only one way for war to end, and that is with you bending a knee to the People's Liberation Army. Like the criminal terrorists who assassinated our great President Yan, you will know no rest until you have chosen to surrender to us."

Without warning, the image of the general cut away to a still image showing an empty Great Hall of the People. As the Chinese national anthem began to play, Spector barked, "Shut that garbage off."

The UCSA President turned back to Christoff. "That's a load of bullshit if I've ever heard it. Terrorists – at least the kind that can assassinate presidents – do not exist in China. And under no circumstances would the Politburo Standing Committee allow a non-member of the PSC to assume the country's presidency."

Pointing at the Ready Room's display, Spector continued, "I'll bet you my best bull, the man on that screen talking just a few seconds ago took over China by killing his own president and then executing what had to be one hell of a well-planned coup."

Spector looked to his left and eyed his national intel lead. "Dave, you said there were some reports out of Beijing about low-flying missiles and explosions. Is that the report or not?"

"Yes, Mr. President. As you say, at around 0900 hours Beijing time, there were several reports of air sirens, anti-aircraft fire, and what were described as low-flying missiles heading into Beijing from the east."

Pausing briefly, Christoff added, "Sir, I do think we need to give ourselves time to get a better sense of what's happened. More data is coming by the minute. By this time tomorrow, we'll have a much clearer picture of what's going on."

Spector leaned forward, placed his elbows on the table, and clasped his hands in front of his face. For a long moment, his eyes stared off into the distance. Finally, after a deep exhalation, he said, "We're losing this war, people. Day by day, our forces are being pushed back. In the north and now in the west. Critical persons who've sat at this table have been snatched away from places that should have been safe. In the streets of our great cities, we've shot dozens of our citizens to keep the peace. And now, we're seeing what could be the end of the Pacific war. Despite his words about enemies surrendering, we can't assume this Wu fellow will continue to fight in Vietnam. For all we know, it's the war in that country that resulted in Yan being assassinated."

Spector's hands came down and rested on top of the boardroom table. "General Hoffman, are we ready to test the new mobile missile launcher?"

The Vice-Chief of the UCSA's Air Force and the man leading the effort to finalize the development of the country's nuclear arsenal met Spector's eyes and said, "The launch vehicles are still several weeks away, Mr. President. Most of the people who knew rocket science fled to California at the beginning of the war. Hurling missiles thousands of miles across the earth's surface remains a challenge, even with near-AI to help us. It's not a math problem in so much as it is an engineering challenge. I..."

Spector's hand raised into the air. "Hold your horses, General. I know your people are doing their best. What about the other delivery option?"

Gathering himself, Hofman said, "Mr. President, as per your direction, we have prepared eight forty-kiloton weapons that can be dropped from the internal weapons bays of the F-35. We have another fourteen ninety-kiloton weapons that can be carried externally on the F-15EX. Last, we have nearly a dozen lower-yield tactical weapons ranging from three to six kilotons that several airframes can deliver."

Nodding his head at the update, Spector said, "I proclaimed we would not lose one inch of Texas or Kansas, and I meant it. If the 1st Marine Division and this so-called Western Alliance cross into our territory, I will give the order to use these weapons, and we'll send a message to our enemies that we're not prepared to accept any further loss of territory and that they'd better come to the table to negotiate a peace and quick. We need to give ourselves more time, and the only way we'll get that time is if we demonstrate that we are operating from a position of strength. We are a nuclear power, people, and nuclear powers don't get invaded. That's the rule."

Half raising one of his hands into the air, Christoff said, "Mr. President, if I may?"

"You may, Dave, but my decision on this matter is made up. We've discussed the plan several times already."

"Yes, and each of those times, I feel like we've discounted the probability that our enemies will strike back at us with their own nukes. I know I sound like a broken record, but Anders-Maxwell already used them against us. If we strike their soldiers in the West, what's to stop them from striking our people or hitting someplace like Houston or Tampa?"

Christoff's eyes shifted to Hoffman. "We have twenty-eight weapons of varying yields, correct?"

The Air Force general nodded, confirming the figure.

Christoff continued. "Between California and the Neutrals, they have hundreds. They could destroy every major city in the UCSA if they wanted to. The Japanese capitulated after only two bombs, and they thought their Emperor was a god.

"Mr. President, I've come to know you well over the past year. You are a rational and thoughtful man. Respectfully, I can't help but think this plan has massive risks that are being ignored. This may be upsetting to you, and perhaps it means the end of my service to the UCSA, but it has to be said."

As Christoff finished giving his assessment, Spector started to nod slowly and, in a calm voice, said, "Dave, there was a moment where my predecessor had a dozen masked and armed men come into a room just like this and have his generals removed and then fired. Perhaps if he had listened to those men, he might not have suffered the fate that he did. For everyone's benefit in this room, let me acknowledge that I understand your position and respect your willingness to raise your concerns. And to be clear, you won't be resigning. Just keep doing what you're doing."

Spector's eyes moved across the table to General Spellings and the colonel who had assumed Parr's duties as they pertained to Operation Sunlight. "General Spellings, I think it's time we shared with the inner circle what the plan is for the possibility that Dave here has bravely brought forward. All of it, if you please."

"Yes, Mr. President," said the UCSA's Army Chief of Staff.

Turning to the younger officer to his right, Spellings said, "Colonel Maynes, could you walk us through the current state of affairs concerning Operation Righteous Standoff."

"Yes, sir," the colonel said promptly.

Almost jumping to his feet, Maynes said, "Bring up map image three."

On issuing the command, the display at the front of the Ready Room divided into three equal parts featuring maps labelled Los Angeles, Oakland, and Sacramento.

Moving to stand beside the screen, Maynes began his briefing. "One month ago, I was tasked with finding ways to covertly deliver three nuclear devices to the locations you see before you.

With the support of a select group of operators from Special Forces Group Alpha, I am pleased to report that, as of two days ago, we completed our mission.

"At the Port of Los Angeles and the Port of Oakland, we positioned one shipping container, each containing two ninety-kiloton weapons. Each has been hardened to withstand the strongest electromagnetic attacks, is equipped with a dozen cameras, and is linked by a satellite quantum connection that will allow us to observe its operations at all times. We transported a similar container with a single ninety-kiloton warhead to Sacramento. All three containers are active and can be set off within thirty seconds.

"Finally, we have covertly located a smaller device in an undisclosed location north of Los Angeles. When ordered, a team of special operators will detonate the device inside or as close as possible to the Diablo Canyon Nuclear Power Plant."

"Jesus Christ, why?" Christoff said, doing nothing to hold back his incredulity.

Maynes did not answer the question. Instead, he only delivered a hard stare toward the outraged intel man.

It was Spector himself who finally addressed the inquiry. "We will not lose Kansas. We will not lose Texas. The Blues and CANZUK will not cross the line between Cincinnati and Baltimore."

Christoff's gaze shifted back to the UCSA president. As their eyes locked on one another, Spector said, "When Sanchez finds out about the weapons, he will have no choice but to force his new allies to come to the table to negotiate."

His voice still holding alarm, Christoff said, "But the risks, Mr. President. What if the Blues or Western Alliance – hell, what if California won't negotiate down the barrel of a gun? Sir, this is like Russian Roulette. I don't care what the models say, the risks we're taking with this plan... well, they're gigantic."

Spector's jaw visibly tightened as the CIB Director's words registered with him, but in a calm voice, he said, "Sanchez will negotiate, Dave. The model says so, but more important than any damn computer, my gut is saying the same thing. He didn't want war in the first place, so sure as shit, he'll make a deal if he knows millions of people's lives are on the line."

"Mr. President, I trust your intuition, but what if you're wrong? What if instead of negotiating, they deliver their own ultimatum or worse?"

"You know the answer," Spector snapped back at the other man.

"No, I don't, actually," replied Christoff, understanding full well he was now on the most dangerous of ground.

Drawing himself up in his chair and delivering his own hard stare at Christoff, Spector declared, "Then I'll give you the answer, Dave. I'll make it perfectly goddamned clear to you what will happen if I'm wrong."

With one of his index fingers poised above the table, ready to drive downward to emphasize points as needed, Spector started to rail, "This country. This fucking country that we've all helped to build was in response to a nightmare. A nightmare so terrible we seceded and have fought a four-year war that has killed nearly thirteen million people. But despite these losses, despite all the pain and sacrifice, in my heart and my head, I know there isn't ten percent of the people left in this country who want to go back to the way it was. There is only one thing down that road. Endless persecution, and not just for those of us sitting at this table. The woke legion that was Menendez and is now that son of a bitch Morgan – the retribution that the Blues will seek will touch every single person, every family, and will go on for a generation or more."

Pausing, Spector's eyes narrowed. After taking in and expelling a deep breath, he continued. "We're not going back to that, Dave. Not while I lead this country, and I said as much to you and every other person in this room when you joined this war cabinet. You always knew it could come to this, so don't you dare – not for one moment – give some horseshit excuse you didn't know I'd put everything on the line."

Specter suddenly closed his eyes and brought his hands together in front of him as though he was about to say a prayer.

When his eyes opened, they'd moved from the CIB director and taken up the Norman Rockwell painting of the Statue of Liberty hanging directly across from him. While staring at the iconic American artwork, he said, "Let me be very clear. If California and the Western Alliance push into the West, I will set off the nuclear weapons in California, and we will drop nuclear weapons on their next six largest cities. If the Blues pass the Cincinnati-Baltimore line, I will destroy their largest cities."

He paused as his gaze left the painting to reacquire Christoff. Unflinching and in a low and menacing tone, the UCSA president said, "If they don't negotiate, I will do whatever is in my power to ensure our enemies suffer. They will suffer until they stop and recognize our nation, or I am dead. God help me – God help us all – that is what I will do if Ricky Sanchez does not choose peace."

***

Ottawa

In what was a rarity in recent weeks, Merielle wasn't suffering from a headache. It was close to 10 pm and she was feeling as good as she had in the past two months. No doubt, the day's events had served to lighten the mental burden she'd been carrying. For once, things had gone CANZUK's way.

Like all others, her day had been filled with meetings. She had met with the military once earlier in the morning to discuss the dramatic events that had taken place in China and then again in the late afternoon. Larocque had attended the second meeting with a pair of experts from CSIS's Chinese desk.

In both meetings, there had been consternation that Canada had not been brought into the scheme to take down the Chinese leader, but Merielle had dismissed the gripes. Australia and the UK were far more engaged in the Pacific than Canada, and everyone understood how pervasive China's Ministry of State Security was in each CANZUK nation. They had played things close to their chests because they needed to, not because they wanted to keep Canada or New Zealand from the extraordinary effort.

For Merielle, the important thing was that Yan was gone, and there was an agreement for China to slowly cease hostilities across Southeast Asia.

Larocque's people had speculated that the change in leadership could also mean a change in tactics by the people running China's shadow war in the Pacific and BC. Merielle could only hope. With each passing day, her relationship with Aziz and his people was becoming more complex. If the Chinese pulled their foot off the gas, so could the White Unit. And if the White Unit could pull back, then perhaps the growing conflict between it and CSIS could be averted.

If things did begin to resolve in the Pacific, it meant CANZUK could put more resources into the fighting taking place in North America. More than ever, Merielle was determined to see the FAS defeat Spector and the Reds. Of everything, this feat would be her legacy.

Based on the latest estimates provided to her by the military, if Canada and Britain went all in with Morgan and the Blues, together, they could push the UCSA from Washington, and within as soon as six months, they could exhaust the Red Faction's ability to fight. Victory, perhaps a total one, could happen soon.

But everyone, including Canada, needed to throw more bodies at the problem. A lot more.

General Kaplan, the Chief of Defence Staff, had said if the money was there and if Merielle's government passed C-23, the *In Defence of Canada Act*, the CAF could have forty thousand new soldiers ready to join the frontlines within three months and another sixty thousand within a year.

The financial aspect of the plan would be addressed tomorrow. Bill C-19 would modify the latest budget, enabling Merielle's government to borrow the necessary funds to expand the country's industrial base. This expansion would facilitate the production of weapons, ammunition, drones, and vehicles required for the new soldiers.

In the past year, both Britain and Canada had dramatically increased their ability to produce war materiel. But more of everything was needed.

In another four weeks, the IDC Act would pass, giving the military the authority to start a lottery to conscript one hundred and ten thousand Canadian males between the ages of twenty-two and thirty-five.

To say that the scheme was controversial would be an understatement of monstrous proportions, but the country needed more men in uniform, and Merielle had a plan to make sure her government could make as many unpopular decisions as were needed so that her country could survive and win the conflicts to come.

Once they were done south of the border, CANZUK would have to turn its attention to Europe. Rank-and-file Canadians would resist, of course, but she would drag the country to that continent to assist Great Britain and do for their ally as the UK had done for them in North America.

Kaplan had already set up a team to look at the European problem. As would always be the case with Europe, it was a complicated mess. Would they support France and Poland in their efforts to confront the Russians or would they only look to support the Nordics? And what was to be done with Germany?

She paused her thoughts when she heard a quiet knock at her door. Turning her chair to the entrance to her office, she saw her executive assistant.

"You have some visitors, Madame Prime Minister."

Forcing a pleasant look onto her face, Merielle said, "Oh, it's late. I would have thought everyone had gone home by now. I trust they're visitors of the friendly kind?"

There was a twinkle in her assistant's eyes as she gave her reply. "It's Irene and Mr. Oyinlola."

Her assistant, like most women who worked on the Hill, had a poorly hidden thing for Oyinlola, Merielle's Minister of Health.

He was handsome, fit, charming, and politically, a big asset for the Conservatives. But Merielle was wary of the man. Whereas Merielle herself or the growing political arm of the White Unit had been able to pin down most of the Conservative caucus' loyalties as it pertained to her leadership, Oyinlola had been elusive. To be sure, the man had been playing a game, but to what end, Merielle had not yet been able to tell.

Irene MacPhail, on the other hand, was a well-known quantity. She had been actively working against Merielle's plans, and on more than one occasion, she had to talk herself out of removing the woman from the complex political calculation she was trying to solve.

But each time, she had convinced herself to keep the Newfoundlander around. MacPhail was Merielle's application of the ancient maxim to keep your friends close and your enemies closer.

Whatever your political persuasion, people across the country trusted Irene MacPhail like they trusted no other politician. Whether it was her career as an unflinching reporter, her East Coast folksiness, or her competence as she tackled and solved one domestic political file after another, Canadians seemed to adore the woman.

It was for this reason that Merielle kept her in the role of Deputy Prime Minister. For the moment, whatever resonance MacPhail had with the people was an advantage that Merielle was more than happy to use.

But for all her charms and abilities, MacPhail remained clueless when it came to navigating the world currently confronting Canada.

Merielle quickly chided herself. Clueless was uncharitable. In truth, MacPhail was quite aware of how the world worked, she was just wholly naïve in terms of how its problems got solved.

Take the Chinese situation as just one example.

Had MacPhail been presented with the opportunity to launch a missile strike to assassinate the leader of the country Canada was fighting a desperate and bloody war with, she would have wrung her hands, spoken with a half-dozen 'experts,' taken a few key colleagues out for coffee to 'sound them out about the opportunity,' and then and only then decide that the extra-judicial nature of the request was against Canadian values and would put Canada's international reputation in jeopardy.

The woman might not admit to it, but she had become one of the stalwarts of the Laurentian Elite, that small but hugely influential swath of Canadians who controlled the country's levers of power, be it in the media, business, or, in MacPhail's case, politics.

It was an intricate and intimate web where well-connected people took quiet meetings with other powerful people and decisions got made.

What decision of the Laurentian Elite was she going to be informed of tonight, Merielle wondered.

"Please let them in, Carmen, and please take any drink orders from them. I'll take a coffee myself. I plan to be another hour at least."

After hearing her executive assistant exchange pleasantries with the two politicians, she stood and got from behind her desk so she could greet her late-hour visitors.

As they walked through the door, the two politicians were all smiles. "Merielle, thank you for seeing us tonight. We're sorry to take you away from whatever you were doing," said MacPhail, her subtle Newfie lilt sounding as pleasant as ever.

Merielle gestured toward the leather couch and chairs that made up the small conference area in her office. "No problem at all. I was just muscling through a pile of briefing notes that have been growing on my desk for the past two weeks. Your visit is actually doing me a bit of a favor. Please, have a seat."

As all three politicians moved to sit down, Merielle's assistant brought in her coffee and handed it to her. Taking the beverage, Merielle smiled and said, "No tea or coffee? We have decaf, or I've something stronger in my desk if you're in that type of mood."

"We'll pass, Madame Prime Minister. We won't be with you long," said Oyinlola.

Merielle's eyebrows raised at the use of her title. Without taking a sip, she put the coffee she was holding on the table in front of her and said, "Okay then, let's get down to business. What's brought you to see me at this late hour?"

It was Oyinlola who spoke. "We know you are working with an outfit called the White Unit. In fact, we know that the White Unit reports to you."

"Is that indeed a fact, Mr. Oyinlola?" Merielle said in a calm voice.

"We are not here to get into the details, Merielle. We are here to tell you what will be happening tomorrow so that you can do the right thing for the country and for yourself."

Merielle's eyes moved from Oyinlola's to MacPhail's. "And what is it that will be happening tomorrow?"

Merielle continued to stare down MacPhail as Oyinlola spoke. "Tomorrow, seventeen Conservatives and the opposition parties will vote against C-19. It will not pass, and the Martel government will fall. Based on discussions with the Liberals and NDP, it has been agreed that a unity government will be formed. It will operate under a two-year supply and confidence agreement. Irene has agreed to lead this new government."

"Has she?" Merielle said, her voice quiet.

"I have," said MacPhail.

Merielle's eyes narrowed on hearing MacPhail's confirmation. She then asked, "And what, pray tell, shall happen to me when this coup d'état takes place? If I look out the window to my office and look to the steps leading to the Peace Tower, will I see them setting up the scaffolding for my hanging?"

"This is why we are here, Merielle," MacPhail said. "You cannot undo what has been done. The vote will take place tomorrow, your government will fall, and you will no longer be prime minister. As for what happens to you, it depends on how you want to play this."

A wicked smile rose to Merielle's face. "Tell me, Irene, how am I to play this dangerous game you've decided to join?"

MacPhail shot back. "It will not be made dangerous by us, Merielle. Everyone understands the sacrifices you've made. Everyone understands the decisions you've made have helped to save the country. You can leave with dignity and full immunity. There will be no questions, no public inquiries. You will retire and live the rest of your life as a private citizen and most everyone in Canada and the rest of the freedom-loving world will adore Merielle Martel. It will not be a bad life."

"Full immunity for what?" Merielle snapped back at the other woman.

"Or we can go in the other direction, Madame Prime Minister," said Oyinlola. "The direction where your government falls, and the new government makes exposing your past actions its chief priority. And you get to take in all of the inquiries and investigations from the confines of a cell. Your career will be over, your reputation ruined, but worse, Merielle, as the sharks that are the media and your political enemies gather around your treading form, our country will be distracted from what it should be focused on."

Merielle's gaze slowly transitioned from MacPhail to her co-conspirator. "And just so I'm clear, Michael, what is it that this country should be focused on?"

"Ending the war in the US, of course. We still want that, Merielle," Oyinlola said. "But if you don't make the right choice – you could ruin everything you've worked so hard to achieve. CANZUK needs to remain cohesive, and Canada needs to be focused on the task that is before it. But it won't be able to do that if it gets embroiled in the scandal that is your involvement with the White Unit."

Merielle nodded as though to signal her understanding of Oyinlola's words. Slowly, she rose from her chair and walked behind it. Placing both of her hands along the top of its back, she said, "You are both fools. Do you have any idea how dangerous the world actually is? You are nothing more than cosseted, privileged elites who would love nothing more than for this country to return to the days when it wagged its pathetic finger at the world's worst dictators, lecturing them as though our words held meaning. You're fucking loathsome."

"Merielle –" Oyinlola began to say, but she cut the man off. Staring daggers at him, she whispered, "I don't want to hear another word from you, Michael, you traitor. Shut your mouth."

As she stared down her Minister of Health, Merielle heard her assistant close the thick wooden door to her office. Assured of their privacy, Merielle's gaze shifted back to MacPhail. "Don't tell me, to get the opposition parties on board, you promised them the IDC Act would be pulled?"

As MacPhail began to give a reply, one of Merielle's hands shot into the air. "No, don't give me whatever prepared bullshit reply you've got canned in that disloyal head of yours. You've sold out this country, and you've sold out our allies so that you could do what? Stop me from making tough decisions? Stop me from doing what is necessary to secure the future of this country for the next fifty years, if not longer? And all because you're afraid Canadians don't want blood on their hands."

As a look of disgust grew on Merielle's face, she added, "You two are worse than loathsome. You're Quislings. The blood in your veins is pathetic *and* treasonous."

Hand still in the air, she pointed an accusatory finger at MacPhail and said, "Do you think for one moment that Mitchell Spector and his gang of thugs can be trusted to exist on this continent for one moment longer than necessary?"

"Bad people and bad governments exist the world over and have for millennia," Oyinlola said in a firm tone, interrupting Merielle.

Raising his voice another octave and pointing his own accusatory finger, he berated, "And who's to say the Spector Administration won't fall if it's left to its own devices? They've had to declare martial law. Their cities are burning. If the Blues and Reds come to terms, the UCSA could collapse in a few months, if not weeks. And it's not Canada's damned war, in any event. We and CANZUK need to chart a new course. We need to look at cutting deals, not implementing conscription programs."

Merielle rounded on Oyinlola. "I thought I told you not to speak."

"I won't be silenced by you, Merielle. You're not Stalin yet."

"Ahh... and there it is." Merielle oozed. "You're afraid I'm to become a tyrant. Is that what's motivating this little traitorous cabal of yours?"

"Merielle, we're concerned about you," MacPhail said in a calming tone. "This White Unit and everything it's alleged to have done. It's not good. And look who you've surrounded yourself with. I sit in Cabinet with you. I've never seen a more complacent bunch of yes-men and women. And the IDC. It is already a disaster in Quebec. The Separatists are going to tear this country apart if you go through with it.

"Michael is right. We need to start looking in the direction of peace, not more war. We've done enough to help Morgan and the FAS. We need to help them find a way to end the war, and then, as a country, we need to start healing. We want you to help us with this healing, Merielle. And you can if you work with us. You've made tough decisions, and we respect you for that, but it's time to pass the torch."

As MacPhail finished her plea, the two women stared intently at one another.

Finally, Merielle dropped her gaze, turned, and walked toward her desk to stand behind it. Looking down, her hand pulled open the top drawer, where she saw the Sig Sauer P229 compact pistol she had come to favor.

It was there. She checked for it every day when she first entered her office. It gave her comfort.

The two people who had just informed her that she would no longer be prime minister deserved to be shot, as did the other MPs of her party who had signed onto this coup. But not right now.

To Aziz's credit, he had foreseen a move of this nature, if not precisely how it was playing out. It was time to send her new enemies away into the night so she could affect their plans. They had underestimated her in giving her a warning. It was yet another example of how soft this country's elite had become.

Her eyes rose from the weapon to reacquire the two politicians. In a calm voice, she said, "I want to thank you for coming to see me this evening. I appreciate both of you for your courage and honesty, and I want you to know that however this process ends, I will forgive you – both of you – and treat you with the courtesy you've shown to me this evening."

Firmly, Oyinlola said, "Do you have an answer for us, Madame Prime Minister? Will you cooperate and support our proposal, or will you resist and put everything we've gained over the past year into jeopardy?"

"I understand your offer, Minister, and I need to think about it," Merielle said. "I will communicate with you before 0500 hours. If I agree to your terms, that will give you enough time to put the finishing touches on this takeover of yours."

It was MacPhail who spoke next. Again, she sounded composed and sincere. "It is the process that our democratic system allows for, Madame Prime Minister. You may not like it, but it is legal. Governments fall in Canada all the time. Keep that in mind, Merielle. What we're doing is allowed. It is our democracy working."

Pointing to the door of her office, Merielle said curtly, "I've heard enough. Leave. Now."

After briefly exchanging looks, the two politicians got to their feet and moved toward the office's only exit. As he reached the massive oak portal, Oyinlola placed his hand on the doorknob and turned to look at his party's leader. Choosing to mirror MacPhail's serene demeanor, he said calmly, "Don't destroy this country. That's not who you are, Madame Prime Minister."

Merielle stared back at him, a faux smile rising to her lips, and she replied, "It is history that will judge who destroyed this country, Minister. Not you or me. Now, get the hell out of my office."

Chapter 36

Ottawa

"What do you mean she's prorogued Parliament?" said MacPhail, green eyes wide with surprise. "I thought you had spoken with the Governor General, and he told you that under no circumstances would he bring the current session to a close."

"He won't answer my calls. No one in the GG's office will. I have a mind to drive over there right now and find out what the hell is going on," Oyinlola said, then quickly unloaded with a few ugly curses.

As the politician's swearing came to an end, MacPhail heard someone speaking loudly in the reception area outside her office. Just as she was getting up to see what was going on, the door to her office opened, and Sandy McNabb, her chief of staff, walked in.

As the woman's concerned eyes connected with MacPhail's, she said, "That was a sergeant with the Parliament Protection Service. They've just received a report of an explosion at the Starbucks on Kent, and someone just called in a bomb threat for the Laurier Bridge. They're locking down the Hill. Everyone is to stay in their office until we're told otherwise."

"Like hell am I staying in this office, Sandy," MacPhail snapped back at the woman.

The room's only television came to life. MacPhail turned to Oyinlola, who was holding the TV's remote. On the screen was Merielle Martel. She was sitting behind a desk that MacPhail didn't recognize.

Just as Oyinlola increased the volume, the prime minister began her address. "Citizens of Canada, it is with the heaviest of hearts that I address you. I speak with you on this day to deliver unthinkable news.

"Late yesterday evening, I was informed by the RCMP and CSIS of an organized plot to displace my leadership of the Conservative Party and of this country. It was and is a Chinese-led plot that involves as many as fifty Members of Parliament, including MPs from all parties.

"In response to this crisis, I spoke with the Governor General early this morning and advised that the current session of Parliament should be prorogued. He has agreed. Parliament will not sit until this emergency has been fully resolved.

"I have also spoken with the Commissioner of the RCMP and the Director of CSIS, and they have assured me they will take whatever steps are necessary to ensure the federal government continues to function normally. As we speak, police and other security officials are moving to apprehend the alleged conspirators and secure federal buildings, including Parliament.

"I have also spoken with the Chief of the Defence Staff, General Kaplan, and..."

The rest of Merielle's words were cut off by a torrent of gunfire that broke out just outside of MacPhail's office. Through the thunderous crack of bullets, MacPhail heard several voices yelling and at least one terrified scream.

Because of the high ceilings of the rotunda just outside the Deputy Prime Minister's office in Parliament's Centre Block, she easily made out the conversation taking place between two opposing groups of people.

"Drop your weapons!" more than one voice was bellowing in English, while others gave the same command in French.

"I said, 'drop it.' Don't do it, or you're dead. Don't do it!" a single voice roared.

Without warning, another exchange of gunfire erupted. Amid the ear-shattering barrage of sound, MacPhail heard someone yell, "I'm hit," while another male voice unleashed a scream of pain that stopped as soon as it had started.

Then, the shooting stopped.

Not far away from the entrance to her office, someone was moaning in pain, but this noise was quickly overwhelmed by the sound of multiple pairs of boots pounding over the Centre Block's marble flooring.

Sandy, standing in the doorway to MacPhail's office but looking outward into the rotunda, gave a quick yelp, turned, and scampered to join MacPhail where she was standing behind her desk. As Sandy passed Oyinlola, he stepped into the middle of the room and put himself between the two women and whoever had entered the antechamber that acted as Sandy's workspace.

Two masked men, each wearing black from head to toe, entered the room. Each had an assault rifle locked into their shoulders. One of the men was pointing his weapon at Oyinlola, the other had zeroed in on MacPhail's center mass. The word POLICE was stenciled across the front of their body armour.

It was then that a third man in black walked into the room. His face was also covered by a balaclava. He, too, was armed, but only with a pistol on his hip. Coming to a stop, he said in a clear and calm voice, "Michael Oyinlola and Irene MacPhail, you're under arrest for treason and other crimes against the Government of Canada."

"Who are you?" Oyinlola demanded.

Oyinlola took a step in the direction of the gunman he was addressing. "You're not the RCMP. We're not going anywhere. In fact, if anyone's committed treason, it's you."

Casually, the officer who had levelled the charges against them reached down to his belt, pulled the handgun from its holster, aimed it at Oyinlola, and pulled the trigger.

But instead of hearing a gunshot, MacPhail heard a loud snap, which was quickly followed by the unmistakable sound of surging electricity.

In front of her, she saw Oyinlola collapse to the ground and begin to shake violently.

Seeing her colleague and friend writhe and then begin to scream in pain, she issued her own panicked words, "Jesus Christ, stop! Stop what you're doing! Please stop!"

After another few seconds, the surge of electricity ended.

"No one move. No one speaks, or the next time, I won't use a taser," the masked man bellowed in a Quebecois-accented voice.

When Oyinlola continued to moan in pain and protest, the solidly built man who'd tasered the politician took three strides forward and delivered a brutal kick to the laid-out man's ribs.

The faux cop roared, "Shut up, or the next time, I promise it's a bullet to your head!"

It was only when Oyinlola collapsed to the ground and grew silent that the man turned his eyes on MacPhail. After staring at her for what seemed an eternity, he moved in her direction and, in a quick movement, held out a phone to her. He snapped, "Take the call."

When MacPhail didn't move, he roared, "Take the fucking call!"

Slowly, she reached for the smartphone and, seeing that it was an incoming video call, held the device upright and activated the comms software.

Merielle appeared.

"Deputy Prime Minister MacPhail. I've just been informed that several terrorist attacks have been launched in and around the Ottawa area and that there's been an attack on Parliament. Are you okay?"

MacPhail's hand slowly came to her mouth and in a soft voice, she said, "Merielle, what have you done?"

Giving a sympathetic nod of her head, Merielle replied, "I understand, Irene. It is a lot to take in. Violence in its purest form can cause confusion, poor decision-making, and even irrational thoughts. Whatever has happened, it's best if you and I and those affected by today's tragic events are brought together so we can talk through what's happened and discuss a plan to make our country safe. By working together, we can overcome this plot. I didn't think they'd ever go this far. Clearly, we've underestimated the lengths to which the Chinese are willing to go to destroy our country."

MacPhail didn't know what to say. Perhaps she was confused. Perhaps she, too, had been tasered, and the intensity of the experience had put her in a dream-like state. This couldn't be happening.

She heard Merielle's voice again. "The men who are with you will make sure you make it to me safely. You, Michael, and others. No one will hurt you. When we're together, I'll go through the morning's events, and it will all make sense. Go with them now. We'll be together soon, and together, we can devise a plan to save Canada. I value your partnership, Irene. We'll talk soon, dear friend."

Then the display went dark.

MacPhail's stunned gaze rose to meet the dark eyes of the man who had given her the phone. He said, "We're leaving, Deputy Prime Minister, and when we leave this room, you will walk by my side. There is a motorcade waiting for you outside. You will not say a word to anyone. You will walk, you will get in the SUV, and you will remain silent the entire time. Is that clear?"

When MacPhail didn't say anything, he repeated his question, only this time his words were loud and laced with aggression. "Is that clear?"

"It's clear," MacPhail said finally, sounding defeated.

"Good, then follow me."

***

CSIS HQ, Ottawa

As Larocque entered the expansive command center buried under twenty meters of soil and concrete at the center of Ottawa's CSIS campus, everyone stopped what they were doing and looked in his direction.

He vividly felt their worried and angry gazes because he, too, was worried and angry.

The attacks across Ottawa had caught them by surprise, but for the moment, they weren't his primary fear. His overriding concern was finding out what happened on Parliament Hill.

As he strode toward the main operations room where his most trusted staff were waiting for him, he replayed the recent conversations he had with both Aziz and MacPhail for the hundredth time.

That this was a Chinese attack as it was being reported in the media was laughable. No, this was the White Unit's doing, and it was now official: Merielle Martel had gone entirely off the rails.

That it had happened so quickly and had taken such a violent turn is what had set Larocque back on his heels.

And he wasn't the only one. Across the government, people were confused, afraid, and looking for answers. The problem was that he didn't have answers yet.

What he did have was unproven speculation. Yes, they had hard evidence that the White Unit did exist, but what they didn't have was evidence linking it to Merielle, and they had nothing to say that it was the White Unit that had set off two good-sized bombs in Canada's national capital and conducted a well-executed raid on Parliament Hill that had killed three people and absconded with a dozen politicians.

The White Unit and its alleged links with Merielle were not something CSIS had widely shared with the rest of government because to do so would have led to anarchy. The idea that Canada's prime minister, in the middle of what was effectively World War III, would try to launch a takeover of the national government to give her dictatorial powers was something straight out of a Tom Clancy novel.

But that's precisely what was happening. At least that was his working theory.

Walking into the room, he saw the faces of the people he had asked to be present. All of them were either on-loan CANSOFCOM soldiers or CSIS folk he was sure he could trust. But more important than the in-person officials were the three faces on the massive display at the front of the space.

Present were General Kaplan, Canada's Chief of Defence Staff, Margaret Kostopoulos, the Commissioner of the RCMP, and the Chief of the Communication Security Establishment, Andre Potvin. More than anyone in the country, these were the people he needed to pow-wow with if this growing disaster was to be averted.

Just as important was who was not on the call. There were no politicians and no senior bureaucrats. Without question, those two groups were tainted, but even if they weren't, speed was what the moment called for. And the one thing Canadian politicians and bureaucrats did not do was move quickly.

"Sorry to be late, folks," Larocque said as he walked to his usual chair.

Sitting down, he faced the screen and said, "General Kaplan and Commissioner Kostopoulos, I understand you took the briefing from my people, and you now know everything that CSIS and CSE know about this situation?"

The RCMP Commissioner spoke first. "I got the briefing, Jackson, and I have questions, but I think events might have just overtaken our discussion."

"Oh, how so, Margaret?" Larocque asked.

"I just got an email from the Prime Minister's Office. She has a new chief of staff. A gentleman by the name of Gary Clarke. Heard of him?"

"I haven't, but I barely know anyone in this town," said Larocque.

"Well, it may not matter. Whatever his background, Mr. Clarke just sent an email out to about thirty different senior officials. It includes my name, Andre's, and yours, Jackson. It says we've been removed from our positions effective immediately and that our organizations will be run by other individuals who are to be named soon."

The RCMP Commissioner quickly added, "General Kaplan, your name doesn't appear on the list."

"This is not good," the Chief of the Defence Staff said. "If each of you pass on your leadership to others in your organization or, worse, to people who might be affiliated with this White Unit, whatever opportunity we have to stop this madness will pass. Whatever is to be done, it has to happen fast and, if possible, quietly. If the country understands what's happening, who knows how bad things could get? And never mind what our allies will think. Christ on a goddamn cross, what a mess."

"CSIS, you called the meeting," said CSE Chief Potvin in a thick Quebecois accent. "Jackson, you and your team have the best handle on what's happening, we're hoping you have a plan. If you do, let's get straight to it. As the General says, whatever we do has to be done quickly."

Larocque nodded. "We have a plan, but we have to remain in our positions for the next twenty-four hours for that to happen. Andre, can your people do something to neutralize that email that Margaret just mentioned? If we can pull it back, discredit it, or somehow confuse the situation, that should give us the time we need."

"That shouldn't be a problem. I'll have my people working up some options, and we'll have something ready to go within the hour, if not sooner."

"Good stuff," said Larocque. "We know the PM and her people are operating out of Harrington Lake. That's where they've taken MacPhail and the others. We need to use their isolation to our advantage. Until we can act, we need to make it so they can't engage with the media or whatever other allies or resources they may want to bring to them. Margaret, can the RCMP block off all the entrances to Gatineau Park?"

"Not a problem. I'll send the word to have it sealed up tight ASAP," said the RCMP Commissioner.

"Excellent," Larocque said confidently. More than anyone else in the room and perhaps in the whole country, he had been involved in these types of fast-moving, high-risk operations and knew what it took to bring people together to act. Having a plan and selling it as though it were as likely to happen as tomorrow's sunrise was the key to getting people – even very senior ones – to buy in. In times of crisis, people wanted leadership, and of all things, decisive leadership was the one thing he could deliver in spades.

"General, I've got two big asks for you," Larocque said, prepping the ground for his request of the CAF. Kaplan hadn't been removed from his role as the leader of the armed forces, and Larocque knew the man had a close relationship with Merielle. How could they not? They'd been working together hand in glove since she'd become PM.

With his usual calm demeanour, Kaplan spoke. "I've had my people look into the evidence you've provided and in the short time we've had, it leads me to believe something has to be done. But more than the evidence, it's clear to me something is wrong with Merielle. I can't put my finger on it precisely, but she's been acting differently in the past month or so. I want to respect the constitution of my country, but with today's events and all the other information, I think we might benefit from a brief political pause so we can sort out what the hell is going on and then set it right.

"All this to say, Larocque, tell me what you need, and I'll do everything I can to make it happen."

In his mind's eye, Larocque executed a victorious fist pump, but in a moderate tone, he said, "First, we need to isolate the PM's ability to communicate with the outside world. Whatever electronic warfare and surveillance resources you can point at Harrington Lake, we should do that."

"Our Vigilance aircraft fly out of Trenton. They can be above the target area within the hour," said Kaplan.

"My people can help with that as well," the CSE chief said, jumping into the conversation. "With Harrington Lake so close to Ottawa, we can limit their ability to connect with the outside world with little trouble. But if they decide to come back to Ottawa, it becomes a much bigger and very public problem to isolate them."

"If the general approves my second request, they won't get the chance to return to the capital," said Larocque.

Turning his gaze back on the CDS, Larocque said, "General, I need you to put the 427 Special Operations Aviation Squadron or whatever parts of it are here in Ottawa at my disposal. I'm going to need helicopters. Every last one you can give me."

As the request registered with him, a thoughtful look came across Kaplan's face. Finally, he said, "Most of SOAS is down south supporting JTF-2 and the SAS, but we've got some platforms at Pet and Dwyer Hill. How many do you need, and when do you need them?"

"As many as you can give, General. I've got just over a company of people that have to be moved."

Larocque then glanced down at his wrist for a time check. "It's 0914 hours. If we can have them ready to roll by 1130 hours, that should give me enough time to finalize a plan."

"To do what?" asked the RCMP Commissioner.

Larocque's gaze moved to the police officer. "Merielle Martel has placed a bet that this country's politicians will do what they always do, which is to prevaricate, then negotiate, and eventually, accept some type of government that will legitimate what has happened today.

"Well, we're not politicians, and I have no intention of letting Canada become the world's next authoritarian regime. By the end of today, the Martel government is no longer, or I'm in jail, or..."

He didn't put words to the third possibility. Instead, he let it hang in the air and waited for someone – anyone – to tell him his proposal was insane, wildly illegal, or both.

But no one in the room or on the call spoke up, and so he said, "The PM and this White Unit think they're the only people in the country prepared to do unexpected and daring things. Things that I daresay are very un-Canadian. Well, with the help of your organizations, they're gonna find out just how unexpected and daring we can be."

***

Washington, D.C.

—

Reynolds walked across the gravel parking lot in the direction of the waiting convoy of armored vehicles and trucks that had a group of approximately a dozen men gathered beside the lead vehicle, a hulking JLTV. Except for a single man who stood out from the group like a sore thumb, the gathering looked like the veteran special operators they were.

It had taken nearly two hundred and twenty million in crypto, but he'd pulled together the team he needed to pull this mission off.

Finding one hundred experienced special ops mercenaries in North America hadn't been the problem. After four years of civil war, there was no shortage of battle-hardened men prepared to take on dangerous work if the pay was right.

The problem was finding men who would keep their mouths shut when they finally found out who their target was. That moment was now.

When he arrived at the collection of hard-looking operators, Reynolds' eyes focused on the brown-skinned, pudgy man wearing blue jeans and a flashy orange golf shirt. To the soft standout, he asked, "We're good?"

"Everyone has been scanned. No one has a private device on them," said the Indian.

"And the other part?"

The Indian gave Reynolds a look suggesting he was annoyed by the question, but he didn't hesitate with his accented reply. "Everything is ready, of course."

That's all Reynolds needed to hear. He had now pulled off five jobs with the Indian and his partner, the Savant. They had failed in L.A. with Sanchez, but just. The lessons they'd learned from that op had been many, and all had been applied to their current mission, so his confidence was peaked. They had the right tech, and they had the right people.

He turned his gaze to the other men. All were professional mercenaries, and each of them and their teams had completed dozens, if not hundreds, of paid missions in support of one side of the war or the other. None of them cared about who won because all they cared about was getting paid. Every last one of them.

But they hadn't been on a mission like the one they were going to do in the next hour. Reynolds' best guess was that of the eleven mercenary captains standing before him, a third would walk away when the little brown man released the mission parameters onto the devices each of them had been given only a few hours earlier.

"Gentlemen, I know you're anxious to learn more about the mission and why I'm paying you so much damn money. Well, that time is now. On the device you were given this morning, there should be a single file called Op 7. Open the file and read the first three paragraphs. When done, I want to see your eyes on me."

It took nearly two minutes but eventually, the eyes of all eleven men had reconnected with Reynolds. The looks on their faces were mixed. Being professionals, half the faces gave no indication of what they were feeling. The other half were split between looks of kid-like excitement or someone who'd just received news of their execution.

After clearing his throat, Reynolds said in a clear and loud voice, "As it says in the document, if you don't want to be a part of this opportunity, that is your choice. If you walk, you get twenty percent of your payout. No questions asked. The only thing you have to do is stay put until you're released. Successful or not, this location will be safe for several hours after the mission. Until you're released, you are to stay in lockdown. You do not get paid until your release."

He paused, giving his words a moment to sink in. When no one gave him a confused or outraged look, he continued.

"The walk-away crypto is easy cash, and while I want all of you to help with this bat-shit-crazy scheme, I won't hold it against any of you if you choose to stay out of it. Because make no mistake, boys, what we are about to do *is* crazy. But all of you know me well enough that I don't do suicide missions. I work to get paid and if we pull this off, all of us are going to get paid, and big-time."

He paused his address again and waited to see if anyone would crack before he asked the question. Canvassing every operator's face, Reynolds now only saw determination. He stepped closer to the group and said, "So, now you know what the score is, and you have a sense of the role you're going to play. It's the moment of truth and times ticking, so I'm only going to ask once."

In his head, Reynolds counted to three and then said, "If you're out, raise your hand."

He quickly scanned the group of men. When no one's hand came up, he began to nod in satisfaction and in a near yell, he said, "Gentlemen, welcome to my crazy train. Today, together, we make history. We get to kill a fucking president."

Chapter 37

Harrington Lake, Prime Minister's Secondary Residence, Quebec

—

MacPhail and six other Conservative politicians were seated in the comfortable living room area on the main floor of the Harrington Lake residence. Until ten minutes ago, she had been sitting in the back of an SUV by herself, trying to work through what had just happened.

The shock of events back in her office had begun to fade at the halfway point between downtown Ottawa and the short journey to the heart of Gatineau Park, where the PM's secondary residence was located.

A pair of masked men wearing ballistic vests and carrying automatic weapons stood at the edge of the room, watching them intently.

MacPhail had been the last of the group to join. When her two minders had walked her into the well-appointed space, she'd been told to sit and not to talk to the others. Having seen what these armed thugs could do, for the moment, she told herself she'd follow their direction.

In the past year, MacPhail had exhibited bravery she didn't know she had, but what had befallen her in her office had devastated her. To see that much raw violence in the heart of Canada's democracy and to know it had been perpetrated by Merielle Martel – well, it was too much.

Looking at the faces of the politicians sitting around her, she surmised the others were also in the mood to comply.

Mala Shandra, a frumpy but delightful woman who hailed from one of the Conservative ridings in the Greater Vancouver Area, had been crying at some point. Her mascara was a wreck, but as her eyes connected with MacPhail's, a look of anger flashed across her face. Shandra was not supposed to win her seat a year ago but had won because her sunny personality turned pugnacious when the moment called for it.

Like the other politicians present, Shandra had signed onto the plan to bring down the Martel government. It had taken some convincing, but eventually, she had signed onto the strategy when she had received a guarantee that Canada would continue to honor its current commitments to the war.

Canada would not cut and run from the fight with the Reds or the Chinese. Shandra and the others who agreed to vote against the funding bill had been unanimous on this point. Under no circumstances would Canada leave CANZUK high and dry, but as opportunities to end the war came about, it should be the Canadian position to push hard for peace.

Just as it looked like Shandra was going to say something, MacPhail heard someone begin to walk down the hardwood staircase that joined the two floors of the residence.

Turning in her seat, MacPhail saw the form of Merielle Martel walk down the stairs. She was not alone. Behind her was another woman whom she did not recognize.

As Merielle's feet reached the main floor, MacPhail turned so she could face Canada's prime minister.

As always, Merielle was attired in a tailored dark pantsuit over an off-white blouse. On her feet were the practical loafers the former RCMP officer wore for all but the most formal occasions. MacPhail did not need to ask why the woman favored these particular shoes. It was obvious. If needed, she could move in them quickly.

The woman who followed her was taller and younger, in her twenties if MacPhail had to guess. Unlike Merielle, she wasn't dressed in business attire. She wore a well-worn pair of jeans and a pair of black high-top hiking boots that offset the dark, tightly knit sweater she was wearing. In front of her body, she was carrying what looked like a banker's box.

Together, Merielle and the nameless woman stopped outside the seating area where MacPhail and the rest of the MPs were now standing. Turning to the two masked soldiers standing along the wall, Merielle said, "You can leave, thank you."

Without uttering a reply, the masked men pulled themselves off the wall and made to leave.

Merielle's gaze returned to MacPhail and the rest of the MPs and, conversationally, said, "I want you all to know that I regret what happened this morning. I will regret it for the rest of my life. I will regret it, but if I had to do it again, I wouldn't hesitate. I am the prime minister of this country with a sizeable majority. All of you know this, but together, you tried to betray me. No, not me, you tried to betray the country. I won't let that happen."

"Merielle –" MacPhail started.

"Stop," Merielle said, almost shouting the word.

"I'm not finished, nor am I here to debate with you. All of you had the opportunity to come to me to raise your concerns, but instead, you chose the worst kind of deception. I want to assure all of you who are here that treason is still very much a thing in Canada. Each of you will be charged with it before the end of the day."

"This is preposterous!" Shandra all but shouted. "I'm a lawyer and a damned good one. Nothing we've done is treason. Everything we've done is within the law. It's called the democratic process. You may not like it, but I'll be damned if I'll let you call me a traitor."

"But aren't you?" Merielle said calmly to the MP.

Shandra snapped back at the question, "Jesus Christ, Merielle, have you lost your mind?"

Merielle turned to the brown-haired woman standing behind her and reached for the box she was still holding. Removing its lid, she pulled out a grey file folder.

Documents in hand, Merielle turned back to the group, walked toward Shandra and held out the file. "Take it," Merielle said.

When the MP made no move to accept the document, she turned to her left and thrust the folder into MacPhail's arms. Having no choice but to take it, MacPhail looked down at the folder as though she was being offered a venomous snake.

Merielle returned to where she had been standing. "I'll leave the rest of the documents for each of you to peruse. I think you'll find them interesting and compelling. But more to the point of this conversation, you'll find out why I had to take the action that I did. As severe as it was and as much as I did not want to do it, I will not stand by as assets of foreign governments try to overthrow the democratically elected Government of Canada."

Hearing Merielle's words, MacPhail opened Shandra's file and quickly scanned the first page of the document. As she reached the end, her eyes came up and found Merielle's. When she spoke, she did nothing to hold back the emotions roiling in her. "You can't do this. This is not right. This is not who you are. This is not who we are as a country."

With a serious look on her face, Merielle took two steps forward so she was on the edge of MacPhail's personal space. "I will not let Canada be subjected to the foreign powers for whom each of you works. Foreign government interference has always been a problem in this country. I just never imagined it could gain such a foothold in my government. This is my shame, but it is also my problem to solve."

Taking her eyes off MacPhail and turning to the woman with the box, Merielle said, "Leave it on the table so they can learn just how much we know of their betrayal."

On hearing the command, the woman walked forward and placed the banker's box on the coffee table in the center of the room's seating area. As she walked by, MacPhail noted the cat-like grace with which the woman moved and saw the handgun holstered at the small of her back.

The files deposited, the silent woman returned to Merielle's side.

MacPhail's gaze returned to the PM as she addressed the small group. "You have the next hour to review the documents. Read them or don't. It will not matter. When we speak again, we will discuss a plan to correct the shameful treason each of you conspired to undertake in the past twenty-four hours."

She took a step backward from MacPhail and when she spoke again, her brown eyes were zeroed in on MacPhail's green. "For most of you, if you're willing to work with me, I'm prepared to forgive and move past what I see as a one-time, if terrible, lapse in judgment. But not all of you. Someone in this group has more responsibility for today's near-disaster. Do not let that person convince you that I am the problem. I am not the problem. I am the leader of our party and the Prime Minister of Canada, and I only want what's best for you and all Canadians."

With that, Merielle turned and walked past the fit, plain-looking woman. As Merielle strode by her, the mysterious staffer, if that's what she was, stared at the group of politicians for a long moment. Only when Merielle began her ascent up the stairway did the woman finally turn and follow the politician who was still in charge of the country.

As the nameless and armed woman walked away, MacPhail turned back to her colleagues.

Looking into each set of eyes, for the life of her, MacPhail had no idea what to say. Clearly, she and Oyinlola had been fools to approach Merielle last night.

Even in the face of Merielle's serious crimes, they had wanted to do the right thing for the party and for the country.

Foolish was nowhere near a strong enough word to describe how stupid they'd been to try and negotiate with Merielle Martel. All their naiveté had done was give her time to hatch a plan that could cost MacPhail her life, as had almost happened with Oyinlola.

She had no idea where the man was, but as her colleagues continued to stare at her and wait for her to say something, she wished desperately for his counsel.

Finally, forcing her gaze to meet Shandra's, she said, "Let's start with the documents. If we're going to come up with a plan, we need to know just how bad or crazy things really are."

**

Washington, D.C.

—

As the convoy of military vehicles approached the last checkpoint before Reynolds and his team of mercenaries passed into the green zone around the White House, he gave a quick update to each of the mercenary captains riding in the vehicles behind him.

"This is Zero One. We're approaching the last checkpoint. It should go as all the others but, if it doesn't, you know what to do. Once I make contact, we are committed. Zero One out."

It still wasn't clear to Reynolds who had contacted him for this mission but at every moment, that person had proven themselves to be a reliable overwatch. At first, he had doubted the promises of the person who said he could get Reynolds and a team of up to one hundred men into the green zone, but in the two weeks he'd been prepping for the mission, he'd been in and out of the area on five different occasions. The encrypted credentials he'd received had been impeccable, and today had been no different.

The battered JLTV he'd been riding in stopped twenty feet from the imposing concrete-and-steel gate that was the last barrier between his assault force and their target. This far into the maw of the beast that was the political heart of the UCSA, he was now well and truly into the shit.

Four regular force Red Faction soldiers came out to meet his lead vehicle while a half-dozen more stayed on the ramparts of the barrier. Immediately behind the gate was a tower that held a Ma Deuce. Its fifty-caliber muzzle was pointed at the windshield of Reynolds' JLTV.

In the back seat, he spoke quietly to the driver, "Stay cool, Cummings. Just like the other two, I've got this."

The man only grunted the non-verbal equivalent of *sure thing, boss*.

Reynolds opened the door, stepped down to the pavement of Constitution Avenue and began to walk in the direction of the soldiers waiting for him. One of the four, a captain by way of the rank on his chest rig, was a few steps in front of the other three men. The officer, probably in his mid-twenties, had a nasty scowl on his face. The three men flanking their leader held their weapons casually, a sign Reynolds took to mean they weren't keyed up for trouble.

"Your orders," the officer said in a growl.

"And a fine morning to you, Captain," Reynolds said cheerily, tapping the screen of the palm-sized tactical pad he was carrying.

"The orders should be on your machine now," he said, holding up the tac pad.

With his right hand, the still-glaring captain pulled a tactical unit from his body armor and, with his fingers, began to manipulate the screen. Finding the document that Reynolds had just flipped to him, he took a moment to read the orders.

Looking up from the screen, the captain said, "Bravo Battery from the 111th Field Artillery Regiment, 29th Infantry Division. It says you guys are drone operators. I would have thought they needed you guys at the front?"

"I just go where I'm told. And besides, based on everything I've been hearing, the front might be here sooner than you think."

"You trying to say we're losing the war?" the captain snapped at Reynolds.

Reynolds made a point of looking at the younger man's name tag. "I'm not saying anything, Captain Dugger. What I am saying is that someone who's way beyond our pay grade told me and my guys to be here, and in the Army I proudly serve in, you follow the orders you've been given. To the letter. And the letter you just saw said my battery is to report to the Flagg Barracks at 0930 hours."

Reynolds quickly glanced down at his watch and then continued. "Based on my watch, that gives me approximately seven minutes to get to where I need to be, and you know the old saying, if you ain't 15 minutes early, you're late."

The officer's face softened a touch. "Alright, hold your horses. We'll get you on your way. The paperwork checks out. We're all just a bit touchy with what we're being told about the front. What have you heard anyway?"

One of Reynolds' eyebrows arched upwards, and he said, "So we're cool?"

"Yeah, man, we're cool. You're the first group in two weeks to get transferred in. All I've heard about up north is the stuff they're letting us hear, and I'm almost certain it's all bullshit."

The officer stepped closer to Reynolds and, in a conspiratorial tone, said, "Is it as bad as they're saying? If they're sending a whole battery of drones to us, it's gotta mean shit isn't going well up north. I mean, the only reason they're sending you here is because they think the Blues are gonna make it this far?"

For several seconds, Reynolds didn't respond, but then he lowered his head and, matching the other man's tone, he said, "Listen, friend, I'll give you all the details I can, but I need to get to my rendezvous on time. If there's a place we can get a drink around here, why don't we meet there and we can trade notes? I've got a guy I'm tight with who's in the 38th ID. I just spoke with him two days ago. I've got the real deal, brother."

For the first time during their conversation, the captain's face revealed a smile. "There is a place just outside the green zone east barrier called the Free State. It's where the junior officers go to hang out. I'll be there for a couple hours tonight starting at six. If you can make it, you'll drink for free."

"I'll be there, brother," Reynolds said quickly.

The captain nodded his head, turned around, and then yelled toward the gate. "Open it up!"

Turning, Reynolds strode back to the JLTV, opened the rear driver's side door and climbed up into the vehicle. Sitting down, he looked ahead and saw the massive steel gate begin to slide to the left.

"We're good?" Cummings asked from behind the wheel.

"More than good, my man. We're aces high."

***

CFB Petawawa

Dressed in combats and wearing his chest rig, Larocque walked in front of the huge screen at the front of the room where he was briefing his people. On the screen were two images.

On the left was an overhead image of the prime minister's residence at Lake Harrington. It was nestled in the heart of Gatineau Park. Provincially owned, the park only had a handful of homes within it and they were only there because they had existed before the Canadian government purchased the 360-square-kilometer area in 1938.

Entirely isolated and surrounded by kilometers of dense virgin forest, the property took the form of a one-hundred by three-hundred-meter triangle, where the narrower base ran along the southern end of Harrington Lake.

The lake was elongated in shape and just over three klicks long. It was across its surface that helicopters from the 427 Special Operations Aviation Squadron would fly before unloading a single wave of commandos from the Canadian Airborne Regiment.

With a trio of Super Griffon gunships flying overhead, four CH-525 Rocs would unload nearly eighty soldiers and a handful of police officers and CSIS IOs on the lake's shore, and with Larocque at their head, they would undertake a feinting assault of the property's main residence, where it was suspected the prime minister and her newly appointed advisors were holed up. Also, there would be the politicians who had been taken from Parliament Hill, including Irene MacPhail.

Three klicks to the west, a ninety-man strike force made up of the Canadian Special Operations Regiment and a handful of JTF-2 commandos had already unloaded out of a pair of Chinooks at the western edge of the park and were now halfway to the point where they'd undertake the actual assault on the cottage.

It was this group of men – all of them highly trained in the art of entering and securing a building –

that would take the PM into custody and, if necessary, kill anyone who got in their way.

It was an imperfect and hugely risky plan, but if they executed it well, Larocque was confident they could capture Merielle and end the day's nightmare before things got out of hand.

The blistering pace of their operation was being driven by an announcement that Merielle's people had made before the CSE could isolate and cut off all communications into and out of Lake Harrington.

Merielle's chief of staff, this Clarke fellow, was still in Ottawa and had advised the media just an hour ago that the PM would be making an announcement from the grounds of the residence at 1400 hours about the attacks in Ottawa, including the incident on the Hill, and that she would be returning to Ottawa after this statement.

Instead of launching their operation in the late afternoon as they'd first planned, they now had to make their move before the reporters gathering at the park's gates found their way past the RCMP and to Harrington Lake.

Gatineau Park was itself a massive triangle, its narrowest point terminating on the edge of Ottawa's downtown core. Its proximity to the nation's capital meant that dozens, even hundreds, of reporters hungry for information on the early morning attacks would descend on the PM's residence, making their takedown impossible if they waited too long to act.

And so, they'd moved everything up. The country's future couldn't wait for the perfect plan.

Standing before the soldiers, cops, and intelligence officers that would be wheels-up in fifteen minutes, Larocque projected his voice and said, "The time for questions is over. It's a quick and dirty plan, but I'm confident it will get the job done. If you have any concerns you want to discuss privately, you have five minutes. I'll be here at the front."

His eyes canvassed the twenty or so faces intently staring at him. The officers and senior NCOs of the Airborne, he trusted with his life. The CSIS IOs present were from the Direct Action Team and could be counted on. The handful of RCMP officers were here because he needed the credibility of the national police force. He would have liked to have kept them out of the op, but that wasn't an option.

Resigned to the make-up of the players on his team and trusting that what they were doing was right, Larocque delivered his final words. "Some historians will call what we're about to do a mutiny or a coup. It is neither.

"I trust everyone in this room because of the importance of what we're doing. Our country's future is at stake, and that's not hyperbole. What happens in the next hour determines whether or not Canada remains a democracy or becomes something very different."

Delivering a hard stare at each of the faces in front of him, he said, "Remember your oath to the King, remember why you joined the service that you're a part of, but most important, remember that democracy and freedom have never been free. Today, we do hard things. Today, we save Canada.

"Task Force True Dominion... dismissed."

Chapter 38

West of Punxsutawney, Pennsylvania

―

From his position in the commander's hatch of his Leopard 2 A7, Major Lange of the Royal Canadian Dragoons watched as all eleven of his tanks from his reconstituted squadron rolled through the mid-season cornfield.

It had been three weeks of intense fighting since they began to push the Red Faction back from Buffalo. In that time, the Dragoons had received nineteen tanks and their crews from the Lord Strathcona Horse, the Canadian Army's reg force heavy armor regiment based out of Edmonton. Fully operational once again, his formation and the other two tank squadrons of the Dragoons would lead Operation Northern Hammer.

With the help of various drone assets, a team of British SAS operators had identified what CANZUK intelligence believed was the field headquarters of the Red Faction's 6th Army Group.

Why the 6th HQ, with its generals and its riches of intelligence, was this close to the fighting was a question for when he had the luxury of time to play amateur historian. Today, the only kind of thinking he had to do was to coordinate his people, blow shit up, and survive.

The voice of the Canadian Brigadier coordinating the Dragoons' role in the upcoming fight crackled through his BAM: "All units, all units, this is Ripsaw Sunray. Northern Hammer is a go. I say again, Northern Hammer is a go.

"Team Grinder, you are a go in five mikes for Objective Golf. I say again, Team Grinder, you are a go in five mikes for Objective Golf. Team Anvil is to take Objective Hotel. Go time is in fifteen mikes. I say again, Team Anvil, go time is in fifteen mikes. Juno and Vulcan assets are inbound and will hit the pre-designated targets per location Romeo-One, Map Alpha. All units are in the pipe and primed. Fight hard, everyone. Today is our day. Ripsaw Sunray out."

Lange looked down at the large tactical display that featured the Royal Canadian Dragoons, its two hundred and thirty vehicles, and the geography they were about to navigate.

It was the most powerful fighting force his country could send against an enemy. Thirty-seven Leopard 2s, seventy-one LAV VIs, fifty-three four-wheeled Tactical Armored Patrol Vehicles, and an assortment of other support vehicles would help the main fighting elements of the Dragoons find and then destroy their enemy.

Following closely behind them in their own collection of LAVs was 1st Battalion of the Royal Canadian Regiment, the RCR, and 2nd Battalion from the Princess Patricia's Canadian Light Infantry, the PPCLI.

Two of the Patricia's four battalions had been rushed from Alberta only two days earlier to help with Northern Hammer, CANZUK's biggest ground offensive of the war.

The same map displayed the enemy Lange, and his soldiers were about to face.

Two days ago, two brigades from the Red Faction 3rd Infantry Division, along with parts of the 30th Armored Brigade, were brought forward to replace what was said to be an exhausted 35th Infantry Division and a ragged collection of Red militia units that had dug in just west of Punxsutawney.

For three straight days, the 35th and the Red militia had fought a dogged eighty-kilometer rear-guard action against the 10th Mountain Division from New York and the 91st Regional Infantry Division out of New England.

The fighting had followed State Highway 322, which passed ten klicks north of the mildly famous town that, in better times, had informed the people of the United States if spring would be early or late by way of an overfed groundhog named Phil.

UCSA sappers and militia volunteers had hastily built a network of trenches and a series of minefields to the west of the town.

The purpose of the Punxsutawney defensive stand was to help protect Pittsburgh.

From within and behind their trenches and minefields, several thickets of Red Faction artillery had been set up to hammer any force that wanted to approach Pittsburgh from the east.

From this same defensive position, the Red's 3rd Infantry Division and the 30th Armored Brigade could foray out to attack the flanks of whatever force tried to move on the City of Bridges.

It was because of this dual threat that Lange, the Dragoons, and the entirety of the 4th Canadian Division, along with the 32nd Infantry Division out of Wisconsin, were driving south in the direction of these dug-in Red Faction forces.

Seeing the tanks in front of him had just passed the designated starting point for the offensive, he activated his BAM and ordered his part of the regiment to stop its advance. In turn, all other units following them would stop their roll.

Everywhere around him, Canadian armor came to a halt. On his tactical display, three klicks to his east, the leading elements of the Blue's 32nd Infantry Division appeared to be doing the same.

Despite the concentration of artillery the Red Faction had four kilometers south, Lange was confident his tank and those surrounding him were not in harm's way.

For the past thirty-six hours, dozens of CANZUK drones, men from Britain's SAS, and the recce companies from both the RCR and PPLCI had worked together to identify and clear out any advanced spotters who could direct the Red's dug-in guns.

As an additional precaution, the Royal Artillery had flown in a unit that specialized in anti-drone warfare.

Operating two dozen Swedish-built anti-drone drones that were fast and loaded with the latest sensors, the unit's operators had been working around the clock to flag and shoot down any flying machine the Reds put into the sky within a ten-kilometer radius.

Effectively, until the Reds saw Lange and the Dragoons emerge from the tiny forests and uneven farmland that was this part of Pennsylvania with their own eyes, their enemies would be blind to their approach.

The border around Lange's tactical display flashed, drawing his eyes downward. In the chat section of the BAM system, Grinder One-Zulu, the 2IC for the 2nd Regiment of the Royal Canadian Horse Artillery, had posted a priority message.

In one minute, the three batteries of the Regiment, two sets of eight M777s and one set of ten CAESAR mobile artillery units, along with all of the guns supporting the Blue's 32nd Infantry Division, would open up to unleash a twenty-minute barrage on those parts of the Red Faction defense the Dragoons and Blues were going to smash into.

Over the rumble of his tank's engine, Lange heard the first of what would be dozens of salvos from the Canadian Army's big guns. Eight klicks to the Dragoons' rear, the first 155mm shells took only twenty seconds to reach their targets.

Ahead, at less than two kilometers, the horizon rumbled as dozens of high-explosive and deep-penetration artillery shells connected with targets that had been designated by a score of high-altitude drones surveying the Red's fortifications.

Based on earlier calculations, it would take the Dragoons and the lead elements of the 32nd ID about fifteen minutes to reach the point where they could begin to engage with the first line of their enemy's defense.

Lange activated his BAM and said, "Open Channel Anvil Group Bravo and keep it open, authorization Lange-India-Six."

"Channel open. Channel will remain open until advised otherwise," advised a synthesized Patrick Stewart, the voice he'd once again designated for his BAM.

To his squadron, Lange said, "Anvil Group Bravo. This is Anvil Bravo-One. All units advance to Line Yankee, staying under twenty klicks an hour. I say again, all units advance to Line Yankee, staying under twenty klicks. We're gonna do this slow and steady. Keep your eyes peeled and watch for hidden missile teams or spotters that have moved up from their lines in the past couple of hours. Our people have cleared from the area, so anything that moves out there is the enemy, so kill it."

Lange paused momentarily as a colossal explosion erupted in the direction where the Reds were being hammered. A bright orange fireball leapt into the sky and immediately transitioned into an oily black mushroom cloud.

To Lange's left, his tank's gunner, Sergeant Bobby Betts, whistled but didn't say anything.

Like everyone in the Dragoons, the Sergeant was waiting for Lange to give the word to start the advance.

Pulling his eyes from the growing column of destruction, the gunner from the outskirts of Saskatoon turned to look at Lange. With a look of determination on his face, he said, "It's time to get this party started, sir. Give the word so we can give 'em hell."

Nodding at the NCO's enthusiasm for the chaos that was to come, Lange reactivated his BAM and said, "Anvil Group Bravo, today we make more history. Today, Dragoons, we fight like hell. Advance. Advance. Advance."

***

Three klicks ahead, Major Varma watched as a flight of eight British AH-64E Apaches split into two separate groups.

In two teams of four, the British attack helicopters had been tasked with providing direct fire support to the Canadian and Blue Faction armor units as they advanced on the Red Faction's outer defensive line.

Each Apache carried a loadout of eight Hellfire missiles, two pods of Hydra 70 rockets, and their legendary chin-mounted 30mm cannon.

Staying well back from the advancing armor, the Apaches would savage whatever targets the soldiers on the ground flagged for them as they started to take fire from hidden UCSA hardpoints.

Varma's headset came alive as the first call came in from the Dragoons to light something up.

Ahead, one of the Apaches attached to the Canadian 4th Division unleashed a single Hellfire. In the distance, a section of brown earth geysered into the air.

Down the line, another of the attack helicopters unleashed what Varma guessed was the entirety of the 2.75-inch rockets it was carrying.

Well beyond the British gunships, a series of massive explosions erupted on the horizon as a batch of CANZUK fighters dropped their bombs on Red Faction artillery and suspected command-and-control positions.

All but blinded by CANZUK's earlier efforts to shoot down their drones and hunt down their forward observers, the Reds' artillery had remained silent until their front-line soldiers began to call in fire missions on the advancing Canadian and Blue armor.

But no sooner had the Red Faction's big guns opened up than loitering CANZUK fighters had swept down from the sky to pummel the now exposed artillery positions.

Amidst this combined arms onslaught, the eight RCAF Super Griffons under Varma's command would be held in reserve, waiting to be directed to that part of the battle where their moderately armed gunships might be able to make a difference.

A female voice with a strong Scottish accent sounded off in his headset. "Saber Sunray, this is Juno Delta. Do you copy?"

"Juno Delta, I have a good copy," said Varma.

"Saber Sunray, we've identified a grouping of artillery that Longsword won't be able to get to. The data should be on your screen now. This is your new target."

"Roger, Juno Delta. I see the data. Team Saber is starting its run now. Saber Sunray out."

Closing off the conversation with the RAF Wedgetail battle coordinator, Varma opened the BAM connection to the other Super Griffons.

"Team Saber, we're a go. Targets should be on each of your displays. In pairs, we hunt in our assigned grids. As we do so, everyone keeps their eyes peeled for MANPADS. Intel says they're still out there. And remember, folks, don't get static. The Brits can sit pretty and pound because they're in an armored tank that happens to fly. We have no such luxury. Fly like butterflies and sting like bees. That is the order of the day. Saber Sunray out."

As Varma manipulated the Super Griffon's flight controls to move in the direction of their assigned target grid, he opened a preset BAM channel to connect with the officer piloting the helicopter that would be his partner for the dance to come. He said, "How are you feeling, Da Silva?"

"Good to be back in the saddle, Saber Sunray. All of Saber Two is ready to give the Reds hell."

Varma grunted. His on-again, off-again love interest would not talk to him on the ground when she'd found out she'd been paired with him for the mission.

A part of Varma knew he shouldn't have asked their Squadron's commanding officer to make the pairing, but the colonel owed him one.

Of course, the woman he loved was perfectly capable of taking care of herself.

Tilly Da Silva was one of the best helicopter pilots in the CAF, but too often, when the bullets started to fly, the woman took chances. That's what had gotten her shot down over Ohio two weeks earlier.

Varma chalked up the risk-taking to her ethnic heritage. The Portuguese might not be as hot-blooded as their Iberian cousins, the Spanish, but they weren't far off.

Whether she was fighting the Reds or quarrelling with Varma, Captain Da Silva could transform into one hell of a spitfire when the circumstances demanded it. She was just the kind of woman Varma couldn't resist.

Through their private comms, he said, "Remember, Till, nothing reckless. Hurt them, but live to fight tomorrow. We're a dying breed, us Canadian gunships."

Her response was sharp. "Cut the chatter, Sunray. We've got a battle to win. Saber Two out."

Varma muttered under his breath, "Damn woman."

His co-pilot, Robins, glanced over. "Trouble in paradise, boss?"

"Oh, nothing. Just... a minor HR issue."

Robins smirked. "The same 'issue' you've been dealing with for weeks?"

Varma returned the younger man's grin with his own and said, "The same."

Without missing a beat, Robins quipped, "Maybe HR can set up a mediation? Heard that works wonders."

Varma chuckled. "You're a real comedian, Lieutenant. Now get us where we need to be. We've got a battle to help win."

***

"Unleash hell, Grinder!" Lange yelled into his headset at the officer coordinating the 4th Division's artillery. "I don't give two shits how close you think you are, don't let up until my guy tells you to. Bichon knows exactly what he's doing, and if he's telling you our guys are clear, then that means there's room. We're getting torn apart, so make it bloody well happen. Anvil Bravo-One out!"

Forty meters ahead, four LAVs filled with RCR infantrymen slammed on their brakes, bringing the twenty-thousand-pound IFVs to a halt. As soon as they had stopped moving, the rear hatches to all four troop carriers began to descend. Three-quarters of the way down, soldiers leapt from the back end of each machine and, in random order, ran to the left and right of the vehicles that had kept them safe until this moment of the fight.

Just as the first soldiers appeared, furious machine-gun fire erupted from what Lange knew to be the second line of the Red Faction's defense. Tucked into the turret of his Leopard, he watched helplessly as soldiers emerging from the LAVs were cut down by sheets of murderous enemy bullets.

As he opened his mouth to give the order to advance to put themselves between the trenches and the exposed infantrymen, each of the LAVs' Bushmaster cannons opened up.

In their effort to whittle down the number of men who could storm their positions, the Red defenders had finally given themselves away. At close range, the armor-piercing rounds of the four LAVs began to chop up the areas where the dug-in gunfire was coming from.

But as the rounds from those locations slowed or stopped altogether, other defensive positions in the area shifted their weapons to the exposed Canadian infantry and the LAVs who had dropped them off.

As with the first defensive line, the Red Faction engineers had done a textbook job of locating their trenches and hardpoints so they could easily support one another. It had been a terrible slog through the first line of defense, but the combination of artillery and almost non-stop air strikes had eventually allowed the Canadians and their Blue allies to move past the first objective.

BOOM! The furthest right LAV in front of Lange's Leopard exploded when an anti-tank missile struck the IFV on its right side. Its backside ramp still open, a massive gout of fire and debris ejected from the vehicle as though it was the mouth of a cannon.

"Betts, find that bastard and put him down ASAP!" Lange roared at his tank's gunner while trying to activate his BAM. Hearing the chime signaling the comms software was ready, he said, "Open channel for Grinder Bravo, priority code Lange Hotel-Victor."

But before the always calm voice of Patrick Stewart could advise him where he was in the queue to speak with the second-in-command for the 2nd Regiment of the Royal Canadian Horse Artillery, he heard the scream of incoming shells.

"About bloody time!" Lange yelled as the first artillery round came down near the Red positions still raking the RCR infanteers.

As Lange's forward observer had demanded of Grinder, for the next ten minutes, the equivalent of three football fields would be pounded by a combination of High Explosive and Anti-Personnel shells by the 2nd Regiment's M777 guns.

Confident the LAVs and their disembarked soldiers would survive the nearby bombardment, Lange lowered himself into his tank and opened a channel to those Dragoons still in the fight. Of the thirty-seven tanks they had started with two hours ago, twenty-five remained in good fighting order and of these, seven had taken flanking positions to his left and right.

On his tactical display, Lange quickly selected those seven tanks, and then ordered the BAM software to create a chat room. In seconds, the seven tank commanders had dropped into the chat.

With no time to waste, Lange started to outline his plan. "I think I've identified a gap in front of us. If you boys are up for it, I want to drive through it and move on to Objective Charlie. It's only a klick away and dollars to donuts, there is little to nothing between us and them. Everything the Reds have is on this line. The footage we have of their HQ says they haven't started to evac. I don't know if their comms suck and they don't know they're about to lose, or they've been ordered to make a stand, but if we move fast, I think we can take the prize."

"And what do we do when we get there, Boss?" asked one of the tank commanders. "We're just seven tanks."

"Leave that to me, Teddy. I just need to know if all of you are down with the plan. I say it's clear, but we could just as easily run into what's left of their armor or more trenches the drones didn't see. As much as this could shorten the fight, it could be a suicide mission, so if anyone thinks it's a stupid idea, speak now or forever hold your peace."

The tank commander named Teddy spoke up again. "It's crazy, but it ain't stupid, Major. For the record, my crew and I are in."

In quick succession, the remaining tanks voiced their support for the risky plan.

When the last commander reported in, Lange said, "Nice. Then rev your engines, Dragoons. It's time to dive into the belly of the beast."

***

"Juno Delta, I just did an ammo check. Four of us can do the escort. Just send the coordinates for where we need to be. Saber Sunray out," Varma said, confirming the request for close-in air support from the high-above battle coordinator flying in the RAF Wedgetail.

He then toggled the BAM to reconnect with the six Super Griffons still in the sky over the battlefield and said, "Okay, people. If you can believe it, we've been drafted into escort duty. Whoever is running this fight needs us to lead the way for an air assault of Objective Charlie."

Da Silva interjected, "The Red's HQ?"

"None other," Varma confirmed. "Turns out some crazy son of a bitch tanker is leading an impromptu charge to take it, and two Chinooks with a company of Patricia's and a troop of SAS are being ordered in to help. The coordinates of where we'll hook up with the Chinooks just popped into your data. The four of us who still have ammo need to link up with them pronto, so let's get to it, people. Saber Sunray out."

***

Beside him, Sergeant Betts unleashed a long burst with their tank's pintle-mounted C-6 machine gun in the direction of a trench that had been in the process of readying an RPG.

As Betts continued to spray the threat, one of the Leopards trailing Lange's tank raced past them to their left and, at what had to be close to fifty klicks an hour, drove into and over a long barrier of concertina wire about twenty meters in front of the trenches that Lange and the other six Leopards were in the process of assaulting.

The advancing tank, an armored juggernaut weighing sixty tons, easily rolled over the two-meter-high razor wire.

On the back end of the Leopard was a two-meter steel arm with a hook at the end of it. As the tank passed over the defensive wall, this same arm snagged the razor wire and started pulling tens and then hundreds of meters of the concertina wire with it.

The driver of the tank, no doubt under the orders of the Leopard's commander, drove the machine toward the same trench that Betts had been tearing into.

As the tank roared by the emplacement, sections of the trailing razor wire dipped into the slits.

Aghast, Lange watched as the writhing bodies of two soldiers were ripped from the trench and dragged behind the still-moving Canadian tank.

Making a sharp turn, the Leopard continued its parade of death as it angled toward another defensive emplacement.

Lange's BAM spoke inside his helmet. "Incoming priority call from Scimitar Three."

Glad for the interruption, he ducked into his tank so he didn't have to continue to watch the horror show of the two Red Faction soldiers being torn to shreds. "Accept the call," he advised the near-AI comms software.

"Anvil Bravo-One, this is Scimitar Three. We are three mikes from your position. What's your status?"

"Scimitar, we're pressing on the west side of Objective Charlie. We're about to move past its outer defenses. Once we get there, we'll form a perimeter and put down red smoke. I suggest you put down within our ring."

"Roger that, Anvil Bravo-One. We'll put down on the red smoke. Anvil, be advised we have four Sabers riding shotgun with us. Any special requests for them?"

Sabers? Lange had to think for a minute. Then it struck him. Super Griffon gunships would be escorting the Chinooks into the LZ. He said, "Nothing special, Scimitar. Let them know it's kinda crazy down here and that anything that's not a tank is fair game."

"Roger that, Anvil Bravo-One. We're now two mikes away. Scimitar Three out."

***

At one kilometer out from the landing zone, Varma adjusted the altitude of his Super Griffon from forty feet to four hundred. Ahead, he could see several plumes of black smoke and the occasional flash of a tank muzzle as it fired its main gun.

They were approaching the objective from the north. From this altitude, he saw a messy circle of tanks bathed in red smoke. Around them was a collection of burning vehicles.

Out of the corner of Varma's left eye, he caught a bright flash. Ahead, one of the Leopards bucked and then exploded.

Shifting his eyes to where he'd caught the flash, he saw a mix of vehicles racing toward the tanks. "There's the cavalry, Robins," Varma told his co-pilot. "Tag and waste the bastards!"

"Done," said the co-pilot calmly. "Targets have been set for those of us still packing."

Varma felt their Super Griffon shudder as the first of its two remaining SPIKE missiles ejected from its launch tube. Less than five seconds later, the missile slammed into the front wheel of a JLTV, forcing the armored machine to flip ass over tea kettle.

Their second SPIKE slammed into an army-green SUV, turning it into a raging column of orange fire. Other vehicles succumbed to missiles launched by the three other Super Griffons.

"We're all out, Boss," Robins said.

Varma toggled open his connection to his flight. "Okay, people, it's a knife fight from here on in. Work in pairs and have your door gunners rake anything that comes within one hundred meters of our people. Saber Two, you're with me. Saber Sunray out."

***

Working the tank's main gun, Lange quickly positioned the Leopard's targeting reticle on the barn that had unleashed the hail of machine gun fire that had killed Betts only two minutes ago.

Fearless, exposed, and working the C-6 like a champion, a heavy-caliber bullet had caught the sergeant on his left shoulder and ripped through the entirety of his upper body.

By the time Lange had pulled him down into the relative safety of the tank's turret to start first aid, Sergeant Betts, the funny and brave son of a farmer, was well and truly gone.

A minute later, as his finger hung over the trigger that would fire the 120mm Anti-Personnel round into the structure hiding the Red Faction soldiers that had killed his friend, he could see men racing out of the building.

As his finger made contact with the main gun's trigger, the tank shuddered as it ejected its spent shell casing and filled with the acrid smell of burnt propellant.

The eleven hundred flechettes he'd fired at nearly fifteen hundred meters per second reached the barn instantaneously, shredding whoever was still inside it.

Not bothering to enjoy the retribution, Lange called out, "Kojo, load another APERS."

As the private began to call out the steps of loading another anti-personnel round, Lange heard the distinctive sound of the tandem rotors of the Chinook helicopter through the still-open commander's hatch.

Rocketing upward, he turned his body to face north and saw the two huge helicopters just as they set down.

From the back ends of both machines, soldiers began to appear.

Lange could immediately distinguish between the British special operators and the reg force Canadian soldiers.

While the SAS wore mostly similar uniforms, they carried an array of different and wicked-looking weapons. And to the last man, their fitness level made it look as though any of them could have moonlighted on one of Britain's national rugby teams.

On the other hand, the soldiers from the Patricia's carried the same weapon, the C-71, and while there were many well-built lads, more than a few sported the body and gait of a younger man who hadn't yet come into his full self.

Regardless of the differences, the two groups of soldiers started their business without hesitation. While the fifteen or so men of the SAS rushed toward the large farmhouse where it was suspected the

6th Army Group's commanders were holed up, the Princess Patricia's divided into formations of twenty and began to clear out the farm's various outbuildings.

As the SAS men approached the farmhouse, a pair of Super Griffons lowered themselves into a position where they could unleash a crossfire into the building if it was requested.

Ahead of him, at about sixty meters, as clear as day, Lange eyed one of the Griffon's door gunners leaning far outside his aircraft to point the barrel of his minigun at the bright yellow door the British commandos were about to breach.

But just as one of the burly British soldiers stepped forward with a battering ram, the entrance to the farmhouse swung open. Slowly, the first Red Faction officer revealed himself. He was in his mid-fifties and was carrying what looked like a white bath towel.

Behind him, more officers tentatively appeared. When the parade of UCSA soldiers ended, half of the UK commandos moved into the building, while those who remained started the process of taking control of their new prisoners.

Five minutes later, Lange heard the order to dismiss the two Canadian gunships still hovering over the takedown.

As one, the helicopters smoothly veered right, turned their cockpits away from the farmhouse, and gained altitude as they flew north.

As Lange's gaze returned to the British commandos and their growing number of prisoners, a relieved voice began to speak inside his helmet. "All units, all units, this is Ripsaw Sunray. Objective Charlie has been taken. I say again, Objective Charlie has been taken. Enemy units are retreating. Do not pursue. I say again, do not pursue retreating enemy units. Operation Northern Hammer will consolidate on our current position. Magnificent work, people. Simply magnificent. Ripsaw Sunray out."

Chapter 39

The White House, Washington, D.C.

—

Reynolds and the convoy of fifteen military vehicles pulled up alongside Freedom Plaza. Still in the back seat of the JLTV, he took a moment to collect himself. They had done it.

He had been to Washington a few times near the beginning of the war. The changes that had been made to the city to turn it into a fortress had been remarkable. No wonder the Reds had decided to use tactical nukes to carve a path to the White House.

In the short time the UCSA had been in possession of the city, their engineers had been busy repairing key defenses. In another month, the former capital of the United States would once again be all but impregnable to a conventional force.

That he and his team had gotten this close was no small miracle. Inside the final ring of defenses, the last obstacle they needed to confront was the ring of fortifications around the White House itself.

From this point on, there would be no subterfuge. They would move fast and strike hard.

Ahead two hundred meters was the Tecumseh Sherman Statue entrance or as others called it, the White House Ground's Southeast Gate. This would be their breach point.

Pressing a button on his wrist unit, Reynolds activated the pre-set comms channel connecting him to the ninety-seven mercenaries that would assault the complex. Divided into nine teams, each sub-unit had a role to play, and in addition to his direction, each team would be connected to the most powerful near-AI tactical program on the planet.

The plan to gain entry to the White House grounds and then storm the building itself had been fed into the program. In minutes, it had spat out a dozen improvements worth Reynolds' time.

And if that wasn't enough, the program would collect and analyze various types of data and make recommendations to support each sub-team's mission in real-time. The near-AI-backed tactical program was so powerful it would even give targeting recommendations to individual soldiers in the middle of a firefight.

To the mercenaries, Reynolds said, "Okay, ladies and gents. We're here. Operation Crimson Fall is a go. Teams Four, Five, and Six, you're up. Execute now."

Reynolds opened the door to the JLTV, stepped onto the sidewalk, and gave a quick look down the street toward the South Lawn of the White House. Before the war, the street would have been littered with parked and moving cars, but now, it was mostly empty except for a few parked military vehicles.

There were still people, however. Washington was still home to a few hundred thousand folk committed to the notion of making government function, whether that was the District of Columbia or the UCSA.

It was these people, along with a few armed soldiers, who were out and about this morning.

In the five minutes it had taken them to drive to their current location, Reynolds had changed from his UCSA Army uniform into attire that matched the civil servants walking the street. He had also adorned his face with the smart glasses he would use to send and receive data from the near-AI tactical program and the Indian.

Just as he grabbed a briefcase from the floor from where he'd been sitting, Team Four reached him. They wore civilian clothing, but unlike himself, the two women and three men didn't have the physicality of special ops soldiers. With credentials affixed to their chests and satchels or briefcases in their hands, they looked every bit like the local bureaucrats he'd seen throughout the city.

They didn't stop to speak with him. As they strolled by, Reynolds took up a position at their rear, and as a group, they casually walked in the direction of the Southeast Gate.

As they walked past the façade of the grand Hotel Washington, Team Five and Six quickly confirmed that the doors to the vehicles holding the drones were open and everything was good to go.

In the convoy behind him were six battered Oshkosh Medium Lift Tactical Vehicles with custom-installed racks that would allow nearly seven hundred drones to spool up and zip to whatever task the Savant had assigned them.

From a barge cruising north up the Potomac, another three hundred drones meant for more robust tasks would also be spinning up their fans.

They were three-quarters of the way along the frontage of the vast Treasury Building on their right and the mounted form of General William Tecumseh Sherman on their left when Teams Ten and Eleven confirmed they'd arrived at their positions near the east and west ends of Pennsylvania Avenue. Fifteen men each, these teams would descend on Spector's motorcade if he managed to escape from the building.

The six members of Team Four were now on the east side of Executive Avenue.

Across the street at the Southeast Gate, he made a quick count, and of the individuals he could see, there were twenty armed police and soldiers keeping watch over a small group of civilians in the process of having their IDs checked.

His comms unit still open, Reynolds said, "Team Four is at the release point. All teams wait twenty seconds."

The two female operators leading Team Four started to walk across the street toward the gate. Reynolds and the three male operators moved to follow them, but on reaching the midway point of the avenue, he and the other two operators unlocked the briefcases they were carrying and let them fall open at their sides.

As the three cases opened, Reynolds instantly heard the high-pitched buzzing of sixty drones as they spun up their fans.

His voice like ice, Reynolds said, "We are active, people. All teams are a go. I say again, all teams are a go."

As the Death Adder micro-antipersonnel drones popped into the air and zipped forward in the direction of the gate, the eyes of police, soldiers, and civilians all turned in the direction of the loud, artificial sound coming from Team Four's direction.

In some cases, a few of the police and soldiers moved to grab or raise their weapons, but it was too late. Flying at a speed of seventy miles an hour, the near-AI controlling the micro-drones prioritized any target deemed to be an immediate threat.

In twos and threes, the Death Adders darted within inches of their targets' heads and detonated their explosive charges, sending a spray of ball bearings into exposed necks and faces.

As Reynolds and the rest of Team Four reached underneath their clothing and pulled out suppressed handguns to take down any targets that survived the sudden attack, he heard more detonations as the drones continued to move through the crowd to eliminate anyone who wasn't one of his people.

Even the soldiers inside the guardhouse beside the gate had not been spared.

Trying to flee the slaughter, one of the cops outside the reinforced building ran to the door to find safety. Reynolds had watched as the DC cop hadn't opened the entrance more than half a foot before a trio of drones slipped through the gap and quickly detonated.

He watched in fascination as the bullet-resistant windows contained the energy of the explosions while also serving as a canvas for the occupants' blood.

As the drones finished off the last of the civilians, the two female operators from Team Four jogged to one of the destroyed soldiers. Removing the man's pass, they moved to the guardhouse and quickly gained access to the space.

Seconds later, Reynolds watched with a huge sense of relief as the bollards in front of the gate lowered into the ground just as the steel-reinforced South Gate began to slide open.

As the entrance to the South Lawn opened fully, Reynolds' ears caught the sound of more buzzing, only this time it wasn't high-pitched. It was a deeper hum he'd heard many times before.

Turning around, he saw the Indian's near-AI flying army. Over the street he and Team Four had traversed only five minutes ago were hundreds of different-sized drones moving in all directions.

Further down the street, he saw the various vehicles of the convoy moving toward them. "Here comes the cavalry," he said aloud as the two male operators from Team Four milled around him firing suppressed rounds into the heads of anyone who hadn't been killed outright by the micro drones.

As the JLTV he had ridden into Washington slowed, allowing him to jump into the back seat, he let his mind give birth to the thought that he and the Indian's plan was working, and beautifully.

If all continued to go well, within the next twenty minutes, history would be made, and he'd become a very rich man.

***

As Agent Harry Greer's eyes struggled to make out the dark specs that seemed to be flying in his direction, his earpiece came alive with the voice of the Agent-in-Charge of the President's motorcade. "All agents, be advised the Eagle's Nest has been breached at the Southeast Gate. Hostiles have gained entrance to the South Lawn. I say again, the Southeast Gate has been breached. This is not a drill. Be ready for tactical extrication of Bull Rider. Rustler Two out."

As Greer continued to look above the tree line to the east, he saw agents assigned to the motorcade come forward to line up beside him out of the corner of his eye. In all cases, each agent had their weapon out or was drawing whatever firearm they had on their person.

From the direction of the South Lawn and on the other side of the White House, he heard a long blast of automatic gunfire followed by several explosive pops that sounded like grenades.

The man to his immediate right, a North Carolinian and former US Marshal, pointed to the airborne objects that were most certainly drones and said, "Christ, those things are moving fast."

Someone else further down the line yelled, "Here they come. Protect the motorcade. Open up with everything you've got!"

The order had come from Hines, the agent who took charge of the motorcade when the formal Agent-in-Charge wasn't present. As the driver of one of the motorcade's armored SUVs, Greer only had his Glock 19 on him.

Quickly, he looked over his shoulder at the line of ten black vehicles that were the UCSA President's motorcade and spied one of the two vans that carried the Counter Assault Team. There, he could get his hands on one of the extra shotguns or assault rifles they carried.

As his fellow agents started to open up with their wide assortment of weapons, Greer yelled, "I'll be back!" and stepped toward the closest CAT van.

Before he had taken his second stride, parts of the top of the van exploded upward. As he took in the scene, he watched about two dozen drones pop into the air and race toward the incoming hostile drone units.

Another thirty strides later, he reached the back door of the CAT van. Throwing open its doors, he grabbed one of the Remington 870 shotguns and a bandolier of extra shells. Chambering a round, he ran back to the firing line.

But he was too late.

The attacking drones – dozens of them – had arrived, and like birds of prey streaking from the sky, the units zipped downward and exploded.

Amid a cascade of bright flashes, Greer watched in horror as every agent before him was turned into a screaming, bloody mess.

Cursing, he raised his weapon and placed its sight on one of the many drones still pouring from the sky.

Units much larger than the drones that had just laid waste to his fellow agents dodged and weaved as they got closer to his position.

Bellowing like a man possessed, Greer repeatedly unloaded his weapon, but just as he connected with one of the elusive machines, causing it to fall to the ground, another of the units streaked over his left shoulder.

Before he could turn to see why the drone had spared him, he perceived a bright flash and felt his body begin to hurtle through the air.

As his mind slowed down time, it managed to record the exact moment when his body slammed into and skidded across the circular driveway leading to the front of the White House. Coming to a stop, Greer blinked his eyes rapidly so he could begin to orient himself.

Hearing furious amounts of gunfire, he looked in the direction of the North Portico entrance and saw perhaps two dozen Secret Service agents and police firing their weapons in the air in all directions.

Above them, drones continued to drop from the sky and detonate themselves, killing the building's defenders in ones and twos.

Despite the pain lancing through his body, Greer rolled himself to his hands and knees. Having years of combat experience as a Navy SEAL, he knew to take a moment to let his body reboot.

As he focused his eyes on the pavement beneath him and concentrated on his breathing, the ringing in his ears started to subside.

With a grunt, Greer pushed himself upward and got to one knee. Once again taking in the pitched battle at the front entrance of the White House, he forced himself to get back on his feet.

Standing, he reached into his suit jacket and drew his Glock. It would be next to useless, he knew, but there was nothing inside of Greer, genetic or otherwise, that would prevent him from doing his duty.

He took one unsteady step forward and then another and another. Gaining momentum, he began to run in the direction of the massive overhang at the front of the President's residence.

He was halfway to the portico when a massive explosion bloomed at the far end of the East Executive Avenue, that long and low stretch of building that connected the White House to the East Wing.

Greer watched in horror as a portion of the drones that had been pressing the defenders at the White House's main entrance suddenly knifed in the direction of the pillar of black-and-grey smoke and disappeared within it.

It dawned on him what they were doing. Aloud, he said, "They've created a breach point to get into the building."

He stopped as the last agents and police at the White House's main entrance retreated into the residence. Outside, there was still an uncountable number of drones flitting underneath and around the iconic portico.

Standing alone on the White House's driveway, he turned back to where he had come from to see the whole of the Presidential motorcade a smoking wreck.

The President's limousine, a lesser facsimile of the vehicle that had driven Gloria Menendez and her predecessors when the country was whole, was a blazing inferno. In front and around the vehicles lay scores of the destroyed bodies of his fellow agents and friends.

Tearing his eyes from the surreal scene, Greer looked toward the West Wing. To the best of his knowledge, that was where the president had been.

After a quick scan of the building, he could see drones covering every entrance. They had even stacked themselves in front of the never-used door that led into the Press Gallery Kitchen.

His service pistol still in hand, he took a step in the direction of the West Wing's north entrance. There were only a half-dozen of the machines hovering outside this access point, and while his brain told him it would be useless to continue the fight, his heart wouldn't let him do anything else.

It was imperfect, but he still believed in the UCSA, and he had given an oath to protect its Commander-in-Chief.

As he got within firing distance of the deadly flying machines, Greer raised his weapon and took aim, but as he did so, two of the drones rotated in his direction. Together, the pair began to advance.

With the sound of an intense firefight coming from the direction of the South Lawn, Greer didn't hear the third machine that had positioned itself at his rear.

Taking a deep breath, he pulled the trigger of his pistol and saw one of the two grapefruit-sized drones approaching him flinch, wobble, and then drop to the ground.

He placed the sight of his pistol on the second drone but didn't get the chance to pull the trigger.

Greer barely registered the explosion behind him as his body was thrown forward.

As he tumbled to the ground, his vision swam and caught fractured glimpses of the sky and the looming shadows of the drones circling above him. He tried to raise his weapon to remain in the fight, but whatever the reason, he couldn't make his arm move.

As he struggled to breathe and as his brain fought to make sense of the monumental pain wracking his body, a strange peace began to settle over him. A peace that, without warning, turned into darkness.

***

As it had been every day since he'd taken up residence in Washington, their lunch would be a working one. Spector sat back in his chair as the orderlies brought trays of sandwiches and coffee into the Cabinet Room.

This meeting, his third of the day, had focused on the incessant challenge of how to get enough fuel into the nation's supply chain so that people across the country could fill up their vehicles whenever they wanted.

It had been a stubborn ongoing problem for the UCSA since CANZUK had entered the war, and it had only become worse since the US Navy had decided to officially throw in with California.

On first joining the war, CANZUK had been able to cause enough damage to the UCSA's own oil refineries that Spector had directed his Energy Secretary to negotiate deals with Venezuela and Nigeria to supplement the country's gasoline reserves.

But no sooner had these deals been struck than British and Canadian submarines began to hunt and sink the tankers transporting fuels and other critical chemicals from these countries.

Because of the neutral status of Venezuela and the others and because each sunk tanker was its own monumental environmental disaster, CANZUK's international reputation had suffered, but this had not stopped them from sinking ships or even going so far as to sabotage the refining capacity in several of the countries trying to support the UCSA war machine.

Eventually, as enough Chinese air defense units were brought into the country, the UCSA was able to repair enough of its refinery capacity that it could keep almost ninety percent of the country's gas stations operating with a three-day reserve of fuel. It had been a major domestic victory for Spector and had gone some distance to cool down the tension growing in most of the UCSA's major cities.

But with the entry of the US Navy into the war, all that had changed. Thankfully, because of crew desertions and maintenance issues, none of the Navy's aircraft carriers in the US Northeast or Europe could be put into service. Early in the civil war, the admirals had consolidated all their trained officers and pilots in California to keep three of its eleven aircraft carriers operational.

As it stood presently, the only aircraft carrier they had to contend with on the East Coast was the Royal Navy's *Prince of Wales*, and it hadn't been able to strike a refinery in weeks.

In contrast to its carrier fleet, the US Navy's submarine force was in better shape. In keeping with its policy to stay out of the war, the admirals had given orders to dock most of its East Coast submarines in the ports of friendly allies and made arrangements with those countries to house their sailors indefinitely.

Canada, for example, had taken in one Ohio-class ballistic missile sub and two Virginia-class fast attack boats, while Britain had taken in no less than seven vessels and their crews.

But within one week of the US Navy entering the war, the number of submarines in the Atlantic capable of sinking UCSA-bound ships or launching cruise missiles at his country's refineries had tripled.

As Spector reached for the ham sandwich in front of him, he looked across the table at his Energy Secretary, Melissa Gardner, and said, "So our biggest refineries along the Gulf Coast are offline for the next six weeks at least, maybe longer depending on when our enemies run out of cruise missiles. Is that correct?"

"That's correct, Mr. President."

"And based on the advice of the military, you agree that we should build up and harden the capacity of several smaller refineries located in Kansas, Tennessee, and northern Georgia?"

"That's my strong recommendation, sir. The refineries along the Gulf are just too exposed. There are two refineries tucked into the Appalachians that would be ideal for this initiative. It'll take us eight months, but once we convert and expand their infrastructure, we can produce up to seventy million gallons of gasoline and diesel fuel per day. This would represent sixty-seven percent of our daily consumption needs."

"And we'd be able to protect them?" Spector said.

As the Energy Secretary started to give her reply, she was cut off by what was most certainly a long rip of automatic gunfire.

Across the table, General Hoffman exclaimed, "Who the hell is firing a weapon?"

Spector's head snapped in the direction of the room's huge windows, but before he could get up to try to see what was going on, the two doors to the Cabinet Room burst open, allowing a half-dozen Secret Service agents to rush in.

As a foursome of heavily armed agents surrounded Spector, it was the Agent-in-Charge who addressed the room. "The White House is under some type of mass drone attack. The President and all Cabinet officials in the building are to be taken to the PEOC in the East Wing. We need to move now!"

As the Agent-in-Charge finished giving instructions, a series of quick explosions shook the room's walls.

Without warning, two of the agents standing beside Spector grabbed his arms and began to pull him in the direction of the closest doorway. As more automatic weapons began to echo outside, Spector made no effort to resist their movement, and though he was overweight, he remained a powerful man who could move quickly when he needed to.

But as they entered the hallway, instead of allowing his protectors to guide him to the right, he tore from their grasp and bounded left into the Oval Office.

As the Agent-in-Charge bellowed for him to stop, Spector reached his desk, opened the drawer, and pulled out a loaded .357 Colt Python revolver.

His father had given it to him just before he'd died. A JAG officer for thirty-four years, the old man had kept the weapon in his desk during the years he'd served as a military judge.

Holding the weapon with its barrel pointed at the ceiling, Spector said to the agents who had chased him into the office, "Sorry, but I'm not going anywhere without this. I may be your president, but I'm also a general and a Texan, and if people are going to try and kill me today, I'll be damned if I don't tag a few of them myself."

With the gun, he gestured to the doorway and said, "I'm still getting to know this place and have no idea where this PEOC place is, so lead the way, gentlemen. This time, I promise I won't leave your side."

***

The JLTV Reynolds was riding in didn't have a turret, but it did have an open space that allowed the person sitting in the middle rear seat to stand and operate a weapon. And to his right, that's exactly what the former Marine was doing as his vehicle, and those from the rest of the convoy slowly rolled forward in a line across the South Lawn.

Using a REAPR .338-caliber medium machine gun, the one-time gunnery sergeant, along with a dozen other similarly armed men, were pouring thousands of rounds per minute into anything moving outside or inside the White House.

At the same time, the tactical drones escorting them were darting forward and exploding themselves in the general vicinity of anything not cut down by the hailstorm of lead being sent forth from the convoy.

Through the bullet-pocked windshield, Reynolds could see men in dark suits fighting and dying along the Truman Balcony and the two sets of curving steps that led to the White House's main floor.

Here and there, he could see slashes of red contrast with the alabaster white of the building's exterior.

As the JLTV came to a stop thirty meters from where they would enter the building, Reynolds said, "Teams One, Two, and Three standby."

He pressed a toggle on his wrist unit to switch to the channel that would connect him to the Indian. "Tiger, we're in place. Time to make history."

"Copy, Lion. Breach is happening now."

From the barge four miles south on the Potomac, two heavy weapons drones, each carrying a pair of multi-purpose AGM-114R Hellfire missiles, had raced into the core of the city the moment chaos erupted around the White House.

Tucking themselves onto the top of a building half a mile south of Reynolds' current location, on the Savant's command, the two drones sprung into the air, and upon reconfirming their respective targets, they launched three of their four missiles.

Through the open hatch where the gunnery sergeant was still firing with his machine gun, Reynolds heard the distinctive scream of the missiles as they traveled the short distance to their targets.

Reopening the channel that would connect with his assault force, Reynolds said, "Teams One, Two, Three. Move. Move. Move."

As he said the last "move' the three missiles struck their targets.

To his right, two Hellfires slammed into the entrance of the White House's East Wing. It was underneath this building that the Presidential Emergency Operations Center was located. A secure and fortified space with supplies and top-tier communications equipment, the PEOC could be defended for hours, if not days.

The information he'd been given suggested that Spector and his people felt safe in the White House and had not made plans to use the out-of-the-way facility.

Nevertheless, the two missiles that had just hammered that part of the complex would make it difficult, if not impossible, for their target to make it to this space.

The third missile had streaked in low over the convoy and smashed into the very center of the White House at ground level. It was through this smoking gash that the three twelve-man assault teams he had just ordered forward would access the building.

As chunks of debris from the missile strikes fell to the ground around him, and as weapons fire from the convoy continued to lash the exterior of the building, Reynolds ran forward to join the group of operators twenty yards from the newly formed entrance.

A dozen feet away from the smoking breach point, a clutch of volleyball-sized drones suddenly fell out of the sky and positioned themselves around the new entrance.

As the drones hovered in place, Team One, with its twelve special operators, positioned themselves to be the first to enter the building.

This was the group Reynolds attached himself to.

All three breach teams were made up of American operators. Unless it were necessary, he would not let any of the foreign mercenaries enter this hallowed ground. In Reynolds' mind, what was about to happen would remain a family affair.

Without warning, the dozen or so Urban Tactics Anti-Personnel – UTAP – drones hovering in front of Team One darted into the obscure interior of the Diplomatic Reception room.

Via the jagged hole, Reynolds heard a torrent of gunfire as the defenders engaged the drones. In response to the attack, some number of the UTAPs released stun grenades or raced forward and exploded within a few feet of whoever was shooting at them. In all, Reynolds heard three distinct detonations.

As he was not the leader of Team One, Reynolds kept his mouth shut for reasons of professional courtesy.

As per the official plan, he was tagging along with Team One to keep an eye on this critical part of the mission. In what remained of their task, he didn't have any more tactical responsibilities. Rather, in consultation with the Indian and the Savant, his only job was to guide the overall effort to hunt down the UCSA president.

As if the man had been reading Reynolds' mind, the former Green Beret leading Team One gave the order to enter the building.

Still wearing civilian clothes but now sporting a chest rig, helmet, and a Colt M5 carbine, Reynolds was the last of Team One to step over the smoking rubble of the new entrance and storm into the White House.

The oval-shaped Diplomatic Reception room was now a chaotic mess.

In what Reynolds was sure wouldn't be the last historic tragedy of the day, large chunks of the cherished landscape mural that covered the oval walls of the space were torn or actively burning.

As he jogged through the room, he easily dismissed the despoilation of his country's cultural heritage. All that mattered to him and to the men who were further into the building was collecting on the hundreds of millions in crypto they'd been promised.

With his weapon at the ready, Reynolds strode into the Center Hall. This was the main thoroughfare that linked the White House to the East and West Wings.

Looking to his left, he saw the mercenary captain of Team One standing in the doorway of what Reynolds knew to be the one and only Secret Service station inside the White House. Arriving at the man's location, he looked inside the hub and saw that, as planned, one of the UTAP drones had detonated itself in the space.

A single body with a destroyed face lay sprawled in the middle of the room. To his surprise, it was a female agent. A shame, he thought. Outside of her mangled face, the rest of her was attractive.

Pulling his eyes from the body, he turned back to the door leading into the Diplomatic Reception room to see the second breach team arrive. As the last of Team Two appeared, it was followed by another clutch of UTAP drones.

Over the next half-minute, two dozen of the killing machines entered the hall. Despite their deafening sound, Reynolds was thrilled by their numbers. It was only because of these units they would be able to get to Spector in the time they had.

The excited voice of the Indian suddenly spoke in his earbud. "We just had eyes on the target."

"Where?" Reynolds said calmly.

"He's in the West Wing. We just got a good look at him through a window. They saw you enter the main building and they know we've destroyed the motorcade. They just tried to leave out of the west-side entrance, but we had it covered. We just killed a half-dozen agents who tried to make a break for it. That was only a minute ago. It's your move, Lion."

"How do their reinforcements look?" asked Reynolds.

"They're organizing themselves. The near-AI estimates you have twenty minutes to get this done."

"I won't need half of that. Lion out."

Reynolds opened the channel for the three breach captains. "The target is in the West Wing on the main floor. As of one minute ago, he was near the west-side entrance. They know they're trapped. Teams One and Two will gain entrance to the West Wing. Team Three will hold this position and act as a Rapid Reaction Force. We need this done in ten minutes. Move, people."

Chapter 40

Harrington Lake, Quebec

―

When the two Chinook helicopters set down on the edge of Gatineau Park nearly sixty minutes earlier, Dune was the first to run down the ramp. Behind him were thirty commandos from CSOR. In the other Chinook were another twenty CSOR operators and a handful of JTF-2 commandos.

CSOR had just returned from California two days before, and if they'd waited another two hours, Dune wouldn't have been available to join the op.

As it was, he and one other CSOR officer, Major Bradford, were the only officers available to lead the mission. The remaining frontline leaders had bugged out of Petawawa for some well-deserved leave. The smaller JTF-2 contingent was being led by their 2IC, Lt. Colonel Collette.

Dune knew of the man only through reputation. It looked like he could bench-press a thousand pounds and was said to be hard-charging but also an exceptional leader of men. Apparently, he'd come from the Royal Canadian Navy's Naval Boarding unit.

The CSOR major and Collette were thirty yards ahead of him.

Together, the officers had pushed the two groups of special operators hard. Gatineau Park was within the Gatineau Hills, and since unloading from the Chinooks, they had set a blistering pace through undulating and dense forest.

It was as they were starting to come down from the most recent elevation that Lt. Colonel Collette's fist rose into the air, bringing the two rows of commandos to a near-silent stop. As the colonel opened his fist and slowly patted toward the ground, Dune and the soldiers to his left and right got down to one knee.

It was then that a hushed voice began to speak into his BAM. "We're three hundred meters out. The ETA of Assault Group Bravo is twenty mikes, so we have that much time to get to the designated attack line. Sniper teams make their way forward. The rest of us will depart in five. From this moment on, no one makes a peep, or I'll personally wreck you and your career when this is over."

The JTF-2 2IC let his threat percolate in everyone's ears for a spell and then continued. "When we reach the jump-off point, on my word, Viper Two will lead the first wave. Viper Sunray – me, will lead the second. If it's needed, Viper Three will lead the reserve. No matter what happens, no matter what confronts us, we take the residence, and we take Target Omega alive. It couldn't be more simple, people. Viper Sunray out."

The moment the JTF-2 officer finished his address, three sets of sniper teams got up and slowly moved into the bush in front of them.

Five minutes later, Dune and the rest of the assault group got to their feet, and like ghosts, ninety of Canada's best soldiers stalked forward, knowing what could happen in the next thirty minutes could be the most consequential use of military force in Canadian history.

***

"What do you mean the RCMP is not letting them pass?" Merielle said into her phone.

After a moment of listening to her new chief of staff, she said, "I don't care what you need to do, but you need to find a way for the reporters to get here. I was told that you know Ottawa as well as anyone, Gary, so make it happen. Now!"

Merielle ended the call, and as much as she wanted to slam the phone into the desk she was standing behind, she slowly placed the device down and locked her eyes on Aziz.

Not flinching from her stare, he said, "We knew this could happen, and we've taken appropriate precautions. Gary is a wizard of Ottawa. He'll get it sorted out quickly enough. We're the ones in control. Trust me, Merielle, there's no one in this country that can move fast enough to stop what we're about to do."

"I wish I felt as confident as you sound," Merielle said.

"We both know this country and the bureaucracy that serves it," Aziz said calmly. "They are still trying to figure out what happened on the Hill this morning, and it'll be another day or two before they can decide on any action. By then, you'll have your

MPs back in line, and those few who won't play along will be taken away. Patience is what we need for the moment, Madame Prime Minister."

Just as he finished delivering his reassurance, Aziz's hand moved to the back pocket of his jeans to retrieve his phone. Activating it, he quickly tapped the screen several times, and as he did so, a look of concern began to emerge on his face.

"What's wrong?" asked Merielle from across the room.

Aziz said nothing. Instead, he moved in her direction and showed her the screen of his phone.

On the display, she saw video of a group of soldiers with painted faces carrying various automatic weapons walking through a dense green forest. The video was taken from above as though it was from high in a tree.

When her eyes came up from the screen, Aziz's index finger was pointing west, and he said, "That way, two hundred meters. Fifty to one hundred men. CANSOFCOM, of that, there's no question."

Merielle's eyes snapped in the direction Aziz had been pointing. "They wouldn't dare."

As she rounded back on Aziz to rattle off the first of a dozen questions, his hand was in the air signaling to her to hold off. His phone was at his ear. As he listened to whomever was speaking, his brown eyes were shifting rapidly.

The phone then dropped from his ear, and with his other hand, Aziz produced a small handset that he'd been wearing on his belt. He depressed the unit's button and said, "Echo-Seven, is your mobile signal dead?"

When only static came as the reply, he repeated, "Echo-Seven, what is your status?"

When no reply came, he dropped the radio from his face and locked his eyes on Merielle. "They're coming. I don't know how many, but we shouldn't stay here. We need to get where the public can see you. They won't move on you if you're surrounded by reporters and the public."

Merielle, instantly appreciating their predicament, said, "The reporters waiting at the park entrance. We only need to make it to them."

"Agreed," Aziz said quickly.

With an urgency to her voice, Merielle said, "Get the vehicles and your people ready. I'll grab the MPs. Let's be ready to move in five, if not faster."

Instead of a reply, Aziz's eyes widened and then moved toward the study's large window that overlooked the lake.

Like a big cat, he surged toward the window and quickly opened it. Tilting his head, he listened for a few moments.

As he turned back to Merielle, she too could hear the sound of helicopters in the distance. Before either of them could speak of the new sound, there was an aggressive knock on the door.

"Come in!" Merielle said in a firm voice.

The door swung open, and one of Aziz's lieutenants barged into the room. Looking at Aziz, he said, "Our comms have been shut down, and helicopters are coming. There are six or so of them flying down the length of the lake and –."

Aziz cut the man off. "We're leaving, Sergeant. I want the motorcade in front of the residence in three minutes. We're gonna run light. I need most of you to stay here to hold back what's coming. You need to give us ten minutes. You good with that, soldier?"

"We're all in, sir," the man said without hesitation.

"Good, then make it happen."

As the White Unit operative sprang into action, Aziz turned back to Merielle. "You may need a few of my men to get your people to move quickly."

Merielle nodded and said, "Good idea."

She then strode toward the study's desk, pulled open its top drawer and withdrew a holstered pistol.

Merielle tucked the weapon into the small of her back. This done, her eyes reconnected with Aziz, and in a voice that sounded like she wasn't screwing around, she said, "Five minutes, we meet you at the motorcade. Go!"

***

The top speed of the three Super Griffon gunships leading their flight was 260 kilometers an hour, and, for most of their trip from Petawawa, that's how fast they'd flown.

A kilometer ahead of him, Larocque spied the three gunships bank right as they transitioned from flying only a few meters above the emerald-green treetops of Gatineau Park to the pristine blue water that was Lake Harrington.

Larocque activated his BAM. "Open Channel Three-Alpha."

"Channel is open," advised his BAM.

"All units, this is Raptor Sunray. Raptor Force is three mikes out. Viper Force, commence your attack in two minutes."

"Roger that, Raptor. We'll jump off in two mikes."

"Solid copy, Viper Sunray. We'll see you on the ground," replied Larocque.

"Hold one, Raptor," said the officer leading the CSOR and JTF-2 assaulters just west of the cottage. "We've got vehicles moving to the residence. It looks like the motorcade is getting ready to move."

"Roger that, Viper," Larocque said coolly, confirming the new info. "It sounds like we've been made. Make your move, Viper. I suggest at least part of your force move to the road to interdict the convoy if it gets underway."

"Roger that, Raptor. I'll send the reserve force that way now. Viper Sunray out."

Sitting at the door of one of the two CH-525 Rocs, Larocque could easily see the PM's secondary residence at the end of the lake. "Open Channel to Cobra Team."

"Channel to Cobra Team open," advised the voice of the BAM.

"Team Cobra, if the motorcade leaves the residence, you are to target and destroy the lead vehicle the moment it leaves the residence grounds. Make it as hard as possible for the rest of the convoy to get on the road. Confirm order, Cobra One."

"Raptor Sunray, this is Cobra One. We have a solid copy on that order. I'll do it myself."

"Roger that, Cobra, Raptor Sunray out," Larocque said, ending the transmission.

Ahead, Larocque watched as the three Super Griffons arrived at the end of the lake. While two of the gunships banked right and climbed into the air, the third turned left and released a trail of flares as a white streak flew into the air from a barn-like structure at the south end of the property.

The surface-to-air missile wasn't fooled by the flares and slammed into the exposed right flank of the Super Griffon, setting off an explosion bright enough to compete with the cloudless morning sun. As the wounded helicopter began to free-fall toward the green canopy below, Larocque unleashed a string of vicious curses.

Ahead of him, his eyes were drawn to the underside of the two Chinooks carrying the bulk of his assault force.

From their bellies, a dozen anti-missile drones appeared and dropped toward the lake. Just before they impacted the water's surface, each small machine came alive and raced ahead of the two lumbering transport helicopters.

From the same location where the first SAM appeared, another white streak bloomed, but this time, it was headed toward the lead Chinook.

At the exact moment the missile had leapt from the ground, half of the air-defense drones raced forward to meet the threat, and as one, they detonated themselves, taking the SAM down.

Just as Larocque was about to open a channel to the two remaining gunships to order them to lay into whoever was launching the surface-to-air missiles, he heard the distinct *brump brump brump* as one of the Super Griffon's door gunners opened up with a fifty-cal.

Satisfied the SAM threat was being taken care of, his eyes returned to the Chinooks. Together, the wheels of the two helos slammed into the well-manicured lawn forty meters from the front of their objective.

With their ramps already down, eighty heavily armed paratroopers from the Canadian Airborne Regiment swarmed out of the bellies of the ugly-looking machines.

Their boots on the ground, the two groups of soldiers raced forward, assumed the prone position and together, trained every one of their weapons on the building to their front.

It was a textbook insertion.

As the two Chinooks began to rise into the air, Larocque tapped his BAM wrist unit, activating the direct link he'd established with his own helicopter's pilot. "Major set us down right behind my boys."

"Roger that, Raptor. We're one mike out."

Before Larocque could acknowledge the update, the helo he was flying in dropped closer to the lake and started to shed its airspeed.

In less than one minute, the two Rocs would do as the Chinooks had just done, but they would unload Larocque, the Airborne's field surgeon team, members of the CSIS DAT, and a handful of RCMP officers. And together, God willing, they'd arrest Merielle Martel.

***

As Merielle walked down the stairs onto the main floor of the residence, she wore a look of tranquillity. Following her were four White Unit operatives, each wearing balaclavas, and the young woman who had been with her during her first conversation with the MPs.

"We are leaving. All of us," she said as she stepped onto the worn hardwood floor.

On seeing Merielle coming down the stairs, MacPhail had been the first to stand and walk in the direction of the PM. But as she squared her shoulders and prepared to address Merielle, Shandra stepped in front of her, held up the folder with her name on it, and said, "This is an outrage, Merielle, and one you won't get away with. None of us are signing anything and certainly, we won't be helping this coup or whatever it is you're doing."

The MP took another step toward Merielle, and in a voice nearing shrill, she said, "None of us. Do you understand?"

What happened next took place with near inhuman speed.

The unremarkable woman flowed past Merielle and stabbed with something in her right hand in the direction of Shandra's diaphragm. The instant the object connected with the MP, there was a familiar crackling sound.

As a cry of pain issued from Shandra's mouth, she staggered backward, crashing into MacPhail, causing the two women to become entangled and fall to the floor.

MacPhail issued a yelp as the full weight of Shandra slammed into her torso, forcing all of the air out of her lungs.

As she struggled to breathe, the woman who had waylaid Shandra moved to stand over the MP and, from her back, produced a handgun, which she pointed in Shandra's direction.

Quietly, she said, "You have one chance to live." Then she fired a single shot into the politician's right shoulder. Shandra screamed in agony as the bullet tore into her body.

Almost at a yell, the woman with the handgun said, "Get up and do as you're told, or the next bullet goes into your skull. And that goes for the rest of you."

When Shandra made no move to comply with the woman's order, MacPhail got to her knees and moved to the gasping woman's side. "She'll come. We'll come," MacPhail said reassuringly.

The woman moved her eyes from Shandra to MacPhail and then back to Shandra. Slowly, she moved the barrel of her pistol so it was aligned with the wounded MP's head.

Before MacPhail could scream in protest, Merielle's voice sounded from behind. "That's enough. They've said they'll come along, so that's what they'll do."

The woman holding the gun gave Shandra a hard stare but eventually stepped back. When she did, the masked men stepped forward. Two gathered up Shandra while the other two helped MacPhail get to her feet.

In a commanding voice, Merielle said, "Bring them to the motorcade. You can address the wound when we're on the move."

Hearing the instruction, the single masked man now holding MacPhail shoved her forward in the direction that Merielle was walking. "Move!" he barked.

As she started to walk, MacPhail heard the unmistakable sound of a helicopter outside the building.

When she tried to crane her neck toward the lake where the sound was coming from, Merielle's henchmen gave her another quick shove. "Eyes front or you'll get the same treatment as your treasonous friend."

Doing as she was told, MacPhail strode forward to a pair of double doors that Merielle had just moved through.

Reaching the outside, she saw eight SUVs, but instead of the RCMP protection detail MacPhail was used to seeing, there were more of the masked men. All of them were armed with assault rifles, and most were looking not in the direction of the residence but toward the forest that bordered the property.

But it was what she saw next that stopped her in her tracks.

On the grounds, in the same direction the guards were looking, MacPhail instantly recognized a score of four-legged machines that she knew had been used on the evening Bob MacDonald had been assassinated. To her untrained eye, they looked like the very same units the CANZUK militaries had encountered in upstate New York and Vietnam.

The name of the near-AI killing machine struck MacPhail just as the same guard gave her another shove to the back to keep moving. As she resumed her walk, she watched as the Hyenas stalked in the direction of the wall of trees less than sixty meters away.

Reaching the SUV she would be riding in, the second to last in the convoy, another masked gunman met her and, without warning, grabbed her arms and then roughly guided her to her seat.

In her ear, he whispered, "Behave, or it's a bullet in your head, you traitorous bitch."

MacPhail, with none of the courage of Shandra, said nothing. Even if she wanted to reply, she couldn't have, because in that very moment, all hell broke loose.

***

Dune had been twenty meters from the tree line when the word came that a pack of X5 Hyenas was prowling toward the CSOR and JTF-2 assaulters. Collette's voice came across the BAM, "Viper Three, take your boys one hundred meters east and set an ambush on the road leading from the cottage. If the motorcade gets away, it doesn't get past you, understand?"

Before Dune could reply, three Super Griffon gunships climbed into the air from the lake, their rotor blades drowning out the sounds of the forest surrounding him. Two of the machines broke left at the lake's edge and flew directly over his position while a single gunship banked right.

He lost sight of the lone helicopter through the trees just as he heard the snap of what sounded like a missile being launched. This was immediately followed by an ear-cracking explosion that came from the direction of where the single Griffon had been.

As his eyes snapped toward the sound, Collette's voice roared in his BAM, repeating his order to get moving, only this time it was punctuated with a string of F-bombs.

"But the Hyenas?" Dune replied, yelling.

"I don't want to hear about the Hyenas. Get moving and set the ambush. Confirm that order, Viper Three!"

"Roger. We're on our way. Viper Three out."

***

Collette, the 2IC for JTF-2, hadn't yet encountered the Hyenas or their near-AI brethren, the bipedal Wraiths, and truth be told, he was hoping it would remain that way for however much longer the war went on.

He'd heard from army intelligence and soldiers themselves how difficult these things were to kill and how quickly they could move.

Ahead, through what remained of the forest, he counted twenty of the bloody things slowly approaching their position. What was a challenging assault on a single building that may or may not have hostages had just turned into a suicide mission.

He looked beyond the PM's cottage and saw the two Chinooks coming in to land the Airborne. They were to assault the other side of the building.

Just as the wheels of the two big helos hit the ground, half of the Hyenas that had been stalking in his direction stopped and, as one, turned their arm-like heads in the direction of the offloading paratroopers. Then, without warning and like they had been shot out of a cannon, their feet tore up the grass they had been stalking across and high-tailed it toward the newly arriving soldiers.

He was now facing half the number of deadly automatons. Above, Collette could hear the whomping of the two remaining gunships. One was armed with a mini-gun, the other a fifty-cal. They also had SPIKE missiles, but those wouldn't be of use in helping to put down what lay between his men and their objective.

Without warning, the air filled with a torrent of automatic gunfire. The Airborne had seen the Hyenas and opened up on the threat.

At the cottage, his eyes caught new movement around the motorcade. People dressed as civvies were being rushed into SUVs by masked men.

It was now or never.

He had a single C6 7.62 machine gun being operated by one of the CSOR men. The commando was only a few feet to his right.

Getting up, Collette moved to the soldier and got on one knee. Ahead, he could see his movement had caught the eye of one of the Hyenas. Its head swiveled in his direction, as did the rest of the autos.

To the CSOR machine gunner, Collette said, "As soon as I give the word, try to make a path for us."

The commando grunted.

Collette stood and grabbed a C13 grenade from his chest rig and bellowed, "Ready grenades!"

Up and down the line, his own JTF-2 assaulters and the CSOR commandos, each with at least two grenades on their battle armor, got to their knees and moved to ready their own weapons.

After a count of five, he bellowed, "Throw grenades!"

Whether or not they'd been told to hold their position or because their near-AI brains couldn't figure out what Collette and his men were up to, the Hyenas arrayed against them only stared in their direction, the weapons on their backs remaining silent.

It was only when the commandos' grenades started to land among them that they began to react. While half the autos opened up with the assault rifles or grenade launchers on their backs, the other half sprinted forward.

As the C6 opened up on full auto below him, at the top of his lungs, Collette screamed, "Charge!"

***

When Merielle stepped out of the cottage, she entered a war zone.

Inside, Aziz had forced her to put on a ballistics vest, and with him and two other masked men in the lead, they raced with their heads down for the fourth SUV.

As she ran, bullets snapped over her head and made a loud smacking sound as they made contact with the wood siding of the residence.

Making it to their vehicle, she scampered into a seat. Looking west, she was floored to see a line of Chinese Hyenas firing their turreted weapons at a line of men wearing Canadian Army combats charging out of the tree line.

As she took in the surreal scene, the ground around the Hyenas exploded in a series of ear-splitting detonations. Merielle flinched as shrapnel from the firestorm slammed into the window she was looking through to create a handful of white divots.

Of the five Hyenas that had been standing and firing their weapons at the still-charging soldiers, only two remained operational, but it was enough. In quick succession, a handful of the human attackers fell to the ground as they were cut down by the Chinese kill-bots.

Behind her and outside the SUV, Merielle heard Aziz bellow, "Move, move, move!"

She turned in his direction, and as he flew into the seat beside her, she growled at him, "Where did those come from, and why are they shooting at Canadian soldiers?"

As the SUV moved forward, Aziz turned to her and snapped, "The autos can be purchased on the black market. The same black market where they'd been purchased to help kill your former boss. They're what I would call insurance."

His explanation paused as his side of the vehicle was raked with bullets. He barely flinched as a line of pockmarks appeared beside his head in the window.

When the rounds stopped coming, he resumed his response. "As for the soldiers, you should have never elevated Larocque. He's coming for you. You may like the man, and he may think highly of you, but I know men like Jackson Larocque. You can't turn a patriot from his country any more than you can get a zealot to walk away from his religion. Let's just hope we get to those reporters. If we can, the initiative will be back in our hands."

He turned away from her and looked forward.

The lead SUV of their convoy was entering the narrow paved road that would lead them in the direction of Ottawa and the reporters at the edge of the park and away from the growing shitshow behind them.

As their vehicle passed into the natural overhang of trees that lined the roadway, Merielle heard a loud tearing sound and a deafening *WHOOMP!*

Ahead, the SUV leading the motorcade ejected high into the air. At its apex, the vehicle and everyone inside it transformed into a sphere of orange-and-yellow fire.

As the explosion's energy rocked their SUV, their driver hit the brakes, as did the rest of the vehicles in the convoy. Aziz unloaded a string of curses, then put his radio handset to his mouth and yelled, "Vehicle two, drive past it. Everyone keep moving deeper into the trees, we'll be safe there. Keep moving, or we're dead!"

But Aziz's order had come too late.

Twenty meters in front of the burning SUV, Merielle caught sight of a massive tree beginning to lean in the direction of their escape route.

Slowly but inexorably, the giant maple gave way to gravity, and with a thunderous roar of snapping wood, it collapsed across the roadway.

Together, Aziz and Merielle looked at one another. Before she could say anything, he opened his door and extricated himself from the vehicle. Turning back to her, he said, "I'm going to go and sort this out myself. Don't move."

"Aziz –" she said sternly, but he had already turned away and was walking to the front of the motorcade.

She watched him disappear around the next vehicle.

Cracking her window slightly, Merielle strained to hear everything and anything happening around the convoy. Behind, she could still hear gunfire and the yelling of voices. The bellows were getting closer. Above was the thumping of helicopters. Ahead, in the direction where Aziz had gone, she heard nothing.

Just as she put her hand on the handle to open the door, the masked White Unit operative in the passenger seat said in an awe-filled voice, "Fucking unbelievable. It's him."

"It's who?" she asked quickly, but as soon as the question left her lips, Merielle knew what the man's answer would be.

The operative pointed to his side-view mirror and said, "Behind us. See for yourself."

Merielle moved forward in her seat, then craned her neck to get the right angle on the mirror.

Once she could see what the operative could, she let loose with a resigned sigh and said, "Stay here."

"But –" the masked man started.

Merielle cut him off. "I said stay put. Enough people have been killed for one day."

She reached to her back and grabbed her pistol. She then opened the door and listened. The gunfire had stopped. Now, she could only hear the sound of yelling voices.

Merielle stepped onto the road, closed the SUV's door and turned to confront the man whom she had been sure would share her vision for securing the country they both loved so much.

Chapter 41

White House, The West Wing

The Indian couldn't manage as many screens or drones as his younger and more talented associate, the man Reynolds called 'the Savant,' but for the number he could manage, he could do some extraordinary things.

On his main display was the live stream from Reynolds' tactical glasses. He was standing behind the soldier in charge of Team One, and together, they were looking across the West Colonnade, which led to the entrance of the West Wing.

In his headphones, Reynolds' voice materialized, and the former Green Beret said, "Tiger, hit the entrance with the heavy stuff. Do it now."

"Confirmed, Lion. The heavy stuff is on its way. It'll be there in thirty seconds," the Indian replied calmly.

On hearing Reynolds' request, the near-AI of the tactical drone management program instantly brought up the targeting stream of the drone carrying the remaining Hellfire.

In his top right screen, he could see the near-AI had already placed the drone's targeting laser on the Rose Garden entrance of what was one of the most consequential buildings of the past one hundred years.

As a non-American, it wasn't lost on the Indian what he was doing to this iconic building. It was as if he were back home firing missiles into the Taj Mahal. It was an architectural crime against humanity, but there was no help for it. The forty-three million in cryptocurrency he was set to be paid if this mission was a success would set him up for life, and being just thirty-two years of age, this was no small thing.

He triggered the weapon and watched as it travelled the short distance from the drone to the entrance Reynolds and the rest of his people would use to start the last and most critical part of their mission.

Switching back to the view supplied from Reynolds' glasses, the Indian could see that the audacious special forces operator was already dashing to the smoking hole he'd created.

By the time Reynolds was halfway across the Rose Garden promenade, a dozen of the Savant's UTAP drones had zipped into the dust-filled gash. Via Reynolds' glasses, the Indian heard several quick explosions emanate from beyond the destroyed entrance.

As Reynolds reached the West Wing, the Indian forced himself to drop the feed. Whether or not they got Spector, it was now his job to ensure the remaining eighty-nine operators in and around the White House had a way to get out of DC.

With a single verbal command, all but one of his screens transitioned to the feeds of the anti-armor drones he'd flown to the tops of various buildings in the early morning darkness. With another command, a tactical map of Washington's core appeared on this main display.

Using a handful of hugely expensive recce drones all but invisible to the naked eye and radar, the Indian could see the various columns of vehicles moving in the direction of the White House. Helpfully, the near-AI program had already prioritized targets for him. He approved the plan.

Aloud, he said, "The barge."

Instantly, the screen to the left of the targeting overlay of DC showed the live feed from the top of the river barge's wheelhouse. Lined up along the length of the barge were three dozen drones, each of which was the size of a small car.

The Indian's fingers danced across the keyboard in front of him. A second later, as one, each of the logistics drones fired up their eight fans, and in ones and twos, they began to rise into the air.

He marveled as all thirty-six units were airborne and started to move north up the Potomac. Of everything that had been pulled together for this world-breaking mission, this was the part he was most proud of. Not even the near-AI had thought to use the drones in the way they were about to be used.

Feeling delighted with all he'd done to get to this point, the Indian said aloud and to himself, "Ladies and gentlemen, there goes the cavalry, and to me comes forty-three million."

***

The explosion on the other side of the building rocked the floor underneath Spector's feet. Tripping as he rounded yet another corner in the labyrinth that was the West Wing, he fell in a messy heap to the ground.

Instantly, a pair of Secret Service agents were on him, trying to get him to his feet. Things had gotten bad enough that they didn't bother to ask him if he was okay. The two strong men simply grabbed at his shoulders and, with a pair of grunts, hauled him to his feet.

To his credit, Spector had helped in the process. He might be overweight, but he had been a general only a year ago and was still spry enough that, with the help of the two younger men, he was back on his feet in only a few seconds.

They were in the hallway outside the Vice President's office, a position he had chosen not to fill. Ahead of him and behind were at least a dozen agents. Looking through the Lobby Room at the very center of the complex, Spector saw the agent-in-charge come flying around the corner from the direction where the explosion had taken place.

Reaching him, in a firm but low voice, the agent said, "They've breached the entrance at the Rose Garden. They'll be in the building in seconds if they aren't already."

As if to punctuate the point, from the direction the agent had come from, there was the roar of gunfire. Over the cacophony, somebody yelled, "Drones! Drones are in the building!"

This was followed by a trio of explosions and more than one terrified scream of pain.

Spector's eyes connected with the agent-in-charge and over the deafening sound of automatic gunfire and still more explosions, the senior Secret Service man said, "Mr. President, we're going to have to take you downstairs. We'll put you in the Situation Room and hold them off until help arrives. It's not as secure as the PEOC, but it's the best we have at the moment. I'll stay here and oversee a fighting withdrawal."

Spector only nodded his head at the man.

The lead agent turned to the two men who had helped Spector get back to his feet. "Move and don't open the door unless someone gives you the right answer to today's challenge."

Together, the two agents said, "Yes, sir!" and pulled Spector through the doorway where a flight of stairs would bring them to the West Wing's ground floor.

With one agent ahead and one behind, Spector quickly negotiated the staircase and came to the relatively quiet ground floor of the complex. A right, a left, and another left and the three of them were walking into the Situation Room. It was empty.

As the door slammed shut behind him, he turned to look at the Secret Service agents who were also looking at the door. Above them, they could hear an intense battle being waged.

It was a mix of yelling, screams, and almost unending gunfire interspersed with explosions that were most certainly frag grenades. As he took in the sounds, a part of Spector's brain refused to comprehend what was happening.

But that refusal evaporated when he heard the fighting begin not far from the Situation Room's entrance. One of the agents turned from the door, pointed to the corner of the space and said, "Please stand there, Mr. President."

Spector looked at the agent and, after a second, said, "Horseshit, son."

He walked to the head of the boardroom table, the place where he'd sat only a few times before and put his big hands on the two ends of its surface.

With everything he had, Spector groaned and heaved the massive solid wood piece of furniture onto its side, causing a loud crash that rivalled the sound of the battle that was getting closer by the second.

Placing his hands on the overturned furniture, he then pulled and shimmied one end of the table to form a barrier between the west side of the room and the three doors that led into the space.

Dodging out of the way of the shifting table, the two agents watched Spector with confused looks on their faces. As he returned their stares, he reached to his back and withdrew the stainless steel .357 Colt Python that had been his old man's.

He took three steps, grabbed one of the room's many rolling leather chairs, and positioned it behind the table that had just become his last stand.

Breathing hard and sweating profusely, he sat down, placed his forearms on the table's edge, and pointed the revolver at the main door leading into the world's most famous boardroom.

His eyes reconnected with the two agents still staring at him.

Knowing surrender or capture could never happen, he said, "Gentlemen, whatever comes through that door, I sure as hell ain't gonna go down without a fight. My suggestion is to put yourself behind this good American oak and help your President when the time comes. Cause if I'm gonna make a last stand, it's gonna be one for the history books."

***

Reynolds stepped over the body of one of Team One's men. He had been shot through the face and died instantly. According to the data scrolling through his glasses, three other operators on Team One were also KIA.

Looking down the stairway to the basement floor of the West Wing, he heard men yelling as they cleared rooms. The gunfire had died down to single shots. No doubt the shots of an executioner snuffing out the life out of those Secret Service agents who hadn't fully died.

The voice of Team Leader One spoke in his earbud. "The floor is clear except for the Situation Room. There are three entry points. All are closed."

Reynolds looked at the time on his wrist unit. Nearly fourteen minutes had passed since the Indian had given him the countdown of twenty. As he started down the stairway, he said, "I'm coming down now."

Reaching the bottom of the stairs, he stopped to look at a portrait of someone who had to be a former president. Reynolds' eyes flashed to the silver plate immediately underneath the painting. John Quincy Adams.

"Just another long-gone white dude," he said as he resumed his walk.

Taking a left, he saw Team One's leader standing with the leader of Team Two.

Reaching them, he raised his fist to the two and said, "Montana and Indiana are in the house, he said, making reference to the two soldier's home states. "I'm glad it's you two."

Both men pounded Reynolds' proffered fist. "How do you want to do this, Ren?" asked the Team Two leader.

"Quickly. All of us need to be on the South Lawn in four minutes. So, breach and get it done."

"Breaching charges are ready to go, Boss," advised the Team One lead.

Reynolds smiled. "Of course they are. Do it."

The two men walked toward the doors their respective teams would blow to access the only place their target could be.

Twenty seconds later, from his position around the corner, Reynolds heard the charges on the two doors blow.

Flash-bangs came next. Then, there was a short tear of gunfire and at least one person bellowing a string of curses.

His weapon at the ready, Reynolds moved forward.

Entering the space, he saw that the room's massive boardroom table had been turned over and tucked into the corner, where it formed a redoubt. A pair of operators were on the other side of the table, pointing their weapons at a person or persons on the floor that Reynolds couldn't see.

He walked up to the surface of the bullet-scarred furniture with his M5 at the ready and peered over its edge.

Lying on the ground on his back was the President of the United Constitutional States of America. He was flanked by two dead Secret Service agents, who each had a bullet through the center of their foreheads.

Spector, however, only had a pair of bullet wounds just below his left collarbone. He was still breathing, if heavily. When Reynolds appeared with the two team leads flanking him, the man's blue eyes shifted from the operators who had him at gunpoint to look at the new arrival.

The UCSA President wheezed in a long breath, then said, "You must be the leader of this motley crew. Well done. Truly. Well done, son."

Spector was then struck with a coughing fit that racked his massive upper body. At several points during the attack, the leader of the Red Faction ejected gobs of bright red blood from his mouth that covered his chin and his already blood-soaked button-down shirt.

The fit over, Spector's eyes reconnected with Reynolds.

With blood all over the lower part of his face, the blue of the man's eyes had somehow become more intense.

When he spoke, Spector's words were weaker than before. "Before you do what you need to do, son, tell me where you're from and what unit you were with before this terrible war started."

Nodding at the question, he said, "The name is Jerome Reynolds, sir, and I was dishonorably discharged two years before the war started. I finished my career with the 7th Special Forces Group out of Elgin Air Force Base in Florida. I was a major until I wasn't."

Spector nodded his head at the synopsis. "Dishonorably discharged, eh? For what?"

Slowly, Reynolds lowered his eye to the red dot sight on his M5 and placed the reticle on Spector's forehead. Quietly, he said, "Goodbye, Mr. President."

After pulling the trigger, he lifted his head from the sight and pronounced, "One minute to take pictures and take his index finger. Be sure to take the wedding ring as well. In ten years, it'll be worth a fortune."

***

As there were limited numbers of the press in Washington and they only produced the news the UCSA said they could, there were no news feeds to watch the chaos at the White House.

Within the first minutes of the attack, Christoff had called everyone he knew to see if he could get details about what was happening, but everyone he'd talked to knew as much as he did, which was to say nothing.

The CIB didn't have any drones of its own, at least not in Washington. That kind of surveillance was the exclusive domain of the military, and everyone he'd spoken to on that side of the fence was clueless or actively trying to respond to the crisis.

It didn't help that in the short time since the administration moved its base of operations to Washington, they hadn't set up a secondary operations site outside the White House.

It also didn't help that Spector hadn't designated a Vice President. On more than one occasion, Christoff had counselled the man to designate someone to fill the crucial role, but the big Texan had steadfastly refused.

He could hear Spector's voice as though he were in the room with him now: *"This country doesn't need a VP. It's a horseshit role, and I'm not going anywhere. Until this war is over, I'm this country's leader, and that's it — end of discussion."*

Aloud, Christoff said, "And how's that working out for us now, Mr. President?"

"I'm sorry, sir, what was that?" asked the Assistant Director for Domestic Security, standing across from him in one of the boardrooms in the former CIA headquarters' expansive operations center.

"Nothing, Bill. I was talking to myself. Do we have anything new from your people?"

The other man shook his head and said, "As of one minute ago, nothing firm. There are only a few countries and individuals in the world that can operate the type of drone-heavy operation we're seeing. Our guess is that it's the same group that tried to take down Sanchez, but we're still working to confirm."

Nodding, Christoff said, "Confirm what you can as soon as you can, Bill. The generals and the others will want answers from us within the hour. You can count on that."

"We won't need an hour. There's only a handful of people and countries who can do this. We'll know soon, sir."

Quietly, he said, "Okay, I'll be back in five. I need time to think."

Christoff turned away from the small group of people he'd brought together to talk through the known facts of the disaster playing out eight miles down the Potomac and moved to leave the conference room. As he opened the door to exit the space, he was forced to dodge right as an analyst with her head down blew past him, no doubt with an update for whichever person in the room was her boss.

The entrance now free and clear, he stepped into what was now the CIB's Operational Command Center and started to make his way to one of the bullpen's exits.

It was one of those rare occasions when he needed to have a smoke.

In 2008, in a callous effort to make the lives of smokers even more miserable, the CIA had shut down the one and only ventilated room the Agency had installed for the very kind of moment Christoff was now experiencing.

He was twenty feet into the corridor that led away from the Ops Center when he said, "Piss on it," and pulled out the cigarettes from his pants pocket.

In a well-practiced movement, he put a smoke in his mouth, lit it up, and took what could be the most satisfying drag of his life. He waited to exhale as a trio of young-ish analysts walked by him, all of them staring at the burning cigarette still at his lips.

Christoff didn't care. That they hadn't heard from anyone inside the White House in the past fifteen minutes was indication enough that the countdown of his life on this planet had begun. Smoking indoors was the least of his concerns.

As he released the smoke from his now-burning lungs, his phone began to vibrate in rapid, truncated beats. His hand stopped moving his cigarette to his mouth. He had set the vibrate function for only a handful of people.

Quickly shifting his smoke to his left hand, his right darted into his pocket to retrieve his phone. Recognizing the number, he accepted the call and said, "Peter, did you do this?"

"I'm sorry, Director Christoff, this isn't Mr. Parr, it's Governor Sanchez. It is nice to make your acquaintance, if only over the phone."

Christoff didn't respond. Instead, he stood dumbfounded as more people walked by him, each of them staring incredulously at the lit cigarette he was holding.

"Director Christoff, are you there?"

Christoff tossed the cigarette to the cement floor and stepped on it. "I'm here."

"Good, we don't have much time, so I need you to listen carefully to me. I've reached out to you because I've been told that of the bunch surrounding President Spector, you're one of the more reasonable. Is this true, Mr. Director?"

"I'm biased, but I'd say that's true," said Christoff, slowly backing himself against the corridor's wall.

"Excellent", Sanchez said calmly. "As of three minutes ago, Mitchell Spector is dead. I suspect this will be confirmed in the next fifteen to thirty minutes by your people. In that time, you will do several things. I won't list them now. There's a document on your phone. Read it and do everything that's laid out to the letter."

When Christoff began to stutter out the beginnings of a reply, the other man said sharply, "This is not a dialogue, Director. Open the document and do what it says. If you're concerned about your legal status after the war, if you do everything that's asked, you will be given immunity. And –."

This time, Christoff said forcefully, "You don't understand. General Spellings and the President –

they've secretly placed nuclear weapons in the Ports of Los Angeles, Oakland, and somewhere close to downtown Sacramento. You don't have the leverage you think you have, Governor. Spellings is a true believer. He doesn't have a conciliatory bone in his body. He'll demand California pull back from its build-up in the West so that we can continue the war against the Blues.

"And before you ask, the nukes cannot be accessed without setting them off. Even if I knew their precise location, which I don't, Spellings and his people have thought through every eventuality. Spector's death does nothing to change that."

Sanchez went to speak, but Christoff cut him off again. "I'm sorry, Governor. There's one more thing. We have more nukes. Upwards of twenty of them and soon we'll be able to deliver them as far away as London. With these weapons, the war could go on for years. Spellings and some of the others – they'll be incensed by what happened today. I'm not sure how they'll respond."

There was a long bout of silence. Finally, Sanchez said, "Listen to me. I'll only say it one more time: the UCSA will lose this war, Christoff. You wouldn't still be talking to me if you didn't know this was the case. You are the director of the CIB, and I know you were intimately involved with Mr. Parr's work, which means you have the wherewithal to do ruthless things. But you have to move quickly. If we work together, we can bring an end to this war. We can end the madness."

"How?" Christoff said quietly as his eyes dodged up and down the conduit.

"You will receive another document on your phone in ten minutes. Follow the instructions."

"And if I don't?"

Sanchez's reply was immediate. "I will not protect you when the war is over. You will live to survive to see your next birthday if you help us and only if you help us."

"And if I try and fail?"

"Then you die at the hands of the regime you now serve, Director. Believe me when I say there are far worse fates."

The connection ended.

Christoff again looked up and down the long hallway. No one was close by.

Dropping his phone back into his pocket, he walked back in the direction of the Ops Room. He didn't know what Sanchez would ask him to do, but one thing he was sure of was that the closer he was to General Spellings and Hoffman, the closer he would be to the next President of the UCSA.

***

Eighty-two operators had survived the attack on the White House. That the number was that high was a miracle.

A miracle that would deliver to him millions in crypto, immunity from his crimes committed before and during the war, and citizenship in the beautiful State of California.

The vehicles of the convoy that had brought Reynolds to the White House were now in a full circle on the South Lawn. At the center of the redoubt, one-third of his operators were waiting and looking in the direction of the drones that were fast approaching from the south.

They were flying low to avoid UCSA radar.

Fighters had been scrambled and twice flashed over top of the White House, but they hadn't done anything. How could they? Their mission had been so complete the Reds would have no idea what had just happened, and in the absence of information, no pilot was going to be asked to strafe or bomb the grounds of the White House.

As the first three drones arrived and hovered ten feet above the circle of vehicles, each released four cables from their chassis. Each of the wires was quickly grabbed by a single operator who immediately affixed it to a harness they were wearing.

Moments later, with their weapons ready, eleven men and one woman ascended into the air while the drones flew back in the direction they had come from.

As the next three drones arrived and extended their cables, a vaguely familiar voice started to speak in his earbud. "Major Reynolds, this is Governor Sanchez of California. I'm sorry for the intrusion at this critical juncture of your operation, but I insisted to our intermediary that I speak with you directly."

For a long moment, Reynolds said nothing. Into this silence, Sanchez said, "I know it's you who tried to kill me at the Anaheim Convention Center. What is done is done, and today, you showed me I made the right decision to engage with your services, even though there remains a large part of me that wants to see you pay for your crimes."

Sanchez paused and said, "Major, can you hear me?"

"Yes," Reynolds finally said.

"Good, then I would ask that you listen carefully. There has been an important development that I would like you to assist with. Of course, I will make it worth your while."

As the second wave of drones ascended with another twelve operators in tow, Reynolds chose not to respond.

Calmly, into the silence, Sanchez said, "One hundred million in crypto is what your assistance would mean."

Reynolds said, "You have my attention, Governor. You have one minute."

"There will be a meeting in DC in the next hour. When we confirm its location, we would like you to be there."

"Who's at the meeting?" asked Reynolds.

"It doesn't matter. All that does matter is that we will have a way for you to attend and leave this meeting with your life intact. At the meeting, you will be required to eliminate one or several people."

"If you're asking me to do what I think you're asking me to do Governor, the answer is no."

"Three hundred million, Major."

When Reynolds gave no reply after ten seconds, Sanchez said, "We're running out of time, Mr. Reynolds. You have five seconds, and the money is off the table. Five, four, three, two..."

Unhurriedly, Reynolds said, "Four hundred million. Three hundred in crypto and one hundred in gold and silver. That's my price, Governor."

Sanchez's reply was instantaneous. "We have a deal, Major. Stay close to your phone. The details of our ask are on their way."

Chapter 42

Harrington Lake, Quebec

It was just as his helicopter was setting down that Larocque saw the ten or so Hyenas jogging toward the Airborne's paratroopers.

The weapon carried by the majority of the commandos was the Army's new C-71 assault rifle. Its 5.56mm round wouldn't be effective on the charging automatons, but they had other weapons, including grenade launchers and anti-armor rockets.

Based on Larocque's calculation, it wouldn't be enough to stop the fast-moving kill-bots. But there was no help for it. They were committed, so the best thing he could do would be to get on the ground and do what he could to minimize the impending slaughter.

As the landing gear of his CH-525 hit the ground, Larocque jumped out of the machine. Wearing a chest rig and helmet over civilian clothes, he waited for the CSIS IOs and RCMP officers from his helo and the second Roc to gather around him.

As he waited and watched the first two Hyenas close within twenty meters of the center of the Airborne's firing line, a lone Super Griffon slid itself directly above the firing paratroopers, where it unleashed the full power of its onboard M134 Minigun.

Brrrrrrrrrt!

Firing three thousand 7.62mm rounds per minute, the two closest Hyenas were instantly shredded into scrap metal.

To the left and further back from the two autos that had just been destroyed, one of the Hyenas stopped in its tracks and raised the grenade launcher on its back to target the lightly armored gunship, but before it could get a shot off, geysers of dirt erupted around it.

Looking up and to his left, Larocque saw the Roc that had just unloaded him.

On full auto, the door gunner was unleashing a storm of .50-cal rounds.

Looking back in the direction of the grenade-launching Hyena, Larocque saw the auto was laid out on the ground and smoking.

He then quickly scanned the battlefield in front of his former regiment.

All of the Chinese autos had been put down. The closest any of the kamikaze robots had gotten to the Airborne's line of attack were the first two Hyenas the Super Griffon had put down with its minigun.

The automaton threat defeated, Larocque saw the commanding officer of the Airborne rise to his feet and bellow for his men to resume their advance to the PM's residence.

It was at this moment when Larocque's eyes caught movement on the roadway leading to the building. A convoy of SUVs was speeding away from the residence to the forested roadway.

He unloaded with a vicious curse and then turned his gaze on the CSIS IOs and RCMP officers who had formed a semi-circle behind him. To the last, each of them had their weapons drawn.

Had the Hyenas made it past the Airborne, these people would have been ready to take up the fight. Brave souls, he thought.

"Eyes on me!" he roared over the sound of nearby gunfire.

Instantly, the eyes of each of the CSIS and RCMP officers locked onto him.

"Half of you will come with me. The other half will join the assault on the residence. Everyone knows their job. You're not here to fight. We're here to arrest. I want the fastest people on me. We're going on a short run. Everyone else, go to the residence. Move people, now!"

***

As bullets slammed into the SUV she was in, MacPhail lowered herself in her seat. From the door leading into the cottage, a man appeared and bellowed for people to get ready to move.

He stepped out of the way, and through the doorway came another two masked men. Between them was a blindfolded Michael Oyinlola.

Her heart jumped on seeing her friend and colleague. He was alive.

The two men trudged him in the direction of MacPhail's SUV.

Reaching the door, they all but threw the MP into the seat beside her.

MacPhail instantly reached out for the man and found that zip ties bound his hands together.

In a pained voice, he said, "Who's that?"

"It's me, Michael. You're alive. I feared the worst."

"Irene. It's good to hear your voice."

"Shut up back there!" roared a voice from the driver's seat. "Not a word, or he gets it. If he gets out of line, I'm to shoot him. That's what I've been told, and I'll happily do it, so keep your mouths shut!"

Another masked man jumped into the front passenger seat. Slamming his door, he said, "There, the lead SUV is moving. See, I told you, we're going to get out of this nightmare."

Their SUV lurched forward.

"Not too fast, man. Stay cool. You've done this before," the man in the passenger seat said.

His voice panicked, the driver spoke, "This is bad, dude. That was the army back there. JTF-2, for sure. And did you see down by the lake? Those were cops. This is crazy. What are we gonna do?"

"I said, stay cool, Ro. I thought you were up for anything. And you're getting paid. The colonel knows what he's doing, trust me."

The man speaking pointed ahead and said, "See, the lead SUV is almost to the trees. Freedom is ten seconds away."

Ahead, there was a sharp bend in the driveway, and just thirty meters beyond the bend was the roadway that would bring them back to Ottawa.

Reaching the turn, the driver gunned the engine, sending the SUV racing forward. The masked passenger said, "Ro, dude, ease up. You need to keep your distance from the next vehicle."

The sudden burst of speed and the turn had forced MacPhail into the door at her left. At that exact moment, she felt Oyinlola's weight slam into her.

As she grunted in surprise, Oyinlola whispered, "Open your door if you can."

She didn't know what made her comply, but on hearing his words, her unbound hands reached for the door's handle. On pulling it, the SUV's notification system started to blare.

From the front of the vehicle, someone started to yell something, but MacPhail didn't catch the words because she had been propelled out the door as a result of Oyinlola himself leaping out of the moving vehicle.

For the briefest moment, it felt like she was flying, but this sensation terminated when her body slammed into what felt like the road's gravel shoulder. On contact, one of her knees turned into fire, while her left elbow made a crunching sound. Pain lanced through her body as though a bolt of lightning had struck her.

Incredibly, she came to a sliding stop with all her faculties in play. Slowly, MacPhail raised her head and saw that she was looking in the direction the convoy was headed. The SUV she'd been riding in had stopped, as had the last vehicle of the motorcade.

Running in her direction were four masked men wearing body armour and guns on their hips. She could only see their eyes. All four sets were narrow and furious.

Glancing beyond them, at maybe thirty meters past where the trees of the park began to enclose the only road, MacPhail saw that the rest of the escaping motorcade was still moving, if slowly.

As the four men reached her, two of the thugs raced past, no doubt on their way to grab Oyinlola.

Grabbing her, her two assailants reefed on her shoulders and hauled her to her feet like she was a child. Because of his bright green eyes, she recognized one of the two operatives as the man who had placed her and Oyinlola into the SUV.

With no warning, his fist plowed into her stomach, driving the air out of her lungs. Her knees gave way, but her captors didn't let her fall. Instead, as she gasped for air, they started to drag her back to the vehicle she had escaped only seconds before.

As they reached the SUV and were just about to throw her in, MacPhail heard a loud hissing noise rip through the air above her. As she was about to look up to identify the source of the sound, she saw the two men holding her were looking toward the departing motorcade. Her eyes followed theirs.

BOOM!

Ahead, where the trees enclosed the roadway, a giant yellow-and-orange explosion bloomed into the air.

As the flames and black smoke began to climb high into the clear blue sky, the man who had hit her cursed and tightened his grip on her arm, but just as he and the other masked man were about to force her back into the vehicle, someone behind them screamed, "Police! Don't move! Everyone's hands in the air. Now!"

Hearing the command, her two handlers stopped, and across MacPhail's frontage, they looked at one another.

"Hands in the air. NOW! I'm not gonna ask again," the same voice bellowed, repeating the command.

Behind her, MacPhail could hear the sound of more booted feet arriving.

Another voice spoke, but instead of yelling, it addressed her captors calmly. She recognized the speaker instantly. "Let her go unharmed, and I'll make sure you don't face charges of treason. Do something stupid, and it's life in jail, or we kill you where you stand. You have three seconds."

The man who didn't hit her released his grip on her arm. Slowly, he turned and raised his hands in the air.

For a too-long moment, the other man didn't move. But then he growled something under his breath and released his hand from around MacPhail's upper arm. Slowly, he, too, raised his arms in the air.

As he did this, MacPhail heard the scuffling of boots pounding over pavement and a new jumble of commands as multiple people closed in on her two captors.

Raising her own hands in the air, she turned to see two RCMP officers and two civilian-dressed men grab and then force the two masked operatives onto the ground. Beyond them was a female RCMP officer and a woman in civilian clothes. Both held handguns and were covering the men who were in the process of handcuffing the men who'd just surrendered her.

Between the two women stood Larocque. He moved in her direction. "Madame Deputy Prime Minister, are you okay?"

Nodding, MacPhail said, "A little banged up, but I'll survive."

She looked over his shoulder and scanned for Oyinlola but couldn't see him. "Where's Michael? Is he alright?"

"It looks like he sustained a concussion. He was woozy when we found him. We've moved him to our triage area, which is where you need to go."

"But –."

"No buts, Irene. It's not safe here," Larocque said, cutting her off.

As if to punctuate his words, another loud explosion came from the direction of the motorcade. Together, Larocque and MacPhail turned their heads to catch the sight of a massive tree toppling onto the roadway.

"Nicely done," Larocque said aloud. He then turned to the woman dressed in civilian clothes who was still covering the arrests of the two men and said, "Alia, take the Deputy PM to the triage."

That order given, he turned away from MacPhail, and with nearly a dozen uniformed RCMP and plainclothes officers she guessed were from CSIS, Larocque began to lope forward to the column of smoke that was the front of the prime minister's fleeing motorcade.

***

"Now!" Dune snapped at the co-pilot of the Super Griffon, who'd sighted in on the lead vehicle of the motorcade.

An instant later, from the direction of the lake, he caught the dull crack of a SPIKE missile ejecting from its launch tube. This was followed up by the ignition of its jet engine, which drove across the eight hundred meters it needed to travel before it sunk into the top of the lead vehicle.

BOOM!

The SPIKE missile must have driven itself into the rear half of the SUV because it detonated its fuel tank, producing a gigantic fireball.

Already connected to the channel with the men under his command, Dune yelled, "Dashney, blow it! Now!"

Out of the Yukon Territory, Master Corporal Dashney was his company's explosives expert. He had rigged twelve feet of detonation cord around the trunk of a single massive maple tree already leaning in the direction of the road.

Thirty meters from Dune's position, the det cord blew. He heard but didn't see the explosion. What he did see was the shifting of forest canopy as the ancient maple crashed past its fellows and landed with a series of cracks and a dull *whoomp* as its massive trunk set down across the whole of the roadway.

"Brilliant, mate. Bloody brilliant!" Dune said over the BAM.

As he started to get to his feet, he issued a new set of orders. "Lads, except Reed and Raz, we're gonna advance. We move on the motorcade together, but as we do so, we need excellent trigger discipline. No shooting unless it's to defend yourself. Anyone who fires a weapon without a bloody good reason is in the shit, and that's no joke. We start with the first vehicle and work our way down in four teams of seven. Two teams left, two teams right. We leapfrog over one another.

To his two sharpshooters, Dune said, "Reed and Raz, follow along from the trees and be ready to shoot if I give the word. Reed, mate, take the left side. Razzy, take the right."

"Let's go, people!"

With the order given, the thirty men under his command got up from the forest floor, formed up, and in their four teams started to advance.

They quickly moved past the burning wreckage of the lead vehicle of the motorcade. Dune peeked inside the SUV as he walked by and saw two blazing corpses in the front seat. He hoped that wasn't anyone important. The word he'd received was that the VIPs had been loaded into vehicles two to seven, but that intel had come on the fly.

When they were twenty feet from SUV number two, he eyeballed masked men in the front seats. Together, they were staring and no doubt assessing their chances against the heavily armed CSRO commandos moving in their direction.

As the eyes of the man in the passenger seat connected with Dune's, he quietly said, "Just sit right there, mate. Be cool."

But just as he finished uttering his plea, the front doors of the SUVs swung open. From the right side, the driver produced a carbine and, through the lowered window, opened up on full auto at the CSOR men just ahead of Dune.

The commando leading the group screamed as he dropped to the ground, but behind him, his mates opened up with a barrage of well-aimed shots, one of which tore through the assailant's throat, dropping him where he stood.

On the left side, the masked man had moved to the rear door and was in the process of dragging someone who didn't want to be dragged from the back seat.

Recognizing what was going on, the soldier in front of Dune began to run forward and to the left to give himself a clear line of fire, but by the time he had the masked man in his targeting aperture, he had extracted his hostage and was holding her in front of him.

Dune didn't recognize the woman. She was of Indian heritage, to be sure. She was wearing a white blouse soaked in blood. A bandage had been tightly wrapped underneath her armpit and shoulder.

Dune whispered, "Reed, do you have a shot?"

"I have a shot," the CSOR sniper confirmed from thirty meters back in the bush.

But before Dune could give the order, a deep voice boomed from behind the masked man holding the hostage.

"Hold your fire! Hold your fire!" the voice roared.

"Hold one, Reed," Dune said, his voice calm.

He moved his eyes from the hostage-taker to a huge man striding forward. He had a black mustache, a thick mat of hair with tinges of grey at his temples, and the chest of a bull. Aloud, he said, "Crickey, I didn't think they made body armor for blokes that big."

The giant stepped beside the hostage-taker and said, "Who's in charge here?"

Dune placed his reticle on the man's forehead and said, "Right here, mate."

The man looked at Dune quizzically.

"I may sound like an Aussie, but I'm as Canuck as the rest of the blokes around me. Identify yourself."

The man didn't answer the question. Instead, he said, "You've attacked the residence and motorcade of the prime minister. Do you know what you've done? It's treason for all of you. Set down your weapons. All of you. That's an order."

"Yeah, mate, I don't think so. Who are you, again?"

"My name is Colonel Mustapha Aziz. I'm with CANSOFCOM, and I'm a special advisor to the prime minister. Now drop your weapons before somebody else gets killed."

"It's him who's committed treason!" screamed the woman with the bloody shoulder. "Him and the PM. They're in it together. If you let them get past you, they're going to implement an authoritarian government. Don't listen to him!"

The man named Aziz took a step in the direction of the woman and produced a handgun that he levelled at her temple. "I'm not going to ask again. Drop your weapons. This is a national emergency and acting with the authority of the prime minister, I'm ordering you to back down."

Quietly, Dune said, "Reed, do you still have the hostage-taker?"

"I have the shot."

Dune took in a deep breath. The reticle of his carbine Colt C-71 had never left the forehead of this Aziz fellow. Still quiet, Dune said, "Reed, take the shot."

As the word *shot* left his mouth, Dune pulled the trigger of his own weapon.

***

As MacPhail watched Larocque charge into danger, the CSIS IO named Alia addressed her, "Deputy Prime Minister, please follow me."

Without looking at the other woman, MacPhail said in a firm voice, "I'm not going to the triage area or whatever he called it."

"Minister, if you don't follow me, I'll call over a couple of my colleagues, and have you carried to the triage, kicking and screaming if necessary."

MacPhail finally turned to face the woman, who might have been in her mid-twenties. "What's your name, by the way?"

"Boulanger," she replied.

"Well, Officer Boulanger, you can call your colleagues, but as you can see, everyone is pretty busy at the moment. So, that gives you one of two choices. You can detain me physically and prevent me from helping the man I was just speaking to –."

"You mean the Director," Boulanger said, interrupting.

Ignoring the clarification, MacPhail continued, "Or, you can come with me and help keep me safe as I try to help the Director pull our country out of the bloody awful nosedive it's in."

The IO didn't reply. Instead, her hand came up, and her index finger danced across the display of her BAM wrist unit.

When her gaze reconnected with MacPhail, she said, "I've sent a message to my colleague saying I need their help. I could detain you on my own, but I won't."

MacPhail cocked her head and said, "Covering your ass so Larocque can't say you didn't follow his orders, eh? Smart woman."

MacPhail turned her back on the CSIS IO and started to limp in the direction Larocque had gone. Over her shoulder, she called back, "Keep up, Officer Boulanger. We have a country to help save."

***

Ahead, Larocque saw Merielle exit from the SUV.

As was typical, she was wearing a power suit and flats. Not typical was the handgun she was holding in her right hand. From afar, her eyes connected with his.

In a loud voice, he said to the CSIS and RCMP officers surrounding him, "Stay here and don't come forward unless I give the word."

With that, he strode forward.

As he covered the fifty or so feet between himself and Merielle, he elected not to draw the gun on his hip. He was determined to see Merielle survive this day.

Not politically, of course. Her career in politics was over, but depending on what happened in the next five minutes, she could still play a part in helping save this country from running headlong into what would be the worst political scandal Canada had ever faced.

"That's far enough," Merielle said when he was ten feet away.

"It's over, Merielle," he said.

"I can see that now," she said, her voice emotionless. "I should have known you would swing into action, Jaks, but I didn't think you'd be able to get the CAF and RCMP to come along. Is anyone else involved?"

Larocque, tamping down his own emotions, said, "It doesn't matter. All that matters is coming up with an arrangement that limits the damage. The bureaucracy, the media, our allies. No one is clear on what's transpired. They only know there was an incident on the Hill this morning, and of course, everyone in Ottawa will know something happened here. We can't hide explosions, but we can set the narrative."

Ahead toward the front of the motorcade, there was a short burst of automatic gunfire. Neither Merielle nor Larocque flinched as the sound of bullets ripped through the air.

Larocque took another two steps forward, but before he could take a third, a form flowed from behind the front of Merielle's SUV and positioned itself in front of the PM.

It was a woman, and she had a handgun that was pointed in the direction of his forehead.

As he took in this new party, the young woman's face, not pretty but by no means unpleasant, tickled a memory inside Larocque's mind.

Finally, it struck him. "Lieutenant Hall. I had tried to track you down after Missouri, but you disappeared into thin air. Now I know what you've been up to."

Larocque's eyes moved back to Merielle. "This private black ops thing you've gotten yourself involved in ends today. All of it ends. Call her off, Merielle."

Once again, gunshots came from the front of the motorcade. This time, it wasn't a barrage from a half-dozen automatic rifles but a pair of cracks in quick succession.

Larocque didn't look in the direction of the gunfire. Instead, he stared at Merielle and said, "Tell this viper of yours to lower her gun so we can talk. I have a proposal."

"A proposal for what, Jaks? Am I to become a nobody and watch people who don't have what it takes to begin to run this country? Am I to become a modern-day Napoleon banished to Saint Helena?"

From behind Hall, Merielle started to shake her head. "The bureaucracy and the politicians won't let it happen. None of what's happened can be kept hidden. As soon as the war down south ends, the elites will wiggle themselves back into power, and they will find out what happened. They'll be relentless, and they'll bring us back to where we were before the war – feckless and unserious.

"War is about to erupt in Europe, Jackson, and you want to hand power over to who? Irene MacPhail? Or worse, you want to call an election allowing one of the other parties to run the country?"

Merielle took a step forward, and as she did so, a look of sadness overcame her face. "Of everyone I've dealt with, I thought you would understand. You've lost so much. So many men have died under your command. You more than anyone know about the sacrifices that must be made."

For the first time in the conversation, Larocque injected heat into his words. "Sacrifices I made because the people elected to run the country gave me orders. I didn't go to Missouri on my own. Nor Washington. I went there because I was ordered to. By Bob MacDonald and by you. That's how this country works, Merielle. There are processes and institutions bigger than both of us."

Merielle took another step forward so that she was standing only a foot behind Hall. "Well, if you're so good at following orders, Director Larocque, I'm ordering you to stand down. Stand down and help me save this country for the generations that are to come. You know I'm right. You know this country is broken."

Forcing himself to moderate the growing anger he was feeling, Larocque retorted, "I can't, Merielle. I won't."

With a face still etched with sadness, Merielle shook her head, and slowly raised the weapon that had never left her hand. She levelled it at Larocque's face. "You are the man who brought together CSIS, the CAF, and the RCMP. You are the glue that's holding them together, Jackson. I knew your leadership would get them to bend to you. I just didn't think you would use them to stop the work that needs to be done."

Merielle closed her eyes briefly and said something Larocque couldn't hear. When her eyes opened and they reconnected with his own, he instantly recognized that Merielle was at peace with herself. She would do what she thought needed to be done.

She said, "They'll unravel without you, Jackson. I still have people who will help me even with everything that's happened. Goodbye, Director."

Larocque opened his mouth to yell for her not to do it, but the words that filled the air didn't come from him.

***

As MacPhail reached the same group of CSIS and RCMP officers who had accompanied Larocque, but for a pair keeping an eye on a handful of men lying on the ground face down, the rest were all staring at the nearby standoff.

She went to step past the group, but somebody – not Boulanger – grabbed her shoulder. When she looked to see who it was, a lean and tall black man with a shaved head said, "I can't let you do that. The Director said he'd call us when he needed help."

MacPhail rounded on the man. "Are you joking?"

"He was very clear, Minister."

"Good, so you know who I am. Then listen up, whoever you are. The Director that you all seem so keen to listen to is about to have his fucking brains blown out."

The man's jaw clenched, but he gave no reply.

"Listen, he can't call for your help because he has a gun in his teeth. Did you ever think of that?"

The man released her shoulder and said, "The Director knows what he's doing."

"Maybe, but also, maybe he's about to take a bullet in the head, and I don't know about you, but I'm not prepared to stand here and do nothing but watch it happen."

Again, the tall man gave no response.

MacPhail turned to find Boulanger and said, "Come with me."

As Boulanger took a step forward, several other CSIS and RCMP officers moved to follow her, but MacPhail rounded on them and barked, "No! Stay here. The last thing we need is more goddamn guns."

Thumbing in the direction of Boulanger, she said, "She'll be enough."

With that, MacPhail turned and resumed her painful walk toward the impending disaster.

Thirty paces later, she pulled up her stride five feet behind Larocque just as Merielle raised her weapon.

***

"Merielle, don't!" Irene MacPhail's Newfie-accented voice sounded off immediately behind Larocque.

Two sets of eyes, Merielle's and Hall's, lifted from him to look over his shoulder. It was the chance he needed.

Lowering himself, he charged toward Hall.

He heard a round go off and felt a bolt of white-hot pain as the bullet ripped through his left shoulder. There was another shot. This one hit his ballistics vest in his abdomen and partially drove the air out of his lungs, but neither shot slowed down his momentum.

Before she could squeeze the trigger a third time, he was on the much lighter woman, and with his right palm, he struck Hall in her sternum with every ounce of strength he had.

Larocque had spent a lifetime hitting things. Though Hall was wearing her own ballistics vest, the force of Larocque's strike drove her backward into Merielle and together, they tripped over one another and fell to the ground.

Larocque drew his gun, took two steps forward and pointed his weapon at Hall's face. She was gasping for air.

Seeing the younger woman was incapacitated for the moment, he shifted his weapon to Merielle but found the PM had recovered and that he was once again looking down the barrel of her gun.

He pleaded, "Merielle, please. Please, for the love of God, we can work this out."

"We can't. I'm sorry. Goodbye, Jackson."

Larocque closed his eyes and waited for the end. A single gunshot rang out, but instead of experiencing blackness or whatever comes with your own death, he only heard MacPhail cry out, "Jesus Christ!"

His eyes flashed open. Below him, lying on the ground, was Merielle. She was staring blankly into the morning sky. A single line of blood ran down the side of her face from the bullet that had struck her above her right eye.

Slowly he turned. There, he found MacPhail with both hands on her hips staring at Merielle's body. Her emerald-green eyes held a profound sadness. Beside her was the CSIS IO he'd told to escort the Deputy PM to the triage area.

Boulanger still had her Glock 19 pointed at her target. Her eyes were wide, and the pistol she was holding with both hands was visibly shaking.

Making sure to stay out of the line of fire, Larocque moved to the young intel officer's side and calmly said, "Well done, Alia. She knew you were there. She wanted this. She did this to herself. Take a deep breath, and just for another minute more, keep an eye on the other one."

As Boulanger nodded her understanding and shifted her weapon to Hall, Larocque's eyes turned back on MacPhail. "We've done our part, Minister. Now, it's up to you and your colleagues to pull this out of the fire. You have an hour at most before you'll have to make some kind of statement."

The politician shifted her eyes from the body to Larocque. "I don't know what to do. This all happened so fast and it's all so unbelievable. But it happened, so we have to deal with it. Any ideas?"

Larocque did have an idea. "Use the Hyenas."

MacPhail's eyes narrowed, and she said, "You mean the robots? What about them?"

With the nod of his head, Larocque signalled for MacPhail to follow him as CSIS and RCMP officers began to converge on the scene.

Once he was sure no one could hear their conversation, he said, "Earlier versions of the Hyena can be bought off the black market. Dollars to donuts, that's where these came from, but the media doesn't need to know that. Tell them it was a Chinese operation. An assassination attempt. A successful one. Tell them it was them who set off the bombs in Ottawa. Get your story set and your people on board. You have an hour, tops."

"No more lies," MacPhail said forcefully.

Larocque glared at the politician and, in a low voice, said, "Listen, this country is still at war and could be for another year or more. The last thing we need now is a political scandal of epic proportions. The second US civil war might be close to ending, but Russia is on the move and –."

MacPhail cut him off. "What do you mean the civil war might be close to ending?"

"An hour ago, it was confirmed Spector was killed at the White House. Details are fuzzy, but it's confirmed the man is dead. As we stand here, the UCSA is on the verge of collapse."

"Jesus, incredible timing," said MacPhail as she struggled to grasp the implications.

Seeing she was pulling together various threads, Larocque pressed her. "You are the Deputy Prime Minister, and I don't know much about politics, but you still have a majority. Rally your party and give the country a year at least. Two would be better. CANZUK needs to help the world get on the right path, Irene. Tearing ourselves apart while the alliance needs us will accomplish nothing."

After a pause to give her a moment to process his words, Larocque added, "The military and security agencies will support this direction. We won't tell you what to do, but we discussed a scenario like this. We all feel strongly this is the way to go."

Her eyes met his. The sadness from before was gone. Now there was anger, or maybe it was determination. The red-haired politician from Newfoundland said, "I need to pull together the MPs that are here. If I can get them on the same page, then I'll see about doing what you propose. If what you say is true about the US, then more than ever, Canada needs to be stable. At least for a time."

Nodding at the statement, Larocque said, "I'll pull them together for you."

But before he could step away, MacPhail's hand grabbed his good arm. "First, get your shoulder looked at. You're an actual bloody mess."

For the first time since being shot, Larocque looked at the wound and noted that most of the rolled-up sleeve on his left arm was saturated in blood.

"I'll do that."

"Good," MacPhail said, tightening her grip on his arm. "When the time comes, Jackson, I won't protect Merielle. The country deserves to know what she became."

It was now Larocque's turn to wear a look of sadness. He said, "I know. The country deserves to know. In a year or two, when the world is done with this madness, we'll tell the country everything. But not today, Irene. Not today."

Chapter 43

North of Baltimore, Maryland

Lange set down his fourth Red Bull of the day.

He didn't know who to thank in the CAF, but if he lived to see the end of the war, he promised himself and others that he would find the person who'd made getting the energy drink a priority so he could put them in for the Victoria Cross. In his estimation, the beverage had saved hundreds, if not thousands, of lives.

Once again vibrating, Lange looked ahead at the battle-scarred Challenger 3 tank fifty meters ahead that held his new commanding officer from the Royal Tank Regiment – RTR.

What remained of the Royal Canadian Dragoons had linked up and been combined with the legendary British armored regiment three days earlier.

With the arrival of the Canadian 2nd Division from Quebec, the 5th Division from Atlantic Canada, and two Blue divisions, the RTRs, along with the other units that remained of the UK Expeditionary Division, had surged out of Syracuse to beat back the UCSA 2nd Army.

As with the Royal Canadian Dragoons in Ohio and West Pennsylvania, the fighting from Upstate New York to Scranton to Philadelphia had been unrelenting and vicious. On the two fronts, CANZUK had suffered no less than eleven thousand casualties.

Four kilometers ahead, he heard the deep rumble of another air strike.

The RAF, RCAF, and Blues' Air Force had been laying waste to the northern reaches of Baltimore, their next objective. The combined air forces had been dropping bombs nonstop since yesterday, while the artillery from all three armies had been saturating the Red-held city for the past six hours.

The pretense of fighting a war that sought to preserve innocent life and infrastructure had been left behind weeks ago.

Lange didn't need to see North Baltimore to know that this perfectly fine city of nearly six hundred thousand people now resembled something akin to Berlin in 1945 or Gaza in 2024. It would be the eighth such city to receive this brutal treatment.

A Scottish-accented voice started to speak in his BAM. It was the CO of the RTR and the man who'd been driving Lange and the twenty-six Leopards and Challengers that remained from the two regiments. "Listen up, lads. New orders have come down, and they're just what we suspected. In fifteen mikes, Squadrons B and C will advance to Objective Hotel.

"Per the norm, whatever resistance is there is to be rooted out and put down. There will be no air support, but you'll have a battalion of infantry made up of the Royal New Brunswick Regiment and The Princess Louise Fusiliers. As the infantry goes, I've been told these lads fight like hell. Concerning the enemy, like every other shite town we've taken in the past week, expect the Reds to put up a fight.

"On my word, Major Lange's A Squadron will push past Objective Hotel and drive to city hall, where a group of Blue militia is holed up. Intel is that they're low on ammo and light on bodies, but they're holding the ground. A Squadron, you'll have a company from 2nd RCR with you. Get there and hold it until we can push in more of the Blue's militia. Two fresh battalions are on their way.

"And before any of you send me a nasty note asking why we don't wait for the goddamned Blues to arrive and fight their own bloody war, the higher-ups have already determined the blokes at city hall can't wait. So, I don't want to hear any pissing and moaning –."

A long, pleasant tone sounded off in Lange's headset. The voice of Sir Patrick Stewart said, "Hold for incoming priority call from Ares Sunray."

Interesting, Lange thought. Ares Sunray was the British Lieutenant General with overall command of all CANZUK ground forces in the Northeast theater.

The General's monotone voice started to speak. "All units, all units, this is Ares Sunray, validation code Victor-Alpha-Seven-Charlie. All CANZUK units will cease hostilities against Red Faction forces at 1500 hours. I say again that all CANZUK units will cease hostilities at 1500 hours. On direction from CANZUK high command, I am pleased to inform you that as of 1330 hours, the UCSA has surrendered. I say again, the UCSA has surrendered."

***

Washington, D.C.

—

Across Washington, Reynolds watched and heard the Indian's anti-armor drones wreak havoc on the Red Faction forces trying to make it to the White House. In the end, all of his people had been taken away to the south of the city, where they would land in a half-dozen different locations, jump into waiting vehicles and disappear into the country-wide chaos that the UCSA had become.

There had only been one change to the plan. Instead of going south, Reynolds and three other members of Team 4 were transported north, where they were dropped off on the shoreline of the densely wooded west side of the Potomac.

After a ten-minute hike, Reynolds emerged from the forest onto a suburban street with five-million-dollar homes to find a lone black SUV waiting for them.

Waiting outside the vehicle was a tired-looking man with a bald head wearing a suit well past its best-before date.

Reaching the man, Reynolds asked, "Elliot?"

Following a single nod, the man replied, "That's me. I'm to take you into Langley. I'm told you know where to go once we're on the campus."

"I do," said Reynolds.

Elliot said, "I have four passes in my coat pocket. I will reach for them now if that's okay?"

"It is," Reynolds replied.

With the passes in hand, the man gave one to Reynolds and each of the other three operators.

Looking down at the card, Reynolds was surprised to see his face on it and said, "The Indian. Is there nothing that sick bastard can't do?"

"Pardon me?" asked their liaison.

"Oh, nothing. These will work?" Reynolds asked.

"For the next couple of hours, yes," Elliott said, quickly adding, "But I don't guarantee anything."

When Reynolds gave the man a hard stare, he shrugged his shoulders and said, "I was given all of fifteen minutes to make this happen. I'm ninety-nine percent sure you'll be okay."

Reynolds only reply was a grunt.

The bald CIB man gestured to the SUV. "Are you ready?"

Reynolds turned from the man to look at the one woman and two men he'd brought with him for this impromptu effort.

Still dressed in the civilian clothes they'd been wearing when they'd breached the South Gate of the White House, he asked, "Are we good?"

As all three operatives nodded their readiness, his eyes shifted to the lone woman. "Remind me how well you remember the Operations Center?"

"I worked there for three years, pulling more eighteen-hour shifts than the country deserved. I know it like the back of my hand."

"Any chance you might get recognized?" Reynolds asked.

The female operator shook her head and said, "It's low-risk. It was ten years ago, and no doubt the CIB has brought in its own people. On the off chance it happens, I'll roll with it."

His eyes moved back to their driver. "Let's do this."

***

Flanked by two of his staffers, Christoff walked into the main boardroom of the CIB's Operations Center and saw General Spellings and Hoffman sitting at either end of the gigantic rectangular table.

Both men turned their eyes on him as he swept into the room. Before either could begin to chastise his tardiness, Christoff said loudly, "It's been confirmed. Sanchez sponsored the operation using a backdoor Parr had into the near-AI that administers Operation Sunlight. It's one hundred percent confirmed."

Spellings' fist smashed into the table's surface, drawing the eyes of the twenty-odd people in the room.

A furious look on his face, he said at a near yell, "An act of war. I say we light up Oakland and tell him he has two hours to reclaim California's neutral status. At the same time, we should target the Blues up north. The bulk of the 10th Mountain and parts of the 42nd Infantry Division are getting ready to cross the Susquehanna at Aberdeen. They're bunched up like cattle at a bottleneck, and there isn't a CANZUK unit within fifty miles. We need to move fast and act ruthlessly. A couple of five-kiloton warheads should do it. We have to set them back on their heels if only to give us a couple of days to sort out who the hell is going to lead this country."

There it was. It had taken Spellings all of one minute to point out the elephant in the room.

Standing behind his chair, Christoff quickly scanned the faces of the key people present. Including himself, six of Spector's cabinet members were in the room, as were nine of the UCSA's most powerful military men. And to the last person, all of them were wearing their best poker faces.

As Christoff expected, it was Hoffman, the Chief of Staff of the Air Force, who responded to Spellings, the leader of the Army. In a calming baritone, he said, "We need to select a new president before we do anything. We can't go off half-cocked without a leadership structure in place. That's only going to lead to more chaos."

Spellings' reply was quick and heated. "Our people on the ground don't need a new leader. They need to see action. They need to see the enemy being driven back. The Army—the outfit that's been fighting this goddamn war, needs to see something dramatic, or it's going to collapse. Mark my words. If we don't do something big, we're going to lose this war within a week—two weeks at the very most. My people are at their breaking point."

Seated, the country's two most senior generals stared at each other like two boxers at a weigh-in.

It was Hoffman who finally broke away from the standoff. "John, I've already got half the cabinet with me, the Air Force and five of the generals in this room. They're with me. I understand where you're coming from, and there's a part of me that wants to act as you're suggesting, but it's too much and much too fast. The situation we face is complex. The worst thing we could do at the moment is to be impulsive and set off a bunch of nukes."

Without taking his eyes off the other man, Spellings slowly got to his feet. "I knew you'd try to make this kind of move, Sid. You've always had your eyes on the prize. Well, I'm not going to make that easy for you. As we speak, units loyal to me are –."

Barking the word, Christoff said, "Gentlemen!"

Cut off mid-sentence, Spellings levelled a baleful glare on the CIB Director.

As Christoff took up the man's gaze, he felt the rest of the eyes of the room turn to him.

To Christoff's left, Hoffman said, "Dave, you have something to say?"

"I do, and I'll only say it once. I have negotiated a deal with Sanchez. Morgan and the Western Alliance have approved the deal. It will grant us immunity from any crimes we've committed, but we must surrender unconditionally by 3 pm today. There are a few other minor details, but they're inconsequential next to the decision to lay down our arms."

"You did what, you son of a bitch?" Spellings roared and started to move in Christoff's direction.

From across the room, Hoffman bellowed, "General Spellings, stand down!"

When the Army general did not let up his stride, one of the CIB staffers who'd accompanied Christoff into the room stepped in front of the intel man. Producing a pistol from underneath his suit jacket, the well-built man pointed the weapon at Spellings' center mass.

Seeing it, Spellings stopped in his tracks.

His face red like a fire engine, the UCSA Army Chief of Staff growled through gritted teeth, "Dave, whatever you think you're doing, it doesn't matter because you're finished. You're a dead man. You're a fucking traitor."

From behind the man with the gun, Christoff said, "Do it."

A single shot rang out and struck Spellings directly between the eyes. Like a marionette with its strings suddenly cut, the man crumpled lifelessly to the boardroom's carpeted floor.

With the echo of the gunshot still ringing, the second staffer Christoff had brought with him produced his own handgun and was pointing it at the other half of the room not being covered by the man who had put down Spellings.

Outside the boardroom, in the Operations Center, there was yelling, followed by a half-dozen gunshots.

At the top of his lungs, Christoff shouted, "STOP! Everyone remain calm. Everyone stay cool and listen to my words because I will not repeat them."

When no one said anything or moved, in his normal voice, Christoff said, "This is not a negotiation. The UCSA is going to lose this war. If we survive, we can do what the Confederacy did after the last war. We can work within whatever new system is negotiated and try to get some of what we've fought for. But if we don't take this deal, all of us – every one of us in this room and many more – will be shot by firing squad or worse. Thirteen million Americans have died. We did that. Us in this room. There will be no mercy. And those aren't my words. They're from Sanchez, and he and his people mean it."

Christoff slowly canvassed the room and, to the last person, saw looks of dismay or hatred. He didn't care. He'd been presented with an opportunity to stop the madness, and that's what he would do, even if that meant his name would live in infamy.

"The following words I speak are important. I know this is hard, but we're doing this. I will lead an interim government that will oversee our surrender and enter into negotiations with the FAS to create some kind of reformed United States. This is the only opportunity we'll have to secure some sort of leverage.

"I'll say this one more time. This is not a negotiation. If you're with me, raise your hand."

"No one do anything," Hoffman said forcefully.

Christoff's eyes snapped to the end of the table where the Air Force general was still seated.

As always, the former fighter pilot's demeanour was relaxed. As his dark brown eyes stared at Christoff, it felt like the man was trying to look into his soul.

General Hoffman said calmly, "Whatever deal you think you've made, Dave, we don't have to take it. Yes, things look dire, and while John's impatience was his downfall, we still have leverage. We have cards to play. Valuable ones.

"But setting that aside, who is it that you think you are that you speak on behalf of an entire nation? A nation that has fought so hard and suffered so much. Dave, for Christ's sake, you're the Director of the CIB. No, no one in this room is going to raise their hand."

After a long pause, Hoffman added, "I guess that means you're going to have to kill all of us."

Quietly, staring into the defiant eyes of the only man in the UCSA who could stop what Christoff knew in his heart and mind needed to be done, he said, "Not everyone, General. Just you."

After a brief pause, Christoff said to no one in particular, "Do it."

Reynolds pivoted to his left and placed the sight of his handgun on the chest of the man sitting at the end of the table. From twenty feet away, he sent three rounds into Hoffman's chest.

His weapon still raised, he strode past the Director of the CIB, past the operative he'd brought with him into the room, and closed the distance between himself and the gasping Air Force general.

A half-dozen feet away, he placed the red dot of his Glock on the man's forehead and just like he'd done with Spellings, he made sure to send General Sydney Hoffman to the hellish afterlife the man most certainly deserved.

As the sound of the gunshot petered out, Reynolds closed his eyes and attuned his ears to listen to the room's stillness. The next five seconds would determine if a massacre would take place.

When all he heard was his own breathing, he opened his eyes and slowly turned to face the onlookers.

Every face was staring at him intently, and on more than a few, he saw what could only be described as looks of relief.

With Reynolds' and the second operative's guns still pointing at them, Christoff said, "It's over. Everyone in this room stays put for the next hour. I'll be back in fifteen minutes, and when I come back, we'll discuss how to bring this war to an end without those of us with gallons of blood on our hands spending the rest of our lives in a jail cell or being strung up."

Epilogue

For the past hour, Hall had been sitting in the *Sukhasana* or the Easy Pose, as it was known to most newbies taking up yoga.

Opening her eyes, she glanced at the food that she placed on the tiny desk that took up the corner of her six-by-eight cell. She closed her eyes and ruthlessly suppressed the urge to gobble up the sustenance.

In the three months she'd been jailed within the Canadian Forces Service Prison and Detention Barracks in Edmonton, she'd lost fifteen pounds. Five pounds for every month she'd been in this soul-sucking place.

Within days of her arrival, she had determined this was how she would save herself. She would starve to death instead of enduring a lifetime in this prison.

She inhaled a deep, calming breath and pushed away her bitterness. It would not help her endure what was to come. Instead, she searched her recollections and found the one truth that fought off the darkness.

She had become an assassin. Or a murderer to those who couldn't appreciate the political nature of the work she'd done. And a very good assassin at that. Her life might end early, but for a brief and intense period, she had done something extraordinary for the country she loved.

Her only regret? Petit. She had not wanted to kill the man. She had argued for some other kind of resolution, but Aziz himself had shut down the conversation and told her to do what needed to be done, or he'd have someone else do it — someone who might not be as proficient.

She had made her choices and knew that when she pulled the trigger to end the life of Josee Labelle in that café in French Guyana, her ultimate fate would be far from pleasant.

It didn't matter. Keeping Canada safe from traitors and international foes was what was necessary, and on those counts, Sarah Hall had done as much or more than anyone else in the country, and no one could convince her of otherwise.

As she let her self-assessed vindication percolate, she heard a door open far down the hallway. As best as she could tell, she was alone in this wing of the barracks. A pair of military police – MPs – would visit her four times a day. Three times to drop off her food and once to escort her to the outdoor exercise area, whereby herself, she was given thirty minutes to do whatever she wanted.

Her lunch had been dropped off an hour ago, while her exercise time had been in the early morning. Her dinner wasn't scheduled for drop-off for another two hours. Perhaps it was another surprise visit from her obese lawyer, Major Gupta.

Her assigned legal counsel had visited three times, and with each conversation, Hall had become more convinced her weight was being transposed to her portly legal representative. Whatever fitness standards the Office of the Judge Advocate General had regarding its officers, it wasn't being applied to the grotesque Indian-Canadian.

The clumping of boots ended on the other side of her door. There was a jangle of keys, and then the door opened. Behind the two familiar faces of her guards, there was a figure, but it wasn't the overstuffed lawyer.

The figure wore civvy attire, and he was lean and fit, unlike Gupta.

The two MPs separated, allowing the civilian to walk into her cell.

As the figure passed the threshold, there was a loud metallic clang as one of the MPs reached forward and closed the steel barrier that kept her in this oppressive, small place.

With neutral expressions, she and the man stared at one another until the MPs' pounding boots could no longer be heard.

When the cell was quiet but for her own breathing, Hall said, "I don't get any news in here. You're still running the show?"

"I am. For now."

Nodding at the confirmation, she continued, "So apparently, my name is Rylee Daniels, and I hold the rank of corporal. Or that's what I've been told by the barrel of lard who's charading as my lawyer. I'm not sure if I should be hopeful or depressed my real name and rank aren't being used?"

She paused, waiting to see if the still-standing man would respond to her prompt for information on her legal status. When he offered no reply, she said, "Edmonton is a long way from Ottawa,

Director. I hope you haven't flown all this way only to stare at me?"

"I've been told you're not eating. Looking at you now, I can see that's the case," Larocque said.

"Yeah, well, as it turns out, I don't have the courage to hang myself."

A slow crease formed at the corner of Larocque's mouth, and his eyes narrowed as he registered her reply.

"Isn't that what you and the government want?" Hall said in a matter-of-fact tone. "To see me waste away and die so that the Government of Canada doesn't have to confront the fact that I killed people on its behalf."

"Some in the government would like that, Lieutenant, but not me."

"Oh, and what do you want, Director? Do you want a public trial so you can further ruin the reputation of the woman who had the courage and temerity to save our country? How does the country fare, by the way? Have the elites already wormed their way back into power? What about McPhail? How badly has that pathetic woman screwed things up?

When Larocque offered no reply, Hall scoffed, pointed outside the cell and said, "I bet you it's a disaster out there. Who is it this time, Director? The Russians?

On seeing Larocque's jaw tighten, Hall said, "It's bad, isn't it? Merielle's warnings have come to pass, haven't they?"

With still no reply from Larocque, Hall continued, "Well, you can't say you weren't warned. You were warned, and you killed the only person who was prepared to save this country. Well fucking done."

As though her rebuke had hit its mark precisely, Larocque almost whispered, "I understand your mother spoke German, Lieutenant, and that you scored high marks in the language during your time at the Royal Military College?"

Hall cocked her head sideways and said, "Is that a question, Director?"

"It is, so answer it, Lieutenant."

Hall didn't answer. Instead, she crossed her arms and delivered a defiant stare back at the leader of Canada's national intelligence service.

But no sooner had her eyes connected with Larocque's than the fit former special operations officer closed the distance between them, grabbed her by her still-crossed arms, and slammed her into the far wall of her cell.

Towering over her and keeping her arms locked in place, Larocque growled, "Listen to me carefully. I will leave you to rot in this cell for a long time, young lady. I will let you waste away because no one knows you're here. The prime minister, Aziz, the White Unit. They're all gone. You are a ghost, Sarah Hall. You exist, but no one can see you."

Releasing her arms, Larocque stepped back and gestured to the tiny space around them. "In this space, your existence will be beyond miserable, and I promise you Hall, I will be only too happy to let you rot for what you've done. You're no innocent. You know what you did was wrong, so don't dare try and heap your pity party on me"

He paused to let his words sink in. "Now, I'm going to ask the question again, Lieutenant, and this time you're going to answer it. You're going to answer it, or I'm going to let you starve or go insane inside this cell. I don't give a fiddler's fig which it is. Do you speak German, Lieutenant?"

Hall closed her eyes and inhaled deeply as the repeated question registered with her. When her eyes finally opened, she said, *"Ja, ich spreche gut Deutsch."*

Nodding slowly, Larocque said, "Good. Now, listen carefully. There's an alternative path that doesn't see you starve yourself to death, but you have to answer the next few questions truthfully. No lies and no games, or I walk out this door, and for the next ten years at least, you remain in purgatory. Do you understand?"

Hall only nodded.

"Did you kill Sam Petit?"

"Yes, I was ordered to by Colonel Mustapha Aziz. I had misgivings, but I did kill him."

"And was it you who killed Josee Labelle in French Guyana?"

Hall hesitated for a moment but then said, "Yes. Once again, under the direction of Aziz."

"How many Chinese operatives did you personally kill?

Although her words were barely a whisper, her hazel eyes looked at Larocque defiantly, and she said, "Four. I killed four of them. One woman. Three men. And I'd do it again if I needed to."

Larocque nodded slowly. "Your parents were informed you died three weeks ago while working a covert CSIS op in Indonesia. Your body was never recovered. To them, the rest of your family and friends, you truly are a ghost.

"Your name is now Mara Bauer, and from now on, you work for me."

The End

Copyright

Copyright R.A. Flannagan Writing 2024
    Published by R.A. Flannagan Writing
    All rights reserved
    No part of this book, Wraith Horizon, may be reproduced, scanned, or distributed in any printed or electronic form without the permission of the author. The author holds exclusive rights to this work. Unauthorized duplication is prohibited.
    Except for referenced or inferred Canadian politicians, this is a work of fiction. Any resemblance of characters to actual persons, living or dead, is purely coincidental.
    Cover design by Ares Jun: aresjun@gmail.com
    Special thanks to my editor: Stephen England. Stephen is an author himself, and he writes a terrific thriller: https://www.stephenenglandbooks.com/
    A very special thanks to my Beta Readers:
    - J. Crough
    - David E. Pickering
    - Darren Bourn
    - Andy Johnson
    - Alex Binnie
    - Bob Flannagan
    Their many helpful comments, edits and encouragements brought Wraith Horizon to the next level.

Afterword

Dear Reader:

Thank you so much for reading Wraith Horizon. I hope you enjoyed it. If you did, I would be grateful if you could leave a review on Amazon. It's pretty easy to leave a star rating, but if you could take a moment and write a quick review, you would be doing me a HUGE favour. Ratings and reviews make a big difference in getting new readers to take a chance on my work.

Regarding the work. Phew!

Wraith Horizon was a huge challenge to write. I had initially planned to create a series of mil-fiction short stories to bridge the gap between Red Blue Storm and what became Wraith Horizon. But the short stories got longer and turned into a full novel. With this much content but still lots of story to tell, I got to thinking I should write two books. But in the end, my muse (and my editor) made Wraith Horizon come out in a single longer story. Despite its difficulty, I'm very proud of it. I think it turned into a decent yarn.

What's Next:

As you'll see from the epilogue, I've set up the story to move to Europe. Book 4 will focus on the UK and its efforts to counter the French, German, and Russian threats. As I'm not British and my forte is Canadian and American politics, I'm going to have to do a fair bit of homework to plot out a realistic and compelling tale. Nevertheless, I'm looking forward to the challenge.

But before I write Book 4, I will be writing a standalone novel. This one has been inside me for a while.

It is untitled as yet, but it will be loosely based on the story of Amanda Lindhout, a Canadian journalist who was abducted in Somalia. She spent over a year in captivity. Her story is sad, frustrating and hugely compelling, and I recommend it to you: A House in the Sky: A Memoir. Amanda was kidnapped with an Australian, Nigel Brennan, and he too wrote about his experience, though I haven't read it: The Price of Life.

Without a doubt, at some point during Amanda's captivity, Canada and Australia's security services thought about trying to rescue their citizens. In this proposed alt-history, that's exactly what's going to happen.

Names, locations, etc will change such that unless you were familiar with Amanda and Nigel's story, you'd have no idea. But this is where the inspiration for this next book came from. As a reader of mine, I thought I'd give you this little but important insight into this next project.

***

How to get in contact with R.A. Flannagan:

It's not hard, and I would love to hear from you regardless of the reason. Here's how you can connect with me:

- Email: raf@raflannagan.ca
- Website: https://raflannagan.ca/
- Facebook: https://www.facebook.com/profile.php?id=100094311130981
- Substack: https://raflannagan.substack.com/

Again, a heartfelt thank you for reading my stories and supporting my writing career.

Sincerely,

R.A. Flannagan

Printed in Great Britain
by Amazon